T0294569

THE FACE OF TIME

THE FACE OF TIME

An Li

translated by

Du Lixia and Zhang Min

edited in English by

Tom Nolan

supported by

the Shaanxi Translators Association

and the Shaanxi Literature Foundation

CHAX PRESS

TUCSON 2023

ISBN 978-1-946104-46-5

Library of Congress Control Number: 2023942141

Chax Press
1517 N Wilmot Rd no. 264
Tucson Arizona 85712-4410

Chax Press books are supported in part by individual donors, the Arts Federation of Tucson and Southern Arizona, the Arizona Commission on the Arts, and by sales of books. Please visit *https://chax.org/membership-support/* if you would like to contribute to our mission to make an impact on the literature and culture of our time.

The American publication of *The Face of Time* is supported by the Shaanxi Writers Association.

Poison tastes sweet, but the antidote, bitter.

This book is dedicated to my parents who gave me life, the mountains and rivers that nurtured me, the earthen cave dwelling that sheltered me from rain and wind, and the village that I have missed so much!

CONTENTS

PART I

1

A steamed bun in the morning and a mug of water in the afternoon. That constituted all that Third Aunt lived on each day.

As Third Aunt related her wretched life, she was sitting in a luxurious restaurant, eating stewed fish. Between every two bites of fish, she would stop to recount her misery, and struggle to squeeze some tears out of her eyes, which resembled two minuscule muddy pools. From time to time, one or two teardrops would descend her cheeks like overripe grapes.

Third Aunt had always been at odds with Taoqi, her daughter-in-law. However, in the last few days their relationship had turned from cold war to red hot conflict. As a result, Taoqi's face bore bloody marks where Third Aunt's three fingers had struck it, while the corners of Third Aunt's mouth were swollen where Taoqi had torn at it. After the battle, Taoqi lay in bed, crying. Third Aunt lay on her *kang*[1] in another room, crying too. Taoqi swore she would live no more; Third Aunt vowed she would put an end to her own life too. After crying for a long while, Taoqi rose and locked the kitchen door with an iron padlock. Peeping from within her room through the opening between the double doors at what Taoqi had done, Third Aunt got off the *kang*, searched here and there, found an old style bronze padlock, and added it to Taoqi's. Taoqi, who was now sitting on the threshold, spat on the ground. Third Aunt had a mind to spit on the ground two times or even three times, but refrained from doing so, because she was afraid Taoqi might think she was copying her. Instead, she cursed a hen hunting for food in the courtyard. She exclaimed the hen was good for nothing except for sale. Given that it hatched no chickens, could it even be called a hen? The hen's face turned red because of the abuse Third Aunt hurled at it, but Taoqi's face didn't redden. Rather, it grew increasingly pale; not with a pure pallor, but with a dark and sallow pallor, like the color of the wrapping paper used in food stores.

Taking a lift on a coal truck, Third Aunt came to the provincial capital and met there her son Dalin, to whom she made a bad report about Taoqi. She urged Dalin to go home and gave Taoqi a good thrashing. He ought to tear Taoqi's mouth apart, and knock the teeth out of her mouth, and send them rolling all over the ground.

Dalin worked as the head waiter in the very restaurant where he was treating his mother to the fish dinner.

Dalin had made a phone call to me earlier in the day, inviting me to come over to eat fish. When I arrived at the restaurant I saw a waitress standing by them with a pair of tweezers in hand; after much effort she had just picked a fish bone out of Third Aunt's throat. Taking the fish bone from the waitress, Third Aunt scrutinized it for a long while, then scolded Dalin for being brainless. As brainless as Taoqi he was, she grumbled. Why had he ordered fish for her? Hadn't there been any other dishes to choose from? Didn't he know fish had bones, which were like a multitude of insidious steel needles waiting their chance to kill? Aya, the fish bones had nearly claimed her life.

Dalin laughed good-humoredly. Though already in his thirties, Dalin looked as innocent as a laughing baby, with a clearly visible dimple in each cheek.

Picking a piece of fish meat off the bones, Dalin put it onto his mother's plate, and said, "Taoqi didn't feed you, that made you angry. I feed you tasty fish, this makes you angry too? I wonder where all your anger comes from. Don't be angry, please. Anger shortens people's life, you know. I'll teach Taoqi a lesson for you when I come back home some day, okay?"

Narrowing her eyes, Third Aunt twitched her mouth, and said, "I want you to come back home *now* to teach her a lesson. Beating makes a good wife, just as kneading makes dough pliant. Harsh discipline makes horses and mules obedient. Taoqi's disobedience is a result of your not beating her hard."

"What era do you think we are in now, Third Aunt? How come you still hold to such out-of-date ideas?" I said.

Third Aunt glared at me with apparent dissatisfaction. With her mouth twisting, she vigilantly picked up her cloth bag from the stool next to hers and hugged it to her bosom, as if it had suddenly occurred to her that an atrocious robber was around and she feared he might seize it. Her bag was as old as Adam, with a faded embroidered image representing Chairman Mao receiving Red Guards. The bag looked pretty soiled all over.

Dalin told his mother to put the bag down and not to let it trouble her dinner.

"No one would attempt to steal it," Dalin said. "Even if you gave it away, no one would have it. Unlike village thieves, who steal cheap things such as towels or door curtains, city thieves are picky."

What Dalin said put a flea in my ear. What did he mean? Apart from him and Third Aunt, I was the only person present. Then who would be the thief? Did he mean I was coveting Third Aunt's bag? Was I the thief in question?

As I was pondering these thoughts, the door was pushed open from outside, and in came a woman who was in her early middle age. The woman was richly decked-out with jewels; the golden threads woven in her long skirt glittered in the lamplight, making me dizzy. Her hair was dyed blond. The skin of her gourd-shaped face was anything but smooth. It was obvious that her face had undergone cosmetic surgery, and the application of a thick layer of make-up hardly covered the scars. Particularly eye-catching was her jaw, which was so remarkably swollen that it looked like a piece of over-baked brown bread fresh out of the oven. Her eyes were two narrow slits, intensely dark with mascara. But the most eye-catching object of all was the necklace hanging round her roughly-scarred neck. The necklace was made of gold and inlaid with two precious stones, one a ruby, the other a sapphire. Both stones emitted a faint infernal light.

Seeing the woman come in, Dalin rose to his feet in a hurry, growing respectful. His face was smiling from ear to ear, but his tongue was stiff. He introduced me to the woman in broken sentences, saying that I was his cousin; my name was Tian Daqing; my nickname was Black Bean.

The woman burst into laughter, with her mouth wide open; her upper lip was much thicker than the lower. She exclaimed that my name and nickname sounded interesting and funny. With extraordinary enthusiasm she said she had learned about me a long time before: wasn't I a big scholar from Mazi Village, whom the entire village took pride in?

"Dalin has mentioned you so often that I couldn't be more familiar with you — by repute, that is. It's my great honor to meet you in person today!" she exclaimed.

These exaggerated remarks, pronounced with flirtatious voice, made me uneasy. One might have thought that I had been sitting next to a hot furnace; dense beads of sweat were gathering on my forehead. I replied, "I'm nobody in my home village. I have a cousin who is only one day older than me. He did his studies in the United States and has American permanent resident status. He is the person in my home village who has really made it."

The woman took a pair of chopsticks. After picking up a piece of fish and putting it on Third Aunt's plate, she picked up another piece and set it on mine. She instructed us to make ourselves at home, laughed dully, and claimed she had heard about my American cousin.

"Dalin has mentioned him often too," she said. "You know, Dalin can never overcome his bad countryside habits. Even though he now dwells in the city, his heart stays in the village. His mind remains narrow. He never talks without saying the village this or the village that."

To console me, probably, she claimed she viewed my cousin's American success as unimportant. "Live in the United States? So what? Does American permanent resident status mean everything? There are beggars in the United States. A toad remains a toad wherever it goes, and a phoenix is a phoenix wherever it dwells."

As she spoke, she produced a business card from her pocket, and handed it to me. I glanced at it and caught sight of a name already very familiar to me due to Dalin's prior effusive references: Li Tiantian.

"Oh, you're Boss Li! Nice to meet you, finally. Dalin has talked a lot about you too," I said with a smile on my face.

Enchantingly, Li Tianian smiled. But her smile vanished from her face as quickly as a meteor falls from the sky.

"Dalin has got a heart that distorts what it shows, a mouth that perverts truth. I wonder what he has said about me. He must've slandered me in front of you," she said.

"He told me you are able and hardworking. He told me your business is prosperous. If these are slanders, he has indeed slandered you," I replied. "He earns a living by your good graces. How would he dare to slander you? He could hardly worship you more."

My words made her taut face loosen and light up.

"Yes, yes," she blurted out. She said she did believe Dalin hadn't spoken ill of her, because even though she had this fault or that shortcoming, at least she could be considered as Dalin's benefactor; when Dalin first came to this city without any friend to turn to, it was she who hired him, cared about him, helped him, and treated him like a treasure; she lifted him up above her own head; she held him in her own palms; she had done her best for him. Given all she had done, if Dalin still spoke ill of her, Heaven would judge and vindicate her without her beseeching.

Without saying a single word, Dalin made efforts to smile, like a kindergarten kid doing his best to look docile and humble in front of teacher. Patting Dalin on the shoulder and pouting her lips at him, Li Tiantian ordered Dalin in a voice that brooked no contradiction to take good care of Third Aunt and me. She said if the present dishes were not enough, we should feel free to order more; if I wanted to drink wine, I should just take it from the bar counter; if we were not well served, she would take Dalin to task.

The moment Li Tiantian left the private room, Dalin's high spirits dropped drastically; he grew depressed and gloomy. He again picked some fish for me and for his mother, but he did not eat anything himself. Instead, he lit a cigarette and smoked thoughtfully. Suddenly I realized that after having lived for years in the city, Dalin's formerly hidden handsome features had started to show: his skin was light-colored and exquisite, his regular, delicate face was good looking; his eyebrows were dark and his black-and-white eyes were crystal clear; his nose had a wonderful shape; his mouth was especially well formed — it turned up slightly and had a cool and arrogant air. If he walked down the street in a designer suit, probably no one would think he came from a village; most people would take him for the son of a government official.

Actually, Dalin had not often talked about Li Tiantian in front of me; on the contrary, he deliberately avoided any topic relating to her. Nevertheless, I had learned about Li Tiantian by piecing together the isolated details he had occasionally revealed.

Li Tiantian had divorced two husbands. In each divorce, the division of the property had occasioned open warfare. The personalities of her two ex-husbands were polar opposites: one had a fiery disposition, the other was dull; one was like a firework that would go off at the least spark, the other was like a rock that made no response even to the hardest kick. But when they divorced, both did the same thing to Li Tiantian, as if they had come to an agreement beforehand. They both threw sulfuric acid on Li Tiantian. They both ended up in prison, one after the other. All things considered, though, Li Tiantian was lucky. Although she failed to dodge fast enough to evade the flying spray of sulfuric acid, which ended up burning part of her skin, she escaped with her life.

Of course, Dalin had mentioned the necklace Li Tiantian wore. According to Dalin, Li Tiantian had it purchased in South Africa; the gold was pure gold, the diamond was high carat, and the entire piece cost six hundred thousand RMB; Li Tiantian always suspected that people were scheming to steal her necklace, and never took it off even when going to bed. The necklace had almost killed her: it had constricted Li Tiantian's throat several times and nearly suffocated her.

I could not help asking Dalin, "What's the nature of your relation with Li Tiantian?"

He trembled, as if my question had shocked him out of a dream. He accused me of groundless suspicions, "What relation can a boss and her employee have? Of course we are just employer and employee."

"Is it really that simple?" I asked. "Does an average boss treat an average employee so well?"

Dalin signaled to me not to go on with the topic. Obviously, he did not want his mother to know too much about it.

But despite Dalin's precautions, Third Aunt caught our conversation. She commented, "How nice your boss is! How pleasantly she spoke! How different she is from Taoqi! Taoqi always wears a long face, like a hanged dead ghost."

2

Dalin called me whenever Third Aunt came to Yuebei. He would say he wanted to treat me to a meal, but as a matter of fact he was finding a place for his mother to stay. He knew that after my divorce I had a big apartment to myself, big enough for her to live in whenever she was in Yuebei. I had no objection to Third Aunt's living in my apartment, and in fact it was interesting to hear her gossip about the village. However, she was such a big mouth, that the moment she got back to the village she lavished praise on my apartment in terms more fit for a palace. That resulted in just about every villager wanting to come and live in it. Finally, patients, cattle dealers, people seeking satisfaction from higher government echelons in miscarriages of justice, even casual visitors — they all ended up dropping by at my place. They would step in, and after a short break, begin counting my doors. Third Aunt told them that I earned quite a lot in Yuebei, and that the apartment in which I lived had nine doors. Until this news came to my ears, I had no idea how many doors the apartment had, but thanks to their continual reminders and repeated count-ups of my own, I found it did indeed have nine doors, if one included the doors to the kitchen and the bathroom. I warmly welcomed every visitor from my village. After all they *were* my fellow villagers. How could I give them the cold shoulder? I had heard their complaints about me: given that I worked far away, my influence in Yuebei, like water far from thirsting mouths, or a piece of steamed bun too far across the table to be reached, had brought them nothing. Were I to come back to Gaotai Township and serve as a vice head or something like that, I would be able to offer a little help when they applied for sites to build houses, or for marriage certificates or for other things of that nature. These words made me feel rather guilty, as though I were defaulting on a debt, so as a kind of compensation, I opened my doors and waited for them to descend on me.

To Third Aunt, the sofa was too soft, so she hated sitting on it. After a short while she would feel pain in her back, and numbness in her legs, which would make her tumble when she tried to get up. She had been accustomed to sitting cross-legged on a *kang*, but I had no furnishings of that kind, I only had a sofa, so she would take the bamboo mat which stood rolled in a corner of my balcony, spread it over the floor, and sit on it cross-legged without taking off her shoes. After doing that she would begin rambling talks on topics as extensive as they were insubstantial, from her grandmother's having made her embroidered shoes, to, without really noticing the transition, the mad woman in our village — Qiuli.

"What a big goose! Ha-ha-ha. She thinks she can grasp smoke!" At the mention of Qiuli, Third Aunt would laugh happily with her mouth wide open.

Who could catch smoke? Baolai's wife Qiuli thought she could! Had she ever caught any? Of course not! Qiuli had tried to, but ended up getting chased all over the village by Third Aunt with a poker in hand. Qiuli used to be a smart woman. When she married Baolai, her eyes were limpid as water, her face round as a full moon, her skin white as tofu jelly, her voice softer than egg white, and her smiles sweeter than honey. Everyone in the village, man or woman, wanted to give her an affectionate pinch when they saw her. One day, Qiuli had a stomach-ache, and was given injections in the village clinic. On the third day when the needle was still in her, she went mad for no apparent reason. She began by uttering mumbo-jumbo, in which could be heard screams mixed with hysterical singing. Later she became violent, smashing a thermos flask with a punch and upsetting the injection rack with a kick. Only after Shuanniu the village doctor had given her two sedative injections could Baolai get her under control and carry her home on a handcart. The villagers streamed in to have a look, yet no one could make it out. How could a person go mad so suddenly? Was she possessed by some ghost? Unlikely! What were the real reasons? After much pondering and guesswork, most villagers began to have their doubts about the medicines in the village clinic. According to them, Shuanniu had been summoned by the public security officials because of selling fake medicines. The odds were ten to one that Qiuli's suffering had something to do with the medicines Shuanniu had used on her. As a result, some people kept on at Baolai to the point where he asked Shuanniu for the return of a healthy wife.

In a storm of rage, and under the watchful eye of others, the timid man stepped out as if he were ready to die together with his enemy. But he had hardly taken a step before he diffidently turned back. He was so afraid of the Shuanniu brothers that before any face-to-face confrontation actually took place his lips became pale and his legs began to tremble. That Baolai had a head as soft as a persimmon on his shoulders was known to all, so someone, having gone home to fetch half a bottle of spirits, urged him to drink it, saying it would embolden him. Without hesitating, Baolai held up the bottle and emptied it.

With the help of the spirits, Baolai's face, red and bashful by nature, now became even more crimson, like a lighted pomegranate lantern. He darted to the gate of the clinic, threw a few curses at Shuanniu, tore the sign board off the wall and flung it onto the ground. He stomped on it, trying to break it into pieces, but failed because his legs and feet were not strong enough. However, his curses and stamps drew Shuanniu out of his office. Shuanniu stood in the doorway, leaning against a jamb, and stared at him with eyes like search lights. On seeing Shuanniu, Baolai, like a fully-inflated basketball pierced by a knife, fell flat at once. He shut his mouth, drew back his foot, and the only thought flashing through his mind was how to get away as quickly as possible. A sinister smile crept into Shuanniu's face, a smile which, in the eyes of Baolai, looked like the cold light of a sharp dagger.

"Well done! Well done! I would like to see you do that again!" Shuanniu sneered at Baolai, with his lips puckered up.

One of Baolai's feet was raised, suspended in mid-air, but he didn't let it fall for a long time. Without another word, Shuanniu turned around, went inside, and brought back a shovel which he launched at Baolai's head. Baolai jumped aside and took to his heels. Although he was not hit by the shovel, he was frightened out of his wits, and out of his soul as well. From then on, Baolai seemed unable to retain his urine, wetting his pants from time to time.

Third Aunt touched on Baolai's story lightly. However, when she talked about Qiuli she couldn't hide her excitement. Even the fish meal could not bring her such excitement. Qiuli's story made her smile broadly, and when she smiled her face looked like a piece of crumpled brown paper. Third Aunt said that Fugui, also known as Fullghost, was totally to blame. Fullghost was the best appellation for him because he, with a belly full of wicked ideas, could come up with one trick after another in the blink of an eye. Fugui had dreamed of having a son all his life, but his wife disappointed him time and again, delivering one girl after another. Over a decade, they had Zhengyue, Yuanyue, Layue, Runyue...some of them tall, some of them short, and forming a considerable group. Fugui sold them off young and cheap except for Layue who he had hoped would one day take care of her parents when they were old. One hundred *yuan*, sometimes less, or even an inherited engraved pipe might be enough to buy a girl from him. The way he sold his daughters was rather casual, and, like vegetable pedlars selling their cabbages, he did not care whether they were bought to be fried or made into dumplings. Thus, his daughters met with various destinies. One, who had been on the streets, was adopted by a kind couple and taken abroad, where she enjoyed a comfortable life. One became an old man's wife after being trafficked many times. One, practically a child bride, was maltreated by the man's family. She was black and blue all over, looking like an old woman although she was still in her youth.

Fugui wanted to find a husband to move in with Layue, the only daughter he had not sold. After a careful search around, he selected Qi Guangrong from the neighboring village, a poor ugly-looking guy with a flat nose and buck teeth. Both Layue and Fugui's wife expressed objections, but Fugui was more than willing and content, even compromised and yielded when Qi Guangrong flatly refused to move in. Everyone said Fugui was a fool, and that he was blinded by chicken shit. He was the only one who knew that he was not. Qi Guangrong's great grandfather, a salt dealer in the reign of Emperor Tongzhi or Emperor Xuantong of the Qing Dynasty, had been given a piss-pot for providing the palace with salt. An emperor's piss-pot — it must be worth something! With this invaluable pot, Layue need worry about nothing for the rest of her life. And if Qi Guangrong could give him, Fugui, in his capacity of father-in-law, even a tiny share in it, he too need worry about nothing the rest of his life.

But what was Qi Guangrong now? He was still digging coal in a small coal pit, although he never forgot to buy his father-in-law a pound of sweets every time he received his wages. Fugui loved sweets, but he never ate them at home, instead he ate them in public places where people were most densely packed. Before eating he would hold one up high, squint, and look at it for what seemed like forever. Throwing one into his mouth, he would chomp and gnash, and lick his lips for another long period, with an intoxicated looks on his face.

No one cared too much about Fugui's eating manner, because what he ate or how he ate was altogether his business and had nothing to do with other people. The only one attracted by his performance was Qiuli. When she saw Fugui eat sweets she would stand still as if her feet were glued to the ground. She gazed longingly and timidly at Fugui, putting her finger into her mouth to suck it. Fugui asked if she wanted to eat. Qiuli nodded. Fugui had no intention of giving her candy, so he made a show of his different eating methods in order to tantalize her appetite. Once in a while when he was feeling generous and benevolent, he would crunch the candy with his teeth and put one small piece, no larger than a grain of rice, into Qiuli's mouth. Qiuli would look as if the candy tasted spicy rather than sweet. As she ate, the muscles on her face twisted and contorted.

At the entrance to the village was a spacious clearing, and it was the Tiananmen Square in the eye of the villagers. People often went there to have a leisurely walk after meals. A stretch of mud village wall, old and broken, had been worn right down by people's feet over the years to the point where it resembled a stage. When December came, the stage was lit up brilliantly, and the opera singing there would not stop until the second day of the second month after the Spring Festival. In addition to singing opera and watching it, the villagers worshiped their goddess as well. In front of the wall was a withering old locust tree which was nicknamed Old Mom. It was said Old Mom had been planted by the distant ancestors of the Mazi villagers, who began to offer sacrifices to it at some unspecified time in the past. Quite apart from festivals and holidays, even on ordinary days people went to kowtow and burn incense to it if their children were suffering from fever or if their old cows were experiencing a difficult labor.

Today, Fugui was squatting down by Old Mom and listening to several guys chatter. On seeing Qiuli dawdle over, he produced a candy from his pocket and held it up high. The moment he saw Qiuli, he put that candy into his mouth, sucking on it with an exaggerated expression. Qiuli stood there staring at him, her eyes steady and empty, her face wearing a yearning, silly smile, and her mouth dripping with saliva.

Fugui winked at her and asked if she wanted to eat. Qiuli's lips spread like a saucer. She swallowed with an effort and nodded hard.

"Go catch smoke from Third Granny's chimney. I'll let you eat my candy!" Fugui took a furious bite at the candy with the tips of his teeth.

Qiuli was still wearing that silly smile of hers.

"Get moving! Catch some smoke from Third Granny's chimney, and the candy is yours!" Fugui stamped his foot on the ground.

Stooping, Qiuli ran to the smoke not far away. She struggled yet failed to catch the gracefully-rising cooking smoke which, stirred by her grasp, dispersed in all directions. Mad about it, Qiuli threw some clods into the chimney. Then, at the instigation of Fugui, she moved a stone slab from far away, panting heavily, and placed it on top of the chimney.

Third Aunt, whose house was built on a lower place, was burning firewood before the kitchen range. All of a sudden, the raging flames began to fade away. Billows of smoke flew backward, gusted out of the range and engulfed her immediately. Her sore tear-streaked eyes could see nothing. Realizing someone might have done something to the chimney, she took a fire poker and went out to have a look. Qiuli, lying prone on the stone slab, was blowing air into the chimney through a cleft left uncovered by the slab. Third Aunt exploded with anger, teeth gnashing.

"Qiuli, you hanged ghost! I'll break your legs, just you wait and see!" she shouted out loud.

Seeing Third Aunt charge at her, Qiuli slipped down from atop the chimney and made her escape. Qiuli led the chase, and Third Aunt followed, fire poker in hand, swearing as she chased her from alley to alley. But Third Aunt couldn't catch up with Qiuli, who ran faster than a hare. Exhausted, she sat down on the ground gasping, while Qiuli stood a few steps away laughing "hee-hee-hee..."

"I don't blame Qiuli. Fugui is to blame!" Third Aunt repeatedly stated that Fugui was responsible when she told me this part of the story. Once she identified Fugui as the instigator, she ran to find him and, when she found him, struck him hard on the leg with the fire poker.

"Silly Qiuli!" Third Aunt prattled on. "A poor woman. She takes off her trousers before other people at the drop of a hat. How embarrassing! She is immune to shame, even if you spit on her face. Pity poor Baolai! How ill-fated he is. A good guy like him does not deserve such retribution! Blind heaven is to blame! If it had opened its eyes it would have brought the Shuanniu brothers to justice, and along the way have had Taoqi's mouth sewn up with needle and thread."

I was not familiar with Baolai. He lived in the northernmost part of the village, and I in the southernmost. When I left Mazi Village for higher education, he was still a pupil carrying a checked schoolbag made of homespun cloth. It was rather his father who had left a deep impression on me. His father Gangan, who had once been village head, had been unshakable in that position for 20 years. If it had not been for an unexpected paralysis, he would have occupied it for the rest of his life. Gangan had a bladder-like dark red face which was always sullen, like the weather before a thunderstorm. However, it was universally acknowledged that he was a born good-natured man. In order to raise money to cure the liver of a villager who was no blood relative of his, he sold all the sheep in his pen, and what was more, he even sold his own blood to the blood bank, which caused him to fall down in a faint. Each spring or autumn, he would lead villagers to build the irrigation system, hoping to divert water from Three-River Bay to the terraced fields. This project had, however, never been completed, and all there was to show for it were the rusty iron pipes on the slope which attracted thieves far and near to dismantle and sell for money. Gangan's thrift was always on the lips of villagers. In a trip to another county to buy tree saplings for the village, rather than ordering nine-cent noodles for meal, he only spent two cents on two bowls of noodle soup, one for himself and the other for the villager in his company. Back home, the villager complained that he was so starved that his chest and back stuck together, and swore he would never again go out on business with Gangan.

3

I was truly surprised when I got a phone call from Liben. Since he left China more than ten years before, he had never returned once, nor did he ever contact me. There used to be a colorful rumor doing the rounds in the village, to the effect that Liben had been run down by a car in America and cremated. Upon hearing the rumor, Liben's sister Lifang cried her heart out, which left her eyes horribly swollen. Liben's brother-in-law Beiqiang was so worried that he could hardly stay put for a single second. Beiqiang came to Yuebei looking for me, asking me to find out what had happened. After making countless calls, I eventually established that the news was fake.

On the phone, Liben told me he was now in Yuebei airport; he hoped I could get a car to pick him up. He had considered the idea of taking an airport shuttle or hiring a taxi to come to the city from the airport, however, after thinking it over, he felt it would be better to be picked up at the airport. It was thirteen years since he had left his homeland for the last time. Now he was back; what he yearned for most was the warmth with which he would be received in his hometown! In addition, a sense of romance would hopefully emanate from his meeting with me, his best friend, at the airport. He particularly instructed me to bring him a bouquet of carnations, his favorite flower.

"Sure, sure!" I promised him. But I felt unsure. It was easy to buy a bouquet, but I had no idea where to get a car. I went downstairs and managed to buy some pure white carnations in the neighborhood. I scratched my head over the car problem.

I got out my cell phone. I dialed Li Tiantian's number, but instantly hung up. She did have a Buick, but was it proper for me to borrow it given that we had only met once? If she refused me, what a fool I would feel!

I hailed a taxi. I consoled myself with the thought that, being one of my own folks, Liben would not mind the anonymous car he would be picked up with. Growing up beside him, didn't I know his background all too well? As small boys, we used to help our families herding goats or collecting firewood. Whenever we saw other people riding in a tractor, we felt sick with envy, wishing we could enjoy such a ride. Even though Liben had travelled round the world and was now returning from abroad, he would not, I believed, have forgotten his background so quickly.

When I got to the airport, Liben was seated on a chair in the arrival hall, intently reading a comic book. I walked round him several times, unsure if he was really the person I had come for. As he raised his head and our eyes met, we were both taken aback. Almost simultaneously we called out each other's name. We hugged; I presented the carnations to him.

He was bald and hunchbacked. The hair at his temples was messily matted, like scrubby undergrowth. A pair of broad gold-rimmed spectacles concealed nearly half of his face. Only his blue-and-white striped suspender pants, which were worn loosely, vaguely suggested some American taste.

Liben paid a visit to a washroom. On returning, he stretched his arms around my head and pressed a forceful kiss on my face. I had not anticipated this, and my face burned. I was not accustomed to being kissed by a man in public, and I struggled to pull myself out of his arms. He laughingly stroked my face, and said, "Too old-fashioned you are! It is a new era, but you are just as conservative as you ever were. You're still like a country boy."

"I just can't help it," I replied. "I grew up on noodles and hominy gruel, not on MacDonald's hamburgers. I'm afraid I can hardly change."

"People can change," Liben said, citing himself as a good example. "Weren't we nearly the same when we were small? We even felt shy and timid when we made a visit to the county town. None the less, these days I travel all round America, so big and colorful, with my head held high and my chest thrust out, don't I?"

Liben did not have much luggage, just a gripsack. But the gripsack was so heavy that I suspected there must be a fat pig inside. As we headed for the car park, Liben walked in front of me. I carried his bag following behind. He was unconscious of how strange his walking posture was, with his legs wide apart, so that he moved forwards like a crab. As we were about to get in the taxi, I cast a stealthy look at his crotch. The sight made me gasp and sent a chill up my spine. Why? Because his crotch bulged, as if a bowl had been placed over his loins, beneath the clothes. What was wrong with Liben? He used to walk straight and square. What had happened to him? What had "colorful" America done to him to transform him like this? Far from walking with his head held high and his chest thrust out, he looked distinctly hunched.

There were homosexuals in America. I could not help wondering if Liben had gone gay. There were drug dealers in America as well, so I wondered if he was a drug smuggler. Anyway, all the news reporting I had been surrounded with convinced me America was a chaotic country. Immersed in such an environment, white cloth would be dyed black, and the sun would fade and become as pale as the moon. Then how can you expect Liben to keep his integrity?

What was concealed in his crotch? This question lingered in my mind. Could it be some drug? This was my first surmise. But on second thoughts, I rejected it as unlikely: if it was a drug, how could the customs officials have failed to discover it? Of course, not all customs officials were sharp-eyed and devoted to their work; there were always some who were slack on the job. While on duty, they yawned, with their eyes half shut, as if they had not woken up yet. Lawless guys liked nothing more than this kind of officials. I wondered how many malefactors had secretly laughed to themselves when dealing with these officials! Moreover, a wad of American dollars would turn a ferocious tiger into a docile cat. I had heard friends who often went through customs when going abroad sigh deeply that some customs officials' appetites were as bottomless as the Pacific Ocean! As these thoughts swarmed into my mind, I could not help thinking to myself: was Liben a fish that had got through the net at the customs?

The taxi started to move, but Liben and I became silent. He turned his head, looking out of the window with wide-open eyes, as if wishing to sweep everything, on both sides of the highway, up into them. We only talked to each other occasionally. Our sporadic exchanges sounded like unexpected gun reports. The air in the taxi felt as cold as in a refrigerator storage cabinet, and my thoughts became crazily active. For some reason, Fourth Aunt's story surfaced in my mind.

When Fourth Aunt was still alive, she had walked in a way a bit like Liben's. She too walked with her legs far apart; her crotch "swelled" high as if an unfurled minuscule umbrella were inside. Every time she moved her feet, she needed to make some effort, and her face twisted with pain.

Fourth Aunt — while she was still young and not yet my Fourth Aunt — used to be a military prostitute. As such she followed the army wherever it went, at the exclusive service of captains, battalion commanders and the like. As a result, she had enjoyed various delicious foods. Her most frequent saying was "Is there anything that I've never seen? Is there any delicacy that I've never tasted?" After the liberation in 1949, she was repatriated to the village. Naturally, she had a feeling of loss. The unbearable thing was that even though she was like a cup of delicious wine, no one came to drink it; even though she was like a fresh flower, no one cared to pluck it. She watched helplessly as time passed by, and no man came by to marry her. If anyone had a mind to marry her, upon learning about her past experience he just shook his head and ran away as fast as his legs could carry him.

Having not been able to afford a bride price, Fourth Uncle remained single well into his forties. A match was proposed by a go-between, who advised my would-be Fourth Aunt to give up on the dowry. Not long after the marriage, they had a daughter whom they named Luobo[2]. When Luobo was ten years old, Fourth Uncle passed away. Almost as soon as he died, Fourth Aunt set about finding a live-in son-in-law. Eventually, after much ado, a man named Song Tongguo entered into Fourth Aunt's home.

At that time, Song Tongguo was twenty-five, fifteen years older than Luobo. Not being a local, Song Tongguo spoke with a strange accent. When he meant to say "have some food," he came out with "have some fuck." Being apprenticed as a blacksmith in the county town, Song Tongguo was a strongly built man; his muscles looked as solid as iron. Fourth Aunt took a liking to him immediately. Before long, she started to regard Song Tongguo as a son rather than an in-law. Since Song Tongguo came home only at weekends, the whole family celebrated weekends as though they were festivals: they would cook pork, fry cakes and make dumplings. Fourth Aunt's face overflowed with broad smiles. Issuing from her house, she would go wherever there were most people. In public she chattered on and on, praised Song Tongguo incessantly, and referred to him as "my son."

"When I can't sleep at night, I move my hand along my son's legs," Fourth Aunt would say. "The tendons in my son's legs feel very hard." She made hand gestures while speaking, with her intoxicated emotion fully present in her face.

Her account revealed to people that Fourth Aunt and Song Tongguo shared the same *kang* at night. This knowledge made many people titter, with their hands covering their mouths.

"Besides feeling your son's legs, what other places of his body have you touched?" Fugui asked coldly.

Fourth Aunt did not seem to care about people's peculiar looks or expressions. She replied, "What other places of his body have I touched?

Well, he's my son. I can feel wherever I want. What has it to do with you?"

Third Aunt patted Fourth Aunt, urging her to go home, with the implied message: Stop your talk! Aren't you ashamed of yourself?

But Fourth Aunt completely ignored Third Aunt's good-willed hints. Actually, she pitied Third Aunt from the bottom of her heart, because Third Aunt had only had one man in her entire life; and what was worse, the man did not keep her company for long — Third Aunt's husband died when the couple's firstborn son Dalin was only six years old. What an unimaginative and silly woman Third Aunt was! She'd rather live as a widow than find a new husband. In Fourth Aunt's view, woman was soil, while man was rain and fertilizer. If soil was not watered or fertilized, in the long run, the soil would harden.

With a glare at Third Aunt, Fourth Aunt went on all the more emphatically, "The tendons in my son's legs felt so hard, as hard as rebar."

"You got the man for your daughter as *her* future husband, or for yourself?" Fugui asked with a long drawl. "You've been fucked by so many cocks. Weren't those enough for you? Don't overdo it. Beware of contracting syphilis," Fugui warned her.

Fourth Aunt had not seized what Fugui was implying until this moment. She rushed to Fugui, threatening to tear his mouth.

Quickly Fugui turned his head aside. Nevertheless, Fourth Aunt's long nails left two bloody traces on Fugui's ears.

Third Aunt had once said Fugui's saliva had poison. Fear a devil, and the devil exists. Unfortunately, what Fugui had said came true. Fourth Aunt ended up getting syphilis, and it turned out to be a serious condition. Her crotch festered day by day; dripping pus drenched all the pants she wore. Before long, people noticed that Fourth Aunt's "down there" began to expand rapidly, from the size of a small tea-cup to that of a huge bowl. As she walked, her legs extended far apart, and she moved in a twisting manner. One month before Fourth Aunt's death, thirteen-year-old Luobo and twenty-eight-year-old Song Tongguo began to sleep under one quilt. That marked their marriage. What, after all, was a marriage certificate? Wasn't it merely a sheet of paper? It did not matter whether they had been granted that paper or not!

Liben nudged me and asked what the place was we were passing by.

Looking out of the window, I said it was the Economic Development Zone of Yuebei City.

"The buildings are so tall!" he exclaimed. "When I left, this was a large stretch of wheat fields."

"You are right," I replied. "Yuebei too has developed rapidly in these years."

Liben remained silent for a moment.

Then he asked me if I felt he was a bit strange.

I confessed he did seem strange. Inadvertently, I cast another glance at his "down there." Noticing my glance, he took the plunge and told me there was a urine bag hung between his legs.

What he said baffled me even more. I asked, "Why was that stuff hung there?"

Apparently, my question touched on an emotional sore-point. Tears rolled down from his eyes. Taking off his spectacles, he wiped his eye sockets with a napkin. Letting loose a long sigh, he said, "What a shame to come back in this condition!"

"What on earth has happened?" I asked. He explained he had come down with kidney stones in America and had to be operated on, but an absent-minded black surgeon had failed to do the simple operation successfully. As a result, the control system to his urethral canal was out of action; that was why a urine bag must be hung inside his crotch.

Like snow water dropping down from house eaves, his urine was dripping drop by drop into the bag, completely beyond his control. The bag had to be emptied every two hours. Whenever he felt his crotch bellied out, he knew the bag was almost full and it was time for him to rush to a toilet and empty it. The most agonizing time was during his sleep time, because he had to get up to dump the urine from time to time. Consequently, an otherwise good sleep was often annoyingly disrupted.

"Can you still have sex?" I asked.

Liben glared at me and asked back, "What do you think?"

"Without sex, can your wife, my sister-in-law, put up with it?" I asked further.

"Your sister-in-law became another man's sex toy a long time ago." As he said this, his face twitched.

4

A call from Dalin set Mazi Village boiling. Liben had come back with a large amount of US dollars! All the villagers would receive their share, ten dollars each! People got busy informing one another, beaming with delight. They hated the fact that they couldn't see Liben sooner, and hated more than anything else that they couldn't get hold of those splendid dollars at once. Pies do rain from the sky! They had heard of US dollars, but never seen any. People said it was more valuable than RMB, at a rate of 1:10. Great, marvelous! Marvelous, great!

Of course, the happiest were Liben's sister and his brother-in-law. Liben had had two elder sisters. One died mysteriously six days after she got married. The other, Lifang, married someone from the neighboring village. She persuaded her husband Beiqiang to move the whole family back to Mazi Village, seeing that no one attended to the property left by their deceased parents.

As a matter of fact, the inheritance was just a dull adobe house in which there was nothing but an earthen *kang* and an old horizontal cabinet. Situated at the west end of the village, the house had a few mud rooms in bad condition, with a collapsing back wall which, standing unsteadily like a drunkard, was propped up by a log to prevent it from tumbling down. The family seldom socialized with their fellow villagers, so naturally few people came to visit them. A flock of sparrows, however, had built an enormous nest under the eaves, unconcerned by the family's poverty. Liben's brother-in-law was a muffled pot of few words, a kleptomaniac with sticky fingers. One midnight he was digging up Shuanniu's paper mulberry tree when he was caught red handed by the owner, who was lying in ambush. Shuanniu ordered him to kneel down, so he knelt down. Shuanniu ordered him to slap his own face, so he slapped his own face. After much humiliation, he was subjected to a good cudgeling. Thwack! Thwack! A bulb-like bulge rose instantly at the back of his head. Later he was sent to hospital and diagnosed with a brain concussion. Back from the hospital, he became more reticent than ever, and like a frost-bitten straw, he bent his back and lowered his head as he walked.

From then on, Beiqiang was unhesitatingly and automatically deemed the prime suspect for every theft in the village. When a family in the east end of the village lost a bundle of firewood, or one in the west end lost a door screen drying in the sun, curses would rise from that quarter, advance inexorably, and finally linger outside the gate of this family.

Come curse him. Curse him as hard as you can, and jump high as you please to curse him. Beiqiang has gone to the fields, so he won't be able to hear, so you may direct all your curses at him. And even if he is home, he will pretend he is not able to hear, so come and direct all your curses at him. Benumbed and accustomed, and as long as you do not break into his home to launch personal attacks, Beiqiang won't blush a bit. What else can be done? Anyway, his parents in the grave have been violated by vicious comments who knows how many times.

The news that Liben had just come back to the village put an end to the neglect of the Beiqiang family, whose visitors multiplied overnight. To the consternation of all, Liu Qi, the township head, like the king of hell, drove his own Santana to the gate of Beiqiang's house, overtaking that of Shuanhu the village head. Tall and fat with a bulging belly, Township Head Liu looked like a pregnant woman carrying a nine-month baby. It was astonishing to see his two dashes of eyebrows, black and bristling, and his two round eyeballs, protruding like two glass beads. Above his lips was a thick moustache which was trimmed into a tidy row of bushes. A former butcher, Liu Qi had been a big shot in his trade. It was said all the pigs knew him, and those who didn't had heard of his cruelty. A glance at him would make them run mad for their lives; if a man wanted to intimidate his pigs, he only need shout out Liu Qi's name. Very effective for sure! Some pigs, complacent as they were, lost heart the moment they heard the two syllables — Liu Qi. One day, he went to see a distant relative who had become a county leader, with a wad of bank notes tucked into his waist on the left and a butcher's knife at his right side. It turned out that this relative of his was very helpful and succeeded in getting him onto the criminal police team. A criminal policeman by nature, Liu Qi soon displayed his talent in interrogating prisoners. Just a glance at his savage face would terrify many a prisoner into wetting his pants. If you refused to confess crimes according to his instructions, he would be doing you a favor if he just gave you a few kicks or punches, tear your ears, or strike your teeth out of your mouth. More often than not he would strip you of your clothes and thrust a burning steel bar into your anus, a method he had actually carried out only once. In most cases, before that steel bar was thrust into their anuses, prisoners — by now as feeble as a thin streak of mud —

would start crying for mommy and daddy. They would confess to whatever they were told in a spirit of total obedience. A story Liu Qi used to boast to his friends was that a certain prinsoner, horrified by the red-hot steel bar, called him "grandpa."

"Did you fuck your mother last night?" Liu Qi asked.

"Yes, I did." The prisoner replied.

"How many times?"

"As many as you please, sir."

"I say you fucked her ten thousand times." Liu Qi roared.

"Yes, I fucked her ten thousand times."

Later Liu Qi learned that the man who admitted he had fucked his mother had in fact lost his mother when he was three years old. This part of the story pleased Liu Qi very much, and the thought of it made him laugh. He laughed again and again. As evidence of his rise to glory, Liu Qi often showed off with this story. However, there did exist some fools who, not knowing to turn back, would run smack bang into the wall. They refused to yield to Liu Qi's tricks. Refused? Very well, perhaps they had not yet suffered enough of the torture. Having killed pigs for years, Liu Qi had come to the conclusion that all animals in this world were afraid of death! Even pigs were, let alone human beings. Therefore, he thrust that red-hot steel bar into the anus of that fool named Jinbing. Once out of the hospital's emergency room, Jinbing proved to be disabled, and he disappeared soon after. The county government transferred a compensatory sum to a special account, in the hope of pacifying him, but he was nowhere to be found. Liu Qi also sent his men out, but fruitlessly. Liu Qi looked for Jinbing to warn him that, if Jinbing dared tattle, not only would Jinbing and his family die, but his sisters, brothers, his mother-in-law, father-in-law, and his brother-in-law's whole family — all would be wiped off from the face of the earth! In spite of this, the fact that one letter of accusation after another was commented by the central government and returned to the province and municipality, showed that Jinbing was still alive, and was jumping up and down like a flea! However, although you knew that he was still in existence, you could never locate where he was. He was like a wisp of pungent odor which had caused you to fall sick or feel like sneezing, but you could neither see it nor catch it. Liu Qi seldom had headaches, but this time he had a headache about Jinbing. He never frowned at anybody, but this time he frowned at a man who had gone into exile in order to hide from him.

In the end Liu Qi was dismissed from the police team, on account of his audacity. If not for his brothers he would almost certainly have resumed his old trade of butchering pigs. Liu Qi had many good brothers. How could they bear to see their Brother Liu come down so far in the world? Xu Yuanyuan, Liu Qi's best brother, was the boss of the Beigou Coal Mine. He had been convicted because of an assault, and it was Liu Qi who had him fished out of the prison. Later, when Xu Yuanyuan competed for the operating rights to the Beigou Coal Mine, Liu Qi stood by his side and drove the original operator away with machetes and clubs. A plum is customarily given in return for a peach, so how could Xu simply look away when Liu Qi was in danger? Xu Yuanyuan and Zhang Shutian, the county secretary of the Party Committee, were brothers — actually, better than brothers. He told others that he had even sacrificed his favorite lover Lin Nan in order to win Brother Zhang's favor. He said he had given Brother Zhang a clear order, demanding that Brother Liu be appointed to a senior position, or at least a township headship. As expected, Liu Qi became the head of Gaotai Township. One word could sum up Gaotai people's feeling toward their township head. Scared! Anyone who saw Township Head Liu, like a mouse seeing a cat, would duck away from afar. When Liu Qi came to Mazi Village, he stayed exclusively at the village head Shuanhu's home. Knowing that Township Head Liu was fond of the bottle, Shuanhu cut the locust trees on a whole slope, sold them and brought back several boxes of Maotai and Wu Liang Ye, for Liu Qi's particular use. Shuanhu's principle was: drink yourself under the table! If you did not drink well, he would regard that a lack of respect for him. As a result, each time when Township Head Liu left Shuanhu's house, he was seen tottering along, soaked right through like a jelly-fish.

Today, however, just because Liben was coming home, Township Head Liu's car went right by Shuanhu's house and stopped at the gate of the Beiqiang family house. This was a puzzle that Shuanhu could not figure out. But Township Head Liu had arrived, so he must go to meet him. Anyway, bitter as he felt, he had to hurriedly walk toward Beiqiang's home.

5

When I picked Liben up at the airport, I felt sorry for him; he looked so desolate and forlorn, all alone with his luggage bag. Far from there being a throng of enthusiastic people to welcome him, there was no-one there but me. The flowers were presented to him specifically at his own request. It was true he had acquired an American green card, and if he'd take one more step he would have become an American citizen. But apart from the green card, what had America given him? A urine bag! A urine bag that he had to hang between his legs! Having broken up with his wife, he only had his own shadow to keep him company. What a lonely and wretched existence!

To my great surprise, a mouse from the United States instantly began to be viewed in China as a mighty tiger. Once Liben had settled down in a five-star hotel, the flow of visitors was steady and endless. He was so busy receiving these visitors that Dalin was kept waiting in the lounge for five long hours before finally getting a glimpse of Liben's face.

Prior to heading for the hotel, Dalin had visualized in his mind's eye the happy scene of imminent reunion. Now that his dear cousin had suddenly returned after a long absence, Dalin thought, it would undoubtedly be the extended family's top priority to have a get-together. However, to his surprise Dalin found Liben surrounded by crowds of strange people. Some offered to take him to a restaurant to have dinner together; some wanted to invite him to a ball room to sing and dance together; some proposed accompanying him to a massage parlour to enjoy a massage and get his feet washed. These invitations, along with all sorts of flattering remarks, flew around Liben, and gave him the feeling that he had been lifted off the ground, floating and drifting in the clouds.

Dalin did not manage to get close to Liben until Liben was about to leave the hotel, eagerly escorted by a considerable crowd.

Dalin, who had been waiting in the lounge, ran forth and greeted Liben. To identify himself, Dalin said he was Dalin from Mazi Village — news which left Liben dazed for a couple of seconds.

"Are you from the house of Third Uncle?" Liben asked.

"Yes, that's right," Dalin nodded.

Not until then did Liben shake hands with Dalin. He patted Dalin on the shoulder, and said, "Oh, I was wondering who you could be! I failed to recognize you. When I went abroad, you were still a primary school kid. You were only this tall then." He gestured to indicate Dalin's height. According to Liben's gesture, Dalin had been as short as a thermos flask.

To Dalin's amazement, those who were inviting Liben to dinner were leading officials in Kaiyang County. Most of these people were unknown to Dalin, but he recognized two of them: Zhang Shutian, the secretary of the county Party committee, and Liu Qi, the township head of Gaotai. He had seen the former on TV, in local news reports. Zhang Shutian was much smaller in real life than he had appeared on TV. As a matter of fact the Zhang Shutian in front of his eyes was no more than a wizened, middle-aged man. As for Liu Qi, he knew all about him. Years back, Mazi Village officials had come to villagers' houses to collect *tiliu* taxes, which were to be placed at the disposal of the township and village governments. Since the villagers felt that too much was being demanded, the majority of them refused to yield the money. Shuanhu made a report to Liu Qi about the matter. Spurred on by the report, Liu Qi commanded four policemen in the township police station to move to the village, with hand-cuffs at their belts and truncheons in their hands. The sight was so terrifying that not a dog in the village dared to bark, and the chickens made no sound. The cats moved stealthily and hid themselves quietly in corners. Most of the villagers were scared to the point of rupturing their gall-bladders. Who had not heard the story of Liu Qi? And now the policemen were at his side and at his service. Even an idiot knew that the blow of a truncheon was not as light as the fall of a chicken-feather.

Given the circumstances, those who could afford hastily handed over the stipulated sum, while others, who did not have the money, did their best to borrow some, so that they could pay too. For a while, people flocked to the village office in such numbers that the room got extremely packed.

Nevertheless, there were still a few people who did not pay the tax: some of them, perhaps, were on account of simple tardiness in carrying out orders; others on account of a skittish disposition and a determination to try their luck. Fugui was one of them. Fugui had believed his tricks would help him get through the crisis — his favorite phrase was "You can capitalize on ideas."

To pull off his trick, he lay on his *kang*, covered himself securely with a quilt, and feigned illness. To his great disappointment, this trick did not work with Liu Qi at all. Liu Qi and his men came up to his *kang*, shouting their commands and ordering him to rise.

"Aiyo. Ai-yo. A-i-y-o." Fugui groaned over and over again, each groan more drawn-out and more miserable-sounding than the last.

The veins of Liu Qi's forehead bulged out one after another as Fugui's moans rose to his ears. Lifting his foot, he kicked Fugui forcefully, and cursed angrily, "You good for nothing old bush! What are you crying for? How dare you behave like a big boss in front of us! Are you sick of living?"

Fugui was beaten half to death. For the next six months, Fugui had to walk with a stick, and then in a twisted fashion once he stopped using it. The villagers laughed at him. A remark made by Third Aunt clouded Fugui's face for days, but inspired Shuanhu and Shuanniu to jeering shouts. What Third Aunt said sounded highly philosophical: "He always lays snares to trap others. This time the snare failed to fulfill its purpose. Instead, it almost strangled the man who laid it."

To tell the truth, Shuanhu had avoided speaking with Third Aunt for a long time, because she had not given her vote to him in the village head election. In spite of the feud, though, when he heard Third Aunt's taunts against Fugui, Shuanhu let forth a hearty peel of laughter. He raised his thumb, saying "Third Granny pisses peculiarly high into the air. She's so peculiar that even the children she bore are not like other people. She's produced a bull-like son."

Shuanhu referred to Dalin as the "bull-like son." It seemed that Dalin and Shuanhu had been enemies even before they were born into this world. From Dalin's early years, as far back as he could remember, he had detested the way Shuanhu swaggered in public. After growing up, he competed with Shuanhu for the village head office. The contest ended with his crushing defeat. He suffered a beating from Shuanhu's brothers. In addition to this, weird things took place in his household, one after another, in close succession. All his pigs and chickens were found dead on a certain night, with not a single survivor; the dense trees growing in his old homestead were chopped down, with only a few left standing there in wretchedness; the crops in his fields were inexplicably harvested and taken away when they were not yet ripe. Dalin reported these cases to the police, but when they learned that he was the notorious Dalin, they nearly put him in hand-cuffs, because Shuanhu had portrayed him to them in advance as a crazy dog. No wonder the policemen's eyes were inflamed with anger when they saw Dalin — the crazy dog!

What could be expected of going against Shuanhu? Nothing but negative consequences! There would be no positive effects at all. Feeling that such a predicament was too difficult to endure, Third Aunt, without letting Dalin know about it, cosied up to Shuanhu's wife Huaihua[3]. From time to time, she either helped Huaihua do some needlework, or gave her some sugar bread as a gift. But when she saw that Huaihua remained lukewarm in the face of her gestures of goodwill, she resolved to give away the pair of silver ear-rings which she had worn on her wedding day. Upon receiving the silver ear-rings, Huaihua finally wore a happy smile on her face.

Huaihua instantly called Shuanhu to her side, showing him the ear-rings, so that he might decide whether they were made of genuine silver or not. Shuanhu lifted the ear-rings and dashed them onto the rock table that stood in the courtyard. The ear-rings tinkled drily and rolled away. Shuanhu picked them up and examined them closely, but did not find any cracks caused by the hard impact. He was thus convinced they were genuine silver.

Smiling all over his face, Shuanhu said, "Third Granny, I understand why you have kept coming over to my place. You tell your bull-like son and let him know that I am a generous-minded person — an exceptionally generous-minded person. If he can come over here, call me 'brother,' and apologize to me, all the grudges and feuding between us will be completely wiped out. We live in the same village. If we were to trace our family trees back to the tenth generation, our ancestors might turn out to be from the same family. So why do we scowl at one another?"

Third Aunt replied, as endearingly as she could, "You're right. You're absolutely right."

Third Aunt called Shuanhu "Number One *most able* person in the village" and "Number One *most reasonable* individual in the village," Which instantly established Shuanhu as everyone's darling. Third Aunt vowed that Dalin would certainly come over to apologize. "Sure he'll do that. Sure!"

But Dalin steadfastly refused to go and apologize. He believed he had not done anything wrong. Why should he apologize? He thought it was Shuanhu, not he, who should apologize.

Before long Dalin paid the price of his stubbornness.

The day Liu Qi led the policemen to Mazi Village to collect the taxes, Dalin was absent: he was doing a job out of the village. Third Aunt was anxious to pay the taxes, but she did not have the money. She pleaded with

Shuanhu for a postponement, and Shuanhu granted her one day — two at the very most.

Unexpectedly, Dalin returned home that very night. No sooner had he put his hands into a basin to wash them than the policemen broke in and took him away. He was imprisoned for more than twenty days. When he came out, the skin all over his body was severely ulcerated.

When Dalin gave me his account of seeing Liben go to dinner with Liu Qi and Liu Qi's men, his animus against Liben became audible. Although we had both agreed to go back to the village in Liben's company, after his meeting with Liben in the hotel, Dalin changed his mind. He would rather not go back in his company! Even if a ton of gold were to be his reward, his heart would not be moved, let alone by American dollars.

6

It was a beautiful day in early spring when Liben set out for Mazi Village. On both sides of the road wild grass was sprouting, and the tree tops were tinged with green. Liben looked out of the car window, with his eyes wide open for fear that he would miss any of the details. As the car drew near to Kaiyang County, I became aware that Liben was breathing rapidly. His whole body shaking, his face contracting, he appeared as if he had been suddenly stricken by a disease. I asked him what the matter was. He did not reply, but went on repeating his instructions to the driver to slow down. Slow down more!

Seeing a farmer and his wife weeding in a wheat field, Liben asked the driver to stop the car by the roadside and got out. He walked over to the couple, and after whispering a few words to them he took the hoe out of the wife's hands and weeded for a few minutes. Back in the car, he said with emotion, that a couple weeding shoulder to shoulder in the field indeed represented the flavor of his hometown. What an idyllic scene! This was the hometown of his dreams — oxen dragging ploughs, donkeys pushing mills, men growing crops, women weaving cloth; the light cast by the oil lamps, the bellows keeping the kitchen stove alive, the superstitious old women burning incense and worshipping the Buddha, the blind old men telling fortunes with the aid of their fingers. Yet none of these scenes could be found in the United States, where everything was done by machines, and people all enjoy themselves. Therefore, people in the United States were lazy and their lives were meaningless.

As he spoke, Liben caught sight of a middle-aged woman who, bearing a pole, with a bucket on either end, over her shoulder, was struggling up a hill by a zigzag path not far from the road. At her side two little kids were staggering forward; each carried the end of a pole from which a third bucket was suspended. The middle-aged woman wiggling her body, the little kids leaning forward, it seemed that they might roll down the slope at any moment. At the sight of this, Liben's face dissolved into tears.

"I never expected that our hometown folks would be as poor as ever, that they would still be living a dog's life," he sighed, wiping the tears from his face.

I disapproved of Liben's blowing hot and cold; I wondered why a few days in the United States had so changed his personality. A typical nervous temperament! One moment he felt nostalgia for such backwardness, the next he was in agony over it.

I could not tell whether Liben had sensed my doubt or not. At any rate, he asked me whether he was being ridiculous or contradicting himself.

"A little bit," I said. "Anyway, it's hard for others to guess what you expect of your hometown — to have changed or to remain unchanged."

Liben said he didn't know either. As far as his feelings were concerned, he wished his hometown could remain as it had been forever, so that after ten or twenty years he could still recognize it whenever he came back; but as far as his reason was concerned, he sincerely wished that great changes might have taken place, because only in this way could its people rid themselves of poverty and lead a more happy and peaceful life. With respect to this, he was perpetually at war with himself. He felt as though he were his own enemy, and, like a small boat drifting on the sea, he knew not where to drop the anchor.

I said that all men were self-contradictory, and that I was no different from him. Although I had stayed in China, I had the same feelings as he did for our hometown. "Everybody wants their hometown changed, but in that case, will it still be your hometown?"

Liben told me that he came back aiming to change our hometown in a positive way, i.e. he had invited an investor from Guangzhou and they planned to build a factory in Mazi Village. In a few days the investor would come to Kaiyang to investigate and survey.

Suddenly it all made sense. No wonder that the leading county and township officials had been in such frequent contact with Liben! They had been attracted by this project which he was about to introduce.

I asked what the project was. Liben said the details had not yet been elaborated; however, the investor was a friend whom he had made in the United States, and who had done so well since his return that he had accumulated several large-sized state enterprises on the strength of very little money. He said because of those billions in assets, his friend had become arrogant, and would hardly, if not for his sake, have agreed to allocate such a large sum of money to such a poor and remote place.

I flattered Liben, saying that he was a really capable man; I laid it on pretty thick. But I advised him to think hard about the potential problems rather than acting impulsively; I warned him that the local officials were very difficult to deal with and that he should be extra careful.

Liben said, "Don't worry. Be assured that the local officials are eager to achieve something and will not stand in the way. Who wouldn't be happy if the project succeeds and they get promoted?"

Instead of going directly to the village, the car headed for the township government complex, which, covering a vast lot, looked more like a billionaire's manor. It was made up of splendid office buildings, well-distributed pavilions and towers, and a patterned gravel path winding away in the direction of more secluded quarters. By the side of a little lake sat an old man with a wolf dog on a leash. One glance at the animal would fix it in your memory forever, because one of its eyes glared while the other was a black hole, as if an ink cap had been inserted there. The old man was dozing off and the dog was keeping watch like a tiger. The screech of the brakes startled the man, and the dog, jumping and barking, dragged at him as it tried to pounce upon us. He shouted at it but could not calm it down even when he used dirty words. He said, "Knife Victim, how dare you go mad like this! Township Head Liu will fix you right once he comes back!" Dogs do understand human speech. No sooner did the dog hear the mention of "Township Head Liu" than it capitulated, barking and jumping no more. Its ears dropped down, and its one good eye revealed a timid look. The old man approached the car and asked what he could do for us. We replied that we wanted to see Township Head Liu. He said Township Head Liu had gone to the Beigou Coal Mine after receiving a telephone call from Boss Xu early that morning but he didn't know what had happened there. I asked the old man what his job was in the township government. He replied that he was a security guard in charge of the safety of the place.

"A security guard should be a young man who is quick in action and strong enough to fight against gangsters. What's more, a young man is not easily wounded!" Liben observed.

Displeased with what Liben said, the old man replied in a tone that suggested smoldering gunpowder, "Why, do you look down on me for my old age? Let me tell you, things get lost here or get stolen there, but never has the township government complex lost a single strand of thread since I and my dog have been here on watch. Thieves are no fools. Once they find out that I am here as a security guard, I bet they would not dare come even if they had five gallbladders."

A young man in his thirties approached while we were talking. He was tall and erect, wearing an old black suit. On seeing him, the old man said, "Township Head Zhao, Township Head Liu is out, I am afraid you've got to receive these people. I don't know where they come from. A bunch of disrespectful fools who have been talking down to me! By the way, if you want to treat them to lunch, just let them have some snacks in the canteen outside. Don't exceed the thirty *yuan* standard."

The young man repeatedly nodded his assent.

After the old man and his dog were gone, the young man asked where we had come from. I gave my name, and introduced Liben to him. The young man became extremely amicable, even a bit excited, saying that Liben and I were celebrities who had grown up in and been produced by Gaotai Township, that he had never expected two such big shots might stand face to face with him, and that he could be so blind as not to have recognized us. Then the young man took out his business cards and presented one to each of us. He told us that his name was Zhao Xiaohui, vice head of Gaotai Township. While thus speaking, he grabbed at our clothes and invited us to his office to have some tea. He said he would treat us to Kaiyang's most famous local snack *wowo noodles* in a few minutes.

We declined his kind invitation, saying that we were not here on business, but were casual visitors on our way to Mazi Village. However, as we got into the car, Zhao Xiaohui squeezed in. After the car was started, Liben asked Zhao Xiaohui, "Who is that old man? He has a strange manner, and speaks as if he were an old Master." Zhao sighed. Before he went on, he urged us not to disclose what he was going to say: the old man was Liu Qi's father, who was actually the second most powerful figure, not in name, but in reality, of Gaotai Township. When Liu Qi was away, he became the boss. Even the township secretary of the Party committee had to report to him. This secretary, finding his condition unbearable, had lain in the hospital for a year and a half, on the pretext of illness, and it seemed that by now he had no intention of leaving hospital again. Zhang Shutian, the county secretary of the Party committee, had talked to the township secretary of the Party committee several times, all to no avail. The latter had pleaded with Zhang Shutian to have him transferred to another township, as a second in command if necessary. But Liu Qi learned about it before any action could be taken, at a time when Zhang Shutian was sincerely considering the matter. Liu Qi told Zhang Shutian that he wanted no one but the present secretary, and insisted that the present secretary wasn't going anywhere. Zhang Shutian, even though he was a superior official as the county secretary of the Party committee, was afraid of Liu Qi. Liu Qi's purpose was that as long as the present secretary stayed where he was, he could conveniently fix him whenever he wanted to, with his objective being to provoke him to death, or at least make the prospect of death attractive to him. Of course, the most hoped-for thing would be for the secretary to fall victim to cancer, or partial paralysis, or something like that. Liu Qi's father was back-seat driving and swaggering around in the place, and people couldn't but nod and bow to him. If you attracted his ire, he only need grumble a few words to his son and you would be doomed, given Liu Qi's explosive temper. You would be lucky if Liu Qi limited himself to making you kneel down before him. More often than not, he would pour a pot of shit or urine down your throat. Liu Qi's father did nothing but idle around, but he had two salaries, one for himself, and the other for the dog.

Hearing this, I felt my hair stand on end, and I believed that Liben was also experiencing a lot of emotional turbulence because he kept asking "Are these things true? Are these things possible? Why don't people stand up and expose Liu Qi?"

Zhao Xiaohui repeatedly reminded us that we should keep this conversation to ourselves. After a long sigh, he said he hated having to stay here any longer, and that several times he had been on the point of resigning, so as to go south to find a job there, no matter how humble the job might be.

"A beggar is happier than a man trapped in this damned place," Zhao Xiaohui added.

7

Outside the courtyard gate of his sister's house, Liben quickly found himself surrounded by villagers. Everyone wanted to see how he looked now he was back from America. They all yielded to the impulse to reach out and touch him. To get a good look at him, some villagers stood on tiptoe, some forced apart the shoulders of those in front of them so that they could peer through, and some children even climbed the tall paulownia tree to get a glimpse.

Those closest to Liben went so far as to take advantage of their proximity: some stroked his face, some tugged his coat tails, some thrust their hands into his pockets and took out napkins and pens, which they scrutinized with interest.

Naturally the villagers talked with one another about him, until their low whispers merged into a drone. They generally agreed that Liben had aged a lot; he had left the village as a youngster who looked as tender as egg yolk, but had returned a beaten man with a beard and a bald head. *How come his forehead is covered with so many wrinkles? Didn't the American environment agree with him? Was it too windy and stormy there? Was it because American food wasn't tasty? Was the work in America too hard?*

Liben was escorted into Beiqiang's courtyard, while the multitude of people remained locked outside the gate. Because Liben had given him a carton of Marlboro cigarettes, Shuanhu appointed himself guardian of public order. He shouted out commands, stopped people in their tracks with outstretched arms, laid about him with a wooden club to pound whoever got within reach. He did all these things with the firm intention of stopping the flood of people from rushing into Beiqiang's courtyard. The clay wall was already on the verge of collapse, how could it withstand the crowd's pushing and shoving? Shuanhu ordered that people form a queue, and that each household delegate one member to stand in line. Those families with no delegate in the queue deserved to lose any benefit. Habitually slow to attend village meetings, they were now sluggish to show up to receive the gift of American cash. They had no one to blame but themselves.

Before long the villagers formed a long queue. Like a Japanese army officer in a war movie, Shuanhu stalked back and forth along the queue, roaring at the top of his voice and waving a wooden staff. Nothing escaped his sharp eyes — if any family had two or three persons in the queue attempting to get more than their fair share of money, he would pull out the offenders; if anyone got out of line, he would beat the offender with his staff. In full public view, Baolai was removed from the queue. But Baolai was not removed because his family had had more than one delegate in the queue, or he had made the queue crooked; he was removed on account of a toothache. His right cheek swelled, and to relieve the pain, he would poke a matchstick into the gaps between his teeth from time to time, leaving disgusting saliva dripping down from the corners of his mouth. A single glimpse of this made Shuanhu flare up with anger.

It did not take long for the crowd to form a neat line, but the gate was decidedly slow to open. Inside the house, Liben and Lifang were hugging and weeping bitterly. Five bundles of American dollars were piled on the *kang*, each bundle containing ten thousand dollars. Squatting on the verge of the *kang*, wetting his fingers with his saliva, Beiqiang counted the dollars out over and over again. Having counted several times, and having calculated with the help of his fingers, he finally worked out the total amount. He opened up the lid of a trunk, and carefully put in one bundle after another, his hands shaking incessantly. Then he closed the trunk and locked it with a huge iron padlock.

Having locked the trunk, Beiqiang said to Liben and Lifang, "Please stop crying. Don't cry any more. The bitter life is past, the sweet life has begun. What's the point of crying?" But far from stopping their tears, his words made them weep more bitterly, particularly Lifang, who cried so hard that she collapsed on the floor. Liben was completely at a loss as to what to do with his sister. He did nothing but gaze at her, his eyes full of tears.

Lifang cried and recounted the family's miserable existence in the past. She started with the story of how their parents were bitten by a dog, as they led them — still children at the time — to beg for food and money. She related how on a Chinese New Year's Day the family had nothing but wild vegetables to eat. She mentioned the old home-made clothes and patched socks Liben wore when he went to college. She gave an account of how their father's leg was broken by a slab of stone when he was working on an irrigation project to earn bread for the family. She blamed their ill-fated parents for not having lived long enough to see their son's return from America.

"Just look, father and mother," she cried. "Look, father and mother. Do you see how rich your son is? If you were living, you would be able to have anything you desire. If you desired to eat delicious food, you could afford it. If you desired to drink spicy drink, you could afford it. If you desired to wear expensive clothes, money would be no problem. You could cough as many times as you felt the need to. You could spit wherever you want. You'd look radiant without having to make up your face. Why did the God of Death claim your lives so early? What a shame! Why does the God of Death not show more discernment? Why does he claim the lives of good people but let the wicked people live on?"

It was not until Shuanhu came in that Liben and Lifang stopped weeping. Shuanhu told Liben that an orderly queue had already formed and that people were running out of patience.

"Let's get on with it, then," Liben said.

"It's better to distribute the money by family unit," Shuanhu suggested. "That's much easier than distributing per capita. A reasonable amount for each family would be fifty dollars."

"Alright. Just as you say," Liben agreed.

Shuanhu went out the gate and guarded it. He kept the door open just a crack, and let people squeeze in one after another to receive the family's share. After getting money, people squeezed out of the crack one after another. In spite of the fact that these people had to bend over and sidle through the crack twice as they entered and exited, they could not conceal their happiness as they came out the gate. Their faces wreathed in beaming smiles, and keeping firm hold of one or several bills, they waved the banknotes in the air. A few people showed their bills to those still waiting their turn in the queue, letting them see how the American bank notes looked. "Look," they said. "It has a picture of a foreign old man on it. He is not good-looking. He has a wrinkled face and some matted hair."

The villagers had found out the exchange rate: one American dollar could be converted into ten Chinese *yuan*. This meant the money given by Liben could buy a calf, or three piglets, or over twenty packs of fertilizer. Not bad. Not bad. Generations came and went, but who in this village had ever been given a single dime for free?

Once they had their cash gift, some hurried back home to hide it in a safe place, some preferred to remain on the ground outside Beiqiang's gate to chat.

When the dollars had been distributed, Liben came out the gate. Instantly he was surrounded by the crowd. Seeing that his eyes had turned red, they all asked him, "What's wrong? Anything wrong with you?"

"Nothing wrong. Everything's fine," Liben replied, keeping his agony to himself.

Lifang came out of the gate, carrying a basket, with tears in her eyes. What surprised the people was that apart from a thick stack of joss paper, some incense, several packs of milk candy and some boxes of cake, there was in the basket a stack of American dollars of considerable thickness. It now dawned on them that the sister and brother were heading for the graves of their parents. But they could not help asking, "Why are you taking so many dollars?"

"To burn them in front of my parents' graves," Lifang replied. "For one thing, we want to let our parents know their son has come home. For another thing, we want to assure them they'll no longer suffer from poverty in the nether world. Now they have these dollars, they can use the money as travel fare to go to America to visit their son when they miss him."

Lifang sobbed again, which made the other people's eyes redden, too.

"Don't be upset. Don't be sad." The villagers comforted Lifang. They said that Liben had now become the No.1 rich fellow among the many generations of people in the history of the village, and that if her parents knew this, they would laugh in their graves.

All the villagers protested at Lifang's burning the dollars. Their voices merged into a bout of babble.

American dollars are expensive, so it's a shameful waste to burn them. And, who knows what currency is used in the nether world? If American dollars are neither used nor exchanged in the nether world, doesn't that mean this thick stack of dollars will become useless paper? It's not a good thing to have too much money, either in this world or in the nether world. Too much money means disaster. People with too much money are likely to be followed and mugged by robbers. If they are unlucky, they may even get killed.

They spoke in an undertone which was louder than words: Liben should divide the dollars among them, the villagers, as well. By so doing Liben would increase his virtue, and this would bring blessings upon his offspring.

Even had they ten thousand objections to burning the dollars, Lifang and Liben's determination to do so could not be shaken a little bit. Looking at the figures of Liben and Lifang as the two vanished into the distance, some of the villagers sighed, some stuck their tongues out, some made faces, and some laughed or cried.

Several women cried. One woman wondered whiningly why her parents had been so foolish as not to have ensured she got through school. If she had completed her schooling, the chances were she might have ended up going to America, too. She had heard people say there was so much money in America that wherever you went you would stumble over it; as long as you were willing to bend down, you could pick up as much money as you wanted. If she could pick up a gunny-sackful of dollars, wouldn't the villagers be as dumbfounded at her, as at Liben?

Another woman asked with a groan why she had not raised a successful child like Liben. To give birth to a big brood of rats was no better than giving birth to one tiger; to work hard for an entire life was no better than sending to America one child who did well in studies. What a hard life Liben had led in school! He studied under the light of a kerosene lamp, which smoked his face and made its skin look like a carelessly drawn grayish map. The water he spat onto the floor was as black as ink.

But most people were not admiring. They consoled themselves laughing: *Does money mean everything? Can't you see that rich people also cry? If you compare yourself with your betters, you'll feel like dying; if a mule-rider compares his condition to a horse-rider's, he's tempted to get rid of his mule. The key thing is to feel good about yourself. As long as you feel satisfied with your life, even the coarsest meals make you happy.*

Having money does not mean possessing happiness! This conclusion met with unanimous approval. Fugui once more cited that big official he knew, as an example. As for how big the official's title was, Fugui had no idea, but he knew he was somebody big, and the main evidence for his conviction was the man's imposingly majestic look. His head looked like a super-size pumpkin, his neck was thick and short, his face resembled fermented dough, and his pot-belly was particularly impressive — as huge as the mausoleum of an emperor. How could a person with such a protruding belly not be a big official? Only those who were big officials could afford to eat the rich food necessary to develop such an enormous belly, which had, as a result, become their emblem. This official had as much money as he desired. He lighted his cigarettes with bills of one hundred *yuan*. Nevertheless, he did not lead a happy life — even a country farmer was happier than him. Why? Because both of his two children had let him down: His daughter was put into prison for defrauding men by marriage, while his son was a cripple, who walked unsteadily.

It was as a result of the big official's daughter cheating Fugui's nephew that Fugui had come into contact with him. This led Fugui to the insight that money does not necessarily mean happiness. The reason why he retold the story about the big official on this particular occasion was to reveal the truth that rich people do not have brilliant offspring. What is money? Money is an intoxicant that poisons whoever drinks it.

What Fugui said gave rise to a hubbub of conversation. Instantly, people were won over to Fugui. Everyone seemed to become hostile toward money.

Of course, there were bound to be some people who did not go along with Fugui. Dapao, whose name meant "cannon," was one such. Dapao had just returned from working on the farm and happened to be passing by, carrying a hoe on his shoulder. Behind him came Qiuli, who wore a tattered shoe on one foot, and nothing on the other. There were several coagulated scars on the bare foot.

In response to Fugui's long homily on money, Dapao commented, "Don't talk balls. You'll never convince me you don't love money. The other day when a corn dealer was here, you kicked up a huge fuss over a ten-cent difference in the total amount. You ended up stealing the weights of his weighing scales. If you don't love money, get your money from your house and give it to me. I'm in dire need of it."

People did not like Fugui, because his words were more flimsy than cloud. People did not like Dapao either, because he invariably talked back no matter what you said — when you said east, he would say west; when you said that a black bird was black, he would obstinately claim it was white. However, today a considerable number of people, one after another, took Dapao's side and argued against Fugui. "Dapao's right. Who in the world has a grudge against money? For the sake of ten cents, you stole the corn dealer's weights. How do you have the brass neck to claim you don't love money? It's enough to make a pig laugh."

Feeling embarrassed, Fugui turned round and kicked Qiuli, and asked her if she loved money. With her tongue stiff, her saliva dripping from the corners of her mouth, her voice hardly distinguishable, Qiuli uttered her most frequently repeated words, "No worry about food, no worry about clothes; all worry is money never enough."

Returning from his trip to his parents' graves, Liben noticed the unkempt-looking mad woman who had joined the crowd. He was both frightened and astounded because she kept drawing close to him. Pulling Third Aunt's coat tail, he asked in a low voice, "Who is she?"

"You don't know her? She is Qiuli, Baolai's wife." Third Aunt answered.

"But what reduced her to this?" Liben asked again.

All the people glanced stealthily at Shuanhu, but none of them answered Liben. Aware of the implied criticism in people's glances, Shuanhu became furious. Addressing Baolai, who was now standing in the crowd, he shouted at the top of his voice, "Baolai, you tell, in the presence of the public, how you reduced your wife to this state. You torture her so that she has become a madwoman, but you shift the blame to my brother Shuanniu. Do you call yourself a man, you dickless wonder? You utterly shameless creature, you keep on making charges against Shuanniu. Do you think you're a heavy-weight challenger? Do you think your cock is hard enough to rupture concrete?"

The more Shuanhu spoke, the more furious he got. His face turned black and gray with indignation. He rushed to Baolai, and punched him in the face. Instantly, blood burst out of Baolai's nose. But Baolai neither fought back, nor argued. He simply squatted down, pressing his nose hard with his handkerchief.

It seemed Shuanhu's indignation had not been altogether vented; he delivered a hard kick to Baolai. Stupefied by the sight, Liben said over and over again, "How can such a thing happen?"

Zhao Xiaohui, the vice head of the township, who had come in our company, showed his extreme disapproval of Shuanhu's behavior. He held Shuanhu's waist with both his arms, and roared, "Don't bully simple people, okay? You are the village head, you are supposed to take care of them, and protect them! It's a disgrace that you act like this!"

Shuanhu angrily glared at Zhao Xiaohui. The look in his eyes seemed deadly, like the chilly, sharp blade of a knife. He struggled out of Zhao Xiaohui's grip, snapping, "Does this have anything to do with you? Who do you think you are? How dare you speak in defense of this unruly person?"

Shuanhu left in anger. Zhao Xiaohui was angered half to death. He turned his face aside, its expression as grave as ice.

Liben talked to Baolai in an effort to comfort him. Afterwards, he went over to Zhao Xiaohui to show his solidarity. He kept saying, "I'm to blame. I am to blame. I shouldn't have come back. If I had known that my return would lead to Baolai's suffering a beating and Township Head Zhao's getting a scolding, I wouldn't have come back."

"This has nothing to do with your return," I said to Liben. "With you back here, it's like this. Without you back here, it remains like this."

8

Mazi Village was unique in Kaiyang, because its topography was different from that of any other place. Only one of its four sides was connected to the outside world, while on the other three sides the earth fell away into valleys. If you made a map of the village, you would find that it was a highly isolated peninsula. People from other villages of the same township had a vivid metaphor for it — a dog's tongue, which, however, was considered a detestable insult by the Mazi villagers. They thought, even if it were a tongue, it should be that of a human being. The question whether it looked more like a dog's tongue or a human being's had thus become the focus of disputes between the Mazi villagers and outsiders. Anyhow, a tongue was a tongue in so far as it had the shape of a tongue, be it a dog's, a human being's, or any other kind of animal's.

In fact, the so-called tongue formed a sloping terrace. The terrace was not altogether regular in shape: narrow at one end, it fanned out at the other, with fertile land all around. It would take nearly half an hour for a middle-aged man walking at a leisurely pace to go from the north end to the south end, whereas walking from the east end to the west end could be accomplished in the time it took to smoke two pipes. The village was huddled at the north end of the terrace, right next to North Valley Village. The villagers always took pride in the fact that it boasted a couple of thousand-year-old trees, which were a proof of its long and rich history to successive generations. At the central clearance stood one such tree. It was an ancient locust tree, so big that several people, joining hands, could hardly embrace it. Its weathered bark was full of cracks, with the biggest one wide and deep enough for a cat to nap in unnoticed. Old and withered as it looked, green sprouts would shoot out in spring. It had been deified and given a nickname Old Mom by the local people. Every Qingming Festival, males in the village, young and old, would come to the tree, each with a shovel on his shoulder. They first kowtowed, then shoveled, in a symbolic fashion, new earth onto the roots. It was said that he who failed to do so would not be blessed in the coming year, so that his pigs would die if he raised pigs, his cows would die if he raised cows, and his family members, too, would be afflicted with all kinds of diseases. Folks from neighboring villages joined in the fun. They kowtowed, burned incense, and tied pieces of red cloth all over the branches. From a distance the whole tree seemed to be ablaze with red peppers.

Even Liu Qi, an outrage to gods and ghosts alike, knew to kowtow before Old Mom. This, undoubtedly, added to the magic power Old Mom exerted on the local people. Having returned to the township and learned from his father of Liben's coming home, Liu Qi followed our steps to the village. Guided by Shuanhu, he went to Old Mom and found Liben hugging her as if hugging a lover whom he hadn't seen for years, kissing her repeatedly until finally kneeling down before her. Liu Qi didn't intervene. He told Shuanhu to fetch a thick stack of joss paper from the village shop, and knelt down beside Liben. Such an act became the talk of the village although few people had actually seen it take place. People tended to shun him as if he were the plague. On hearing his car approaching, they would run away as quickly as possible. Quite a few went home, closed their doors and bolted them. They did not even dare make a sound as they coughed up their phlegm.

Walls have ears. The detail of Liu Qi's kneeling down had been embellished and talked about for a long time — of course this took place later. On the very day, after the two finished the ceremony, Liu Qi shook Liben's hand and didn't let go for a long time. He addressed Liben as "brother" again and again, and repeatedly apologized. He said he had not expected that Liben might take him by surprise, and such an important guest as Liben should have received the cold shoulder in his own hometown. He loudly rebuked Shuanhu in the presence of Liben and me, blaming him for dereliction of duty, since he hadn't organized the villagers to sweep roads and alleys, paint the broken walls, and drive pigs and cattle back into their pens. "Look! There is bull dung and chicken shit on the ground everywhere, bumps and potholes on roads everywhere, old clothes and shabby socks drying everywhere. What kind of impression does this make on someone just returning from abroad?"

It had been Liu Qi's plan to send a drum and gong team to the county town for the purpose of welcoming back Liben. Just as they did for the celebration of festivals, they could set up a gift desk at Liben's brother-in-law Beiqiang's home and call on the whole township to make contributions — 100 *yuan* per household. The village would have no claim on the gift money, all of which would be left in the charge of the township. However, this didn't mean that the township could embezzle the money. Most of it would be used to build a new house for Beiqiang — a three-storey one, with glazed tiles on the roof, ceramic chips on its outer walls, and the same interior decoration as a hotel. And the money left over would be used to invite opera singers. He had contacted the county opera troupe, so that its once famous actors and actresses could be summoned to sing their heads off. Once shining stars of the stage, they were now down and out like dog shit, some mending shoes or selling fruit on the street, some babysitting as nannies, some singing at weddings and funerals in a makeshift troupe. Only Shi Yafen, who had played the role of Liang Qiuyan[4], had been wise enough to throw herself into an official's arms and was appointed the director of the county foreign affairs office. For a woman, a pretty face was equivalent to a fortune. A man could have whatever he wanted so long as he possessed, and was willing to take advantage of, power; and likewise, a woman could have whatever she wanted so long as she had a pretty face and at the same time did not mind opening her legs. Having said this, Liu Qi laughed. So did Shuanhu, whose face had been stern up until then, and also Zhao Xiaohui, who had been standing silently nearby. Liu Qi said Liben would definitely meet Shi Yafen sooner or later, and warned him that whereas it was all right for him to flirt with her, he should not go so far as to make a pass at her. Still, given his power in Kaiyang, it would be as easy as to take a piss for him to get Liben any number of girlies cuter than Shi Yafen. All Liben would need was a rock-hard cock.

Liu Qi instructed Zhao Xiaohui to take good care of Liben, offering his excuses that he would be heading to the county town to prepare some "night snacks" for Liben. What were those night snacks? They were not the sandwiches which Liben had eaten in the United States, nor the coffee he had drunk there. They were, as a matter of fact, beautiful women. He wanted Secretary Zhang of the county Party committee and Commissioner Tang of the county public security bureau to join with Liben in enjoying the night snacks. The best way to turn a leader into one's servant was to treat him to "night snacks." After three or four times, he who had been a hungry wolf to the masses, would be converted into a tame hare before you.

Liben was terrified when he heard Liu Qi was arranging "night snacks" for him. His face turned puce; a vague plea appeared in his eyes. He raised both hands in sign of surrender, "I can't. I can't do that!" Liu Qi patted him, "Don't be pretentious! There are no CPC branches in the United States, so I am wondering what you learnt there to change you into such a block of wood? What don't they get up to there? Although I haven't been to the United States, I've watched lots of their videos. What a mess! They even fuck animals."

Liben whispered a few words in Liu Qi's ear, making his face light up with a bizarre smile which lent it an extremely hideous expression. He looked at Liben's crotch, head slanting to one side, and as if still unconvinced, reached out his hand and suddenly gave it a flick.

"So it's true then!" Liu Qi yelled out.

In alarm, all eyes were diverted to Liben's crotch. He didn't know what to do, his face as red as an inflated crimson balloon. His first instinct was to try to cover that area, a response he regretted the very next moment, for it only stimulated more curiosity. Shuanhu yielded to temptation and gave Liben's crotch a quick flick, too.

"A soft lump! Where is your little brother? How did you come to lose your little brother, Liben? What have you been up to in the United States all these years? How can you lose your little brother? I heard people can sell anything in the United States. You didn't sell your stuff, did you?" Shuanhu burst into a guffaw.

This time Liben was really offended. With a face as black as thunder, he turned his back on the people present, and departed. He headed for Three-River Bay, alone. After signaling Shuanhu and Zhao Xiaohui to follow him, Liu Qi jumped into his Santana 2000. The car roared away, leaving a black column of smoke behind it.

9

I slightly regretted having come back in Liben's company. My regret derived not just from the fact that Liben was the center of people's attention, which was something I used to enjoy: I wilted like an obscure leaf beside a brilliant flower whenever I was with him. Actually, I did not much mind being a leaf, the problem was that I was in a bad mood — whatever I saw and heard seemed to stain the word "hometown" and cover it with a thin layer of dust. As Liben got sullen, I shared his sullenness. But we differed in that Liben retained his child-like simplicity of mind. Although he would from time to time pout in anger, all it took was somebody to give him candy and he would cheer up quickly. But I was more intractable. When I was sullen, a complete candy factory could not cheer me up, let alone one piece of candy.

Liben toured every corner of the village, feeling every inch of the weather-beaten walls with his hands, howling forth a peal of wails at his parents' graves. During the trip, the site which intoxicated him most was Three-River Bay, which lay east of the village. The bay formed a deep cavity where three narrow gullies met to create a broad basin. The three creeks winding out of the three gullies converged here, forming a lovely, clean and clear stream. Viewed from afar it looked like a silvery snake as it flowed past the middle of the basin. The most amazing thing about the bay was its six fountains gushing crystal clean water. One of them shot out from a crevice above a gigantic protruding rock. It was the only fountain given a name by the villagers: Breast Nipple. Below Breast Nipple, a huge pit had been cut by the spraying waters which backed up to form a beautiful pond, so clean that its bottom could be seen clearly. In winter time, the villagers' cisterns would be waterless, so they had to go the one and a half kilometers to Three-River Bay to fetch water. Some people simply placed their buckets straight below the nipple to catch water, but before the bucket was full, they would get wet all over due to the splashing water. Other villagers simply hung their bucket onto the hook at one end of their shoulder-pole and sank it into the pond. When the bucket was full, they would forcefully press down the pole at the near end to make the bucketful of water at the far end swing over to their feet. One can say with justice that for the villagers, the nipple was the source of all drinking water.

As small kids, the place we frequented most was Three-River Bay —

sometimes for the purpose of collecting green fodder for livestock, sometimes for the sake of fetching water, sometimes just for fun. When in primary school, I often went there with Liben in secret to swim during the noon break when we were supposed to be having a nap at home. I was a poor swimmer. On two occasions I sank down and found it hard to surface. The pond was irregular in shape and depth. Since the water was so clean and transparent, the pond looked fairly shallow. You would not realize the measureless depth of that water until you jumped into it. At the critical moment of the first accident, I was pulled up by Liben; at the critical moment of the second one, I was rescued by the old secretary of the village Party branch.

The old secretary of the village Party branch was Baolai's father, of whose real name I was then ignorant, though I knew all the villagers called him Gangan[5]. He was so nicknamed because he was tall, thin, and shaky. The major impression he left in my mind was that of stubbornness: he often argued heatedly with people for the sake of a word or a sentence. One debate he had had with Shuanhu made the villagers laugh so hard that their sides ached horribly.

"The earth moves around the sun," Shuanhu said.

"Of course not. The sun moves around the earth," Gangan said.

"The earth moves around the sun. Both Copernicus and Bruno announced it," Shuanhu insisted.

"I don't care who announced it," Gangan retorted. "What I know is that the sun moves around the earth."

The villagers split into two groups. Most of them supported Shuanhu's view, the rest backed Gangan's. Neither side could convince the other. Consequently, they went to the school to seek the teacher's judgment. The teacher, who was teaching in the classroom, was called out to decide the case. Without hesitation the teacher took the side of Shuanhu. Returning to the classroom, the teacher mocked Gangan and called him a stiff-necked, stubborn, stick-in-the-mud — a Number One stiff-necked, stubborn, stick-in-the-mud! Using Gangan as a counter example, the teacher gave us a warning lecture with an expression of disdain on his face: "Look! This is the result of not studying hard in school."

Gangan saved my life. But he claimed a high price for that. No sooner had he pulled me out of the water than he began striking my face. He struck Liben's too. My nose was comparatively sturdy and it withstood the blows.

But poor Liben's nose was not as sturdy; blood spurted out copiously. Later, Gangan reported on us to our teacher and parents, accusing us of polluting the village drinking water. If the parents' harsh scolding was bearable, the teacher, who took the village head's words at face value, punished us ruthlessly. He ordered us to compose a written self-criticism, in addition to doing three days' classroom cleaning.

The most extraordinary sight around the Three-River Bay was the wild ducks all over the place: some squatted on rocks, some perched on trees, and some swaggered leisurely on the banks with the air of a newly promoted government official. They had no fear of humans — they even seemed to have an impulse to make fun of visitors. They often played tricks on people who went there to fetch water. They might peck you on your foot, or fly up and knock off your straw hat. The funniest incident occurred during one of Fugui's visits. He had in his pocket a piece of steamed bread, which lured three or four wild ducks to peck it, and he had a hard time fighting with them before he won the battle by a narrow victory. One duck had the habit of showing off — not just its beautiful feathers, but also its voice. The usual scenario was that, whenever a visitor drew near, it would quack, which would rouse all the other ducks to join in its quack. Then the quacks, in turn, would induce frogs to croak at the top of their voices. The quacking of ducks and croaking of frogs would complement one another and form a melodious symphony in the valley.

After such a long time in the city, the visit to Three-River Bay made me realize how charming it was! The murmuring river with pleasant ripples, the swaying willow branches, the wild flowers that spread everywhere, and the lush bushes that grew freely. Fish swam leisurely, bees and butterflies danced around flowers. Occasionally one or more rabbits dashed into the woods nearby.

Liben had a romantic mind. Sitting on a rock, he hated to leave. He not only recollected his wonderful memories of the past but also fantasized about the future of the place. All of a sudden, a bold idea erupted from his mind: turn Three-River Bay into a tourist site, so that city residents, sickened by urban pollution, could come here to enjoy the nice view and breathe the fresh air.

"Forget about it!" I said to him. "Wherever city residents go, they bring pollutants along. If you wish to see Three-River Bay as it is now during your next trip back from America, you'd better not do anything to it. The bay is like a beautiful girl. She will maintain her purity and simplicity if she is kept isolated and in solitude. Once she goes into the world, it's hard to tell how she will be transformed. The beauty of a prostitute and that of a maiden are not the same thing."

Liben agreed with me. Still, he argued, "If a good thing cannot become a productive power, its value fails to be fully realized. Our fellow villagers have a treasure at hand, but they live as meagerly as beggars. A solution must be worked out, to change this condition!"

Simultaneously Liben and I remembered how stubborn Gangan had been. During the period when Gangan served as Secretary of the village Party branch, an educated urban youth took the manager of the county's water plant to the bay. After touring around and tasting the water, the manager went straight to get Gangan for a talk about a joint venture. At that time, drinking kvass was just coming into vogue. The manager was planning to make use of Three-River Bay water to open a kvass-production factory. They did find Gangan; however, before they could describe their plan in full, they were driven out of the village. Holding a spade in his hands, Gangan ran after them, making a shoveling gesture while hooting at them. In this way, the manger of the water plant was scared away, and the youth escaped from the village too. Gangan would not allow anyone to get their hands on Three-River Bay. "We'd do better to sell our underwear for money than ruin the good *fengshui*[6] left to us by our forefathers."

Naturally, Gangan was condemned by the whole village, who called him "Dead Stubborn Ghost." What a rare chance it was that a factory leader, like a god of wealth, was willing to cooperate with the village and give money to villagers! But the dead stubborn ghost failed to recognize the god and drove the god away. The villagers said Gangan was to blame for their poverty.

It so happened that when the time came to campaign in the election for the post of village head, Shuanhu made full use of the water factory event. Both on private occasions and at public meetings, he launched vicious attacks against Gangan, hurling various names at him, such as "Old Stubborn Chap," "Stupid Jerk," "Disgusting Dog Shit." Stricken by these invectives, Gangan fell ill and became paralyzed. He was confined to bed and was never able to get up again. When he looked bad enough and started to vomit blood, his son Baolai carted him to a hospital for examination. The test result took Baolai aback. Baolai wept loudly, "Oh dear! My dad has got liver cancer. It's already at the advanced stage."

When Qiuli became insane, many villagers claimed that it was definitely the result of Gangan's past sin in connection with the water factory event. "A retribution!" they judged.

"The more I think about the matter, the more I feel Gangan was a good man," I said to Liben.

Liben agreed with me. "In the United States," he said, "Gangan would be called an environmentalist. He would be respected by the general public." With this he took pity on Baolai and said he would try his best to help him, as he deserved justice.

"Justice?" I laughed. "To hell with that! What justice can you get in a world like this? You are like every scholarly type. You won't survive unless you turn a blind eye to evils, call white black, and live like a dim-wit. Don't attempt to do what is beyond your ability! The world is an immense and exceedingly hard rock. We people are no more than vulnerable eggs. If an egg knocks itself against the rock, it's simply asking to be destroyed."

What I said somewhat irritated Liben. "If everyone is chicken-hearted, even afraid of being hit by a falling leaf, how can our society make progress?"

I responded to his question with a laugh. I had intended to debate with him; however, seeing how naïve he was, I swallowed my words. Instead, I suggested visiting Gangan's grave to show our respect. He happily accepted my suggestion.

10

Dalin and I were sitting in a private tea room of Li Tiantian's restaurant. Li Tiantian kept us company for a while, then instructed Dalin to take good care of me, and left. Dalin arranged for me to meet Xiaolin, his younger brother, hoping that I could help him find a job. Having completed his army service, Xiaolin went to the south, eager to find a suitable job, but found that it was by no means a place full of opportunities and strewed with gold and silver, as he had imagined. After many tries and failures, he called Dalin in a tearful voice to say that he wanted to come back. At this very moment, Xiaolin was already on the return train. He would get off in about half an hour and would arrive at the restaurant about an hour after that.

From what I had said, Dalin concluded that the chances of the project, which Liben intended for the village, were ten to one against it, and that it would most likely end in failure.

I asked him why, and told him that the county had listed it as a top priority, and that before I returned to the provincial capital the county had asked Liben to stay for a meeting to deal with the matter. Secretary Zhang had said while patting his chest to inspire confidence, "Anyone who attempts to block this project will be removed, without appeal, from his or her post!" In China, things suffer from negligence from above. Once the authorities start taking them seriously, they are bound to succeed.

Dalin smiled. He said of course it would be a good thing, and that he hoped that it might succeed, because his younger brother might find something worth doing there — no need to run around hunting for a job anymore. According to Dalin, if the factory prospered, he himself might pack his bag and make his way back, too.

"Dailin, you are too pragmatic," I said. "All you think of are your own interests."

A shadow of gloom passed over Dalin's face. He frowned and, considerably embarrassed, explained that he was a contradictory mixture, sometimes romantic, sometimes pragmatic. His reason for wishing to return to the village was the same reason which had motivated him to come to the city — to flee, before from Taoqi, now from Li Tiantian. Having issued several ultimatums, Li Tiantian had given him a deadline to divorce Taoqi and hold a wedding ceremony with her, Li Tiantian, soon after. She became increasingly forward, going so far as to call him "hubby" in the presence of his colleagues. She had promised that she would buy the most luxurious villa in Yuebei once Dalin married her, and that Dalin would not need to work. All he would have to do was live off her, enjoying a comfortable life in the villa. If he felt lonely, she could buy him a dog and a cat to be his friends. There was only one condition: Dalin would not be allowed to meet anyone, even members of his own sex.

"Isn't that great? To just enjoy life, without doing anything! How many people have it so good?" I asked with a laugh.

"Isn't that doing time in prison? Isn't that being under house arrest? Li Tiantian is an envious woman, and can easily fly into a fit of jealousy. It is exhausting to live with her." Dalin's mouth twitched.

With a sigh, he asked me what he should do.

His mobile phone rang before I had time to reply. He picked up his phone. "How come he is in the police station?" he shouted in a panicky voice, his face contracted, his muscles tight. I could barely hear the mumbles coming from the phone. All I heard was Dalin's "I'll come immediately" when the conversation drew to an end. Switching off the phone, Dalin stood up, as though he was to go at once. I asked him what had happened. Dalin said his younger brother had been arrested and sent to a police station. I asked him how that could have happened. Dalin said he didn't know the details, but a policeman told him that Xiaolin had had a physical altercation with urban management officers, giving one a bloody nose, so the police had detained him for interference with public function.

I advised Dalin, first of all, to calm down. I said fighting was not a serious matter; all the police station wanted was this! — I mimicked the counting of bank notes with my hand. Dalin understood what I meant. He took out his wallet, and after a brief look said that a trip to the police station would cost at least five thousand, but he had only a few hundred *yuan*. I took out mine and found there were just over a thousand inside. I gave him the thousand, and kept what was left over. Dalin took the money, his eyebrows still knitted tightly. He walked out of the tea room without a word, and came back a short while later, followed by Li Tiantian, who was blaming Xiaolin for being a stubborn bastard who would take a blow rather than a hint, a fool who would rather walk into a brick wall than turn aside in time. She said she would have let Xiaolin work in the restaurant, which was in need of a buyer, if he had been endowed with the slightest flexibility. But Xiaolin was way different from his older brother! He talked with the force of a cannon firing shells. "Who can bear such a thing? Character is destiny, and it sometimes does kill a person."

With this, she took out her phone and called a friend, of whom she had always been very proud, whose name was always on her lips. Every time I sat and talked to her, within five minutes she would divert the topic to this friend of hers. From her intermittent comments, I came to know a lot about this man, although I had never met him. His name was Ye Zhonghua, and he was a division chief of the municipal public security bureau. Everyone was in awe of his very powerful backing, for behind him stood two great mountains. One was his father, a retired vice chairman of the provincial committee of the CPPCC[7]; the other was his father-in-law, still vice governor of a certain southwestern province. Ye Zhonghua was a distant relative whom Li Tiantian had managed to catch up with after many twists and turns. She could call him "uncle" in line with his clan seniority, but Ye Zhonghua found the title rather awkward, and wanted her to regard him as a friend. To run a restaurant required a protector, otherwise various disturbances would cause it to close within a day. Ye Zhonghua was a protective shield in Li Tiantian's hand. Numerous departments, such as the department of taxation, the department of industrial and commercial administration, the department of city image maintenance, the department of environmental protection, the department of sub-district administration, etc., had intended to milk her for all she was worth, but the moment they heard she and Ye Zhonghua were relatives, or saw her take out her mobile phone to call him, they all retreated like a sinking tide.

However, there were moments when Ye Zhonghua displeased her. One day, he brought his younger sister with him when he came to dine at the restaurant. His sister was very ugly. How ugly? In Li Tiantian's words, a pig would be scared out of its senses and run away as fast as its legs could carry it if it saw her. Her mouth was twisted due to a stroke she had suffered, a front tooth stuck out of her lips, one cheek bulged like a ball while the other was sunken like a ditch. Her eyes were awry and of different sizes, one large as a ping pong ball, the other small as a soybean. She proved the truthfulness of the old folk saying: ugly persons love to make trouble. This spinster named

Ye Lihua fell in love with Dalin at first sight. Her goo-goo eyes never left Dalin during the meal, which gave Li Tiantian the disgusted feeling that she had eaten a fly. After the meal, she even asked for Dalin's business card, shook Dalin's hand and invited him to visit her at home. From then on, Dalin was bombarded by her telephone calls and messages in which she told him right out that she had taken a liking to him and that she hoped they might become the best best best best best…friends in the world. She had used twenty "bests" in succession, angering Li Tiantian almost to death. Li Tiantian had the habit of censoring Dalin's messages, and when she read the passionate words sent by Ye Lihua, she kicked up a tremendous fuss about them. Dalin quit his job, but Li Tiantian kept back his salary. He stayed in my home for a few days, during which period Li Tiantian, in desperation, was combing every corner of the city for him, almost burning out my telephone with her incessant calls. Only after she had made an apology did Dalin reluctantly come back to the restaurant with her. Once back, Dalin was kept under her strict control. She not only changed his phone number but prohibited him from answering phone calls from anyone but her. Whenever there were in-coming calls, she would be the first to listen, so as to identify the caller. If they were from Ye Lihua, her tone would become very harsh. She told Ye Lihua many times that Dalin had quit his job and had gone home to take care of his wife during her post-natal confinement. Her implied meaning was that Dalin had long since been a married man, and that Ye Lihua should not waste time on dreams, like a toad that wanted to swallow a swan! It was said that a woman would become stupid once she fell in love. Ye Lihua was a case in point. She continued as before to call the restaurant reception, and inquired about Dalin's new phone number as well as the name of his hometown village. One day, when she could stand it no longer, she went to the restaurant, but to no avail. As they had been previously warned to do, the staff all claimed to know nothing when questioned. Li Tiantian pushed Dalin into the storeroom, with the cabbages and white gourds.

Li Tiantian was not afraid of Ye Lihua, and was, on the contrary, full of self-confidence, because compared with Ye Lihua she was nothing less than a fairy. But she had scruples about Ye Lihua's family. If they did challenge her to a fight, it would be like arm-wrestling against Mike Tyson, and ten Li Tiantians put together would not be equal to the struggle. Wherever one turns a fearful eye, there one sees a ghost. As expected, Ye Zhonghua called her in person about his sister and Dalin. He said Ye Lihua had fallen in love with the young man working in her restaurant, and was having a fit at home because she could not find him. His sister had smashed several articles of furniture, and had gone on hunger–strike as well. Ye Zhonghua asked Li Tiantian to help find the young man, and to act as a go-between or match-maker for them if necessary. He was very pleased with the young man, having seen him on several occasions. Promises slipped glibly from Li Tiantian's mouth, but after she hung up she went into the manager's room, closed the door, and wept bitterly by herself.

11

By the time Dalin and I hurried to the police station next to the railway station, Ye Zhonghua had already called ahead. It was the head of the station who received us. He was warmly courteous, making tea for us and offering cigarettes. He gave us his business card, from which we learned that his name was Han Weiguo.

"How did you get to know Director Ye? What's your relationship to Director Ye?" He persistently asked these questions, eager for information. "Usually, if there's anything Director Ye wants us to do, he just has his subordinates call us. He has never bothered to call in person."

Sheriff Han described the sincere reverence, indeed the awe, which he felt for Director Ye. Apparently, he wished us to pass his homage to Director Ye. He said among all the division directors in the public security bureau there were few that he really revered. Most of them were promoted to their leading positions on account of their connections. They had neither talent in writing nor eloquence in speaking. But Director Ye was different. He had real ability. He didn't speak often, but when he did he could talk for four or five hours without a written draft. Listening to his speech was like enjoying a symphony. What a joy it was! His utterances, even insignificant words like 'this' and 'that', sounded authoritative, rhythmic and melodious. They couldn't have produced that effect without ample practice. In fine, Shriff Han's admiration for Director Ye was unparalleled.

Han Weiguo had his subordinates take Xiaolin inside. Xiaolin looked somewhat like Dalin with the same fine features and the same tall and handsome stature. But he differed in that his sword-shaped eyebrows were exceptionally black, and his hair stood up straight like a wire brush. In my memory, Xiaolin was still the naughty boy he had been when I last saw him, but here stood before me a young man with a light beard, and this quite took me aback. But what surprised me much more was that he had obviously undergone some severe physical abuses: two of his jacket buttons were gone; the front of his jacket was torn open; the exposed part of his chest seemed to have been hurt by some sharp tool, which had left two long bloody scars there; his trousers were torn into strips; his shoes were nowhere to be seen, leaving his feet bare and dirty.

Raising his eyelids, Xiaolin threw a glance at me and Dalin, then let his head droop, biting his lips with an air of defiance and disobedience.

As Dalin started forwards, stretching his hands out to support Xiaolin, Sheriff Han stopped him peremptorily, his amiable countenance giving way to a stern, tough look. He said to Xiaolin, "Do you know your wrong-doing was a violation of criminal law? In view that this is your first violation, we have exercised our discretion as policemen, and decided not to charge you. However, that doesn't mean you are guiltless. Do you understand?"

Not raising his head, Xiaolin remained silent, but his teeth bit his lips harder than before.

"You must confess your guilt now," Sheriff Han went on. "If you confess your guilt, we'll release you right away. But if you don't, we'll have to hand you over to a detention house."

Turning his head to Dalin and me, Sheriff Han continued, "You don't often see one as stiff-necked as this! He is as stubborn as a mule. Since coming into the police station, he has never once confessed his wrongdoing. He'd rather die than confess. In wartime, he would make a stalwart revolutionary hero. What a pity it's peace time now! If he chooses to behave like a mule in peace time, sorry, he is doomed to suffer. Nothing good can come of it."

Both Dalin and I urged Xiaolin to admit his wrongdoing. If that could win him his freedom, why not?

Xiaolin glared at me with furious hatred. His eyes emitted angry flames while he spoke in a low but firm voice, "Why should I admit a fault I never committed?"

Sheriff Han shouted at Xiaolin with an explosive voice, "You are a boiled duck whose body turned soft while the beak remained hard. You say you haven't committed a fault? Do you mean it is us, the police, who have committed a fault? You have the guts to challenge and contradict our national authorities? I'd like to see who gets the upper hand. I'll call Director Ye right away. I don't mind going to him in person to take his punishment. I don't mind being removed from my office, even. I have twisted numerous people as if they were dough in my hands for me to knead. Don't imagine I can't crack open your pig-head!"

Sheriff Han picked up the receiver of the phone on his table and was ready to call Ye Zhonghua. Dalin and I spontaneously lunged forward to grab the receiver from his hand. We explained and apologized in turn, saying that Xiaolin was still too green to know the real nature of society; that he was aiming at the moon with a sling-shot, but didn't know the weight of things or the size of the world. "You are a magnanimous person. Please don't bother with him. We confess his wrongdoing and apologize to you on his behalf."

"To me?" Sheriff Han glared at us with wide open eyes. "Are you implying this is something personal? You make it sound as if I held a personal grudge against him. It's no use to confess his wrongdoing to me. He must confess to the law."

"Yes, yes," both Dalin and I consented in unison. "He should confess to the law. You are enforcing the law. You are just. You are disciplining him. It's for his own good, so that he'll afterwards walk in the paths of righteousness. We are particularly and extremely grateful to you."

In the midst of the conversation, I winked at Dalin, who instantly opened one of Sheriff Han's bureau drawers while his attention was elsewhere and thrust an envelope containing three thousand *yuan* into it. Sheriff Han, though he had seen all this from the corner of his eye, maintained an air of innocence. But his facial expression underwent a change from "overcast" to "overcast with occasional sunshine." His voice had become much smoother too. You could even say he sounded somewhat kindhearted despite the fact that his words continued to be harsh as before. He said, "Is it too much to ask of a person guilty of a criminal offense that he should admit his wrongdoing?" He claimed that at first he had planned to put Xiaolin in prison and have him stay inside for three to five years; so now unless Xiaolin admitted his wrongdoing, he, even as the head of the police station, could actually do nothing to solve the problem.

We tried once again to persuade Xiaolin to confess that he had done wrong. We said, "If you feel embarrassed to make an oral confession, a written one on paper still counts." But when Dalin put a pen and some paper in front of him, Xiaolin's attitude remained the same. Dalin was so infuriated that he walloped Xiaolin. This did not work either; Xiaolin remained unyielding.

From afternoon till evening, three or four hours had passed. But there was no sign that Xiaolin's obstinate attitude had slackened a bit. Sheriff Han received a telephone call from someone who invited him to play cards. Taking a look at his watch, he began showing his impatience — he appeared to be in a hurry to leave. Consequently, he let Dalin write a confession on behalf of Xiaolin and sign Xiaolin's name on it. After Dalin pressed his fingerprint on the signature, Xiaolin was released from the station.

Dalin went to a store and bought a pair of shoes for Xiaolin. He took off his coat, and put it on Xiaolin. Seeing the wounds on Xiaolin's body, he could not help weeping.

"What happened?" I asked Xiaolin. "Whatever possessed you to fight with urban management officers?"

Puffing heavily, Xiaolin said angrily, "I detest their behavior. They do nothing but bully people. They are sons of bitches."

"Bully who?" I asked.

Xiaolin said after issuing from the exit of the railway station, he set about finding a telephone booth to call his brother Dalin. Before he managed to find one, though, he saw a group of urban management officers beating an old man who had stood his moveable cold drinks stall on the curb of a pavement. The officers kicked the stall over and surrounded the old man to give him a sound thrashing. Such a sight was more than he could bear, so he went to question them, "How could you beat him like that?" To his astonishment, this mere question led one of the men to punch him in the face. What shocked him more was that all the other officers fell upon him — there were six or seven in all. They beat him up under many watchful eyes. Among them, some punched him, others kicked him; and one odd guy thrust his hand into Xiaolin's crotch and took hold of that thing between his legs, with so much force that he almost pulled it off. Although Xiaolin had practised boxing in the army, which might have enabled him to overpower two or three people at a time, it was really too much for him to confront six or seven attackers. Moreover, these fellows were all reckless young creatures. Overcome by them, Xiaolin, lying on the ground, was abused and insulted at their will. After they had beaten him to their hearts' content, they grabbed his clothes and pushed him into their van so as to take him to the police station.

At first, Xiaolin had fancied the police would do him justice, thinking the police station should be a place for reason. But against all his expectations, the policemen gave him an additional beating without asking him a single question about what had happened. Sheriff Han, head of the station, was nothing but a bastard. He searched in Xiaolin's pockets and took away all of Xiaolin's money, which amounted to two hundred *yuan*. He was so nasty as to even take out the letter written by Xiaolin's girlfriend for a read, tore it into pieces, and dumped the pieces into a dustbin.

"Does it make any sense that the party in the wrong didn't apologize to the party in the right, but that the party in the right was forced to apologize to the party in the wrong?" Xiaolin burst out angrily, his look showing that he had been badly wronged.

"A wise man knows when to retreat," I said to Xiaolin. "Once you apologize, you'll get released. Can't you weigh the loss and gain?"

"Stubborn, you stubborn mule!" Dalin rebuked Xiaolin. "Is it so difficult to apologize? Would it have made your eyes drop out? Would it have severed your tongue?"

"Don't you see, to apologize would mean confessing to have done wrong?" Xiaolin replied. "I havn't done anything wrong, why should I say I am in the wrong? It is they who should apologize to me! It is they who should apologize. I don't think justice can't be found in this world."

"You are too naive," I replied. "Do you really think there is justice in this world?"

12

Xiaolin slept in his brother's room for a night and disappeared the next day. No one knew where he had gone. Dalin called everyone he knew, and looked in many internet bars, but found no trace of him. I consoled Dalin on the phone, "He's an adult, so leave him alone. He is free to go up into the sky or down underground as he chooses." But Dalin was still worried, fearing that his younger brother would make more trouble. Xiaolin was like a needle sticking in his heart. Its least movement would leave him feeling hurt for half a day. Whatever he found his hands doing, he did it in an absent-minded way. He had been restless all day long, which greatly annoyed Li Tiantian.

No news came until three months later, when Fugui and Third Aunt arrived at the provincial capital and located the restaurant where Dalin worked. On seeing him, Third Aunt burst into tears. With a shaking hand, she produced from her pocket a paper with a red stamp on it. Dalin was struck dumb for a long while, his legs wobbly, his face deadly white — it gave notification that a decision of reform-through-labor[8] had been passed, and it was phrased as follows: In consideration of the fact that Tian Xiaolin has violated the criminal law by interfering with civic administration and threatening public security officers, it is decided that he shall be subjected to one year of reform-through-labor, etc.

Third Aunt sat in the hall weeping. She wept so bitterly that her tears, like bubbles, oozed out drop by drop, and her snot, peeping out of her nostrils, was ready to run. She said she would die if Xiaolin were not bailed out! What meaning would her life have if her son were suffering in jail? Death would be better than such a prospect! And wasn't it Dalin's fault that his younger brother had been put into jail? If Dalin hadn't invited him to the provincial capital, would Xiaolin have been detained by the police?

Third Aunt's weeping attracted many onlookers. Those who were dining in their private rooms came out to the hall to see what was going on. Quite a few thought that the restaurant executive was bullying an old woman from the countryside; some began to criticize Dalin while others tried to appease Third Aunt. Seeing herself become the focus of so much attention, Third Aunt produced from her breast a certificate of merit to show them. The certificate had been sent home when Xiaolin was serving in the army. On it was clearly written that he had been awarded a Citation of Merit Second

Class for his outstanding exploits in fighting the floods and relieving the victims. As people passed the certificate around, Third Aunt went on to say that a model soldier with merit had been locked up in prison, how could that be?

Most people were perplexed and did not know what the certificate was good for, who had been in prison, and what the restaurant had to do with the certificate and the imprisonment. Just then Li Tiantian came back. She was getting out of her newly-purchased Toyota, when she heard a lot of noise coming out of her restaurant. She trotted into the hall, and seeing Third Aunt, sitting on a fountain step, wipe away her tears, she felt anger flare up inside her. Black clouds darkened her face. Her eyes were full of contempt and scorn. She questioned Dalin furiously, "What are you doing? Do you want to ruin my business? For what purpose? Where's your conscience? If you don't want to continue to work here, get out of here immediately!"

At first, Dalin did not pay much attention to what Li Tiantian was saying, but when he heard her shout "get out of here" his face went as red as an electric iron. He dragged Third Aunt up from the fountain step, and out of the restaurant. Fugui made no utterance, but merely followed Third Aunt like a shadow — he went wherever she went, stopped wherever she stopped, his face convulsed by her wailing rhythm.

After they left, Fugui remembered that when he arrived he had had with him a plastic bag in which were three steamed buns and a fortune-telling book. He turned to fetch it, but came back empty-handed. A waiter said the bag had been given to a garbage-collector. Fugui was unhappy, grumbling that the steamed buns were unimportant but that the book was of vital importance to him. He had planned to set up a fortune-teller's stall. Without the book, how could he fool people? As he had a weak memory, and the contents of the book had not yet been absorbed, didn't he risk losing face when the moment of truth arrived? He followed Third Aunt to the city, hoping that she would convince her son to give him, Fugui, a foothold. There was no need for Dalin to arrange his meals. All he wanted was a place to put up at night. A corner of Dalin's sleeping bed would be enough. It would be wrong of Dalin to reject him; on the contrary, Dalin should feel proud to share his bed with Fugui, who was no ordinary man. Yes, he had a strong conviction that he was extraordinary, and his intuition told him that he was going to make a lot of money, as he had once dreamt that he would — colorful bank notes were dancing before him like snowflakes. If he had a pot of rice, would he let Dalin starve? He was not a stingy man, and he was more than willing to part with a dipperful. He had calculated that Dalin's outlook was poor, especially when he succumbed to the influence of bad women. And look, all his calculations had been proved correct! At home Dalin had Taoqi, a glaring serpent, here he had this woman boss — a weird-looking tigress, so far as he was concerned, no matter how much Third Aunt praised her generosity to Dalin. Fugui told Dalin he could dispel his bad luck by sleeping in the same bed with him, and that for three years at least — maybe even for five — no demon or ghost would bewitch him again. Fugui was a threat to all demons and ghosts. Troublesome as they were, at the mention of his name, they would fall a-trembling! Among people he went unremarked, but he was very famous among ghosts. When they saw him, they knelt down before him, treated him to wine, and even bribed him with money. Well, if he did say so himself, he was an upright man, and those demons and ghosts who gave him money would be repaid with bloody curses, or with a good punching and kicking, instead of with his favor. There was no way he would let anyone soil his life-long good name! Of those wild ghosts, there was no one who had escaped being sorted and tamed by him.

Dalin led Third Aunt and Fugui to my work place without calling me in advance. Whenever he was confronted with problems, he was soon at the end of his tether. And he had realized that the best way for him to solve such problems was to turn them into mine. I was pondering whether or not to resign, having had a quarrel with Xue Yulu, the director of the editorial department. A woman with a mind as narrow as the mouth of a tiny wine glass, Xue Yulu was still in her early thirties, but was nonetheless an experienced player in officialdom. She and President Sun of the press house were like daughter and father, although no one actually took them to be such. In the press house, she was too hot for anyone to handle. An improper word, or an untoward joke, would trigger disasters. You would hardly have to wait till lunch time before an accidental utterance made in the morning had made its way into President Sun's ear. And when she snitched to President Sun, she never repeated what she'd heard verbatim, but would instead add oil and vinegar, transforming a slingshot into a missile with a three-thousand-mile range.

Bad luck served me right, fair and square, when it so happened that Xue

Yulu became my higher-up. She was like a queen, treated like an older sister by woman reporters and editors with sweet tongues and unctuous lips, some obviously older than she was. They honored her with small favors or gifts, buying her such things as fashionable luxurious shawls, sending her things like perfumes and bracelets, or entertaining her with tea or performances. If they attended a press conference, they would invariably demand a red envelope[9] for her as well. Luo Xiao, the only woman reporter with a backbone, was sick of Xue Yulu's style. She used to yell at Xue Yulu, and then had to live with the consequences. For three successive months she was not allowed to finish her tasks, and had to live with seeing herself "failed" on her appraisal form each month. Aware that this could go on no longer, she had a fierce quarrel with Xue Yulu and resigned. Luo Xiao, who was a capable young woman, then opened and ran a beauty salon. After she left, she still kept in touch with me, but seldom talked about the press house. She encouraged me to introduce customers to her; one would earn me a 200 RMB kickback, and two would earn me 500.

There were two male staff members in the social news office, me and a young man whose name was Xiang Wenhua, whom people called Xiao Xiang. A muddle-headed youth, Xiao Xiang appeared lethargic all day, as if he had never really managed to wake up. He kept out of sight in the office during daytime, and did not trudge in untill it was time to knock off in the afternoon. Once he came, he would spread out a newspaper from elsewhere and begin copying news from it. He need only change the place name, so that a Chengdu newspaper article "A Chengdu Rat Bites Pedestrian on Street" became "A Yuebei Rat Bites Pedestrian on Street," and a Hefei newspaper article "Hefei Illegal Ads Become a Plague" became "Yuebei Illegal Ads Become a Plague." But Xiao Xiang was never criticized. He even won the Prize of Reporter of the Year on an annual basis. He was favored like this not because he had been sucking up to Xue Yulu. Rather, it was because he had a solicitous father who had become one of the provincial leaders. It was through Xiao Xiang's father that Xue Yulu had been able to find a job in the provincial government for her younger brother Xue Lihan, an ex-armyman. Xue Lihan often came for Xiao Xiang, with girls in heavy make-up in tow. It was said he had been running a nightclub downtown, and the girls were from there.

The departure of Luo Xiao was a great loss for me. I had been the second to last outsider in the department, and now I was the last. A man in his forties, bossed about by a young lady, already has reason to feel embarrassed. In this case, the lady — far from behaving like a normal young woman — had the fiery temper of a spinster. It seemed that she could only prove she was my superior by finding fault with me. The news which I got by much effort, was dismissed by her with scarcely a glance, but with a big cross and for no reason. I had tried to improve my relationship with her, but this led her to take me for a lecher with designs on her. As a result, she despised me more than ever. Shortly before Dalin, Third Aunt and Fugui showed up, I had finished a long news report on the incidence of suicide among migrant workers and handed it in, only to receive a "death sentence" from her on the pretext of my undermining of social stability. Unable to bear any more, I had a quarrel with her, which I knew she would soon report to President Sun. As far as President Sun knew, I was just someone with a bad record of long standing. When he saw me, he lowered his eyebrows and tossed his head to one side, so that the two or three strands of hair flapping on his gourd-like bald head appeared particularly laughable.

As I sat listlessly at my desk, thinking about whether or not to write my resignation letter, a woman reporter came in from outside to tell me that someone wanted to see me, but was stopped at the gate by the security guard. I walked out and saw Dalin, his mother and Fugui. At the sight of me, Dalin could not contain himself, and said he was determined to quit his job at Li Tiantian's restaurant, because she had stormed at his mother, making him lose face in public. He would never go back. Never, never, ever!

13

After our divorce, my ex-wife moved out, taking with her our only child and all the money in the family. I was left alone in the house as sole occupier. Generally speaking, to live alone is lonely. But my case was the exact opposite: I often had visitors, who made my house a mess. As a matter of fact, my apartment became a free hotel for them. Whoever came to the city from my home village felt free, it seemed, to come over to stay at my house. They simply informed me of their arrival. There were times, then, when my house was packed with people; I was forced to spread cushions on the floor as makeshift beds in order to accommodate those for whom I had not enough real beds, so that I was no longer master under my own roof.

As always, Dalin, Third Aunt and Fugui stayed in my house. Third Aunt was observed admiring the natural gas cooker in my kitchen. "What a magical thing! At the turn of the knob, fire comes out. You don't need to feed dry firewood into the stove, and there is no smoke choking you to tears or making you cough."

Third Aunt declared that people in the city looked much cleaner and whiter because they were not exposed to suffocating smoke or scorching fire while cooking their meals, as the country people were.

Fugui was obviously fond of using my toilet. He visited it at very short intervals, but he never flushed it after he had done his business. The most unbearable thing about his behavior, however, was that he was a chain smoker. He never smoked without coughing, and never coughed without spitting. Instead of going to the toilet to spit, he spat straight onto the floor no matter where he happened to be. Then, in accordance with his habit, he would wipe his sputum with the soles of his shoes, spreading disgusting dirt over a wide area.

The thought of Xiaolin would make Third Aunt burst into a flood of tears. She rebuked Dalin, demanding that he get Xiaolin out of the detention house. She said she would be ashamed to go on living if Dalin did not manage to get Xiaolin out. Every time when Third Aunt began her ceaseless nagging, Dalin went out; he would walk around the courtyard for a while and come back claiming that he had found someone who would help and that this person was looking for yet more persons who could help out. I knew he was lying, but Third Aunt had absolute belief in his words, so that when she listened to them the light of hope for Xiaolin's release would appear in her face. When her moods turned a little upbeat, she would chat with Fugui about matters in the village. They both let out sighs for Qiuli's gloomy future. They both cursed Shuanniu and his brother Shuanhu, and wished a horrible death on them. They both commended Liben for his great success, for his transformation from a snotty little boy to the richest person in the townships far and near.

"How few people in our township have seen a county magistrate or a county secretary of the Party committee! But Liben is one of the few. Not only has he seen both, he has shaken hands with them."

"More than that! He has dined and taken baths along with them. He even knows the very size of that thing between their legs!"

In their eyes, Liben was the equal of the sun, which casts its light wherever it appears. Even his brother-in-law Beiqiang changed because of him. Beiqiang used to walk with his head drooping down, as if he were looking for a lost needle. But he never walked now without humming merrily, as though his heart were enjoying a comfortable massage. The world was changing. A dog could become a wolf. A pig standing on its hind legs could pass for a powerful leopard.

Judging from what they said later, I knew that the villagers had learned about the failure of Liben's medical surgery in America, and that they had also learned Liben's big money had come as compensation for the medical accident. The villagers' attitudes toward Liben were complex, a mixture of scorn and envy. They were scornful that Liben's fortune had resulted from the damage to his body, the more so because the part ruined was not an unimportant one, but the core of cores. Its damage meant he would be heirless and his family line would come to an end. What was the use of money to such a person? But they were envious that Liben had got money at all. Piles of ready money, as valuable as gold! Who in the world would turn his nose up at money? Who would not smile broadly at the prospect of it? The thought of the hardship involved in the making of money made Fugui and Third Aunt sigh with emotion: the flesh people consume by hard work isn't worth its weight in pig meat!

They recalled a Niu family at the north end of the village. The wife came down with kidney problems. Because they had no money for medical treatment, all four people in the family swallowed pesticide and fell dead together. After their death, no-one offered to bury them. Shuanhu saw to it by forcing some villagers to bury them. After that, Shuanhu repeatedly claimed that the Nius' property was not enough to cover the burial expenditures he had paid, and that he had had to pay the bill with his own money. Did he pay with his own money? He might fool a ghost, but no living man would believe him! Many villagers were there to help. Anyone could work out what the cost must be. To bury them was no more difficult than to bury some dead rats. It was only a matter of digging a pit, dumping the dead bodies into it, and then filling it back in. Given the Niu family were all dead, Shuanhu took possession of their house and property. He thought he was absolutely justified in taking their things.

No one cared that he took them. Anyway, the Nius did not have anything valuable. The house was clay-walled. On rainy days, raindrops dripped through the roof. There were few possessions: the pots were without lids, but simply covered with straw hats; the grain in the barn had been almost totally sold to buy medicines; the only thing that might be regarded as a modern convenience was a black and white TV set — but even there, though, the images would shake and twist as if the figures on TV were having cramps.

The Niu family were not the only poverty-stricken people. There were many others like them. That was why the young men and young girls left one after another to find jobs in the cities. But of course, work in the cities was far from easy money. Numerous people had paid a heavy price. Some lost their lives in coal mines. Some got their legs hurt in construction work. Some were compelled to steal or rob when they couldn't collect their overdue salaries. These people were therefore pursued by public security bureaus, and some of them were still in prison. The worst thing was that a girl named Jidan[10] ended up becoming a sex worker in the city. Her parents were to blame for not having given her a decent name. Weren't chicken eggs from chickens? After being hatched by a hen, chickens came out of the eggs in their turn. By becoming a real chicken[11], Jidan had lived up to the name given to her by her father Shuanhu.

A man values his face as a tree does its bark. A barkless tree cannot live long. A shameless person's life is not worth living. If a person does not have a sense of shame, even God can do nothing for them. The most contemptible thing was that instead of feeling ashamed, Jidan felt proud. She behaved arrogantly whenever she saw people from our village. Her face never blushed with shame. Of course, even if her face were to go red, no-one would know, because she hid her face under a thick layer of cosmetics. She used so much makeup that she looked like a ghost. Always her eye sockets were ghostly black and her lips blood-red. Her clothing barely covered her back or breasts. As she walked, she deliberately swayed her protruding buttocks from side to side, with a strong smell of lust emanating from all over her body.

Because of Jidan, the Shuanhu family became the first in the village to build a two-storied house. Also because of Jidan, Shuanhu's wife Huaihua began to lilt tunefully in her pride. Huaihua was plain as a piece of mud, but she curled up her tongue to make her voice crooked, and she even uttered some exotic words from time to time. Her exotic utterances sounded so funny that the villagers put their hands over their mouths and laughed uncontrollably. Huaihua loved showing off. What she showed off about changed rapidly and regularly. She bragged about the magnetic therapy pillow Jidan had bought for her. She said the pillow made her feel like she was afloat while sleeping, as if she were flying in an airplane. But she had never taken a plane in her whole life! A moment later she grumbled that Jidan had bought her too many shrimps; for the sake of finishing the shrimps she had had to stuff her stomach. Her stomach was so fully stuffed that it took her days to digest them all.

Many villagers were so enthusiastic about coming up and paying court to Liben, greeting him, flattering him, saying sweet words to him. Didn't they hope to get some money off him? Many people invited him to dinner. To prepare the dinner, they traveled a long way to the market and bought pork and lots of vegetables. Baolai killed his fat hen to treat Liben. This made Shuanhu and his brother Shuanniu very unhappy with Liben. Sending someone to spy on him, Shuanhu discovered that the hospitality Baolai showed him had another purpose — that of requesting Liben to pass his appellant materials against Shuanhu on to Beijing, and to submit them into the hands of a high-ranking official. What a pleasant illusion Baolai was indulging! Didn't he know who the boss of Mazi Village was? The sun could light the entire universe, but a single cloud could cast its shadow over a small area of water and land. Hadn't Shuanhu himself said he was a cloud? No matter how tremendously able Liben was, even to the point of being able to fuck heaven, wasn't he still connected to Mazi Village, either in this life or the next? Was he 'able' enough to escape from Mazi Village forever?

According to Fugui and Third Aunt's account, no sooner had Liben come out of Baolai's gate than he was dragged into Shuanhu's house. Shuanhu gravely warned Liben, and asked him to make out who was the sheep and who was the wolf. He told Liben to consider the consequences beforehand: to sue Shuanniu would mean suing Shuanhu himself, and to sue Shuanhu would mean suing Gaotai Township Head Liu Qi, and to sue Gaotai Township Head Liu Qi would mean suing Kaiyang County Secretary of the Party committee Zhang Shutian, and to sue Kaiyang County Secretary of the Party committee Zhang Shutian would mean offending officials of all the higher levels, because all these officials were interconnected, and to offend one would lead to all the others falling upon him. Shuanhu later bragged to the villagers that Liben had become so terrified that he made three or four visits to Shuanhu's outhouse. In addition to his "tough" tactics, Shuanhu also used some "soft" strategies. One evening, he prepared some dishes and wine in honor of Liben, and invited Liu Qi to come over to dine and drink in Liben's company.

The villagers competed to invite Liben to their houses for meals. They did that for purposes different from Shuanhu's. Some in the hope that Liben could take their children abroad — they did not mind a bit if their children were hired to do washroom-cleaning, firewood-collecting, or livestock-herding. Anyway, they thought, foreigners were rich and it was far easier to earn money in a foreign country. If Liben had got so much money in compensation for a surgical failure, it was likely that other people could expect such good things as well. But more villagers invited Liben to dinner for the sake of getting a place in the factory which Liben was planning to set up in the village. Word had gone round that once the factory was built, many workers would be hired. Who would not want to get a good position in a firm so close to home?

According to Fugui, he had just had an unpleasant time of it with Song Tongguo. The unpleasantness had derived from the fact that Fugui liked to work as the factory's warehouseman, and so did Song Tongguo! A warehouseman's job was easy to do. And also at the warehouse you could skim a little something off the top. Those who live in mountains live from mountains. Those who live near rivers live from rivers. Wasn't it natural for a warehouseman, who kept a warehouse of goods, to take stuff home in secret? Fugui once worked as a warehouse keeper for a short time at a period when people were organized in production teams. While the hungry villagers collected leaves from trees for food, his family had long, white, tasty noodles to eat. Fugui well knew the various benefits of the job. But to his annoyance, Song Tongguo forestalled him by letting Liben know he had the same wish. When Fugui made his request, Liben shook his head rapidly from side to side. Fugui did not know why his request was declined. When he later discovered that the problem lay with Song Tongguo, he flared up with anger. Not that he was a narrow-minded fellow, but who would not have become angry in this situation? He ran to the ground by Song Tongguo's courtyard, throwing out loud curses and insulting remarks. When Luobo fought back, he called her "the bastard daughter of a military prostitute," which distressed Luobo so much that she began weeping loudly. At first, Song Tongguo kept a low profile. But when Luobo started crying, Song Tongguo rushed out of his gate, iron hammer in hand, his face looking as black as thunder. The moment Song Tongguo raised his hammer, Fugui got so frightened that he ran away as fast as his legs could carry him. A clever man will not fight when the odds are against him. Fugui knew very well that the blacksmith's hands were powerful. If he were hit by the blacksmith, a bone fracture at least, somewhere in his body, would be the result, even if his life was spared. The value of life! Without his life, could he still come to the provincial capital along with Third Aunt? Without his life, could he still sit in my drawing room to gossip?

Anyhow, Fugui could not understand why a blacksmith insisted on taking care of a warehouse instead of striking iron. As he was in the middle of expressing his doubts, Fugui suddenly shifted to a new topic. Seeing that the Americans were so generous in offering compensation, he also — but unlike Shuanniu who beat others with impunity — had hit on the idea of going to America. If no accidents happened, Fugui said, he would definitely use his brain and force one or two to happen. In this way, he would make plenty of money for his children, grandchildren and great grandchildren to spend during their lives. Specifically, he would contrive to be the victim of traffic accidents; he was ready to lose one leg or arm, or to have the stuff between his legs run over by a car, like Liben. Anyway, he was old now. That stuff of his had retired from active service — it had become useless. If its sacrifice could bring in a large sum of compensation money, it would at least be accredited with turning dross into gold.

14

Third Aunt and Fugui had stayed in my home for four days before I could fully figure out why Xiaolin had been sent to the reform-through-labor farm after we had managed to fish him out of the police station. Was this not the result of Xiaolin's stubbornness? Sheriff Han had been so merciful as to set him free, but he refused to admit he was wrong, and would take a yard when given an inch. He went to the police station again and again, demanding an apology.

The police apologize to you? What a novelty! How funny! Who do you think you are? Do you think you are the son or grandson of a king, or you are a relative of the provincial governor, or you are the second uncle of a provincial department's director? Such an act is deemed too odd even by Laoyu who has been working in the police station all his life. What is a police station? Isn't it a place specially for torturing people? Locking you up with handcuffs, punching you with fists, kicking you with feet, seizing your hair and bumping your head against the wall, forcing your mouth open to pour shit and urine down your throat…these things are not only common enough, but are part of the police's daily routine. If they apologize for these things, they will never have time to do anything else, as they will have to make apologies without end.

There were ten policemen in this station, and they all believed that Xiaolin was mad — either from water on the brain or from an electric shock. Who would be so foolish as to jump into his own grave and invite others to bury him? Xiaolin found the policeman who had attacked him, but the latter could hardly remember who he was. When the policeman finally realized that he was the block-head sent in by the urban management officers, he gave Xiaolin two slaps. Xiaolin glared at the policeman, his hair standing on end.

The fourth time Xiaolin stepped into the police station, he decided not to pick on that policeman. He decided instead to see Sheriff Han. Sheriff Han was not in, so Xiaolin waited outside the gate of the police station. Not until dusk had fallen did he see Sheriff Han's car drive into the court. He dashed over. Once out of the car, Sheriff Han threw a few curses at him, dirty and harsh, concerning the reproductive organ of his mother. Having been informed by a certain policeman on the phone of the trouble Xiaolin had been making in the police station, Sheriff Han exploded like a land mine.

He had freed this son of a bitch for the sake of Director Ye Zhonghua, but he had been repaid with resentment instead of anything good. It was one thing that he was ungrateful, but quite another for him to come making trouble all the time. Such a person must be taught a lesson!

"Why do you police swear at people?" Xiaolin challenged with glaring eyes.

"Do you think they should not dare to do so? Police fuck people as well. You are a half-baked product of your mother's womb!" Sheriff Han disdainfully cast a sidelong glance at him. "I swore at you, so what?"

"I will report you to your superior," Xiaolin threatened.

"You fathead, you want to report on me? Who do you think you are to report on me? What are you going to report about me? What have I done that you, fathead, could report?"

"You swore at people, and you took bribes as well. I saw you accept a stack of money from my brother. Don't think I didn't."

Sheriff Han was exasperated. He turned and gave Xiaolin a heavy punch so that two red streams shot from his nose. Another punch sent one of Xiaolin's teeth flying to the ground. He shouted to the policemen nearby to handcuff Xiaolin. They came at the double, seized his arms and handcuffed him with his hands behind a big iron pipe. As his nose bled, he thought: bleed, bleed, bleed; bleed to the last drop!

Sheriff Han took out his mobile phone and called Director Ye Zhonghua, to whom he explained with much exaggeration how Xiaolin had disrupted work at the police station, how he had punched a policeman, and how he had run so wild as to smash two flower pots and a fish bowl. Before Sheriff Han could suggest what to do next, Ye Zhonghua had already given his instructions: the only thing to do was to send him directly to the reform-through-labor farm!

In this way Xiaolin became a member of the reform-through-labor farm. When she was informed of this by the farm, Third Aunt made her tearful way here. Third Aunt wanted Dalin to get his younger brother out. She would lead him home and never allow him to wander away again. Xiaolin had to be released from the farm, or she would put an end to her life. But she would wait to see Xiaolin walk out of the farm with her own eyes, certain that if she died before then she wouldn't be able to close her eyes in the grave.

I found it increasingly unbearable for Third Aunt and Fugui to live in my home. The phlegm spat by Fugui had left spots here and there on my floor. He even wiped his nose and rubbed his fingers with sticky snot on my wall. What was worse, Li Tiantian was calling me from morning to evening, regardless of whether I was busy or asleep. After Dalin left her restaurant, she seemed to have lost her soul. She called Dalin, but he refused to answer her, for love or money, so she seemed to have decided to exhaust my phone's battery. She guessed that Dalin was staying in my house, or that at least I must know where Dalin was. I said I didn't know where Dalin was. I begged her not to call me again. I said, "I want to steer clear of the affair between you and Dalin, and I'm begging you not to drag me into it, okay?" But Li Tiantian replied, "Who else can I call but you? I know Dalin very well, and that there are very few people in this provincial capital on whom Dalin can depend. I'm sure you must have hidden him. If you refuse to hand him over, I have no choice but to keep calling you." Her words sounded more and more absurd. She asked me with whom Dalin was associating. I said I didn't know. She asked me if Dalin had been associating with any women. I said I didn't know. She asked me if Dalin had recently been associating with Ye Lihua, and if he had called her, and if he had ever mentioned the name of Ye Lihua in my presence, and if he had, what was his facial expression? And the conversation kept on like that. I just kept saying that I didn't know, I didn't know, I didn't know...Li Tiantian even entrusted me with the task of smelling Dalin's underwear and then telling her whether it smelled of woman.

"Boss Li, what do you think I am? Am I a spy in your pay? I feel the shame, even if you don't." I was greatly offended.

I felt myself to be in such a tight corner, as to switch off my phone, which was, however, against the regulations of the press house. If Xue Yulu couldn't get through on my phone, one hundred *yuan* would be subtracted from my salary for that month. Xue Yulu had an innate obsession with regulations, and she often went over those which piled up on her desk. For her nothing could beat the occasional pleasure of catching someone out who had violated the regulations, as this gave her the chance to show off her authority. She often called to check if I had my phone on, hoping that one day she might hear "The subscriber you have dialed has switched off power" or words to that effect. Nevertheless, she kept a corner of the net open, through which those in her favor might escape, Xiang Wenhua in particular. She gave him her best care and protection. I had only been caught once. She subtracted the money, reported the matter to President Sun, and mentioned it every time we held an office meeting. I asked her if she found it amusing to continually harp on the same problem like that. She smiled without losing her temper, against all my expectations, and said "yeah." I asked, conversely, if it wasn't boring for her to stir-fry old rice in this manner. Still smiling, she said "nope."

Two hours later, my home landline rang. When I picked up the receiver, I heard Xue Yulu's voice. How did she know my home telephone number since I had never told her? So far as I could remember, the only person in the press house who had been told my home telephone number was Luo Xiao, but Luo had left the press house. Had Xue Yulu called Luo Xiao? Thanks to Xue Yulu's fanning the flames, everyone in the press house knew that I had been on intimate terms with Luo Xiao. For some time Xue Yulu had been suggesting that Luo Xiao and I were lovers, and a story went round as if this were actually the case, saying that on the evening of a certain date someone spotted me and Luo Xiao hugging and kissing each other in the shade of a tree in the city wall park, one of my hands thrust into the latter's collar to hold her breast tightly.

Xue Yulu asked why I had turned off my mobile phone. I lied that I was ill and needed sleep, and was afraid of being disturbed. She said I should know the regulations of the press house, and that money would be subtracted from my salary if I was caught with my mobile phone switched off. I said she might subtract as much as she liked. She then got me to make a trip to the press house, saying someone was looking for me. I asked her who it was. Xue Yulu refused to say, only urging me to go without delay.

I did not know who was looking for me until I stepped into the office building of the press house. From afar I heard the shrill voice of Li Tiantian, coming from Xue Yulu's office, and echoing in the whole corridor. Xue Yulu's office door was open. I stood outside for three or four minutes, but they took no heed of me. They sat face to face, and talked animatedly, as if they had been friends for years. Li Tiantian seemed to be saying that Dalin was missing, having taken a large sum of money from her restaurant, and that the only person who knew his whereabouts was Black Bean — Tian Daqing in the press house. Xue Yulu was laughing her head off. She said it was the first time that she heard Tian Daqing called Black Bean. Black Bean, hse-hse-hse! The mere thought of it would make people laugh themselves into a state of idiocy. Xue Yulu decided that Black Bean was Tian Dalin's accomplice, and urged Li Tiantian to make a report at the police station. Tian Dalin was nowhere to be found, but Black Bean was at hand. Black Bean, hse-hse-hse!

Xue Yulu laughed till her neck twisted like linen thread. And it was while she was twisting her neck that she caught a glimpse of me. She stopped laughing immediately, and sat erect, looking every inch the self-disciplined leader. Li Tiantian saw me too. She sprang up, rather agitated, tears shining in her eyes.

"Brother, I beg you to tell me the place where Dalin is hiding. I am almost crazy," she pleaded endearingly.

"What do you mean, 'almost crazy,' you've been completely crazy! Why do you have to call me every day and ruin my peaceful life? Dalin is not me, and I am not Dalin. Why badger me when Dalin is the one you are looking for? Do you mean to drive me crazy too?" I pulled a long face.

Li Tiantian, whose face wore a very aggrieved expression, said, "Brother, I apologize, okay? Just consider me crazy, and ignore my crazy actions, okay? I came to where you work because I saw no other way, but it turned out, to my surprise, that Director Xue is like an old friend of mine, so warm-hearted, so generous. Brother, how lucky you are to have come by such a good leader."

With a cold grin I said, "Am I indeed? To call her a good leader does not do her justice. The fact is that she is a *great* leader."

Perhaps Li Tiantian sensed the irony in my words, for she came over and walked me out. As we were going, I asked protestingly, "Is Xue Yulu really as good as you said? What do you know about her? How can you determine whether she is good or bad, since you just met her a few minutes ago? Are you all-seeing Buddha, or almighty God? She is finding fault with me on the pretext of helping you. So you get what you want, while I get pushed into the abyss. I am Black Bean, but what's wrong with that name, after all? Is he who is named Thunder and Lightning really thunder and lightning? Is she who is named Rain and Dew really rain and dew? Does the woman whose name Yulu means "rain and dew" have the least trace of the tenderness which rain and dew have? She is nothing but hail!"

Li Tiantian said she had no idea about the grudge between Xue Yulu and me, and that she had meant nothing malicious. All she wanted was to see Dalin. She missed him very much. She would die for the lack of him. In real earnest! When she had lived cheek-by-jowl with Dalin all day long, she never knew how much he had meant to her, but once he left, she felt that her soul was lost, and that her brain was like burning hay in a pit. She asked me to send a message to Dalin, containing her apology and hopes for his return. Without him, she was so bitter that it seemed a cat was scratching at her heart with its paws from morning to evening. What torture!

"Don't you know Dalin is the husband of another woman, by the name of Taoqi?" I warned Li Tiantian.

"Why do you mention that name? That woman, Taoqi, is no worthy wife for Dalin. Their marriage is in fact a mistake, and mistakes must be corrected!" Li Tiantian replied with a scornful smile, heedless of my warning.

I cast a glimpse at Li Tiantian. Her acid-burnt face was as ugly as ever, although it had been restored and beautified many times. I didn't say anything, but I was thinking to myself: if the marriage between Taoqi and Dalin is a mistake, what about the affair between you and Dalin? Have a look in the mirror before you criticize others for their ugly mugs.

Li Tiantian dragged me to a corner of the courtyard. She took out a stack of bank notes from her pocket and insisted on my taking it, in compensation for the trouble she had caused me. I resolutely refused and pushed it back into her pocket. I told Li Tiantian Dalin was having a bad time these days, and that his head was like a bomb about to blow up.

With a deep sigh, Li Tiantian said that she had guessed Dalin's bitterness long before. How could he, who was so infatuated with her, not feel bitterness for putting her in a bad mood? To lovers, one day without seeing each other seems as long as three seasons! Probably he was experiencing the same thing as she was. Dalin didn't answer her calls because he feared loss of face. But she knew he was deeply in love with her. As he was missing her badly, how could his head not explode?

"You do flatter yourself! Why not ask him why he has been upset recently, before asserting that he is love-sick for you? You are rather a curious character," I said.

"Who else could Dalin be upset for? Who is that person, I ask you? Is it Ye Lihua, who is funny in the head?" Li Tiantian appeared somewhat surprised and bewildered, her head slanting to one side.

I told her that person was Dalin's younger brother, and gave an account of the sentence to reform-through-labor passed on Xiaolin, and of the tearful scene performed by Third Aunt. Li Tiantian burst into tears at once, sighing again and again over Dalin's sufferings. If Dalin suffered, the agony she felt would be ten thousand times greater than anything she suffered on her own account. If the wheat awn pricked Dalin, her heart would ache to death, as though a sharp knife were stabbing it. How silly to hide such an important matter from her! Was it easy for a stranger to the city like him to get Xiaolin out of the reform-through-labor farm?

Li Tiantian implored me to call Dalin so that she could meet him. She would like to treat us to tea in a newly-opened teahouse. One of its speciality teas, with the name of Great Red Gown, was priced at five hundred *yuan* for one cup, but she would not so much as blink if it were served for Dalin's sake. The teahouse provided all-in-one services, so that customers could eat in, if they felt hungry. She must have a good talk with Dalin. A good talk, to be sure. She had the ability, as well as the determination, to rescue Xiaolin from the reform-through-labor farm. One thing was certain: in Yuebei, Li Tiantian was somebody!

15

On returning from Mazi Village, Liben phoned me. From what he told me, I could tell he had had a busy time meeting lots of people. He had been received by a vice governor of the province; the construction work he proposed had been shortlisted as a model for the New Village Reconstruction Project.

He repeatedly said he was exhausted; that he had never imagined that attending dinner parties could be tiring to the point of inducing collapse; that his heart ached while seeing a tableful of dishes costing thousands, tens of thousands, or even more. "So much time is consumed by attending dinner parties. Isn't it an utter waste of life?" he complained.

On the phone, Liben gave an account of his itinerary over the past days. After leaving the village, he spent some days in the county town, then returned to the village again along with a team of geological prospectors to obtain geological structure samples. With the samples in hand, he went back to the county town again to discuss the use of village land with the leading officials. After several rounds of discussion, an agreement was struck, which allowed the factory to use the land rent-free, on condition that the village would move en masse to a new locality designated by the government. In the new settlement, the villagers would live in houses designed and built by the government with non-governmental funds. The houses would be villa-style buildings, whose construction cost would mainly come from funds raised by Liben, whereas the factory would be responsible for the infrastructure construction.

Additionally, Liben expressed his wish to help Baolai get justice. He said if necessary he would have the villagers elect a new village head to replace Shuanhu, who had been too insolent and whose presence was not only as oppressive as a mountain over the villagers' heads, but was also a negative factor influencing the factory's prospects.

I advised Liben that he should not be impetuous, and that he should think carefully about the consequences. But it was obvious my words displeased him greatly; we nearly came to the point of shouting at each other. He got so agitated that his speech began to falter. He said it was because of cowardly people like me, fearing wolves ahead and tigers behind, too timid to take any action, that the social atmosphere in China was deteriorating; if a malignant tumor was not removed as early as possible, it would be too late to remove it when it grew big; if we dared not fight against an evil which we hated, we would become its accomplices.

"I'm afraid you are too naïve, Liben," I said to him. "Living abroad for so long has made you a simpleton."

Infuriated by my remarks, Liben replied, "I'm willing to be a simpleton. Is there anything wrong with that?"

"It's up to you whether you listen to me or not," I said to him. "I offered my advice for your good, don't you see? Why do you flare up? Is it that you are stuffed with explosives?" I hung up then.

I did not get a single call from him for almost ten days after that, nor did I have any desire to call him. Probably, he was genuinely angry with me. Well, if that was the case, it would no doubt be better to leave him to himself. *I saw that you were about to throw yourself off a cliff, so I pulled you back out of the goodness of my heart. Instead of appreciating my kindness, you became angry with me. How senseless!*

One afternoon I received a phone call from him. He said he would like to invite me to tea in a teahouse named Alibaba, on Defu Street. I said I would be happy to join him, but if there were to be any officials present at the get-together, I'd rather not attend; I felt extremely uncomfortable meeting officials, for those officials, each with an air of complacency, behaved and spoke as if they were emperors; although I was nobody, I hated serving them. Liben assured me that no officials would be around, that he would like to have some rest, and that he wanted to chat and relax with me. I said that sounded very nice, and I would be there for sure.

When I arrived at the Alibaba Teahouse, Liben was already there. He was sitting in a private room taking a nap. He looked fairly tired. I woke him up. Wiping the saliva drooling out of the corner of his mouth with a piece of paper napkin, he yawned and apologized, saying he was really tired. Taking a seat opposite his, I asked him how the project was going. He said everything was going well, and that he could have a little bit of rest these days — though it might not last long; at present he was in Yuebei expecting a Mr. Michael from the United States; as the president of American Pacific Winnie Co., he was to fly here in order personally to conduct an investigation before deciding whether to invest, as well as to establish how much to invest if the decision was favorable. Mr. Michael was busy as a bee. Acting as a guest professor at a number of internationally famous universities, he was often invited to give lectures across the world. It was estimated that as soon as Michael arrived, there would appear in Yuebei floods of people desperately eager to associate with him.

Liben asked after Dalin, saying we'd better invite Dalin to come here. I said Dalin was in trouble. He was almost out for the count. How could he be in the mood to join us! He had spent fifty or sixty thousand *yuan* in order to get his brother Xiaolin out of jail. However, there was no visible sign of success.

"What's wrong with Xiaolin?" Liben asked.

I explained how Xiaolin ended up twice in the police station.

I had thought Liben would be shocked and infuriated with the inconsistency of the law, since that had been his usual reaction to other occurrences which, for us, took place so commonly that we could no longer feel shocked or infuriated by them. But unexpectedly, this time Liben focused on Xiaolin.

"Xiaolin is a marvelous young man with great potential," Liben exclaimed. "He has a great character."

Liben demonstrated enormous interest in Xiaolin and could not wait to see him. He would like to have a face-to-face talk with Xiaolin, the veteran, to see if he was really as I had depicted. If he found it to be true, he would assign Xiaolin important tasks. He believed if all Chinese people were like Xiaolin, the social atmosphere would be remarkably improved.

Being careful not to show any approval of his remarks, I laughed and said, "A normal person's mind has two routes, but Xiaolin's only one."

"How many routes do you think my mind has?" Liben asked me.

I refrained from answering him. But he insisted that I answer the question. I had to speak honestly, "Your mind has one and a half routes. Less than two but more than one."

Liben burst out laughing, saying "I never imagined that was my image in your eyes."

Fearing he might get angry with me, I said in a hurry, "I was kidding. It was a joke. Your mind has three routes. If not, how could you have been able to go abroad and get your degrees there?"

A young and handsome waiter came in, served us tea and a plateful of fruit. With smiles on his face, the waiter asked in a low voice, "Do you need anything else? Would you like to book any special service?"

"What special service do you mean?" I asked.

"It means you can chat with a naked waiter or waitress," the waiter replied. "If you, the client, have other needs, the waiter or waitress can provide for them too."

"To chat with a naked person of the opposite sex? Is that what you mean?" I asked.

"If you prefer a male, a waiter will be sent to you. But if you prefer a female, a waitress will be placed at your service. It's up to our clients to decide," the waiter said.

"A sexual encounter between members of the same sex? Isn't that homosexual activity? That can be done here?" I was amazed.

"Yes, of course," the waiter replied with a smile on his face.

"Do you also chat with a client in your nakedness?" I asked the waiter.

With a shy reticence, the waiter shook his head. With firmness in his voice, he claimed he never dealt with that kind of thing.

I was skeptical of the truthfulness of what the waiter said of himself. Could a person wallowing in mud remain clean? Who in the world would believe it? As I scrutinized the young man in front of me, a weird feeling arose in my heart: there are tens of thousands of professions in the world to choose from, why do some people choose this disreputable business? Your body was given, in a broad sense, by God; in a narrow sense, by your parents. Do you have a right to misuse it? A person's dignity is an integrated whole; therefore, it involves the dignity of the body. It's a distortion of life to turn one's body into a commodity for other people to enjoy themselves.

"What's your name?" I asked the lad.

"Call me Larz," he replied.

"Isn't Larz the name of the protagonist in the Indian movie *Vagrant*? Is this your real name?" I asked.

The youth said it was his stage name.

I asked him if he would like to take a different job somewhere else.

"Of course," he said. "But I wonder what I can do if I leave here."

Liben looked pretty impatient while listening to the conversion between Larz and me. He motioned Larz to leave the room. No sooner had Larz stepped out, than Liben started to scold me for engaging in such a long chat with a waiter. "What's the point of talking with a waiter?" he grumbled.

"As a journalist, I need to know more about society as it really is. Defu

Street is a well-known teahouse street. But today for the first time I learned that there are sexual transactions going on here. I'm about to do some secret investigations and do a report on it."

"My goodness! There's so much filth in this great country of ours!" Liben said. "It is simply beyond me that China should have become like this! What a shame that there's hardly any clean spot left in the nation. Hair salons serve as places for prostitution, foot-wash-and-massage houses are places for prostitution, singing-and-dancing bars are places for prostitution, so-called health-care massage has become a cover for prostitution. Now teahouses are on the way to becoming whore-houses. Even though China is not yet a well-developed nation, the sexual capacity of the Chinese people has been remarkably improved. What a miracle!"

Just then, Liben's mobile phone rang. He answered the call. After saying hello into the phone, he left the room.

Before long, the door opened and in came Larz to add water for us. He smiled at me as if I were a longtime acquaintance of his.

"If your don't mind, Sir, could you please give me your business card?" he pleaded softly.

I hesitated for a moment before I handed over my business card.

He said "Thank you," and retreated from the room, walking backwards.

Before long I regretted having given him my business card, because I recalled a story of one of my friends, who was a book-dealer. He had been to a dance hall once, and the most unusual thing he did there with a girl was to touch her hand. Unfortunately, he gave her his business card. Sometime later, the girl was caught by the police for prostitution and his business card was found in the girl's pocket. This card transformed him into a whoremonger. Even with eight mouths to mount a defence, he had no way to clear himself. Not only was he warned and fined by the police, but the scandal led directly to three years of strife between him and his wife which ended in their breaking up.

I was still in this state of regret when Liben returned with a woman in tow. He introduced me to her, saying that though my stomach was solidly stuffed with books, I failed to apply the knowledge acquired from them to my real life; if these books were not digested, they could only hurt me and make my stomach ache; the fact that I viewed this with distaste and that with disproval was a symptom of my dyspeptic condition.

I felt so embarrassed that I wished I could hide myself behind a *pingfeng*, a standing screen in the room. Teased by Liben's remarks, the woman tittered cheerfully and said, "How humorous you are, Liben! You're as interesting as ever."

"You're getting a name for yourself as a comedian through mocking me. What a heartless person you are!" I said to Liben with some displeasure. I looked away, towards a wall, too shy to look into the lady's eyes.

"I'm kidding. It's just a joke," Liben said. "I didn't think you would take it to heart."

Liben introduced the young lady to me. I cast a glance at her. She impressed me as a "big" woman — everything about her was big. She had a big stature, a big face, a big nose and a big mouth. And biggest of all were her breasts, which protruded like two dominating hills threatening to burst open her shirt.

"Her Chinese name is Kang Yuanyuan," Liben said. "Her English name is Coris. She got a master's degree in social science from Stanford University."

Kang Yuanyuan had been travelling the world and had published several books. The thing most deserving of mention about her was she declined an offer to work in a university but instead went alone to Africa to help AIDS victims in Namibia. During her stay in Africa she nearly became the prey of a leopard. Since returning to China, in spite of her enthusiastic desire to help others, she could not find an appropriate place to do so. She took a disabled old woman home from an old people's nursing center. She looked after the old woman, fed her and washed her feet for her, but what she got in return was constant interference from the old lady's children. They broke into her house, smashed her belongings, and called her "cheat." They said she had acted in the hope of getting the old woman's estate. They charged her with having lured the old woman into making a will. Therefore they compelled her to present the will to them. But how could she give them the will when no will actually existed? Since she could not hand it over to them, they harassed her incessantly. She would have loved to open an orphanage. With that desire in mind, she went to various administrative departments to make enquiries and applications, which received no responses. When she argued with the staff, they concluded that she was a mad woman.

As Kang Yuanyuan talked about her past experience, tears flowed from her eyes. Liben handed a paper napkin to her, but she did not take it. Rising to her feet, she went to the washing room. During her absence, Liben told me under his breath that Kang Yuanyuan used to be his lover. He said they had dated for a while, however, because Kang Yuanyuan lacked femininity but abounded in nervous temperament, he proposed to break up. With pity in his voice, he exclaimed Kang Yuanyuan would make an ideal friend, but not an ideal wife. In the meantime, he asked me to look for a life partner for Kang Yuanyuan, the sooner the better.

"In the United States, even if a woman is unmarried in her sixties, no one gossips about it. But in China, if a woman remains single in her thirties, people point at her back," he said.

16

Dalin arranged for Xiaolin to live in my home after the latter was released from the reform-through-labor farm. I sensed from Dalin's talk, though he was not explicit, that I would no doubt have my work cut out keeping an eye on his younger brother.

Third Aunt and Fugui had left my home a few days before. To tell the truth, it was I who drove them away. I could not bear Third Aunt's tears, which never dried up and made me feel as though I were trapped in a long, wet monsoon; but the worst thing was Fugui's dirtiness. As if dissatisfied with his own efforts, he summoned his daughter and grandson to join him in turning my home into a garbage dump. Fugui, unbeknownst to me, used my landline to call his daughter Layue, telling her how wonderful Yuebei was — tall buildings, speeding vehicles, kaleidoscopic colors, women in shirts without sleeves, and men in shoes without heelpieces; how comfortable Black Bean's home was, with a daily bath, a soft sponge bed, with deep-fried dough sticks served as a staple food, milk as plentiful as water. By this, he meant to invite his daughter, who had never yet strayed far from home, to come and enjoy this life, and to tour the city, too.

So it was that Layue came, taking her four-year-old son by the hand, and me by surprise. Layue was thin and tall, like a long-legged mosquito, seemingly unable to resist a gust of wind. For some unknown reason she had, as a young girl, taken a fancy to me. Whenever I was back home on vacation from university, she would loiter in, gazing at me fixedly with strange eyes. She stuck her finger into her mouth as if she were sucking an ice-cream, unaware that saliva had dripped out of her mouth and onto her collar. Her mother would come in search of her, and shout at her to go home and feed the cow, but she made no response, still gazing at me fixedly with strange eyes. Only after the angry mother gave her two kicks would she tearfully go away. Her mother came to see my mother, proposing that I should marry her daughter, saying that the reason that Layue frequented my home was that she had lost her soul there, and that she was always mumbling about how good-looking my eyebrows were, how white my teeth were, or how erect I carried myself when I walked, like a poplar tree without any branches. Her father, however, believed that she had been possessed by a ghost. He made a pile of wood in the courtyard, lit it and hardened two rattan strings above the flame, and then whipped her on the back with them. He whipped her very hard, thinking that only in this way could he make the ghost yield. Layue was beaten black and blue, her back crisscrossed with red scars. She fell ill and lay in bed for half a month, but it seemed that the ghost remained despite the repeated blows of Fugui's rattan. She showed no sign of recovery. Shortly before school started, Layue arranged to meet me by a pile of firewood, where she gave me a pair of insoles. I shook her hand to thank her. She blushed to the tips of her ears and breathed as rapidly as if she had received an electric shock.

Awkwardly, Layue said she hadn't meant to come, and that she had hesitated for two days, and had only made up her mind after hearing that once she came she could see me and live in my home. She confessed that she had almost forgotten what I looked like, and was very curious about what I was like now, and that she was, of course, envious of that woman of mine — how lucky that woman was to be able to marry me; she wondered what precious incenses the woman had burned in her previous life. She made a point of saying that in that period of infatuation she had behaved crazily enough to make one suspect that she had taken an aphrodisiac, but eventually she had come to her senses, and now the thought of me was no more extraordinary to her than the thought of her pig at home. She loved Qi Guangrong, her husband, as he did her. Look, the little kid called Langwa was the result of their love. Qi Guangrong was good in every respect, except that he made no money on account of his honest simplicity. Whereas other villagers had built their houses with bricks, his family was still living in its old adobe house, which was hardly fit for humans to live in — leaking so hard on rainy or windy days that the crops in the barn often went moldy. Worse still, mice dug holes in the walls, making them soft and loose. One of them was tilting, supported only by three logs and could collapse at any moment. Layue didn't care what might happen to the wall, but she did care that Langwa and she might be buried alive.

At this point, tears began to run down her face. Fugui angrily dismissed her tears as so much horse piss. It was destiny that determined one's wealth or rank, and heaven one's life or death. Who was to blame if you were born with a beggar's destiny? However, Fugui had predicted that Layue's day would come, but as to when, he was not yet certain. Anyway, someday Layue would come out on top. He had not blindly forced Layue to marry Qi

Guangrong. He had done it out of foresight and careful consideration. An ordinary man could only see as far as his toe, but he could see further than six thousand miles. Naturally, those who saw only as far as their toes could not understand him. This was what Chairman Mao meant when he asked in one of his poems, "How can a sparrow understand a hawk's ambition?" Fugui had heard rumors about Qi Guangrong's great grand-father providing salt for the imperial court of the Qing Dynasty. As a salt dealer, Master Qi had raised a tall chestnut mare and shuttled with the animal between north and south, east and west. It chanced once — only once — that Master Qi chivvied his mare into the palace yard. What was a palace? Was it a place open to ordinary people? Who from Kaiyang County had ever been admitted in there? Master Qi brought back a treasure which was said to be the emperor's piss pot with urine stains on it. A stingy man, he hid the pot away the moment he came home. No one had ever seen it, but that did not mean it wasn't there! It definitely existed, though it had yet to be found. Qi Guangrong's grandfather hadn't found it in his life time, neither had his father. Third time lucky! In Qi Guangrong's generation, the pot would automatically turn up even if no effort was made to find it!

"Don't you believe me? Wait and see! Can you imagine, my silly child, how much it is worth? There are those who wish to lick an emperor's urine, never mind urine that has become a historical relic. Can an emperor's piss pot be made of clay or enamel? No, no, it must be made of gold. Gold is precious in itself, but palace gold! Wait, because the good days to come are worth waiting for. When you have your fortune, I hope you will still remember your dear mummy and daddy, and will no longer blame your daddy for having married you to a block of wood." Fugui's words made Layue's face blossom into a smile.

Leaving her kid in the drawing room, she began sweeping, wiping, washing and cooking, like a hostess just back home from a business trip. She even offered advice and suggestions on the items displayed on my shelves. For example, the stone I considered a work of art should, according to her, have been thrown away, and the porcelain bowl on which I had spent a thousand *yuan* should have gone to the kitchen, and used to feed chickens, if ever I were to own any. As it was cracked in two places it would, even in the countryside, have been thrown into the gutter a long time before. Although my mouth said "yes," my heart was muttering "What do you know? That bowl is a historical relic!"

Langwa was the most unbearable. He would pee once in a while, and when he peed he would part his pants and take direct aim at the floor. Thick sticky liquid kept flying out of the kid's nose, and each time Fugui would catch it in his hand and wipe it on the sole of his shoe, so that when he walked, the liquid stuck to the floor, leaving dirty marks all over the place. Langwa even got into my study, tore one of my books to pieces, and knocked one of my frames to the ground, severely distorting its shape.

I was reluctant to scold Langwa, but merely sighed over the frame, saying that it was a prize of great sentimental value I had won, and that after all, it was normal for kids to be naughty. However, Layue did not think so. Hearing the crash, she rushed in, seized Langwa by the hair and gave him a good hiding. Langwa howled hysterically. I told Layue not to beat him, that tact was needed in the education of children. She said that no good child escaped a beating now and again, and that I should know the saying — "Spare the rod and spoil the child."

The day following Layue's arrival, I decided that they would have to go, for they really were more than I could stand. Once, when Dalin criticized me for having alienated myself from working people, I had protested; but now I couldn't agree with him more. The truth was that they had had my sympathy, but not my fellowship. What were the people, after all? They were a blurry concept in my mind, but somehow different from Fugui, Third Aunt, Layue and Langwa. Who were the people, then? The people as a totality were a hotchpotch which included all kinds of human beings — gentlemen, villains, the rich, the poor. Those who stole, robbed, raped, killed or murdered, on what grounds were they not of the people? Of course, I too was one of the people, a grain from the sand-dune of the people!

I lied to them, saying that a couple of far-away friends were coming to live in my home, so due to limited space I had to beg their pardon and ask them to leave, in the hope that they might be kind enough to help me out. Third Aunt saw through my ruse, and her face went as black as thunder. She said she would leave the moment Xiaolin was out of the reform-through-labor farm; thereafter she would not stay even if she was asked to. Who would think she enjoyed staying in my home? No, it was like doing time in a prison! She said Xiaolin's suffering made her heart hurt, just as though it were being cut by a knife. Sitting on the sofa, she said she felt uncomfortable, just as though she were sitting on a fire. What's more, she had other matters to worry about. Taoqi, in her absence, might have transported who knew how many goods to her maiden home. A thief with an innocent face, Taoqi used to smuggle goods to her maiden home. Third Aunt was the warden, and one of her responsibilities was to guard against Taoqi. Nevertheless, there are moments when cats doze off and rats run wild. If Taoqi was brass-faced enough to do this, how could she stop her?

Fugui was quite satisfied with life in my home. He said the biggest gain for him was to have learned how urban people led their lives. He had never suspected that they relieved themselves sitting, a fact which enriched his store of knowledge. Layue laughed at her father, saying she could have guessed that was true although she had never been to the city. A younger brother with the same family name as Qi Guangrong had worked in the city and told her all about such novelties. She had longed to sit on a toilet bowl, but once sat on one she had felt so awkward that it took her half a day to pee, and even then, she wet her trousers. On stepping out of my door, Layue expressed her hope that I would come to her home when I returned to Kaiyang, that she wanted to give me a pair of insoles, and make *cuocuo noodles* for me — her best dish. How delicious! Layue licked her lips, her face beaming with sweet and happy looks.

17

Since first he came to my house, Xiaolin had confined himself to his small room. Day in and day out, he stayed inside, almost never going out except to use the toilet. I had attempted to have a talk with him, or at least to see what he was doing in the room, but as I pushed the door, I found it was locked from inside. I shouted Xiaolin to open the door, but there was no response. I shouted again, but still there was total silence inside the room.

Fearing Xiaolin might commit suicide, I rang Dalin, urging him to come over to have a talk with his brother. I said if anything should happen to Xiaolin I was not able to live with the consequences. At the other end of the line, Dalin muttered something I did not quite catch — perhaps he would come; or he would be too busy to come.

I knocked at the door furiously. After a long while, the inside knob turned. The door opened.

"What are you doing?" I asked Xiaolin.

Wordless, Xiaolin looked at me with his dull eyes. His unkempt look and the twisted quilt on the bed suggested that he had probably just had a sleep. Taking hold of his arm, I dragged him out of the room, and having sat him down on a sofa in the sitting room, I asked him to talk with me. He sat still, his eyes looking straight ahead, but his mouth tightly shut. Noticing that his nose was a little crooked, I asked him what had happened to it. At first, he refused to answer, but after I asked more than ten times, he replied, "Of course it was beaten into that condition. Do you think sleep can make it look like that?"

"Who beat you?" I asked.

He glanced at me, with a look which seemed to say I was pretending not to understand an obvious matter.

"A watch-guard beat me," Xiaolin said impatiently.

"Did they beat people often?" I asked.

Xiaolin let out a chilling peal of laughter. After a long pause, he said that "watch-guard" was a euphemism; actually, it just meant "goon;" a watch-guard's job was to beat people; they had become used to beating people; they had devised various beating methods; they had become addicted to it, like some people who became addicted to drinking or smoking; they would feel unbearably uncomfortable if they did not beat people at least once a day.

"How did the guard beat you?" I asked. "Tell me about it so I can investigate the matter. We can expose their deeds to the public."

Xiaolin cast a glance at me. Twisting his mouth, he looked at me skeptically. Nevertheless, he related some of his experiences in the reform-through-labor farm. As he told the story, there was neither excitement nor fury in his voice, but only indifference. I felt, emanating from every inch of his body, the chilly gloom that only deep caves normally produce.

According to Xiaolin, generally speaking a new prisoner had to go through several trials before he could settle in. The first consisted of torments from those prisoners who had arrived previously. Anyway, as a new arrival stepped into a jail, what he encountered first would be a beating. Every jail had a big brother figure nicknamed the "top dog." Of course, a top dog rose to his place through bloody fights. Only those who were physically strong and violent, with a heart remarkable for cruelty and hardness, could win this title. The reason why they were so reckless and unscrupulous was, of course, that they had got the watch-guards' acquiescence. Since the watch-guards did not wish to confront prisoners directly, they entrusted the task of watching the prisoners to the top dog, who had much in common with a monitor, except that he was ten thousand times more domineering. When meals were sent in, all prisoners were obliged to offer some of their own share to the top dog. The new-comers were even completely deprived of theirs. If a newcomer was displeasing to the eye of the top dog, all the others would fall upon the newcomer at his order of "Beat him!" They would punch and kick him until his skin split, his flesh tore, and he cried bitterly.

The top dog would devise ever new methods of tormenting people. He derived the most pleasure from torturing a prisoner's private parts. Obviously, it was old hat to strip a prisoner of his clothes and make him masturbate in front of the crowd, or to make a prisoner crawl on the ground and bark like a dog. What pleased him to his heart's full content was to thrust a rod into a prisoner's anus, or to burn a prisoner's reproductive organ with a red-hot iron wire to listen to him scream in bitter agony. All new arrival prisoners had to go through this hell-like "trial." This had become an obligatory process for all those who stepped through the prison door.

Xiaolin's account made my scalp tingle. He claimed he had been spared such an ordeal. According to Xiaolin, the watch-guard who led him into the jail was a baldy, over fifty years of age. With two front teeth gone, his mouth looked like a dark mine. Blinking his eyes toward the top dog, the guard referred to Xiaolin as "a connection" and offered the top dog a cigarette. The top dog hit Xiaolin with his fist, but this punch signified good-will. Xiaolin was filled with heartfelt gratitude toward the watch-guard, thinking that he had been fortunate enough to encounter a good man. But that very night Xiaolin discerned the reason why the baldy had helped him: the creature was a sexual pervert; as such, he dreamed of having an affair with every handsome young man who came along — for, viewed from whatever angle, Xiaolin could be considered a handsome man.

As it happened, the baldy was burning to see Xiaolin. He chose to interrogate Xiaolin at 1:00 a.m. Xiaolin was led to the dormitory of the bald man, who proceeded to do his utmost to lure Xiaolin. He offered Xiaolin cigarettes; he offered Xiaolin fruit; he turned on his DVD and played American videos for Xiaolin. The video programs were pornographic and the people in them were no better than beasts: there were displays of man-man fucking, of woman-woman fucking, of human-human fucking, of human-beast fucking. These images were so despicable that it was only with great effort that Xiaolin refrained from vomiting in the presence of the bald man. So Xiaolin was already feeling extremely sick, when the baldy grabbed his waist from behind and thrust his hand into his crotch from beneath his belt. Taking hold of that thing of Xiaolin's in his hand, the baldy squeezed it with force, making Xiaolin feel both pain and embarrassment. Using all his might, Xiaolin struggled out of the bald man's hold. Tremendously displeased, the baldy abruptly pulled a long face. But in a moment, his face was all smiles again. He pleaded with Xiaolin in a pitiable manner, as if he had been a tiny creature just hurt by Xiaolin. He made an oath to Xiaolin, saying he would take good care of him and would try his best to let him leave this hellish prison as soon as possible.

Turning his back on the bald man, Xiaolin paid no heed to whatever he said or did. Seeing that Xiaolin's attitude showed no sign of change, the baldy let out a sigh.

"Well, well," the baldy said. "If I cannot have the joy of eating any meat, could you let me at least drink some meat soup?"

This was the baldy's way of pleading with Xiaolin to shit in front of him; he enjoyed seeing a handsome young man shit. But again Xiaolin, his face full of contempt and indignation, refused to yield. Having no better option, the baldy moved his hands over the clothes covering Xiaolin's body. Then he brought Xiaolin back to his prison house.

The following day, at the work place, the baldy called Xiaolin aside to admonish him. He asked him if he had thought it over and changed his mind. Xiaolin replied he hadn't. The baldy asked if Xiaolin was willing to render him some service. Xiaolin replied he was not. With his face turning crimson with anger, the baldy warned Xiaolin, "Don't reject a face-saving request! If you refuse a toast, get ready to drink a forfeit."

Thereafter, Xiaolin got a beating every other day. The baldy always had Xiaolin come to his own dormitory so he could beat him there. As an overture to the beating, the pervert would more often than not order Xiaolin to take off his clothes. When entering the room, Xiaolin would find the man armed with an implement of torment that would vary from time to time, such as a wooden stick, an iron pole, a burning cigarette, or a thin needle. Though small in size, it was such tiny things as burning cigarettes or needles that were most horrifying. Wherever a live cigarette burned on Xiaolin's body, a bruise appeared. Xiaolin had so much pain that sweat came out all over him. A soundlessly inserted needle instantly brought up a bone-crushing pain. Xiaolin's bottom ended up with numerous holes and wounds, looking like a sieve.

One day, when Xiaolin was once more called to the bald man's room, he noticed his baleful expression and the bloodthirsty look in his eyes. The baldy had a butcher's knife in his hand, which shone with chilly light. He ordered Xiaolin to stand up straight and remove his own clothes.

Hardly had Xiaolin unfastened his belt and rolled down his trousers when the knife started to flit between his thighs. After feeling some fleeting numbness which spread all over him, Xiaolin felt deadly dizzy. If he had not taken hold of a table in time, he would have thumped down heavily. What a pain! It was as if his heart had just been gouged out. Blood trickling down his thighs reddened his trousers and drenched the floor tiles.

Realizing that the bald guy had just been cutting his pubic hair and in carelessness had hurt his scrotum, Xiaolin burst into a rage. His hair stood on end; the blood vessels all over his body were about to burst. He had no wish to go on living. If you received nothing but disgrace, what's the meaning of living? He wanted to end his life and take the bald rascal with him. This would give his death some value. It would help potential subsequent victims if he could make this old rascal, who had power to insult other people, vanish from the world. Taking hold of a desk lamp, Xiaolin pulled with so much force that the wire broke. He lifted the lamp and dashed it against the bald rascal's head. The baldy dodged his head to one side. As a result, the lamp struck his shoulder rather than hitting his head. Meanwhile, the alarm rang out loudly; the two wolfhounds tied at the entrance of the jail barked vehemently. Xiaolin lifted a chair. But before he had time to throw it, he had already been brought under control: someone held his waist from behind, another man snatched the chair from his hands. A gang of men broke into the room and pressed Xiaolin onto the floor, at which point he fell into a coma due to loss of blood.

As Xiaolin woke up, he found himself lying in a bed in the clinic, with the baldy sitting on a stool next to his bed. The baldy smiled at him; he even lowered his voice muttering apologies, saying he was about to request the authorities to show clemency to Xiaolin. According to the baldy, the detention house would sue Xiaolin and charge him with the crime of attacking a policewman, and the case would be transferred to the procurator for sentence, but he had talked twice with the warden, expressing his hope of making Xiaolin's offense sound less serious. The baldy described his pleading with the warden in the following terms: "It's normal for a young man to be impetuous and commit some faults. All of us used to be impulsive young men. Can you find a young man who has never had one moment's impetuosity? Let's not make a big fuss about it, please! Let's just verbally criticize the young man and give him an opportunity to repent and atone."

The baldy asked Xiaolin what he thought of him? Wasn't he gracious enough? Wasn't he kind enough? He had been so widely known for his kindness in the reform-through-labor circle that the warden had criticized him for excessive kindness, calling him the farmer in the fable *Farmer and Snake*.

Looking at the unparalleled ugliness of the baldy's face, all Xiaolin wanted to do was kill him. However, he did not even have sufficient energy to sit up; he was extremely tired and feeble; and his crotch was in pain. With all his might, he strove to expectorate some spit, hoping it would land precisely on the baldy's face. Because of his insufficient strength, though, the spit landed on the sheet covering the verge of the bed.

Not realizing that the spit carried Xiaolin's scorn, condemnation and denouncement of him, the baldy attentively took out a paper napkin and cleaned it up. He told Xiaolin he was here to take care of him — he was responsible for feeding Xiaolin, for giving Xiaolin enough to drink, for helping Xiaolin when he needed to piss or shit. Whatever Xiaolin wanted, he should just let him know. His warm and thoughtful service would make Xiaolin feel he had had the good luck to come across a living Lei Feng[12].

18

Xiaolin made me promise not to tell his mother, his elder brother, or anyone else about his maltreatment at the reform-through-labor farm. He asked whether or not I could do that. I replied that I could, but I wanted to know about his motives. It was understandable that he did not want his mother to learn about it, because she was too old to bear the blow, but as for his elder brother Dalin, who had loved and cared for him so much, there should be no reason for him to be kept in the dark.

Xiaolin said he was afraid to hurt his elder brother again. He had brought too many troubles on his elder brother with his inconsiderate actions. Now Dalin had become Li Tiantian's sex slave. To get Xiaolin out of the reform farm, Li Tiantian had spent one hundred thousand *yuan*, and invited those who had a hand in the matter to drink tea, to have their feet washed, and even to go out whoring. Li Tiantian was no fool, so why was she willing to spend so much money? Naturally, because she had calculated that it would turn to her advantage. She forced Dalin to sign an agreement, the thrust of which was that Dalin should divorce Taoqi within half a year to marry her, Li Tiantian, and that, if Dalin kept his promise, the debt would be magicked away. Otherwise, though, the debt would be doubled with each passing year — twenty thousand the second year, forty thousand the third year, eighty thousand the fourth year, etc. Such an agreement was hardly acceptable for Dalin, but he signed in the end because he was eager to rescue his brother.

I wrote a summary of Xiaolin's story. As a reporter, I felt drawn to carry out an investigation into this matter. I felt that I had a responsibility to help him counter this injustice, to make the world in which we were living a cleaner and brighter place. A reporter had to advocate good while denouncing evil, and a little heroism was needed to "stop a crime in progress with a loud shout." What's more, the harm inflicted on Xiaolin had been inflicted on the whole of society, along with its legal system and legal authority.

Xiaolin laughed at me. Adopting a sophisticated tone, he criticized me for believing, with all my experience of the world, that there were any laws in this society. If the existence of laws remained a question, what was the point of talking about the legal system and legal authority? I said that I thought he had gone to extremes, and that he shouldn't look at everything through distorting spectacles. Xiaolin replied that he didn't want to, but he was just compelled to, in fact, by Sheriff Han in the police station and the baldy on the reform-through-labor farm. After being released from the reform-through-labor farm, he saw everything in different colors. Even the sun in the sky had lost its radiance, dimmed by a dark cloud.

Xiaolin tried to dissuade me, insisting that there would not be any positive result. He wanted to solve the problem on his own. I asked how he would be able to do so. He said he had been cogitating, during the sleepless periods in my home, ways to get revenge. He had devised two plans, the first of which was to buy two packs of explosives on the black market, one for blowing up the police station, the other for blowing up the reform-through-labor farm, like Palestinians suicide-bombing Israelis. The second plan would be to kill the baldy's whole family, but before he killed the baldy he would cut off his reproductive organ and throw it to the dog. In order to carry out this plan, he would have to buy a sharp knife, and fulfill some other indispensable conditions. He had bought Tibetan knives as gifts while serving in the army, so he would mail-order another like them, if he decided on the second option. The knife must be one of those curved like a new moon, with saw teeth on its edge, so that he could finish him off with a single cut. Of course, he would have to locate the baldy's home first, and check if there were any security guards or watch dogs in the neighborhood. But neither would bother him. With the combat-skills he had acquired in the army, he could mow down two or three of the guards like so many stalks of wheat. As for the dogs, he only needed throw a piece of poisoned meat, and they would be finished. Since the baldy often stayed in the dormitory of the detention house, away from his family, there would be some difficulties in killing him. It didn't matter though, as he had already found the solution — which was to slip in and kill the baldy, and then go back to eradicate his family.

I shuddered at Xiaolin's accounts. I could barely recognize the young man standing before me. How was it possible that a sweet and innocent lad had turned into a demon in such a short time? He sounded like a professional killer when talking about murder, with looks so cold and cruel, without fear or confession on his conscience.

"Xiaolin, can you think wisely? You are now at a dead end; if you do not retreat quickly you'll make a big mistake! Listen to me, I should go first to investigate the matter as a reporter, and if this does not solve your problem, you'll still have time to talk about killing them. Why must you resort to force if things can be settled peacefully? Is killing such a happy thought? Have you ever considered the consequences? Yes, you'll be out of it, knowing nothing with your eyes shut, but what about your mother? Won't she be driven to death by the pain? What about your elder brother? Won't he be involved in your case and despised the rest of his life? Did you come to this world just for killing a few people before you leave? It's rather pitiful, isn't it?" I reasoned.

Xiaolin dropped his head, speechless, but I could sense that he was experiencing a life-and-death struggle in his heart. After a few seconds of silence, he turned hysterical.

"Why don't you let me die? Tell me how can I go on with this life? Do I deserve to go on living, humiliated like this? I live like a damned pig!" he shouted at me furiously, plucking at his hair, his face distorted. He raised the mug from the tea table, his hand shaking, as if he was weighing whether or not he should throw it onto the ground. I urged him to do so. I knew the passions welling up in his belly needed to find an exit, and if a mug was the price of calming his brain, its sacrifice would be worthwhile. However, he finally gave up the idea and gently put it back on the tea table, an act which told me that he was not totally insane, that the morality in his heart had not completely collapsed.

A thought struck me. I must bring him to the Christian church. He needed find a fulcrum to stop his soul from sinking. As he was standing at a crossroad, not knowing where to go, I could not bear to see him heading in the wrong direction. As to how to save him, I had in fact no idea. All I knew was that right now he could neither tell the taste of sweet sugar, nor that of hot pepper or bitter poison. His heart had been bewitched by a wicked belief, and religion was perhaps the only weapon to drive it out, and most probably the last straw.

The church was only five minutes' walk from the neighborhood where I lived. Whenever I was passing by that slim Gothic structure, I would consciously or unconsciously have a look at the high-rise cross on its top. From it Bible chanting could be heard which, like a cloud of fragrant mist, would disperse in my head, dazzling me to the point where I got lost in a world of fantasy. I had enjoyed going there, whenever my heart was in knots, although I was not a Christian. I used to sit in a dark corner silently for two or three hours. Overwhelmed by the solemnity of it, I had to breathe carefully, and would feel guilty if I let out a cough. I did not know what the Christians were whispering, but the sight of their devoted faces set my bound body and heart free. It was in this church that I became acquainted with Minister Gao. A persistent man, with a conspicuous nevus on the nose, he had been trying unsuccessfully to convert me from time to time. Christ in my eye was no more than a vague notion. I found it unbearable for an animated man to creep into a notion, to let it control one's life and wrap one up like an airtight bag. An aimless man, I hated being directed by a force from outside.

The door of the church was locked. The prayer would begin at seven in the evening, but now it was only four in the afternoon. I called for the door-keeper, and he opened the door for us. The great difference between a church and a museum was that a museum's door was open only for ticket buyers, while a church's was open for all. All were equal and pitiful children of God, whether you were an official or a tramp; and it would open whenever you needed to come in, without too much explanation, even if it had been locked.

To my surprise, the church was very dark with all its lights turned off, but a shaft of light from above shone down on the twisted body of Jesus, and freed other places inside from the reign of darkness. Locked as it was when viewed from outside, surprisingly there were quite a few Christians inside. An old lady was standing at a corner, head lowered, facing the wall and murmuring something; a middle-aged woman was sitting on a bench, holding a *New Testament* with both hands and reciting it in low voice; a young man, in fashionable clothes, was kneeling down on a bench, praying or contemplating. Rows of coarse benches, for Christians to sit or to kneel, were so empty and desolate. The church, like an auditorium, was now as deep and vast as a ravine.

Xiaolin and I were sitting on one of the wooden benches. Neither of us spoke — language seemed superfluous and cumbersome in such a place. Looking at the committed Christians and the crucified Jesus suspended in mid-air, I suddenly felt that I had been hollowed out. The mess in my brain drifted away, and the viscera seemed to have disappeared from my belly without a trace. The inside and outside of the church, though separated by a single door, were two different worlds indeed!

After we had sat for about twenty minutes, my mobile phone rang. The other world was calling me, so I poked at Xiaolin, who was still in a daze, and we walked out of the church together.

It was Dalin. He asked where I was and where Xiaolin was. He was now below my apartment building. He had just been up and knocked at my door for a long time, and was terrified to find that no one answered. He knew that I might have gone out to work, but what about his brother? His hair was standing on end by the time his brother stepped through the door. Xiaolin couldn't afford to court any more troubles.

On entering the courtyard, I saw Li Tiantian's car near my apartment building. Dalin was standing beside the car, anxiously looking toward the gate. When he saw us, he ran over. Ignoring my smile, he threw an arm round Xiaolin's shoulders, asked him how he felt, whether he was doing better than he had been, and how he was eating and sleeping, etc. To each question, Xiaolin just replied "not bad."

Li Tiantian got out of the car. She wore a white dress, which made her look graceful, and a pair of red high-heeled shoes, which resembled two little crimson birds. She was smiling, and the scars on her face under the sun were even more conspicuous.

"Sorry for the trouble, brother. Xiaolin is a tough nut. He lets a platoon of people move around him, and no one can have peace." With this, she turned her head to Xiaolin. "Xiaolin, have you learned your lesson this time? Without my help, you would still be doing time in the reform-through-labor farm. How is it that you are here, enjoying your freedom? Listen, Xiaolin, you are not a kid any more, and you should have learned something about this society. It's a high-speed train. If you pit your fragile flesh and blood against it, aren't you setting yourself up for a train accident?" Li Tiantian's lips twitched as she said those words, apparently proud of her status as a benefactor.

Xiaolin was as numb and insensible as a block of wood. Dalin got his brother into the car, and told me that he was sending him back to the village. Third Aunt couldn't wait any longer. Her tearful daily phone call had been making Dalin feel terrible for the rest of the day, from morning to evening. I said he might as well send his brother back; his mind needed a rest, and the fields in the countryside might be more suitable for him.

After Dalin left, I took out my mobile phone to have a look at the clock. It was time for most people to knock off from work. Unlike them, however, newspaper men and women usually knocked off at midnight, so I needed make a trip to the press house. Once there, I went directly to Xue Yulu's office. I needed to inform her of my intention to investigate the abuses of detainees in the reform-through-labor farm, for without her consent all my efforts would count for nothing, no matter how well I did my job. Access to publication was in Xue Yulu's hands, and she could sentence an article to death as easily as killing a mosquito.

To my astonishment, Xue Yulu was very supportive. She had never been so agreeable since becoming my superior. She had always been hesitant and reluctant to assent to whatever interview plan I proposed to her, leaving me the impression that she was always fault-finding. I was not accustomed to receiving a satisfactory answer so promptly. After all, there was something odd and mysterious about her smile.

In the corridor outside Xue Yulu's office, I met Xiang Wenhua. He was enjoying a sausage with obsessive relish. I asked him what he was up to these days. All agog, Xiang seemed to be full of curiosity. It was natural that he would feel like that, for in spite of the fact that we worked in the same department, we had seldom spoken with each other. Xiang replied idly that he had been busy with the usual tripe. I said I would like to have a private talk with him.

"When?"

"This evening."

Xiang Wenhua declined because Xue Lihan had invited him to a karaoke bar that evening. He asked if I had a lot to say to him, and I answered not really — just a few words. He suggested that we go to the meeting room.

"I have the key to it," he said.

Xiang Wenhua really was a special figure in our press house. I would never have guessed that he had the key to the meeting room. For journalists like me, the meeting room, which was furnished like a splendid palace, was not accessible to ordinary men. Xiang Wenhua opened the outer door and led me to that of the inner room. He kicked it open and, pointing inside, said that it was the place the press house had specially arranged for him to rest in; he often slept away whole afternoons there.

I cast a glimpse into the inner room, and saw that it was fully furnished — there was a bed with spring mattress, a sofa, a DVD player, a computer, golf clubs, etc. Amazingly, there were women's articles, such as perfume and sanitary napkins. Before I could make any inquiry, Xiang Wenhua began to complain, saying he was often unable to access the room, to which he was entitled by name, even when he was drowsy with fatigue; and that President Sun had been so mean as to occupy it at will, neglecting to put his things away when he left. Once when Xiang Wenhua went in to sleep, he found the floor covered in slippery dirt, whose foul smell almost turned his stomach.

"Has Xue Yulu ever come here?" I asked.

Xiang Wenhua looked around and lowered his voice, "Why not? Of course she comes so long as President Sun is here!" Realizing he had said something unworthy, Xiang Wenhua asked me not to disclose it to others. Anyhow he was dependent on the good offices of President Sun and Director Xue, so he must keep the matter a secret for their sake.

Sitting down on the soft sofa, I began to praise Xiang Wenhua, saying that, although he and I had not had much contact, I still found him to be an exceptionally nice young man, neither inclined toward gossip nor involved in other people's business, neither snobbish nor arrogant, despite his being the son of a senior official. Xiang Wenhua said he should have long since gone abroad. He had a younger sister in Canada who repeatedly urged him to go, saying that the air there was fresh, and that people lived longer as a result. A businesswoman in Canada, his sister had a fairly bulky purse and had bought an apartment for him. The apartment remained unoccupied, however; and in order to guard the furniture in it from worms, a white person had to be hired. As manpower in Canada was expensive, they had to pay that person more than 10,000 RMB each month. Of course, hiring a Chinese Canadian would have been cheaper, but the whole family opposed it, saying that they would trust anybody before Chinese Canadians — for they had sticky fingers, and couldn't keep a secret.

I said it would be his best choice to immigrate to Canada straight away. Canada was a developed country, and in almost every respect better than China, which was still a developing one. Xiang Wenhua frowned and, after a sigh, said "Who could refuse such a prospect?" However, he was not a good learner when it came to English. He had entered numerous training courses, but the words which had lodged in his memory were no more than twenty. He wondered who had invented English; with sounds like "ji-ji-gua-gua, wu-li-wa-la," it sounded just like the chirruping of birds. What a mess! Xiang Wenhua had failed to acquire the English language, even though he had spared no effort in trying to learn. Would he not become a blind and deaf man, if he could not speak the language of the country where he was planning to go? Nevertheless, he would emigrate one day. Not many people with the means to leave wished to stay at home!

I changed the subject. I asked Xiang Wenhua if he would like to join me in an interview. Xiang Wenhua told me not to mention jobs in his presence; the mere mention of them would make him start to drop off. Interviews, writing, etc., were the most monotonous things in this world. Why should all these burdens be pushed onto him? How inconsiderate his father was! He had chosen journalism for him from so many possible jobs, in the hope of improving his writing skills! It was like driving a duck onto a chicken rack, or using a bamboo pole for a crossbeam. Wasn't that ridiculous?

Still, Xiang Wenhua asked what kind of interview I had in mind. I told him how Xiaolin had got his scrotum hurt in the reform-through-labor farm. Xiang Wenhua asked if I was making it all up, with his eyes glaring large and round, and his face full of surprise. I said I would not speak ill of the reform-through-labor farm without first having acquired solid evidence. What did he think, that I was sick of living? Xiang Wenhua seemed to be getting very agitated, or rather, very excited. Rubbing his hands he said, "Let's go, let's do the interview, let's terminate the mother-fuckers!"

Xiang Wenhua asked when we could go. What he meant was to go as quickly as possible. Given his habitual failure to find any material of his own worth writing up, he could do nothing but lift copy from other newspapers. "Hse-hse-hse, ha-ha-ha, got his scrotum hurt…just the thought of it makes me laugh. What a bizarre subject! How funny it is! If written out, it might shock the whole world! Or win a prize, you never know!"

Xiang Wenhua also made it clear that he did not wish to do the writing, and was not interested in the payments either. I should write the article and sign my name before his. He would just follow me, and would prefer to be regarded as my bodyguard! His father was particularly keen that Xiang Wenhua should never say whose son he was, wherever he went.

I agreed to everything. I invited him to tea to celebrate the wonderful cooperation between us. Casting a look at his watch, Xiang Wenhua said that he had kept Xue Lihan waiting too long and had to go. I said I had a word of advice for him: that he had better keep away from Xue Lihan, who was a street hooligan and would someday have him ruined. Xiang Wenhua stood up and stretched his back, saying, "You don't understand: only hooligans ever achieve anything great! Don't you see how many former hooligans have now become big shots? This is a society for swindlers, and everyone is swindling! Big Brother, do you not know the times you are living in? How can you go on being so block-headed?"

"All right, all right, let's say no more about it," I said. "As per our agreement we will set off tomorrow."

"No problem," replied Xiang Wenhua. He then asked, "Is the reform farm far away? If it is I will try to order a car."

"You can if you really want to!" I said; and then warned him again, "For the time being, there is no need to let Xue Yulu know that you are going with me."

"So what if she knows? Is she able to stop me?" Xiang Wenhua said casually as he went out.

I shook his hand in farewell, and made my way back on my bicycle. Bearing Xiang Wenhua's company in mind, I felt confident of justice for Xiaolin. Xiang Wenhua knew what he was up to, when he limited his own role to that of my bodyguard. Had he seen through my intentions? I had involved him for just that purpose. With Xiang Wenhua's backup, we would have green lights all the way.

19

Guankou Farm, meaning *Narrow Pass Farm*, was the name of the reform-through-labor farm where Xiaolin had been detained. It was a four-hour ride by car from Yuebei. The narrow road zigzagged through the mountains, with towering crags on one side of the road, frighteningly deep valleys on the other side. In the valleys, a winding creek ran reluctantly between grotesque stones. Our car bumped along the rough road, threatening to throw our intestines into confusion.

The reform-through-labor farm was located in a valley, which, surrounded by multiple ranges of mountains, had a wide stretch of open land in the middle. Several rows of brick-built houses formed a clustered settlement. It looked like a deserted military barrack. Two watchtowers loomed above the houses, which were surrounded by a wall covered with dense iron nets. A loudspeaker fastened to a tree was shouting something from time to time.

I woke up Xiang Wenhua, who had been sleeping all the way and snoring more or less loudly. Opening his eyes and looking out of the window, he said, "What a hellish place it is here!"

Xiang Wenhua made the driver stop the car, saying he wanted to piss.

Getting out of the car, Xiang Wenhua hastily urinated on the ground. He had hardly tied up his belt when he started to run after a wild rabbit. In the race, Xiang Wenhua was obviously the slower of the two. However, he ran a long way after it, his stout figure swaying among the bean crops. Naturally the rabbit kept beyond his reach. As he returned, Xiang Wenhua was waving a handful of newly plucked wild flowers.

When we arrived at the gate of the reform-through-labor farm, the guard stopped us from entering. The guard was fairly young. Standing straight at his post, he looked very much like a puppet. As he looked at us, his eyes rolled back and forth, but his head remained motionless, as if it had been firmly fixed in place.

"We'd like to see the warden of the detention house," I said to the guard.

"He's not in," the guard said.

"If the warden is not available, we'd like to see the vice warden," I said.

"The vice warden is not in either," the guard answered.

"Then we'd straight away like to see a bald watch-guard who is around sixty years old," I said.

"What's his name?" The guard asked.

Stuck for an answer, I just stressed that the watch-guard that we'd like to see was a bald man.

"There are several bald men here. How can I know which one you're looking for?" the guard said.

Having run out of options, I produced my press card and showed it to the guard. With his head held still, the guard took my press card and lifted it high into the air. Narrowing his eyes, he scrutinized it for a long while before handing it back to me. Smiling hesitantly, the guard said, "I can't let you in."

"Why not?" I asked.

Twisting his mouth, the guard said, "Haven't you heard the phrase: 'Beware of fire, thieves and journalists'?"

Annoyed by his remark, with fiery anger in my tone, I said, "You have no right to stop journalists from conducting interviews."

The guard replied, "This institute stipulates that no journalist should be permitted to enter."

Greatly infuriated, Xiang Wenhua pointed at the guard with his forefinger, shouting, "Who do you think you are that you dare to stop us journalists? Are you sick of living?"

While Xiang Wenhua was shouting his denunciations, the guard hastily rushed into the guard's cabin and pressed the emergency button. All of a sudden, the noise of the alarm bells burst out. The bell noises were mixed with grotesque human shouts. In less than two minutes, a police car whistled out of the courtyard and arrived at the gate. No sooner had it pulled up than five policemen got out, asking the guard, "What's up?"

Pointing at me and Xiang Wenhua, the guard said, "These two men who claimed to be journalists are trouble makers. When I refused to let them in, they found fault with me and even threatened to beat me."

Taking one step forward, Xiang Wenhua argued, "Why not let us in? We have every right to do interviews. Why do you stop us?"

Hardly had Xiang Wenhua finished his words when one of the policemen took hold of his arms forcefully. Snatching the wild flowers from Xiang Wenhua's hands, the policeman dashed them onto the ground and stamped upon them heavily. Xiang Wenhua shouted out the command, "Let go of my arms!"

But the policeman paid no attention to his words. Turning his head around, Xiang Wenhua strove to bite the policeman on the back of his hand. Outraged by Xiang Wenhua's attempt, the policeman gripped Xiang Wenhua even more tightly, and, to vent his fury, kicked Xiang Wenhua several times in the shank. Grabbed by two policemen, Xiang Wenhua was dragged into the police car. Immediately afterward, I was dragged and pushed into the car, too.

Sitting in the car, Xiang Wenhua's face was as black as thunder. He made only one remark, "You'll regret what you've been doing to me!"

Hearing this, the policeman who had kicked Xiang Wenhua, spat in his face, so that half of it was covered in spray. In spite of the burning anger erupting from his eyes, Xiang Wenhua closed his mouth, arguing no more. I took a paper napkin from my pocket and cleaned Xiang Wenhua's face of the spittle.

Showing no sign of either regret or timidity, the policeman shouted, "I will regret? What nonsense! I've never known regret in my life! You fucking journalists! I've seen plenty of journalists before! You come here to make a show of authority? Why don't you open your fucking eyes wider and see clearly what sort of place this is? I don't mind telling you that too many fellows, even more stiff-necked than you, became meekly compliant, after staying here only a couple of days. But you'd like to show you're more formidable than them? Who do you think you are? I advise you to bear it in mind: my name is Zhang Zheng. I'll wait and see what you can do to me."

After both Xiang Wenhua and I were pushed into the police procedural office, all the policemen who had escorted us left. In the room sat a young policeman, whose attitude was more reasonable.

"What's your purpose in coming to the reform-through-labor farm?" he asked.

Turning his head aside, Xiang Wenhua disdained to talk with the young policeman. I handed my press card over to the policeman. He took and viewed it.

Rolling his eyeballs, the policeman asked me, "Have you contacted our leader beforehand?"

I shook my head.

"What do you want to find out with your interview? Is it for a positive report or for negative fault-finding? If you are here to find fault, you'd better leave as soon as possible," he warned us.

"It's not a matter of a positive report or negative report, but of an objective investigation into a case," I replied.

"What case is it?" the policeman asked.

"As for the particular case, there's no need to reveal it beforehand," I said. "We'd only like to see the warden of the detention house and the watch-guard who has a bald head."

"The warden is not in. As for the bald watch-guard, what's his name?" the young policeman asked.

I thought hard. After some while I suddenly recalled Xiaolin had once mentioned that the bald man had a deformed ear, resulting from having been bitten by a dog. Hearing this, the young policeman let out a hearty laugh, and said, "Can it be Song Laowan[13] that you'd like to see? His name perfectly matches his personality: he is as dull as an old bowl. I wonder what it is that makes him worthy of investigation?"

While talking with us, the young policeman picked up the office telephone to make a call to the warden of the reform-through-labor farm. The call got through successfully, but the warden's attitude sounded very tough: he would not accept any interview. The warden said he himself was in the middle of attending a meeting in the city, but that he had decided he would return at once.

At this moment, Xiang Wenhua spoke again, "You are illegally detaining us, you do know that, don't you?"

The young policeman looked surprised, and said, "I'm receiving you. You are not in custody with handcuffs. Why do you call this 'illicit detainment'? What nonsense you're talking!"

Taking out his mobile phone, Xiang Wenhua said he was about to call the Party secretary of Yuebei municipal politics and law committee. In his call, Xiang Wenhua addressed Secretary Huang as Uncle Huang, claiming that while he was conducting an interview together with another correspondent in Guankou Farm, he had not only been barred for no valid reason, but had also been beaten up; now he was still being detained illicitly, deprived of his fundamental right to freedom.

While Xiang Wenhua was on the phone, I noticed that the policeman's face changed from florid to pale. Overwhelmed with horror, the young policeman rose to his feet and got two cups to pour some water for us. His hands were shaking; some overflowing water wetted Xiang Wenhua's pants.

Before the policeman handed my cup of water to me, the telephone on the table rang. Obviously the incoming call was from the warden. With fiery anger in his voice, the warden asked the young policeman, "Who has beaten up the correspondents?"

With a quaking voice, the policeman emphasized repeatedly that he hadn't done any beating, and that his attitude had been excellent. Probably, he wanted us to hear, or perhaps his shaking hand allowed the words to escape from the telephone handset; at any rate, I could clearly hear the voice of the warden at the other end of the line. He said he was rushing back in a great hurry; before he arrived, the correspondents must be received with a maximum of warmth and generosity; whatever the correspondents wanted must be granted unreservedly.

Hanging up the phone, the policeman endeavored to smile at us. But it seemed all of a sudden he did not know how to smile; his smile looked extraordinarily stiff. I smiled back at him, but Xiang Wenhua did not pay any attention to his flattering smiles. The policeman went out and was away a long while. Upon returning, he was followed by two policewomen who were carrying a tray of fruits and a beverage. On the tray were some bananas and pears. The beverage was lemonade. A policewoman courteously peeled some bananas and handed them over to us.

The policeman who had identified himself as Zhang Zheng came too. His former bursting wrath now completely gave way to smiles, which were overflowing from every pore in his face. He took out a Chunghwa cigarette and proffered it to Xiang Wenhua, but no matter how hard he tried, he could not successfully deposit it into Xiang Wenhua's hand, because Xiang Wenhua swung it from one side to the other, evading the proferred cigarette. As a last resort, Zhang Zheng attempted to insert the cigarette between Xiang's lips. However, with Xiang Wenhua firmly closing his mouth, the cigarette simply could not get in. Sitting down right next to Xiang Wenhua, Zhang Zheng incessantly called Xiang Wenhua "Brother," claiming that the incident had been caused by a misunderstanding; nothing more and nothing less than a misunderstanding; he himself was entirely and solely to blame; he was too impetuous; he had got eyes but could not see; he should be damned, yes, he truly should be damned; he would like to apologize; he would sincerely apologize; if apologies were not enough, he hoped Xiang Wenhua might beat him; yes, he meant it — Xiang Wenhua could beat him in whatever way he pleased; Xiang Wenhua could beat him as hard as he wished; while beating, Xiang Wenhua should think of him not as a human, but as a crazy dog that had just bitten him; if Xiang Wenhua didn't want to get his hands dirty, he wouldn't have to. Instead, he could spank himself in front of Xiang Wenhua's eyes. Did this sound okay?

Xiang Wenhua, with contempt on his face, remained oblivious of Zhang Zheng. Zhang Zheng stood up and planted himself in front of Xiang Wenhua, spanking himself. As he spanked for the fourth time, Xiang Wenhua roared like an outraged lion, "Get away from here! How disgusting you are! Get away!"

His face still wreathed in smiles, Zhang Zheng retired from the room, nodding and bowing all the way. Shortly after Zhang Zheng left, Song Laowan entered. Paying particular attention to Song Laowan's ears, I found that the right one was curly, looking like a misshaped and shriveled leaf. And in fact a part of it was missing. In contrast to the way I had imagined him, Song Laowan was extraordinarily small. With crooked legs and a hunched back, he looked pretty pitiable. He appeared peaceable and nice, showing no sign of violence or brutality at all. I suspected that there might have been some mistake, because according to Xiaolin's portrayal, Song Laowan was an unpardonable villain.

Throughout, Song Laowan's face overflowed with smiles, which never left his face for a single second. He added water to my cup and to Xiang Wenhua's cup in turn, then, with great caution, seated himself on a stool opposite us, as if he had been a relative of ours. I asked him if he knew a Tian Xiaolin. Song Laowan nodded and said he did; that Tian Xiaolin used to be a prisoner in this place, and now was outside. Before I could ask any more questions, Song Laowan asked me if I knew Tian Xiaolin too. He said Tian Xiaolin had had a good time at his hands; under his protection, he had not suffered many beatings; on the contrary, he had eaten well and slept well; how many fellow prisoners had envied him!

"I have done my utmost for this lad. Yes, I have done my utmost for him," Song Laowan added.

All of a sudden, Xiang Wenhua shouted at Song Laowan, "Then who cut Tian Xiaolin's scrotum? Tell me, was it you who did it? You old rascal, why do you pretend to be a good man? Tell me now, was it you who did it?"

Song Laowan's face twisted slightly. Nevertheless, he went on looking as amiable as he always had.

"What are you talking about? I don't understand you," Song Laowan asked Xiang Wenhua.

Xiang Wenhua seemed to intend going on with his denunciation of Song Laowan. But when he noticed I was winking to him, Xiang Wenhua closed his mouth. I opened my interview notebook. Taking out my tape recorder, I pressed the recording button. Having done all this preparatory work, I embarked on a chain of questions addressed to Song Laowan.

"Did you often call Tian Xiaolin to your office in the middle of the night?" I asked Song Laowan.

Turning his eyelids upwards, Song Laowan adopted an air of contemplation. Finally, it seemed that with an immense effort he managed to recall a long lost memory.

"It seems I did call him to my office," Song Laowan answered.

"Please don't use the word 'seem' when answering me," I said to Song Laowan. "Say in plain words, 'Yes' or 'No.'"

"Yes," Song Laowan answered.

"How many times did you call him to your office?" I asked.

Song Laowan turned his eyelids upwards again. Scratching his head, he muttered, "Once or twice. I can't remember precisely."

"According to the regulations made by the reform-through-labor farm, can you call a captive to your office on your own?" I asked.

"It is against the regulations to do that," Song Laowan answered. "However, Tian Xiaolin's case was an exceptional one. He had a stomach-ache. Out of my concern for him, I called him to my office." He claimed that he had called Xiaolin to his office for the purpose of using the massage therapy passed down from his forefathers to ease Xiaolin's stomach-ache. He said he had done that on his own because he hated to bother the clinic doctors in the middle of the night.

"You touched and felt Tian Xiaolin's body with your hands, didn't you?" I asked Song Laowan.

"'Touched and felt'? What do you mean?" Song Laowan asked. "I have told you I massaged Tian Xiaolin's stomach with the method passed down from my forefathers. I only did that, and nothing else. What I need to point out is that I massaged Tian Xiaolin through his clothes, which were rather thick."

"But according to the complaints we have received, you summoned Tian

Xiaolin to your office in the middle of the night on eleven occasions," I said to Song Laowan. "And you carried out sexual assaults of great severity on Tian Xiaolin. A more shocking thing was that, when you were alone with him, you cut Tian Xiaolin's scrotum. I wonder how you explain these strange things."

Wearing a bitter smile on his face, Song Laowan said with a sigh, "A good man received an evil reward. There is nothing more to the story than this."

Song Laowan claimed he had summoned Tian Xiaolin to his office twice in all, and it was on the second occasion that Tian Xiaolin took up a knife and attempted to hurt himself so that he could be bailed out of the reform-through-labor farm to receive medical treatment. Thanks to his prompt pressing of the alarm, the clinic doctors had been informed of the accident and had arrived quickly, which had saved Tian Xiaolin's life.

"Look at this chap Tian Xiaolin!" Song Laowan deplored. "It was okay that he didn't thank me. Anyway, I have never expected other people to repay my kindness when I do good things. But how could Tian Xiaolin repay good with evil? How could he wrong me with evil fabrications? I have helped an evil tiger! I have helped an evil snake! A good man received what a bad man deserved. A good man was not repaid with good. How I have been wronged! What wrongs fall to my lot! Do you know why Tian Xiaolin was allowed to receive medical treatment on the reform-through-labor farm? Wasn't it due to my pleading with the warden for permission? I'm about sixty, almost as old as Tian Xiaolin's father's generation. I enjoyed a pure reputation for most of my life. But in my old age I am the victim of this kind of false accusation. What a shameful life is ahead of me!"

Just as Song Laowan was crying out his grievances, Mo Shaoqiu, the warden of the reform-through-labor farm, came back. I would rather say Mo Shaoqiu dashed into the room. As he learned the opulent lad sitting on the sofa was Xiang Wenhua, Mo Shaoqiu's one leg knelt down onto the floor in front of him. Taking hold of Xiang Wenhua's hand, with tiny flecks of spittle overflowing the corners of his mouth, Mo Shaoqiu kept saying, "I'm sorry, Brother! I'm really sorry, Brother! You have to forgive me, who am your brother! Whoever beat you, I swear I'll find out. I'll deal with him most severely. I'll not stop punishing him until you feel content. I give you my oath: I'll definitely remove the black sheep from the police ranks."

20

After a bumper feast was over, Xiang Wenhua staggered to his feet, and was dragged away and pushed into a Hummer SUV by Mo Shaoqiu, who was also staggering and said they would go hunting in the mountains.

I was sent back to the press house in a Santana. Upon getting out of the car, the driver gave me a plastic bag, which he said had been entrusted to him by Sheriff Mo. Back at my office cubicle, I opened the bag and found in it a stack of bank notes. I licked my finger and started to count. There were ten notes altogether, amounting to one thousand *yuan*.

Immediately the plastic bag in my hand was like a piece of burning coal. I didn't know what to do with it. Should I take it back home, or return it to the detention house? Or should I give it to the press house in order to show my integrity, and in the mean time lay the foundation for future investigation and publication of this case? I had decided to continue investigating Xiaolin's grievances, but I had the vague suspicion that things were far more complicated than I had originally thought. During the feast, Mo kept talking about one of his uncles. It was because of this wonderful uncle, the husband of his paternal aunt, that he had encountered no difficulty getting a job in the public security bureau after he was demobilized, and that he was made head of the detention house four years later. A gentle cough from his uncle, who was secretary to a senior official, was sufficient to frighten his subordinates into a cold sweat. His uncle cared for him very much indeed! The reason that his uncle cared about him so much was that he had a good paternal aunt. A fierce tiger outside, he was a tame one at home, and dared not turn his head to the west if his wife said "east!" If ever he neglected to help Sheriff Mo, Mo was ready to fly a thousand miles with prepared tears in his eyes to cry them out before his aunt. Once he cried, his aunt's heart would become sodden and wilt like a piece of paper exposed to rain; she would storm at her husband — shouting, stamping, throwing teacups or pen-pots, even bumping her head against the walls! His uncle, whose mouth was as unyielding as a woodpecker's beak at the beginning, could not withstand such a fuss, and after two or three such episodes would give in, and to hell with his principles!

In fact, what worried me most was Xiang Wenhua. He was certainly the leading light at the feast. Sheriff Mo managed to drag him to sit by his side, addressing him again and again as "Brother." Sheriff Mo frequently poured wine for him, put the food on his plate, and praised his father in the most flattering terms. He said that Governor Xiang was the greatest governor the province had ever had; that Governor Xiang had a fine square face and a wart above his right eyelid, which was the sign of a great man; that Governor Xiang was a good person, and just one look was enough to see that he was a person of rare and superlative quality; that it was an honor for him to be acquainted with the heir to Governor Xiang, and it was the good karma he had accumulated in three previous lives, nay, in eight previous lives; that being the governor's son, Xiang Wenhua didn't put on airs, which was very unusual!

Sheriff Mo proceeded to claim that he had studied *I Ching, i.e. The Book of Changes.* He studied Xiang Wenhua's face for a while, asked about the precise time of his birth, and then declared that Xiang Wenhua was most favorably blessed, and insisted that Xiang Wenhua was connected with him by destiny — could it be that they were twins in a former life! The only difference between the two was that Xiang Wenhua, who had been diligent in his former life, had been reborn in a rich and noble family, while he, who had been less diligent, was reborn in a poor farmer's family. His father was useless and knew only how to dig fields with a hoe, or to lead cattle to pasture by the rein. In spite of this, he was lucky to have a good aunt, and even more lucky to have an uncle whose brilliance filled Sheriff Mo's face with great pride.

"Older Brother Xiang," that was how Sheriff Mo, who was in fact much older, addressed Xiang Wenhua. "How could you insert bricks under your brother's pillow like that? I think this must be the result of somebody else's conspiracy, not your intention! Think it over, Older Brother Xiang. How is it possible for such a thing to have happened in a place under your brother's jurisdiction? What will be the consequence if this is attributed to your brother? Won't your brother be removed from his position? Song Laowan is only a temporary employee, a short, old man who has always behaved himself, as you've seen; and his hand trembles if he is asked to kill a mosquito! I might be convinced if you said others did this wicked thing; but I will die before I believe he did it."

Sheriff Mo showered curses on Zhang Zheng, for being so blind as to have failed to recognize Older Brother Xiang, and for being so reckless as to have attacked people! Zhang Zheng was not in his good books, absolutely not — always crossing him, and always coveting the position of warden! Zhang Zheng had delivered a blow to Older Brother Xiang, but Sheriff Mo felt the pain too. Zhang Zheng's assaults on Older Brother Xiang were tantamount to slapping Sheriff Mo in the face. Zhang Zheng was happy to take a dump, but expected Sheriff Mo to help wipe his ass. He probably thought he was smart! Unfortunately, his smartness had bitten him in the ass — he had lifted a rock, only to drop it onto his own feet! As for the real purpose behind his hitting Older Brother Xiang, wasn't it to ruin the good name of Sheriff Mo? What should we call an organization which dared hit the vice governor's son? The mafia, or an Al-Qaeda training camp? Who led it? Shouldn't he be removed from his position? Look, the rascal, or rather the villain, with his wicked intentions, was nothing less than a ravenous wolf. "Fuck—" Sheriff Mo's mouth twisted as he spat out a dirty word. With a face as dark as thunder, eyes glaring with the ghostly light of a serpent's, he forced out a few more words between his teeth, "The question is, which of the two of us will get screwed into the ground!"

I hardly uttered a word during this whole tirade. It seemed as if I didn't exist, although I sat there at the feast-table. As they shouted toasts, I raised my cup high above the table to let it clink against the others'. Xiang Wenhua didn't say much either, but the pique which had been pent up in his heart seemed to have gone. When Sheriff Mo praised his father and him, his face turned an intoxicated red. He had already come to appreciate Sheriff Mo's qualities as a person, and said that he was a real man, like a knight as described in western novels. Xiang Wenhua took out his pen and wrote down Sheriff Mo's uncle's name and telephone number, which he said would be given on his return home to his father, for strengthening contact with Sheriff Mo's uncle. He seemed to be competing with Sheriff Mo for the title of best drinker. Gulping down one mouthful after another, they began to flatter each other — one said the other was good, too good for words; whereupon the other said his interlocutor was not bad either, good enough to be a brother, to judge from the way he drank, and, what was more, to be a friend both in need and in deed. Hearing Xiang Wenhua was praising him, Sheriff Mo got so excited that on at least three occasions he clasped his head and kissed him on the face.

They went out hunting, and instantly became brothers who appreciated each other. What did this situation mean for me? I thought for a while, and decided that this was not an auspicious omen. The feast was undoubtedly a Hongmen Banquet[14]. Xiang Wenhua had been suborned by Sheriff Mo, and if he turned his coat, he would turn against the investigation as well as me. I should win him over and remind him of his mission, and of his conscience as a journalist. Xiang Wenhua was a pure man, pure almost to the point of being simple. In a way, he had become a weight, and the balance of the scale was dependent on which side he stood.

I called Xiang Wenhua, but his phone was powered off. I sat in the cubicle, senseless as a block of wood, my hand grasping that intoxicating stack of bank notes, my mind pondering whether or not I should turn in the money.

21

Xiaolin made a phone call to me, asking me to go back to the village. I asked him what had happened. Xiaolin was on the point of saying something, but thought better of it. Upon my return to the village three days later, I learned that a big event had just happened: Taoqi was dead!

With regard to what had claimed her life, there were different accounts: one was that she died of the humiliation Li Tiantian had afflicted on her, the other was that she committed suicide due to her womb cancer, which had made her so hopelessly miserable that she took her own life. In both versions, the episode of the fight between Li Tiantian and Taoqi was an indispensable element.

It was said that though Li Tiantian had come to the village in Dalin's company, Dalin did not bring her to his house; instead, he set her up in Beiqiang's house. After that, Dalin went back home with Xiaolin. At the sight of Dalin, smiles abruptly appeared on Taoqi's perennially livid face. After greeting Dalin with the words "You haven't died outside yet" Taoqi went into the kitchen to prepare some food. Shortly, sounds of a knife cutting something on a cutting board resounded in the kitchen.

Third Aunt sneaked to the kitchen door and took a stealthy look inside. She returned, reporting to Dalin that Taoqi was mincing meat, which meant she was probably planning to make dumplings. Third Aunt's peace of mind was deeply disturbed; she grumbled that whenever Dalin was home, Taoqi always tried her utmost to impress him favorably, but that in her usual life she was as lazy as a pig, and that she usually cooked food as if she were making pigswill.

It was Dalin's wish that Li Tiantian should hide herself inside Beiqiang's homestead, avoiding any exposure, in case she were seen by the villagers or should become the object of scandal. However, Li Tiantian was anything but an obedient person willing to remain unnoticed. Her greatest joy was to show herself to the world. She was exceedingly vexed by Dalin's attempt to hide her away as if she were personal property. Li Tiantian did not think that she was a secretly dug-up relic, much less a cargo to be smuggled. Then why should she be kept from public view? Moreover, her visit to the village had two motives: apart from her wish to look at the environment where Dalin had been born and brought up, Li Tiantian dearly wished to make it known to the villagers that he had got a new love. She hated being Dalin's concubine, and wanted to be his legally acknowledged wife. Li Tiantian was ready for a face-to-face confrontation with the woman named Taoqi. She would urge her to leave Dalin and to go her own way. If Taoqi were so unwise as not to take her advice, Li Tiantian would use vicious language to ridicule, humiliate, and curse her. If need be, Li Tiantian would use her hands too, in addition to her sharp tongue. She was willing to go as far as to pick a fight with Taoqi. She would not stop until Taoqi died of vexation.

Of course, Li Tiantian was not solely to blame for straying from Beiqiang's courtyard. It happened that just as Li Tiantian was about to remove her earrings for Lifang to look at, and while she was eloquently telling Lifang about how she had got them and what the price was — she revealed to Lifang they had been made in Italy and had cost her sixty thousand Chinese *yuan*, a kid ran in, telling her Qiuli was spitting on her car. When she went out, on the heels of the kid, Li Tiantian discovered a fairly large crowd of people, the majority being children of various ages. The crowd stood around her car, observing a boisterous scene, though it was hard to tell whether it was the car or Qiuli that they were watching. Having elbowed the crowd aside, Li Tiantian did see a disheveled woman spitting on her beloved car. Egged on by the crowd, the woman even conceived the idea of pissing on the car. Qiuli had already pulled her pants down to her ankles, exposing her hairy private parts. Though Li Tiantian had guessed this woman must be Qiuli, about whom Dalin had told her a lot, she still felt quite terrified as the insane woman stood in front of her in person. None the less, she screwed up her courage and kicked Qiuli, who became dazed for a moment, and then uttered a horrifying howl like a terrified beast confronted by a hunting rifle. Drawing up her pants, Qiuli ran away.

Taking out some paper napkins, Li Tiantian cleaned the dirty marks from her car. Someone started to talk to Li Tiantian, asking her if she had come from America, in what way she was connected to Liben, and how much the shiny new car had cost her. Straightforwardly, Li Tiantian told the people she was Dalin's girlfriend.

Luobo, as one of the onlookers, put in, "Girlfriend? Dalin has a wife, doesn't he? How could he have a girlfriend? If you are Dalin's girlfriend, what is Taoqi to Dalin?"

Li Tiantian replied, "Is Taoqi a fit match for Dalin? He has made this trip to deal with the divorce papers."

Twisting her mouth into the shape of a flat bean, Luobo said, "Divorce Taoqi and marry you? What else do you have except money? Have you looked at your own face? With that scarred skin, it makes people's blood run cold!"

Li Tiantian did not heed Luobo's words. Taking out a pair of sunglasses, she covered her eyes with them and proceeded to take a stroll about the village. Wherever she went, Li Tiantian invariably attracted people, who would point at her and exchange comments among themselves. She paid no attention to these boring people, but she understood that this procedure was necessary in order to gain the villagers' recognition. What was more, as a person coming from a big city, additionally, as a rich boss, she wanted no conflict with the village women, who had never experienced the outside world. Weren't these the people popularly dismissed as the lumpen-proletariat?

As Li Tiantian stepped onto a broad threshing floor, without warning a woman came running toward her from the opposite direction. The woman, who had a bulging belly, fell upon her like a ferocious wolf. Grabbing her hair forcefully, puh, puh, puh, the woman spat onto her face. Though not in the least prepared for this, Li Tiantian managed, with considerable effort, to struggle free, and started to exchange insults with the woman. Li Tiantian concluded from what the woman was saying, that this was none other than her rival Taoqi. Taoqi's shape resembled a stuffed gunnysack. Her width seemed to exceed her height. Were Dalin's eyes covered with chicken shit when he chose to marry this woman? The thought of Dalin having slept with such a woman made Li Tiantian feel very uncomfortable.

In Dalin's mother's opinion, nobody in the world was lazier than Taoqi. But when it came to calling bad names, Taoqi's mouth was as busy as it was diligent. Like a blazing machine-gun, it shot forth a wide variety of vicious and dirty words. She called Li Tiantian bitch, prostitute, the result of her mother having been fucked by a dog, or a donkey, or a horse. In the mouth of Taoqi, no ancestor of Li Tiantian's was a decent individual: her grandfather was a whoremonger, her grandmother a seductress, her father a bastard, her mother a trashy woman unwanted by any man and with a cunt full of maggots. To make the situation worse for Li Tiantian, someone with no stake in the matter chose to get involved. Immediately behind Taoqi stood Luobo, who was assisting her to fire off her curses. Undoubtedly, it was

Luobo who had delivered the information to her which brought Taoqi here now. Luobo's neck was wiry, while her head was oblong. This disproportion made her head sway from one side to another. It was as if a frond of bamboo were supporting a bowl on its top end, making you fear it might fall off at any moment. Luobo spared no effort to invigorate and encourage Taoqi, so that her anger flamed more violently. Whatever bad names Taoqi was calling Li Tiantian, Luobo would repeat them like a parrot. The two women formed a duet, with the lead vocalist singing at a high pitch and the backing singer following at a low pitch.

Of course Li Tiantian fired back too. But she was a civilized person who hated to use vulgar words. She wished to look like a well-educated person, even when it came to brawling. So she said, over and over again, "Why don't you talk reason? How can you be so ill-mannered? Don't you feel that those nasty names you call other people really apply to yourself?"

Many more onlookers were gathering on the threshing floor. Some sniggered, covering their mouths with their hands; some tried to mediate a truce; others laughed so much at this spectacular combat that their eyes were reduced to narrow slits. Life was too boring. A quarrel or a fight lent an additional hue to its tedious routine. This being the case, who would not have felt happy at such a sight?

But there were people who did not like to see any disturbances in the village. Shuanhu was such a person. Having stood on the verge of the threshing floor and watched for a while, Shuanhu went right up to the women. Assuming the voice always adopted by village-heads, he ordered the women to stop, "Aren't you ashamed? Mazi Village has been mentioned in our province's newspaper. The investment project has reached a critical moment. There are visitors in the village almost every day now. What a disgrace it is to quarrel like this!"

Shuanhu had just participated in a study program at the county town. The county magistrate had shaken hands with him — the magistrate's hands were very tender, as soft as sponge. How comfortable the feel of the magistrate's hands was! It must be even more comfortable to feel the hands of the provincial governor. His next goal was to feel the provincial governor's hands. To tell the truth, the experience of feeling the county magistrate's hands had made Shuanhu feel so happy that he turned from side to side in bed and could not get to sleep for several nights afterwards. At first, Shuanhu had only calculated mentally how much kickback the project would bring him, and whether he should buy a bulldozer or some other machines to prepare for contracting the project. It had been quite beyond his expectations that the project could bring him other benefits as well — he had never imagined it could enable him to become acquainted with so many officials! Anyway, it did not do for his daughter Jidan to earn an indecent living in sing-and-dance halls for her entire lifetime. That way of making money, quite apart from its indecency, was not even hygienic. After he got to know the officials, would it be so difficult for Jidan to accomplish a transformation and become a golden phoenix envied by everyone?

To tell the truth, Shuanhu had not been happy with Liben. When he learned that Liben had associated with Baolai, he could not help an unspeakable wrath from rising and erupting.

"The bastard son, Liben! You will plead with me for mercy someday!" Shuanhu cursed Liben in his heart. "How dare you set yourself against me? You idiot bed-wetter. You mark my word. If I set a little obstacle in your path, you'll fall on your face. You have the backing of the provincial and county leaders, but then what? Haven't you heard the saying 'A higher ranking official has less to say than the person who's actually in charge'? Will you present each and every of your complaints to those officials and wail for their intervention? To wail once or twice is okay. But if you keep on wailing, they'll get tired of you and think of you as a worthless wretch."

Of course, though there still were wrathful flames flaring in his heart, on the whole Shuanhu had become calm and peaceful once again. Liu Qi had instilled in Shuanhu the notion of "open the door and welcome them as guests, then close the door and beat them like dogs." At first, Shuanhu could not understand the purport of this utterance, but now he comprehended it as meaning: they should open the door and warmly welcome a dog as a guest, then close it and build high walls, so that the dog could not run away no matter how much it wanted to. When that day came, they could treat the dog as they pleased. They could extract its oil if they wished, they could skin it if they wished, and if they wished to boil or fry the dog, that would absolutely be up to them.

The funny thing was that after the completion of his study in the county town, apart from an unhappy story, practically nothing else remained in Shuanhu's memory. The story went as follows: A certain place was endeavoring to attract investment from outside. The negotiations had been on the verge of a successful outcome. However, for no better reason than that the landlord spat on the floor in front of the investor, the investment project, with a value of perhaps hundreds of millions RMB, was cancelled and came to nothing. The moral of the story was alleged to be: Good image is money. Good image is productive power! Now in broad daylight, and in the public sphere of the village, if the scene of the two women brawling and fighting was seen by a passing official, how disastrous would be the consequences!

In response to Shuanhu's bellowing, Li Tiantian shut up and made her way to Beiqiang's house. But Taoqi did not give up. Running at Li Tiantian's heels, Taoqi continued hurling nasty words at her. Luobo kept lending assistance and companionship to Taoqi. Li Tiantian retreated to Beiqiang's place and shut the gate from inside. Facing the door from outside, Taoqi shouted her curses incessantly. Then someone pointed at the car parked near the gate, trying to let her know it was the very car that Li Tiantian had driven here. Immediately Taoqi ran to Luobo's place and came back with a sickle, with which she energetically slashed the car tyres. The sickle, being rusty and blunt, could not cut through the tyres, and merely left white marks on their surface. Just as Taoqi was raising the sickle for another assault, her wrist was firmly seized by someone, who took the sickle away from her.

It was none other than her husband Dalin. After snatching away the sickle, Dalin freed one of his hands. With his free hand, he struck Taoqi forcefully on the face.

22

Taoqi did not care much about the slap, but she found the word with which Dalin had abused her almost unbearable, for after dragging her home, and having reached the courtyard, Dalin had declared that she was "shameless." Taoqi picked up on this word and demanded in a high voice that Dalin explain how she was "shameless." Had she ever done anything immoral? She was not a street walker, seducing one man today and flirting with another tomorrow. How was she shameless? Married in name, widowed in fact, she had withstood endless torture from Third Aunt. In what way was she shameless? Had Dalin ever asked about her feelings when she was carrying his sinful seed? How come she was called shameless?

"Tell me, Dalin, you son of a bitch, tell me how has Taoqi betrayed you? In what way am I shameless? Shame on you! It's one thing for you to get involved with sluts far from here, but you shouldn't have brought a shameless ugly whore back to our village! Don't you know that you have brought shame on your ancestors? It's you, you son of a bitch, who are really shameless. Isn't it shameful of you, when you say that others are shameless?"

In the midst of her bawling, Taoqi leaped at the window and, seizing the half bottle of pesticide there, poured it down her throat at one go, like a city-slicker guzzling down mineral water. She had sunk down to the ground before people realized that she had swallowed poison. Horrified, Dalin hurried to get her to her feet. He sat on the ground, holding Taoqi against his chest, incessantly calling her by her name. Third Aunt was horrified, too. She shouted at Xiaolin to send for the village doctor Shuanniu at once.

A few minutes later, the news that Taoqi had drunk poison had spread around the whole village. Some were already watching the quarrel between Dalin and Taoqi while others who had just learned of the news were hurrying towards Dalin's courtyard. For a while people, clustering as thick as huckleberries, besieged the courtyard and filled it with all kinds of noises and chaos.

On hearing what had happened, Fugui abandoned the job in hand and rushed toward Dalin's home. He had rescued a newly-wed woman from the neighboring village in similar circumstances. He was very proud of the method he had used on that occasion, and, considering it valuable experience, mentioned it in front of others from time to time. Taoqi's drinking of poison was another great chance for him to show his competence. How could he let it pass? The value of a man depended on his ability to make the people around him aware of his utility. A turd might be welcome to crops. But if a man lived no better than a turd, then he was good for nothing; how could he enjoy life? Fugui fetched a bowl from the kitchen, and went directly to the outhouse — he was looking for a freshly shat turd! However, Dalin's outhouse was very clean, and even if there were any down there, they were thickly covered with new yellowish earth. As he couldn't find what he wanted, he pulled down his own trousers, squatted down and struggled to defecate. Having pulled up his trousers again, he put the turd into the bowl and darted to Taoqi who was then in a coma. Horrified by what Fugui was doing, people at once stepped back to give him a wide berth. Taoqi's face was a bluish purple, with lips tightly shut, teeth gritted, a blackish yellow liquid trickling drop by drop out of her mouth. Fugui knelt down on the ground, tried hard to force Taoqi's mouth open, and fed a handful of his shit into it. The crowd exploded with sound and fury. Their faces expressed different degrees of surprise and disgust. Some put their hands over their eyes, some over their mouths and noses, and some spat incessantly onto the ground nearby.

Taoqi showed no response, even though her mouth was full of shit. Fugui had meant to induce her gag-reflex and vomit what was in her stomach. Once the poison was vomited, would she not recover? However, the motionless woman was causing him a great deal of embarrassment, and with everyone looking at him, he could find nowhere to hide his face. He was no ordinary man in this village! Taoqi was naughty in name and deed. Naughty and worthless, she was refusing to help save Fugui's face. Embarrassed, and keen to get rid of his embarrassment, he declared that Taoqi was possessed by a ghost, a woman ghost who had led a loose life and died of an immoral venereal disease, with an oozing blister larger than a bowl between her legs. And who could this ghost be, if not Fourth Aunt? Fugui's words outraged Luobo, who pointed at his nose, and denounced him bitterly, saying that he must be blind and evil-hearted to fabricate such a charge against her mother, and that obviously, it was the coming of the slut that had driven Taoqi mad and into drinking poison. "Fugui, you're a motherfucking old bastard. You'll be hanged, and you'll get retribution in heaven!" — but Fugui turned a deaf ear to Luobo's yelling. Hands clasped, eyes half-closed, face twitching, he began murmuring; and after he had finished murmuring he heaved a long sigh. He had been chasing the ghost out of Taoqi.

Shuanniu shambled, slowly and listlessly, in his down-at-heel shoes. Apart from a squint, his face was void of any expression. Shuanniu's grudge against Third Aunt's family was known to everyone in the village. While running for the village leadership, Shuanhu went from household to household, addressing everyone he met as uncle or aunt, discoursing so sweetly that he seemed to have a honey-coated tongue. In addition to making promises, Shuanhu actually delivered several hundred bags of washing powder, one for each family. Third Aunt received one, but she didn't vote for Shuanhu. How could Shuanhu and his younger brother Shuanniu not feel angry? On the next day after Shuanhu was elected, Shuanniu went to those who hadn't voted for his brother, and demanded the return of the washing powder. Third Aunt, however, had opened the bag and used some of it. Knowing Shuanniu was finding fault on purpose, she insulted him in terms as cutting as the teeth of a saw. She offered to buy a new bag of washing powder, but this offer was refused by Shuanniu, who insisted on the very one his brother had given her. Third Aunt said she was ready to pay with money instead, but Shuanniu still refused and would accept nothing but the original bag of washing powder. Seeing no alternative, Third Aunt first squabbled with Shuanniu and then stuffed fifty *yuan* into his hand. Shuanniu left, grumbling and cursing, while Third Aunt wailed loudly — that she had been as deeply wounded by the banditry of this robber, as if a knife had cut a piece of meat out of her. Later, when Qiuli went mad due to Shuanniu's inappropriate treatment, Third Aunt stood by her. Baolai's lawsuit against Shuanniu was the result of a group of rabble-rousers, of whom Third Aunt was an indispensable member. When Third Aunt said something, it would soon be amplified and come to the ears of Shuanniu and his brother. In this village which was no larger than the palm of a hand, with houses scattered here and there like urine drops, the stamp of a foot at the west end was deafening at the east end.

Shuanniu approached Taoqi. He felt her pulse, drew up her eyelids to have a look, and then declared to the crowd, "Taoqi is dead! She is already stiff!" In panic, many people began to run toward the gate of the courtyard.

Good grief, Taoqi was dead! In the blink of an eye, she had turned from a human being into a ghost. Ghosts bewitched human beings. Who would expose themselves to the risk of Taoqi's bewitchment, given her reputation?

They had to get moving as quickly as possible. And the farther the better! It was said ghosts were afraid of the color red, so they must fetch a bundle of dry hay to light up outside their own gates once they were back home, so that her ghost could not peep in. Of course, even if they wished to return to the entertainment, they must first ensure that they wore something red about their bodies. They might wear a red belt, a pair of red shorts, or apply some red ink to their foreheads.

Third Aunt was the first to cry out. Her arms supported by others, she walked out of her house and over to Taoqi. She pounded Taoqi's body with her fists so fiercely that you would think she was pounding her laundry to clean it. "Taoqi, O Taoqi, how could you die on a sudden like this? You're still young, why did you go down this path? Poor Taoqi, ill-fated Taoqi, you lost your mother at an early age, and you were brought up by your father, who now lies paralyzed in bed, but now that you are dead, who's going to look after him?" Third Aunt began to recall Taoqi's virtues, saying that she was a good daughter-in-law, obedient and hard-working, and that it was for the family's sake she had been so economic with her own food and clothing. Suddenly, according to Third Aunt, Taoqi had become everyone's favorite flower!

Dalin sat on the ground, hugging Taoqi, and seemed as senseless as a block of wood. His pupils were as motionless as two rusted iron rivets.

23

Before Taoqi's dead body could be encoffined, her brother came to the scene. Taoqi's brother, who worked as a coal miner, seemed to have hurried here without taking a bath beforehand, and had traces of black on his face. He stopped them from putting Taoqi's body into the coffin, claiming that he had no objection in principle to doing so, but that Dalin must demonstrate his accountability before Taoqi could be encoffined.

Following the suggestion of Fugui and some other people, Dalin knelt down before Taoqi's brother, who, however, said that this was not what he wanted. What he wanted was: Dalin must compensate him with money. Consequently, Fugui and Beiqiang, acting as Dalin's representatives, set about negotiating with Taoqi's brother. The three men ducked into a lumber room, made all the people in it leave, then closed the door from inside. Pouting, Taoqi's brother said his piece, with long intervals between his words. His utterances were reminiscent of the way a lazy man chops wood, who, after one downward stroke of the axe, rests for a long while before commencing another stroke. Taoqi's brother said Dalin was obliged to compensate him lots and lots of money.

Fugui said, "Dalin agrees to money compensation, but you must name a figure. How much is 'lots'?"

With recourse to his fingers, Taoqi's brother strove to figure out an amount. He calculated how much the necessary bricks would cost, how much the necessary rebars would cost, how much the necessary cement would cost, how much the necessary sand and lime would cost, how much the necessary lumber would cost, how much the necessary craftsmen would charge him, how much the necessary masons would charge him. He calculated for a long while. But the sub-totals got messed up. He had to start all over again. He calculated. He calculated over and over. But he couldn't work out a figure. He bent down. Picking a piece of firewood, he scratched with it on the floor to help him with the calculations. All this perplexed Beiqiang, who couldn't help wondering: we are talking about the issue of compensation for his sister's death, but he seems to be calculating the cost of building a house; has this lad's brain gone wrong?

Prompted by his puzzlement, Beiqiang asked Taoqi's brother, "What are you calculating?"

"Can't you see what I'm calculating? I'm calculating how much money Dalin should compensate my family," Taoqi's brother replied impatiently.

It was obvious Beiqiang's question had disturbed the lad's calculations, whose brain was getting into an ever messier condition — even messier than a tangled mass of hemp. He couldn't successfully add up all those complicated numbers to reach the correct total. As a result, he had to delegate the job to Fugui and Beiqiang, instructing them, "Just let Dalin pay the sum a house costs. As for how much money building a house costs, you calculate. The amount you calculate will be the sum Dalin should give me."

Fugui and Beiqiang felt this was a rather difficult task. Were houses to be regarded as being all the same thing, just because they were all called the same thing — "houses?" Some houses cost less than twenty thousand *yuan*, while some others cost more than fifty thousand *yuan*. Without a blueprint, how could they calculate the cost? Fugui lit a cigarette and took two puffs. Seeing that Taoqi's brother was yawning more and more often and showing less and less concentration, Fugui gently kicked his leg and said, "I just did the calculations. To build a house such as the one you describe needs no more than ten thousand *yuan*. Here's my suggestion and let's see if you think it is okay. I'll get Dalin to be generous and accept some loss. Let him give you eleven thousand *yuan*. Isn't that good enough? Anyway, Dalin remains your brother-in-law."

With an exuberant smile animating his face, Taoqi's brother said, "This is acceptable. This is okay. What good could my sister do even if she were living? She'd do nothing but waste food. But now her death turns out to be worth a lot of money. Her death is worthwhile. It is worthwhile! Every person is doomed to die. Some people die without benefiting anyone by so much as a cent, but some other people's deaths, aha, can be transformed into a fortune."

Although he had claimed that the proffered amount was "acceptable" and "okay," nevertheless, Taoqi's brother requested some additional money, because when building the house, he would take the opportunity to rebuild the pigsty. Could Dalin give him a few extra hundreds, so that he could buy some asbestos shingles for it?

Before Fugui had time to say anything, Beiqiang gave his consent. "Okay. It's a deal. No problem. You get an additional two thousand *yuan*. In total, that makes thirteen thousand *yuan*."

Taoqi's brother said, "It won't cost that much. There's no need to give so much."

Paying no attention to the signal Fugui winked at him, Beiqiang responded, "You can buy your children some new clothes with the spare money. Let's strike the deal."

In the wake of the negotiations, Taoqi's brother was escorted to one of the tables to eat alongside relatives and neighbours, who had come to attend the wake. Fugui called Dalin, who had been kneeling in mourning apparel in front of the coffin, to a quiet place outside the gate, and reported the results of the negotiations. Hardly had they spoken two sentences when Fugui and Beiqiang began to quarrel. Fugui kept grumbling that Beiqiang was a traitor, ready to help the opposition, offering a hand when a foot was asked for, offering a head when a cap was asked for. Fugui ridiculed Beiqiang by raking up his disgraceful past, "Concerning the two thousand *yuan* increase you conceded at the end, if you were still in your old condition, how many goats would you have had to steal in order to make that much money? How many trees would you have needed to chop down in secret? How many times would you have needed to burgle other people's houses? You just tell me, how many times would you have had to suffer fear and anxiety in order to get so much money?"

Provoked by Fugui, Beiqiang went red in the face. He said to Fugui, "You think you are clean? Why don't you piss a puddle and use it as a mirror to see yourself in? Your face is full of pockmarks, and yet you laugh at other people for their blackheads. Who the fuck do you think you are? Have you forgotten the scandalous thing you and that woman from the neighboring village did in a corn field? Her husband carried a chopping knife and squatted at your gate every day, while you hid out in one place after another. Was it a pleasant experience? You were born to be hit with a brick!"

With eyes red and swollen, Dalin asked how the negotiations had gone on. Fugui gave a brief, general account of the results, emphasizing that if he had been the only representative to deal with Taoqi's brother, one thousand *yuan*, as he estimated, would have been enough to settle the problem. In view of his extraordinary talent and Taoqi's brother's half-witted brain, he would have been able to hold him down to a more favorable price. It would have been as easy as bending to tie his own shoelaces, or as raising his hand to scratch his own head. He wondered why he had been given an assistant.

Was it because he was considered untrustworthy, or was it something else? The worst thing was that the assistant didn't know his place, and insisted on trying to dominate. The assistant thought he could represent his principal Dalin. This assistant was a typical traitor! A traitor just like Wang Lianju in *The Red Lantern*. "What a shame that this is how some people do things. The moment his life shows the least sign of improvement, he starts thinking so highly of himself that he believes he can break the high heavens with his tail. He has a single wad of American dollars in his pocket, and already he sees himself as the American president," Fugui said sarcastically.

Fugui's words of denunciation against Beiqiang rushed on in ceaseless torrents, but Dalin was getting pretty impatient, because from time to time shouts of "Dalin, Dalin" could be heard coming from the courtyard.

Dalin interrupted Fugui, saying, "Stop it, please. I'll indemnify Taoqi's family to the tune of twenty thousand *yuan*. If less is paid, I'll have an uneasy conscience. I feel sad for her. That she should die like that, leaving her paralyzed father behind."

Instantly, Beiqiang expressed his support for Dalin, saying, "You're right. Her family people lost her to death. Confronted by this loss of life, how can we have the fucking heart to haggle over the amount of pecuniary compensation? No matter how much money you give her people, her life cannot be restored. Moreover, we shouldn't take advantage of her brother and deceive him just because he is dimwitted. A proper indemnity would show our generosity. This is much better than the guy who fucked another man's wife but ended up writing an IOU for him."

Beiqiang looked at Fugui out of the corner of his eyes. In his heart he felt very happy that he had taken the opportunity to deliver a fatal attack against him. There had been a rumor that Fugui and a woman from a neighboring village had performed an adulterous deed in a cornfield. The rumor became so widely circulated that in the end it came to the ears of the woman's husband. The husband, who had looked as soft as a noodle, became all of a sudden hard and tough — very hard and very tough indeed. Taking a knife, he went to Fugui's place, and threatened to cut off Fugui's head. Pursued by the woman's husband, Fugui had difficulty finding a hide-out. He ended up huddling in a deserted cave half way up a valley cliff. Unbearable hunger forced him to put ants and dung beetles into his mouth. In the pitch darkness of a waning night Fugui sneaked back into the village.

He knocked at Gangan's door and asked him to be a go-between. Gangan, a righteous man, was utterly disgusted by adulterous behavior. He regarded Fugui's request that he mediate as disgusting, no matter whether or not he would handle it. Gangan denounced Fugui bitterly, saying that he had made all the villagers lose face and had made his face — the face of the head of the village — burn with shame. In great fury, he took up his brick pillow, which happened to be near at hand on his *kang*, and dashed it at Fugui mercilessly.

Under the mediation of Gangan, Fugui was able to return to the village to lead a normal life. But he needed to pay the woman's husband a compensation of two thousand *yuan*, which was by no means a small sum. How could he raise so much money? He sold the family's goats. He sold the family's chicken. Almost all the wheat and corn in the house was sold, but nevertheless amounted to only eleven hundred *yuan*, and that was nine hundred *yuan* short. Having no other alternative, Fugui had to write and sign an IOU for him. Naturally, Fugui's wife did not forgive him. Having suffered a loss both of face and fortune, how could one expect her not to flare up with anger? She got into a three-round fight with Fugui, during which her rake-like fingers left five bloody lines on Fugui's face. Then she declared a separation from Fugui. She shrieked her order that Fugui move out, which Fugui did not obey. In Fugui's view, he was the boss of the family, and as such how could he listen to a woman, who had long been called "a long-haired but short-sighted creature?" How could he let a woman dictate his movements? Since Fugui refused to move out, his wife did. She moved into a deserted place which used to be the barn of the production team to which the family belonged. She had been living in the barn for the last three years.

That Beiqiang had dug up this disgraceful conduct naturally displeased Fugui. After exchanging several rounds of sarcastic remarks with Beiqiang, Fugui angrily left.

Dalin asked Beiqiang to call in Taoqi's brother, who was in the middle of wolfing down food at the table they had arranged for him to join. Patting him on the shoulder, Beiqiang summoned him to the presence of Dalin. Seeing Taoqi's brother coming in, Dalin immediately knelt down, saying "I'm indebted to Taoqi" and so on.

Passing his tongue over his lips, Taoqi's brother said, "Why do you say that? The food is so rich and delicious. It's pretty nice. It's altogether nice."

24

When someone died, the village would remain in a state of excitement for several days. I didn't really get involved in Taoqi's funeral, being eager to get away. The funeral was so lengthy and drawn-out that it was wearing out all those who were connected with it. Therefore, when Shuanhu invited me to his home, I showed not the least hesitation and followed him. Shuanhu was very happy, because my visit seemed a reward to him. Of course, he grumbled a few words against Dalin. "Isn't he a disgrace? That a nice guy, which is what he used to be, should screw around with a slut from the city! Isn't it a bad sign that someone has perished at such a critical moment just when the village is going all out to attract business and investment? Dalin and his family are the sort of people who bite the hand that feeds them." Shuanhu claimed to have done all he could to show himself humane and dutiful to them, but how had they repaid him? Only with curses and grumbles. The one they called "Third Aunt" was a real gossip, with a mouth like a loud speaker and slandered him wherever she went. Because he was a man of the world, he scorned to react to an old woman's gossiping. Otherwise, he would have punched her, or slapped her slandering mouth until it was relocated behind her ears!

Shuanhu lived in a two-storey brick house, the interior furnishings of which were obviously better than those of most families in the village. A dog, chained to the family's mulberry tree, aroused my curiosity. It looked somehow familiar, but I could not recall where I had seen it before. It had a tiger's back and a bear's waist, and two large ears drooping down like two huge fans, and a very ugly, horrible and ferocious face. One of its eyes was a dark hollow while the other burned with the bloody light of hatred. It was restlessly turning in a circle, its paws digging into the ground from time to time, its mouth letting out moans of piercing sadness.

Seeing that I was interested, Shuanhu told me the dog's story. The dog had been given to him by Liu Qi, who had named it "Knife Victim." Knife Victim was the guard dog of a family that lived in the northern mountains of Gaotai Township, and Liu Qi spotted it while he was passing by that family's house one day. Liu Qi used to kill pigs, but he ate no pork. He knew that pig breeders fed pigs with hormones, and pig slaughterers applied chemicals to the pork. What was more, given that pigs hated butchers so intensely, was it possible that they would rest peacefully in a butcher's belly? What if they revolted in his belly like Monkey King[15] who fought against heaven? That would be more than he could stand. But though he rejected pork, Liu Qi was keen on dog meat. The reason that he had his eye on Knife Victim was that it looked stout, and that its thick, solid fat looked as if it would taste particularly succulent and delicious. He wasted no time in talking to the family, with the intention of taking the dog away at once. However, the head of the family was as stubborn as a block of rotten wood, and would not part with it.

Liu Qi identified himself, and said that he would gladly pay or barter; but the old man never stopped shaking his head while Liu Qi made his proposal. Liu Qi had thought the mention that he was Liu Qi, never mind that he was the head of Gaotai Township, would be enough to soften the old man's resistance. But, apparently, the old man was so ill-informed that he had never heard about him, to the great surprise of Liu Qi's driver. Liu Qi was displeased. This refusal to give up Knife Victim annoyed him greatly, but that someone should be ignorant of his authority was worse. The situation was insufferable for him.

Liu Qi was amenable to gentle persuasion, but not to determined opposition. If you toed the line, and gave him a mile when he asked for an inch, he could be very decent, very humane, and would reward or recompense you proportionately; but if you tried to be his boss or his master, when you didn't know your station in life, then, sorry, Liu Qi wouldn't be able to oblige, and would convince you in short order that it was a fallacy to assume that wolves do not eat people. The old man who kept Knife Victim was so completely insensible that he turned down every opportunity to save face, and refused a toast — only to then have to swallow a forfeit. All right, Liu Qi would show him who had the last laugh in Gaotai or even in Kaiyang.

Liu Qi had been on the point of solving the problem in his own way, i.e. to beat the old man, right there and then, until his bones were broken and his skull fractured, when suddenly County Secretary of the Party committee Zhang Shutian's "patent advice" occurred to him — Liu Qi more than once mispronounced "patient advice" as "patent advice" in meetings large and small, and no one dared correct him, although sniggers were audible on each occasion. Once upon a time, he had beaten a self-employed doctor half to death, and the doctor's family had appealed to Zhang Shutian, who arranged to talk with him. Zhang Shutian, grave in manner and severe in tone, admonished him to look to his behavior, because as an official, how he behaved could adversely affect the public image of officialdom in Kaiyang County. How unruly and impulsive it was to beat people up arbitrarily and with one's own hands? However, what impressed and inspired him most was Zhang Shutian's final words, "No wisdom, no strategy, brutal force is all you know. The wise, when they want to stitch someone up, will borrow a knife for the kill, and leave no incriminating evidence in the hands of their victims."

Liu Qi had been unhappy with Zhang Shutian, thinking that the latter looked down upon him all the time. Zhang Shutian had appointed a woman as the director of the urban reconstruction office. And what had she managed to do? After a year working on the task, she had still failed to demolish a three-hundred-meter long street of houses. Unable to withstand pressure from reluctant-to-move households, the so-called "nail households," she had even hidden herself away in a hospital, on the pretext that she had been ill. Liu Qi offered himself as a replacement for the woman, who was good for nothing but weeping. He pledged to Zhang Shutian to make all the nail households disappear from the street in two days! Laws, reasons, and so on were just so much flatulence! No need to reason with the unreasonable! Fists were the greatest laws and reasons. To his disappointment, Zhang Shutian enlisted no talent like him, rather he relied on the service of a woman with impressively large and pendulous breasts! Liu Qi felt that he had not met a discerning leader, so by and by he developed a grudge against him. However, Zhang Shutian's suggestion that he "borrow a knife for the kill" had enlightened him to a certain degree, and from then on he began to harbor an almost positive opinion of the secretary.

Liu Qi left the house of Knife Victim's master. On stepping out of the gate, he grinned coldly. Two days later, the old man came in person and presented Knife Victim to Liu Qi. Liu Qi made no mention of the tactic he had employed for this purpose, and no-one else was aware of it.

At first, Knife Victim raised its leonine head and paid little attention to Liu Qi, as proud as if it were the relative of some senior official. Tut-tut, many a man had been crushed into a ball of piss-soaked earth in Liu Qi's hand, let alone a wretched dog. How dare it look down upon Liu Qi! Who the fuck did it think it was? Liu Qi asked for the dog to be taken to his office, where he was going to teach the untamed bastard a lesson.

With the help of others, Liu Qi pierced, or rather, sewed the lips of Knife Victim together with iron wire, so that the dog wouldn't be able to bite. After Knife Victim was chained to a desk leg, Liu Qi fetched an iron hammer, and struck the dog as he pleased — on the head, on the back, on the leg, on the paw, and even on its reproductive organs. Knife Victim wailed miserably, its eyes showing a faint light of timidity and fear.

Liu Qi took out a shining knife, and waved it in Knife Victim's face. He stuck the knife into its body randomly, and let it bleed all over until its yellow and white fur was reddened patch by patch. Knife Victim huddled down on all fours, shaking constantly. Liu Qi cut its reproductive organ until it was attached only by a piece of fur, poured gasoline on it, and threw the cigarette butt that he was smoking onto it. With a boom, Knife Victim was on fire! The dog rolled on the ground, the fire engulfing almost its whole body. Liu Qi would not allow it to be burned to death, as he had not yet wrung the last drop of satisfaction from this little game. He lifted the fire extinguisher, which had been prepared beforehand, and extinguished the fire on the blazing beast, which by now was almost dead. Its yellow and white fur had turned altogether black, relieved only by patches of crimson; pus oozed out of the wounds. Liu Qi had it dragged away, with instructions that its wounds should be treated at the vet's.

On the third day, when Knife Victim had recovered a little and had begun to feed, Liu Qi sent for it to be brought once again to his office. This time, before taking any action, he verbally assaulted the beast. The arrogance that Knife Victim had demonstrated at its first arrival was gone, and now it was a timid and shy dog. Its mouth was no longer sewn up with iron wire, but it kept it tightly shut anyway. Liu Qi began to abuse, scold and curse it with the most vulgar and nasty words at his disposal. From beginning to end, Knife Victim let its ears and eyelids droop, as if it were listening respectfully. It seemed that it understood human language. When Liu Qi called it a whore, it had a nervous seizure. When Liu Qi threatened to peel off its skin and then fry the body in a wok, it shivered all over, as though on the verge of tears.

Obviously, verbal abuse was not enough to satisfy Liu Qi. Again he took the knife out of a drawer, thrust it, without a moment's hesitation, into Knife Victim's left eye and, despite its struggles, dug the eyeball out, employing the special skill he had acquired as a butcher. But for the announcement that someone had come from the county, which interrupted proceedings, it would be really hard to tell whether the other eye would have gone the same way or not.

Knife Victim shriveled completely. It still barked at visitors from outside, even pretending to be very ferocious. But whenever it heard anyone say "Township Head Liu," it would be utterly disheartened. From then on Liu Qi habitually frightened it and took delight in its deference and obedience. He even boasted to visitors from outside how he had kneaded a dog into the shape he wanted.

A man was no different from a dog! A dog was made obedient through kneading, so was a man! Liu Qi often imparted to his friends in officialdom such experience and secrets.

25

Hearing Shuanhu's account, I suddenly understood why the dog had looked familiar. It dawned on me that, last time Liben and I visited the township government, the dog we encountered was none other than this one — Knife Victim by name. Though the dog had lost its aggressive spirit, nevertheless its appearance remained intimidating. I had truly been scared by it.

Shuanhu recalled the long-standing and deeply rooted friendship between our two households, reminiscing about how his mother, when she was still alive, had taken good care of my family. He said once upon a time, as he was about to dump his shoes on account of the holes his toes had made in them, his mother stopped him. Grabbing the worn-out shoes from his hands, she went to find a tangle of hemp cords. Pulling one cord from the tangled mess and threading it through the eye of a steel needle, his mother sat down in the courtyard and began mending the shoes. After sewing a couple of stitches, she took the shoes to my house and made my father wear them. Being well aware of the difficulties that menaced my family, his mother had always been concerned that my family should have warm clothes.

"How kindhearted my mother was!" Shuanhu exclaimed.

Shuanhu asked me if I was aware of these things. I answered yes.

He asked me if I had forgotten these things. I answered him, "How could I forget?"

"I'm happy to hear it," Shuanhu said.

He said what he despised most were ungrateful people. He said there were some people who, having just tasted ice cream for the first time, instantly pretended to be elegant and have good taste. "I can't help kicking the buttocks of these people!" he said.

Shuanhu made some remarks specifically to flatter me. He said Mazi Village produced two big shots: one was Liben, the other was me. He said in the common people's eyes, Liben was above me due to the obvious fact that while I merely had a footing in the capital city of the province, Liben flew extensively out of China; while I earned Chinese RMB, Liben earned American Dollars; and while Liben's money was countless and inexhaustible, I could only afford to wear the same old coat which I had worn the last time I came back to the village. And so on and so forth. However, Shuanhu declared he could see things other villagers could not: the villagers only saw a person's skin, but Shuanhu could see right through the person's internal organs; the villagers only knew the differences between a horse and a mule, Shuanhu knew *why* a horse was different from a mule. Shuanhu continued to say that actually, in his eyes, it was obvious that I was smarter than Liben given that I was a low-key person, while Liben was like a high-pitched speaker; that I smiled at every person I came across, while Liben's eyes and mouth turned upwards when he met people.

I said, "People's personalities differ. People's dispositions differ. What's more, Liben is near-sighted. He has to get right up close before he can recognize who someone is."

Shuanhu was reluctant to take my words on board. Instead, he slandered Liben good and proper. He said even though Liben had become an American, he still looked down on him. "It is true Liben has become an American. So what? When he was a Chinese, he still had all his organs. But after he became an American, he lost the biggest treasure a man owns."

"Without that treasure, can a man still be called a man?" Shuanhu continued. "Isn't such a man termed an 'androgyne'?" Shuanhu exclaimed that the sight of Liben, who was now neither a man nor a woman, disgusted him.

Shuanhu went on with his remarks, "Liben claims he has taught at an American university, but none of us can go there to check if he has told the truth. Who knows what he did in America? America is a chaotic country. Terribly chaotic! In America, there are men who prostitute themselves to make money."

According to Shuanhu's conjectures, there was a ninety percent chance Liben had engaged in prostitution.

"How could Liben have got so much money? No matter how wildly you might conjecture, you couldn't come up with an answer," Shuanhu went on. "If a medical accident could enable him to get such a huge fortune, does that mean the boss who ran the hospital had a problem with his brain? The hospital boss's brain must have had a red hot iron pole poked through it."

Shuanhu speculated that Liben, as a male prostitute, must have had an affair with a married woman, and in time the affair must have been discovered by the woman's husband. Who can tolerate his own wife doing the deed with another man? In great fury, the exasperated husband sharpened a knife used by pig-butchers and cut off Liben's "tackle" — which, after all, had caused the trouble.

Although the story was no more than a hypothesis, Shuanhu claimed it as an undoubted fact. He asserted that Liben had got AIDS. He said Liu Qi had invited him, on several occasions, to go and take a bath with Liben, but he never went a single time; he feared to be infected with the disease carried by Liben; he was smart, and if anyone took him for an idiot, there could be only one explanation: that the guy's eyes must have been smeared with chicken shit!

After his remarks about Liben, Shuanhu made some comments on Americans, "Americans, like all other people in the world, have two arms and two legs. They don't have three heads or six arms, do they? How come they act like tyrants and dictators, criticizing this, rebuking that? Aren't they like toads that leave their own territorial borders to catch their prey? In what universe are China and America alike? If America is a mountain with tigers on it, China is a huge pigsty. Pigs are foolish and greedy. Just feeding pigs is a difficult job." Shuanhu seemed to be pretty unhappy with the practice of elections. He said, "Why bother with elections? Aren't elections simply the performance of a fixed set of procedures? Moreover, the procedures are chaotic. People feel tortured — some snuffling with their noses, some squinting with their eyes."

Shuanhu made a phone call to Liu Qi and held a whispered conversation with him. Hanging up, he said that Township Head Liu had asked me to go to the township government.

"Get me out of it. I mean it," I said.

But Shuanhu turned a deaf ear to my request. He insisted that I must go. He said if I didn't go, he would lose face — because he had made an oath to Liu Qi that he would escort me to the township government. He said Liu Qi had more than once mentioned he would like to meet me and befriend me.

"Really? I can't promote him to a higher office. Nor can I help him make money. In his eyes, I must seem a good-for-nothing sort of guy. What has he to gain by becoming acquainted with me?" I asked Shuanhu.

Patting me, Shuanhu said, "You think too much. People don't necessarily make use of each other. The key thing they value is a compatible personality."

When we arrived at the township government, Liu Qi was sleeping in his office. Liu Qi did not open the door until after Shuanhu had knocked for a long time. His eyes were bloodshot. Massaging his face with a towel, Liu Qi explained he had stayed up the whole past night playing mahjong. Shuanhu asked Liu Qi whether he had won money or lost money in the mahjong game. Instead of answering the question, Liu Qi said, "Given my good luck, could I possibly have lost money? Of course I won. But I didn't win much. I only won about three thousand *yuan*. Is three thousand *yuan* even worth calling some money?" Liu Qi said that when he worked as a pig-butcher, he had considered one *yuan* some money, but now, even if he saw a one hundred note somebody dropped on the ground, he wouldn't care to bend down for it.

"Of course, who would complain about having had too much money?" Liu Qi continued. "Money doesn't bite your hand. Nor does money burn your hand. Who does not like money? Those who have obtained one *yuan* wish to have two *yuan*. Those who have obtained ten million *yuan* wish to have one hundred million *yuan*."

According to Liu Qi, his goal was to have one hundred million *yuan* within ten years. "This goal is not very easy to accomplish," Liu Qi acknowledged. "Without performing wondrous tricks, how can such a huge gap be filled? Do you know what the most profitable job is in China? Government officials make the biggest money! Robbers, thieves, pig-butchers, goat-butchers, even those who open factories to do business, they are all foolish. They keep busy all day long no matter the wind or rain. Their minds are always troubled with fear and worry. But what do they gain? No one ever offers them the secret to success. As a result they have no idea how or what to do. Given that they have never had any experience in official circles, naturally they do not understand the rationale of 'getting promotion and growing rich.' Getting promotion and growing rich! Yes, there is no doubt about it. If you get promotion, you end up growing rich even if you don't want to! Those who toil do not make big money, and those who make big money do not need to toil. Work more and get more — that is what we are taught, but to hell with that lie! Even a ghost would not believe in work-more-and-get-more."

Zhao Xiaohui entered the room. After giving a warm greeting to me and to Shuanhu, Zhao Xiaohui took out some paper cups and poured tea for us. He also poured a cup of tea for Liu Qi.

Just as Zhao Xiaohui was about to retreat, Liu Qi glared at him sidelong and hooted, "What are you good for? I dispatched you to the County

Forestry Bureau to get their approval for a logging quota. Two months have passed, and you only got a permit for fifty cubic meters of lumber. If you are not qualified for the vice head office, get away from this courtyard!"

Zhao Xiaohui assumed a smiling face, but his smiles were worse than cries. He mumbled, "Fifty cubic meters is the maximum the county's bureau of forestry is authorized to approve. Application for more than this amount needs to be filed with the provincial forestry bureau."

"Ai-ha! Ai-ha!" Liu Qi cleared his throat, and immediately his sputum flew toward Zhao Xiaohui's face.

Zhao Xiaohui dodged. As a result, the sputum landed on his collar. With an embarrassed smile still on his face, Zhao Xiaohui hurriedly made his way out the door.

Liu Qi shouted at Zhao Xiaohui's back, "Those policy rules are fucking pubic hairs! Policy rules are dead, but humans are alive. How can live humans be so cornered by policy rules? Which guy says quotas are required for tree-logging? Quotas, too, are fucking pubic hairs. If they don't grant the quota, I will cut down trees just the same. Dare the forestry bureau bite off my cock? If you, forestry bureau, reject this face-saving request, you, forestry bureau, will be given a donkey cock to suck!"

Shortly afterward, Liu Qi's father ran in. With livid face, the old man asked Liu Qi if he had again bullied Vice Township Head Zhao.

Banging the table with his palm, Liu Qi responded, "Here is Elder Liu Qi's kingdom! If anyone does not serve me, Elder Liu Qi, well, I, Elder Liu Qi, will give him a hard time. What do you mean when you say I bullied him? I dispatched him to handle a tiny, sesame-sized matter. Even at that he failed! Remembering the presence of my guests, I haven't dangled him from a tree to whip him. That counts as sparing him, doesn't it? And yet you charge me with bullying him. To hell with it!"

Liu Qi's father said, "Vice Township Head Zhao is, at any rate, a leader in the township government, yet you make him whine and sob on a regular basis. Is this a decent thing for you to do? The lad is good enough. I can't bear to see you treat him so fiercely."

Waving his hand at his father, Liu Qi said to his old man, "What do you know about this kind of thing? Isn't it for his own betterment I have treated him like that? I've told you before not to meddle in my professional affairs. I've advised you to pretend you're deaf, dumb, and blind in my workplace.

Why don't you listen to me? How come you simply cannot hold your tongue? Well, well, come on. Off you go! I and my guests have other things to tackle."

After his father left the room, Liu Qi told me that the old man's lively concern for Zhao Xiaohui was purely because he dearly loved his would-be son-in-law.

The story was that under intense pressure from Liu Qi and his father, Zhao Xiaohui had begun getting used to the idea of courting Liu Qi's younger sister. As a matter of fact, Liu Qi despised Zhao Xiaohui from the bottom of his heart. Liu Qi's initial intent had been to marry his sister to the boss of Beigou Coal Mine. Xu Yuanyuan was the name of the boss, who, though once again single, after divorcing his third wife, was surrounded by a crowd of women. None of Xu Yuanyuan's former wives had ended well — with one becoming disabled, another mysteriously disappearing, and the third going mad as a result of being intimidated. In Liu Qi's view, a man should live his life like Xu Yuanyuan.

Liu Qi strongly admired Xu Yuanyuan, whom he regarded as a rare hero! However, Liu Qi's father had no opinion of Xu Yuanyuan. The old man dreaded that his own daughter might suffer a similar tragic ending. Liu Qi, as a filial son, had to obey his father and even helped his father to persuade Zhao Xiaohui.

Liu Qi's father had kept on suggesting the match in front of Zhao Xiaohui for months, but the latter simply smiled, neither agreeing nor disagreeing. Seeing that his father had got nowhere with the matter, Liu Qi took up the job himself. Making use of his spare time during a certain supper, it only took Liu Qi ten minutes to settle the problem. "Do you, Zhao Xiaohui, have any good reason to feel self-important? Aren't you just a vice township leader? It is true you look as handsome as a movie star, but what's the use of good looks? In brothels, good looks count, but in officialdom, it is tricks that count. Is there any problem with my sister? Why is my sister an unsuitable match for you? Even though my sister has the defect of a harelip, she still outmatches you by far, Zhao Xiaohui! You don't agree with the match? You dare not to agree? If you don't agree, we'll wait and see what comes out of it!"

It turned out that the very next day after Liu Qi had talked with Zhao Xiaohui, Zhao Xiaohui broke up with his girlfriend.

"Beating is an expression of affection, rebuking signifies love," Liu Qi said.

According to Liu Qi, it was for Zhao Xiaohui's good that he had spat in his face; to some extent, that was a way of showing concern for his future brother-in-law. Such a method could achieve two ends. One was to make Zhao Xiaohui permanently fear him so that he would not dare to be less than devoted to his sister or divorce her for light reasons, let alone abuse her. The other purpose was to train Zhao Xiaohui and enhance his development. Viewed from this perspective, Liu Qi claimed that he himself was no less than a PhD supervisor to Zhao Xiaohui, who was like a graduate student learning under his instruction.

"With his overcautious style and hesitant behavior, Zhao Xiaohui can never assume a full-leadership position," Liu Qi said. "To be a supreme authority, a man must have a heart as hard as steel, a hand as unyielding as iron. Just think about this: if a cat is without authority to hold mice in awe, how can the cat have an easy time?"

26

As a matter of fact, Liu Qi was not so arrogant in his cups. In the dim light, he looked kind of shy if viewed side-on. He talked about his childhood, and tears came into his eyes. He said that due to the shortage of food, he used to pluck wild grass from hill slopes and eat it. He didn't know which plants to eat and which to avoid at all costs. Once he was so starved that he saw stars swirling before him, his stomach was as empty as a wheat flour bag, and his bowels contracted like withered wheat straws. He ate whatever he could find in addition to wild grass, ranging from ants to dung beetles. Before he was back from the hill side, his stomach had begun to ache terribly. At death's door, he was sent to hospital, where the doctor said he had been poisoned. He was in mortal danger until eight days later, when he left the hospital. A fifteen-year-old lad, he weighed barely over twenty-five kilograms when he got out. His father carried him home, weeping all the way.

Liu Qi said his greatest regret was that he had had little schooling; but he respected scholars. With this he clinked his cup with mine. The reasons that he chose to be a butcher were various, he said. First, he couldn't find other jobs because his family was poor and looked down upon. Second, fond of meat from childhood, he found his mouth watering at the sight of it; but born to a poor family, he was unable to eat it from one year to the next, with the exception of spring festival, on which occasion he would be given very small slices, which, before he could savor the flavor of the meat, had disappeared down his throat. Third, to be a butcher strengthened one's fortitude, and he who was used to killing pigs could outface anyone, no matter how powerful they were. A man did not differ much from a pig, since both were afraid of being knifed! Of course, the profession of butcher had had a great negative impact on him, because the word "butcher," like a birthmark or his own shadow, was indelible, and could not be amputated. Wasn't Jin Bing, who had been pursuing him legally here, there and everywhere, taking advantage of his butcher origin? Furthermore, the gentlemen and gentlewomen of the county congress, who regarded him as an eyesore, had proposed to depose him several times, saying that a butcher was not qualified to be a township head. Who were those fuckers to shit on his head? Liu Qi was not afraid of them, and sooner or later he would be pleased to see the old fogeys who had stood in his way bite the dust. Until then, he would regard them as mere lice which could do nothing more harmful than make him itch; but if these lice were not sensible, and took a mile when they were offered an inch, they would be doomed!

Liu Qi asked if I was acquainted with any provincial officials. I hesitated for a moment, not knowing how to reply. On an impulse, I mentioned that Governor Xiang's son and I worked in the same organization. Shuanhu was very excited. He clinked his cup with mine and helped Liu Qi with the dishes, his eyes blinking as though to brag, "Now you see, the person I have brought to you is not good-for-nothing."

Liu Qi, however, remained impassive. He seemed not much interested in Governor Xiang's power. A piece of dog meat got stuck between his teeth, and he failed to get it out although he kept at it for long time with toothpicks. In desperation he had to call for waitresses. He first berated them for the poor cooking and for the undercooked dog meat which had caused him to suffer so much, then he asked them to help with that stubborn piece of meat which was sticking to his teeth. One of them took a toothpick, and dislodged it without much trouble.

In full swing by now, Shuanhu encouraged Liu Qi to use me as a go-between to establish a relationship with Governor Xiang as quickly as possible. Once the connection was made, things in the township would be handled more easily, and so would things in the village, as would, naturally, the private concerns of Township Head Liu. A senior official was like a rich gold mine, whose profitability was dependent on whether or not you were willing to dig, and whether or not you were a good digger. If Township Head Liu got promoted for the sake of his righteousness as a principle, would he forget his little brothers who had served and followed him so faithfully? When Township Head Liu ate meat, he could let them gnaw on the bones, at least. When Township Head Liu ate noodles, he might leave them the broth the noodles had been cooked in. When Township Head Liu slept with young girls, it was not bad for them to flirt with widows. "Township Head Liu, you have access to a rocket launch-pad, and if you are willing to step onto it, and sit on the top of the rocket, one touch of the ignition key will be enough to send you high into the sky."

Shuanhu stressed again the old friendship between the two of us, repeating how his mother had handed down old shoes to my family; he exhorted me to have the hard integrity of firm rock, and not be like Liben who was as untethered to reality as a big soap bubble. Shuanhu urged me to be a bridge between Governor Xiang and Township Head Liu, saying, "If Township Head Liu rises to power, could he be so ungrateful as to forget you — Black Bean? Once the black bean grows and sprouts, it will be black no longer."

It seemed that the meeting had nothing to do with establishing a relationship with Governor Xiang. Rather, Liu Qi had his own plan, which was not disclosed until the last dish was served. He admired the head of Willow Valley Township, who, with a pair of gimlet eyes, had exploited the media so well that he had become a national role model worker, going into and coming out of the People's Great Hall with a red flower on his bosom, as cocky as a punter who had just had sex with a whore. Liu Qi claimed that compared with the head of Willow Valley Township, he had been remarkably naïve; that he didn't realize how smart that guy was until recently, having always looked down upon him. Liu Qi didn't live in a vacuum, and knew that his reputation was a poor one — something which he attributed to his righteous character. He was, in fact, too righteous, like an unbendable stick, and had in consequence attracted a pack of mad dogs, big and small, running after him. He had, in the municipal discipline commission, an acquaintance who often called to tell him to watch his speech and behavior, hinting that there were constant accusatory letters against him. Liu Qi felt greatly wronged; sometimes his chest became constricted, and his belly felt as tight as a fully filled gas tank which might explode at any moment. From time to time he had the impulse to use his butcher's skills to kill people. Of course, he was well aware that to kill pigs was not against the law, but that to kill people was! What were laws, after all? Laws were wires, sometimes buzzing with electricity, sometimes not. Some people were safe no matter how they touched the wires, while others would be scorched to carbon at the slightest touch.

Well then, to cut a long story short, Liu Qi was in effect asking me to be his publicity manager. As a famous journalist, I would have a lot of resources, and would be familiar with the trade. Doing the right thing wasn't as good as saying the right thing, and saying the right thing wasn't as good as exorbitant bragging. In an out-and-out bragging contest, he who bragged best got the best of it. All that is gold does not glitter, but all cattle dung shines if packaged in tin foil! Having seen through the world, Liu Qi decided that he would be naïve no longer, and that he must do something. His ambition was to wear a red flower on his bosom, and go into and come out of the People's Great Hall, with airs to overwhelm the gimlet eyes from Willow Valley Township.

I said journalism was not an idyllic world either, subject to corruption, too. Liu Qi patted the table with his hand, saying "Good! Good! The darker, the better! In fact, darkest is best! I'm only worried that it is not dark enough." He claimed that in the dark there was room to move about undetected, and only in troubled water could big fish be caught. According to him, Xu Yuanyuan had already promised to set aside one million to make him presentable and push him into the highest position in the county in a few years! Xu Yuanyuan had a son who wished to enter the public security bureau, but was excluded in spite of the money which Xu had spent and the ways that Xu had explored. With anger pent up in his chest, Xu Yuanyuan was determined to send his son through that door. If Liu Qi became the head of the county, it would be a piece of cake!

27

When I returned to the press house, I sensed that everything was strange somehow. At the sight of me, all my colleagues instantly got out of the way, as if they were avoiding a SARS patient.

In front of his desktop computer sat Xiang Wenhua taking a nap, with his head on his arms and his saliva trickling a long way down from his mouth, so that it had wetted his trousers and socks.

I patted Xiang Wenhua on the shoulder.

Opening his dazed eyes, Xiang Wenhua glanced at me briefly, then resumed his sleep. I could not help saying to myself, "I wonder why he is so sleepy. If sleeping were a craft, he would absolutely qualify to take part in a contest and would probably win a gold medal."

Xiang Wenhua had once told me what vexed him most was how hard it was for him to wake up from his sleep. By contrast, what troubled me was that I found it hard to fall asleep — for me, trying to sleep was a cruel torture. How I envied him! It seemed that his brain was densely enveloped in smog. Or perhaps for him, sleep was like a silted-up deep abyss. No matter how hard he struggled, it was hard for him to free himself from it.

Eventually Xiang Wenhua woke up. It was his mobile phone clipped on at his waist that woke him up. After repeatedly saying "hello" into his cell phone, Xiang Wenhua looked straight at me with his dull eyes, as if bemused by the fact that I was sitting next to him. He yawned several times. He stretched his body. He then again bent over the table and rested his face on his arms.

Glancing at me out of the corner of his eyes, which his arms left uncovered, Xiang Wenhua asked me in an extraordinarily cold tone, "What's up?"

"Have you forgotten what we two have done?" I asked him.

"What?" Xiang Wenhua asked me.

Glancing around and having found no one else nearby, I said to Xiang Wenhua, "The two of us have been investigating the abuses the prisoners suffered in the detention house, haven't we?"

It seemed that he had long since utterly forgotten the matter. Staring at the ceiling, his eyes blinked again and again; he was striving to recollect. At last, he remembered, and yawned deeply — this being a sure sign of his recollecting something.

"Oh, you mean that thing! Hasn't it already been finished?" Xiang Wenhua asked me.

"How can it be finished?" I asked.

Abruptly Xiang Wenhua regained his vigour. Picking up a pen, he knocked it against the table, and said, "Why do you reckon it's not finished? They entertained us with fine food, with nice drinks, and with gifts. What else do you want to do to them? Are they mud that you can squeeze as you like? That guy Song Laowan, no one could be better than him! But you got him fired. Wasn't that enough?"

"Xiang, please don't get so excited," I said to him. "I'll not give my judgment whether Song Laowan was a good creature or a bad guy. As a journalist, I only investigate whether the thing he is accused of actually happened. It is true the detention house authorities treated us with delicacies and drinks. They even pressed a red envelope on me in secret. But they did all these things for their own underlying nefarious reasons. We never extorted those bribes from them. If they didn't have wicked deeds to hide, why would they fear so much?"

Xiang Wenhua burst into a rage, which was quite unexpected. The impression he had made on me was that of a muddleheaded yes-man. He accused me of having deliberately led him into a trap. He interrogated me about what my scheme was. He said Xue Yulu had once advised him against having anything to do with me, but he had scolded her for meddling too much in his affairs, calling her a dog that attempted to catch mice and do a cat's job; but now he understood at last that she had warned him for his own good.

Xiang Wenhua said that thanks to President Sun's heart-to-heart talk with him, he, an inexperienced person in the world, had woken up, and now he realized how foolish he had been in the past.

"What President Sun said was absolutely true," Xiang Wenhua said. "I have indeed been used by someone who approached me with evil intent."

I said, "Xiang, if that's what you think, I'll say nothing more."

I turned around and was about to leave, when Xiang Wenhua called me to wait. His facial expression and his voice now changed considerably. With a tone that showed his concern for me, Xiang Wenhua said, "You'd better pay attention to your personal safety, because the policeman named Zhang Zheng — the one who pulled me violently at the detention house gateway

— has been fired. Do you expect him to just swallow his resentment? He has been inquiring about your home address. Obviously, he has been considering the idea of taking revenge on you."

Xiang Wenhua said it was up to me whether I would take his advice or not. Anyway, he advised me to lay low for a while, or to hire some bodyguards!

I replied, "Would hiding be a solution to the problem? Hiding for one day is feasible. But can I hide every day? Let him do whatever he wishes. Anyway, I haven't reached my present age by indulging fear."

Issuing from Xiang Wenhua's room, I headed straight to Xue Yulu's office. It turned out that her office door was locked. I knocked on it for a long while in vain.

A fellow journalist passing down the corridor seemed to have learned about my embarrassing situation. Winking at me, he said under his breath, "She is not in. She has been picked up by a rich boss. She will be having fun in the Entertainment City run by her brother." The journalist finished his remarks with a meaningful shake of his head.

Just as I was turning round to leave, I heard a whistle behind me. Turning around, I found the journalist winking at me once again. I went up to him. Having glanced about and having found no other eyes or ears upon us, he said, "Xue Yulu has just taken a new lover. Did you know about it?"

I replied, "No, I didn't."

The journalist continued, "The young man is very handsome. He is only in his early twenties. Wherever she goes, Xue Yulu always takes him along. She tells people he is her cousin, however."

I responded, "Really? What a curious thing!"

The fellow journalist instructed me not to broadcast it, but to keep it to myself. Afterward, he left in a hurry.

I knew very well from experience that once Xue Yulu left her office, it was highly unlikely she would return shortly. So I decided not to wait for her. Even if I had waited for her, a row was the only outcome that could be expected. No matter how much I was in the right, I wouldn't get the better of her, because she had a considerable crowd to back her up. She was not formidable on her own account, but on account of the power structure she fitted herself into.

It turned out that Xiang Wenhua's warning came true that very day. When I returned to my neighborhood, I saw, from a distance, a guy wandering back and forth outside the gate of my residential complex. As I got closer, I couldn't help shuddering: the guy looked familiar, and I soon remembered he was none other than Zhang Zheng. But he looked desperately down and out, without the least sign of the aggression and arrogance he had had last time I saw him, at the reform-through-labor farm. He wore a suit of worn-out western style clothes and a pair of leather shoes which had not been cleaned for a long time. His hair was unkempt, his face wan and sallow, and his eyes were red and blood-shot, as if he had not slept for many days and nights. He carried a knife in his hand, which shone with a faint, chilly light in the evening twilight.

Zhang Zheng fixed his eyes on me. He stared at me for a long while, but he could not ascertain whether I was the Tian Daqing whom he was seeking. Seeing his confusion, I took the initiative and spoke to him.

"Are you Zhang Zheng?" I asked.

At first dumbfounded, after a couple of seconds he asked me, "Who are you?"

"I'm the very person you're looking for," I said. "Aren't you looking for Tian Daqing? I am Tian Daqing."

He was taken aback. I noticed the hand with the knife in it was shaking, as though he were considering if he should raise it and strike at my head.

I offered him a cigarette, which he declined.

"Take it and smoke it," I said. "Feel free to kill me after smoking it."

Zhang Zheng looked shy and embarrassed. He took the cigarette and lit it. While smoking, he said, "You appear to be a good-natured person. But you have a heart as evil as a wolf's. The tricks you have mastered are the ruin of others. Now I have been fired, and I wonder what benefit that could be to you? If I can't survive, why should I let you live in peace? How can you be so cruel-hearted? When I cannot support my son and my wife, I'll bring them to your place. You shall feed them for me! You son of bitch! Because of you, I became the first policeman to be fired in this city in the last twenty years. Do I still have the face to go on living in this world? I want to die. But I'll not die in vain. I'll kill someone before I kill myself so I can use their dead body as a cushion."

I said, "You think you're the only one that's tired of living? I'm even more eager to die. I'm now looking for a way to end my life. Your assistance would truly be appreciated. If you like, act now. Anyway, life for me is no fun. I'd rather die and know complete relief. Nothing more to see of this world, nothing more to trouble my mind. After we die, even if the earth exploded, it would have nothing to do with us!"

Squatting down, Zhang Zheng glared at me with his blood-shot eyes, which seemed as large as ping-pang balls. He interrogated me as to why I had given him such a hard time.

"Have we been foes in this life or even in a previous life? What on earth was the reason? Why has all this happened?" He said he wanted to know why; he'd like to figure out these things; otherwise, after his death he would become a muddle-headed ghost.

I replied, "It was purely because you displeased the warden of the reform-through-labor farm. That was why you were fired. There were people who had been planning to get rid of you. This event was the perfect pretext to use me as a weapon. In the end I served as their scapegoat, and you, just as they hoped, did indeed point your knife at me. Do I have the power and authority to fire you?"

Zhang Zheng said he had known that the warden hadn't been happy with him. The displeasure was due to his being a straightforward person, and whenever the corrupted atmosphere permeating the detention house got too much for him, he shot off his mouth. According to Zhang Zheng, Mo Shaoqiu had indeed long thought ill of him and had sold him short in such things as salary and promotion.

"But I defied him," Zhang Zheng continued. "Who did Mo Shaoqiu think he was? Apart from fawning on his superiors, what was he good for? He was nothing but a mean-spirited man whose mind was narrower than a match box."

"You should make an analysis of the true reason why you were fired," I advised him. "Before carrying out an assassination, you'd better figure out what are the roots of this case, and what are simply the leaves; what is the external skin and what are the internal organs."

Rising to his feet, suddenly Zhang Zheng gestured at me with his knife. He accused me of wanting to look like a saint.

"Don't you bear any responsibility in this issue?" Zhang Zheng challenged. He said that without my having given Mo Shaoqiu this pretext, how could Mo Shaoqiu have executed his plan so easily? Without my having proffered Mo Shaoqiu a knife, how could Mo Shaoqiu have eliminated him? Zhang

Zheng exclaimed that my bringing a vice provincial governor's son to the detention house was tantamount to bringing the plague to it, leaving whoever encountered the vice governor's son in dire straits. He said if I hadn't brought Xiang Wenhua to the detention house, Mo Shaoqiu would never have dared to fire him. Mo Shaoqiu had been looking to give him a hard time since long before; so why did Mo Shaoqiu not do so earlier? Why had he been so slow in carrying out the plan? It was not because Mo Shaoqiu hadn't wanted to do it, but because it had not been possible.

"It is not that easy to fire a policeman," Zhang Zheng said. "But it was you who created a good opportunity for Mo Shaoqiu to get rid of me. It was all because you had taken Xiang Wenhua to the detention house."

According to Zhang Zheng, if I had informed him of the identity of Xiang Wenhua before he actively started to push him, then that would have been manly behavior on my part; if he had known that the fat chap he had been keeping out was Xiang Wenhua, he wouldn't have dared to push him, even if he had had the guts of ten thousand people in his belly.

"I don't mind telling you," said Zhang Zheng, "that Xiang Wenhua looked too commonplace. It seemed that he hadn't taken a shower for many days, and he was too careless in his personal grooming. Judging from his appearance, I naturally took him for a jobless man's son."

"Why didn't you reveal his identity to me?" Zhang Zheng asked me in an accusing tone. "Why have you deliberately let me leap into a fatal pit? What type of evil plan did you have in your mind?"

Zhang Zheng claimed that according to his information, it had been due exclusively to my incitement and instigation that Xiang Wenhua had agreed to go to the detention house to cover the story.

"Well, you tell me what to do next," I said to Zhang Zheng.

"The account must be settled," Zhang Zheng said. "You must compensate the loss I have suffered."

"You can kill me if you want — the knife is in your hand, after all," I said.

After saying those words, I left as quickly as possible. Surprisingly, Zhang Zheng remained motionless.

The church bell was ringing. Its faint sounds were permeating and spreading in all directions, like smoke coming out of household chimneys. Suddenly I had a strong impulse to go to the church.

28

Minister Gao was presiding over a mass. He stood at the altar at the furthest end of the church and whispered prayers which I could not comprehend. Believers knelt in serried ranks on wooden stools, most of them were women, but there were quite a few men, too. The majority of these believers had devout expressions on their faces. After the manner of someone leading a work song, Minister Gao would sing his phrase, whereupon members of the congregation would respond with theirs. I did not understand what they were singing, but I could hear them repeat one word again and again: Hallelujah!

I sat in a corner, like a spectator watching a play. Tired, I gradually got lost in the prayers which sounded like a lullaby. I felt as if I were sinking into a bottomless abyss.

Although usually a poor sleeper, I fell sound asleep on the wooden stool. I did not know how much time had passed, when I suddenly realized that someone was caressing my hair and my neck. I opened my eyes and saw Minister Gao by my side, smiling at me. Minister Gao was only a few years older than me, but he addressed me as "child." He said, "Child, I know sooner or later you will throw yourself into the arms of Lord Jesus!" I asked why he called me child. In a measured tone he said in the eyes of Lord Jesus, all people were children in need of help.

Apparently, the day was drawing to its close. The church was getting dim. Most of the congregation were gone, but some chose to stay, so unreal and unsubstantial in appearance that they looked like ghosts. A few of them still sat in silent prayer, their heads lowered. I asked when the church would close its doors. Again, in a drawn-out tone Minister Gao said the church would always open for anyone who knocked; God's door was always open. I asked, what if a thief should break in? He said thieves were also children of the Lord, and it was just that they had gone astray. They might take whatever they wanted, and the Lord would still forgive them — poor children!

As he spoke, a number of people were filing into the church, who were ignored by Minister Gao. One look at them was enough to know the identities of those new-comers. They were either peddlers or ragpickers; a very few of them, looking like beggars, were accompanied by their wives and children. Carried on in their hands or on their backs were bamboo baskets, in which were leftover vegetables, fruit, cheap cloth, shoes, socks, dirty plastic bottles, paper boxes, and the like. A skinny little old man had, in his basket, a piglet, which, no bigger than a cat and bound with ropes, was struggling desperately and screaming hysterically, as if trying hard to escape.

I asked if these people were going to spend the night here. Minister Gao said they could if they wanted to, and could leave at any time if they didn't. I asked if the church would not become an asylum in that case. He said in the eyes of the Lord, men were not divided according to their wealth or rank, and all men were His children. They gathered around the Lord in the same way they did their parents. He felt sorry for urban management officers because they were not blessed with the Lord's enlightenment. They were pitiable, because they were children blinded by the devil! These unenlightened officers often dealt with peddlers rudely, kicking at their fruit until it rolled along the streets; smashing their tricycles out of shape. The peddlers had to run for cover wherever they could find it, as if they were fugitives. These officers were not to blame. They hadn't had the opportunity to listen to the Lord's teaching. They were just a group of poor children who had lost their way. Those peddlers who were pursued and who could find nowhere else to hide took refuge in the church. Whenever they heard of the coming of the urban management officers, the peddlers would run toward the church as though for their lives.

Once more, Minister Gao sought to convert me to Christianity. I said for the time being I did not wish to submit my soul to his Lord Jesus. I said, "I am a man of this world, and with dirt all over my body, so it is uncertain whether your Lord Jesus will accept me or not." Minister Gao answered slowly, "Lord Jesus will forgive anyone as long as he is a true believer. Sin is not the really dreadful thing. What is dreadful is when someone sins but does not know that he should confess and receive absolution."

I asked if the paradise which had been depicted by Christianity really existed. Minister Gao smiled and said, "How could it not exist? But not everyone can go there. There are conditions: one must always bear good will and perform good deeds in this mortal world." I said, "In this mortal world there are wide-spread evils. If we repay evil with good, aren't we encouraging them?" Minister Gao said, "Once a man converts to Christianity, he turns away from evil and towards goodness. Lord Jesus advocated repaying evil with good because goodness is the only effective measure against evil."

"Has Liben been coming here recently?" I asked.

"Liben came here to pray the day before he returned to the United States," replied Minister Gao.

"If Liben is a committed Christian, why is he promoting economic investment in the secular realm? Isn't this a kind of blasphemy?" I wanted to know.

Shaking his head, Minister Gao said, "The Lord will never prevent his children from getting the good things they want. By the grace of God, they can become president, professor, worker or farmer. The Lord is omnipotent and omniscient. He looks down from on high at his poor children, busy on the face of the earth. His divine light shines on all the creatures of this world. If his children believe in the Lord, they will be taken care of by the Lord, and whatever they do will be supervised by Him. Unbeknownst to them, the Lord will provide them with guidance and strength, and help them succeed. However, you don't have to come to church in order to believe in the Lord, because the Lord is everywhere, and He knows what everyone is thinking in their hearts."

"If that is the case, then everyone must be completely naked before the Lord," I said.

Raising his head, Minister Gao replied decisively, "We need not cover ourselves before the Lord. What can we do that the Lord should not know? In the eyes of the Lord, each of us is born sinful, and only by confessing our sins to Him can we get close to Him and, with His support, ascend step by step to paradise."

Minister Gao's harangue went on, but I was beginning to feel too tired to pay attention. I closed my eyes, hoping that he would go away. He eventually did, but immediately returned. He patted me on the shoulder, placed a *Bible* in my lap, and walked away smiling. In the dim light, his lanky body looked like a drifting wisp of cooking smoke.

When we were young, we used to read in our textbooks such sentences as "Religion is the opium to benumb the people," which, having haunted me since then, kept me on my guard against any religions. No sooner had Liben arrived in Yuebei, than he started looking for churches, anxious to find a place to pray. I asked him if he really thought that a church was really so important. He replied that it was as important as a canteen, if not more so. I laughed at him, saying his many years in the United States had made him neurotic. However, he took no notice of what I said, and would run to a church as soon as he had time, and he quickly became acquainted with Minister Gao. On one occasion, Liben went so far as to bring his fellow Christians to my flat. Once in my drawing room, Liben and his three fellow Christians began to babble with lowered heads, making me want to drive them away. Later Liben apologized to me, saying that he tended to forget everything around him, whenever he became animated by his mission from Jesus — his explanation as to why he had forgotten the core issue: that I was a non-religious outsider. No, I did not have faith in any religion, nor did I have faith in anything else in this world. But irreligiosity did not help me solve the problems I faced. I could find nothing to satisfy my desire to benumb myself. One could take drugs to relieve bodily pain, smoke cigarettes to relieve nicotine addiction, or drink wine to relieve alcohol addiction, but what could one turn to when one's spirit went wrong? Now I was badly in need of something to benumb myself, but I could find no sleeping pills. Was the Bible that Minister Gao gave me a sleeping pill?

I had not seen Dalin for months. When I met him again, he looked like another person. His face was strikingly thinner, his jaw sharper, his cheekbones stuck out. Faint wrinkles had appeared at the corners of his eyes. To my relief, his eyes were as clear as always, although that clarity was tainted with a just discernible trace of melancholy.

Dalin said that he had been haunted by guilt for the last several months, because he had wronged Taoqi — he had truly wronged her. He had expected her brother to give him a hard time and beat him up during Taoqi's funeral, but it did not happen. Since getting the money, Taoqi's brother had been very happy and Beiqiang himself had seen him with his own eyes singing while pissing in the outhouse.

To show his sincere regret, on the eighth day after Taoqi's burial, Dalin visited her father, who had been confined to bed by paralysis. Taoqi's father was already a bit delirious and would not stop complaining about the old story of the mutton, which he said Taoqi did not cook enough.

Though Taoqi had not treated Third Aunt very well, she could not have been nicer to her own father. Knowing that her father had always loved mutton, she once asked Dalin for twenty *yuan*, with which she bought 1.5 *jin*[16] of mutton. Without wasting a moment — she did not take even a minute to wipe her sweat — she took the mutton to him. As soon as she arrived at her father's place, she went straight to the kitchen to cook the mutton for him. When it was done, she scooped it into a huge bowl and served it to him. Her father ate with relish, with oily liquid dripping down from the corners of his mouth. While he was enjoying the mutton, Taoqi leaned against the door frame and bit on a dry and hard steamed bun. In order that her father might eat to his heart's content, Taoqi had not taken even a single bite of the mutton. Her father finished the mutton. But suddenly he started to complain about his stomach, "It aches! It aches terribly."

Her father suspected that what he had swallowed was not mutton, but rubber. Taoqi immediately took her father by the arm and led him to the clinic. The doctor diagnosed that her father had over-eaten, and prescribed a laxative for him. But, oh dear, the laxative was so powerful that he had to run to the outhouse again and again. Actually, he could not manage it even at a run. Feeling the first faint signal of an internal convulsion in his gut, her father would make a dash for the outhouse. He did not have time to squat properly before the contents of his guts had already soiled his trousers.

The strange thing was that her father became paralyzed the following day and never recovered, something which left Taoqi feeling extremely guilty. Even though this incident had made Taoqi very depressed, her father never stopped bringing it up. No matter whom he met, he would mention this matter to rebuke Taoqi. The old man believed Taoqi had not cooked the mutton long enough. He even thought Taoqi had done it intentionally, in order to hurt him. This had made Taoqi weep a lot, leaving her eyes so swollen they would take a considerable time to return to normal.

Dalin did not have a good time back home with Third Aunt, before he returned to Yuebei City. He complained that his mother had been too hard on Taoqi and had always found fault with her. It was hard for Third Aunt to tolerate her son's rebellion. She wondered how come her formerly obedient son had suddenly become so defiant and rude to her. She thought and thought about it, but she could not figure it out. Eventually she came to believe that Dalin had been possessed by Taoqi's spirit. She felt it was not Dalin that she was facing, but Taoqi's ghost.

Third Aunt had always been hard on Taoqi. Unquestionably she would be much harder on Taoqi's ghost. If today she dealt with Taoqi's ghost with forbearance, tomorrow the ghost would once again possess Dalin. If the ghost did not let Dalin go, or even abducted Dalin to the nether world, what should be done? To find out, Third Aunt turned to Fugui for help. She begged Fugui to come to her place. Fugui first lit a stick of incense, then lit some paper with magic symbols on it, and then waved it in a circle round Dalin's body. Not wishing to displease his mother, Dalin pretended to be asleep. But the discussion between Third Aunt and Fugui was really intolerable. It was obvious that Third Aunt did not want him to marry Li Tiantian. She had a firm belief that city people were unreliable, and that Li Tiantian — who used too much cosmetics, which made her look like a ghost — was particularly so. "A single glance would be enough to show at once she is not a good creature," Third Aunt declared. Naturally, Fugui kept adding fuel to Third Aunt's blazing fire. He spared no effort in vilifying Li Tiantian, saying that her facial features were not auspicious, that her looks signified misfortune on any man who married her, and that it was one hundred percent certain she would bring misfortune on Dalin. "Li Tiantian's mottled face looks uglier than a boiled pig foot,"

Fugui claimed. "I wonder why Dalin became enamored with Li Tiantian. Has Dalin been enchanted somehow?"

Speaking passionately, Fugui urged Third Aunt never, on any account, to consent that Dalin should marry Li Tiantian. "Think about it, Third Granny. Taoqi came from a poor family in the countryside. With a country woman like that for a daughter-in-law, what kind of life did you have? A loaf of bread in the morning, a mug of water in the afternoon. If Dalin marries a flirty city woman, will you have the least chance of survival? I'm afraid you won't even have bread or water to keep you alive."

Fugui talked on and on. His endless speech could be summed up in one sentence: if Dalin were to marry his daughter Layue, that would be a most proper match.

Fugui's suggestion was based on the following considerations. The village was soon going to expropriate land for Liben's project. Wasn't it true that the sooner Dalin married Layue, the sooner Dalin's family would have one more member? Actually not one more, but two more! Because if Layue married Dalin, she would of course bring along with her his grandson Langwa. If she brought Langwa, Dalin's household would then have two additional members. Two additional members would mean two more shares of compensation. It had been said that each person could get thirty thousand *yuan* relocation money.

"Let's work it out," Fugui began to calculate. "Two times thirty makes sixty. My goodness, sixty thousand *yuan*! Dalin will have to stifle his laughter! Third Granny, you too may hide under your quilt and laugh when you are alone! And of course, good things must be shared. Only then are earthly law and heavenly principle satisfied."

According to Fugui, Dalin mustn't take for himself the whole sixty thousand *yuan*. No matter how ruthless Dalin was, he was bound to take his own father-in-law and mother-in-law into consideration. Sixty thousand *yuan*! It would be entirely reasonable if Dalin were to give half of it to his parents-in-law.

"By divine edict, Layue is destined to bring prosperity to her husband," Fugui asserted. "Though her life at the moment is not prosperous — it is in fact financially tight — Layue is not to blame. The only person to blame is the great grandfather of Qi Guangrong. Why didn't he follow some other, nicer trade? Why did he become a salt dealer?"

"You see, salt is salty," continued Fugui. "It has salted all his descendants' fates, which have been correspondingly bitter. Fortunately, his great grandfather left them a treasure — the piss pot of an emperor!"

According to Fugui, the piss pot still bore some urine stains of the emperor. Whoever got to smell it on a regular basis would live several decades longer. But damn it! Though it had been said that Qi Guangrong's family possessed such a pot — it was the reason why Fugui had urged Layue to marry Qi Guangrong to the point where Layue broke down in tears — it had never been seen by anyone. Fugui said that Layue was an idiot and more stupid than a pig.

When she got the secret from her father, Layue put all her energy into her search for the piss pot. She had made full use of every minute. When Qi Guangrong was not in the house she turned it upside down looking for the pot, not leaving one single mouse hole unsearched. She was so devoted to the job that she did not rest even when she was drenched in sweat. However, despite all her efforts, she was disappointed. Each disappointment brought forth another sigh, each heavier than the last.

But Layue refused to give up. She would never give up her efforts until the piss pot was found. She even went so far as to carry a hoe outside to excavate. She dug by the household's cornfield verges. She turned the soil under old trees. She even left no stone unturned in the family's cemetery. But despite all her efforts, she had remained empty-handed.

Fugui conceded that Layue had not found the piss pot yet, but even though she had not found it today did not mean she would never find it. When she found it, she would certainly take it to Dalin's house and hide it in the wooden trunk at the head of Third Aunt's *kang*. If Third Aunt smelled it twice a day, her life span would increase from seventy to over one hundred years.

"If Qi Guangrong learns about it, we have nothing to fear," Fugui assured Third Aunt. "He had Layue with him for more than ten years, how could he refuse to compensate her for her wasted youth? The piss pot will serve as compensation for Layue's lost youth."

Of course, Dalin was not happy to hear what Fugui was saying. He did not like Layue at all, and Fugui even less. If he had ever in the past had the intention of marrying Layue, why would he have waited till now? And so he sat up from his reclining position and denounced Fugui fiercely — fiercely after Dalin's fashion. The most vicious language Dalin used was "How shameless you are!"

Casting a glance at Dalin, Fugui exclaimed that he had been wronged by him.

"How terribly you wronged me!" Fugui groaned.

Fugui said that in order to give Dalin a complete family, he hadn't hesitated to dismantle his own daughter's family. But what did he get in return? Instead of being thanked by him, he had not only been insulted by him, but also rebuked. Nevertheless, Fugui said, in view of the fact that Dalin was still a "young idiot with a big head who doesn't understand anything," he, as an aged man, was not going to argue to no purpose. Fugui emphasized that in the future Dalin would eat from the same cooking pot and snore under the same quilt as Layue, so how could he, Dalin's soon-to-be father-in-law, be at odds with his own son-in-law?

As a matter of fact, Fugui had his eye on Dalin only because he had heard that he was going to buy a flat in the capital city of the province and would thereafter settle down there. Otherwise, do you think Dalin had anything attractive in Fugui's eyes? If his daughter could get a foot-hold in the city, he, while visiting the city, would no longer have to encounter Li Tiantian's donkey face. Actually, Li Liantian's face looked even worse than a donkey's. At least a donkey's face had no scars, but Li Tiantian's face looked like it had been bitten and kicked by a donkey.

Dalin smoked a cigarette. After that, he changed topic, from Fugui to Li Tiantian. He told me that all Taoqi's funeral costs had been paid by Li Tiantian. At first, Li Tiantian was very happy with the way the situation had turned out. She said that initially she had expected only that Dalin would divorce Taoqi, and that she had never thought that her trip to Mazi Village would lead to Taoqi's disappearance from the world. Not bad! Quite nice! It was good that Taoqi was dead — really a good thing. The happiest thing for a woman was to see with her own eyes the disappearance of her rival! If Taoqi had not died, who knew — given Dalin's indecisiveness — how many more months or even years it would have taken for Dalin to divorce Taoqi? If Dalin couldn't divorce Taoqi, what would she, Li Tiantian, do? Hire someone to kill Taoqi? If she had taken that risk, chances were that the murder would have been discovered. In the event the murder were discovered, what prospect could she look forward to? Could she still get

Dalin? No way! She would stay in prison, staring at its high walls, with tears welling up in her eyes and rolling down her cheeks.

But Li Tiantian's initial excitement did not last long. In time she came to the conclusion that Dalin was like a bank cheque securely locked in her safe; unless she opened the door, Dalin could not fly away. Consequently, Li Tiantian seemed a totally different person to Dalin. All day long she would pull a long face and twist her mouth. She spoke at a sharp pitch, which resembled the sound made by a knife cutting glass. Her old sweet words had been replaced by harsh rebukes and complaints. Behaving like an abandoned woman resentful at her husband's neglect, Li Tiantian seemed to have a store of complaints as high as the heavens. She recited endless complaints about Dalin's shortcomings. And she always enumerated the kind-hearted favors she had done for him.

Again and again Li Tiantian said that when Dalin first came to the city as a migrant worker hunting for a job, it was her, Li Tiantian, who took him under her wing, and gave him a position as a duty manager at her restaurant. From a beggar he had become a handsome fellow of acceptable appearance. Had Dalin ever tasted any delicacies in the past? Had he ever eaten swallow nests soup? Had he ever eaten Wuchang fish? Had he ever eaten swallow abalone? Had he ever eaten a table of dishes that cost thousands of *yuan*? But now he had eaten and tasted all of that. Had he ever reflected or thought about who introduced him to all of that? Nevertheless, Dalin often blew his top at her, or disappeared without any pretext. Did he have any right to do so? If it had not been for her, Li Tiantian, who had put in so much money and effort, Dalin's younger brother Xiaolin would still be in jail, facing and enduring grievances. The issue of Taoqi was another one that she, Li Tiantian, had helped out with: hadn't she helped Dalin rid himself of an annoyance? But what was the reward she got? She was not only defamed but had to face the loss of money. Did her money fall from the sky? Didn't it come from the sweat of her brow?

"Dalin, oh Dalin, you should press your hand over your chest and think deeply," Li Tiantian had protested. "You should ask yourself if you have treated Li Tiantian fairly. What do you have? Apart from your handsome appearance, what else do you have? Do you have university degrees? Do you have money? Do you have social status? There're many people who are much more handsome than you. You only look attractive externally, but internally you are as worthless as donkey dung."

If Li Tiantian had spoken these words only once or twice, Dalin might have pretended that he had not heard them at all; he would have swallowed hard and have given these words no more thought. However, Li Tiantian repeated those words over and over, day after day, intolerably; even in the presence of customers she bombarded him with reproaches and barbed remarks, rubbing his face in the dirt, so that he had no place to hide. The most unbearable shame was that Li Tiantian decreed that at night he must bow down to her on the bed, with his top naked.

What was more, Li Tiantian had written a promissory note in his name and forced him to sign it. The letter of engagement mainly involved three terms: first, after marrying Li Tiantian, Dalin must unconditionally obey Li Tiantian and there should be no violation of Li Tiantian's will; second, Dalin must keep his distance from all the waitresses working in the restaurant and he should never ever look them straight in the eye; third, Dalin must break all connections with his ancestral village, and no one in the village, including Third Aunt, should come to the restaurant to look for Dalin, nor should Dalin go back to the village to visit them.

After reading this letter of engagement, Dalin refused to sign. Tearing it into pieces, he angrily left the restaurant.

30

That the rural civic school run by Liben and Kang Yuanyuan had recruited no members worried Liben very much. The farmers thought it a fraud that they should be asked to study without receiving money in return. They claimed that they were not as easily fooled as the farmers of twenty years earlier. Liben and Kang Yuanyuan went from household to household to persuade them, but all their efforts were to no avail. The word "enlightenment" on the lips of Kang Yuanyuan was ridiculed and thrown back at her by the farmers. Did she think they were fools? Alright, she maybe knew more, but did that mean they knew nothing? And if she did indeed know more, could she tell them whether to grow wheat before White Dew[17] or after? What was the proper row spacing between two corn shoots? Ah, she didn't know? Were people who could not answer simple questions like those qualified to give lectures to farmers?

"Well, well," they responded to her urging. "We farmers do not need to learn the 'great principles' you intend to put into our heads. They are of no use. Should heaven threaten to collapse, there are more lofty intellects to hold it up. What we need to know is how to grow crops."

At their wits' end, Liben and Kang Yuanyuan had to make a promise: anyone who comes to the lectures would be given a towel. On the day this news got out, the courtyard of the village office was teeming with people. Bedridden old ladies were carried in by their offspring, lads and lasses working not far away were called back by their parents, and those who were visiting their relatives scurried along in a muck sweat. That a mere towel could exert such a strong attraction dumbfounded Kang Yuanyuan. When the last towel was given away, though, the crowd dispersed, and could not be dragged back, and the courtyard appeared empty and forlorn. Only four of them, who had a connection with Liben, remained on their stools looking toward the rostrum. Third Aunt, in low spirits, had come, but not to attend the lectures, only to ease her mind. Baolai had an ulterior motive, and was counting on Liben to help him with his wife's compensation claim. Beiqiang was sitting there simply because Liben was his brother-in-law, and he must pretend to be listening with maximum attention even if he had no interest at all. The last one was Xiaolin who had wholeheartedly been supporting the school and whose watchword was almost the same as Kang Yuanyuan's,

"Ignorance is worse than poverty!" Of course, Kang Yuanyuan had praised Xialin more than once in Liben's presence, so that Liben promised that he would appoint Xiaolin to a most important post once the industrial park was set up.

Liben called me to ask for advice on how to get the farmers to gather. His voice sounded near to weeping on the phone. He said he hadn't expected that the farmers were such short-sighted numskulls as only to care for such petty profits. I said, "Ah, I see the penny has dropped! In the United States your learning increased, but so did your ignorance. Do you know the contemporary China? Do you know China's farmers? Do you think it is possible to succeed in Mazi Village without knowledge about China and its farmers?"

Liben asked what I meant by "knowledge about China and its farmers." He believed that he had sufficient knowledge about China and its farmers. He knew very well what meals farmers ate, what clothes they wore, in what manner they talked, what dreams they had, even what toilet paper they used to wipe their backsides. He knew how frequently they took a bath, how many fleas swarmed in their clothes, and the like. I said it was no use to know things of that kind. He should learn from Lu Xun to anatomize the spirit and soul of contemporary farmers in the way Pao Ding[18] had done with an ox.

"Is it that complicated?" Liben asked.

"If you want to successfully invest in China, you have to know whose words farmers are most willing to follow," I replied.

"Whose words are farmers most willing to follow?" he asked.

"Needless to say, it is the government whose words carry most weight with them. If you want to accomplish anything in China, you must cooperate with the government." I replied.

Liben said he wanted to cooperate with the government, but he hated to cooperate with officials like Liu Qi and Shuanhu. He lamented his bad luck: there were so many good officials in Kaiyang, however, his bad luck had led him to such a man as Liu Qi — a butcher by trade. Cooperation with him would inevitably mean deviating from the original aim of the civic school. What Kang Yuanyuan and he wanted most eagerly to talk about in class were the obligations as well as rights that a citizen had, and how to fulfill these obligations and fight for these rights, etc. The basic reason for their hard life was that the farmers did not know what their innate rights were, in addition to not having received a good education! How could a person with a rope in hand to bind the farmers be willing to cooperate with a person who tries his utmost to undo the binding knots? Wouldn't the latter become an accomplice if he acts under the former's orders?

I laughed. I said, "Liben, you are not simply ignorant. You have reached a state of stupefaction! How naïve you are! So what, if farmers do know their rights? Who do you want them to fight? And what will be the result? In your impulsiveness you are throwing a piece of porcelain against a concrete wall, only to break it! You wish to save them, but I am afraid you can't even save yourself. Do you think you are a savior, a Buddha liberating all creatures from sufferings, leading farmers toward the light? Snap out of it, and stop while there is still time. If you cannot wake up by yourself, I am right here begging you to do so. Do not lead our poor villagers over a flower-covered cliff-edge!"

Liben got very angry. He said he had thought I was an upright intellectual that had a backbone, and he hadn't expected that I, like most intellectuals in China, was an invalid paralyzed by calcium deficiency, a cripple not just in body but also in mind. A civic society, in the real sense of the term, could not be established in China unless farmers woke up, and China would have no future unless civic society was established! Take Mazi Village as an example. Though everyone in this village was utterly pitiable, they seemed to be loathsome to the same degree. Why were they loathsome? Why was the kindness in their nature receding ever further, while their selfishness was spreading like wildfire? Was it not because they were denied a good education? Was it not because they were wholly lacking in basic civility?

I said, "It's one thing for you to come back and invest. But why must you involve yourself in such matters? They are a trap that you will never be able to pull your leg out of."

It was evident that Liben had had enough of me. The "du-du-du" noise suddenly emerged from the phone. He had hung up without even saying goodbye.

One month later, I received a call from Kang Yuanyuan; her low voice betrayed her mood. She kept sighing. I asked her how the civic school was going. Kang Yuanyuan said the school had attracted attention from the different levels of government, and from the media as well. It had made great progress, but not in the right direction. I asked her what she meant by "not in the right direction." Kang Yuanyuan said Liben had indeed taken my advice and turned to local officials for support. The villagers were an odd lot: they were suspicious of favors but amenable to harsh treatment, and became docile sheep on the order from the local government. Township Head Liu and Tian Shuanhu were in charge of the work. They stipulated that those who were late once would lose two hundred *yuan* from their land requisition money; those who were absent once would lose one thousand *yuan*! Damn! One thousand *yuan*! That was an enormous sum for a farmer. Who would not feel anguish at such a loss? With these rules, no one had dared to come late or leave early, or go to the outhouse during the lecture. Even the migrant workers returned from the city in a hurry. But there were drawbacks; the major one being that Township Head Liu seemed to be in love with his own voice, not knowing when to put down the microphone once he had got hold of it. A poor speaker, he would let his illogical speech wander randomly and shout at whomever he found objectionable. Township Head Liu was doing more swearing than speaking. Dirty words would tumble from his mouth for four hours at a stretch. Inside his mouth there was much invective, but only foam came out. All Township Head Liu's vocabulary revolved around the male and female reproductive organs, and almost every sentence contained a "cock" or a "fuck your mother," at which some maiden faces reddened like a soldering iron.

While Township Head Liu was delivering his speeches, Shuanhu stood on guard by his side with Knife Victim. As its name suggested, the dog kept its one apprehensive eye on the audience, its bloody tongue lolling out. It would bark at anyone dozing or whispering. Then Shuanhu would quickly walk over, take out his notebook and jot down that person's name, and would shout at him or her to stand up. The first time this happened, Liben and Kang Yuanyuan talked to Shuanhu in private, and asked him to stop doing that. But Shuanhu preferred to listen to Liu Qi, who gave him a high five and praised his deeds.

Liben was deflated. The villagers, who used to greet him with a smile, now viewed him as if he were an enemy; they either walked away from him, or they scowled at him, or to relieve their feelings they pointed at the mulberry and swore at the locust in the most profane terms. They found appropriate curses for everything: the pig should be slaughtered, the hen should die of a foul plague, and the sparrow should crash into a branch. That these innocent animals were reviled in his and Kang Yuanyuan's stead upset him very much.

Not only animals but Liben's brother-in-law got drawn in. From the time when he had received those thick stacks of colorful US dollars in public, it seemed that the thief hat had been removed from Beiqiang's head. He carried his head high and walked with a straight back. And people who had never before talked to him began to frequent his home. However, after Liben started the school, Beiqiang gradually became isolated from the rest of the villagers, who were no longer willing to walk by his side, or to respond to his words. Even if he ran after them to greet them, they would turn up their noses. This had been going on for some time, when a series of incidents took place. One night, a bundle of joss paper was burned outside his gate, leaving a pile of ash drifting in the wind. The next night, bricks and broken beer bottles were thrown over the wall into his courtyard, the shattered glass cutting Lifang's heels. Another morning, when Beiqiang opened the gate, he found it covered with shit, a sight foul enough to turn one's stomach. Persuaded by Liben, Beiqiang swallowed with difficulty the anger welling up in his belly. Just as the wind never lets the tree rest in peace, one more outrage followed. One day, having been humiliated by Shuanhu in the civic school, Fugui announced that he had lost a hoe and did not know who had been so shameless as to steal it. This immediately stirred up a heated discussion among the villagers. Many a voice rose in accusation, "Who else could it be? Who is the most notorious thief in this village?" Aflame with indignation, thirty or forty villagers, young and old, shouting and cursing, moved in unison toward Beiqiang's home. The locked gate was knocked open, the table in the courtyard was turned upside down, the water vat in the kitchen was smashed into pieces, and the TV set in the bedroom was deprived of sound and image by the blow of an iron bar. Beiqiang wrestled with this group of people, but greatly outnumbered he fell down and was stamped on by numerous feet…

As a result, the whole family of Liben's sister held a grudge against him. Lifang began to protest at his opening such a school, and furthermore protested at his investing in a factory which would be set up in their village. She wept and implored him to go, back to the United States, and never to return. What was the point of investing in the village? Six folks out of every half-dozen in this village were mean-spirited wolves who, if you cut out your heart to feed them, would reject it as being too salty or too spicy.

31

I revisited the village at Liben's request, after he had made a total of six calls asking me to give a lecture to the villagers. I had many scruples about this. On the one hand, I had no desire to get involved in the complicated situation initiated by Liben. On the other hand, I wanted to keep my distance from Liu Qi, Shuanhu and the like. For all these reasons, I was unwilling to go back to the village on this occasion.

Another concern of mine was that in the eyes of the villagers I would forever be the runny-nosed creature named Black Bean. In no case would they listen to lectures from me. In their eyes, I was no more resourceful than Fugui, no more daring than Shuanhu, no more sharp-tongued than Luobo. I might be slightly better than Qiuli, but compared to her I had one defect: I was not as brass-necked as her. Qiuli dared to strip off all her clothes in public, did I dare to do that?

But I went back to the village in spite of my unwillingness. The major reason was that I had heard Liben say that a public bathhouse had just been built in the village. According to Liben's description, the bathhouse was pretty luxurious. It would help to break the villagers' habit of not taking baths, which had lasted from generation to generation through the entire history of the village. Liben said this novelty would really subvert the farmers' traditional lifestyle.

I was fascinated by the bathhouse — not because I wanted to take a bath in it, but because I wanted to see whether it would make a good news-story. Since I had conducted the interview at the detention house, no news report written by me had received Xue Yulu's approval. Like a conscientious goalkeeper, she was determined not to let any ball that I kicked with such great efforts shoot into the back of the net she was guarding. Under these circumstances, what else could I do but quarrel with her? She forced me to, so I did.

I accused her, "You have been finding fault with me, creating difficulties for me, and backstabbing me."

Xue Yulu replied, "Yes, I have been finding fault with you, creating difficulties for you, and backstabbing you. So what? So what? What's the problem?"

I said, "Narrow-minded people tend to have a short life span. Your allotted portion of life will be cut short due to the wicked deeds you have done."

Xue Yulu wailed aloud, saying that she was in danger of being killed. Didn't my judgment that her life would be "cut short" imply that I wanted to stab her with a knife? What an unjust reward she had received! For the sake of work, her life was in danger.

As a matter of fact, I would not have cared about whether my news reports were published or not, or how many of my reports were published, if a journalist's pay was not dependent on his press publications. Publishing or not publishing made a big difference to my livelihood. According to the press house policy, any journalist who ranked last in terms of published stories in a six-month period would lose his job.

In view of the fact that each day brought me closer to getting sacked, how was I supposed to remain calm and composed? Wasn't it natural that I should struggle desperately? Xue Yulu was just a hand pushing me towards the cliff edge. I hated to quarrel with her, but did I have a choice?

Quite unexpectedly, I met Xue Yulu in Mazi Village. It turned out that upon learning from the Internet about the civic school opened in Mazi Village, instead of sending a journalist to cover the story, she came here herself. After arriving she found, quite to her surprise, that it happened to be her colleague Tian Daqing's hometown. This discovery, instead of making her decide to give up the interview, on the contrary, made her intensely interested in the village. Led by Shuanhu, Xue Yulu visited every corner of the village. She went out of her way in order to visit the house where I had been born and raised. It was a three-roomed adobe building whose eaves had fallen in here and there, with moss growing rampant along the roof tile ridges. The courtyard was overgrown with wormwood. On the crooked wooden door hung a rusty iron lock, which was as big as a human fist.

Xue Yulu soon found favor in Shuanhu's eyes. Shuanhu viewed Xue Yulu as an astonishing person. First of all, even though she was a big-shot journalist from a big city, Xue Yulu did not put on any airs; she talked and laughed; she called a spade a spade; she did not mind dirt soiling her feet; she did not mind thistles piercing and tearing her clothes; she took a carrot offered by a villager and had a bite of it without checking whether it was clean or not; she entered an outhouse fearlessly. She was truly amazing!

You bet that Shuanhu told my story to Xue Yulu. The tale he told of my ancestors left nothing out, such as my great grandfather being a drug addict, my grandfather struggling to do a good job as a hostler, my father often wearing his pants inside out, my mother braiding her hair into the shape of a blackbird's nest. In brief, none of my ancestors, male or female, had lived a decent life. As for me, there were too many funny things for him to enumerate. For example, as a kid I could not tell the difference between males and females, and having seen girls squat to pee, peed in the same manner. Or to take another example, while working in the production team, I fastened a yoke to a cow on the wrong side, which enabled the beast to struggle off the yoke and run away madly, and while I chased after it I stumbled into a dry cistern, which happened to house a hornets' nest, and I ended up being stung so badly my face swelled all over.

As Shuanhu gave these accounts, Xue Yulu giggled heartily. The only exclamation she uttered was, "Why was Daqing so ill-starred?"

When I caught sight of her, Xue Yulu had just come out of the bathhouse and was drying her hair with a towel. To my astonishment, a young lad followed her. He was very handsome and extremely fashionable. At his wrist there was an eye-catching blue tattoo. Before Xue Yulu saw me, the lad's eyes met mine. He looked familiar to me, but I could not remember where I had seen him before. I searched my memory, which was suddenly illuminated, as though by a flash of lightning, as I remembered who the lad was. Wasn't he the waiter I had met in the Alibaba teahouse? I remembered I had asked him what his name was and he had told me his stage name was Larz.

I wondered why he was here and how come he was with Xue Yulu. Was he Xue Yulu's toyboy, as rumor had had it?

I was not sure if Larz had recalled who I was, but I could detect that he felt I looked familiar, at least, because his face turned faintly red. Shuanhu, who had been waiting for Xue Yulu outside the bathhouse door, was the first to accost me. He tugged Xue Yulu's lappet to alert her as to who was coming. At the sight of me, Xue Yulu was so immensely surprised that the shock twisted her face. Quickly she resumed her normal look. Smiles which she had rarely worn in my presence rippled over her face. Her smiling face brought into my mind a sentence I once read somewhere: "At last she looked faintly like a woman."

She asked me when and why I had come back. Was it because my heart sickened if I hadn't seen crops for days? Taking a joking tone, she reproached me, and wanted to know why I hadn't asked her for leave, and was it because

I didn't regard her as my boss?

Turning to Shuanhu, Xue Yulu claimed that in the department under her leadership, everyone else obeyed her rule, that I was the only insubordinate person, and that I always set myself against her. Was it because I had eaten too much limestone during my childhood due to not being able to eat my fill of food? She enumerated the details of her kindness to me. She said if it had not been for her, I would certainly have been kicked out of the press house long ago, like a bad apple picked and thrown out of a fruit-basket.

Xue Yulu exclaimed she would have felt okay if I simply hadn't shown any gratitude to her; unfortunately, not only had I severely misunderstood her but had also set myself against her; how badly I had got her wrong!

"It's a good job that I am a broadminded individual, otherwise I would have died of anger several times over," Xue Yulu declared.

While listening to Xue Yulu's charges against me, Shuanhu nodded constantly. Patting me on my shoulder, Shuanhu scolded me, "How can you bully a female comrade? Are you in the habit of picking on tender-hearted individuals, just as people choose a soft persimmon to squeeze and eat?"

Then with smiles on his face, Shuanhu said to Xue Yulu, "From now on, don't you show any mercy to Black Bean. Teach him a lesson whenever necessary. And if he should prove incorrigible, just let me know. I'll pin back his ears for you. Even a reinforcing bar can be bent, how much easier it is to straighten the neck of a human!"

In Shuanhu's opinion, the most effective thing would be to hand me over to Liu Qi, who was like a steel foundry furnace, capable of instantly transforming pig iron into dug iron.

"In this world, there are inevitably some people who are hard to handle," Shuanhu said. "But they are no longer hard to handle once they encounter Liu Qi's steel-making furnace."

On the way to the village office, Xue Yulu introduced Larz to me, referring to him as her cousin. She laughed while saying that Larz was about to become Shuanhu's live-in son-in-law. Shuanhu was so pleased that he could hardly keep his mouth closed. With uneven teeth looking like odd-shaped rocks, his open mouth resembled a broken pomegranate.

Shuanhu confessed he truly liked Larz. "Look at the young man!" Shuanhu said. "How pleasant he looks! He is so handsome, with such a fine nose, fine eyes and a fine mouth. What fine hands and fine feet he has!"

Shuanhu claimed that he felt well-disposed toward Larz, that he had his eye on Larz for his daughter, that his daughter Jidan and Larz were a perfect match, like the union between a phoenix and a swan, a rose and a peony, a tomato and a green bean. He said though neither Xue Yulu nor Larz had ever seen Jidan, it did not matter. It was enough that they heard his description of her. Hearing was seeing. Though Jidan's name, meaning "chicken egg," sounded rustic, she looked very pretty, as pretty as a doll. Impossible to see her without wanting to kiss her. Jidan's face was round, Jidan's eyes were round, so were her hips and her body. Her skin felt like an egg, so smooth.

Larz was silent, his face betraying slight shyness. Though Xue Yulu refrained from laughter, she eventually failed in her effort. Like a swollen balloon pierced by a needle, she bent over with outbursts of laughter.

Thunderstruck, Shuanhu asked her, "Why do you laugh? What's so funny?"

Pointing at Shuanhu, Xue Yulu said Shuanhu was so-o-o humorous; how could he have described his daughter in this way?

As Shuanhu was walking Xue Yulu to a car that was parked near the school gate, I turned to enter the bathhouse. I wanted to see how the bathhouse looked, on the construction of which Liben had invested so much effort. I was curious to see how the farmers, who had never taken a bath in a bathhouse before, would wash themselves there.

The exterior of the bathhouse did not look attractive — its wall was rough and uneven. But its entrance looked very spectacular: a ferocious-looking cement tiger was opening its enormous mouth. The tiger mouth served as both the entrance and the exit of the bathhouse. The interior looked pretty luxurious, just as Liben had told me. The floor was marble, the walls were covered with green ceramic tiles. There were well-ordered wooden cabinets. There were well-ordered couches covered with plaid bed sheets. From the ceiling hung a flowery lantern. When turned on, the lantern looked like a brilliant flower in full bloom. The most fascinating thing about the bathhouse was a line of words on the front wall. The words read: "Change begins with taking a bath!"

Xiaolin worked as watchman at the bathhouse. Since no one was taking a bath right now, he sat on a couch reading.

"What book are you reading?" I asked him.

A shy look appeared on Xiaolin's face. Closing the book, he waved it in my direction.

Approaching him, I found it was Sun Yat-sen's biography.

"Do you think reading such a book is useful?" I asked Xiaolin. "It may be more practical to read handbooks on raising chickens or growing apple trees."

Xiaolin smiled to me. He shook his head and said he had no interest in such insignificant trifles; he just could not force himself to take any interest in them; he'd rather die than force himself to do that. Even if he could raise good chickens and fat pigs, what was the good of such work beyond earning some money? The money thus earned could only be exchanged for cooking oil, salt, soy sauce, vinegar and other necessities. Could the money change his fate? Generations and generations of people had fulfilled a similar fate in a similar manner. Wasn't it sad? Now that he had come into the world, he didn't wish to live like a sheep or pig, without a clear goal in life.

Xiaolin said his goal was to commit himself to the reform in China, and to lead an active life. It was this goal that had motivated him to read the book about Sun Yat-sen, so that he might be inspired by the experiences of the great mind.

I advised him against thinking so naively, and said, "Is there any comparison between Sun Yat-sen's time and ours?"

I told Xiaolin I had once felt huge admiration for Lu Xun, but by now my faith in him had plummeted.

"Lu Xun harshly criticized the times he lived in, but without those particular times, how could he have made a name for himself?" I asked Xiaolin. "He was a fruit produced by the times he lived in. Suppose he had been born into a different historical period, regardless of the thoughts he might have conceived, he would have had no way to get them published. Or even worse, he might have been deprived of his right to life. I once despised the fictional character Ah Q he portrayed in his work, but after years of personal frustrations, I eventually understood Ah Q."

"It's undeniable that Ah Q's 'spiritual consolation approach' is pitiful," I continued. "But let's view this issue from the opposite angle. If Chinese people lead their lives without this spiritual consolation, what will become of them? Do you mean the poor common people are supposed to collapse and be fragmented, like glass yielding to the blows of a hammer? Or should they be left to commit suicide? The spiritual consolation approach is an effective way to comfort oneself. It can save people from desperate disappointment or a complete collapse."

Waving his hand, Xiaolin stopped me from making further observations. He said he didn't want me to pour cold water onto his boiling hot blood; that if everybody behaved like a tortoise, the world would no longer be a human world, but a paradise for insensible tortoises.

In turn, I asked Xiaolin, "Don't you think the world today *is* a paradise for tortoises? Actually, far from being a paradise, in my opinion, it is more like a hunting ground."

32

As I had expected, funny things began to happen one after another after the construction of the bathhouse. When Liben told me about them, the expression on his face was so indefinable that you could hardly tell whether he was on the point of crying or smiling. By contrast, Kang Yuanyuan was in good spirits, though she did complain about the mountain she had had to climb to educate these farmers. Luckily, the bathhouse had been built, so her stay at Mazi Village had not been in vain. Kang Yuanyuan went on and on, trying to prove that the bathhouse was the natural result of the civic school, so that she could take a share of the credit for it.

Problems followed hard upon the opening of the bathhouse. No villagers bathed there, because they were afraid of being charged afterward. Officials had a face more capricious than the weather in summer, which might change at any moment. There was no certainty that they would not one day call on villagers to collect their money, sweet as their words sounded now. The villagers had experienced such things so many times that even brain-damaged Qiuli was wise to them. Furthermore, there were no screens; how embarrassing it was to undress in the presence of others, who were able to have a full view of your completely naked body! A decent villager would never go to bathe there. If you went to take a bath there, you would be a hooligan!

The real problem, though, was not the villagers, but Liu Qi and Shuanhu. The day the bathhouse opened for business, Liu Qi was the first person to take a bath right after he cut the ribbon; the township vice head Zhao Xiaohui and the village head Shuanhu stood guard at either side of the "tiger-mouth" entrance. Liu Qi bathed in a hurry, and came out spluttering in anger. "No sauna, no jacuzzi, no rubdown, no massage, no dancing show, no singing show. Call that a bathhouse? No, it's only a puddle, a smelly ditch!" What displeased him most was that there was no private room for him. What nonsense! Their skulls must have been packed with mud to build the bathhouse without considering where Liu Qi, with his exalted rank, should be accommodated. In his own territory he couldn't find a suitable place! How could he not be angry? Why shouldn't he simply turn on his heels and walk away?

After Liu Qi left in a huff, Shuanhu summoned Liben to a meeting; under a persimmon tree, he discussed the bathhouse with him in a serious way. Shuanhu focused on two issues. First, the bathhouse must be remodeled. There must be three private rooms, one small and two large, all with deluxe decoration, for the exclusive use of leaders at the village, township, and county levels. Leaders at the county level might not often come, but if they did come, they could luxuriate in all the comforts so that they would be deeply impressed by the village. The small room could be assigned to village leaders. Were village leaders not leaders? A distant dragon is less dangerous than a nearby snake; village leaders were the Buddha that really needed to be carefully worshipped, but unfortunately many people did not grasp this point. Village leaders could be wolves or rabbits, depending on how they were treated. Second, the bathhouse must really be a bathhouse, in other words, profitable. How could it make profit? Liben, as the clever man he was, should cotton on without Shuanhu being explicit. But, if Liben was going to feign stupidity, he would have to give him straight-forward instructions — specifically, to hire a group of hot and sensual girls to provide special services. The arrival of the girls would bring many benefits; they could kill two birds with one stone — indeed, up to eight birds! The girls could not only satisfy different ranks of leader, but would attract punters from near and far, and as a result, the bathhouse might be able to charge them as well as the girls, to whom the village housing could be let, while well-to-do families could start country style restaurants, and so on and so forth. If they followed this plan, how could the Mazi villagers fail to get rich? The village was certain to become the wealthiest in Kaiyang County even if it did not want to. Was finding girls the problem? Ha-ha-ha-ha, how could that be? Like locusts they were everywhere, and you could get a handful just by reaching out your hand. Oh, others might find it difficult to look for them, but to Jidan it was as easy as spitting. Was there anything that Jidan couldn't do? If you gave her the commission, she would procure as many as you liked, as sexy as you wished. The girls she mingled with were not only beautiful but particular about hygiene, absolutely free from any exotic diseases. In Jidan's words, those girls washed their nether regions with medicinal water every day, and had excellent professional ethics.

Liben flatly rejected Shuanhu's ideas and demands. He turned and went away before Shuanhu could finish talking. He wondered why there always had to be people who tried to change something good into something else.

Why did they always want to divert every good thing from its original course? He got angry, though he did not want to. He said, "I never suspected you, who are the village head, of having such base ideas. If you go on like this, there's no possibility but that you'll lead the village astray."

I said, "Liben, you needn't feel surprised at anything you've seen here. When Shuanhu said a distant dragon is no match for a nearby snake, he was in fact hinting something to you. Do you understand what he meant?" Liben answered that he was not scared! If he were scared, it was inevitable that Shuanhu would lead him by the nose. Shuanhu and Liu Qi dared not challenge him to that extent; on the contrary, they had to curry his favor. And for why? The money he had raised attracted the attention of the provincial government, which had listed it as a model project of the province; Governor Xiang was going to take charge of it in person. Liben had met Governor Xiang, and had had dinner with him as well.

Having said all this, he looked at me for a while before mocking me and saying that I was pretentious, and that I was so tight-lipped that it was not possible to force open my mouth even with iron pliers. I was rather bewildered, and asked what my pretentions were supposed to be.

"You know what they are," Liben asserted.

"Believe it or not, I really do not know what you are talking about." I confessed.

Liben asked if I was acquainted with Governor Xiang. I said how I could be acquainted with Governor Xiang? Among the thousands with whom he had been acquainted, could Governor Xiang tell me from Adam? I only knew his son, and that was all. Liben said that when he told Governor Xiang about the talents who had emerged from Mazi Village, he mentioned my name and lavished praise on me, then Governor Xiang asked him if I was the one who worked in the press house, who was fond of writing essays and the like. He said that Governor Xiang told him I wrote good articles which told the truth, and that Governor Xiang liked me so much that he could even recite the titles of certain articles of mine. I asked dubiously, "Is that so? Does he have leisure to read essays, with official documents piling up like mountains in front of him?"

Liben shifted the topic to the ways in which the villagers bathed. They were so funny that you did not know whether to laugh or cry. At the beginning, Liben had not planned to employ a door-keeper, but he soon found that he would have to. Some people bathed their sheep, some women washed their clothes basin by basin, some disassembled the taps to sell as waste metal, and some were so nasty as to shit in there, not knowing whether it was a bathhouse or a toilet.

However, the question of whom to hire led inevitably to a clash with Shuanhu. Liben had wanted Baolai, who had a poor family to support, a sick wife, Qiuli, who needed medical treatment, and petition offices to visit. As a door-keeper he could earn five hundred and fifty *yuan* a month, paid by Liben and with nothing to do with the village. Shuanhu was angry about such an arrangement, because he found it unbearable to see Baolai grinning with his yellow teeth although there were so many that he disliked in this village and so many that he sent away with a flea in their ear whenever he saw them. He felt greatly encouraged by the sight of Baolai's sad face, and would be tempted to slap him if he saw him smile. Baolai had been complaining everywhere about him and his brother; first about his brother Shuanniu's practicing medicine without a license, and then about his embezzlement of money from the grain-for-green project. "Ho-ho, Baolai, you are astonishing indeed! It's obvious that you've got a hard wooden club between your legs! Sooner or later you will find out that Shuanhu is not a dead pig on the ground, inviting you to give it a kick as much as you please."

The first strike came from Shuanhu's wife. On the second day after Baolai had become the door-keeper of the bathhouse, Shuanhu's wife ran out of the bath, with her uncombed hair still in a mess, and seized Baolai's collar. She cried and yelled that just now when she was bathing Baolai, the hooligan, had stolen a glimpse of her body through the slit in the cloth curtain! How could she go on with her life? How could she face the world? Her crying attracted other members of the Shuanhu family, young and old, men and women, thirteen or fourteen of them in all. They held him down and gave him a good beating until his head was covered with blood, his mouth torn, and his crotch swollen like a loaf of bread. But for Xiaolin's stopping them and calling 110[19], it was hard to tell whether Baolai would have survived.

Liben repented of his charitable act. He should not have let Baolai guard the bathhouse. Nevertheless, he was more than ever determined to topple Shuanhu. He was prepared to sacrifice himself to get rid of such an imperious village tyrant — as he said between gritted teeth.

33

I delivered my talk one afternoon. The weather was anything but pleasant. Some grayish clouds were drifting in the sky. Irregular gusts of wind, swirling like the skirts of a waltzing dancer, blew intermittently, sometimes violently, sometimes gently, through the audience. Some handkerchiefs were swept off the heads of the aged grannies present by the wind.

I seated myself behind a desk. Before me was a microphone that functioned only intermittently. After announcing the dos and don'ts of the program, Liben withdrew. Kang Yuanyuan sat next to me, taking notes conscientiously.

Right at the beginning, as Liben was making the introduction, there was an unexpected development. Naturally, Liben praised me to the skies, presenting me as a figure of some eminence, as an upright and learned man. And it was at this point that unrest broke out among the crowd, with laughter rippling back and forth:

"Isn't he just Black Bean? Why is he spoken of so highly? As if he were a *white* dung beetle fallen down from the heavens."

"Quite right! How funny it is to pretend to be a somebody after only experiencing the city life for a few days! Don't we know how many inches tall he is?"

"As a small boy, Black Bean often couldn't untie his belt. As a result his pants were often wet with urine. In winter time, his pants were as hard as iron tablets."

"Black Bean loved eating red bean soup most. Without red bean soup, he rolled back and forth over the floor, raising a ruckus. Phew! Black Bean didn't love black beans. He loved red beans."

"Don't we know Black Bean? Why bother introducing Black Bean to us? Even if he were burned to ashes, we could still recognize him at first sight, from the ashes."

Feigning that I heard nothing of their remarks, I took out my lecture transcript and began the talk. Its topic was "On the Moral Codes of Village Residents."

I had hardly completed a couple of sentences when Song Tongguo's loud bawls disrupted me. He cursed Qiuli at the top of his voice, accusing her of having put a caterpillar down the back of his collar, so that he was feeling terribly itchy all over. Song Tongguo picked up a brickbat, intending to hit

Qiuli, only to discover she had run out of range.

Qiuli, keeping her distance, paid no notice to Song Tongguo at all. She repeatedly spat onto a tree, pouting and mumbling, as if she were quarreling with the tree.

Song Tongguo claimed the caterpillar was wriggling like mad on his back; this was more than he could bear; he had to go home to apply some ointment to the stings.

Shortly after Song Tongguo made his departure, a young woman loudly announced that she had to leave in order to breastfeed her baby. Patting the dust off her buttocks she left too. In close succession, people left one after another. Those who remained sat impatiently, and complained, "Those people have left to make money. Why are we made to sit here wasting our time? Why make us stay here to suffer?"

After about twenty minutes, only a dozen people were left sitting here and there in front of me. Undoubtedly, they chose to remain out of kind consideration for my mood. Among them, one woman made this point explicitly — she used to be on good terms with my mother, so she couldn't bear seeing me have no audience.

Among those who remained, some took a nap, some chatted at low volume about catching wild rabbits. Wild rabbits feared humans very much. They hid in caves in day time. At night they stealthily went into the fields looking for food; they chewed corn cobs or nibbled bean-crop leaves. Some unlucky rabbits would be caught by villagers lying in wait. The villagers would strangle them on the spot, and take them home to skin them. After that, they would poke the furless rabbits onto a wooden stick and carry them to the county town to sell to hot pot restaurants. Since the price rose and fell unpredictably, the restaurant owners often fooled the villagers, who were not well-informed about the market situation. Naturally, the villagers, whenever they gathered together, would ask one another about the going rate for rabbits.

In spite of everything, I went on with my talk on the subject that neighbors should learn to be mutually considerate and tolerant. Even I myself regarded this kind of lecturing boring. I felt sleepy. How I wished I could find a bed to lie down on. Just then, Third Aunt spoke, "Black Bean, you stop your talk. No one is listening anyway. Look, you are even tiring yourself out!"

Fugui wholeheartedly agreed with Third Aunt, "Exactly! Your talk is useless. Let the village neighbors who want to quarrel, quarrel. Let those who want to fight, fight. If they did not quarrel or fight, could you even call them neighbours? Without quarrels or fights, where is the spice of life?"

"That's right! That's absolutely right!" Luobo agreed. She claimed she quarreled and fought with Song Tongguo almost every day. If a day went by without a quarrel or a fight, they seemed to feel something was missing, and that their hearts were empty.

Turning to me, Luobo said I had no insight into the minds of the villagers. She said I was to all intents and purposes a blind man attempting to learn about an elephant by touch, or, a blind cat attempting to catch a mouse, but getting bitten by it instead. She said money was what the villagers were thinking about!

"Give money to them, or give them a lecture as to how to turn a penny," said Luobo, "you'll see how they flock to attend it."

Fugui did not approve of what Luobo had said. He thought of himself as the sage of the village. So he challenged Luobo, "What do you know about the matter? You, a conceited, silly and undiscerning young person! You think all the villagers are totally obsessed with money, money, money? You're wrong. Out of every ten, nine are obsessed with wishing ill on their neighbors: if you have money and I don't, I hope some thief steals all your earnings; if you have a new house and I still live in an old cottage, I hope an earthquake razes all the buildings in the village, new and old alike, to the ground, so that everyone will be on an equal footing again. If your son marries a beautiful wife and my son remains single after endless travails all over the place, I hope your son's beautiful wife either gets cancer or gets run over. In brief, I feel happy when others have bad luck, I sing happy songs when others cry, I cheer when others suffer."

Luobo took what Fugui said seriously. She suddenly recalled how Fugui behaved when her mother was sick. In those days, Fourth Aunt's crotch swelled to the size of a small water melon. The worse thing was that the water melon seemed to be festering, with ulcerous liquid oozing out incessantly. Fugui made fun of Fourth Aunt in public. He hummed a song he had made up, which went: "Fourth Aunt's bubbling spring flows without end, without end…" Though Luobo was not happy with Fugui during that period, she failed to realize he was ridiculing her mother; she thought he was only playing a joke.

Now Fugui's remarks suddenly made her see what she had missed so long ago. It dawned on her what an evil man Fugui was! Luobo began looking daggers at Fugui.

As a school girl, Luobo failed in every subject. However, her ability to curse was top-notch. Really, the Ministry of Education was to blame for not including cursing in the curriculum. If it had been an examined course, Luobo would have got full marks in every test. Nothing could so offend the ear as the curses Luobo hurled at Fugui. Sometimes she combined Fugui's family's male and female sexual organs in her curses, sometimes she divided those organs and made use of them separately; and sometimes she mingled male and female sexual organs together; and finally she hacked a given person's organ into pieces. Everyone present turned their heads aside, and twisted their mouths. Some of them covered their mouths with their hands and laughed slyly. One after another, people rose to their feet and left. Fugui stood up, with a facial expression somewhere between laughter and tears, and then left unhurriedly. Eventually only Luobo remained in the auditorium. Up on the platform Kang Yuanyuan and I sat as before, numb with embarrassment.

Glancing around, Luobo saw there was no one left to listen to her. So she stopped swearing. Rising to her feet and stretching her torso wearily, she explained to me that her bad words were not meant for me, and that she had been compelled to shout them.

Waving my hand to her, I said, "The talk is over. You can go now. Feel free to go."

Showing no hurry to leave, Luobo expounded her philosophy to me. She said, "In a rural community you need either an iron fist, or a set of steel teeth. You have to be tough. If you aren't, you are certain to be bullied! If you give an inch, you'll be bullied forever!" She exclaimed that her husband Song Tongguo, as an outsider without local connections, had always been regarded as insignificant and invisible. If she herself hadn't been tough, wouldn't other people have ridden rough-shod over her shoulders, shitting and pissing as they did so?

I cut her short, "Luobo, please stop it. Speak no more, please! I understand you. Everybody needs a special talent. Cursing is evidently yours."

Luobo laughed and left. All of a sudden, I seemed to suffer a total collapse. I did not have a single ounce of strength left, and I could not even summon the strength to rise to my feet. The failed lecture came down on me like a hammer, breaking every joint in my body, which seemed to fall into pieces — never to be put back together again. At the same time, a fire was smouldering in my chest. Naturally, I directed my anger at Liben and Kang Yuanyuan. Since Liben was not present, Kang Yuanyuan had to bear the fire shooting out of my mouth.

"Kang Yuanyuan, so this is what the talk you invited me to give has come to?" I said angrily.

Failing to see what I was driving at, Kang Yuanyuan assured me that I would be paid at the full rate — not a single cent would be deducted. Even though my talk had lasted for less than forty minutes, she would pay me as per the originally agreed four hours, i.e., she would pay me four hundred *yuan*.

Kang Yuanyuan unzipped her handbag, in preparation to counting out the cash for me.

"Do you think all I care about is the money? What kind of person do you think I am?" I asked angrily. "Why did you get me here with you, to lose face? I didn't want to come, but you two both urged me, on the phone and in person, to come and deliver a lecture. Well, now I have. How did it work out? Were the villagers educated? Were they enlightened? You are from Yuebei, and if this school fails, you don't need to come back and face the music. But can I do that? This is my home village. Do I still have the face to come back again?"

Kang Yuanyuan kept her temper. She told me that when she first set about the work, she tended to become furious like me. But after having experienced so many frustrations and encountered so many rebukes and taunts, her face had turned to rubber — if you spat on it, it had no feeling; if you struck it with a rock, the rock would bounce back; even if you cut it with a knife, it would not bleed. She said she was not as discouraged as I was; on the contrary, she was as optimistic and confident as before. She claimed that my experience at the lecture strongly supported her view that it was absolutely necessary to improve the farmers' spiritual quality. Then, she repeated a saying I had become sick of hearing: "Without the modernization of farmers' intellectual consciousness, there'll be no real modernization in China!"

34

When I went back to Mazi Village, I gave my apartment key to Dalin, who thereafter lived in my home. Having decided to cut all connections with Li Tiantian, he changed his phone number, and shut himself in from morning to evening.

However, I discovered on returning home that no matter how hard I knocked on the door, no one came to open it. Not a sound could be heard from inside the house. I tried to phone Dalin, but received no answer. Someone switched the phone after it had rung twice. Something unusual must have happened. I called Li Tiantian, but she seemed not to recall who I was and who Dalin was. She said she did not know me nor Tian Dalin, and warned me not to call her again and not to interfere in her life from then on. Her queer tone added to my belief that Dalin was under her control, and having a hard time of it.

Street lamps began to go on. Without access to my home, I did not know where to turn. I sat on the steps of the church, and chain-smoked. The smoke seemed to swirl out of my mouth into my head. I felt that my brain had become clouded.

Wondering who to call, I took out my phone and randomly flipped through the address book but none of the names and numbers had anything to do with Tian Dalin or Li Tiantian. Suddenly, my eyes lit on one of the names — Ye Lihua! Among the multitudes of people in the city, she was perhaps the only one with an interest in Dalin, who was also acquainted with Li Tiantian. I dialed the number, and after the ring tone, a woman's giggling became audible at the other end of the line. I said I was looking for Ye Lihua. The woman continued giggling, asking why I was looking for her. I said it was not me who was looking for her; it was Tian Dalin. Hearing the name of Tian Dalin, she wailed bitterly, saying that he was dead. "What a pity! What a pity! What a pity!" she went on saying so, over and over again.

I shuddered as a ghostly chill ran down my body. I interrupted her exclamations of "What a pity!" and asked how she came to know that Tian Dalin was dead. After a loud belch, she told me it was Li Tiantian who had informed her of Dalin's death. I asked when Li Tiantian had told her that. She first said "last year," then "the year before last," and finally "next year." She was obviously talking rubbish, so I told her that Tian Dalin had not died, and that Li Tiantian had lied to her because she feared her as a rival. I told her that Tian Dalin was alive and well, living in Li Tiantian's restaurant. Bursting into tears, Ye Lihua asked me if it were really true. I said, "Yes. What reason do I have to lie?" I advised her to go to Li Tiantian's restaurant at once and get Dalin out. After another belch, she said she would go with her brother, who had a gun!

I sat outside the main door of the church for three hours, without receiving any news. I felt a little fidgety, worrying about where I could put up for the night. Seeing believers come out of the church, heads lowered, and disappearing into the dusk after they had finished their prayers, I suddenly had an impulse to walk into the church myself. So I stepped into the church. I sat in the back row, blankly staring at the statue of Jesus on the cross. Bound on the cross for more than a thousand years, suspended high in mid-air, with that twisted posture and agonized facial expression, what message did He want to convey to his followers?

Quite a few believers were still at prayer. Some lowered their heads, while others kneeled, their murmuring mouths emitting a noise like the buzzing of flies or mosquitoes. A few fruit and vegetable pedlars, with bamboo baskets on their back or shoulders, came crowding into the church. They put down their burdens, took out bowls or mugs, and went in twos and threes to the boiler outside the church to draw water.

The believers and the peddlers formed two completely distinct groups. They were physically near to each other, but seemed miles apart. They were each busy with their own affairs, unconscious of one another's existence. The vegetable peddlers discussed loudly the day's profit, and whenever something amusing came up, they burst into a guffaw. A woman peddler shared her story of playing hide-and-seek with urban management officers, in front of whom she had taken off her trousers, to frighten them away whenever she was cornered. A man boasted how he took advantage of customers by manipulating the scale. He took out a magnet the size of a nail and showed the others, saying that he was in the habit of placing the magnet on the back of the pan, so that one *jin* of vegetables seemed to weigh one *jin* and three *liangs*[20].

Minister Gao went past me without noticing me, probably taking me for one of the vegetable peddlers. I was pleased because I did not want to talk to him. What if he asked why I was sleeping in the church? I would find it difficult to answer. The Bible which he had given me was still lying under my pillow. I had turned a few pages, but I had yet to read it carefully. In my mind, the Bible was an unfathomable mire. I was afraid that I could not pull out once I got trapped in it. Was Jehovah, so abstract, so far away from me, able to help me solve the problem of getting articles published, of bonuses deducted for being late for work, or of losing all footing in the organization due to my failing to flatter its leaders? I was not Liben, with a copy of Bible in one hand, and a wad of dollar bills in the other — or one moment dressing up as a saint, the next moment assuming the role of a businessman comfortable in this dirty mortal world.

The lights in the church were never turned off. The dim light was like yellow varnish, tinting each face in the church with an orange color. Certain people were swaying back and forth like ghosts. Some believers remained there long into the night: they either prayed incessantly or dozed off while leaning back against the pew. All these believers occupied the front part of the nave — they were always inclined to stay near to Jehovah. The rear part of the nave was occupied as a sort of asylum by various kinds of people — tramps, beggars, peddlers, odd-jobbers, human-traffickers, burglars, robbers, and so on, among whom some were neatly dressed, some in shabby clothes, some with four limbs, and some without arms or legs. They spat and urinated at will, dropped foul-smelling litter, and were very noisy. One or two of them even imitated dogs barking and wolves howling, letting out bizarre and indescribable sounds. And the rest of them, having fallen into deep sleep, in a corner or under a chair, emitted snores long or short, thick or thin.

I was lying on a bench awake, pretending to be asleep. I abandoned myself to wild fancies, imagining that I was a fish struggling in a muddy swamp, hoping that God might see me and save me. Where was this God? Why couldn't I see him? In my imagination, heaven was like an imperial court, with God sitting at the center, surrounded by flatterers eulogizing His grandeur, glory and justice in the most effusive and excessive terms, in the expectation that He would bless them with official posts and ranks. Because God had already been intoxicated by all these songs of praise, and by all the power and luxury, He had lost the ability to tell the true from the false. "O God, have you followed the example of human beings, or is it the other way round?"

I became suddenly aware that a hand was sliding into my pocket. Obviously, someone was trying to pull my wallet out of my pocket. This person must have been new to the profession, as I guessed, with neither skill nor finesse. Because the pocket was too small, the wallet, which was somewhat large, got stuck; but the hand continued its attempt by application of brute force instead of subtlety. Although I had realized that my pocket was being picked, I pretended I had not noticed. I kept my eyes closed on purpose, afraid that if I opened them, it would hinder his business. However, to my surprise, this foolish thief wanted to take a mile when I offered him an inch. He patted me on the shoulder, muttering to me to change my position. He was so audacious that I sprang up in irritation, shouting at him, "What are you doing? What are you doing?"

Deterred by my shouts, the thief stepped back two paces and fell onto the bench. He looked at me in stupefaction, as if he could not understand why I had made such a fuss. I looked back at him, only to find that he was a mere child, fifteen years old or so, whose skinny body was dressed in old and shabby clothes, and whose eyes were so terribly large that the eyeballs seemed on the verge of popping out of their sockets. I had a good mind to scold him or give him two slaps, but his miserable appearance made me swallow my anger and stay my hand. In line with my profession of journalism, I was always tempted to investigate the underlying causes of things, such as "What brings a person to such and such an end?" But unexpectedly, on this occasion, I had lost all interest in questioning the child in front of me. In this world, there were many unfortunate people. But they all had one thing in common: different as were their appearances, experiences and stories, these people were all very miserable. Listening to their stories, looking at their tears as they poured or trickled down, I felt as if I were walking into rainy weather, with my heart suffocating in the grip of mania, like a city besieged by black clouds. After I had encountered so many such people, a subconscious need to flee began to make itself felt – "out of sight, out of mind." I was not almighty God; I could not help these people, and risked ruining my sleep and my digestion to no avail, so why should I bother? "O God, why do so many people have to suffer the hardships and pains of this world? Why do you let the world you have created become an endless sea of bitterness? Why wouldn't you endow this world with flowers alone? Medicines can cure the body, but there is none for a broken heart!"

I went back to sleep. I was ready for a good sleep. "As water extinguishes fire, sleep extinguishes smoldering thoughts," I thought to myself. But just as I was dropping off, I heard someone say "ay-ay" to me. I opened my eyes and found that the little thief was looking at me curiously, lying on the bench opposite mine. It was he who had made that sound.

"What are you doing?" I asked.

"Why don't you beat me?" he asked.

I was amazed, "Why should I beat you?"

The little thief said he had been mentally prepared to be beaten when he set out to steal, and the fact that he had not been beaten made him feel quite uneasy.

I was even more amazed, and asked if he was quite right in the head. Why did he wish to be beaten?

The little thief said he had wanted me to beat him to death. Yes, he had always wanted to be beaten to death by someone. Nevertheless, seeing that he was only a child, no one wanted to give him a good beating; and this forbearance disappointed him very much.

I was very baffled — this was a mysterious world indeed! Why were there people who wanted to be beaten? Was beating a blessing rather than a harm?

Suddenly, I became wide awake. I wanted to figure out what had happened to the little thief standing in front of me.

35

I was burning to learn what was wrong with the kid named Xiaomao. I wondered what could have happened to him, that he wished to be beaten to death like that? I asked him several times, using various tricks; however, he was unwilling to tell me.

I asked him who his father was.

Indifferently, he replied, "Dead."

I asked him who his mother was.

With equal indifference, he replied, "Dead."

I asked him if he had any relatives.

He replied as indifferently as before, "All dead."

I asked him where his hometown was.

He said, "I don't know."

I asked him how he ended up coming here.

The answer remained the same: "I don't know."

But Xiaomao seemed to be interested in criminal gangs. When I asked him who he liked most, to my surprise, he said Bin Laden.

I rebuked him, "You're only a little boy, how come you like a terrorist leader?"

As he listened to my question, his formerly absent-minded countenance gave way to a faint concentration. Instantly, his big eyes seemed filled with a spark of light. Unprompted, Xiaomao talked about his ideal life in the future: he would like to become a powerful figure in gangland; the people he admired most were those wearing black suits and sunglasses; there were many such figures in films made in Hong Kong and Taiwan, and whenever he saw them in movies he couldn't help shivering with excitement; they conducted beatings and killings, and they chopped off a human head as if they were cutting a green onion — oh, how enjoyable!

Xiaomao asked me, "Where can I find these people?"

I answered, "They are fictional characters. They do not exist in real life."

Xiaomao laughed at me, deriding me for not even knowing the existence of Yellow Shawls.

"What do you know about the world? How inexperienced you are!" he scoffed at me.

He said such people did exist in real life, even around him. He also said if

I was interested in knowing them or joining them, he would introduce them to me; his only condition was that I give him a treat of mutton kebab next day; however, he must inform me beforehand that these people, unlike the black-suited people in movies, didn't dress up in their normal life, instead they fastened a yellow shawl around their arms only when they conducted a collective raid.

"Wherever they go on 'business,' anguished cries and screams fill the air," Xiaomao said. "They chop and kill. They are really awesome!"

"Where do these guys hide out?" I asked.

A mysterious look appeared on Xiaomao's face. Shaking his head, he said he wouldn't tell me their whereabouts until I gave him a treat of mutton kebab.

Seeing that he had shown a willingness to chat with me, I struck while the iron was hot and asked him why he wanted to die.

He said, "Life is worse than death."

I asked, "Why is life worse than death? Is it good after your death?"

He said, "To live is meaningless."

"Is it meaningful to die?" I asked.

Xiaomao said if he wanted to live, he had to steal when he was hungry. But Big Brother hated thieves most of all.

"If Big Brother knows that you steal, he kicks you with his leather shoes, he burns you with an iron, and he stabs you with a knife," Xiaomao said.

I asked him who Big Brother was.

He said that Big Brother was a gangland figure. However, he steadfastly refused to tell me his name. "I won't tell you. I won't tell you on any account," Xiaomao said.

I asked Xiaomao, "Are your parents really dead?"

He said he had no idea; he had never seen his own parents; he had never stopped looking for them. He claimed that upon finding them, the first thing he would do was ask them why they had deserted him; and after finding out, he would do the second thing, i.e., kill them.

His words shocked me profoundly. Even though his parents were to blame for abandoning him, when I heard him say he would kill them, a chill wind seemed to rise in my chest.

I asked Xiaomao, "How did you grow up? Who adopted you after your parents deserted you?"

He scolded me for being nosy. However, tricked by my roundabout questions, he related his short life story as follows:

Having been abandoned at a rubbish dump shortly after birth, he had been adopted by Grandpa Mao, who made a living by ragpicking. Grandpa Mao had never got married and was childless. Since then the two had lived a hard life together.

Xiaomao was ill-fated. When he was nine years old, a disease claimed Grandpa Mao's life, which left Xiaomao a homeless child. In order to survive, Xiaomao tried various means, including ragpicking, stealing, riding a three-wheeled rickshaw to make meager money, robbing trains, living in a cement pipe, where he had been attacked by a wild dog and seriously wounded.

Later he was cheated into doing slave labour at an illegal brick factory. There he was left almost disabled after being beaten up. Some time later, he met the so-called Big Brother by chance. It happened that in the course of an economic dispute between Big Brother and the brick factory boss, Big Brother led a group of his minions to attack the kiln. It was during this turmoil that Xiaomao made his escape. But he did not run far; instead he hid himself behind a wall and watched furtively through an opening. There he witnessed with his own eyes just how powerful Big Brother was.

Big Brother, wearing sunglasses, and standing in the middle of the yard with arms akimbo, gave out his orders. His hotheaded minions, each with a yellow shawl around an arm, carried out the orders. Some chopped with knives, some hit with clubs, some kicked with their feet, some beat with their fists. In a short while, the kiln foremen, who had been swaggering around half an hour before, lay here and there in total confusion. The sight really thrilled Xiaomao, who henceforth regarded Big Brother as a hero.

Rushing out, Xiaomao entreated Big Brother to accept him as one of his followers. Big Brother had Xiaomao kowtow three times. Then Xiaomao bit one of his fingers till it bled, and swore an oath that the blood was a sign of loyalty to Big Brother. Then Big Brother received Xiaomao.

Xiaomao's wish was to do active service — in the form of vigorous fighting and bloody killing — in the front line. However, Big Brother arranged for him to work in the supply lines as a trafficker. Big Brother was very kind to him, providing him with good food and drink, and buying clothes for him.

Big Brother's "stuff" was mysterious. Big Brother always told Xiaomao to conceal the stuff inside his clothes. Xiaomao did not know the stuff was heroin until he got caught by the police. Of course he had looked stealthily at the stuff tucked into his belt; it was white and in a small bag. It looked like salt or sugar or soda powder. Since he had never opened the bag, he had no idea what it tasted like. Xiaomao claimed that if he had known it was drugs, he would have secretly opened and tasted it, for sure.

"Wasn't it a great pity? To live without ever savouring the taste of drugs!" Xiaomao sighed.

What Xiaomao couldn't forgive himself for, was that he had betrayed Big Brother. He told me that the public security people were dreadfully frightening. They banged the table; they twisted his ears; they beat him and kicked him. He would rather have died than surrender, and he might have succeeded in his wish. However, when they alternated harsh treatment with soft soap, Xiaomao revealed all to them. He had betrayed Big Brother. He was unworthy of Big Brother. Would Big Brother suffer him to be at large with impunity? Big Brother's men were as numerous as stars in the sky. They must be chasing him. He had been hiding out wherever he possibly could. He had been fearful, hungry, and thirsty. This was why he wished to die as soon as possible. He craved death to the utmost. He feared death to the utmost too. He couldn't imagine what it was like where the dead dwelt. Was it very dark? Were there uncountable hideous monsters and wandering ghosts?

I told Xiaomao that his exposure of Big Brother was not treacherous, but a just deed. I told him how much harm drug abuse did to society. But Xiaomao did not listen to me at all. On the contrary, he scolded me for not understanding what the code of brotherhood meant. He said he felt truly guilty, and the sense of guilt made him want to depart this world. He said his death would serve two purposes: on the one hand he would free himself of guilt; on the other hand he would gratify Big Brother with this token of penance. However, before he died, he would visit Grandpa Mao's tomb for the last time; he would burn joss paper for Grandpa Mao; he would buy a bottle of wine and bury it in the soil of Grandpa Mao's grave. He claimed he had never cried in his fifteen years of life except when Grandpa Mao died.

"A man, who really was a man, cried. Would people laugh at me for that?" Xiaomao asked me.

I had been feeling sleepy, and while Xiaomao was still telling his story, I fell asleep.

When I opened my eyes again, I saw a beam of sunlight penetrating the church's black curtain and shining on Xiaomao. It appeared as though a golden ribbon were extending from his body. Everyone else was gone. Only Xiaomao remained, sound asleep, saliva dribbling from the corner of his mouth.

I got a phone call from Dalin; I could leave the church immediately to go home. However, I did not leave, because, overnight, Xiaomao had become an object of concern to me. I could not bring myself to leave him unattended until I was sure he had somewhere to go. I set out to find Minister Gao; I believed he might grant my plea to keep the homeless lad in the church. I would be willing to set aside a portion of my salary to cover Xiaomao's accommodation in the church.

36

Dalin was taken into custody by Li Tiantian, as expected. The night when, summoned by Kang Yuanyuan, I went to Mazi Village, several stout men from Li Tiantian's restaurant came and knocked at my apartment door. Their minivan was parked by the neighborhood gate; Li Tiantian was inside, telephoning orders to the men. At first, Dalin did not want to open the door, but he had to when they threatened to open it by force. He knew who most of them were; the man in charge was Mr. Hu, the kitchen chef. Mr. Hu was a fat man; his belly bulged like Mount Taishan, and his face was like a big red tomato. When Dalin offered him a cigarette, Mr. Hu refused it; when Dalin offered to make tea for him, Mr. Hu turned that down, too. When Dalin invited him and his men to sit, Mr. Hu refused and so did his men. Chuckling "hey-hey-hey," Mr. Hu said he had to abide by the orders of whoever was employing him. Then, he signaled his men to take action at once.

Seeing that among Mr. Hu's men, there were some carrying iron hammers, some nylon rope, and some adhesive tape, Dalin understood they had intended to knock him out, tie him up and carry him away. He knew that he was in the process of being kidnapped, and that that night might be his last. He implored Mr. Hu to hold off, begged him to remember that it was he, Dalin, who had introduced him to the restaurant. Mr. Hu repeated that he had to abide by the orders of whoever was employing him. And that was Li Tiantian, not Tian Dalin; so between the two he had to stand by Li Tiantian.

Dalin agreed to go with them, but he expressed his hope that they would not tie him up. Mr. Hu said Li Tiantian was worse than an empress. An empress had at least to sit behind a screen when she listened to state affairs, but Li Tiantian had no need for such discretion. Li Tiantian believed that she was always correct, and that whatever she commanded in the restaurant it would have an authority equal to that of Chairman Mao. If her will were thwarted, there would be severe consequences! During the staff meetings she convened after Dalin left, she showered them with insults; she even garnished their wages. On one particularly bad occasion, she had reduced the wages of a waitress to nothing. Mr. Hu said he would have to tie Dalin up, but he could loosen the rope a little bit, in consideration of their friendship. It ought to look real, even though it was just a show.

So it was as a bound captive that Dalin went with them. No sooner did he get into the minivan than Li Tiantian began slapping him in the face. "Bah! Bah!" She swore at Dalin vehemently, and repeatedly demanded that he cough up whatever he had eaten of hers, return whatever he had taken of hers, and pay compensation for whatever he had damaged of hers! "Run away? Humph! Turn tail and run away like a hare! No way! A hare has four paws, but how many do you have, Tian Dalin? Can you run to the end of the earth?"

Dalin endured Li Tiantian's beating and cursing in silence. The minivan drove to the restaurant, where Dalin was pushed into Li Tiantian's office. Li Tiantian signaled the men to untie him and to tear the adhesive tape from his mouth. After they retreated, Li Tiantian slammed the office door shut, and shouted, "Tian Dalin, you just sit there and reflect. Has your heart been eaten by dogs? Hide from me indeed! Where on earth can you hide from me? Do you think things will be settled between you and me if you see me no more?"

"As we are not a good match, it's better that we part company. Work out how much I owe you. I am no swindler. I'll pay you back!" Dalin murmured.

"Pay me back? How? How can you pay me back? A pauper, a beggar, you wouldn't have enough money to pay me back even if you sold yourself into slavery," Li Tiantian screamed.

Li Tiantian took from a drawer a list itemizing what Dalin was supposed to owe her —

Loans: one hundred and sixty thousand;

Daily expenses including meals and clothing: eighty thousand;

Burial of a wild chicken: fifty thousand;

Wasted youth: three hundred thousand;

Total: four hundred and ninety thousand RMB.

After a glance at it, Dalin gave two snorts of derision. "Burial of a wild chicken!" Was that not being deliberately insulting? Taoqi was dead after all, and Li Tiantian's insults in her regard were more than he could bear.

"If Taoqi is a wild chicken, what are you?"

Li Tiantian grimaced, and said that she had wanted to write down her name, but it made her sick. "Is her being called a wild chicken so insulting? As a matter of fact, it is the chicken who has the right to feel insulted, not her."

Dalin knew it was useless to go on arguing with Li Tianian, so he switched topics. He asked, "What is meant by 'wasted youth?' Who on earth suffers from it? Who on earth should pay for it?"

Li Tiantian became once more as furious as a lioness, alternatively weeping and yelling. "It was my youth which was wasted, of course! Who else's? Could it be yours, Tian Dalin, you peasant?" She said that because she was born in the city, she was naturally superior to him, and that if she had not been mutilated, she would have been more fragrant than a carnation, more charming than a magnolia, more graceful than a primrose. Her beauty had originally been such that it might have caused a kingdom to fall. Many a man had not been able to take another step until he had looked back at her three times! Many a man had emitted sparks of lust at the sight of her! What a pity that such a beautiful flower had been placed in a cow pat that, hard and evil smelling, had mercilessly ruined her dainty face. If her face had not been ruined by that bastard, Tian Dalin would never have been able to enjoy her — he would never have had a chance! It was already lowering enough that she, a successful boss, a woman with a sensuous body, in spite of an ugly face, should have mixed with a farmer-turned-worker! A lady-like woman who used to eat Japanese cuisine and Korean barbecue every day, now had to hold a broken bowl filled with corn porridge. What was that if not a humiliation?

Dalin said, "I only wanted to work in your restaurant. Did I force you to have that affair with me? Aren't I the victim? Didn't you drive me crazy? Aren't you ashamed of talking about your wasted youth? How ridiculous!"

Li Tiantian took the calendar from the desk and dashed it at Dalin's head, cursing him all the while. Dalin stood up to leave, but Li Tiantian seized him by the collar and shouted, "Help! Dalin is trying to rape me." A group of men, led by Mr. Hu, rushed in and immediately pinned Dalin to the ground.

Dalin was locked up in a dark room, emptied for this purpose. He was kept in captivity. The door had two locks; outside men were stationed to keep watch. A jug had been left in the room so that he might relieve himself. Meals were sent in regularly, but he suspected that there was a soporific in them because he felt sleepy all day long. It was very difficult to stay awake!

Thanks to the fact that Ye Lihua made trouble at Li Tiantian's restaurant several times within a day, Dalin was finally set free. "Release Dalin! Release Dalin!" she demanded. Li Tiantian flatly denied that Dalin was in the restaurant. She exhausted her eloquence, but Ye Lihua hardly listened. Li Tiantian was quite unprepared for Ye Lihua's involvement. Who did Ye Lihua think she was? What gave her the right to stick her oar into Li Tiantian's and Tian Dalin's business? Although Li Tiantian was very angry, she could not afford to provoke Ye Lihua's brother Ye Zhonghua! His support was necessary to the continued smooth running of her restaurant. A well-known saying was that "Behind every successful man stands a great woman." Likewise, it could be said that behind every prosperous private enterprise stood a few powerful officials. A leopard's courage would not be enough for Li Tiantian, if she wanted to brave Ye Zhonghua. But her readiness to compromise achieved nothing. Instead, Ye Lihua became even more aggressive. From Ye Lihua's nostrils two streams of sticky, yellow liquid flowed constantly, which she habitually wiped away with her hand and rubbed off on whatever was close by. On this occasion, she pinched off some of her snot and rubbed it off on the cloth covering the service desk. The cloth was, in fact, for decoration. Li Tiantian told her not to, on the ground that it was hideous to behold and killed the appetite. As there were napkins everywhere in the restaurant, why should she rub her snot on this beautiful cloth? Far from dissuading her, Li Tiantian's words reminded her how much she cared about whether the cloth was clean or dirty. Very well, Li Tiantian cared about the cloth, but she, Ye Lihua, did not. She wished to spoil whatever Li Tiantian cared about!

Ye Lihua kept pinching off her snot and rubbing it onto the desk cloth, her hand shuttling back and forth like a fan, fast as lightning. Pinched, rubbed, pinched, rubbed, incessantly. As Li Tiantian squinted at her, she could feel waves of nausea disturb her stomach. Finally, unable to bear it any longer, Li Tiantian gave Ye Lihua a warning tug. Ye Lihua was confounded for a few seconds, then repaid the tug with a punch to Li Tiantian's chest. A brief physical altercation took place. Ye Lihua was crying, and so was Li Tiantian. Customers in the restaurant ran over to see the two weeping.

Ye Lihua called her brother, and told him that she had been hit so hard that her arm had turned the color of sugarcane. Ye Zhonghua asked who had struck her. Ye Lihua answered, "Only that tigress Li Tiantian!" Ye Zhonghua said that he would come at once. From the phone, his angry voice could be heard, asking, "What's wrong with Li Tiantian? Has she lost the plot? How dare she bully me, Ye Zhonghua?"

Ye Lihua was bending over the bar as she made the phone call. The gesture she made was very peculiar, like a ballerina's. At every sentence, she pirouetted. While Ye Lihua was complaining tearfully to her brother, Li Tiantian started preparations in anticipation for Ye Zhonghua's arrival. She signaled to the lobby manager to come over, and whispered a few words to him, whose facial expression showed his immediate comprehension.

The lobby manager took the key secretly given him by Li Tiantian and opened the door of the room in which Dalin was locked up. The manager led Dalin to the back door of the restaurant and let him slip away. Assuming an air of importance, he said to Dalin that although it seemed it was Ye Lihua's trouble-making that had forced Li Tiantian to set him free, as a matter of fact, it was the result of his own diligent persuasion. He had worn his lips thin to persuade Li Tiantian, and their cracked skin was a solid proof of this. At the same time, he made a point of intimidating Dalin, saying that Li Tiantian had wanted to call in the public security forces to get rid of him, and that her hatred of him was as hard to put out as a forest fire. Li Tiantian had alleged to the police that Dalin was a great swindler who had defrauded her of sex as well as money. So the police would come to arrest him in a few minutes; they were on the way to the restaurant.

37

The farmer enlightenment school founded by Liben and Kang Yuanyuan turned out to be a flash in the pan. It was closed shortly afterward. It was not that they wanted to close the school; they were forced to leave.

One day, Kang Yuanyuan invited an expert from the social sciences academy to deliver a lecture. Liu Qi sat next to the expert as a companion. The expert had hardly spoken a few sentences when Liu Qi forcefully grabbed the microphone, insisting in the presence of the whole audience that the expert was too soft, that his speaking style was too tender, that treating farmers in such a polite way would spoil them and give them delusions of grandeur.

As though to demonstrate how to do it properly, Liu Qi started to make a speech. Torrents of rough language and dirty words poured out of his mouth incessantly. There was no sign of Liu Qi' speech ever coming to an end.

Liu Qi's behavior truly annoyed Kang Yuanyuan, who burned with so much fury that her face convulsed and her whole body quivered. When she felt she could not stand it any longer, she interrupted Liu Qi, snatched the microphone from his hand and handed it back to the expert. Struck dumb by what Kang Yuanyuan had just done, Liu Qi looked utterly shocked. However, he did not lose his temper. Rather, he walked out with livid face.

That evening, a long train of cars entered the village. A huge crowd of people got out. They went straight to Beiqiang's house and knocked at the door. They asked Beiqiang where Liben was.

"May I ask who you are, please?" Beiqiang asked them.

The bald man at the head of the crowd told Beiqiang that he was Hao, a department director of the county education bureau. Director Hao declared he had received a report alleging the activity of an illegal school in this village, and that was why he was leading his men here to investigate. He claimed that the guilty people were alleged to dwell in Beqiang's place, and said he hoped Beiqiang would cooperate and hand over the outlaws.

Beiqiang argued with Director Hao, claiming that there was no question of the school having been opened illegally; that Teacher Kang had come to Mazi Village with a letter of introduction issued by the provincial Political Consultative Committee; that the letter carried the committee's red stamp, which he had seen with his own eyes; even though he was not a great reader, all the words in the letter were within his comprehension; it was not good to make groundless charges.

Director Hao told Beiqiang not to waste his breath, but to hand the people involved over to them.

"Do you think I, a well-informed department director at the county education bureau, do not understand the policy as well as you, a farmer, do?" Director Hao asked.

So Beiqiang and Lifang went off in different directions to look for Liben and Kang Yuanyuan. Liben was found in Baolai's house. He had contacted a mental hospital in Yuebei on behalf of Baolai. They had been preparing to take Qiuli to the hospital for medical therapy one of these days. With this in mind, he had given Baolai twenty thousand *yuan*. Actually, he had made over the money with a minimum of publicity, since he did not want anyone to know about it. Unfortunately, Baolai had a big mouth that leaked wind. Whenever he ran into someone, he would praise Liben's kind generosity.

Baolai's extensive praise of Liben had created some problems. Before long, a storm of rumors had blown up over the village — rumors to the effect that it was not for Baolai's sake but for his own that Liben wanted to help Qiuli receive medical treatment, because as a young boy Liben had desired Qiuli, but had not fulfilled that desire — how could a toad win over a swan? — therefore, Liben now intended to take advantage of Qiuli's insanity to fulfill his long cherished evil wish. According to one vivid account, a certain woman, being well hidden behind the piled-up maize straw belonging to the Luobo family, had once seen Liben touch Qiuli's lower private parts.

Liben had been exasperated by this rumor, swearing he would find out who the rumormonger was. But Third Aunt advised him against this course of action. Third Aunt said she was pretty sure the rumor originated in Shuanhu's house. If the rumor could be compared to a whirlwind, its source was the tongue of Shuanhu's wife. The first person that heard the remark was Luobo. Because Luobo's mouth was without bar or latch, but rather had lips like winnowing fans, casting and throwing arbitrarily, so that the rumor circulated around the whole village. So what? Some villagers believed, while others did not. Those who disbelieved, disbelieved on account of this calculation: if Liben wanted to have fun with a woman, couldn't he have found a blue-eyed, blond-haired foreign woman to play with? With so much money at his disposal, why suppose that a foreign woman's heart wouldn't be moved? Did he need to have an affair with a crazy woman with lice all over her body?

Kang Yuanyuan was found chatting with Xiaolin in the watchman's room of the bathhouse. The only person in the village Kang Yuanyuan regarded with favor was Xiaolin. She enjoyed talking with him about international issues, such as the Palestine problem, the Middle Eastern geopolitical issues, and the prospects of black people. While Xiaolin admired Mao Zedong most, Kang Yuanyuan thought Martin Luther King was the best of all. Xiaolin claimed he admired those who brought changes to the world. But Kang Yuanyuan said change wasn't necessarily a good thing, likewise remaining unchanged wasn't necessarily a bad thing; what mattered was whether the leader led society forwards or backwards. According to Kang Yuanyuan, the awakening of the soul and the germinating of people's intellect were prerequisites of change; it was true Mandela had brought changes to South Africa, but he neglected to train the black people to be modern citizens; as a result, once black people rose to power, corruption thrived, nepotism became prevalent, to the point where South Africa had become a safe haven for all the criminality in the world.

Kang Yuanyuan returned to Beiqiang's house earlier than Liben. As soon as she saw Director Hao, she began arguing fiercely with him.

She asked Director Hao what law she had violated.

Director Hao replied, "You opened a school illegally."

Widening both her eyes till they were as big as light bulbs, Kang Yuanyuan said, "Director Hao, you mustn't make groundless charges against us. We opened the school illegally? What do you mean? We have, in our hand, a letter of introduction issued by the provincial Political Consultative Committee, and we have the support of the provincial authorities. How can you say we opened the school illegally?"

Taking a document out of his handbag, Director Hao unfolded it and pointed out a couple of lines to Kang Yuanyuan, who did catch sight of some sentences to the effect that before opening any type of school in the countryside, the operator must get a permit from the county level authorities in charge of educational affairs.

"This means," Director Hao said, "an approval from Kaiyang County Education Bureau is a necessity for opening and running the school in Mazi Village. Without an approval from Kaiyang County Education Bureau, the so-called enlightenment school in Mazi Village is an illegal school. Therefore, it must be closed down."

Kang Yuanyuan did not give in easily, even though she had viewed the document. She kept on arguing with Director Hao. She said that before she set up the school, she had consulted Township Head Liu Qi, who told her that Director Hao, in charge of such work in the county education bureau, was his sworn brother; and that, as long as he informed Director Hao of the matter, no obstacle would arise at all.

"Hasn't Liu Qi informed you of the matter, Director Hao?" Kang Yuanyuan asked.

Director Hao laughed and said, "It was just because Liu Qi informed us, that we were able to learn that there was an illegal school here. That's why we have come to investigate. As sworn brothers, Liu Qi and I have intense mutual friendship, but mutual friendship cannot outweigh the law!"

While they were arguing, Liben entered the gate and heard what they were saying. Liben, tired of running such a meaningless school — it pained not only the operators but also the lecture attendants — said to Kang Yuanyuan, "Stop arguing please! Now that they forbid it, let's close it. What does it matter?"

Kang Yuanyuan was pretty unhappy with Liben's attitude. She almost burst into tears. In a sobbing voice, Kang Yuanyuan said, "Is this some trifling game that one can begin and end arbitrarily? It took us a lot of efforts to start the school. Now the villagers' hearts are united. If we give up, what will we have to say for ourselves?"

Rubbing her eyes, and then her nose, Kang Yuanyuan suddenly raised her voice to reiterate her point that the school would not be closed. She exclaimed she would go and see the county secretary of the Party committee the following day, and if push came to shove, she'd request one of her fellow classmates, who worked in the provincial government's office, to make a phone call to the county secretary of the Party committee.

Director Hao flared up. Black veins bulged in his forehead. Stamping his feet, Director Hao said to Kang Yuanyuan, "You speak of the county secretary of the Party committee and the provincial government's office again and again. Do you mean to wield their power to frighten me? Do you think I have grown strong by sucking up intimidations?"

The officials who had come along with Director Hao started booing and hooting. They said Kang Yuanyuan must have eaten too much glue; which was why she was so befuddled. They rhetorically asked Kang Yuanyuan if

Director Hao could have been promoted to the director's position without the backing of a protector — so shortly after working in the county education bureau, and in the wake of his military service? Without a *big* tree to protect him with its shade, could this have been possible? In order to emphasize Director Hao's heft, one of the men explicitly said Director Hao was connected to a leader in Yuebei municipal government: Director Hao's beautiful sister was married to his beloved nephew.

Director Hao seemed to have lost patience with the confrontation. After answering a sexy-voiced cell-phone call from a female, he gazed absentmindedly. He instructed one of his subordinates to hand over a penalty notice to Kang Yuanyuan, and then swaggered off with all his men.

Following their disappearing figures with her eyes, without even a glance at the penalty notice, Kang Yuanyuan tore it into pieces and threw the bits on the ground. Liben picked up the bits and pieced them together to see what was written there, only to find that the notice was like a heavy hammer coming down on his head. The blow nearly made him faint. The notice not only identified the school as an unlawful assembly, it also declared a penalty of five hundred thousand *yuan*. It decreed that within ten days of receipt of the penalty notice, the sum must be submitted to the finance department of the county education bureau. Otherwise, the education bureau would invoke the law court to enforce the execution of the ruling and to take compulsory measures against the offenders.

Liben spent a sleepless night. So did Kang Yuanyuan. While Kang Yuanyuan turned from side to side in her bed in vexation, Liben was contemplating what to do next. In view of his New Village Project, Liben had no wish to become deadlocked with the local government officials. Kang Yuanyuan, on the other hand, deemed that these people's blatant declaration of her guilt in running an illegal school was a wicked way to set her up. She vowed never to forgive such evil conduct. "I won't let them get away with it," she swore. "No way will I ever forgive them." She wanted to appeal to the media; she even wanted the media to make it known to the whole world so that she would get justice.

On the following day, in accordance with Liben's advice, Kang Yuanyuan went to the township government in Liben's company: they wanted to ask Liu Qi to intercede with his sworn brother Director Hao, so that the county education bureau would revoke the verdict; or at least get the penalty cancelled. Given that the school was not a commercial enterprise, but purely a public service project; given that the necessary funds had been raised only with great efforts, why was a monetary penalty imposed on them? Where would they get the money to pay it? But they did not find Liu Qi at the township government. The only person around the place with any authority was Zhao Xiaohui. Hearing what their intention was, he shook his head and advised them against trying to realize it, given that it was Liu Qi himself who was behind this drama.

It turned out that Liu Qi had been infuriated by Kang Yuanyuan's grabbing the microphone from his hand. After returning to his township government office, Liu Qi immediately convened the leadership team to discuss how to drive away Kang Yuanyuan and abolish the school. During the meeting, in front of everyone, Liu Qi made a phone call to Director Hao, asking him to get onto the case at once, and to impose the heaviest possible fine. Hanging up the phone, Liu Qi furiously grumbled that Liben and Kang Yuanyuan had been going about their funny business on his territory, however they had never treated him to a meal at a restaurant, let alone greased his palm; that in view of the media attention on Liben's project, he had forced himself to swallow his anger; but who could imagine this cheap woman could have gone so far as to snatch the microphone from his hand? If he hadn't taken her sex into consideration, if the ancient precept "good men do not fight with women" hadn't prevailed on his mind, he would have yielded to his impulse and spanked her. From the start of the meeting to the very end, Liu Qi never stopped cursing Kang Yuanyuan.

As a matter of fact, Kang Yuanyuan had so infuriated Liu Qi, that many other people had become targets of Liu Qi's invective. Inevitably Zhao Xiaohui had received the strongest abuse: he had been called a dog, a pig, a pile of useless trash.

Zhao Xiaohui exclaimed he couldn't bear it any longer; he wanted to run away. The main reason for this was because Liu Qi had imposed his own deformed, ugly-looking sister on him. Whenever he saw Liu Qi's sister, he was seized with nausea. Although he had tried to force himself to accept her, his biological instincts were not to be overcome, even with the assistance of reason. He just could not bring himself to accept that ugly woman! His life was hell! This was a true dilemma. He was in agonizing pain, agonizing pain! Liben said to Zhao Xiaohui, "You have a say in your own marriage. Why listen to Liu Qi? There are various national laws to protect your rights. What can Liu Qi do to you?"

Kang Yuanyuan, too, encouraged Zhao Xiaohui, "Be braver! Don't be timid."

Zhao Xiaohui asked Liben and Kang Yuanyuan to look for job opportunities for him. He fancied that someday he would be like the rolling Yellow River that rushes to the East China Sea without ever turning back.

38

Liben returned to Yuebei, but he did not come to see me. He shuttled between the design department and the planning department. He said the planning department's blueprint needed to be altered. Though he didn't come to see me, he called me; he spoke to me on the phone, sighing in regret over the difficulty of getting anything done in China, and over the greediness everyone had shown so far. He had had to kowtow to everyone and to burn incense at their feet as though they were the Buddha. He couldn't help thinking of Li Bai's poem — "The path to Shu[21] is difficult, more difficult than going up to the azure sky." I suggested that Liben change his point of view and his state of mind, so that he could see things from a Chinese perspective, and deal with them according to the Chinese mentality. If he did so, he would find that things which had looked unusual would now seem as normal as the sun rising in the east. One disabled person among a million healthy people catches your eye, but if you live among a million disabled people long enough, you no longer notice their physical defects, and find them so normal that it is the healthy who seem strange.

Apparently, Kang Yuanyuan had suffered an even more severe blow. Liben had wanted Kang Yuanyuan to train laborers into qualified workers, but she, in contrast to him, had a nobler aim in mind; her ideal was to enlighten and impart wisdom to the farmers.

Once back from Mazi Village, Kang Yuanyuan, anxious that the Kaiyang education bureau might locate her and fine her, changed her telephone number. She shut herself up for five days to write "On the Gain and Loss of the Enlightenment School." After the article was printed, she called me to sort out two matters. First, as I was more familiar with Mazi Village than she was, she asked me to judge whether her description matched the true thing. Second, she wanted my help in getting such an in-depth article as she had had in mind published by the newspaper I worked for. During the phone call, I agreed only to her first requirement — to check whether her pen-portrait of Mazi Village matched the one of my experiences. Anyway, it seemed like a good thing that someone should write about the village in which I was born and brought up.

I met Kang Yuanyuan at the Alibaba teahouse. She said she would have preferred to meet me at an academy, whose atmosphere was intoxating.

Indeed, she had attempted to find academies in Yuebei. However, she had discovered that the ancient Yuebei Academy had retained nothing of its former self, except for the name. Now it was a wholesale marketplace for clothing. Inside, the most striking thing was a fat sheep barbecue restaurant, whose strong smell of mutton was enough to knock out a passer-by.

So, if academies were out of the question, then places like tea-bars had to be considered. At least, a tea-bar or a teahouse would be more romantic than the noisy streets. Kang Yuanyuan said she had been seeking a romantic and a poetic lifestyle to adopt. A person with romantic and poetic tastes was like a mountain with misty clouds above, babbling brooks below, and birds twittering all about, but she seemed to have failed to find anyting of the kind. Art galleries had turned into market places for the selling of paintings and calligraphy, song-and-dance halls had turned into theatres of erotica, and concert halls had turned into places for naked bodies to wriggle instead of for music to play. As for men of letters, some of them, with black or brown briefcases under their arms, rushed to and fro to write marketing plans for entrepreneurs, while others, in order to promote themselves, treated powerful guests to feasts…who wanted to sit quietly at a scholar's desk to do studies? Kang Yuanyuan could not help agonizing over this state of affairs. All those who returned from their overseas studies were liable to this feeling of agony. It was all very well for them to agonize, but reality was still reality, no matter how they felt.

At the Alibaba teahouse, we chose the private room in which she and I had first made acquaintance. To our surprise, the waiter was still that handsome young man Larz. Hadn't he been acknowledged by Xue Yulu as her cousin? She had an impressive public presence, so why hadn't she promoted his status beyond that of waiter? How could she bear her public standing to be overshadowed by her cousin's remaining in such a place?

There was nothing unusual in Larz's behavior in spite of the fact that we had met before. Courteous, respectful and sanctimonious, he served us tea and fruit on a tray, never wavering in his reserve. I said, "Larz, we are already acquaintances. Just relax and take it easy." Larz smiled, and showed a mouthful of neat white teeth. I asked what he thought of my village. He smiled and nodded, saying it was a nice place. I told him that in a few years, when he could go there once again, he would find it completely different, with dazzling lights and scenes of conviviality, almost the same as a city. He said he knew that, and he had seen the blueprint of the village. I said my village head wanted to be his father-in-law, and asked him if he was agreeable to that, and ready to love sincerely Jidan, my village head's daughter. He flushed, saying, "It was nothing but a joke on the part of your village head. How could your village head's daughter fancy me? What am I that she would fall in love with me?" I said, "It looked to me that my village head was not joking. He looked like he meant it." Pouting, Larz said, "He knows very little about me. If he knew me, I think he would be scared away."

While Larz was showing Kang Yuanyuan to the washroom, I bent over the tea table to read her article. To be frank, I was shocked by her naivety. I felt Kang Yuanyuan, who had claimed to be saving the ignorant, was more ignorant than those she meant to save. Kang Yuanyuan's ignorance took the form of attributing the farmers' ignorance to their own lack of qualifications. Was this not like emphasizing only the yellow leaves of a tree without checking its rotten roots? It was true that the farmers were ignorant, but were they themselves the cause of that ignorance? If they were undereducated, why were they undereducated? If they thought study useless, why did they think so? If weeds grew in the fields, could you simply blame the weeds?

Of course, the analysis that Kang had done of the status quo in Mazi Village was not wrong in all respects. She divided the villagers into five types. The first was "tiger/wolf" — bad-tempered, domineering, stubborn, and terrifying to most people, such as the Shuanhu brothers. The second was "mouse" — timid, well-behaved on the surface but digging holes in walls when it got dark, such as Beiqiang and Song Tongguo. The third was "bee" — sweet-looking, but ready to sting at any moment, such as Fugui. The fourth was "sheep" — meekly submitting to adversities, and suffering losses in silence, such as Baolai. The fifth was "calf" — pure and persistent in character, and with momentum enough to break old fetters and to achieve something, such as Xiaolin. Kang Yuanyuan held a negative view of the first four types, more or less, but she spoke highly of the fifth type represented by Xiaolin, saying that this type of people was like a brilliant beam on a morning cloud, and that they would eventually transform the rural areas in China.

I laughed as hard at the portraits Kang Yuanyuan had drawn of the Mazi villagers as if someone was tickling me under the armpits. Was Song Tongguo as timid as a mouse? I would not think so. To my mind, he was just the opposite, with the guts of a leopard! Was Fugui, who acted like a god or a ghost, a bee that looked beautiful? Additionally, in Kang Yuanyuan's article, no female was mentioned. I was keen to see into which type she would classify Third Aunt and Luobo, but I could not find any trace of them. Kang Yuanyuan must have been daydreaming. How could such an article get published? For one thing, Tian Xiaolin had long since been blacklisted as a bad example by Xue Yulu and some other people. For another thing, would Shuanhu and his like take it lying down, if criticized and defamed in newspapers?

It was quite a wait before Kang Yuanyuan came back. When she did, she appeared as excited, and as red-faced, as Bruno must have been when he discovered one more celestial law. I had wanted to talk about her article. I didn't expect that she would be so eager to talk about Larz, or that, once she started talking about him, she wouldn't be able to stop. She said that, when she was outside just now, she had had a chat with Larz and found him to be a good lad. "Really, I am not kidding. He really is a good lad." She said Larz told her that his father died of disease when he was six years old, and he had been brought up by his mother; that he had hoped to repay his mother at some point in the future, when he would be in a position to do so, but it had never occurred to him that his mother would have fallen ill the year when he had just begun his junior high school; that his mother had been seriously ill with nephropathy, which by now had deteriorated into renal failure, so he had decided to quit his studies, look for work and earn money to help with his mother's treatment. She said, "It is admirable that he is only willing to work hard for money, and his body is not for sale. Various people — females, males, bosses, officials, gays, divorced middle-aged ladies, or young women who are looking for an affair —have hinted they would keep him in luxury, but he invariably turns them down."

I said, "Miss Kang, should you take the word of some guy working in a tea-bar as gospel? They are all excellent actors, and an actor is only one step away from being a swindler. If he is pure enough, what about that matter between him and Xue Yulu? Is that just a rumor? We saw with our own eyes how intimately Xue Yulu was holding his hand."

Kang Yuanyuan said she had asked Larz that very question. Larz told her that, on the recommendation of a mutual acquaintance he had gone to see Xue Yulu in the hope that she would write about his family problems, and thus raise donations for his mother. Xue Yulu seemed to have had her own preoccupations, though, which had led her to invite him to parks, dinners, theatres, and a village named Mazi in Kaiyang. He had not totally accepted these invitations because he had to work in the teahouse and go back home to look after his mother in his spare time. Xue Yulu's discontent with him grew day by day, and they finally broke up after he refused her demand of *that* kind. On the night before the article concerning his mother was to go to press, Xue Yulu booked a room in a five-star hotel and invited him for a drink. He went, but Xue Yulu asked him to sleep with her straight away, and without a word about drinking. He refused, declaring that he was not a gigolo and then left the hotel. The next day, Xue Yulu angrily tracked him down at the teahouse, her face as long as a sponge gourd, and demanded that he return the expensive platinum bracelet that she had bought for him. However, the bracelet had already been sold to cover hospital expenses. Larz had no choice but to write an IOU, which said he had borrowed from Xue Yulu three thousand *yuan* RMB for his mother's treatment. As a matter of course, Xue Yulu cancelled the article appealing for donations with a phone call.

As she talked, Kang Yuanyuan became very agitated. She said how much she valued such a youth — who was upright and conscientious, who kept his integrity no matter how difficult the circumstances were. She had even pledged to him that she would save his mother. It seemed, to judge from the way she gesticulated with her hands and feet, that Kang Yuanyuan had found a new mission at last. She said she wanted to establish a non-governmental relief organization, but did not know where to get a license.

39

Since her visit to Mazi Village, Xue Yulu's attitude towards me appeared to have become a little bit friendlier. In spite of this, she ridiculed the backwardness of my hometown. She made particular mention of the unsanitary condition of the outhouses. She said that, as a person who felt unbearably itchy if she did not take a shower each day, there was no way she could get used to the outhouses.

She said that once during her stay in Mazi Village, she badly needed to answer the call of nature; she visited more than twenty adobe-wall surrounded outhouses, but none of them was fit for purpose. Among the outhouses she had visited, some had walls which were too low, so that any passersby could see her private parts; some were unbearably dirty with piles of fly-infested dung; some emitted a pungent bad smell strong enough to knock someone over. All in all, no outhouse was even close to being acceptable to her. As a last resort, she had had to go to the bathhouse to relieve herself.

Xue Yulu gave an exaggerated account of the flaws of Mazi Village. Seasoned with her fiction-making talent, this account of her adventures was vividly dramatized. In time, a whirl of interest gathered force in the press house, to the point that quite a few editors and journalists wished to visit my hometown: they mainly wanted to see what the world's most backward village was like. And naturally, they wanted to see what the world's dirtiest outhouses were like.

Some busybody colleague mockingly took hold of the bottom edge of my coat and smelled it, trying to ascertain if I smelled of the outhouses of my hometown. In a spirit of irony, I told my colleagues that my hometown's outhouses had the miraculous quality of curing and preventing various diseases. "Every time I visit my village, I roll around in an outhouse in order to prevent hypertension," I said.

Of course, I was joking. However, Xiang Wenhua, who, disturbed by our laughter, and just woken from his nap, took what I said seriously. Raising his head, he looked at me blankly with his dull eyes. When he heard that rolling around in an outhouse could prevent and cure diseases, his eyes instantly lit up, as if two electric bulbs had been turned on.

"Is that true?" Xiang Wenhua asked me.

"Yes. It is true," I said.

Of course, I was once again joking. But he said he would like to go with me and do some on-the-spot investigation. He explained that his maternal grandma, who was over eighty years old now, had always had health problems. Her legs ached, her head ached, and her abdomen ached in turn. Whenever she suffered from any ache, she would groan. Aiya. Aiya. Aiya. The groans seemed, like cat's paws, to scratch the family members around her. He sincerely wanted to visit his grandma, but due to her constant "aiyas," he dreaded to do so. Brought up with the help of his grandma, his love for her was deeper than the sea and higher than the mountains. Now that his grandma was in agony, how could he regard her sufferings with indifference!

Taking a dictionary from the table next to his, Xiang Wenhua consulted how people could make use of dung. In a low voice, he whispered to himself, "If left for a sufficiently long time, dung can produce methane gas. But what can methane gas be used for?"

He proceeded to research the use of methane gas, murmuring his findings: "Methane gas can burn, and be used as industrial and household fuel." But after he had busied himself for a long while, he still failed to figure out how dung could be beneficial to human health.

I said to him, "I'm afraid even scientists cannot come to a satisfying conclusion on the uses of many mysterious things. Naturally, a mere dictionary will not help you discover these secrets."

Closing the dictionary, he cupped his chin in his hands, with his eyes on the ceiling. Looking blankly for a moment, he stressed that he would definitely visit my home village.

"No problem," I said. "Any time is okay with me. But I cannot guarantee all I've said is true."

Glaring at me with his wide-open eyes, Xiang Wenhua asked me if I didn't want to help him.

I replied, saying, "I was kidding. You just think about it. How can dung cure human diseases?"

Having acquired the firm belief that dung could cure human diseases, Xiang Wenhua thought my denial indicated only that I did not want to offer my help. Offering me a cigarette, which was a thing he had rarely done before, he emphasized that, one way or another, he would definitely go to Mazi Village and do some investigating. "It's settled," he said.

After leaving the press house, no sooner had I caught a taxi, than I received a phone call from Shuanhu. His voice sounded very genial. Addressing me as "Brother," he asked me, "Where are you? Are you busy? How have you been lately?"

After answering his questions one by one, I politely asked him about his whereabouts.

He said he was in Yuebei, staying in Jianguo Hotel; he was with the township head Liu Qi, who had come specifically to see me; they had brought me some gifts, which were specialties in my hometown. Shuanhu meant I was expected to go to the hotel to meet them.

I had a moment's hesitation, then I decided to go to the hotel. My taxi was heading west, whereas the hotel lay to the east. After I gave directions to the taxi driver, the taxi turned around and drove towards the hotel.

As a matter of fact, Shuanhu and Liu Qi had arrived at Yuebei the day before, and Zhao Xiaohui, too, was with them. Incidentally, Zhao Xiaohui's perpetual courteous manner was what Liu Qi disliked most about him. Liu Qi had grumbled that such a man had no great prospects. In Liu Qi's view, a man should behave like a wolf or a tiger; it was the ability to kick and bite which made a man a true man. Like a boxing coach, Liu Qi had vowed to train Zhao Xiaohui to be a first-rate pugilist. Only then could he deliver his sister into his hands with tranquility.

As I arrived at Jianguo Hotel and entered the lounge, I chanced to see Liu Qi rebuking Zhao Xiaohui.

Liu Qi sat on a sofa with his legs crossed, his feet bare, one sock on the sofa, the other one lying on the floor beside one of his shoes. Undoubtedly Liu Qi had sweaty feet — I knew that because his shoes and socks gave off a strong and unpleasant smell.

There were quite a few foreigners in the hall. One senior white lady stumbled over Liu Qi's shoes. Though she did not fall down, she got a real scare. Turning around, she looked at Liu Qi in great shock.

Liu Qi was reprimanding Zhao Xiaohui while scratching a corn on his foot. He yelled at Zhao Xiaohui, calling him a maggot in an outhouse, a bug on a persimmon tree, a worm in wheat bran. "Who do you think you are? How dare you tell me what are good manners and what are bad manners? The man big enough to give a lecture to me hasn't been born yet!"

Standing next to Liu Qi, Zhao Xiaohui's face turned red. He looked extremely embarrassed.

I asked Shuanhu, who was trying to calm things down, what had happened. Shuanhu led me behind a pillar and said it was nothing serious; it was Zhao Xiaohui who was to blame. Last night Liu Qi summoned three *xiaojie*[22], which frightened Zhao Xiaohui so much that he ran away and hid himself, because he thought one of the girls must have been booked for him — and he would never allow himself to mingle with call-girls. Actually, it turned out that Zhao Xiaohui had misunderstood: after all, how could Liu Qi have permitted his sister's prospective husband to go with a call-girl? If he had let his sister's husband-to-be go with a call-girl, how would he face his own sister? The truth was that Liu Qi enjoyed frolicking with a posse of call-girls simultaneously. Only group play of this kind was sufficiently stimulating for Liu Qi.

To tell the truth, Zhao Xiaohui's retreat was just what Liu Qi desired. But he was still displeased. His displeasure derived from his finding out how timid and cowardly Zhao Xiaohui was! Were the call-girls scorpions that had poisonous needles? Or were they boas with venomous bites? If harmless call-girls could frighten Zhao Xiaohui so much, what big things could he be expected to achieve? For this reason, a certain resentment against Zhao Xiaohui had accumulated in Liu Qi's heart. And it showed restraint on Liu Qi's part that he had not flared up last night.

Today, seeing Liu Qi take off his shoes and socks while sitting on a lounge sofa in the hotel, Zhao Xiaohui made a fuss about it. He seemed to be asking for trouble, as though he did not feel comfortable if he went unreprimanded. After all, wasn't it a common enough thing which Liu Qi had done out of habit? None the less, Zhao Xiaohui advised Liu Qi to put his shoes and socks back on, saying that in such a high class hotel it was not appropriate behavior to take off one's shoes and socks; that if this was seen by any foreigners, they would laugh at it; and that, though to be laughed at might be a minor matter, it would be a major one if the image of the Chinese people should suffer among the international community.

"Fuck it!" Liu Qi yelled loudly. He lost his temper. How could he not lose his temper? Criticized by his inferior and younger sister's fiancé, how should he not flare up? He poured torrents of nasty words upon Zhao Xiaohui. In Liu Qi's opinion, even if he were guilty of thousands of misdemeanours, Zhao Xiaohui should never utter a single word of disapproval. Who did Zhao Xiaohui think he was? Even Liu Qi's own father would examine his son's face carefully before venturing to offer advice. Moreover, Liu Qi did not consider he had done anything improper. On the contrary, he believed his behavior would help boost the Chinese people's confidence. How come? Why had the Eight-Power Allied Forces dared to bully the Chinese people in the 1860s? Wasn't it because they had seen that the Chinese were extremely obedient and docile, so that they got the impression that China was the Sick Man of East Asia? Liu Qi thought the removal of his shoes and socks would serve to change the image of the Chinese people in the eye of foreigners. In his view, his behavior was a patriotic act, showing that Chinese people were no longer slavishly obedient creatures, or timid individuals who dared not act on their own decisions. He even had the notion of taking off his coat to bare his chest, thus presenting a Chinese male's robust chest to the foreigners. Of course the ideal way to manifest his patriotism would have been to carry the knife he used to use when working as a butcher, and stalk back and forth in the hotel hall, to see if the blond-haired, blue-eyed foreign phantoms would panic.

While saying this, Liu Qi rose to his feet and slowly paced toward a group of foreigners standing in the middle of the hall, engaged in talk. As he passed by a wiry young man, Liu Qi stamped on his foot. After that, Liu Qi continued his stroll as if nothing had happened, with his head swinging from side to side and his mouth whistling.

Apparently, Liu Qi's stomp hurt the young man considerably, given that he lifted his injured foot and shook it incessantly, with his mouth uttering painful sounds. Turning around, Liu Qi retraced his steps. As he passed by the young man, Liu Qi was ready to stage a confrontation with him; he wanted to beat the young man up and then report the matter to the police, accusing the young "foreign ghost" of initiating the conflict and of having beaten him — if necessary, he would knock his own head against the glass door to wound it, and then he would claim the wound had resulted from the foreigner's attack. When the police showed up, wouldn't Chinese policemen show favor to Chinese people? How unlikely to suppose that Chinese policemen would believe what a foreign ghost might say!

However, to Liu Qi's disappointment, these foreigners were just paper tigers. The young foreigner, whose foot he had just stomped on, grinned at him, and even went so far as to nod at him. This response not only surprised Liu Qi but also annoyed him. Under such circumstances, could he resort to his fists? Of course not! With nothing better to do, Liu Qi returned to the sofa and sat down again.

Sitting on the sofa, Liu Qi smoked and bragged, claiming that he had just avenged the Chinese people who had been oppressed for centuries.

"Ah!" he deplored. "It doesn't work if only one Chinese shows himself to be brave. It is indispensable that all Chinese people show themselves hard and tough. We should become as hard and tough as a penis strengthened by Viagra. If all Chinese people become hard and tough, we will surely knock the Americans' teeth out of their mouths, leaving them to pick them up off the ground. Likewise, the Japanese will be beaten so hard that their bodies will fall to pieces, with their torsos abandoned in Tibet, their heads in Heilongjiang. As for the British, we will set their legs and feet adrift in the Pacific Ocean while their arms will be dropped in the Atlantic. Ha-ha-ha, foreigners aren't that formidable."

Liu Qi concluded that compared to him, foreigners were all as soft as *toufu*.

After listening to Shuanhu's account of what had happened, as well as to what Liu Qi had just said, I wanted to laugh. However, there was no way I could permit myself to.

Going nearer to Liu Qi, I told him to calm down.

"Look, many people are looking this way," I said to him.

Thank goodness, Liu Qi followed my advice. A smile appeared on his face. Though dismayed, Zhao Xiaohui greeted me and asked me to be seated.

Sitting next to Zhao Xiaohui on a sofa opposite Liu Qi's and Shuanhu's sofa, I asked them how they were doing, if there had been any rainfall back home, and whether the apricots had grown as big as human thumb tips.

As Zhao Xiaohui was answering my questions, Liu Qi cut him short, announcing abruptly that he and Shuanhu had come for two purposes. One purpose was to give a gift to an official in the provincial government — that official was very close to Liu Qi; now that his son was going abroad, Liu Qi had come to present a red envelope to express his good wishes.

The other principal task was that he would like to meet Governor Xiang.

His idea took me aback. Was Governor Xiang the sort of figure that anyone could meet who wished to?

40

Governor Xiang was not an easy person to see, but his son Xiang Wenhua was accessible without much difficulty. I could not afford to refuse the task which the township king of hell and the village local snake had both asked me to perform. At the moment, I was so full of self-reproach that I really wanted to give myself a few slaps. It was my own big mouth which, for a momentary satisfaction, had let slip the one thing which I should have kept secret at all cost — that I knew Governor Xiang's son.

At dawn, the moment I got out of bed, before I washed or brushed, I phoned Xiang Wenhua. He said he had a toothache and swollen gums, apparently the result of "internal inflammation." A friend had invited him to go hunting, but because of his condition he decided to rest at home. The doctor would visit in a few minutes. Nevertheless, he had not forgotten about making a trip to Mazi Village. He said that when he told his mother about the purported medicinal properties of the dung in Mazi Village, she had said nothing, but their nanny had ridiculed the idea, saying "Someone has been taking the piss out of you." In spite of all these discouragements, he still looked forward to this trip, for he really wanted to have a look at cattle and sheep, and the crops in the fields, or even to go catching a few hares. I said, "Great. You can go whenever you wish to, even right now. Wenhua, your trip to Mazi Village will surely be sensational news in Kaiyang County. Which of its officials, from the most powerful to the least powerful, does not want to meet you? But you should concentrate on those with immediate power — not figures of distant authority. And, avoid those who would involve you in their troubles, with the exception of the township and village leaders. You see, they've heard that you'll be at Mazi Village, so they have come to Yuebei to see you."

Xiang Wenhua heaved a long sigh. "I want to do things on my own, why should local officials get involved and ruin my visit?" He did not want to meet any of them. He had no interest in meeting municipal leaders, let alone the small fry from the township and the village. I said, "Wenhua, do me a favor and meet them." Xiang Wenhua hesitated for a while, and after many an um and ah, he finally agreed to meet Liu Qi and the others.

Liu Qi held a banquet in the restaurant of Jianguo Hotel, in honor of Xiang Wenhua. He ordered whatever was expensive, and dishes of mynah meat, leopard paws, braised white rabbit, steamed monkey brains, were served one after the other. He also ordered a bottle of Remy Martin, but it tasted so queer that everyone stuck out his tongue. Liu Qi urged Xiang Wenhua to enjoy the food, and frequently served food onto his dish. The plates before him were heaped with all sorts of delicacies, but he didn't tuck in; he seemed to have no appetite. Xiang Wenhua claimed that his mother, who believed in Buddhism, had asked him to become a vegetarian so that he could go to paradise in his next life. Liu Qi was contemptuous of this claim. He said, "I used to kill pigs for more than a decade. Does that mean I won't be able to go to paradise? I don't think that's right." Liu Qi claimed that he strongly approved of the maxim: "Political power grows out of the barrel of a gun." He said, "This is the truth, the absolute truth! Properly interpreted, it means that he who is ruthless will make it big. The panorama of Chinese history teaches us that of those who reached the apogee of power — who was not a mass killer? What was a hero? Are not the so-called war heroes merely those who have killed the largest number of people?" Therefore, Liu didn't think it wrong for him to kill pigs. However, he had a taboo of his own — he would eat no pork.

Shuanhu had his doubts about what Xiang Wenhua's real identity was, and suspected that I had introduced an imposter to them. Xiang Wenhua looked more like the son of a redundant worker than of a senior official. He stared at the fat slovenly young man in front of him and found nothing special about his clothes, or appearance — his ears were ordinary ears and his nose was an ordinary nose. His hair in particular, was shaggy, like clusters of matted grass on his head. Good grief, he even had sleep in his eyes! How could a governor's son have sleep in his eyes?

Shuanhu, while remaining respectful of Xiang Wenhua, none the less interrogated him about this or that detail of Governor Xiang's life. He seemed very interested in Governor Xiang's personal life, about which he asked many questions, such as, did Governor Xiang go home often? When did he go to sleep and get up? Did he carry a pistol on his waist? How many bodyguards did he have? Was the toilet paper he used imported? Was the toilet bowl on which he sat inlaid with gold or plated with silver? Etc, etc.

At first, Xiang Wenhua was willing to answer these questions, but he soon became impatient. He either limited himself to an "mmm" or kept altogether silent. I winked to Shuanhu to stop, however, he failed to catch my drift and continued persistently as ever. In the end, Xiang Wenhua could bear it no longer, but knew better than to make a break for it there and then. He said that he wanted to go to the toilet, and as he stood up, discreetly grabbed my leg. I followed him out. With a sullen face, he asked if this was what I meant by "treating him to dinner." This was stuffing him with dynamite, and he was on the point of exploding! I hurriedly apologized to him. I said my village head was a lowbrow farmer who didn't know how to express himself; and I hoped that he would not mind. Xiang Wenhua grimaced. He said he thought that Shuanhu with his vulgar and irrelevant questions, was not quite right in the head. I apologized to him repeatedly. Xiang Wenhua said that was all right, but he had to be going.

Xiang Wenhua was on the point of leaving, when Liu Qi walked out of the room. The moment he heard Xiang Wenhua say farewell, he caught him by the sleeve and said that he must not go, which would be tantamount to a slap in the face; that Xiang Wenhua ought to follow them to Kaiyang County, and Gaotai Township as well! Although Kaiyang was not a wealthy county, it could still afford to receive him in style.

Up popped Shuanhu and Zhao Xiaohui to echo Liu Qi's invitation. Shuanhu realized that his language had offended Xiang Wenhua in some way, so he hurriedly apologized to him, saying that what he had done was a consequence of curiosity, not of ill will. He had been entranced by the mysterious quality a governor's life must have. Xiang Wenhua said he could not go with them. No, really not! The day after the next was his birthday, and his friends had been waiting too long, and were now shouting that they wanted to give him a special grand celebration. Liu Qi asked, "Wouldn't it be more meaningful to celebrate your birthday in Gaotai?" The honor guard of Kaiyang could be invited, as could the opera troupe of Kaiyang, and the travelling circus troupe from Henan Province. A large-scale celebration could be held, with farmers from Gaotai kneeling before him. Xiang Wenhua smiled, "Wouldn't that make me a deity?" Shuanhu said Xiang Wenhua *was* a deity; no, far greater than a deity! A deity was invisible and intangible, and could bring them nothing; they dismissed it by, at most, burning a few stacks of paper and a few sticks of incense on holidays. But they worshipped Xiang Wenhua with heart and soul!

"No, no. I have other business to attend to," Xiang Wenhua declined.

Liu Qi kept calling Xiang Wenhua "Brother," and in a beseeching tone which was rare for him, asked Xiang Wenhua to go with him in any case. When Xiang Wenhua went to the toilet, Liu Qi followed him to the toilet. But Liu Qi did not enter; he and Shuanhu stood guard on either side of the door. Liu Qi wanted me to help persuade Xiang Wenhua, saying that since an effort had been made to catch this big fish, how could it be allowed to escape at this point?

The moment Xiang Wenhua came out of the toilet, Liu Qi grabbed his arm. Annoyed a little bit, Xiang Wenhua protested and threatened to call the police. But far from loosening his grip, Liu Qi kissed Xiang Wenhua on the cheek. "How can you say that, my dear brother? Your older brother won't let go, because he loves you. Do you think your older brother would ever harm you? Come with your older brother, and he'll show you the depth of his fraternal feelings."

So saying, Liu Qi thrust a stack of bank notes into Zhao Xiaohui's hand, and signaled to him to pay the bills with them, while he himself kept holding Xiang Wenhua's arm. Although he was pulled and pushed all the way to the gate of the hotel, Xiang Wenhua remained as determined as ever. Liu Qi produced another stack of money from his leather bag, and forced it into Xiang Wenhua's pocket, saying it was just a small token of appreciation for his presence. Several times Xiang Wenhua tried, unsuccessfully, to take the money out and return it to Liu Qi. So mournful was the look on his face that one would have thought that he was being marched to an execution ground. With a deep despairing breath, he got into Liu Qi's car. Liu Qi rolled down the window and waved his hand to me. The car rumbled away like a gust of wind.

41

One week later, Xiang Wenhua made an appointment with me, asking me to meet him at the Alibaba Teahouse. He said he had something to hand over to me.

When I got to the teahouse, I found Larz busy about his work. Seeing me, he nodded in recognition.

Though he had a discount card with the teahouse, Xiang Wenhua rarely visited the place. Whenever he came, he always went to Silver Palace, which was so called because its walls were covered with shiny silver. Silver Palace patrons were charged less than Gold Palace patrons; nevertheless, it was still pretty expensive.

There were two charming waitresses in Silver Palace. In the midst of making tea, they kept casting lustful eyes at us. After the fruits and drinks which he had ordered were served, Xiang Wenhua gave each waitress a 100-*yuan* bill, instructing them to stay outside and not to enter unless they were asked to. With broad smiles on their faces, they promised they would do as they were told.

Taking his bag off his shoulder, Xiang Wenhua hugged it close to his chest and looked at me strangely for a long while. Suddenly he laughed loudly for no obvious reason.

After the pause, Xiang Wenhua said that he had never expected I would set a trap for him; that he had fallen into it now, and it was difficult for him to struggle out.

With a show of simplicity and innocence, I asked him, "What are you talking about? I don't understand what you mean."

He blurted out that being a gentle-tempered person, he did not know how to decline other people's requests for help; but once he embarked with them on their *black freighter*, he was completely at their mercy for the rest of the voyage.

Of course, I knew what he meant. I repeatedly said sorry to him, explaining that those guys were bigwigs in my hometown and therefore I could not afford to displease them. "I had no choice," I said.

Xiang Wenhua scolded me for having told lies. "Didn't you say the dung in Mazi Village outhouses had healing power? What nonsense!" he said.

He exclaimed that his poor grandma, in her miserable infirmity, and with her heart full of hope, had waited, like a fool, for him to bring back good news.

"I merely made a joke. I didn't think you'd take it seriously," I said.

Waving his hand, Xiang Wenhua said, "Stop it! You stop it! Don't make excuses."

Although he grumbled bitterly about being misled in this way, his subsequent remarks gave me the feeling that not everything had made him furious during his visit to my hometown; it seemed that there had been some happy moments. Although he harbored ill feeling toward Shuanhu, it appeared that he was well disposed toward Liu Qi. He called Liu Qi an able and enterprising man; it was only a pity that Liu Qi was so straight-forward in speech and so inclined to use coarse words. He said, "Such people are likely to give offence, but they are generally good-natured."

Xiang Wenhua related the story about how Shuanhu had closely followed him, telling him again and again about his daughter, who went by the name of Jidan and who was portrayed by her own father as a beautiful fairy unrivaled for prettiness in this world, as if she were Xishi[23] reborn and Diaochan[24] reincarnated. Actually, the father's intent could not have been more obvious: he was scheming to use Xiang Wenhua's influence to have Jidan assigned to a decent job position. Was such a person still worthy to be a father when he shamelessly told Xiang Wenhua that Jidan would be his if he could procure a good job for her? Shuanhu had claimed that if Xiang Wenhua wished to marry Jidan, he would be more than ready to give his approval; if Xiang Wenhua had no interest in marrying her but only wanted her to provide that kind of service on a long-term basis, not only would Jidan be more than happy to do such things, he himself would also approve without hesitation. All in all, if Xiang Wenhua was willing to say a helpful word, he would be able to enjoy swan's meat, i.e. Jidan's body. How many men had desired Jidan's body! Wasn't this a good deal for Xiang Wenhua?

"Just think, Xiang Wenhua," Shuanhu had said. "Whenever you wish to enter a happy cave, the door will be opened to you. And the moment you enter it, you'll enjoy yourself to your heart's content."

Having been pressed by Shuanhu so hard and having nowhere to escape to, Xiang Wenhua had to compose a note to Kaiyang County Secretary of the Party committee, whom he had become acquainted with during this very visit.

The secretary had invited Xiang Wenhua to accompany him in his public activities and had given him a top class mini-video camera, which he had declined persistently but in vain. Shortly after the video camera had been pressed on him, Xiang Wenhua donated it to Gaotai Middle School. But this displeased the county secretary of the Party committee: Liu Qi told Xiang Wenhua that Kaiyang County Party Committee Office called Gaotai Township Government Office the day after the donation, demanding that the video camera be taken back from the school and returned to the county secretary of the Party committee. Despite being no bigger than a cigarette case, it cost many tens of thousands of *yuan*. How could such an expensive item be given so randomly to other people? While taking the video camera from the schoolmaster's hand, Liu Qi harshly reproached him, saying "What a nerve! How dare you receive a gift without considering who the giver is?"

Having become keenly aware of how incapable some teachers at the school were of doing the right thing at the right time to the right people — they didn't know they were supposed to nod and greet the township government leaders when they encountered them — Liu Qi had on one occasion been to the school to deliver a talk entitled "The Cultivation of Correct Behavior." In this speech, he instructed the teachers to tuck their tails firmly between their legs and behave themselves; he warned them against raising their tails; he threatened to chop off the tails of any people who raised theirs; he threw dirty words at those teachers who behaved badly in this respect, and he reprimanded them one after another. It turned out that the training produced remarkable results: the teachers who used to walk with their heads held high in front of Liu Qi lowered their heads in the same way that hunted game does before the shotgun. One teacher who had been working in the profession for thirty years offered a particularly amusing example — ever since this occasion he became well known for his dread of Liu Qi. At the sight of Liu Qi, his belly would start to rumble as if the sight triggered a conditioned reflex in his stomach. Whenever he saw Liu Qi, he would dash for the outhouse. However, he rarely made it. Many times he ended up shitting his pants, soiling them horribly.

The training program had been a hit. Although it happened years earlier, the villagers still loved to talk about it. That was why you could hardly find anyone in the neighborhood who did not know about it. People kept mocking the old teacher who could not hold his urine or shit at the sight of Liu Qi.

Of course, Xiang Wenhua had learnt that the county secretary of the Party committee was not happy with him due to the video camera incident, but, tired of Shuanhu's nagging, he overcame his unwillingness and wrote to the secretary asking that Jidan be placed in an inconsequential post. To tell the truth, he wrote the note only for the sake of getting the issue off his hands and out of his head. Therefore, he did not use any strong or earnest words in his writing. He imagined that the secretary would not even bother to read it; that more likely the secretary would crumple the note into a ball and throw it into a trash bin.

It turned out that Liu Qi did keep his promise — he did hold a grand birthday celebration for Xiang Wenhua in the township government square just as he had said he would. The program was so full of variety as to dazzle the eyes.

A stage, its four sides colorfully decorated, was erected in the centre of the square. Two enormous loud speakers were placed at the front corners of the stage. The rumbling noises from the loud speakers mingled with the squeaking shouts from the organizers' small hand-held speakers. These noises made people's ears tingle unbearably. At the top of the stage hung a horizontal poster with the words "A Warm Celebration in Honor of the 35th Birthday of Xiang Wenhua, the Grand Savior of Gaotai People." Grand Savior? Whose idea was it to use this title? Spotting these words, Xiang Wenhua nearly fainted, as if someone had knocked him over the head with a club. He protested to Zhao Xiaohui, who was accompanying him, and asked him to tell Liu Qi to make sure that the epithet "Grand Savior" be changed, because it would definitely arouse disapproval. But Zhao Xiaohui gave a helpless look, saying that he had already pointed out his disapproval when the poster was being created; that as a matter of fact, he was not the only one who had expressed disapproval. Everyone present, except Liu Qi, had deemed the term improper — they thought the inclusion of the term might even be a serious political mistake.

However, no one could stop Liu Qi from going ahead with it. If Liu Qi thought snow was black, even if the whole world insisted that it was white, it would do no good. Liu Qi never tired of repeating his favorite cliché: "Just as every word Chairman Mao said was held to be absolute truth throughout China, every word I say will be regarded as truth; one sentence of mine has the weight of ten thousand sentences from other people's mouths."

Although Zhao Xiaohui, like the others, had not agreed with the use of the term "Grand Savior," what could he do? He could not argue with Liu Qi. If he did, the result would not be a change in the wording. Instead, a disaster would befall him.

Under these circumstances, Xiang Wenhua himself went to find Liu Qi, and asked him to remove the poster. But Liu Qi insisted on keeping it, and claimed that it was his temperament either to refrain altogether from doing something, or to make a big splash with it. He wished to make a big splash in Kaiyang County, so that its leading lords would acknowledge him as a capable figure, and that other township leaders would admire him for the backing he had. In this isolated county, how many people could successfully invite a province governor-level official's son to pay a visit? Who but he could have achieved this glory? Liu Qi aimed to make those who had gossiped about him die of frustration. He would like to make their intestines twist painfully in their bellies. He would like to make their brains fall apart utterly. He would like an enormous malignant tumor to grow out of the body of every one of them.

No matter what had motivated Liu Qi, Xiang Wenhua insisted on the removal of the poster. How could he be a savior? Even his father did not dare to view himself as such! He threatened that he would leave right away unless the poster was removed.

So Liu Qi gave in and had the poster removed.

Making use of Xiang Wenhua's visit, Liu Qi had successfully applied for funding, on the strength of which the celebration became as grand and merry as a fair. There were opera performances, in which well-known actors and actresses from Kaiyang County and Yuebei City were hired to perform. There were films full of images of men and women playing lustfully in bed. It happened that a circus troupe of some sort was passing by the town. Besides its male and female monkeys, the troupe also boasted some girls, whose shoulders and arms, thighs and legs were all naked. The troupe's performance was composed of two sections. The performers in Section One were monkeys. A number of male troupe members with naked tops and whips in hand, whipped the monkeys so hard that they groaned; then the monkeys were forced to mate in front of the audience. The performance in Section Two went on in a hidden place. Those who had viewed it kept calling it obscene and pornographic as they came out. Some viewers even spat on the ground to show their disgust.

The troupe had erected a tent. Then its members called people to the entrance, saying there were treasures inside; it would be a great pity to lose the chance to view or touch such treasures.

In the end, no one came out of the tent without a look of disgust on his face. They claimed there were several naked girls inside for visitors who paid extra money to touch. Each batch of people was allowed to stay inside for five minutes. Those who simply viewed were charged 5 *yuan*, but whoever touched the girls was charged 20 *yuan*.

What an amazing thing! Lots people entered the tent. Of course, Liu Qi's entry was free of charge. He would not be satisfied until he brought in his guest. He pulled Xiang Wenhua with great force.

Knowing what was going on inside, Xiang Wenhua adamantly refused to enter. Seeing this, Liu Qi complained that Xiang Wenhua was hard to please.

42

I never expected Xiang Wenhua to introduce Liu Qi to his father. According to Xiang Wenhua, his father had talked, in his own office, with Liu Qi for half an hour, and once home asked him about Liu Qi. From his father's words, he gathered that he had a low opinion of Liu Qi, though he limited himself to saying that work at the grassroots level was arduous, and not easy, and the like. His father warned him not to casually bring people to see him, and above all, not to do anything untoward in his name, so on and so forth.

At Alibaba's Silver Palace, Xiang Wenhua entrusted me with a few articles to hand over to Liu Qi. One by one he produced, from an enormous bag, the articles — eight bundles of money, one piece of porcelain of unique shape, and an ancient statue of Buddha.

I was somewhat stupefied. To my consternation, my heart began thumping nervously. The bundles of money in particular, heaped on the table in front of us, were so dazzling to the eye.

Xiang Wenhua said these things had been presented by Liu Qi to his father, who, exasperated, ordered him to return all of them to the owner as quickly as possible. However, to return something was never that simple; it was not as though one had total freedom of action in such matters. If he called Liu Qi to pick them up, Liu Qi would surely obstinately refuse. If he drove over to deliver them, it was probable that Liu Qi would still shun him. What should be done? Probably the father and son had concluded that the safest way to handle this matter was through me. There were two reasons. First, if I had not acted as go-between, neither Xiang Wenhua nor Governor Xiang could, by any chance, have met Liu. It goes without saying that he who fastens the bell is the best one to unfasten it! Second, I could be considered a witness in this matter. The money and other articles could be returned in such a way as to prove that Governor Xiang had nothing to do with the whole matter. And even if Liu Qi were to become a randomly biting mad dog, a sound explanation would be provided. Xiang Wenhua took this opportunity to show his father in a good light, saying that he was a good official, with no blemish either as a man or as an official. People queued to present gifts, some many times more valuable than Liu Qi's, but his father kept none of them. How to reject money and gifts had thus become a problem that caused the biggest headache for his father. Luckily, his father had a resourceful secretary who, aware of his worries and brimming with ideas as well, had helped him a lot in this respect. In officialdom, being a good official was very difficult. Your colleagues didn't like you because your purity highlighted their impurity. Your subordinates didn't like you because they could not profit from you. The bosses who turned to you for help didn't like you because you wouldn't, in your effort to hold onto your integrity, do anything against the law and the regulations, and when they failed to get what they wanted to — who would they hate more than you? Governor Xiang himself had come to the conclusion that in the end a man like him would be abandoned by the whole world. None the less, Governor Xiang was determined as ever to be a good official. Whether he was a good official or not could be seen from his attitude toward his son. Xiang Wenhua remained an ordinary, obscure journalist, and it was a miracle that he had never been promoted, not even to the position of departmental director.

Xiang Wenhua had nursed a faint dissatisfaction with his father. A joint stock bank had wanted to appoint him as assistant to its president, with a yearly salary of 400,000 *yuan*, a villa and a limousine, but his father was dead-set against his going. His father was certainly not helpful; on the contrary, he was doing everything he could to stand in his son's way, going so far as to call the bank in person, to say that it was not good for a young man who had made so little effort to reach such a high position; it was comparable to a house without a solid foundation, or, a seedling being pulled up to help it grow. "Alas, what a time we live in! But he still clings to such ideas. Is a young man only promising after he has climbed snow-capped mountains, crossed grassy marshes, and eaten tree bark?" Xiang Wenhua grumbled.

But generally speaking, Xiang Wenhua was supportive of his father. He kept saying that his father deserved pity — surrounded though he was by people, he felt lonely, and without friends. Those who claimed to be relatives or friends, with their honeyed tongues and shifty eyes, were in fact trying to exploit his father — trying to redirect his power for their own selfish interests.

I laughed. I said that if a governor was worthy of pity, then everyone must be. Were laid-off workers not worthy of it? Were migrant workers not worthy of it? Were those who couldn't afford their children's tuition or their parents' medical fees not worthy of it?

"Well, well," said Xiang Wenhua with a dismissive wave of the hand. He claimed that it looked like I could never understand him, that while he was talking about noodles, I changed the subject to herbal medicine. What a mess! The two things were as incongruous as a horse's jaw and an ox's skull.

Xiang Wenhua let me count the money and check the articles. I hesitated. I was afraid that by doing so I was allowing a noose to be slipped round my neck. My inaction almost made Xiang Wenhua jump up in anger. He accused me of introducing unworthy people to him who had brought troubles upon him and his father while I stood at a safe distance, arms folded, looking on. Was I really so cruel as to refuse to return some goods on their behalf?

"Okay, Okay, Okay! Stop bothering about the matter. I'll deliver them. Let's drink tea. Here we are, sitting in a luxurious private room, in a place specially designed for drinking tea, and we've talked so much that we have forgotten to drink tea! Look, our lips are dry and chapped," I said.

Having poured a cup of tea for Xiang Wenhua, I stood up and walked out. I asked the waitress to get me a few paper bags and two black plastic ones. Xiang Wenhua was leaning back in the sofa, eyes half-closed. I stuffed the money on the table into the paper bags, and the paper bags into the black plastic ones. I was about to pack the statue of Buddha when I was struck by its familiarity. A closer look told me it was the Six-fingered Buddha the people in Kaiyang were so proud of and so often talked about. Research suggested that the statue was an image of Buddha made in Northern Wei Dynasty[25]. It was slightly damaged, with a mottled face, but its body was smooth and complete, and its six fingers clearly visible at the end of a slightly raised arm. It was said to be the only one of its type in China — indeed, in the whole world, and was regarded as a real national treasure. Legend had it that it had been kept in the Confucian Temple, not accessible to any visitors. A glimpse of it was only possible when a small number of domestic or foreign VIPs showed up. However, most people in Kaiyang had seen it — not in reality but on TV. When it was stolen, the TV had given the crime substantial coverage. Later the case was solved; it turned out that two ignorant middle school students had done this mischief — they had climbed over the wall into the temple, broken the lock on the door and stolen the statue for fun. Thus the cultural relic was lost and found, and Kaiyang people of every social class unanimously applauded. So the question arose: how had such a treasure of treasures been passed, via Liu Qi, into Xiang Wenhua's hand?

I gave Xiang Wenhua a nudge, and he opened his eyes. I held up the statue and asked whether he knew what it was. He looked bewildered, and shook his head, saying, "Who knows? Isn't it a broken statue of Buddha?" I asked him whether he had heard of the Six-fingered Buddha. He pondered for a few seconds, and then said that he seemed to remember having heard of it. I said the Six-fingered Buddha was a national treasure and enjoyed a great deal of prestige. Xiang Wenhua asked in surprise, "Is it?" Then he added, "Where is it now?" I said it was right before his eyes. Now wide awake, Xiang Wenhua grabbed the statue from the tea table and examined it from every angle with wide-open eyes, conceded with a sigh that it did have six fingers, and wondered why he hadn't noticed that before. I gave a brief account of its cultural value, causing him to grab it even more tightly. He said he was going to keep it, in spite of the fact that he believed in neither Buddha nor Christ. A rare, world-renowned treasure, how could he let such thing slip away? What's more, his mother believed in Buddhism and had arranged a special room at home to enshrine more than twenty statues of Buddha, large and small, making it look very much like a small temple.

Having caressed the statue for a long time, Xiang Wenhua returned the Six-fingered Buddha to me, and sighed that it was against the law to withhold national treasures. What's more, his father would get mad if he got to know about it. On taking his leave, Xiang Wenhua said he would call Kaiyang County to remind them to keep an eye on the whereabouts of the Six-fingered Buddha and guard it from the rapacity of ne'er-do-wells.

43

Of course it was not to Liu Qi's liking that Governor Xiang should return the money, but it was a fact he had to accept. He insisted that Governor Xiang had declined the money because it was too small a sum.

Liu Qi said he had read some reports about corrupt officials; he found some people drove pickup trucks loaded with multiple boxes of money to deliver to the officials they wished to bribe.

"It's true, this is a small sum," Liu Qi admitted. "But this is merely an 'exploratory sum.' This is like scouts during a military campaign, who will be followed by large battalions later on. Governor Xiang is too greedy, isn't he? He regarded eighty thousand *yuan* with scorn! Why couldn't he have waited with a bit more patience? Well, well, well! Now I know how big Governor Xiang's appetite is, next time I'll give him a bigger sum!"

It was in a restaurant that I met with Liu Qi, who was in the middle of dining with a crowd of people. Obviously he had drunk excessively; his face was as red as the setting sun. I called him away. Then he escorted me to a corner, where there was nothing but a set of connected chairs. Liu Qi sat down on one of them. I remained standing, for it seemed that two maggots were wriggling on the unoccupied chair.

I asked him when he had arrived at Yuebei. With his tongue twisting in his mouth, he muttered something unintelligible; he seemed to say *zuotian*, yesterday, or *qiantian*, the day before yesterday. He said he had come to the provincial capital to look for Zhao Xiaohui.

"This asshole prostitute Zhao Xiaohui!" Liu Qi said. "After he returned from Yuebei, he ran away and disappeared. His mobile phone was off. He was nowhere to be found."

Liu Qi told me he and his township government men had broken into Zhao Xiaohui's office; in the wake of a careful search, they found that Zhao Xiaohui's departure had been well-planned: the room was empty except for a cabinet, a desk, a bed, and a chair, with all the other things gone.

"Aha, he ran away?" Liu Qi continued. "Did he fly to the moon? As long as he can't fly to the sky, I'll find him."

Liu Qi said his sister had been crying, but he told her not to, promising that as long as he lived, he would capture Zhao Xiaohui, and he swore that even if Zhao Xiaohui had been dismembered, he would bring the dismembered parts back to her.

I was shocked. I felt anxious about Zhao Xiaohui. Although I had heard him sigh and groan, but it had never occurred to me he would run away. He had impressed me as a nice fellow. What could make such a nice fellow do this? Seeing those bulging blue veins on Liu Qi's forehead, I knew how angry he was. Fueled by his anger, he would show no mercy to Zhao Xiaohui once he found him. I really worried for Zhao Xiaohui.

Liu Qi told me those who were dining in the room were public security personnel from Kaiyang County; with all these people combining their efforts, he felt sure Zhao Xiaohui would be captured, though for the time being he had disappeared like evaporated water. According to Liu Qi, hunting down Zhao Xiaohui was no longer a personal matter, but rather of crucial importance to Kaiyang County. Now that a vice township head of the county had disappeared — and neither his living form nor his dead body could be found — how would the leaders of the county not burn with restlessness? They had issued their unconditional command that the public security bureau must, at all costs, find Zhao Xiaohui and get him back.

As Liu Qi was receiving the black plastic bag from my hand, I proposed that he count the money, to see if it fell short of the expected amount, which was eighty thousand *yuan*. Pulling the bag abruptly from my hand, he held it firm without counting the money. Instead, he protested at my making such a fuss.

"Why waste so much breath over a matter as trivial as a fart? Is there any need to count it? Does it matter if it is less or more?" he exclaimed. He said even if I had taken some notes from the wads, it did not matter at all.

Immediately afterward, Liu Qi began to speak highly of Governor Xiang, saying that he was amiable and friendly. He also told me that the county secretary of the Party committee had had a talk with him; that the secretary had been amazed to discover Liu Qi was acquainted with Governor Xiang; that the secretary had struggled to divine how Liu Qi was related to Governor Xiang. Given that it was not easy even for the county secretary of the Party committee himself to maintain an intimate relationship with the governor, the secretary wondered how come this insignificant township head had managed to be received in the governor's office. The secretary asked if Liu Qi had got to know the governor through the governor's son, but Liu Qi shook his head. He made up a story, according to which Governor Xiang's grandfather had been his late grandfather's friend — implying that his family and the Xiang family had had long standing close ties for generations.

I asked Liu Qi how come Kaiyang County Secretary of the Party committee got to know about his relation to Governor Xiang. He said Kaiyang County Secretary of the Party committee had been instructed by his superior, Yuebei City Secretary of the Party committee, to take special care of Liu Qi for the sake of Governor Xiang.

Liu Qi exclaimed that as a matter of fact he hadn't expected Governor Xiang to do much for him. He would be very happy if Governor Xiang could make him a standing vice magistrate of the county. If that was difficult, it would be a nice consolation to be made the head of a profitable bureau in the county government. He had little interest in heading any bureau but the bureau of finance or the bureau of land management. Even fools knew those two bureaus were good. So many people tried their utmost to get a leadership position in them. Just think about it. The bureau of finance took charge of financial matters. What a huge sum of money a county disposed of! Moreover, if he, Liu Qi, became head of the bureau of finance, on a par with the heads of the other bureaus in the county, who would not bend to his will? When he, Liu Qi, seized the power of allocating funding, he would place grants only when he wished to, and he would refuse to give his approval if he was not in the right mood. As for those who would not bow down before him or offer tributes to him, how were they to get funding? Once he became the head of the bureau of finance, he really would be a somebody, body and soul; his neck would stand as straight as a tree-trunk; his eyes would gaze up at the sky; so far as he was concerned, those around him would be no better than ants.

Liu Qi had once forcefully declared that his keenest wish was to be an emperor for a fixed number of days — there was no need to stay in the position for long; it would suffice to fully experience the imperial existence; being emperor for one day would be better than the full life-span of a commoner, whose life was worse than that of dogs or pigs. Liu Qi believed Li Zicheng[26] had done the right thing to drive away the Ming Dynasty emperor and to make himself emperor. He also considered Yuan Shikai[27] to be a person of great discernment. He, Liu Qi, was not a greedy man; he only wished to be an emperor for two years; he had no wish to emulate the behavior of those emperors of antiquity, who in their old age greedily hung on to power without any intention of abdicating, and yielded the throne to none other than their own son or grandson when they died. How grand those emperors looked! They sat on an elevated dragon-design throne. No matter what commands they issued, all the courtiers who stalked and swaggered so arrogantly in their everyday lives, would kneel down before them in a throng. They could kill anyone they wanted to. Furthermore, an emperor could sleep with any woman he liked. An emperor's concubines were innumerable. When an emperor went out, oh boy, gongs were beaten ahead to alert people to give way, and armed guards rode on horseback to provide protection. What a gorgeous scene! But alas! He could never expect such a dream to come true. Nevertheless, getting his hands on the county's bureau of finance would not be so bad! Aha, bureau of finance! As long as he played his cards right, wouldn't the county's bureau of finance become his own money box?

Before long, Liu Qi began to vow to me over and over again that he was not an ungrateful person. He swore an oath that if his dream came true, he would give me a car as a gift.

Liu Qi said there was no need to explain why it was also his dream to become the head of the bureau of land management: these years had witnessed a peak in land acquisition and a peak in the demolition-and-removal of urban housing. These peaks meant money! Who could get the land they wanted without offering a bribe? Moreover, Liu Qi felt himself to be the most proper choice to lead the county's bureau of land management. It was the county secretary of the Party committee who was to blame! The secretary was so blind and stupid that he had not recognized Liu Qi's talent; as a result, Liu Qi's talent was not used to the full, which in turn had prevented Liu Qi from getting that position. One of tasks the bureau of land management performed was to handle house-demolition and resident-relocation. Liu Qi had the strength to do such things. If Liu Qi were put in charge of such work, it could be guaranteed that there would be no resisters. No matter how stubborn a household might be, upon hearing the name of Liu Qi, nine out of ten would piss themselves with fear. They would do as instructed without a murmur. As for the one-in-ten households which refused to move, and which had eyes but could not see, well, just let them wait till their arms and legs were broken. Then they would cry their hearts out.

"Did Zhao Xiaohui give any sign before he disappeared?" I asked Liu Qi.

Liu Qi picked a tiny bit of meat out from between his teeth and dashed it onto the ground.

"Bah! Bah!" Liu Qi spat twice onto the floor, then replied that there had been no sign of any kind; however, some days before he disappeared, Zhao Xiaohui had borrowed five thousand *yuan* from the township government treasurer under the pretext that his mother had fallen ill. Zhao Xiaohui had written the treasurer an IOU, which bore Liu Qi's signature to show his approval. However, prior to coming to Yuebei City, Liu Qi had torn the note into pieces and had reported to the public security bureau, claiming that Zhao Xiaohui had run away after stealing public funds. Was five thousand *yuan* too small a sum to justify a serious punishment to which Zhao Xiaohui would be condemned? Don't worry! Liu Qi knew how to increase the magnitude of Zhao Xiaohui's crime — it would be all too easy. Without needing to bother himself to do anything, the matter could be carried out perfectly. His pal Xu Yuanyuan, the coal mine boss who was whole-hearted in his support of him, would show up at the court when the time came, and testify that Zhao Xiaohui had extorted bribes from him. As for the amount Zhao Xiaohui had demanded, would that be a problem? Xu Yuanyuan could say any amount he wanted: he could say one hundred thousand, or five million. As to the actual figure, it would be determined by how many years he, Liu Qi, would like Zhao Xiaohui to be imprisoned. Only this and nothing more! Even if his whole body had been covered in mouths, Zhao Xiaohui would not be able to lick himself clean of the charge. Zhao Xiaohui might well assert he had never extorted a bribe, but what would his assertion count for? It was the judge's verdict that would count. But weren't judges human? If you could identify their desires, you would have power over them. The purpose of Liu Qi's bringing the public security personnel in to hunt for Zhao Xiaohui, was to put Zhao Xiaohui, the ingrate, into prison. Would Zhao Xiaohui have an easy time in jail? Of course not! He, Liu Qi, was intimately close with the personnel watching over the prisoners. Whenever they met up with Liu Qi, they humbly addressed him as "Brother Liu." As soon as Liu Qi gave them a sign, they would certainly dismember Zhao Xiaohui.

Shortly after I parted with Liu Qi, my mobile phone rang. The caller's number was unfamiliar, nevertheless I answered. The voice at the other end was very faint, like the buzzing of a bee. But I could tell it was Zhao Xiaohui speaking. He said he was outside the gate of my workplace right now, right next to a yellow-painted trash bin.

"I'll be there right away. I'll get over to see you," I said to Zhao Xiaohui.

But when I arrived at the trash bin, looking to right and left, I could not find Zhao Xiaohui anywhere. Just as I was beginning to feel perplexed, I heard someone calling my name. Turning around, I realized there was a person sitting next to the trash bin, and he was calling me. But far from it being Zhao Xiaohui, he was someone I had never seen before.

This person looked like a beggar in every respect. He was unkempt and in ragged clothes. He sat on the ground as if he were paralyzed, with one leg bent inwards. Every time he advanced a single pace, he had to stretch both his hands to the ground to support himself, which he did with great effort; all of which rendered his deformed face, with its gnashing teeth, even more twisted. As a result, it was hard to tell what the expression on his darkly mottled and shriveled face truly signified. It seemed that he was smiling at me. But it also seemed he was crying. With great difficulty, he moved a couple of paces towards me and called out "Black Bean."

Taken aback, I asked him who he was. He turned out to be quick of speech, replying that he came from Kaiyang, and that his name was Jinbing.

Jinbing? The name sounded familiar! But before I could figure out his history, he began to introduce himself. He was surprised that I had not known who he was, given that he had been well known in Kaiyang. He said I should think about this: apart from him, who else had dared to rise up against Liu Qi in public? He had spent all year filing a protest against Liu Qi. As a result, from the county government officials all the way down to the street vendors, who did not know him, Jinbing? In order to pull Liu Qi down from his position, he, Jinbing, had had the guts to go everywhere that occurred to him, and he had forced his way into the highest administrative offices, and he had been bold enough to buttonhole any high-ranking officials he needed to. Officials of various levels would disappear at the first sign of his approach. Even the mention of his name gave these officials a headache.

I asked Jinbing what on earth he thought I could do for him.

Jinbing told me it was Zhao Xiaohui's idea that he should turn to me for help. Zhao Xiaohui wanted him to ask me to publish in my newspaper the story of how he had been disabled as a result of being beaten by Liu Qi, so that Liu Qi's various evil doings would be exposed to the public. Since Zhao Xiaohui had told Jinbing that the provincial governor's son was one of my colleagues, Jinbing conceived the idea of contacting the governor's son through me, so that he could tell the governor's son his grievances. Once these grievances moved the heart of the governor's son, then the governor's heart would be moved too. If necessary, Jinbing would plead with the governor's son to introduce him to the governor. Jinbing claimed that the governor was well-known as an upright official, who would surely feel indignant upon hearing his story. If Governor Xiang burst into anger, Liu Qi would certainly be doomed.

"Hee-hee, how many pigs Liu Qi has slaughtered! Eventually it will be his turn to meet his doom," Jinbing declared, with irrepressible excitement on his face, as if Liu Qi had been tried and he were watching him go to the gallows.

Jinbing said Zhao Xiaohui, the former vice head of Gaotai Township Government, had now degenerated to the point of being closely linked with him — like two grasshoppers tied by one cord, they were bound together; for a common goal, he and Vice Township Head Zhao had joined forces. Their common goal was to pull Liu Qi down through impeachment; they would not stop until Liu Qi was put into prison — in accordance with Liu Qi's guilt. Once sentenced to prison, Liu Qi would have little hope of coming out.

"Where is Zhao Xiaohui?" I asked Jinbing.

Jinbing laughed eerily and did not answer me.

44

It was not long before I met Zhao Xiaohui again. I did not know why, but my heart was crying out to help him. It would be easy for Liu Qi to locate him, given Liu Qi's power to mobilize the public security forces, so I was very worried, because there could be no future for any young man who fell into Liu Qi's hands.

I kept phoning, time and again, the number on which he had called me, but his phone was switched off. On the sixth night the line was open and the call was put through at last. Zhao Xiaohui said that he was in the Alibaba Teahouse, that with the help of Larz, he had become a staff member there. He explained that he had got to know Larz in Kaiyang when the latter visited it. He had at first taken Larz for something of a hooligan, but after associating with him, he came to the conclusion that Larz was an upright, good-natured young man, and in a few short days he and Larz had become close friends. I told Zhao Xiaohui it was very dangerous to stay at Alibaba and that he had better move out since it was one of the most famous teahouses in Yuebei, with people of all walks coming and going, and he would not have a chance to run away once someone recognized him. Zhao Xiaohui said calmly and slowly that he was all right and was learning foot care in the pedicure parlor; that there were not many people around, but for a master with two apprentices including him, and these two people had not the least idea of where he was from and what he had done. I told him he was a fool! The people in the parlor itself might not do him any harm, but those whom he served might. They were the ones whom he should guard against. Zhao Xiaohui just repeated, "Don't worry. I am all right. Who can do me harm?" I asked if he was aware that Liu Qi was hunting for him everywhere. Zhao Xiaohui said he wasn't, but he had suspected that Liu Qi would be looking for him. He swore at Liu Qi in passing, saying he was a base man, too base for him to put up with. To work with him was excruciating, a fate worse than death!

I said Liu Qi was not looking for him in the usual way. He had mobilized the police forces of Kaiyang. Liu Qi would dig three feet into the ground if that was what it took to find him, and had vowed that when he did find him, he would torment him to within an inch of his life.

Zhao Xiaohui became silent. After a long pause, he said he would like to see me, and asked where he could meet me. I said, "Let's meet at the entrance of the church!" I gave him detailed information about the bus route, and suggested that he had better be careful and wear a pair of sunglasses.

The sun had set. In the deepening darkness, the street lamps were lighting up like stars. Standing below an electrical cable pole, I kept my eyes open for Zhao Xiaohui, but he was nowhere to be seen. The church bell was ringing so languorously, as to be sleep-inducing. Peddlers with bamboo baskets on their backs and shoulders began to stream in through the portal. Instead of rushing without more ado into the nave, most of them gathered in the courtyard, each enquiring about the other's income for that day. Some sighed over the profits that certain of their number had made, while others took delight in their own ability to sell their customers short measure.

Just as I was about to give up, Zhao Xiaohi appeared. He had acted on my suggestion and put on a pair of sunglasses. I was amused by his programmatic behavior. When I told him that he should put on sunglasses I had meant in daytime, but who would have believed that he would do so in the evening! I asked why he was so late. Zhao Xiaohui said that he had got off the bus when it stopped by the provincial discipline inspection commission, that he had gone there to present his letter of accusation a few days before, and that he had looked in today to see if there had been any response. If there had been none, he would have given them a push. "Good grief! There are so many letters of accusation that gunny sacks have to be used to contain them. If you don't give them a push, you'll be waiting till the cows come home."

Zhao Xiaohui was carrying a travel bag, and wore an expression on his face less bitter than I had expected. He said he had quit the job in Alibaba, and would take my advice as to where to go next. Pointing to the church, I said that that was the asylum I thought of for him. Zhao Xiaohui looked surprised, and asked if I meant to make him believe in Christianity, which, I should note, he deemed to be a superstition. In the face of any problems, he would rather put his faith in the words of "The Internationale" — we want no condescending saviors to rule us from their judgment hall. I said that one did not have to believe in Christ to go to church. His top priority now, I said, was to find a place to hide. Zhao Xiaohui hesitated, doubting that the church would give him shelter. What was more, he worried that one would become a little silly after hiding out in the church for too long, without contact with the outside world. I said that it was unlikely to happen.

Was there not a movie named *Comings and Goings in Heaven*? In fact, there were plenty of people coming and going even inside the church. There was no need to worry about losing contact with the outside world.

It was time for prayer, when Zhao Xiaohui and I went in. As usual, the nave was occupied by a variety of believers, all of them extremely devout, apparently. Minister Gao was not the officiant on that day. He was just standing beside the officiant. We took a seat and pretended to be one of their number. Zhao Xiaohui was very curious, looking around surreptitiously like a peeping Tom. After a cursory glance around, he lowered his head and asked me in a low voice where these people came from, what jobs they used to do, why they were so committed, and many other questions. As it was not appropriate to start up a conversation in such a solemn and grave atmosphere, I told him that he would understand everything if he stayed here for a few days.

When the prayers were over, after the majority of believers left, a scattered handful remained seated, praying with lowered heads as before. As Minister Gao was about to make his exit from the back door, I dashed over to grab him by the corner of his gown. He paused for a moment, turned round and regained his composure when he saw it was me. I told him one of my friends was in trouble — he was being hunted down, in fact; I hoped that he would lend a hand and let him stay in the church, and so on and so forth. Minister Gao made the sign of the cross before his chest, and on his forehead, saying that the Lord would save him.

I led Minister Gao to where Zhao Xiaohui was, and introduced them, especially emphasizing that Minister Gao had been a postgraduate scholar. Then, turning to Minister Gao, I said that Zhao Xiaohui was a good young man who had been framed, and that the guy who had framed him would follow him till there was nowhere left for him to hide. Zhao Xiaohui had come to seek refuge in the church.

Zhao Xiaohui was not wholly in agreement with what I had been saying. He claimed that he could not stay quietly in the church; he still had a mission to accomplish — i.e. to make charges against Liu Qi at the government offices. His life would be over if Liu Qi was not toppled. When he used to work in the township government, he had had to eat humble pie, but that did not mean that he was weak and easily bullied. I said that no one in the church would care what he did, and that, likewise, he would have to see to his own safety!

I felt something weighing on my foot. I lowered my head to see a little foot stepping on and off mine. When I raised my head again, I saw Xiaomao standing by my side smiling complacently. I patted him on the head, and asked if he was happy here. He nodded, saying that he was happy so long as there were meals for him. I asked if he would go on stealing. He shook his head. He would not, but he himself had been robbed. He told me his former little companions had come to see him to tempt him to continue stealing in the streets, only to be refused by him. So, when they left they stole the bronze cross in his trouser pocket. The cross had been given to him by a believer who claimed to be a university professor. The believer-professor was very kind, and every time he came he would bring Xiaomao something — food, drinks, and a bear hug. Xiaomao enjoyed nestling in the old man's arms, which made him feel as though he were nestling in his own parents', warm from head to toe. His biggest wish was to be adopted by this believer-professor as his godson, and to sit on his shoulders. He was not greedy, and would be content to sit on a father's shoulders just once! During his childhood, how he had admired those kids who had been able to sit on their fathers' shoulders!

"Xiaomao, if that is all you wish, you can sit on my shoulders this once," I said.

"Really?" asked Xiaomao, eyes wide open.

"Yes," I replied. "And so long as you do not steal, I agree to be your godfather!"

Before I could speak anything more, Xiaomao was already preparing to climb onto my shoulders. I squatted down, and he rode on my shoulders as if he were riding a donkey.

45

Dalin had just returned from his visit to Mazi Village. Third Aunt made him bring me two bowlfuls of green beans as a gift; she deplored that this would probably be her last harvest from her own field. With this in mind, she had insisted that some green beans be given to me, in case there might be nothing more of the kind to express her goodwill in the future.

The land in the village had been commandeered. Watching people in the neighboring villages sow their fields, the Mazi villagers could not fail to notice all the farmland lying waste in their own village. Having got used to doing farm work, the villagers were not accustomed to such circumstances. From time to time, they would make a tour of the farmland and meet up with one another to discuss the matter. In the past when they worked the fields, they grumbled a lot about all the hard work. Now when there was no fieldwork, they suddenly felt bored, not knowing what else to do. Live like a city dweller? But how? No one knew. It seemed that the prospects ahead of them were all dark. They wondered whether the route Liben had determined for them would lead to doom or to blessing.

The land requisition had brought about other changes. The most palpable phenomenon was that people from villages near and far within the district were hoping to marry their daughters into Mazi Village, even if no dowry was offered to the girls' families. This made Mazi villagers feel truly exalted. Despite those outsiders' genuine wishes, since the day when a group of county government officials came to hold a mobilization meeting for the land requisition, Mazi Village's household register had been put on hold. At the meeting, the officials declared "the door has been closed firmly." But no-one was foolish enough to believe their words. Well, the door might indeed have been closed, but it was not closed firmly — there was still a narrow opening. Liu Qi's nephew, along with a number of relatives of some leading officials in the county government, had secretly had their households transferred to Mazi Village. Learning about this, of course the villagers were unhappy. They deemed that the entry of these people would result in their losing some of the compensation money which was rightfully theirs. Anyway, no one in the world liked to see other people snatch money from his own money box. But what could the villagers do about it? The best they could manage was to grumble and complain. Other than this, what else could they do? Since all these people enjoyed considerable influence, how would the villagers dare take any practical action against them? If the villagers annoyed these people with more than one cursory glance, they might throw bricks at the villagers in return.

The villagers had not yet received any compensation money — this was what worried them most of all. In spite of the fact that Liben had sworn an oath that he would issue money in person, Shuanhu claimed it was he who had the books with such details as each household's land area as well as the quality grade of each farmland plot, so that it was he who would have the final say regarding both these things; that Liben was dreaming if he imagined that he could issue compensation money to the villagers without him Shuanhu having a say in the matter.

Shuanhu was a wolf. Who among the villagers did not know it? If the issuing of the compensation money was under Shuanhu's control, what prospects did they have? If the compensation money was a bowl of noodles, the villagers understood well enough that after Shuanhu had fished out the noodles and stuffed himself full, very little would be left over for the villagers to divide among themselves. Moreover, Liben's helping Baolai to sue Shuanhu and Shuanniu was no longer a secret. This meant that a fierce confrontation between Liben and Shuanhu was inevitable. Would Liben be a sufficiently tough opponent? If Liben lost the battle and ended up leaving for good, the villagers would be in great distress, and there would be no one to hear their grievances.

The villagers contacted one another in secret, hoping to evict Shuanhu from his office. Song Tongguo, who used to be a close follower of Shuanhu, now allied himself firmly with Beiqiang and Fugui. Song Tongguo had his own scheme: he was plotting to take the place of Shuanhu. He was well aware that the village headship was a juicy position — the position was very juicy indeed, quite exceptionally so, and it would be even more so after the factory was set up. Yes, after the factory was set up, the village head would be like a ruler of a little kingdom. Even the God of Death, dauntless and fearless as he was, dreaded the God of Land, so how much more would the investors in Mazi Village dread Song Tongguo when he became the village head! After investing many millions of *yuan*, the investors would surely seek the favor of the village head (local representative of the God of Land) in order to recover their costs and make money.

Song Tongguo was pretty crafty and full of tricks. Even though Fugui was well-known for abounding in crafty ideas, compared to Song Tongguo, he was only a green hand — in a conflict with Song Tongguo Fugui was like a small sorcerer in the presence of a great one. And in fact, by this time, Fugui resembled a monkey clinging to a wooden pole lifted by Song Tongguo, dancing to the rhythm Song Tongguo whistled. Song Tongguo instructed Fugui to mix some poison with honey, to sandwich the resulting substance in steamed bread, and then to throw the bread into Shuanhu's courtyard so as to kill the vicious dog named Knife Victim. Knife Victim had previously wounded Song Tongtuo, so he hated the beast. Who could have guessed that Fugui, at two or three o'clock on a moonlit night, would, like a man without eyes, throw the bread over at the wrong point of the wall, so that it landed in Shuanhu's pigsty. Thus, instead of Knife Victim getting lethally poisoned, it was Shuanhu's pregnant sow which died.

Was Shuanhu a man to let such a matter go? Now his sow had been lethally poisoned, he was bound to be outraged. Thinking that it must be Baolai who had been responsible, Shuanhu and his family naturally directed their anger at him. Shuanhu's wife was at the forefront of the attack. Standing by the gate to Baolai's courtyard, she hurled her curses into it, her feet jumping up and down in anger and her mouth repeatedly invoking with the dirtiest words both male and female reproductive organs. But this did not soothe her anger; on the contrary, the more she cursed, the more furious she grew. So she began kicking the gate and knocking it with her knees. She used so much force that her knees began to swell.

It so happened that Baolai had just got up and had not opened his gate yet. He had no idea about what was going on outside. Having developed an instinctive dread of Shuanhu's family, and hearing their recriminations, Baolai concluded that another one of his impeachment letters must have been transferred back from a superior level of government, and that by some misfortune the letter must have fallen into Shuanhu's hands. Whenever such a letter fell into Shuanhu's hands, he would flare up like this, as if he were having an epileptic fit. Each time Shuanhu had such a fit, Baolai could do nothing but endure it. But what agony he felt as he did so! Hearing those vicious curses shouted, Baolai felt as if his heart were being ironed with a red-hot flatiron. It was more than he could bear.

Indeed, it had been all getting so unbearable that he had wanted to give up his impeachment campaign. However, Liben would not let him slacken his efforts. To Baolai it seemed he was on a vehicle which at one time had been steered by him, with Liben responsible merely for clearing the obstacles lying in the way. But now it was as if Liben was acting as the driver, while he himself had become a passenger who had no control over whether the vehicle would stop or not.

For Liben, upholding justice was a secondary consideration; his selfish motive was to make use of Qiuli's accident to get rid of the tiger standing in his way.

As Shuanhu's wife almost exhausted her supply of verbal abuse, all the other members of Shuanhu's household came out to launch a more physical campaign. Carrying clubs in their hands, they marched like a military company to the portal of Baolai's place. Breaking into Baolai's courtyard, they first clubbed the two goats to death, then rushed to the chicken-pen and left the chickens either limping or half dead. After these acts, they forced their way into the inner house and set about Baolai and Qiuli with their clubs. It happened that Jidan had come home in the company of a strongly built man, who appeared to have practised martial arts. The man, all violence and no mercy, seized Baolai by the neck. Instantly, Baolai's face turned blue.

The turmoil attracted the whole village to the spot. They all looked on, but no one tried to stop the fight — anyone attempting to would have been regarded as Baolai's accomplice and would have been deemed as a thorn in the side of the village head Shuanhu.

Unable to stand it any longer, Third Aunt put her own life at stake. She shouted "Help them! Or they will be beaten to death," and rushed forth to stop Shuanhu and his people from further abusing the poor couple.

Third Aunt's efforts made all the difference. The fight came to a stop. But the couple, already black and blue, were half dead by this time. Baolai lay on the ground unconscious, with white foam flowing from the corners of his mouth. Qiuli huddled in a corner, her body red and purple all over, and a blister as large as a green walnut bulging on her forehead.

Beiqiang loudly called people to rush Baolai to hospital. But Fugui and Song Tongguo wondered who would pay for the medical treatment? By which they meant that the police should be called now, so that they could come and see how the brute-like village head had beaten the poor couple.

The onlookers grew quite excited.

Some of them remembered the good things Baolai's father, the former village head, had done for the community:

"What a nice man Gangan was! Above all, how many trees he grew! Many hillsides became green."

"Though he looked cold, what a good-natured man he was! No matter who asked for his help, he never turned them away."

"He never embezzled one cent from village funds. And he never skimmed off one cent from individual villagers."

Remembering their former village head, the villagers demonstrated great anger at the horrible injury his son had suffered. Spurred on by the scene, Dapao[28], who was in the crowd, took the lead and shouted, "Down with Shuanhu! Down with the vicious bully!" All the people around him shouted in indignation after him, "Down with Shuanhu! Down with the vicious bully!"

Xiaolin was no longer in charge of the bathhouse: Shuanhu had sacked him, in order to replace him with his own wife. But Xiaolin refused to turn over the bathhouse key to Shuanhu. Liben backed up Xiaolin, telling him not to yield in this confrontation. But Shuanhu said that, as the head of the village, he was the boss; he had ways to fix the matter. After damaging the door's internal lock, Shuanhu bought a padlock as big as an egg-plant and locked the door with it.

As the new manager of the bathhouse, Shuanhu's wife started to collect money from everyone taking a bath: one *yuan* per person. My goodness, who would be willing to spend one *yuan* for the sake of washing the dirt off their body? Consequently, the villagers just viewed the bathhouse from a distance without using it. With no one taking a bath, Shuanhu's wife sat at the entrance, purposeless and bored. As a result, the bathhouse was closed, with the internal equipment being left there to rust.

Shuanhu had declared he would transform the bathhouse into a song-and-dance hall; street girls from across China would be hired and put under the direction of Jidan. The song-and-dance hall would attract city officials and rich men to enjoy its services. Anyway, it would be safe for the officials and rich men to enjoy themselves here. At least the air in the countryside was much better than in the cities.

Given that Xiaolin was unemployed, Liben had advised him to make use of the time to read some books about economics. Claiming that he would soon send a group of people to study in the United States, Liben had promised Xiaolin he would be one member of the group.

Following Liben's advice, Xiaolin had bought some economics books. But every time, before he could finish a couple of pages, he would doze off. He felt what truly interested him remained European and American philosophies.

The very day when Baolai and Qiuli were abused, Xiaolin was reading *Capital* by Karl Marx. He was scratching his head over a difficult economic concept on Page 126 when he overheard the tumultuous noise of people running quickly. Coming out of his house, Xiaolin saw them rushing in the direction of Baolai's place. Hot on their heels, he headed in the same direction, wanting to find out what was going on. Upon arriving, he found Baolai unconscious and Qiuli bruised all over.

Xiaolin felt things had become intolerable. His blood rushed like roaring torrents of the Yellow River. Emulating Dapao, Xiaolin shouted "Down with Shuanhu! Down with the vicious bully!"

46

From the time Baolai was beaten, there was no peace in the village. Several fights took place and several people were sent to hospital. Beiqiang was beaten into hospital, and so was Fugui. Luobo, whose mouth injuries required four stitches, lay in the ward weeping, and threatening to end her life. Xiaolin got one of his arms bandaged up, but he did not stay; instead, he went back to the village and to his normal routine.

It was of great importance that the whole family of Shuanhu moved into the hospital. Shuanhu said he could not stop urinating, because Beiqiang had given his crotch a kick. His wife claimed to suffer from headaches, and complained tearfully to everyone in sight. She said that one moment she would hear a *tcheng-tcheng* sound in her head, as if someone was fluffing cotton with a huge bow inside it; the next moment it felt like a watermelon which had been smashed to pulp on the ground. Jidan lived in a psychiatric ward, where she laughed and wept by turns. When she wept, she wailed in a tone drawn out a thousand miles long, but when she laughed she quacked like a crowing pheasant, so horrible to hear that it brought one out in goose bumps. It was said that thanks to her a pregnant woman in the neighboring ward gave birth prematurely to a poor baby which would not stop convulsing. Jidan insisted that some villager had lifted her skirt to reveal her secret place, a deed so insulting that she felt she could not face the world any more.

It went without saying that Liu Qi would be on the side of Shuanhu. Mid-Autumn Festival was on the fifteenth day of the eighth month by the lunar calendar. During the festive season, while others tried their best to please Liu Qi, Shuanhu did it in a perfunctory way, taking for granted that he was on good terms with him already. Could anyone guess what present he gave? A sack of potatoes! Yes, a lowly sack of potatoes. Liu Qi was worth more than a mere sack of potatoes, wasn't he? Most annoying was that the sack of potatoes left Liu Qi boundless space for interpretation. He apparently thought that the potatoes were there just to cover the really valuable stuff hidden deeper in the bag. In the still of the night, when Liu Qi was alone in the room, he dug his hand in among the potatoes. He mined and mined, but found nothing else; however he assumed that Shuanhu must have buried it even more deeply. So he simply poured out all the potatoes, examining them one by one. He picked up the sack and shook it hard, but still could not find the valuable present he was expecting. Suddenly, he lost his temper. He kicked and stamped, while the potatoes looked as if they were in great pain, some bumping against walls in their flight, some against windows, and some against wooden cases, while others shed tears as they fell into pieces. But all this was not enough to ease his anger. He woke up his father, made him knock at front doors one by one, and get anybody who worked for the township government out of bed. He wanted to hold a meeting. At the meeting, he gave everyone a dressing down, using the dirtiest of words. Zhao Xiaohui was not present, but that did not stop Liu Qi from calling him names, wishing him to be run down by a car when out walking, or to be choked by water when drinking, or to suffer from emphysema when smoking, and to get AIDS when playing around with women. Those assembled all kept their heads down, like frost-bitten saplings. After that, Liu Qi gave them an opportunity to blow the whistle on each other as to who had gossiped behind his back. No one said a word. Liu Qi made them stand in a row to think about their situation, while he himself went to sleep with his head on the table.

Liu Qi briefly entertained the possibility of replacing Shuanhu, but he dismissed it and decided to stand by him as ever before, in view of the consecutive fights in Mazi Village. There had to be an agent who could work on behalf of his interests, and in Mazi Village, except for Shuanhu, everyone was an ungrateful creature. Who else could he rely on but Shuanhu? Liu Qi reported the happenings in Mazi Village to the county public security bureau, and submitted a list of troublemakers. However, the public security bureau did nothing to them: the public security bureau followed instructions from the county government. Given that the county government had set Mazi Village up as a model for new rural community construction, and that this had been extensively reported on by the media, the only thing it could do about the consecutive fights was suppress any news about them. Liu Qi was exceedingly dissatisfied with the county government's attitude. At a wine table, Liu Qi denounced Zhang Shutian, claiming in the presence of Zhang Shutian's secretaries that their boss had a piss-pot for a head.

Zhang Shutian had long been dissatisfied with Liu Qi, but he had had to refrain from showing his anger for fear of Liu Qi's despotic power, and didn't take any actions against him. However, Liu Qi offended him time and again, while turning the township government into a gulag, with officials fleeing one after another, and letters of complaint flying in all directions. If such a situation continued, Zhang Shutain himself wouldn't remain in place for long. What was more, large-scale construction was set to be carried out in Mazi Village, but Liu Qi, ensconced in Gaotai Township like a tiger with its bloody tongue hanging out, stood in the way. Zhang Shutain might never get a piece of the action — he would neither lead away the cow nor even make away with the post it was tied to. Moreover, Zhang Shutian had made a promise to Liben when Liben was complaining that the environment was unworthy of human dignity, and was wavering on investment, pledging that he would transfer Liu Qi from Gaotai once Liben's first investment was in place. It would be as easy as brushing dust from his clothes for a county secretary of the Party committee to remove a township head from his office. But, in fact, he found it rather hard to do so, because Liu Qi, with his fiery and despotic temperament, was no ordinary township head. He would have to plan carefully; otherwise he might lose his own life. After all, the county secretary of the Party committee was not made of steel but an ordinary man. A brick on his head would break it, and a knife in his chest would make it bleed. He had been pondering for a long time whether or not the incident in Mazi Village should be exploited as a heaven-sent opportunity. In other words, might he get rid of Liu Qi — the poisonous tumor, by means of the villagers' hands?

Summoning personnel from the county's relevant departments to a meeting, Zhang Shutian made arrangements to deal with the incident in Mazi Village. He stressed that no force should be used against the masses, no matter what they did, within the territory of Kaiyang; that the officials should not match the masses oath for oath, fight for fight; that the officials should maintain strict discipline and be lenient on the masses when conflicts occurred between them; that the group fight incident in Mazi Village had its origins among officials, and a certain mischievous official in the township government was accountable.

The meeting concerned Liu Qi, but he was intentionally denied an invitation. When Liu Qi learned what had gone on at the meeting, he took a butcher's knife and headed for Zhang Shutian's office. Zhang Shutian's attitude was somewhat frosty, his face snow-pale, and it seemed he would no longer receive Liu Qi in the same way as before — as evidenced by his getting his secretaries to pass him cigarettes and to fetch him water the moment Liu Qi entered his office, while showing no inclination to extend his hand, lest Liu Qi demand a foot. Liu Qi questioned Zhang Shutian as to why he excluded him from the meeting, why he attacked him by making insinuations at the meeting, and why he entrapped and harmed him when he had always benefited by his service. "Damn! If you don't go easy on me, don't expect things will go well for you, Mr Fucked-by-a-donkey! You'll be meat for the butcher's knife!"

Liu Qi took the butcher's knife from his waist and banged the blunt edge down on Zhang Shutian's table. Hearing the roars and knocks, Zhang Shutian's secretaries rushed in, guarded him with their bodies, at the same time doing all that they could to dissuade Liu Qi. Before long, the office, inside and outside, was crammed with people. All of them tried to pacify Liu Qi, but none dared to denounce him. Liu Qi left with a chilling word of warning, "I killed pigs for six years or more, and there's a fat one I wouldn't mind adding to the tally!"

Liu Qi went directly to the hospital. He walked into Shunhu's ward, then, without a word, raised his nose to blow out a thick streak of mucus at him. After that he turned and made for another ward. It chanced that Luobo caught a glimpse of him through the slit of the door when he passed by in the corridor, and at once let out a long modulating wail. Such inauthentic crying was more than he could bear. He went over, intending to spit in her face, and slap her as well. Seeing Liu Qi come in, Luobo sprang up, and looked as if she was about to hang herself from the window with a rope. Liu Qi was driven near to frenzy. It was due to Luobo's gossip-mongering that the conflict in Mazi Village had grown gradually greater, and that he had become a target for Zhang Shutian, the county secretary of the Party committee. Now, his brains totally blank, his eye beaming with fire, he drew out the long knife from under his clothes and poked it right into Luobo's throat, from which a stream of blood spurted out like fireworks, reddening the wall, the sheet, the table, the chair, the floor, and what not.

47

The news about the manslaughter committed by Liu Qi travelled far and wide in Kaiyang. But Liu Qi was nowhere to be found. So long as he was still at large, everybody felt anxious. The public security officers were divided into four groups to search for the culprit. Alongside the public security men went a formidable body of armed police officers, with machine guns in hand and tear-gas grenades at the ready. But apart from a note discovered in Liu Qi's office, they found nothing else of use. Apparently, the note was meant to intimidate. It listed all the people he vowed he must kill, with Zhang Shutian receiving top billing. In all, over twenty people were listed, including the head of the county bureau of finance, the head of the county bureau of land management, Liben, Fugui, Xiaolin, Dapao, and Baolai. At the end of the list was a postscript: "Do not look for me. You won't find me!"

How extremely happy many people felt to learn that Liu Qi had committed manslaughter! Broad smiles beamed from their faces. Unable to restrain their joy, quite a few people bought firecrackers and fireworks. However, because Liu Qi was still at large, none of them dared to set them off.

Liu Qi's fall was an enormous blow for Shuanhu. Along with his wife, he secretly went back home from the hospital and stayed indoors with the gate firmly shut. Jidan returned to Yuebei as stealthily as possible.

Did Shuanhu's shutting himself indoors mean that he would be left alone and at ease? No way! On the evening of the following day, a mourning shed consecrated to the memory of Luobo was set up outside the portal of his courtyard. The premature death of Luobo, a creature who used to be a dab hand at calling names, aroused the whole village to tears — people cherished a fond memory of Luobo and eulogized her. As people talked about Luobo, she was suddenly transformed into an exceptionally brilliant person.

"Luobo, ill-fated Luobo, how could you depart the world so unexpectedly? You left Song Tongguo a widower and your daughter an orphan to get up to who knows what? How will they get on in the world?"

"Luobo, warm-hearted Luobo, you used to help others while they squabbled, though it was none of your business. Now that you are no more, we'll never again see you so courageously intervene when squabbles begin."

"Luobo, how greatly you miscalculated! We Mazi villagers are on the threshold of a good life, we'll be able to eat meat every day, but you are no more. Why didn't you wait till the compensation money was secure in your hand, so you could eat and drink extravagantly in the county seat for once before you left the world?"

In sum, the villagers all thought that it was not Luobo who should have died; that those who ought to have died had not, but she who ought not to have died had. Was it that Heaven had taken the wrong life?

A black tent was erected outside Shuanhu's courtyard gate. At the back of the tent lay a coffin with Luobo's dead body inside; in front stood a broad table, on which were displayed some of Luobo's belongings alongside some fresh and dried fruits as a sacrifice. Though she had passed forty years of age, Luobo had never had her individual photo taken; the only photo with her image in it was that pasted on her marriage certificate, in which she was side by side with Song Tongguo. Given that there was no portrait to revere, a soap case, which was Luobo's favorite item, substituted for it.

The soap case, made of pure silver, had been a gift from a Kuomintang army officer to Fourth Aunt, who bequeathed it to Luobo. Naturally, Luobo cherished it dearly. Deeming that such a valuable soap case was too good to hold cheap soap, she had locked it up in an iron box, and fastened the only key to her belt — suspicious as she was of her husband, Song Tongguo. Her primary anxiety had been that he might steal it and take it to his own ancestral village, which was far away. Many people had alerted her that she had better be really on her guard when dealing with an outsider, in case she were taken advantage of.

Well, what they said made sense. When looking at Song Tongguo's eyes, Luobo had observed that they blinked quickly, and cast furtive glances from time to time at the key tied at her waist. As a result, Luobo had never slept soundly again; her sleep had become light, shallow and short. When she slept, she would often be awoken by nightmares, in which people were robbing her of the beloved soap case.

Of course Luobo was not the sort of stingy creature to keep a good thing for herself. Almost every month she would take the soap case out of the iron box, and carry it aloft around the village to show it off. After all, whose household in this village had a pure silver soap case? Probably no other family had an item of such great value. The antique treasure in Shuanhu's household was just a bronze lamp. To begin with, it looked dirty, and secondly, it was bent out of shape. Moreover, only fools mentioned silver and bronze in the same breath; only idiots deemed copper to be more valuable than silver. Just listen to how the two metals were traditionally described: "genuine gold and silver" and "scrap iron and bronze." Silver was classified with gold, as one of the precious metals. If an equivalence was established between metals and human beings, gold and silver would correspond to prominent officials and nobles. By contrast, bronze was classified with iron, both metals being trash which no one would bother to pick up from the roadside. They corresponded to beggars and tramps in human society.

Now that the soap case, which had given Luobo so much pride, was serving as a substitute for her portrait, who would not feel sad at the sight of it? In front of the soap case, several rows of incense sticks and some candles stood inside an incense burner. The light from the burning candles was reflected in the faces of those who stood before the table, turning their faces the color of tomatoes. Smoke from the incense sticks curled upward and permeated the tent, making the people present look ghost-like.

In mourning wear, Song Tongguo and his daughter knelt down in front of the broad table, behind which lay Luobo's coffined body. A musical band composed of a handful of players was desultorily playing mourning music with *suona* horns, *bangzi* clappers, gongs and drums.

Still playing, one drummer stepped into the mourning tent, and went up to the silver soap case. He picked it up, and scrutinized it again and again. This brought out Song Tongguo's extreme touchiness and antipathy. Approaching the drummer, he snatched the silver case from his hand and thrust it into his own pocket.

Song Tongguo's behavior was, in turn, reproached by folks from the Tian clan. They said the silver case should either be placed in Luobo's coffin, to be buried with her, or should be kept by someone from the Tian clan for Luobo's daughter, till she grew old enough to determine her own fortune; when that day came, the silver case would be given to her. This treasure, which had been passed down from the Tian family, should by no means end up in a Song family member's pocket — to make the thing worse, this particular Song family member was not even local, and he would most probably take the soap box away from Mazi Village.

During this argument about who should possess the soap case, noises were heard coming from Shuanhu's courtyard: Shuanhu's wife was swearing at the top of her voice. It sounded like she was cursing Knife Victim, but closer scrutiny convinced the people that under the pretext of abusing the dog she was hurling bad names at all the villagers. How could this be tolerated? People piped up with their opinions:

"You, the main cause of Luobo's death, haven't been taken to task yet. How dare you bring things to a head like this?"

"Luobo's mourning tent should have been set up in your courtyard! Her body should have been placed on your bed!"

"We people have shown you mercy. We have done you an unheard-of favor by erecting the mourning tent at your gate rather than inside it, but you do not know a good thing when you see it. We've managed to save your face, but you don't mind losing it by provoking a conflict like this. What do you think you're doing? Are you sick of living?"

Again Dapao took the lead and shouted "Kill the family of the bullies!" Whereupon, Luobo's kinfolk and the villagers, male and female, old and young, all launched an attack on Shuanhu's place. People began by dashing stones and broken tile pieces into Shuanhu's courtyard. Then a few people knocked forcefully at his iron gates, some with fists, some with bricks, some with iron sticks. The sounds carried quite a long way. In the meantime, a group of people knocked against his courtyard wall with combined force. With a bang, part of the wall collapsed, and a large opening appeared.

As the wall fell, Knife Victim dashed out. To evade the dog, the people who had attacked the wall scattered in all directions. Knife Victim threw itself at the crowd, snapping at people's heels, and leaving them bleeding. As Knife Victim was raging so ferociously, Song Tongguo picked up a shovel from Shuanhu's next-door neighbor's place and hit the dog with it. The shovel hit the beast precisely on the neck. With a howl, Knife Victim lay down on the ground.

Some people had rushed into Shuanhu's courtyard, picking up spades and hoes to hit him and his family. Seeing that the intruders were too many for them and that they were doomed to lose the battle, Shuanhu and his family escaped through the back door.

In no time, Shuanhu's place was smashed right up, with the chickens and pigs lying in their blood on the ground, half dead.

When the police showed up, the situation had calmed down, except for a group of people arguing how to dispose of the dog's cadaver. The group consisted of Beiqiang, Song Tongguo, Dapao, Fugui and Third Aunt.

Fugui insisted that the dead dog be brought to his house — he would send it to his daughter Layue. His grandson Langwa had got anemia. Having heard that eating dog meat could help with the production of human blood, Fugui wanted to take possession of the dead dog solely for the sake of his grandson. His selfishness provoked the strong resistance of all the people present. They wanted to know why he should have the dog to himself, "Is it because you can spout your piss higher or is it because you can shoot your shit thicker?"

Song Tongguo claimed he was the person the dead dog should go to, rather than anybody else. Without his having sacrificed his own wife, without his daughter's having sacrificed her own mother, would there be any dog meat? Bearing in mind that he had suffered the loss of a human being, how mean people were being! How could they have the heart to take the dead dog away?

Beiqiang said he felt that his legs were weak lately, which seemed to be due to calcium deficiency. Having heard a doctor say that dog meat was warming food that could supplement calcium, he wanted to take some back home. As a matter of fact, Beiqiang was not greedy. He had no intention of taking the whole dog. He only wanted one leg of the dog.

Third Aunt was not fond of dog meat. To tell the truth, she was not fond of any meat, let alone dog meat. The smell of blood made her faint — and if not faint, at least feel like vomiting uncontrollably. It was for Baolai's sake that Third Aunt had asked for the dog meat. In her eyes, Baolai was more pitiable than Luobo: the poor thing was still lying in hospital. It was true he was still alive, but no one could foresee how his condition would develop. According to Third Aunt, the real problem with Baolai was not the cerebral edema caused by the abuse; rather the root problem was his personality. Wasn't there a saying "A nice donkey is more likely to be ridden; a nice man is more likely to be bullied?" A fatal weakness with Baolai was his timidity. To change this, Baolai must be given some wild beasts' meat to eat, so that his internal character would be altered. It was said that people looked like whatever animal whose meat they ate: if they ate wolf's meat, they would look like a wolf; if they ate dog's meat, they would look like a dog; if they ate pig's meat, they would look like a pig; if they ate snake's meat, they would look like a snake; if they ate scorpion's meat, they would look like a scorpion, and so on. Third Aunt harboured no doubts with regard to this maxim. She used to take Taoqi as an example, declaring that she must have eaten scorpion's meat when she was small — that must be why Taoqi's heart had been so vicious. After Taoqi died, Third Aunt ceased citing her as an example, but picked Shuanhu as an illustration instead. As a small boy, Shuanhu loved to eat crabs and often went to the river to catch them. He used to string up the crabs he caught to carry them home. How many chains of crabs he had carried home! He either grilled them with fire, or fried them with oil. Sometimes he even ate a live crab raw. Thanks to his crab-eating habit, one of his front teeth was damaged and gone. However, he had no intention of giving up this hobby; he was as obsessed with eating crabs as ever. Looking back, wasn't it right to say that Shuanhu's peremptory personality and unusual code of conduct had resulted from his having eaten so many crabs? In line with this principle, Liu Qi must have eaten wolf's meat and drunk wolf's milk. Otherwise, why had he had so many wolf-like idiosyncrasies in his character?

If the dog had been a silly dog, Third Aunt would not have bothered with its meat. But because it was a wolf-dog, she could not wait to have its meat for Baolai. Moreover, it was not a common wolf-dog, but one that had been trained by Liu Qi — consequently it had acquired some of Liu Qi's traits: cruel, ferocious, and crafty. Third Aunt wanted to take a part of it home; she would boil the meat; she would make some sticky soup; and she would have Xiaolin deliver the food to Baolai.

In shifts with another villager, Xiaolin had been taking care of Baolai in hospital. Qiuli lay fixed to her own *kang* in the house, with a dark cloud of flies as her only companions. These flies were so fat and so numerous! They flew up and down, as thickly packed as bees in a beehive. What a terrifying scene! Third Aunt did not dread the terrible stifling smell in the house. What she really dreaded were those astonishingly large black flies. Nevertheless, Third Aunt did not yield to them — she sent two meals each day to feed Qiuli. Every three to five days, Third Aunt would clean Qiuli's shit and urine strewn on the floor.

48

I was astonished to discover that Dalin and Ye Lihua were now on the threshold of marriage.

Dalin said that Ye Lihua's rescuing him from Li Tiantian had meant only that he had been transferred from one prison to another. Ye Zhonghua had carried him to the foot of East Hill, and locked him up in a villa there. All right, "locked up" was a bit of an exaggeration, but it was not far from the truth. East Hill was located on the southern rim of Yuebei, about thirty kilometers away.

A brook ran out of the deep vale of East Hill. Weeds grew and wild flowers bloomed brilliantly on both banks, the eastern of which had been lately developed into a settlement of villas. Creamy in color, on terraces high or low, these villas were built along the hill slope. Ye Zhonghua's villa stood highest amid luxuriant woods and verdant grass. Pheasant cackles frequently disturbed the quiet here, and at times a boar would appear. Boars walked with a special gait, their feet pointing outwards and their heads swaying, always puffed up with pride. They were evidently rather nosy, because they often sneaked along the walls and peeped in, as if eager to learn who their neighbors were, where they came from, what backgrounds they had, and whether they would be easy to get along with.

Most of the residents were bosses; certainly, there were some officials, too. Ye Zhonghua's villa was bestowed on his father by the president of an enterprise. It was thanks to his father that this entrepreneur had turned from a mechanic into a billionaire. However, Ye Zhonghua's father didn't like living in it. He visited it only once, but could not sit on the sofa in the drawing room for more than five minutes together. As he suffered from heart disease, he had to send for doctors frequently. But if an emergency occurred in a remote place like this, death would carry him away before any doctor arrived. By now the father listened only to the advice of his primary care physician. If the physician asked him to sit down, he dared not to stand up. If the physician asked him to stand up, he dared not to sit down. If the physician asked him to eat slowly, he would nibble on a deep-fried dough stick from sunrise to sunset. He slept on his side as the physician advised, and as a result the right side of his body grew a thick callus, hard as an iron sheet.

Though the villa had been done up like a palace by Ye Zhonghua, he did not live there except on those weekends when he left home on the pretext of investigating cases. He would come with some young lady. He had a suspicious wife who used to call the villa at the drop of a hat, to make detailed enquiries as to whether Ye Zhonghua was in, or had been in, and if so, whether he was alone or with others. Ye Zhonghua thought that was disgusting. It was said that he had proposed divorce, but that the idea had been utterly rejected by his wife. She knew how much he was good for, and it was a lot. Ye Zhonghua looked, at first sight, exceedingly shabby. You would have thought he was still living in the era of the Red Guards, what with that old green-fading-to-yellow bag with the words "The Red Army fears not the trials of the Long March" printed on it, hanging aslant from his shoulders. Only his wife knew how extravagant his daily life was. In the company of others, he smoked Lanzhou cigarettes, which sold for two *yuan* a pack, but in private he smoked the expensive paper-wrapped Chungwa which he kept in his pocket. When he drank, he only drank Remy Martin, domestic wines and even Maotai being too cheap for him. He had a pair of briefs, made by a famous Italian company, which cost over a thousand *yuan*. In his wife's eyes, Ye Zhonghua was a shining gold mountain. She was not a fool; her brains had neither been shocked by electricity nor drowned in water. Why would she give it up without a fight? As time went on, she shifted the focus of her supervision and control from the man to his wallet. Each day she would check it, but what she didn't know was that her almighty husband's head was not made of rock either. Ever since she had begun checking his wallet, Ye Zhonghua had two, one for his own use, and one for her check.

At first, a maid had been hired to take care of the villa. A polio victim, awfully deformed and somewhat scary to look at, she was ushered into the villa, after going through the hostess' strict selection process. Among those who had competed to serve Ye Zhonghua, many were dressed to the nines, and quite a few had their faces made up — all afraid that they would fail because they were lacking in the good looks department. Little did they know that the last thing Ye Zhonghua's wife wanted was beauty; and it was the polio victim, whom they had almost all mocked, who was chosen. Ostensibly just a maid, the polio victim was in fact the real hostess of the villa. As the Ye family seldom came, she was the only one who lived there permanently. Once she had cleaned the whole house, which she did every three days, and once she had mowed and watered the lawn, she just stayed indoors and enjoyed life. She could watch foreign movies on the luxurious projector, or go through the great pile of porn DVDs. With hot spring water available twenty-four hours a day, she might even sleep in the bath tub. The sofa and bedding of high quality were a new experience for her. More wonderful was that there was a mountain of expensive articles kept in two of the rooms. Ye Zhonghua seemed often to bring in goods, but not to count them. Perhaps he himself was not sure what had come in and how many things there were. The polio victim, though short of physical strength, had a full complement of brains. She knew how much a Rolex watch was worth, and that a gold *ding*[29] was much more valuable than ten tractors put together. The dazzling gifts, the exquisitely-packed cigarettes and wines and cognac, hadn't been inventoried at all. The wines and cognac were always kept intact, while the cigarettes would not be disposed of until they nearly went moldy. The cigarettes were never counted when they were stashed. Even if a carton of Marlboro dropped off the minibus, Ye Zhonghua just cast a look at it and made no effort to pick it up.

Ye Zhonghua's attitude toward these things had evidently been picked up by the polio victim. She knew that there were no records of the cigarettes and wines, or of anything except the Rolex watches and gold *dings*. The room would seem as packed full as it had been before if as many as ten cartons of cigarettes were removed. A wicked idea occurred to her. She first stole a bottle of Remy Martin, then let her father drink it at home, only to see him hospitalized as a result. She couldn't help lamenting the destiny of the poor. "You want to give them a taste of the high-life, but most likely end up killing them." The first theft was only to test Ye Zhonghua's response to the loss of the cognac. Her judgment of the matter was confirmed. In the following months, Ye Zhonghua had been in and out of the room three or four times without noticing that a bottle of cognac was missing.

So the polio victim stole a carton of cigarettes each month and sold it to the store outside the villa area. The proprietor was a middle-aged fat woman, willing enough to spend a hundred *yuan* on a paper-wrapped Chungwa offered by the polio victim, but no more than that. If only she hadn't, as she did on one occasion, suspected that the carton of Chungwa which the polio victim was trading was fake, their business arrangement would have gone on forever. But the purchaser insisted that it was fake, while the seller thought this was an attempt to blackmail her. So far as the polio victim was concerned, it was impossible for fake cigarettes to exist in Ye Zhonghua's home. She muttered in her mind, "Humph! Do you think I don't know what you are up to, replacing the real with the false? Do you think you are the only wise guy in this world?"

But it turned out to be the store-owner who was the more stubborn of the two. She reported the polio victim's deeds to Ye Zhonghua. But Ye Zhonghua didn't denounce the polio victim; instead, he gave her some money and told her to fuck off back to where she had come from.

When Dalin moved in, the polio victim was still the keeper of the villa. Knowing that Dalin was Ye Lihua's boyfriend, she flattered him with her honey sweet tongue, telling him that he was very much like Jang Dong-gun, the Korean actor. Dalin, out of courtesy, returned the compliment by praising her as "infirm in body but firm in will." However, they had lived under the same roof no more than three days before the polio victim was dismissed. Ye Zhonghua told Dalin he had intended to hire another maid, but now he had given up on the idea. He would give the key to Dalin, and let him take care of the villa. Ye Zhonghua made a point of looking around the room in which the most precious goods were kept, and said to Dalin, "Take whatever you like when you want to smoke or drink, but do not pawn them for money." And then he added that, as a matter of fact, he had long since discovered the goods in this room were diminishing, but he feigned ignorance for fear of disgracing the polio victim. Chaotic as they were, the goods in the rooms were itemized, with the inventory kept in his computer.

In this way, Dalin became the villa's housekeeper and security guard.

49

In the months following Dalin and Li Tiantian's separation, I did not hear anything from Li Tiantian. But one day, out of the blue, I got a phone call from her. She claimed she was almost dead with anguish; she was bitterly aggrieved; she didn't want to live any longer; she was about to commit suicide; but before she died, she would like to see Dalin so as to settle their affair completely — after all, she hated to bring her regrets, complaints and grievances to the underworld. She emphasized that the so-called settlement was not a monetary settlement, for she well understood that poor Dalin could not pay her the money he owed even if he were to sell himself into slavery. She said what she would like to settle was their emotional entanglements.

I had no soothing for her to hear. What a volatile woman! She might look like a sunny and cloudless sky one minute, and hurl thunder and lightning the next. Who in the world could endure her?

I shouted into the receiver, telling her never to call me again. I said, "I have nothing to do with Dalin, and nothing to do with the conflict between you and him."

Li Tiantian cried at the other end of the line, saying that I was insulting her.

Having no interest in hearing what she was about to say, I hung up. When she called again, I simply switched off my mobile phone in exasperation.

I learned from Dalin that in the period when Li Tiantian was giving him a hard time, she also managed to procure a young lover — who was in his twenties and impressively handsome. Very soon, Li Tiantian's passion for the young man burned fervently. She treated him as her beloved treasure; they went as a couple to teahouses, movie theaters, and song-and-dance halls; he slept with her in her house at night. Life went on like this for about two months, when one morning she woke up to find him gone. He had vanished like melted ice. At first, she did not take it seriously. She did nothing more than look around and ask after him. But as she discovered that the jewelry box on her dressing table had gone, she really panicked, because in addition to a diamond ring, the box had also contained a bank savings book with a total of 80,000 *yuan* deposit. Strangely enough, she had revealed the password to the young man. This is how it happened:

One day, as they were chatting, her young lover said he would like to check whether her love for him was genuine or not: if she really loved him, she would not hide anything from him. At that moment, Li Tiantian must have been enchanted, being so deeply immersed in her fanciful and wonderful illusions that she altogether lowered her guard. She told him how much money she had in her bank account, when her birthday was, and what type of men she liked. Unconsciously, she revealed the account password. She regretted for a short while leaking the information, but then she consoled herself, "Anyway, he has already agreed to marry me, so what is there to fear? Money is what he needs, and money is what I have; the only way to win him over is with money."

Hoping against hope, Li Tiantian rushed to the bank to report the loss of the bankbook, only to find that the money had been withdrawn on the afternoon before her young lover disappeared. She mobilized dozens of people to search for the youth in the railway station, the bus station, the intersections of the streets and other places, but the search was fruitless. She cried and cried, however all this crying failed to bring her lover back to her. Then she remembered Dalin; she recalled how nice Dalin had been to her; she even recollected the romantic and sweet moments when he made love to her. Dalin had a special smell which was tremendously alluring to her. Whenever she thought of the smell, all the pores of her body would warm and dilate, making her feel faintly intoxicated.

As a matter of fact, before calling me, Li Tiantian had approached Ye Zhonghua, asking him to give Dalin back to her. She enumerated various shortcomings Dalin had, implying that even though Dalin was good-looking, his bedroom skills were not good. Ye Zhonghua grew impatient with Li Tiantian's conduct. With an angry face, he told her never again to come to his workplace. Li Tiantian sat down on a sofa and began sobbing; she pleaded with Ye Zhonghua to ask, out of pity for her, his sister Ye Lihua to give up Dalin, saying that if she did, she was ready to accept whatever conditions they proposed, including offering a sum of money to Ye Lihua.

"What is money? A mere superficial possession," she said.

Ye Zhonghua corrected Li Tiantian, declaring that she was wrong. He said, "To those who have money, money is a superficial possession; but to those who don't, money is life!"

Li Tiantian said flatteringly, "Your thoughts are profound, like a philosopher's. You're truly worthy to be called a leader! You have so much insight!"

Ye Zhonghua corrected Li Tiantian once more, saying that his words were quoted from a magazine he had read, and were not his own original creation.

Li Tiantian failed to get what she desired from Ye Zhonghua. She even failed to get Dalin's new mobile phone number. It was then that she remembered me.

After I switched off my mobile phone, she called me many more times. She also went to my workplace to look for me. Since I did not go to my office often, she frequently had occasion to open Xue Yulu's office door. There, in my workplace, she gave a tearful account of her misery in front of several people. Having finished her account, and finding that her tears had failed to move Xue Yulu, she adjusted her strategy — she started to denigrate me, claiming that I had courted her, and that, for no better reason than that I had failed to win her hand, I had been trying every means to ruin her relationship with her fiancé. She said that I had an evil heart and evil bowels, and that I was completely responsible for the break-up between her and Dalin.

As Li Tiantian's account touched on this matter, Xue Yulu's interest was abruptly aroused. Again and again she checked with Li Tiantian, asking her "Is that true?" The look in Xue Yulu's eyes was as drifting fog driven by a swift wind. Both corners of her mouth lifted with excitement.

Having worked together with Xue Yulu for more than ten years, I knew her pretty well. Apart from talking about clothes and money, the only joy in her life was other people's misfortunes. As a media person, she could not care less about domestic issues or international events. If you talked about the Palestine situation with her, she would ask you, "You're not going there for a holiday, so what does it have to do with you?" If you talked about Freud with her, she would blurt out, "That old guy was a rascal." If you talked about Churchill with her, she would put on a disdainful look and say, "Churchill was too ugly-looking." Only the misfortunes of certain people she knew, or of people she knew of, could really stimulate her interest. When Liu Xiaoqing was imprisoned, she delighted in the news for days; she could not help humming songs while walking; as she chatted with people she would switch the topic as quickly as possible to Liu Xiaoqing, announcing that she had long ago conceived a dislike for her, that she had not only hoped but also long foreseen that Liu Xiaoqing would experience a crisis. "And now look, hasn't it happened as I predicted?" she said. The way in which she made her declaration gave the impression that Liu Xiaoqing's imprisonment had not been the result of her tax evasion and fraud, but had been the outcome of Xue Yulu's inexhaustible curses.

When Luo Xiao was still working for the newspaper, if she and her boyfriend had a row, and if Xue Yulu learned about it, she would invariably feel extremely happy. She would sing; she would call out cheerfully; her laughter would echo back and forth down the whole corridor. The break-up of Luo Xiao and her boyfriend delighted Xue Yulu so much that she could not stop talking about it. She invited all the colleagues to a dinner, at which she got well and truly drunk. Poor Luo Xiao got so annoyed that she fainted and collapsed on the floor, and ended up hospitalized for days. After resigning from the job, Luo Xiao opened a beauty parlor, thinking that in this way she could manage, eventually, to steer clear of Xue Yulu. But things did not turn out as Luo Xiao had hoped. Xue Yulu paid special attention to Luo Xiao's business. She asked her "brothers and sisters" working in the Industry and Business Administration circle to "see to" Luo Xiao's business. Accordingly, her "brothers and sisters" "saw to" Luo Xiao so effectively that Luo Xiao could hardly survive. Every eight or ten days, Luo Xiao's business would without fail be closed for one or two days. Xue Yulu took great pleasure, whenever Luo Xiao's parlor was closed, in not only knowing precisely when it was closed but also in knowing the exact offense which caused the closure. Additionally, she knew what penalty had been demanded from Luo Xiao, how she had argued with the Industry and Business Administration personnel, and how she had cried. The days when Luo Xiao cried were those when Xue Yulu would lift her cup high in celebration. How much happiness Luo Xiao had created for Xue Yulu!

I got a phone call from Xue Yulu, who asked me to go to the press house. According to her, someone wanted to meet me there. I asked her who it was, but she refused to say.

I hurried to the press house. As I pushed open the door to Xue Yulu's office, I identified Li Tiantian at once, and instantly, with boiling blood rushing to my head, backed out. Running after me, Xue Yulu grasped my coat sleeve, and strove to drag me back into her office.

"What's the matter? What's up?" she asked me.

"The woman sitting in your office is crazy. Why do I need to see her? I have nothing to say to her!" I replied.

Just then, Li Tiantian dashed out of the room. To my utter surprise, without saying a single word, she fell to the ground, firmly holding my legs.

I yelled loudly at her, "What are you doing? Shame on you! Instead of behaving like the boss you are, you look just like a soaked-through wet hen!"

Instead of answering me, Li Tiantian merely raised her voice to its top pitch and howled as loudly as she could. People came out from every office to look. They looked and asked one another, "What's the matter? What's going on?"

The guard was drawn to the scene too. Having divined Xue Yulu's intention, the guard simply stood around to watch, the smile on his face showing his great delight in this misfortune. Faced by the puzzled eyes of the people, I was at a total loss as to how to resolve the situation, my face turning red with embarrassment.

Seeing that so many people were around, Li Tiantian cried more loudly. She called me a bad man who had violated her.

My goodness! How could she have invented such a shameless charge! Being unable to control my temper any more, I lifted my hand, and gave her two blows.

50

I complained to Dalin that whereas he was happily living in the villa and was about to marry a girl from a senior official's family, I had become something that was neither a human being nor a ghost — having been bitten by a mad dog that he had provoked. Poor me!

Dalin smiled bitterly. He said everything was his fault...everything his fault. He didn't know what destiny had decreed that such a group of women should intrude into his life, each as sticky as paste oozing out of a pot. To cheer me up a little, he passed me a cigarette and apologized again and again, saying that it was his bad fate to blame, and affected by his bad fate, my life too was doomed to be overshadowed by black clouds. I said, "Oh, come off it. From now on, don't tell me about the woman you have just hooked up or broken off with."

In fact, Li Tiantian's behavior on that very day had a pretty negative impact on me. Within a day, the story had circulated throughout the whole press house. Almost everyone was told that I had raped a restaurant boss, who, though disfigured, was very rich, and, what was more, one of our clients. Some were whispering behind me, others were pointing at me when they saw me, and still others were enquiring about who I was. Even Master Worker Kang, the boiler maintenance man, came to the department in which I was working, and peeped in at me. He wanted to know what I was, and whether or not I looked like a hooligan.

It seemed that colleagues in my own department were trying to shun me. At first, I felt a little frustrated and embarrassed, but I made that famous dictum of Wang Shuo[30] — "As a hooligan I fear none!" — my own. Yes, since I had become the famous hooligan of the press house, what did I have to be embarrassed about? What did I have to hide? I wrote with a brush "As a hooligan I fear none!" on the front of my desk to warn all who saw it: Don't provoke me, or I'll fight you at the cost of my life!

Xiang Wenhua had no idea what was going on between Li Tiantian and me. He had been absent for quite a few days. No one would inquire about the cause or causes of his absence. It was alright for him to be absent forever. Who would deduct his allowances and bonuses, just because of his absence? And there was no reason why he should fail to accomplish his monthly publication task, since the publication statistician was President Sun's niece, and she had been keeping a close eye on it. If she discovered Xiang Wenhua might not be able to finish his monthly task, she would report to higher authorities, level by level. As a result, leaders at different administrative levels would put their heads together to come up with solutions for him — to have his name signed on articles written by other journalists, or to designate someone else to write in his stead. And there would, of course, be green lights all the way from the initial censor to the final publication. In addition, the statistician would count a five-hundred-word article as one of eight hundred. A rumor that Xiang Wenhua was going to work as assistant to the general manager of the provincial electric power company caused great panic among heads big and small in the press house.

It was inconceivable that Xiang Wenhua might leave the press house! He must not leave, absolutely not! If he left, would they still be able to get Governor Xiang's help? There was no doubt that due to Xiang Wenhua people in the press house had benefited enormously, especially the heads to whom nothing was denied. To have Xiang Wenhua was like having a stout and robust tree. When you shook it during difficulties, it would drop whatever you wanted. For example, during the professional appraisal season, the press house would be able to acquire a few quotas more for senior positions each time, not to mention quotas for foreign travels: it seemed that the sun had never ceased shining on the press house, for there were always places for its employees whenever the municipality, the province, or some subordinate department organized a delegation to go abroad. A cow as precious as that, who could see it go with equanimity? The press house had long been planning to promote him to the post of division director, and had talked with him several times about it, but, to general consternation, he had not the least interest in such a position, rejecting it as too exhausting, too troublesome, without any freedom. Most unbearable to him were meetings, at which a newspaper or a document would be read for what seemed like an eternity; just as one leader, with a superhuman effort, ended his lengthy contribution at long last, another leader would pipe up with supplementary comments, and still another would add that there was something he wished to emphasize — he would rather cut his throat with a knife than endure such tedium.

That very afternoon saw Xiang Wenhua, who had not been spotted for a long time, saunter into the office and toward his desk. All of a sudden, his eyes brightened as they lit on the words I had written on the front of my desk. He halted, squinting at them in momentary astonishment. Ages seemed to pass, but he still did not seem to have figured out what they meant. As he stared at the words, I in turn stared at him, but he showed no sign of wishing me to speak. Hitting his forehead twice with his fist, he slumped listlessly onto a seat.

Xiang Wenhua's comings and goings attracted no attention from his fellow colleagues. It seemed that he came for the sole purpose of sleeping. As usual, he bent over his desk and fell asleep straight away. In no time his snores could be heard coming from the office, heavy and loud, like rumbling thunder.

No one made a fuss about Xiang Wenhua's snores which, like ambient music, had become part of community life for four or five years. There were times when his colleagues would have felt a bit lonely without his snores. The arrival of Xue Yulu attracted all eyes, because she had seldom entered this spacious office, even though she was director of it. If she needed to talk with someone, she would just shout in the doorway, and the one who had been named would follow her to her office. Of course, it was Xiang Wenhua who was most frequently summoned, but he was not at all grateful for this distinction, and his face invariably wore an impatient expression. Today, instead of shouting loudly, Xue Yulu walked stealthily up to him and patted him gently on the shoulder. Xiang Wenhua opened his bleary eyes and looked blankly at her. Xue Yulu did not speak, but waved her hand at him in a conspiratorial fashion. After Xue Yulu left, Xiang Wenhua straightened his back and walked out.

A few minutes later, Xue Yulu's loud voice sounded down the corridor. She was calling me, and there was a note of real contempt in her voice. I walked out of my office, asking her why she had shouted so loud like that. Xue Yulu's face, pink a moment ago, immediately turned eggplant-purple. She first frowned, then pouted her lips toward President Sun's office, and said President Sun wanted to see me.

It was as though the sun had risen in the west. In the thirteen years, since I had first stepped through the gate of the press house, this was only the second time that President Sun had summoned me. The first time had been eight years earlier, when President Sun was still an editor-in-chief, subordinated in the hierarchy to an enemy of his. In order to overthrow this big shot, Editor-in-Chief Sun sent for me and asked me to sign a letter of petition.

I remembered that he had smiled very sweetly, his mouth cracking like a stuffed steamed bun which had not been kneaded well, his face radiant with warm, soft beams. He praised me in the most exaggerated terms, saying that I was highly gifted, but it was a shame that I, as a steed which could run a thousand miles a day, had not met with Bo Le, the master horse appraiser; that once he became the first chair, he would employ my services; that with my character and competence, I should at least be appointed a departmental director or something like that. I did not take his words seriously, although I signed the letter of petition, as he asked me to. A few months later, with a shake, Editor-in-chief Sun magically changed into President Sun, who, to my great surprise, seemed to have entirely forgotten his commitment, and from then on his once beaming face congealed into a cold cement wall. I greeted him when I met him, but he answered only with a low buzzing snort, without looking at me. Soon he put an end to the old game, and redisposed the pieces as he wished. Of course, I was not a piece on his chessboard, and later I heard stories about the many people who called at his home, about the leaders who wrote him messages, and the staff members who shed tears over their failure to secure an important position. What a tough job! Too many eyes were watching, and too many mouths were eager to talk. In order to pacify the rolling wave of saliva, and to prove that he had only appointed people on their merits, he changed his plan and arranged for his nephew to be the vice director of the distribution department, instead of the director of the advertisement department — a post sought after by everyone.

On this occasion, President Sun was seated behind a large desk, which, like a mountain plateau, lay between him and me stranded on the opposite side. Cold air seemed to emanate from his face whose expression was like iced fruit jelly, while a few lonely strands of white hair trembled on his bald head. His eyes, hidden behind a pair of glasses, were like two deep caves, and it was very hard to see clearly whether or not there was any happiness in them.

President Sun glared at me. His mouth worked, but made no sounds. His heavy breathing was indicative of extreme indignation. Indeed, he was furious! He threw a document at me, which landed on the sofa where I was sitting. I picked it up. It was an internal report issued by the higher authorities, which listed, in great detail, events in the publishing establishments over a six-month period, and which named and criticized the administration of several units. No doubt, our press house was on the list. To my surprise, I found my name in a paragraph that criticized our press house. I could not help but shiver. I felt dizzy, hot and dry, as if my whole body was on fire; drops of sweat rolled down from my forehead and wet my trouser legs. I managed to calm down, and read the paragraph carefully once again, and finally realized that it was about my interviewing the temporary worker Song Laowan of the detention house. In the document I was said to have intimidated the litigant and blackmailed the concerned institution with fabricated accusations. How ridiculous it was! In what way had I intimidated Song Laowan? In what way had I blackmailed the detention house? The detention house hid money in the fruit basket given to me, and I had handed the money over to Xue Yulu. Could this be called blackmailing?

I said, "He who does not investigate has no right to speak. Heeding only one party can all too easily confuse the facts." President Sun spoke at last, but his voice was distorted with anger. He said there was to be no argument, no explanation, because he had no interest in listening. What he cared about was that the prestige of the press house had suffered greatly, and all its efforts for a whole year had been brought to nothing on account of me — the fly in the ointment. I said, "Didn't I hand over the money given to me in the fruit basket?" President Sun impatiently waved his hand for me to shut up. He made me leave his office to reflect on my mistake, and be prepared for a legal investigation and whatever the judicial tribunal decided. No sooner had I stepped out of his office than he followed up with a few soft emotional words, to the effect that he had no intention of throwing me into prison, because both he and the press house would be dishonored if any of its employees were imprisoned during his term of administration. He would with might and main build a dam to stop the advancing torrential flood.

51

After exiting from President Sun's office, I tried to call Xiang Wenhua, but failed to reach him.

When evening closed in, he finally answered my call and said he was in the song-and-dance hall run by Xue Yulu's brother Xue Lihan.

"Are you there singing songs?" I asked him.

"No. I'm here for something else," he said.

"Could you come out? I'm eager to see you," I said.

"What's wrong with the world? Have people been possessed by ghosts during these last few days?" Xiang Wenhua sounded quite impatient.

He complained that so many people were making appointments to see him, and all of them claimed they had urgent things to discuss. Not having the magical ability to divide himself into multiple Xiang Wenhuas, how could he deal with the situation?

"I understand very well how busy you are," I said. "But what I want to discuss with you is no ordinary thing; otherwise, I wouldn't have bothered you so late in the evening."

"Okay, then," Xiang Wenhua said. He agreed that, after having handled the issue at hand, he would see me. I suggested we meet at Alibaba Teahouse.

I hoped I could meet Larz at Alibaba. I wanted to ask how his mother was. I even wanted to introduce him to Liben and ask Liben to give him money for the sake of saving his poor mother's life. Anyway, 100,000 RMB would be an insignificant sum for Liben.

I seated myself in a room, when in came a waitress. I told her I would like Larz to serve me instead. With downcast face, the waitress said she didn't know who Larz was, and then left. In a minute, the head waitress came in and explained that the waitress was newly hired, and therefore didn't know Larz.

The head waitress told me, "Larz has quitted his job here. There was a middle-aged woman who came almost every day. Finally, one day she came and took Larz away." Grimacing, the head waitress snorted, then said under her breath, "An old cow hungry for tender new-grown grass!"

After ascertaining the middle-aged woman's figure and features, I felt quite sure that she must be Kang Yuanyuan.

Strangely enough, at the very moment when Kang Yuanyuan's image flashed into my mind, my mobile phone rang. The number showed the caller was none other than her. I asked Kang Yuanyuan if she was with Larz.

"Yes, we are together. Is there anything wrong with that?" she asked.

"I'm now at Alibaba. They told me Larz had run away with you."

"I have something serious to tell you," she claimed.

"What is it?"

Kang Yuanyuan told me that through her efforts, the provincial charity funds committee had allotted twenty thousand *yuan* for Larz's mother to receive medical treatment; in addition, she herself had donated fifty thousand *yuan*; and her six classmates in the United States had each donated thirty thousand *yuan*. So money was no longer a problem for Larz's mother's kidney transplant. The only problem now was that a suitable kidney could not be found. Kang Yuanyuan asked me to publish a report about Larz's mother: it was probable that my report would get some dying people's attention and that they might be willing to donate their kidneys to her.

On the phone, Kang Yuanyuan emphasized Larz's filial piety in taking care of his mother day and night, without anyone else to help — with the result that Larz had been reduced to a gaunt figure with haggard features.

"By now he is nothing more than a walking skeleton!" Kang Yuanyuan said.

"I can't do as you ask," I replied. "At least for the time being, I cannot."

"Why not?" Kang Yuanyuan asked.

"I can't explain it clearly to you now," I replied simply.

I hung up the phone. The document which President Sun had showed me suddenly surfaced in my mind, as did his twisted face.

I called Xiang Wenhua once more. He answered, "I'm afraid I can't come over to see you tonight. Whatever issue you have, let's wait till tomorrow."

As though from an electric shock, my brain echoed with a big "Bang!"

"Why can't you come? We have made the appointment, haven't we?" I asked Xiang Wenhua.

In a tone similar to the one I had assumed when I spoke to Kang Yuanyuan, Xiang Wenhua said, "I can't explain it clearly to you now."

After I asked him again and again, he reluctantly let drop four words, "Xue Lihan killed someone!"

"Really?" I asked.

I really wanted to hear more! But Xiang Wenhua had already hung up.

I set down my phone. As though I were a wicked man taking delight in seeing other people suffer, I felt an irrepressible joy surging up in my heart. Although I had never touched alcohol, I suddenly had the impulse to have a good drink. Ordering a 250 ml-bottle of liquor, I drank every drop of it. To me, the neon lights outside looked exceptionally charming tonight, and the liquor seemed delicious. Boy, I really felt exhilarated!

The following day, even though I had no plausible reason to go to the press house — since my work duties had been suspended — still I went there. I wanted to see if Xue Yulu, who habitually laughed heartily at others' misfortune, would laugh heartily when her own brother was in trouble. To be honest, I went there hoping to see her in tears. I hoped to see grief break her heart. I hoped to see her cry so hard that she lost her eyesight.

But Xue Yulu was nowhere to be found in the press house. The journalists who had been dispatched to report the incident had long been back. They had worked out a detailed report, but President Sun had prohibited its release. According to President Sun, at this crucial moment when Yuebei City was going to host a Hong Kong & Macao investment invitation conference, the publicity of this case would damage the city's image, jeopardizing the prospects of investment.

By now the violent act committed by Xue Lihan had become a widely discussed topic around the city, and you could tell from the expression of the press house people's eyes they were eager to talk about it. It seemed that everybody was on guard not to betray a secret, while involuntarily wishing to reveal it, and then exchange their views. Everywhere in the press house — in the offices, under the shade of trees, and by the gateways — there were people in pairs or groups talking in the manner of secret agents. Once they sensed that they were being spied on, they instantly dispersed.

I wished to join them and share the happiness I had waited so long for, but without success. They were on their guard against me; they were skeptical toward me. It was as if I had been a notorious traitor. When I approached them, they gave the impression of wanting to run away as fast as their legs could carry them. When I button-holed them to ask about the stabbing, they kept shaking their heads, saying that they didn't know much about the matter, or, alternately, that they had never heard about it at all. Their attitude was a huge blow to me, making me feel that I had been removed not only from the press house but also from people's hearts. I seemed to be a bird without a branch to perch its feet on, or a dog wanted by no one.

I eventually found a person who could inform me of the way events had transpired. That person was Xiang Wenhua, who had just arrived at the press house, to which he had driven in Xue Lihan's BMW. He parked the car by the gate without turning off the engine or locking the door, then got out and hurried to his office. He was here to pick something up, and wanted to leave immediately afterward. As he was about to depart, I accosted him. Putting on an air of sincere concern, I asked, "How is Xue Lihan now?"

Though a little impatient, Xiang Wenhua did not evade the question. He said, "Xue Lihan was jailed last night. But what he did might be considered justifiable self-defense."

"How so?"

"Because the victim waved a wine bottle at him and threatened to beat him with it. So he took out a knife. However his intention was not to kill the guy, but to intimidate him and force him to back off."

I had many more questions to ask, but Xiang Wenhua struggled out of my grasp and quickly left. Suddenly I felt a keen sense of loss, as though I had been abandoned by the whole world. The tiny hope I had cherished of watching Xue Yulu in trouble, with a helpless look in her tearful eyes, was about to collapse. Why had Heaven turned against me?

I did not go to work on the following day. Instead, I wandered about the church gate. I felt like entering it to see if Zhao Xiaohui and Xiaomao were still there; I wanted to know how they were doing; I wondered if I should join them. While I was hesitating, an old newspaper-peddler passed by me, and his shouted advertisement contained a reference to the song-and-dance hall murder case. I hailed the old man, asking him which newspaper carried a report on the case. He took out a newspaper, which turned out to be one published by my press house. I paid for it and quickly discovered the article, on the 2nd page. The name of the author was of particular interest: Xiaolu, which was the pen name of Xue Yulu.

The truth was that Xue Yulu used her real name most of the time. It was only when she encountered cases that needed a pseudonym that Xue Yulu would become Xiaolu.

Reading the article, I learned that the victim was a migrant worker.

According to the report, after having enjoyed himself with a *xiaojie*, the migrant worker refused to pay, complaining that he had been charged too much, and alleging that the parlor was blackmailing him. He ended up grappling with the headwaiter in the lounge. He was waving a beer bottle in the air, with the intention of killing the headwaiter, when Xue Lihan, courageous boss that he was, summoned up the courage to stop the violence. Seeing that the bottle was about to hit a young lady on the head, Xue Lihan took out his knife to frighten away the migrant worker. But much to everyone's surprise, the migrant worker threw himself onto the knife. Xue Lihan endeavored to dodge, but unfortunately he failed to do so quickly enough. Consequently, the knife thrust into the migrant worker's heart. If it had not been for Xue Lihan's timely valour, God knows how many people would have lost their lives to the rage of the crazy terrorist.

My goodness! Xue Lihan had been portrayed as a hero! Congratulations! One more great hero had emerged out of the blue!

PART II

52

I had had a discussion with Liben about the meaning of time. He seemed keen to know what it was, but neither the Chinese nor the English dictionaries he had consulted had provided an exact answer. Not that these dictionaries were lacking in explanations, but that Liben regarded them as too mechanical. He liked books, but was opposed to taking what he read on trust. Not until he had cudgeled his brains for what seemed like an eternity did he think of a slogan which had been popular in China for a long time: Time is money!

Making a point of disputing this, I asked Liben if he could calculate how much an hour was worth in US Dollars. Liben criticized me for being too captious, saying, "It is only a metaphor. Why look at it from a pragmatic perspective? Lost in pragmatism, one would become vulgar, and such a profound aphorism would be redolent of the stink of money." Nevertheless, Liben provided illustrations through citing examples, saying that for an idler time was worth nothing, but for a Wall Street investor one minute might harvest a million or ten million US dollars. I asked if harvesting that much profit had a meaning. Would the investor live forever with that much money? Liben said of course it had a meaning. How was one to display the value of one's life? Was it not measured by the money one earned? I challenged him, saying, "Is it meaningful to live in this world? Every person is just a lonely traveller in this world. In order to console themselves, people endow their deeds with this or that significance, but isn't life a vain dream in the end?"

I was recalling this debate between Liben and me because I had indeed been experiencing the flight of time at first hand. In a blink of an eye, six years had passed, and nothing was what it had been, just fragments left by time as it went its fugitive way, some of which, clear or blurry, were picked up by my memory. Mazi Village was gone. The whole village had been relocated to a terrace five kilometers away, its peninsula-shaped site vacated to make room for Meiteng Enterprise Ltd — a newly established Sino-US joint venture. It seemed that the company had encountered some problems, to judge from its chimneys which, though they had been standing high for quite some time, discharged smoke only intermittently, stopping every few days before resuming their function again.

The former Mazi villagers had been collectively moved to a newly established village with the weird name of Sakelu Park. The name was given by Liben who had wanted the village to make a clean break with its past, and its people to draw a line under theirs. At first, the villagers could hardly get used to it. Liben told them that there was a famous village in the United States named Sakelu Park. Its people lived by farming sunflowers, their houses were surrounded by flowers, and it attracted visitors from all over the country. He had the same ambition — to construct a Chinese Sakelu and turn it into a tourist paradise, so that the villagers, who had been farmers for generations, would be able to lure visitors with the beauty of their hometown. Gradually, the villagers accepted the new name and took pride in it. Ah, how uncouth the name of Mazi Village sounded! Those who knew the origin understood that the village was named after the hemp-planting tradition its residents had long had, however, to those who didn't know the origin, the name seemed to suggest that everyone in the village had got a pock-marked face[31]. Now, with this novel and exotic name, no matter where they went they could denigrate the people who lived there, by interpreting their village names, with their references to a ditch or to a horse's mouth, to determine that the villages themselves could not be uglier or more rustic! How could they aspire to be Sakelu's peers? The more they thought and talked about the name, the happier they were with it. Who would not be happy to lead almost the same life as people in the United States? Although in the minds of the villagers the United States had a negative image, as an embodiment of evil, they had also learned from watching TV that the United States was the wealthiest and most powerful country on earth. Anyway, whenever the poor sat side by side with the rich, it was the former, not the latter, who had cause to feel honored.

The new village was built on the land possessed by a village named Xijiayuan, meaning Household Xi's Tableland. The requisition of the land had caused quite a few conflicts. The village head of Xijiayuan was strongly supportive of granting the land because the township government had agreed to get his son work in Meiteng. But the villagers were not. They divided themselves into two groups, each made up of two hundred people or so, men and women, young and old, and with a shovel in hand, took turns to guard their land day and night. Zhao Xiaohui, the new township head, so hated open conflict that he went to speak to them time and again, and as a consequence was taken prisoner. The villagers pointed at his nose, swore at him, and someone even spat in his face.

"Township Head Zhao, if you do not agree to this condition, we will not agree to give away our land. The condition is that each villager must have ten thousand *yuan* compensation! What do you mean 'That's too much?' On the contrary! We haven't opened a lion's mouth and asked one hundred thousand for each; we ask only ten thousand *yuan*. Still too much, you think? Say that again, and we will increase our demands. You will soon see whether an arm wins over a leg, or a leg over an arm."

At the command of Zhang Shutian, the county dispatched its public security police and armed police to rescue Zhao Xiaohui. Although nine villagers from Xijiayuan had been arrested, the fire animating the villagers had not been extinguished. They claimed that they would appeal to the higher authorities, and would not stop their complaints against Zhang Shutian until he was taken down. At this point, quite a few Mazi villagers began to miss Liu Qi. If Liu Qi had remained as the township head, would land requisition be a problem? Liu Qi needed only to stand there, shout, stamp twice on the ground, and no one from Xijiayuan would have had the guts to make trouble. To tell the truth, Liu Qi had been a talent. In the present society, without a figure like him, it was hard to push anything forward; every new enterprise was as heavy as an elephant's buttock.

Having struggled for two months, the Xijiayuan villagers were finally exhausted. It seemed that the saying "The crying baby gets the most milk" was not applicable in this case. They had cried, and rolled on the ground, but got no more milk. What was more, the ring-leaders had to lie on the bed they had made for themselves. So far, eighteen of them had been arrested. Others, like vultures, gradually drew their heads in. Doing time in the detention house was really tough. When villagers went to visit their kinsfolk in custody, grown men as they were, the prisoners dissolved into tears, as malleable to torture as wax is to heat. Some were inflicted with bedsores, some were as thin as rakes because of dysentery, and still others were unable to stand on a now paralyzed leg. Those who returned from the detention house played up its horror, and admonished others to give over agitating and climb down the ladder provided. After all, they had only one head each, and should not put it to the trial of an encounter with a blade. Before long the county and the village representatives came to a written agreement. The public security bureau released the villagers in custody, and every household in Xijiayuan was compensated to the tune of two thousand *yuan*, half provided by the county treasury and half by Meiteng. This decision set the whole of Xijiayuan Village boiling. What was this, then? Money distributed per household instead of per capita! Wouldn't that force villagers to split their families? And in fact families splitting up was for a while a fashion in the village — one into two or into three being a frequent choice, and even divorces between husband and wife were quite common. Zhang Shutian could not help but curse with anger. He said it would take at least ten thousand years for Chinese farmers to be transformed from barbarians into civilized human beings; they were ready to throw away their sense of shame for a meager sum of money. Zhang Shutian therefore issued an order to freeze the household register. Compensation would be based on present households, and no newly-split households would be taken into account. Seeing the authorities outwit them at every move, and having struggled in vain for so long a time, the villagers had to succumb to reality, with much reluctance.

According to Liben's conception of the place, Sakelu would have its doors open to all. Its residents might come and go as they liked, and people from other villages might tour the park free of charge. What a harmonious picture! However, the wish was not equal to the reality, which was far more complicated than he had wished. During the construction stage, setbacks happened one after another. Six strong workers were not enough to watch over the building materials. Sacks of cement disappeared unnoticed. Rolls of rebar were lifted onto an unlicensed agricultural three-wheeler by an unidentified group of people. More egregious still was that some people even pulled down a newly-built wall in order to make off with the bricks.

There was no choice but to build a winding wall round Sakelu, high, deep, and with dense barbed wire on top. After the park was completed, the whole population of Mazi Village moved in. Liben proposed pulling down the wall, but was strongly opposed by most villagers — who, after all, had their arguments. During its construction, folks from neighboring villages, like evil mosquitoes, had come for a bite from time to time, flagrantly sucking blood. Now that the construction had been completed, who knew but that worse things might follow? As the beautiful houses offered a stark contrast to the shabby villages nearby, how could those living in the latter not be green with envy? A rich man living in a poor quarter, surrounded by a populace in rags, could he sleep sound? If the rich wanted safety, they had better build high walls. Another reason the Mazi villagers wished to be separated from the outside world, one which they found too embarrassing to declare, was: since we now enjoy the American way of life, how can we condescend to associate with people from those poor villages?

Indeed, each family now owned a two-storey house built in the western style. They were twenty meters away from each other, with a pinnacle on top. The yellow outer walls adorned by blue lines were extremely eye-catching, and the panes of the aluminum alloy windows emitted a dark blue effulgence in the sun's rays. The insides were simply decorated, with painted walls, and floors paved with tiles. A few articles of furniture were given as gifts — a TV set, a gas stove, and so on and so forth.

The Mazi villagers were satisfied with being able to move into Sakelu Park. They apparently could not have felt more satisfied. The pleasures of moving into new homes dissipated the resentment of those who had been angry about land compensations. In less than a year, one could easily sense that the atmosphere of the village had changed considerably for the better. Quarrels and gossip were less common, and even mutual home visits grew rare. The territory of a family or household was clearly marked with iron fences, and disputes over boundaries no longer occurred. When villagers happened to encounter one another, they only lavished praises on Liben. They even thought to make a sculpture for their benefactor by pooling their money. Yes, it was Liben who had changed their destiny for the better. He was a red sun in their book!

53

As it happened, the statue of Liben was erected near Sakelu Lake, which had been created in the center of Sakelu Park. To tell the truth, the lake was fairly small, with a total area of three to four average-sized rainwater pools; the water in it was not plentiful. The idea for its construction had been proposed by Liben, according to whom, "The presence of a body of water would add liveliness to the place; only when a place has land and water coexisting side by side, with land beside water and water beside land, is it a place to be treasured, with good *fengshui*."

In Liben's opinion, it was not enough merely to improve the living conditions of the villagers; their character should be changed as well. To achieve this end, the only way was to ensure that the villagers' offspring had better schooling, so that more children could pass college entrance examinations to receive higher education. In order for the village to produce more college students, the chief thing was to encourage the children to strive harder at their school work, nevertheless, the secret support of *fengshui* was also absolutely necessary. Although the lake had been built under the pretext of making the park more beautiful, in actuality, Liben's real concern had been for *fengshui*.

The construction project for Liben's statue was handled exclusively by Song Tongguo. After Luobo was entombed, the township government gave her family thirty thousand *yuan*. In addition, Liben gave Song Tongtuo thirty thousand *yuan* out of his own pocket. So immensely grateful was Song Tongguo that, with tears in his eyes and in the presence of the whole village, he knelt down before Liben. Thenceforth he exclaimed to whomever he met that even though many years of smithying had hardened his heart — his heart had grown harder than iron, and he had forgotten what it was like to cry, and even his wife's death had failed to draw a single tear from his eyes — what Liben had done made his tears run in torrents.

Ever since then, Song Tongguo had been absolutely obedient to Liben. Of course he did that for the sake of his personal interest as well. As a matter of fact, he had intimated to Liben that he wished to be appointed to a middle-rank administrative post in Meiteng. He had heard that a middle-rank administrator in Meiteng Corporation, once it started production, would earn a monthly salary of 8,000 *yuan*, on top of the annual bonus of over

10,000 *yuan*. And this was the reason it had become his prime concern to win Liben's favor with whatever means he had at his disposal. That was why when some people proposed to build a statue for Liben, Song Tongguo welcomed the proposal as a good idea; he regarded it as an ideal opportunity to show his goodwill to Liben.

Song Tongguo visited one house after another, encouraging the villagers to pay a contribution for the construction of Liben's statue. He said if each household contributed 50 *yuan*, the total amount would only suffice to build a gypsum statue; but if each household contributed 200 *yuan*, the total amount would suffice to build a stone statue. "120 households at 200 *yuan* each makes 24,000 *yuan*," he calculated. He said it was clear that 24,000 *yuan* would not be enough to purchase a block of high quality marble, but fortunately he knew a mason who would agree to charge a very low fee for the sculpting work.

The final sculpture turned out to be made of gypsum, due to the fact that Shuanhu's household and a few others were unwilling to pay their share. As a result, the collected money was only sufficient for a gypsum figure.

Ever since Shuanhu stopped acting as the head of the village, his gate was always closed; his family did not associate with any people in the village; the first thing his wife did when she caught sight of a villager was to spit onto the ground — bah, bah, bah, as if she had just swallowed a fly.

To be honest, it was unjust to blame Shuanhu for failing to donate the money. Shuanhu had never refused to donate the money. The truth was that Song Tongguo had hated to go to Shuanhu's house to collect it. Given that Shuanhu had had a part in Luobo's death, how could Song Tongguo, her husband, not be hostile toward Shuanhu?

In spite of everything, the final product — the gypsum statue — was gigantic. It was at least five times bigger than Liben himself. With eyes looking into the far distance, Liben's statue, like that of a great personage, stood akimbo on a square rock base, which was surrounded with flowers.

But Liben's statue was left in peace for barely one month; thereafter disapproval emerged. The first person expressing unhappiness was the county secretary Zhang Shutian. Immediately after conducting his inspection of Sakelu Park, Zhang Shutian summoned the township head Zhao Xiaohui to his office. There, the secretary criticized Zhao Xiaohui harshly; the secretary's face was as dark as a storm-laden sky, with black clouds rushing and fierce winds raging. The glances of the secretary, like lightning bolts cutting open the dark firmament, struck terror into Zhao Xiaohui's heart.

The implied thrust of Zhang Shutian's message was: Who was this Liben? Wasn't he simply a fellow who provided funding for the construction of the park? Look at Sakelu Park residents! Were their eyes covered with chicken shit? What did they mean by behaving like beggars, happy to call anybody mom or dad who threw a couple of coins into their bowls?

"Isn't that a serious problem? Is anyone who breastfeeds you really your mother? Is anyone who has milk to feed you your mother? Does it mean that a chicken should regard a weasel that brings him a gift as mother? It is undeniable that Liben has made considerable contributions to the establishment of the park. But without the good policies of the government, no matter how strong his wish to better his fellow villagers' life, how could he have made his wish come true?" Zhang Shutian asked Zhao Xiaohui.

"One understands that common villagers are not very discerning," Zhang Shutian continued. "But how can you Zhao Xiaohui have allowed such a thing to happen? You just think, and then answer me this question: Was Chairman Mao great? He could be regarded great in every sense, couldn't he? But he placed his own portrait behind those of Marx, Engels, Lenin, and Stalin. Why? It was not merely a matter of good manners, but also a matter of politics. First is first, second is second. If the third transgresses his boundaries and takes the place of the first or the second, that comes to a usurpation of the Party's power. Those ignorant people are fearless, but fearless people are inclined to make serious mistakes. It shocks me that the Sakelu residents have forsaken all those great political leaders, as well as the leading officials of various levels of the government; instead they have set up a statue of a fake American fellow. To make things worse, the fake American's statue is larger than the usual statues of those great world-leaders! What on earth did the Sakelu people think they were doing?"

To Zhao Xiaohui's bitter discomfort, Zhang Shutian repeatedly compared him with Liu Qi. The thrust was that Township Head Zhao was less competent than former Township Head Liu, who had been laid low in the earth. This was certainly a signal that Zhang Shutian was about to depose him. Of course Zhao Xiaohui was not worried about the security of his office; he had never been keen on it in the first place. He had been dragged out of the church to assume this office when he seemed to have developed a vague fascination with dear God.

After having listened to Zhang Shutian's rebuke for two long hours, Zhao Xiaohui finally grasped the real reason why the secretary was so indignant: it was because the statues of the leading officials at various levels of government had not been set up.

Zhao Xiaohui was always disdainful of the practices of officialdom. On his first day as the head of the township government, at the inauguration meeting, he announced he would do away with the bad habits prevalent in official circles. He proclaimed that meetings would be held only when absolutely necessary; that purely routine inspections would be avoided as much as possible; that officials from superior levels of the government would not be entertained with meals unless unavoidable. Liu Qi had thrown away money as though it were nothing but paper. As a result, a debt of at least six million *yuan* had been bequeathed to the township government. After Liu Qi was sentenced to death, all the debtors were scared out of their wits. They flocked to the township government to reclaim their debts. Not having money to settle the debts, Zhao Xiaohui, as the new head of the township government, had to hide out as if he had been a criminal boss.

Zhao Xiaohui had paid a visit to the statue. Personally, he had no objection to it. If the villagers wanted to express their gratitude in this way, then let them do so. There was no law against people setting up a statue of a person to whom they were thankful. But in Kaiyang County, Zhang Shutian was the Number One boss, always ready to take the law into his own hands. How could Zhao Xiaohui dare to act against him?

Zhao Xiaohui went to see Xiaolin, the interim keeper of Sakelu Park. He wanted to hear Xiaolin's opinion. They talked over a simple meal. They agreed that Sakelu had become a weird monster of problematic nature. Regarded as a village, the problem was it had no farmland for people to work; but regarded as a bunch of urban streets, the problem was it had no fundamental businesses to pursue.

According to Zhao Xiaohui, the solution to the statue crisis was either to move Liben's statue into a room or to set up a group of other people's statues next to Liben's. From his pocket, Zhao Xiaohui took out a list of names of the people whose statues were supposed to be set up — a list which he had made after careful consideration, and the number of the names came to over thirty.

Looking at the list, Xiaolin chuckled.

"It would be a terrifying sight indeed if one statue were to be set up for each of these people!" Xiaolin said. "My goodness, some township government officials are included too? Surely they themselves know well what they look like in the villagers' minds."

After glancing back and forth across the list, Xionlin asked Zhao Xiaohui why Township Head Zhao was not on it. Zhao Xiaohui replied that he had no intention of standing next to the rainwater pool to be blown by the wind and burnt by the sun.

Xiaolin crumpled the list of names into a ball. He told Zhao Xiaohui he would rather move Liben's statue into the management office of the park than take so much trouble erecting statues for these dull officials according to their rank. Xiaolin said, "Suppose their statues were made, who would pay? I'm sure they themselves would not pay. Would the county finance department allocate the funds? The pay for the artisans alone would amount to between one hundred and two hundred thousand *yuan*, not to mention the outlay for materials."

"Many more troubles will emerge as time passes," Xiaolin continued. "These officials are hard to please. Once the statues were done, huge piles of complaints would arise: this statue has a slightly crooked nose; that statue has a rather curly ear; this one's legs are too long; that one's arms are too short. You think you've done a good thing for them, but that does not mean they will be pleased. There are too many examples of thankless efforts. If one of these officials is displeased, I, as the park's interim keeper, will definitely have a hard time. So, it's better to do less than to do more. I'd rather displease them by not doing anything for them than displease them after having taken enormous efforts making their statues."

Zhao Xiaohui went along with Xiaolin in this matter. He made some casual remarks in praise of Xiaolin, saying Xiaolin was mature now, unlike in the past, when he had been filled with futile zeal and passion, and had given the impression of being reckless and impetuous. Xiaolin responded that this should not be called maturity; rather it signified his fall. Xiaolin exclaimed that in the past he couldn't tolerate having one grain of sand in his eye, but now even if a whole desert were piled up in his pupil, he would get used to it by and by. Xiaolin said he had been warning himself over and over, "You oughtn't to act like this! You shouldn't behave this way! Don't let yourself fall into the mud! Don't let the mud devour you."

Casually, Xiaolin spoke ill of Song Tongguo, "This fellow Song Tongguo is a match for Fugui. No, he surpasses Fugui by far. People call Fugui Fullghost, meaning he is rich in odd ideas. Actually Fugui has only petty tricks — tricks which are not only trifling but also shallow. Shallow water cannot hide big fish. Even people who are almost blind can see fish scales clearly. But Song Tongguo is different. He is wily, but assumes an innocent appearance, as though he were easy to see through. He plots one thing in his heart but speaks another with his mouth. Song Tongguo should by no means be taken lightly. Liben is too credulous, failing to withstand Song Tongguo's blandishments. Song Tongguo's proposal to build a statute for him is intended to push him over the edge of a cliff."

The day after Zhao Xiaohui and Xiaolin discussed Liben's statue, it was taken away by the urban management centre personnel who came over from the county town: a truck moved into Sakelu Park, then a dozen young men got out of it; without giving any explanation, they set about demolishing the statue.

A villager brought Xiaolin over. When Xiaolin tried to hinder them, they pushed him around. One lad thumped Xiaolin in the stomach. The fat guy in charge introduced himself, claiming that his name was Duan Dingding and that he was co-director of the urban management centre. On learning that Xiaolin was the park keeper, Duan Dingding told him that the park had been incorporated into the urban management system, and that therefore the urban management centre was in charge of superintending the park.

Duan Dingding claimed that because Sakelu Park had set up the statue without prior approval from the urban management centre, the park was in violation of regulations, and the statue must be demolished. Additionally, a penalty of five thousand *yuan* must be submitted.

Xiaolin rang Zhao Xiaohui, informing him of the matter.

By the time Zhao Xiaohui arrived in his car, the truck carrying the statue was gone, leaving only Duan Dingding, along with his driver, behind; they were bargaining with Xiaolin in the latter's office. Duan Dingding looked pretty enraged. He patted Xiaolin's tea table with so much force that the sound irritated the ear. He shouted that he had dealt with some stubborn fellows in his life, but none as stubborn as Xiaolin.

"Nevertheless," Duan Dingding said, "I'm not afraid of stubborn fellows. I'm an expert at breaking stubborn people of their stubbornness once and for all."

The focal point of the debate between Duan Dingding and Xiaolin lay in whether Sakelu Park was a village or an urban locality. Xiaolin insisted it was a village, and as such it was beyond the control of the urban management centre. But Duan Dingding emphasized that it was an urban locality, because its residents lived in villas and these residents neither worked any farmland nor raised any cattle or pigs. "What else can it be but an urban locality?" Duan Dingding asked Xiaolin.

Zhao Xiaohui was acquainted with Duan Dingding. After briefly rebuking Xiaolin, Zhao Xiaohui invited all three men to the best restaurant in Gaotai. Before the meal was served, Zhao Xiaohui had made Xiaolin buy two cartons of expensive cigarettes and force them onto Duan Dingding, who accepted without demur. After that, Duan Dingding's spirits lightened considerably. His face was soon wreathed in smiles. Patting Xiaolin on the shoulder and addressing Xiaolin as Sage Younger Brother, Duan Dingding said, "Out of blows friendship grows. From now onward, if Sage Younger Brother needs any help, feel free to tell me, your brother. On the territory of Kaiyang, your Brother Duan can be counted on as a powerful person."

After quaffing down half a bottle of liquor, Duan Dingding demonstrated his magnanimous character. Waving his enormous hand, he shouted at the top of his voice, "The monetary penalty is cancelled. It's cancelled. Not a cent is needed, as long as I, your brother, can have liquor to drink and cigarettes to smoke whenever I come to Gaotai and Sakelu."

54

The news that the provincial leaders would visit Sakelu Park made its residents at once happy and busy. After all, how many people, including those who had lived in Mazi Village for generations and those who were now living in Sakelu Park, had ever seen a county magistrate in person? Now they had seen both — the county magistrate and the county secretary of the Party committee. On the day when Sakelu was opened, the two of them had come and sat on the stage. Though the villagers could not see them clearly at a distance, they had at least seen them. And soon they would be able to see the provincial leaders too. What was not to like? Leaders from the province! Big shots, not the kind of bureaucrat you could see anytime you wanted to. Never mind the actual sight of the provincial leaders, the mere thought of it thrilled them as much as the Spring Festival.

As for the actual date of the visit, the villagers had a lot of trouble arriving at a consensus. It was a problem which persisted in spite of the many discussions and enquiries. Without a specific date, all they could do was wait longingly, but they kept themselves busy in the meantime. As a matter of fact, they were fully occupied — rehearsing a *yangko*[32]dance performance, organizing the honor guard, purchasing uniforms, decorating the reading room, cleaning up repeatedly, and watering the lawns again and again. Hard as the *yangko* dance was in and of itself, it was even harder when there was no coach on hand to help rehearse it. Shuanhu had sung opera in his childhood, acquiring a name in towns and townships far and near. However, since he was deprived of the village leadership after Liu Qi was executed, he began to bear a grudge against Liben, and refused to participate in any activities connected to him. Xiaolin had a talk with him. He replied he would be happy to oblige, but only on condition that Liben apologize to him in person and kowtow to him three times. Xiaolin left, greatly annoyed. Then Xiaolin called me to ask who could come and help out. I knew that after Larz had lost his mother, Kang Yuanyuan sent him to Yuebei Arts Academy, where he was said to have learned singing and dancing. I had not seen him for years, so I did not know where he was now. I called Kang Yuanyuan, who claimed that Larz was in the south, however she did not know his specific whereabouts either. She only knew that he was adrift in the world, here today, gone tomorrow. Nevertheless, Kang Yuanyuan gave me Larz's most recent phone number, and told me to call him directly.

The call went through immediately. To my surprise, Larz still remembered my name when I mentioned it. He said he was roaming about in the south, without a regular job, and not earning any money. I disclosed to him that Sakelu was in need of a *yangko* coach, and asked if he was willing to take on the job. He hesitated, especially when he learned that there would not be any financial compensation. I told him that he should come anyway, on the grounds that he might attract Meiteng's attention if he did a really good job of it. Having attracted Meiteng's attention, he might be asked to stay and work in an actual paid position. Until the time when the production actually began, Meiteng would be in need of a large number of workers. Larz said "All right, I'll act on your advice."

Larz came to meet me soon after he returned to Yuebei. He had obviously changed a lot. In my memory he was a handsome boy, pure and innocent, still wet behind the ears. The man standing before me now was an older version of that boy, though he retained his original countenance. A moustache was beginning to appear round his lips, and wrinkles were beginning to climb his weathered cheeks. His speech and behavior revealed a certain air of frivolity. He passed a cigarette to me while putting one into his own mouth, and related with a complacent expression on his face how one girl after another was courting him. I asked whether he had seen Kang Yuanyuan. He said he had, and it was Older Sister Kang who had come to pick him up at the railway station. He had almost no money but he had managed to buy her a piece of Burmese emerald, only to be scolded by her because she thought that he was too prodigal and that he did not know how to cherish money. He added that Older Sister Kang would accompany him to Mazi Village — Sakelu, I corrected him.

The next day I handed Larz over to Xiaolin, who had made the trip to Yuebei solely for the purpose of receiving him. On seeing Xiaolin, Larz asked about the transformation of Mazi Village. As Xiaolin described Sakelu to him, he opened his eyes widely, eager to have a look for himself. He began, as it seemed, to flatter Xiaolin, saying that if Sakelu was as good as he had described, he would like to be one of its gardeners, for he had acquired a fairly good deal of knowledge of gardening.

Later, I heard that Larz's coaching in Sakelu was a great success. At first, the villagers felt that he was a city dandy, and dared not approach him, but within a few days almost all the villagers had come to like him, dragging him by the arm to dine at home with them. Of course, Larz worked very hard and he never lost his patience. More importantly, he never laughed at anyone, no matter how awkwardly they danced. Third Aunt took a particular fancy to him. When she heard that his mother had died, leaving him alone, she held his hand tightly, nearly hugging him in her arms. She shed tears of pity for him and offered to be his godmother. In a spirit of fun, or perhaps of sincerity, Larz did accept Third Aunt as his godmother. He knelt down in front of her in the presence of witnesses and called her "Godmother" in a drawling tone.

Shuanhu and his family isolated themselves from the rest of the village people, but when he heard that the coach of the *yangko* team was Larz, whom he had chosen to be his future son-in-law, he came to look him up. Larz remembered this village head, so he exchanged hearty pleasantries with him. Shuanhu said Jidan was at home, and he hoped that Larz could come and be their guest. But Larz had no interest in seeing Jidan, having long before been informed of her trade. His mouth responded with several all-rights; however, he took no action, even after Shuanhu had invited him three times. With no way out, Shuanhu had to swallow his pride and, together with his wife, started bringing lunchboxes to him, big and small, each filled with such home-cooked delicacies as chicken and fish, delivered to the administration office of the park.

Larz's tongue was softened under the effect of Shuanhu's meals. When there was no-one else around in the house, Larz would address Shuanhu as "Uncle," who felt thereby emboldened to speak of his own exploits. Shuanhu denigrated every one of his fellow villagers in turn, which could be summarized as "all those who lived in Mazi Village were bad guys," in a parody of "no good guys lived in Hongtong County," a libretto from the opera *Courtesan Yutangchun*. He made a point of warning Larz not to get close to people like Song Tongguo, Third Aunt, Xiaolin, or Fugui, saying that they were all scorpions, poisonous in and out, each with a poisonous heart and a pair of poisonous claws. Unlike most of the villagers, he was not bullish at all about Sakelu's prospects, thinking that sooner or later it would all end in tears, although everyone was grinning from ear to ear right now, and he wished the day of reckoning would come soon! For others it would be a bitter day, but for him it would be the happiest of days! It was easy to imagine the future which awaited them when they had used up all their land compensations — a mere sixty or seventy thousand per family — within a few years. Now that they did not grow grain, they had to buy it, as would their offspring too, generation after generation. A body of standing water, served out with a ladle, would be exhausted eventually, even if it was a sea. In his estimate, in less than two years there would be some in the village who would find it difficult to subsist, given that at least three or four families had paid their debts with the land compensations, and one — he did not specify which, but he was in fact referring to Baolai — was spending the money to cure his wife's illness. The hospital door was a tiger's mouth, eating human flesh without spitting out bones, and it could not be satisfied by any amount of money thrown into it. As for the future of Meiteng, no one knew, but in Shuanhu's judgment it was doomed to go bankrupt in the end. And even if Meiteng ran well and was in a position to employ the surplus manpower of the village, would it actually do so? Would they pay wages to people for doing nothing — given that they had neither crafts nor skills?

Shuanhu summarized his point, saying that a wise person would prepare for his future in good time. Why had he been interested in Larz all this time? Because he thought the marriage between Larz and Jidan would be very profitable. And at the end of this detour, Shuanhu came back to Jidan's profession. He intended to open a song-and-dance hall — so called because it sounded harmless to passers-by — but who did not know it was just another name for a brothel? As chickens lay eggs, or cows breed calves, money made money! If the song-and-dance hall was successful, they could enlarge its scale, extend its range of activities, and open a casino.

Shuanhu was absolutely sure of his judgement. For at least the next five or six years there would not be a second Sakelu in Kaiyang. In other words, during the five or six years ahead, Sakelu would be the main attraction for people in Kaiyang or even beyond it, and would as a result become the focus of numerous visits and tours. The over-fed inevitably went looking for fun, but where was the safest place? Sakelu, of course; it was far away from the county town, out of sight of leaders, wives and acquaintances! There would be no need to worry about attracting customers, as prices here were cheaper than those in the county town. Once business started, the more private rooms available, the better. Only when there were ample private rooms could demand — which was bound to be enormous — be met. And one might go a bit farther. Once the production in Meiteng was at full steam, thousands of workers would be crowding in here. Would they, perchance, be chaste monks and nuns? Or would they be castrated and free from the sex drive? Desire burned like wild fire, but how could it be extinguished? In a song-and-dance hall, of course! Was there a better place than a song-and-dance hall in this world? Therefore, business was bound to boom, and things were bound to get as red-hot as an oilfield on fire. If you earned enough money, you could go to the United States or to Australia, and eat or drink whatever you liked. If you wanted to drive a BMW, you drove one; and if you wanted to sit in a stretch-Lincoln, you sat in one. Whoever stood in your way, you glared at him or just cut him up. By the time you were that rich, you could buy a villa in a big city, and if you found it unsatisfactory, you could buy another. Who would regret leaving this shabby Sakelu? When the song-and-dance hall opened, Larz would be the proprietor, Jidan the proprietress, and Shuanhu himself the management counselor! The proprietor was responsible for management, the proprietress for collecting money, and the counselor for soliciting customers. As long as they cooperated harmoniously, the world's money would fly merrily to them like iron filings to a magnet.

So entranced was Shuanhu by the reeling off of these details, that he remained totally unaware when Kang Yuanyuan came and stood by them, having entered from outside. Shuanhu's words twisted her heart into a knot. Unable to bear it any more, she let out a cough. The moment he saw her, Larz invited her to sit down, but Shuanhu gave her the cold shoulder. With a sullen face, Kang Yuanyuan walked back out of the door. Hardly had she disappeared from the doorway when Shuanhu said to Larz, "That woman is a freak. Just leave her alone!"

Kang Yuanyuan had evidently heard Shuanhu's words. Near as they were, she took out her phone to call Larz, and told him to come out for a word with her. Shortly thereafter Larz came out, followed by Shuanhu, who walked away into the distance. Kang Yuanyuan was waiting for Larz by the lake. The moment she saw him, she roared at him like a lioness. She was shaking all over, so agitated that she was almost unable to speak. She pointed at Larz's nose and denounced him for sinking so low as to befriend such a dirty man. To hear what Shuanhu had been teaching! Hadn't he been trying to tempt Larz into a sucking pit?

Larz could not understand why Kang Yuanyuan was reacting like this. He said that he had done nothing but listen. Why was she losing her temper like that? Was it necessary? Was it even serious? This retort exasperated Kang Yuanyuan almost to the point of vomiting blood. She slumped down onto the ground, gasping heavily, and swore to cut all ties with him. Larz went over to grab her by the arm, and to get her up. Still shaking violently, Kang Yuanyuan refused to stand up. A little annoyed, Larz turned and walked away. He picked up his bag from the administration office, hailed a passenger trike and got in, without informing anyone. As soon as he reached the county town, he jumped off the trike and made for the bus station.

55

Kang Yuanyuan almost burst into tears as she told me about Larz. She kept saying, "I'm angry enough to die. I'm angry to the point of death! How can a person like this, who can't tell good from bad, even exist?"

I soothed her, saying, "After all, Larz is still very young; it is inevitable for a young man in his twenties to be capricious. In no time, he'll seek your company again."

But Kang Yuanyuan said that she could not wait; that she wished to find him right then and there to rebuke him, so that the anger pent up in her chest could be vented. Otherwise, she would die of anger.

After condemning Larz, Kang Yuanyuan calmed down a little. She exclaimed that if Larz regained his senses and wanted to associate with her once more, she would continue to view him as her brother as she had before, but if he kept to his foolish path and followed the instigations of Shuanhu and his like, she would completely break with him.

Massaging her chest, Kang Yuanyuan said that, as a matter of fact, she seldom got mad; that she understood anger harmed health; that even though she didn't want to get mad, she couldn't help it — recently, so many unpleasant things had been frustrating her. Just look at what she had encountered after she returned to China! She came back with the intention of devoting herself to the service of the motherland, but all her enthusiasm had gone like the waters of a fast-flowing river. She hadn't accomplished anything, and now felt mentally burnt out and frustrated. She would do better to hang herself with her own hair! She did not understand why people simply couldn't appreciate her goodwill. Whatever she had done for people, she used her own personal funds as well as her American friends' financial aid. She did not need people to pay her back; all she expected was their understanding and cooperation. However, she harvested nothing but frustration and deceit. She was almost at the point of having no trust in anybody.

She said she had helped with the construction of an orphanage. However, as soon as the operational funds entered into the bank account of the orphanage, the director ran away with all the money, leaving the poor orphans uncared-for in cold weather. She reported the case to the police. The policemen bustled about the matter for days without catching the culprit. After that, the case was neglected altogether.

She told us another story, which concerned one of her cousins. This cousin of hers had rarely associated with her family in the past. But on learning about her return from America, the cousin phoned her, claiming in sobs that she could not afford to send her two kids to school, and that the kids' father, her husband, had attempted to hang himself several times. Kang Yuanyuan asked her cousin how much money she needed to complete the children's schooling, and generously offered to provide the kids with tuition. Her cousin seemed to have integrity. Declining Kang Yuanyuan's offer, her cousin claimed that her family possessed some ancient paintings, but, for fear of being swindled by conmen, her folks had not dared to put the paintings on the market; considering Kang Yuanyuan's experience of the world, she wished to entrust her with the management of their sale. According to the cousin, once the paintings were sold, all her difficulties would be solved. At that point, would paying for the kids' schooling still be a problem?

Knowing little about painting, Kang Yuanyuan asked her cousin when they had been painted. Her cousin said they had been painted during the Ming Dynasty; in all, there were four of them, each one worth between six hundred thousand and one million *yuan*. Kang Yuanyuan asked her cousin and her cousin's husband to bring the paintings to Yuebei, but they declined on the pretext that it involved a long journey and that they were worried about the paintings' safety, because they were both country-folk who had never travelled far from home. After a short hesitation, Kang Yuanyuan promised she would come to them instead.

Her cousin's family dwelt in a village in Northeast China. Though that was her ancestral village, Kang Yuanyuan, who was born in Yuebei, knew little about it. Cherishing the desire to deliver her cousin's family from its difficulties, Kang Yuanyuan set out. Not lacking for money, she had no wish to make money for herself through selling the paintings. She went there by air, with a bank card in her pocket. When she reached her cousin's place, she noticed that the house looked pretty, and that it was well furnished inside. However, her cousin started to cry the very minute they saw each other, groaning about various hardships and difficulties — oh, the daughter was ill with leukemia; without money for medical therapy, the poor girl had to stay in bed; oh, the son loved to go to school, but since the family could not afford the tuition, the poor boy had to stand outside the classroom, looking in through the window longingly.

Kang Yuanyuan went into the inner room to see the daughter; the girl was lying in bed under the bed clothes, shivering franticallly. Without staying for long at her cousin's place, Kang Yuanyuan left, taking the paintings with her. She went to a nearby town along with her cousin's husband.

Finding a bank, Kang Yuanyuan withdrew one hundred thousand *yuan* and consigned it to her cousin's husband — this amount served as the cash pledge for the paintings she was taking away for sale. The paintings might not be sold in a short period of time, and the girl must be treated without delay. Once the paintings were sold, Kang Yuanyuan would give every cent to her cousin and her cousin's husband — she would help them with the sale and she would charge no commission. As they parted at the bank, Kang Yuanyuan again and again instructed her cousin's husband, who was carrying a bagful of cash, to be extremely careful on the return trip.

Having done all these things, Kang Yuanyuan rushed to the airport and took a flight bound for Yuebei. As the plane landed and she turned on her mobile phone, she received a call, which shocked her tremendously. The call was from her cousin, who told her that during her husband's return journey, the money had been stolen.

Kang Yuanyuan was so shocked that it was as though someone had just knocked her on the head with a club. What could she possibly do about this? The only thing she could do was advise them to report it to the police.

The very next day, after she returned to Yuebei, she went to see a friend who collected valuable scripts and paintings, and asked him to help contact people interested in purchasing the paintings. The friend told Kang Yuanyuan to bring the paintings to his place, so that he could estimate a price. Fearing that the paintings might get lost or be stolen, Kang Yuanyuan requested Larz to go along with her. On the way, they were both exceedingly careful — looking right and left, they were wary of anyone passing by.

As he unfolded the paintings, her friend was knocked for six. He loudly called Kang Yuanyuan an idiot. Far from being paintings drawn during the Ming Dynasty, they were just worthless trash! They were photocopies of paintings.

"This can be easily detected at first sight," her friend declared. "Are your eyes for breathing instead of seeing? How could you have failed to notice these problems?"

Realizing that she had fallen into a trap, Kang Yuanyuan made a call to her cousin, only to find that the number was no longer in service.

This affair delivered a harsh blow to Kang Yuanyuan. She felt a heart-breaking sorrow, as if a thick iron needle were piercing her heart one stroke after another. The sorrow did not simply derive from the fact that she had lost a large sum of money; more importantly, her faith in life had been shaken. She was ready to give money generously to her relatives if they needed it. But this unfair way of carrying on was more than she could put up with.

Kang Yuanyuan said she had returned to China with two missions, two missions which she had taken to heart. Mission One was to help those who needed help; Mission Two was to provide enlightenment to those who had little schooling. But her cousin's behavior made her uncertain as to who really needed help and who feigned to. Even more disappointing was the question: how had it come about that these decent-looking Chinese, whose dignity she had fiercely defended before foreigners, had grown so ugly?

On the other hand, so Kang Yuanyuan thought, her cousin's fraud had strongly emphasized the necessity of carrying out her enlightenment program. She said, "Look, these people have degenerated to the point of becoming beasts. If no intervention is implemented now, they will become nothing but beasts. To stop people from degenerating, the only reliable remedy is education. But education can be towards good or evil ends. Benevolent education leads people in the direction of virtue, reason and humanism. But malevolent education takes falsehood as its banner, subdues people's thoughts, transforms them into senseless believers, and makes them act like puppets. In brief, benevolent education removes the blindfold that covers people's eyes and lets people enjoy light, vigorous life, freedom, and love; while malevolent education blindfolds the eyes of people who are already struggling to make out anything in darkness, making people genuinely blind and deaf. It is not the case that only farmers need to be enlightened. It may be true that those with Master and PhD degrees have mastered the required professional expertise and skills, yet their academic degrees are no guarantee that they are not ignorant. Neither the duration of a person's schooling, nor the amount of knowledge acquired through that schooling, can prove that he has rid himself of ignorance. The core point lies in whether the education you have received is benevolent or malevolent. If it is malevolent, the longer you receive it, the more poison you will absorb, and consequently the more taste you will have for poison. This is comparable to eating. Eating more is not necessarily good for health; the key point is what you eat."

The big talk Kang Yuanyuan engaged in was not groundless. She had conducted, as a researcher for a non-governmental organization, a survey among a circle of high level intellectuals. The findings surprised her: few of those intellectuals lived in their own times; with regard to the majority, there was no telling which era they were living in; many people's thoughts were not consistent with the values of the modern world; on the contrary, their thoughts were in the same mould as those of Dong Zhongshu[33], who lived before the Common Era.

Kang Yuanyuan said she had made up her mind to open a civic school in Sakelu. She thought that now the conditions to set it up were much more favorable than in the past. Those who had strongly opposed it were no longer in the way: Liu Qi was dead and Shuanhu had been removed from office. At least Xiaolin and Zhao Xiaohui would give a green light for the setup of the school.

In spite of her elaborate explanation, neither Xiaolin nor Zhao Xiaohui could understand what kind of institution the civic school would be, and in what way it would be different from a national education school. They took Kang Yuanyuan for an investor in a training business. Accordingly, they proposed that she open a vocational school specifically aimed at training the rural females to do embroidery work. They said that embroidery was a promising industry, that if the project succeeded, all the products could be exported abroad and lots of American dollars would be earned for Kaiyang County.

56

I learned from Xiaolin's phone call about all the pomp and circumstance which accompanied Governor Xiang's visit to Sakelu Park. Xiaolin praised the governor profusely because he had shaken hands and had his picture taken with him. He talked for an hour and a half on the phone, describing the governor's trip in detail.

Governor Xiang's trip to Sakelu Park was a seismic event in Kaiyang's history. Followed by a couple of departmental directors, and surrounded by a large throng of reporters, the governor's motorcade drove in massive array into the territory of Kaiyang County. The county heads had been waiting some distance away, and now they joined in to form an even more magnificent motorcade. Leaders of the public security bureau took on the role of bodyguards, closely following the governor, and a troop of motor trikes carrying police station sheriffs sounded sirens to clear the way ahead. Seven years before, while he was still a vice governor, Governor Xiang had visited here but the county heads then had not given him an adequate reception. And now he came as the principal governor — a daughter-in-law who had endured all kinds of hardship and injustice had turned into a mother-in-law at last! If Kaiyang failed to take him seriously this time, it would suffer greatly. The Kaiyangers were no fools. They knew that a governor was worth much more than ten gold mines.

Soon the Kaiyangers experienced Governor Xiang's swift and resolute working style. No matter how hard people tried to persuade him, he refused to go to Kaiyang Hotel, which had gone to the trouble of changing its carpet in his honor. There were rosy smiles on the beautiful faces of the stewardesses who stood by the doorway, but it was all in vain due to the absence of anyone to see them. The governor first went to inspect Meiteng, where he gave orders, on the spot, to the provincial government head-office to coordinate, within a definite time frame, all the departments concerned, in order to solve the problems that had been troubling Meiteng. He then headed for Sakelu. But the trip did not go smoothly, and the motorcade had to stop from time to time. Sitting in the car, the governor naturally did not know what was happening on the road ahead. The leading officials of Kaiyang lied to him, saying that a few cows grazing at the roadside had meandered into the middle of the road, and that the policemen, so humane that they would not resort to violence, were slowly driving them away.

The fact was, a group of people had come out of nowhere and stopped the advance of the motorcade. They knelt down on the road, all of them, men and women, young and old, with a banner carrying the words "We want justice!" on it. The narrow road was completely blocked. An investigation conducted by the director of the county government head-office revealed that they were people from Beigou Coal Mine, some of whom had been savagely beaten by Xu Yuanyuan's men to the point of disabling them; some had waited for months or even years without receiving any messages from their family members who had disappeared while working underground; some had worked in the mine for several years and never got paid, unable to demand their wages without the risk of getting beaten. So they had come to stop the governor's motorcade because they felt so cornered. They believed that the policies established by the higher echelons were in principle well-designed, it was just that the officials on the ground, like a grimacing monk reciting sutras, deviated from them.

After arduous efforts, these people were coaxed to make way! However, the motorcade did not move far before it came to a stop again. There turned out to be a big pit in the roadway near Sakelu, and the leading motor trike fell into it, leaving the rider with a bad facial injury. The fresh earth in and around the pit proved that it had just been dug. Who could have been so wicked as to want to ruin the image of Kaiyang on purpose? Yesterday the public security bureau had sent men to scrutinize the route three times and they had not discovered a hole like it! The commissioner of the public security bureau declared on the spot that he would order an investigation into the case, catch the skulking criminals responsible, and ruthlessly crack down on them. The head of the courthouse seconded the idea, saying that once the case was cleared up and the suspects arrested, the court would sentence them as quickly and as severely as possible.

Unable to sit in his car any longer, Governor Xiang decided to walk to the spot for a look. Pointing at the hollowed-out area, he asked what had caused it. All those who were present gave a unanimous answer, claiming that the road surface had collapsed half an hour previously. Looking toward the cottages in Sakelu, the governor asked if there were any alternative routes. The county magistrate replied that the county had planned to build one but had found itself short of money. The governor turned to the chief of the provincial transportation bureau, saying, "Old Zhu, can you explain why there isn't a decent road leading to our model village? Sakelu will welcome inspectors from the United Nations in a few days. If we do not speed up the reconstruction, this road will cause the province to lose all face!" Chief Zhu responded at once, saying that he would allot a special sum of money for the road, but Kaiyang County would have to submit a report, with a budget table attached.

A workgroup was summoned from the neighboring village to refill the hollow. When they learned that the man they could see in the distance pointing here and there was Governor Xiang, the same Governor Xiang who had been inspecting work and doing speech on TV the whole year round, they worked even harder. They spoke among themselves, saying how lucky they were to see a real governor, that it was a great honor which would make them look good in the eyes of their relatives and friends for quite a while to come — all thanks to the job they were undertaking. However, the pit could not be refilled in a short while, and Governor Xiang's time was as precious as gold. How could he be kept waiting in the sun? So the county magistrate made the snap decision to instruct the motorcade to make a detour through the grain fields alongside the road. If the farmers complained, the county had the financial wherewithal to compensate them. Corn was cheap anyway. A hundred stalks combined were not enough to raise the money for a cup of tea in a teahouse. Kaiyang as a big county could as easily spare such a small sum of money as nine yaks could spare a hair.

The governor, however, was adamantly against running over the grain. How lovely the vivid green corn saplings were! They were the sweat and blood of the masses. As a result, he did not get back into his car until the great hollow was completely refilled.

Governor Xiang got out of the car at the entrance of Sakelu Park, and walked into the village, where a hubbub was already gaining momentum. Popping firecrackers, deafening gongs and drums, dazzling flags and slogans on both sides of the road, and the parade of the *yangko* dancers dressed in gaudy colors, all these took the governor a little by surprise. Zhang Shutian, as he walked along by the governor, saw a touch of disapproval on his slightly pale face. The county secretary of the Party committee appeared to be so frightened that he could barely move his arms. Cameras snapped and lights flashed, but the governor did not have much of a smile on his face.

Instead of entering the reception room arranged by the local officials, Governor Xiang took a walk in the courtyard. After his tour of it, he stood in an open area and delivered a speech to the masses. He first praised Sakelu, saying it could serve as a role model in the development of rural China... then he changed his stance and declared that Sakelu was not perfect. Why? He had received letters of accusation from some of the villagers. What did these letters reveal? They showed that there were black spots hidden under the surface polish, and contradictions lurking beneath the seemingly universal harmony. How could these contradictions be resolved? Of course, it was necessary for governments at different levels to care for the common people, to prioritize their interests, and so on and so forth.

The governor's words were so moving that the Sakelu people began wondering under their breath how such a wonderful governor could exist. No sooner had the governor ended his speech than a tsunami of people surged forward to engulf him. Even the policemen could not stop them or drag them away — though one of them was dragged to the ground, while another had the clothes torn from his back. The police had no choice but to join hands in a hundred-strong circle to block those who continued to rush toward the governor. The circle, stretched like a rope, was vulnerable to the impact of the human tide; it wobbled, swayed and changed shape. One moment it was an oval, but the next it was twisted into an eggplant. Those blocked outside the circle cried and shouted, thinking that they were not receiving equal treatment.

"Why are we the only ones to be prevented from going in, while the people in there can have close contact and have their pictures taken with the governor? And, what's more, the police were taking bribes in full view of the public. A short policeman was seen taking a pack of cigarettes offered by Song Tongguo and allowing him to slip in between his legs! Is Song Tongguo's face whiter or bigger than ours? Why should he go in while we have to wait outside, worried and helpless?"

The crowd round Governor Xiang was totally out of control as though it were a hornet's nest which had been poked by a stick. They seemed to have forgotten that it was the head of the whole province in front them, and that their behavior was bound to seem shocking to those standing outside watching them. Some felt the governor's clothes, some his tie, and some even pinched the governor's cheek twice with their dirty fingers. Third Aunt was also standing at the governor's side. From time to time she lifted a corner of the governor's jacket to her nose to smell it. Fugui was the first to propose having his picture taken with the governor, who readily agreed — to the consternation of all. Who would have thought that a farmer, a shabbily-clad redneck, should have had an idea so audacious that none of the many county escorts would have dared to consider it? Ignorance was dauntless indeed! More worrying was that, once Fugui had kicked it off, others quickly followed his lead and competed to have their picture taken with the governor, so that the governor, who did not want to refuse any request, was kept as busy as a bee. For a time there, he was sweating in buckets.

Zhang Shutian tried his utmost, all the while offering tissues to Governor Xiang to wipe the sweat off his face, to stop people from approaching him. However, on an occasion like this, no one was going to take a mere county secretary of the Party committee seriously. With Mount Taishan towering above them, other mountains looked like molehills! Nothing could stop them from having their picture taken with the governor. Absolutely nothing! An opportunity like this came once in a month of Sundays, were they going to let it slip away?

In order to put an end to this chaos, Zhang Shutian whispered a few words both to the governor and to the commissioner of the public security bureau, whom he beckoned over. The commissioner nodded again and again, as though he had taken Zhang Shutian's point. After Zhang Shutain left, four policemen squeezed into the circle. They approached the governor, roughing up the encircling villagers as they went, and before the crowd knew what was happening, had lifted the governor into the air. While the policemen in front cleared the way with clubs, the ones in the rear bore Governor Xiang away.

57

Governor Xiang's visit focused the press's attention on Sakelu. In addition to the provincial and municipal media titles, some national ones came too, in close succession. This attention gave Xiaolin a sense of pride, but also exhausted him badly, because the attention would result in more than the arrival of the journalists. In addition, there would be the cost of receiving them all.

It would not be going too far to entertain the reporters with a feast at a restaurant. However, the cost of each feast might easily be eight hundred or even one thousand *yuan*. The reporters all seemed to have the habit of demanding two cartons of expensive cigarettes to take away. A more annoying thing was that some reporters openly asked for a gift of money in red envelopes. If refused, they would threaten to shine a light on Sakelu. Sakelu was not perfect; its defects were clearly visible. For instance, it did not have its own drainage pipes, which was the cause that waste water had flooded a large piece of the neighboring village's farmland. This, in turn, provoked the passionate protests and complaints of the inhabitants. For another example, instead of being elected by its residents, the keeper of the park was appointed by the investor. Was not this a violation of China's village electoral law? A further problem was that discord had arisen among the residents — since some villagers could afford meat, while others had only coarse food to fill their bellies. The gulf between rich and poor triggered brawls from time to time. It was in fact a reporter's threat to shine a light on Sakelu that had brought Xiaolin to Yuebei. As we had agreed, he was expecting me at the portal of a hotel.

After we met, I led him to see the reporter.

Actually, the reporter in question was only a temporary employee working for a minor newspaper which seemed on its last legs, housed as it was within a bunch of low and shabby one-storeyed rooms. Though this newspaper's circulation was small, the reporter had a belly for something big.

The reporter turned out to be a rough young man who had a very broad forehead but a pair of excessively narrow cheeks. His office was unbearably untidy, with a thick layer of dust covering his table.

Seeing us, the reporter blurted out to Xiaolin, "Eight thousand *yuan* will put an end to it. Otherwise, no matter who you turn to for help, it won't do any good at all."

The reporter's grim face did not soften a bit until Xiaolin furtively stuffed two cartons of cigarettes into a drawer of his office table. It was then the journalist explained that he had been compelled to do what he had done, since he must submit five thousand *yuan* per month to his newspaper. Nevertheless, the reporter expressed his strong displeasure for Xiaolin's having not received him attentively. According to him, when he got to Sakelu and introduced himself, Xiaolin responded with a curt "I'm busy" and then left him there alone.

To set us an example, the reporter gave Xiaolin and me an account of how he had been grandly received in a certain county — the head of that county's department of publicity had walked to the outer gate to welcome him; he had been treated with Maotai liquor at the subsequent feast. After sharing the story, the reporter interrogated Xiaolin as to his official rank and how it was that Xiaolin could have been so self-important. "You're no more than a village head. Who do you think you are?" the reporter said.

Xiaolin explained that the day when the reporter showed up in his office, he had just returned from a round of collecting water and electricity utility fees from the Sakelu Park households. Since many households had refused to pay, he had been in a lousy mood — if the fees could not be collected to pay the power supply firm, the firm would cut the power off. If the power was cut off, the villagers would surely curse him to death.

The reporter said, "Don't bother to say more. Your coming is as good as a frank confession of your fault. Therefore, I'll offer a waiver of three thousand *yuan*. Give me five thousand *yuan*, and there's an end to the matter. For you people who live in villas, is five thousand *yuan* anything?"

After enumerating a long list of difficulties faced by the Sakelu residents, Xiaolin said, "Beautiful-looking shoes do not necessarily mean that the feet feel comfortable in them. People who do not live in Sakelu cannot understand the difficulties it has."

I lent Xiaolin my support, saying, "The villas in Sakelu are utterly different from urban villas. In cities, villa dwellers are rich people, but in Sakelu, villa dwellers are poor rural peasants, who neither have a salary nor do any business; how can they have money? What's more, Xiaolin is only the interim keeper of the park. Without any public funds to access, how can he possibly raise this sum?"

The reporter said it was none of his business. He insisted that Xiaolin give five thousand *yuan*. He said that he had conducted interviews in the adjoining village and they called Sakelu Park a disaster and threatened that if Sakelu did not compensate them for the damage it had caused, they would create a disturbance and even go to Yuebei to launch a collective petition.

I winked at Xiaolin, to make him stop arguing with the guy. When the two of us withdrew from the reporter's office and reached the corridor, Xiaolin's mind was still obsessed with the matter. He asked me whether he should go back and give the guy five hundred *yuan*, for what that might be worth.

"No need to do that," I said. "I have figured out a way to deal with him."

"What is it?" Xiaolin asked.

"I'll tell you as soon as we get out of the gate," I replied.

Something else that had brought Xiaolin to Yuebei was his mission to fetch pictures for the Sakelu villagers. The villagers had competed with each other to have pictures taken with Governor Xiang, however they had no idea who the photographers taking them were. After the event, all the villagers came to Xiaolin, to entreat him to look out for their photos. The one who had visited him most often for this purpose was Song Tongguo, who had explicitly stated that he would pay Xiaolin for the trip: the picture with him standing next to the governor was so important for him that he couldn't wait to have it — his mouth seemed to snatch after the picture like an eager hand.

Who could have taken the pictures?

The reporters of course!

Given that tens of reporters had bustled around Governor Xiang, Xiaolin had no way to know who they were. Fortunately, he had recognized one of them as Xue Yulu, whom he had met before and whose appearance he still remembered.

Xiaolin recalled that Xue Yulu had positioned herself right in front of Governor Xiang, and her camera's light had flashed incessantly. So he was sure that Xue Yulu definitely had some pictures with the villagers and Governor Xiang in them. However, he was not certain whether Xue Yulu would be willing to give him any.

In the taxi on the way to Xue Yulu's office, I said to Xiaolin, "As long as we can obtain one picture that has Governor Xiang and you in it, we can show that picture to the troublesome reporter's press house. Then they won't have the guts to expose Sakelu's problems."

Only half believing what I was saying, Xiolin asked me, "Can a picture have such great power?"

"Absolutely!" I said. "Let's wait and see."

Xue Yulu had been the vice president of the press house for three years. President Sun, who kicked the bucket last year, had strongly recommended her to the higher level authorities. However, after she successfully secured the position, she so exasperated President Sun that he died of chagrin.

After retirement, President Sun continued to deem that he still had as much influence as he had had in the past. He accepted a large sum of money offered by a big firm. In return for the money, he composed a lengthy report about the firm, which would fill a whole page of the newspaper. He hoped to get Xue Yulu's approval for its publication. In President Sun's mind, Xue Yulu was a dog he had raised and fed; as such, what else could she do but give her approval with a grateful heart? However, to President Sun's surprise, something utterly unexpected came to pass — as he went to see her, Xue Yulu met him with a face colder than ice; she could hardly have been more reluctant to talk with him. When he brought up the purpose of his visit, Xue Yulu responded in a completely businesslike tone, stating that for the publication of such a lengthy report, normally one hundred and twenty thousand *yuan* must be charged; after a favorable discount for him, the amount would not be less than one hundred thousand *yuan*. The old man spoke in a near-pleading voice, but Xue Yulu answered curtly, "No way! I mean it!"

As the old man left her office, Xue Yulu did not bother to look up or say "Good bye."

The minute he was out the press house's gate, the old man's tears flooded out uncontrollably. That same evening he rang her, but she pointedly did not answer his call and then switched off her mobile phone.

That night, the old man was rushed into a hospital emergency room due to a heart attack. Three days later, he departed the world.

Making an excuse, Xue Yulu did not attend President Sun's funeral. She could cite solid reasons for her decision. She exclaimed that President Sun had been a "sex wolf," a play-boyish person in spite of his advanced age. She said she had hated him so vehemently that she wanted to make him die of exasperation.

I did not enter the press house with Xiaolin; I made him go alone to ask

Xue Yulu for some pictures. Unexpectedly, she granted his request without hesitation. Xiaolin was out of the press house in no time with a large envelope in his hand. Leading me aside, he took out the pictures for us to view.

These pictures were amazingly good and well taken. The one with Third Aunt and Governor Xiang in it looked especially nice. Viewing this picture, we could hardly keep from laughing. In the picture, Third Aunt was catching the Governor's lappet, with her head turned aside, her mouth wide open, and her eyes narrowing into two thin slits; Governor Xiang was smiling too, but with an air of dignity.

In contrast, Xiaolin and Governor Xiang looked pretty formal and serious in their picture. The two men seemed to be father and son who were physically close but spiritually divided.

Xiaolin said Xue Yulu had expressed enormous surprise with the transformation of Mazi Village into Sakelu Park. He quoted her as saying, "A transformation from hell to heaven — is it really that easy? It's so incredible."

Based on the remarks Xue Yulun had made, Xiaolin concluded that she would like to have a villa of her own in Sakelu — not necessarily a ready-made one; what she wished for was a plot of her own, so that she could have a villa built on it; when she had her villa in Sakelu Park, she would not spend much time in it; rather she would go there only during holidays for relaxation. She said she wanted to own a villa in Sakelu mainly because she was fond of the pleasant environment. Far away from factories, it was not polluted and there was plenty of fresh air.

Xue Yulu had asked Xiaolin whether he had seen me lately.

Xiaolin answered her, "Yes, from time to time."

Xue Yulu said, in an outburst of emotion, that actually she had been pretty nice to me, but due to my stubbornness and disobedience, we had become estranged; nevertheless, as a gracious and magnanimous person, she had never borne a grudge. She told Xiaolin that it was her firm opinion, now as in the past, that I was a talented journalist, and that it was a great pity so few people in the press house could compose smooth sentences like me.

I smiled at what Xiaolin was telling me, and did not take seriously what Xue Yulu had said about my talent.

I urged Xiaolin to take the pictures to the press house where the reporter worked who had threatened to expose Sakelu's problems. I advised him to go straight to see the chief editor and show him the picture with Governor

Xiang and Xiaolin in it.

"In the meantime, brag a little in front of the chief editor," I said to Xiaolin. "Claim that you are a distant nephew of Governor Xiang."

Xiaolin refused to do so, "It doesn't pay to cheat people, I'm afraid."

I replied, "Why, given that you live in a whorehouse, are you so obsessed with chastity? There are traps laid everywhere. Will you get anywhere if you refuse to do likewise? You'll go nowhere!"

Xiaolin did not go along with me in this respect. He believed that society was like a fruit-bearing tree; that most of the fruits it bore were good; that it was normal that there should be some misshaped fruits or worm-eaten fruits on the tree.

Xiaolin accepted my advice, so he went to see the chief editor and show him the picture. However, he refused to pretend to be the governor's nephew. In no event would he do that!

Just as I had predicted, Xiaolin came out of the press house with a big smile on his face. The hunch-backed chief editor accompanied Xiaolin all the way out of the gate. While bidding him goodbye, the chief editor bowed down to Xiaolin again and again; the flattering smiles on his face were overflowing disgustingly, like pork lard boiling over.

As soon as he saw me, Xiaolin gave me the thumbs-up. He kept praising me, "Your trick was superb! It was truly superb! With the help of one photo, a potentially troublesome event was completely eliminated."

Xiaolin gave a detailed account of the story:

The chief editor had not given Xiaolin the slightest attention until he showed him the picture. Seeing the photo, the chief editor's attitude changed radically: in a second, the warmth in his demeanour soared from 100 degrees above to 100 degrees below zero. Actually the chief editor became so fierily enthusiastic that his figure seemed to shiver. Xiaolin had never imagined that a photo could have the capacity of transforming a frightening tiger into an obedient cat.

The chief editor eagerly shook hands with Xiaolin. While pouring water for Xiaolin and offering him a cigarette, the chief editor said, "We are pals. There must have been some misunderstanding. Yes, a misunderstanding."

The chief editor promised he would deal with the journalist severely.

After making this oath, the chief editor passionately praised Governor Xiang, claiming that the governor not only had good character but also had strong qualifications. He called the governor "the most respected governor" in the province since the founding of the People's Republic of China.

Of course, the chief editor asked Xiaolin how it was that he had had a picture taken with Governor Xiang? Were they closely related? Could Xiaolin act as a middleman to put him in touch with Governor Xiang?

To all these questions, Xiaolin replied as vaguely as possible.

58

Yesterday — it was yesterday that Liben called to ask me to recommend someone who might take over Meiteng's agency in Yuebei. I hesitated a long time before finally plucking up the courage to ask what he thought about me as a candidate. Liben said that, as a matter of fact, he had actually considered me, but dismissed the thought on the grounds that I would not look twice at such a job — which would obviously be a waste of my talent. In his eyes, I was a proud man of letters, while the agency job was a vulgar, pragmatic matter. I said I had long since been of a pragmatic frame of mind, and that I could not afford to be proud any more. Since getting sacked by the press house, I had been turned down by all reputable organizations. Even when I made a good first impression on them, they had changed their mind after inquiring into my case. I was now outside, on society's door-step, like an unwanted bowl of left-over rice. The most important thing for me now was to actually get a bowl of rice, or I might starve to death!

Liben said it would be me, then. The matter was settled. I said, I heard that the general manager's family name was Wang, and I did not know what he would think of me. Liben said that General Manager Wang was unfamiliar with the local situation; up till now, at least, everything was referred to his, Liben's, decision. General Manager Wang was like an amputee, and Liben was his walking stick, without whom he would find it difficult to advance even an inch. I said Wang had invested a large sum of money here, and unlike public funds that no one cared about, it was the result of his own sweat and blood, so Liben should not let it go down the drain! Liben said he was well aware of that. As a special counselor he would never do anything without careful consideration. I said that that was how it should be. After that Liben drew a tempting picture for me, saying that as a staff member of an American enterprise, I might make at least one trip to the United States. And if I made a good job of my work, I might even commute between China and the United States, flying back and forth day after day. Furthermore, I might even become a citizen of the United States sometime in the future!

The establishment of Meiteng Agency in Yuebei was marked by the renting of two offices and the making of a plaque. After I moved into the office, the first few days were peaceful, too peaceful, in fact, for me to feel at ease, as I took the salary Meiteng was paying without doing anything; but that peace was abruptly ended on the sixth day by people from the tax office. There were three of them, two men and one woman. The moment they arrived at the agency, they took down the plaque which had been hanging outside and, without further inquiry, threw it down on the ground, and stamped on it with their feet. I rushed out hastily to ask "What's the matter? What's the matter?" With taut faces, they did not answer me directly; instead they roared at me ferociously that the agency was suspected of illegality with regard to the formalities of tax registration. Not only must it be shut down immediately, but I was going to be fined fifty thousand *yuan*. I knew that my real offense was not to have honored them as gods and burned incense in their honor. I knew it was not difficult to appease these people. All they wanted was some pocket money. If I offered them several cartons of cigarettes every now and then, invited them for a drink from time to time, and a modest sum of money stuffed inside a red envelope into their pockets, then everything would be all right. Whether something was legal or illegal was entirely up to them.

I asked them to sit down, but they refused. I invited them to drink tea or smoke cigarettes, but they again refused. They just stuck to their demand of fifty thousand *yuan*. Fifty thousand *yuan*, and not a cent less! With no other option, I had to use Dalin as a shield. So I asked them whether they had ever heard of Dalin, vice-captain of the tax inspection team. Their expressions became irresolute, and their eyes were full of doubt: "How do you know Captain Tian? What's the relationship between you and Captain Tian?" The woman asked straight out about my connection to Captain Tian. I said Tian Dalin was my younger brother. Taken aback, she wanted to know if he was my real brother in the literal sense. I said Tian Dalin was my uncle's son.

In short order, as if prompted by the text of a slide show, they made a 180-degree turn, their eyes beaming with sweet smiles. One of the men even picked up the plaque from the ground and brought it into my office. They sat down on the sofa, and this time accepted both tea and cigarettes. They talked with me about Captain Tian, and all agreed that he was a good man, decisve and competent, while inquiring now and again whether Tian Dalin's father was really my uncle, or if his father and my father were blood brothers, and so on and so forth. They were not downright skeptical, but that they knew that swindlers were everywhere. In a fraud case just cracked in Yuebei the other day, it transpired that the convict had posed as the nephew of some state official, had swindled two hundred million *yuan*, and seduced a large number of young girls. Nowadays people were so reckless as to try to pass themselves off as relatives of central government leaders. Was there such a thing as law in their eyes?

In order to convince them, I dialed Dalin's number. Dalin spoke in a changed tone; even his voice sounded strange to me. I seldom contacted him at that time because he was always complaining about how busy he was. At that moment he happened to be in the Republic of Korea, so he told me — but after hearing from me that some tax collectors were picking on me, he had a few words with one of them. As these people were from a low-tier tax office, they were only acquainted with Dalin by name, not in person. The fat man who seemed to be in charge took the phone, his eyes narrowing into slits, smiles erupting onto the surface of his face like soap bubbles. A stout man, he spoke with such softness as to tickle one to death. He flattered Dalin most fulsomely, instantly portraying Dalin as the bright sun. He said he would lead the whole office to welcome him at the airport when he came back.

After a few civilities, Dalin asked them to take good care of me, and so on and so forth. Putting down the receiver, the fat man gave me a firm handshake, and insisted that we were a family. He reproached me for not having disclosed my relationship with Dalin soon enough, which had almost resulted in a misunderstanding. He invited me to drink with him, and lost no time in bragging that though he had just completed his military service, thanks to his protector, he had been able to enter the tax bureau. And who was that protector? Sorry, it would be indiscreet to tell me.

The fat man dragged me into a restaurant for a drink, admitting that he expected me to put in a good word for him with Dalin for the good meal he was about to treat me to. I said there was no need for them to bother. Dalin was only a vice captain of the tax inspection team. As a farmer's son, could he really have much power? The woman, who had been silent all this time, finally spoke, her mouth twisting like a fried dough twist. She laughed at my ignorance of Dalin's backgrounds, which proved how far I was from being a properly qualified brother. Dalin's canopy might not be broad, but his roots were sturdy and deep! The expressions on the woman's face flickered capriciously like neon lights. She pulled me outside and whispered in my ear to ask whether I had been informed of Dalin's recent affair. I was rather shocked, and asked her about Dalin's immediate past. Although the woman spoke in a mosquito buzz, the meaning of her words was a cosmic revelation to me. Dalin was divorcing his wife Ye Lihua! The daughter of an official in Beijing had fallen in love with him, or was it that Dalin had tempted the official's daughter? All in all, the two had an unusual relationship; they flirted with each other. The daughter of the big official stayed in Yuebei for three quarters of a year, creating disquietness and unrest in the Ye household. It seemed that they would get married soon. Ostensibly an honest man, Dalin was in fact more cunning than a common thief. He knew that once he married this official's daughter, his luck in officialdom would soar like the morning sun. Who, in the whole tax system, did not know of Dalin's affair?

"Really?" I said. "Can a man really change so much overnight?"

59

To tell the truth, I would not have called Dalin if I had not been harassed by the tax office personnel. I could not remember for how long I had not contacted him. Indeed, for months on end, his name had not flashed in my mind for a single time. The Dalin who had disturbed my peace of mind was currently no more than a vague symbol, whereas the previous impression had been vigorous and lively; but with the passage of time it had been withering continually, until eventually it had become as dry as an old stick.

Dalin's marriage with Ye Lihua had gone against the wish of each and every one who knew him. It was against his own will, too. The reward Ye Zhonghua had vowed to give him was really alluring: once he married Ye Lihua, his *hukou*, i.e., his registered social security account, would be changed from agricultural to urban; he would possess two estates, including one villa; he would have a Buick limousine to drive; he would hold a decent and enviable job.

In the face of the conditions offered by Ye Zhonghua, Dalin wavered. He came to see me, asking my opinion whether he should take them or reject them. Instead of making a decision for him, I advised him to think carefully before taking any action. I told him, "The huge fortune owned by Ye Zhonghua may have been acquired improperly. If anything happens, you may not be able to keep the wealth."

As we parted, Dalin articulated something that left a long-lasting impression on my mind, "First I'll get those things and later I can divorce Ye Lihua — then the whole fortune will be equally divided between us."

What he said took me aback. I could hardly believe that such vulgar and materialistic words had come from Dalin's mouth.

Since he had moved into that villa, Dalin's thoughts had gradually undergone a remarkable change. In his conversations with me, the topics about past rural life gave way to things such as: how much top brand cigarettes cost; what liquor brands were genuinely appealing; how many types of Rolex watch there were; which brand of car had better functions, BMW or Benz; how to determine the quality of jewelry; what had enabled a certain official in the provincial or municipal government to secure a promotion, etc.

"How is it you have become so vulgar, Dalin?" I asked him. "You were not like this in the past."

Wearing a puzzled look on his face, Dalin replied, "Am I vulgar? To pay attention to oxen as they pull the plow or to chickens as they scratch for food is not considered vulgar, but to pay attention to fashionable commodities is called vulgar?" His face reddened a bit. Firmly denying he was vulgar, he claimed he was faithfully following the progress of the times.

Dalin and Ye Lihua's wedding ceremony had been fairly simple. Only five guest tables were ordered — one table for Ye Lihua's parents, uncles and aunts; one for those connected with Ye Lihua; one for those connected with Ye Zhonghua; one for Dalin's relatives and friends; and the last one for any people who might unexpectedly show up. Even though Ye Lihua had never gone to work, there was an institution where she was nominally employed: she had been receiving her salary in due time every month from Jiaotong College. At the end of each year, when the bonus went into Ye Lihua's bank account, her brother Ye Zhonghua would invite the Jiaotong College leaders to a restaurant to have dinner together. On the wedding day, the table reserved for Ye Lihua's guests was taken by the Jiaotong College leaders; the college principal and vice principals made up eight of the party, and the college secretary and vice secretaries of the Party committee made up the remaining three. To tell the truth, there were barely enough seats for them.

Dalin had had a hard time deciding whom he would invite. He discussed with me for a long time over the phone, but we failed to come to an agreement.

I said, "Ye Zhonghua's wish is that the wedding be held quietly, and no one but the guests should know about it."

This was Ye Lihua's third marriage and Dalin's second marriage. The Ye family did not think the affair was anything to be proud of, and neither did Dalin for that matter. He had no desire to invite his own relatives. Lacking close friends, he wished only to invite Zhang Shutian, Kaiyang County Secretary of the Party committee. This act was intended to kill two birds with one stone — first, he would establish a connection with the secretary; second, he would request the secretary to pave the way for Xiaolin's future development. Hadn't there been a popular story about the power a county secretary of the Party committee assumed? In the story, two people are arguing how large the sky over a county is. One of them claims, "It is as large as the palm of our county secretary of the Party committee." The other person scorns that answer, forcing the first speaker to explain why the sky over a county is as large as the palm of its county secretary of the Party committee. Then the first person replies by asking two rhetorical questions, "Haven't you heard of the idiom 'One hand of an authority can conceal the sky?' In a county, isn't its secretary of the Party committee the Number One authority?"

Dalin had been aware that he himself could not sit side by side with Zhang Shutian. However, he knew the Ye family could! It would be a great honor for Zhang Shutian to dine with Elder Ye.

Dalin did not want Third Aunt to attend his wedding, because she had adamantly objected to the match. The mother and son had been at odds with each other.

To tell the truth, initially Third Aunt had intended to receive Ye Lihua when she was told Ye Lihua was a retarded woman. In Third Aunt's eyes, it wouldn't have mattered much even if she had also been deaf or dumb — a woman was no more than a tool to bear babies; as long as Ye Lihua could bear her a grandson, who had a weenie between his thighs, Third Aunt would regard her as acceptable.

But after having taken a trip to Yuebei to meet with Ye Lihua, Third Aunt had become unshakable in her opposition to the marriage. The sight of Ye Lihua mopping her running nose with her own sleeves from time to time had really got on her nerves. That day, Ye Lihua held a paper box full of grapes firmly within her arms, fearing that Third Aunt might grab some grapes from it. While eating the grapes, Ye Lihua spat the grape skins with so much force that some landed on Third Aunt's feet. What annoyed Third Aunt more was that as she motioned Dalin aside to have a word in his ear, Ye Lihua ran like mad at Dalin's heels. Throwing the grape box onto the floor, she howled as if her parents had just died. Then and there, Third Aunt forced Dalin to break up with Ye Lihua. But could Dalin break up even if he wanted to? Being well aware of the influence of the Ye family, Dalin realized that a common person like him could not afford to displease them. Moreover, Ye Zhonghua's treatment of him was really not bad; he had received lots of gifts from him.

In great fury, Third Aunt left Yuebei for Kaiyang, where she fell ill. She was hospitalized; she nearly ended up in the hospital's mortuary. Third Aunt whined tearfully to whomever she came across, saying, "Dalin must have been struck blind, otherwise how could he choose an idiot when there are countless normal women in the world? This idiot is even worse than Taoqi. It is true Taoqi ruined her reputation by calling people bad names. But wasn't that one of her talents?"

Third Aunt favored Layue, Fugui's daughter. She dispatched Xiaolin to ask Dalin to come back and date Layue.

Xiaolin did take a trip to Yuebei, but he had not succeeded in seeing Dalin, though he had managed to find his way to the Ye family address. Their courtyard, surrounded by a forbidingly high wall fenced with barbed iron, was securely guarded. The sentry who guarded the gate glared balefully at Xiaolin, as if Xiaolin were a scoundrel. He almost went to the point of arresting him.

When she learned that Layue was passionately attached to Song Tongguo, Third Aunt grew more anxious. But what could she do? Dalin's mobile phone number had changed; she could not find him anywhere.

Layue had divorced her husband Qi Guangrong and had moved out along with her son Langwa to live in her parents' house. As a matter of fact, the court had decided that Langwa live under his father Qi Guangrong's care. However, his mother hid him away and would not allow his father to take him. Layue declared that Qi Guangrong could have Langwa back on the condition that he give up the piss pot in exchange.

Dalin had invited me to attend his wedding, but I did not go — I made an excuse, saying that on his wedding day I would be out of town on a business trip. I used to care for Dalin very much. When he first came to Yuebei, he spent one and a half years at my place, living and eating together with me. How pure he had been then! In those days, the sight of lovers walking hand in hand along the streets would prompt him to make a negative comment. Now, as I saw Dalin going more and more astray, I no longer wanted to associate with him. He had made up his mind to choose a cliff and to jump off it — he took the falling for flying, and derived an unparalleled excitement from it. Even though I had sincerely wished to take firm hold of him, and prevent him from falling, it was beyond my power to draw him back. All I could do was tear the invitation into pieces and drop the bits into a dustbin.

Liben attended Dalin's wedding. After the event, he visited me, spending half a day at my place. He told me that to his surprise, Xue Yulu had turned up at Dalin's wedding; she sailed charmingly around the place, her brittle laughter heard intermittently here and there. Liben could not help wondering at what point in his life Dalin had associated closely with Xue Yulu. This question baffled me, too.

According to Liben, no ceremonial rites had been performed on the occasion. The guests had been there to attend a feast rather than a wedding ceremony. The whole thing had been pretty dull. Dalin hardly smiled and Ye Lihua did not say anything as if she had been instructed to be quiet. Old Mr. Ye sat squarely like a sculpture, with a dominating look in his eyes. Under such circumstances, all the guests behaved with careful respect and talked in whispers.

"To tell the truth, Xue Yulu was the only person who could be considered lively," Liben said. "However, her liveliness created nothing but profound displeasure on the part of the Ye family."

The story was that while Xue Yulu was persistently urging Dalin and Ye Lihua to drink a "loving cup" of wine with entwined arms, for no obvious reason Ye Lihua started wailing. She collapsed onto the floor, her legs kicking frantically, her hands patting madly. She cried at the top of her voice, her tears and snot smudging her cheeks. This spoilt the entire feast. Those who attempted to calm her down failed in their endeavors. None of their tricks worked.

Initially Old Mr. Ye showed no sign of wanting to intervene. But, seeing that the row his daughter was making showed no signs of ending, the old man staggered toward her. When he got close to her, Old Mr. Ye suddenly lifted one foot to take off his shoe. This created the impression that he was about to beat her with it. Instantly, Ye Lihua's howls came to a stop. She bounced up and rushed towards the other end of the hall. Ye Zhonghua followed his sister, only to see her disappear into a washroom. With great effort, he dragged her out of it.

Upon finishing the story, Liben heaved a sigh, and said, "How could Dalin take such an idiot woman to wife?"

I said, "This idiot woman may not bring happiness to Dalin, but she can definitely bring him material benefits. Of course, this nuptial tie satisfies the vanity deep in Dalin's innermost heart."

60

The trip to my hometown was an enraging experience. On my father's birthday each year, I would pay a visit to the tombs of my parents, a practice which I had followed for fifteen years. But when I came back this time, I was surprised to find that my ancestral tombs were gone.

The site on which Mazi Village had once stood was occupied by new buildings, large and small, of different shapes and colors, between which were set concrete roads at right-angles, along with lawns and gardens. A newly-built square, enhanced by a playground, was surrounded by a cluster of buildings. The square, home to a small artificial lake with colorful surging fountains, had yet to be completed, and workers were in the middle of installing tall street lamps.

Was this Mazi Village? Apparently not! Then what was this? That a rustic village should have been turned into a modern town, in such a short time, was a miracle — a miracle which amazed me for a moment, but which then left me trapped in nameless distress. I was supposed to be back in my hometown, but I could find none of the fellow villagers I had once been familiar with. All I saw were strange faces. I tried to talk to them, but they seemed uninterested in talking.

With a bamboo basket in hand I struggled to find a way through the village, and I almost got lost. The hillock I could remember, on which hare grass had spread in luxuriance and morning glories had quietly bloomed, was altogether gone. A sizable persimmon tree, at least three or four hundred years old, had stood not far from my family's ancestral tombs. However, there was no longer any sign of it. Over my family's tombs there had grown five or six cypress trees, in addition to a plum tree planted by my father in his childhood. There used to be a nest on top of the plum tree, where flocks of birds had raised their chicks, and flown in and out. Where were all these trees? Where had all those birds gone?

The sacrificial offerings in my basket consisted of a bottle of quality wine, two packs of choice cigarettes, a box of exquisitely-packed cakes, three deep-fried dough sticks, a string of firecrackers, and a thick stack of joss money. My father drank little when he was alive, but only because he simply could not afford it, as I thought, since all men were fond of the bottle; while cigarettes were my father's favorite indulgence. It had been a pity that he could only afford to smoke dry tobacco which he grew for himself, and which was so strong that it often reduced him to hysterically choking and coughing. The deep-fried dough sticks were bought for my mother who once, on returning from town, said that folks there ate deep-fried dough sticks as if they were a staple food, and had, over many days, spread that news in the village. Although a deep-fried dough stick sold for only five cents, she had still been reluctant to buy one for herself. But meanwhile…where were their tombs? Where must I burn the stack of joss money?

I was in a dilemma; but at that moment, thank heaven! I caught sight of Song Tongguo who, in a western suit and leather shoes, with the airs of a big boss, came out of the office building and got into a Santana. I stood in front of the car, blocking its way. Upon seeing me, Song Tongguo got out. His face seemed to have been heavily made-up, because it looked very bright. He smiled sweetly, and warmly greeted me. He obviously could not wait to tell me that he had become a middle-rank executive of Meiteng Company, a real one that had been approved at a board meeting and announced in a company document officially issued. According to him, his appointment to such an important post stirred up a lot of envy in Mazi Village — Sakelu, as it was called now! A lot of people refused to be convinced. So be it, and to hell with them! At least Liben and other high-level executives of Meiteng Company recognized that he was — not just a talent, but an outstanding talent! At first, many people wanted to compete with him, Beiqiang in particular, who fancied that he could fuck a hole in a millstone with his soft cock! Then why had he failed? He thought that Liben would be biased in his favour because he was his brother-in-law, but Liben was such an upright man that he would only appoint the competent; he had seen through Beiqiang and decided that he was a useless puddle of piss and mud.

I asked Song Tongguo what his duties were, specifically. After adjusting his tie, he straightened his neck and said that he was temporarily in charge of recruiting workers, and would probably be put in charge of making purchases in the future. Did these two positions not constitute real power? Right now, he was on his way to the human resources bureau of the county, to apply for the employment quotas. To be frank, at present he no longer needed to worry about food and drink wherever he went, because people were lining up to invite him to dine. The queue was longer than the Great Wall. Arrogant officials like the chief of the human resources bureau or the director of the organization department smiled obsequiously at the sight of him. What a glorious life he was leading now! He had not lived to no purpose, he really had not. He had not come to Mazi Village in vain, and he had not been a live-in son-in-law in vain. It was very valuable, he believed, to be Luobo's husband, no matter how he sliced it! Valuable, really valuable, extremely valuable! Of course, Luobo had done her part before she was dead. She had died for a good cause. An ill-favored woman, with a widow's peak, she would no doubt have stood in the way to his prosperity if she had lived. It was her death that drove his bad luck away, and illuminated the way ahead of him!

Song Tongguo asked me whether I knew of anyone who would like to work in Meiteng. If I did, I should let him know. Given that he was a door keeper, might he not open it a crack for my sake? Anyone else who wanted in would have to give a present, but in view of my friendship with him, I would not have to. Song Tongguo was not greedy. By no means!

I told him that I had come back to visit family tombs, but unfortunately I could not find them. Song Tongguo laughed at my superstition, saying that tomb-visiting was a form of delusion. How could I believe such nonsense? He said his father had been buried in a valley at his hometown, where, it was said, a flood had washed his bones away. He had not gone back even once, but was he not still living very well? He had an old mother at home, nearly ninety years old, an old oil lamp about to run out of fuel, but seven or eight years had passed since he last saw her. What would the economic returns of visiting her be? None! In today's society, nothing but economic returns counted.

Nevertheless, Song Tongguo took me in his car to look for my parents' tombs. The car travelled in all directions, north and south, east and west. Whenever we stopped somewhere, we would get out, verify our location and spend a moment trying to recall if this was the right spot or not, only to eventually shake our heads in disappointment. At first, Song Tongguo was very patient, but gradually he began checking his watch from time to time, evidently eager to go away. After searching for half an hour, the car took us back to where we had started. As I was getting out of the car, Song Tongguo told me to pick out a random spot to symbolically perform the rituals. "Why make a fuss for everything to be one hundred percent precise?" he asked.

Standing outside the gate of the office area, I felt rather sad. Suddenly, a faint hatred against Liben rose in my bosom. Why had Liben done all of these things? The Mazi villagers had moved into villas at the cost of losing their ancestors!

Just as I was getting to the end of my tether, Fugui drifted in front of me like a leaf in the wind. He was strangely attired, wearing a colorful paper hat on his head and a string of beads on his chest; he clapped his hands the moment he saw me, and mumbled "May the Buddha preserve us." This terrified me so much that I stumbled backward a few steps. Once he was back in his right mind, he asked me when I had come back, and why. I answered each of his questions, and asked him why he carried a woven bag. After repeating "May the Buddha preserve us" again, he said he was here for Song Tongguo, who had married Layue but who had refused to live with her. Song Tongguo would rather stay in his office than go home. Song Tongguo claimed that he was busy busy busy, but that was just an excuse. The real reason was that Layue had married him without the emperor's piss pot, and that was what displeased him. Now, while it was true that Layue had promised to bring the piss pot as part of her dowry, it was also true that she admitted the pot had yet to be found. A fight between them took place on the very day they got married. Song Tongguo punched Layue with his iron fist so hard as to give her a suppurating ear. Was Song Tongguo any kind of a husband? Was he even a human being? Hearing that Song Tongguo had hooked up with a modern woman in the city, Layue hid under her quilt and cried every night. If her mother had not had such a deft hand and such a sharp eye, she would have jumped into Sakelu's artificial lake. Of course, as the lake was shallow, she would not have drowned, even if she had jumped into it.

That was the reason for Fugui's visit — to persuade Song Tongguo to change his mind, go home and continue his conjugal life with Layue. How cute Langwa was! He was endowed with a sharp tongue although he was a kid barely more than ten years old. Everyone acknowledged that Song Tongguo's late wife had been spirited in quarrels, but even if she were still alive she would not be Langwa's rival. When cornered, Langwa would drop to the floor and take a bite of the opponent's foot.

I asked Fugui what the woven bag was for. He told me that he was collecting garbage. As the factory was about to go into operation, stuff was littered all over the place. A quick round up could be exchanged for enough money to meet his daily needs. He stressed that he only picked up what had been abandoned, and that he would never climb walls to steal things because that sort of thing was disgusting and would bring shame to Sakyamuni. Fugui asked if I had heard that he had been converted to Buddhism. I replied that I had not. Wrinkling his nose, he began to tell me how he had become a Buddhist just a few days before. Seized by a sudden headache, he had fallen asleep with his clothes on. Soon after, he had a vision in which a rainbow-colored beam of light shot down vertically, and wavered before his eyes. In the light appeared the face of Sakyamuni who held out an edict and pronounced Fugui to be the Buddha of Shining Virtue missing for three hundred years. Originally enshrined in Sichuan, the Buddha of Shining Virtue had been demolished in a farmer's revolt on a certain day of a certain month of a certain year, and since then the Buddha of Shining Virtue had been in exile in the boundless universe, unable to find a human body for shelter. Considering that Fugui had a merciful heart, Sakyamuni made the Buddha of Shining Virtue perch on his shoulders. Sakyamuni instructed Fugui to concentrate on Buddhist activities, saying He would cast sacred light over Fugui. The moment when he woke up, Fugui immediately set up a tablet for Sakyamuni in his house, burned incense, and knelt down to worship. From that day on, Fugui became a divine being, whole-heartedly devoting himself to Sakyamuni. He gave himself a monastic name — Shining Virtue.

I did not want to listen any longer. The scorching sun reminded me that there were no tall trees to give shade, and that Mazi Village, which had once been so green, had been replaced by a bare concrete jungle. I asked Fugui whether he could recall the site of my parents' tombs. He raised his hand to point straight at the Meiteng office building, and said that they were buried right under it.

"Are you certain?" I asked.

"I couldn't be more certain!" Fugui replied.

On the day the office building's cornerstone was laid, almost all the villagers came to watch the ceremony. My ancestors' bones were dug out by excavators, and got so scattered that a heated discussion sprang up among the villagers. Fugui would never forget the scene, as if it were incised on his brain. How could he be less than certain?

"What happened to the bones in the end?" I asked again.

"Reburied, of course." Fugui said. "Crushed into the foundation."

I had an impulse to cry out loud. My chest seemed to be exploding into flames like a petrol bomb. Notwithstanding the security guards' efforts to stop me, I went directly to the Meiteng office building, knelt down on the ground, emptied the basket in one go, and ignited the joss money. The security guards kicked me, but I refused to obey their orders to stand up. Kneeling all the time, I wailed hysterically at the top of my voice.

61

I had a fiery exchange with Liben in Third Aunt and Xiaolin's house, where he was temporarily living — for, even though he had helped build Sakelu Park, Liben did not have a single inch of estate there.

Before I had a chance to vent my anger on him, Liben rebuked me harshly. He exclaimed that my act of burning joss paper in front of Meiteng's office building had shocked all the staff members, from top rank leaders all the way down to common employees.

"What a bad omen for the firm!" Liben shouted at me. "Production work had not yet begun, and already you were burning joss paper in its yard."

Liben told me that Wang Dawei, the general manager representing the Chinese investors, had called him into his presence and flared up at him; and that Wang Dawei had wanted to report the case to the public security bureau, but thanks to his, Liben's, earnest pleas, Wang Dawei eventually gave up the idea of making the police hold me accountable for my criminal behavior. Wang Dawei had ordered that I be removed from my office and that my position as the director of Meiteng's Yuebei Office be taken over by someone else.

Third Aunt had prepared a nice meal, which included my favorite thousand-layer bread. I had hardly taken two bites when Liben began recounting this matter. I expected him to offer me loads of apologies on behalf of Meiteng. But instead of confessing their faults, they accused me of misconduct.

"How ridiculous this is! What ridiculous nonsense!" I shouted angrily. "Is there no justice in the world?"

In fury, I dropped my chopsticks. But all my exasperation had not yet been vented. Lifting my bowl, I dashed it on the floor. If it were not that Liben looked pitiably small, I would have liked to rush at him, grab him by the collars and beat him up without mercy.

Pointing at Liben's nose, I shouted at him, "Where are my ancestors' tombs? Where have they gone? I can live with not being office director, but I can't bear the loss of the tombs containing my ancestors' bones! I want to get them back! I am their offspring, but I failed to safeguard even their tombs. I have nowhere to go to mourn my ancestors. What shame I have brought on them! How unworthy I am!"

Liben seemed to be baffled by my anger. Stupefied, he looked at me as if I were an alien from outer space. Turning to Xiaolin, he asked in a low voice whether I had been given compensation for the loss of my ancestral graves. Having thought for a while, Xiaolin replied that it seemed I hadn't been compensated. Liben then complained that the person in charge of this work had been too careless. Rising to his feet, Liben walked over to me. Patting my shoulder, he forced me back into the chair. In a soothing tone, he said to me, "Don't flare up. Calm down. I'll have them issue compensation to you. If they have any objection, I'll pay you myself."

Third Aunt was cleaning the mess on the floor. While carefully collecting the scattered food into a plastic bag, she murmured that it could be used to fertilize the flowers she planted.

I was breathing heavily on account of the enormous fury I felt. It seemed that a heavy tablet were lying on my tongue and something were blocking my throat, so that I could not articulate anything. In the meantime, Xiaolin and Liben were arguing with each other, each claiming that it was his own duty to pay me the compensation. Xiaolin said he would compensate me with part of his salary, but Liben insisted he himself should compensate me, because he was better off than Xiaolin.

Their prolonged arguing made me feel sick. Was it for money that I had flared up? If I obtained a wad of banknotes in exchange for my ancestors' bones, how would I have the heart to spend them? Nevertheless, I could not help asking about the amount of compensation. Liben replied, "Ten *yuan* for each grave."

"How many graves did your family have?" Liben asked me.

Bah! I spat onto the floor, and said, "Ten *yuan!* A compensation of ten *yuan*? That's a further humiliation for my ancestors! Are our ancestors so valueless that they are only worth ten *yuan* each?"

Thinking that I was displeased with the low amount, Liben explained to me that actually the so-called grave compensation sum hadn't been budgeted for initially. Later on, because some villagers wouldn't rest unless they were compensated, the investors had to make some concession and promised to give some symbolic compensation. "Otherwise, even this tiny amount of ten *yuan* would not have been offered," Liben added.

I said, "Even if one hundred thousand *yuan* were offered to me, I wouldn't accept it. Let alone ten *yuan*. All I want is my ancestors' graves. I can't bear that they should be lost on my watch."

Liben said that he knew well it was not money that I wanted, however, now that the matter had reached this pass, were there any other means to compensate me? "After thinking over and over again, money is the only solution," Liben concluded.

Liben and Xiaolin were discussing the possibility of recategorizing a piece of land in Sakelu Park for me, so that I could build my own villa on it. After all, in addition to my ancestors' graves, hadn't he also caused the loss of my ancestral house?

"Have you only now realized this? What do you think you have done?" I asked him. "What you did was nothing less than a crime!"

Liben did not seem annoyed by my words. He said that before the demolition of the village, he had asked a photographer to come to Mazi Village, and the photographer had taken pictures of it; that the pictures had been made into a book and every household had been given one copy of it as a keepsake.

Liben confessed that whereas it was he who had encouraged the villagers to boldly transform themselves, to bravely step into a new life, and to break with ignorance and backwardness, now he felt neither bold nor brave; he had been missing Mazi Village from time to time.

Liben complained that he was getting old, as evidenced by his sense of nostalgia. He said, "Even though I'm not very old in years, my soul is already worn and weary."

By nighttime, my mood had calmed down considerably, so I got on the same bed as Liben. I chain smoked while Liben coughed continually. I could not go to sleep, and neither could he. We started chatting. Liben said that he had exhausted his energy during the eight years since he had returned to China; that he grieved he had made it his mission to shoulder so many responsibilities.

"But grieving is useless," Liben said. "Now I'm like a person aboard a speeding train. The train is moving at full speed. The railway is precarious, with a precipice on either side. It's impossible for me to jump off the train."

Lots of things were on Liben's mind. Of course, his greatest anxiety was: what should he do if Meiteng failed in this investment venture? He said if that really happened, the situation would be beyond tears; perhaps the only way out would be suicide.

"After all, in America Meiteng is not the kind of big, rich firm, which would not care about a loss of hundreds of millions in investment," Liben said. "Meiteng is merely a small corporation. By concentrating all its resources and raising all the funds it could, it had eventually obtained the needed amount for investing in Mazi Village. If anything bad happens, everybody will be caught in a deadly trap."

In a self-mocking manner, Liben claimed that he had become extremely vulgar; that he used to deem it blasphemy to talk about money in God's presence, but now he made a point of visiting the church in the county seat to pray, and one of his first prayers was to ask God to bless Meiteng, so that it could make money — make lots of money!

I responded, "It will be fine. There'll be no problem. Now that the provincial government has listed it as a key project, the authorities will not just let it collapse, will they?"

Liben burst out in another fit of coughs. After going to the washroom to spit, he returned to the bed, and said, "Is there anything in the world that can't collapse? The Tang Dynasty used to be so prosperous, but didn't it decline and fall? Hitler used to be so overwhelmingly conceited, but didn't he perish? If *they* could collapse, then how much more a firm with no solid footing! Meiteng is like a gigantic ship under construction. Though not yet fully built, it has already been hit by one tempest after another."

Once again, Liben deplored the villagers' mores. He said, "The once hard-working farmers have now been reduced to idlers. They used to live in shabby houses, but now they dwell in gorgeous villas. In the past, some villagers could not afford five *yuan* for their children's medical treatment, but now every family has tens of thousands of *yuan* in their savings account. Aren't those the changes that have taken place? Yes, definitely. However, one thing remains unchanged: the villagers' mores remain the same. They remain short-sighted and narrow-minded."

I said, "A change of clothing does not mean the alteration of a person's personality. Does dressing a beggar in an emperor's suit mean you can make an emperor of the beggar? If a person's mind remains the mind it was, if his flesh and blood remain the flesh and blood they were, and if his bones remain the bones they were, how can you expect to reform him by changing his living quarters and environment? Isn't your idea too naïve?"

But Liben believed in the precept "Education changes all." He believed that Kang Yuanyuan's efforts would produce positive effects on the villagers. According to him, Kang Yuanyuan had been successful in the United

States; while in America, Kang Yuanyuan had worked with both Chinese communities and black communities to carry out her so-called "Citizen Self-Awareness" experiment and program — yes, "Citizen Self-Awareness" was the actual name Kang Yuanyuan had given to the educational program she had implemented in the USA. "Her American program had produced an unexpected effect," Liben claimed. "In the black communities concerned, criminality dropped remarkably, and the children's school enrollment rate rose considerably. Those old blacks who for most of their lives had engaged in violence, became church goers one after another to receive God's teachings."

"Kang Yuanyuan is fairly well-known in the United States," Liben continued. "She was interviewed by the *Wall Street Journal,* and a large picture of her was posted on the first page of the newspaper."

I asked Liben, "Have you ever heard the saying 'Orange trees growing in the South produce good oranges, but those growing in the North produce fruit that's not fit to eat?' Environmental differences will lead to different results. Using an American model to shape a Chinese village will get you nowhere, that's for sure. Revolutions were carried out in America. Revolutions were carried out in China, too. But the revolution led by Washington gave birth to a brand new citizen society; whereas the revolution led by Sun Yatsen gave rise to a disintegrated China, in which warlords fought with one another, leaving the common people struggling to survive. China and America vary in soil, in cultural heritage, and in religious belief. Their national genes differ even more. Simplistically analogizing China and America is an act of blatant irresponsibility."

"Far from being the truth, what you said is a complete fallacy," Liben argued. He was getting a little angry, his tone becoming quite unfriendly. "It is just because of the existence of a large host of people like you, that China has been so slow in moving forward."

"America is the world's America, not just America's," Liben continued. "America has made an experiment for the whole of mankind, and the experiment has been a success. The Americans have beaten the path to success. This will spare other nations both the trouble of exploration and the setbacks it causes. Isn't it a pleasant thing to follow the American route and be spared the trouble of path-finding? There's only one universal value in the world; there's no such a thing as 'This universal value suits only America but not China.' China has never tried to practise this universal value, how can you conclude that it does not suit China?"

I retorted, "Hasn't Kang Yuanyuan practiced it? What has come of the civic school she ran in Mazi Village? Has she succeeded in improving any villagers' mores? The only outcome she harvested was to transform herself into an inexhaustible laughing-stock among the villagers."

Liben stopped debating with me. He turned around to face the wall, with his back toward me, as if he would like to go to sleep. However, his horrible coughs made it hard for him to nod off.

62

On the second day, Liben went to the county hospital for a check-up. There were thin strands of blood in the phlegm he had spat earlier that morning. Third Aunt shivered with fear. Long experience told her that he must have been seriously ill. She said Liben was a fool and began to reprove him without reserve. Had his head been pecked by chickens? Had his brain been crammed with the leftovers of a meal? How could one achieve anything great if one was careless of one's health? How could a butcher kill pigs or sheep if he did not have a sharp knife? How could a young man carry a 100-kilo bag of grain if he was not strong enough? She followed this up by strongly urging him to go to hospital immediately! Liben was unwilling to comply, saying that he would recover from the coughing in a few days. She scolded him with a face as black as thunder, with words so fierce that he could not but promise to go.

Once Liben was gone, Third Aunt burst into tears. She shook out all the age-old stories concerning Liben. She started with Liben's parents, with the inadequacy of their diet, with their eating leaves and bark, all of which had resulted in constipation. It was constipation that had killed his father. Unable to feed him and his sisters, his mother had led them to beg for a living. During his bitter childhood, Liben had never worn an undamaged article of clothing, his shoes were given to him by other people, and would shed their heels in a few days. Just like his mother, he had suffered from the cold, had been bitten by wild dogs, and had had stones and tile pieces thrown at him by children from the neighboring villages. He was often seen with injuries and scars here and there on his body. No-one had expected that such a beggar would make his way to the merry United States, and would return with such a big fortune. He must have gone through all kinds of hardships! He had, however, hardly had a chance to enjoy life — just a few days — before he got that bad illness. One could not help feeling sorry for him. Oh, how silly Liben was! He had so much money that even if he spent it like water it would never run out. What had brought him to such a pitch of self-denial, as to bring money back to feed the ungrateful wolves? A wolf at least knows to wag its tail when it gets fed, but those on whom he had bestowed his gifts were not at all grateful. And not content to be ungrateful, they even stabbed their benefactor in the back. Most of the Mazi villagers were ungrateful wolves, and often spoke ill of him behind his back.

Third Aunt's nattering had finally worn down my patience. I asked Xiaolin if he could show me around. Sakelu was about to be transformed into a scenic spot, but it was still strange to me. Xiaolin said that was no problem, as he was just thinking the same thing.

The tour had only succeeded in filling Xiaolin's belly with anger. Just the sight of rubbish in the court was evidently enough to work him up into such a rage that he had to shout at the villager on duty. The village households took it in one-week turns to keep the court clean, sweeping twice a day and at the same time clearing the rubbish away. The rota was posted on the billboard, and provided each household with its own copy as well. However, some villagers dragged their feet, so that time and again the rubbish accumulated like mountains. Right after this we came across a pile of something repulsive as we were walking on the high street. It had originally lain at the roadside, but it had expanded to occupy almost half of the road width, and dirty garbage was littered and flung along the road for a dozen meters. In the sun, meal leftovers, watermelon peels, even faeces exuded foul smells, which attracted swarms of buzzing flies.

Back at his office, Xiaolin checked the timetable. A Dali household was responsible for the present week's sweeping and clearing. He waved his hand to me to keep up with him, and headed in a rage towards Dali's home. I followed him, keen to see what was bound to be an operatic performance.

From a distance one could hear the shuffling sound of mahjong mixed with laughter and shouting coming out of Dali's house. Its gate had been left ajar, and opened with a gentle push. As expected, a group of people sat round a table playing mahjong, four players, three on-lookers. Dali and wife were at the table, discussing the previous set as they played. It was obvious, from their complaints and sighs, that in the previous set an opponent after expecting a single tile to form the pair in order to win, had therefore made it on his own. Dali's wife attributed the loss of the game to her husband, abusing him and claiming that his brain seemed to have been paralyzed. He still claimed the character to match a triplet, even though he knew that the opponent on the right was already waiting for the winning tile. If only he had refrained, the opponent on the right could not have won by the necessary circle himself!

When Xiaolin and I arrived, it did not arouse any interest in the group who, after raising their eyes to have a brief look, continued doing as the game dictated. Xiaolin thwacked the table with his palm so hard that a rack of tiles were sent bumping and jumping. Dali's wife's eyes showed their whites as she stared at Xiaolin in puzzlement.

She snarled, "What's the matter? What's the matter? Are you crazy?" Xiaolin roared at both Dali and his wife, "Tell me who's on duty today! Go and have a look outside. How can all that rubbish be piled there?" Dali cut in and said, "What are you roaring at? It's none of our business, even if it is heaped up like the Himalayas. I haven't had a lucky hand like this for a long time. Did you come to make trouble? Get out! Get out!"

Dali rose and pushed Xiaolin toward the door. Xiaolin got pushed as far as the doorway, but he managed to come back. This time, he took a more conciliatory tack, almost imploring them to stop playing and get the rubbish removed as quickly as possible. Dali said it was the Shuanhu family who had not cleared the rubbish the previous week, and the hill of rubbish was already there when Dali family took over. Why must the Shuanhu family's work fall to them? Had they eaten so much that they needed to do some extra work for the good of their digestions? "Fair's fair, Xiaolin. You only know to pinch the soft and bully the honest. Why don't you go reproach Shuanhu? Confront him if you have the guts!"

Dali impatiently gestured to Xiaolin to leave, because others were waiting for him to draw tiles in the game. Dali's wife seconded her husband, saying, "Wait until we finish the game if there is anything else you want to say. When the game is over, we can quarrel or fight — that will be up to you! But you mustn't interrupt us while we are playing. If we lose because of you, you'll have to pay." Xiaolin had to back out from Dali's house, grumbling as he went, "He was named Dali, so he is supposed to be reasonable[34], but he does not live up to his name. He is utterly unworthy of his own name!" I asked if there were any solutions available if the Dali family refused to observe the rules. Xiaolin sighed. How could there be any? They were not paid salaries from which money could be deducted, and these infractions were such trifles that the police would not want to get involved. How could he take the matter further? As the interim keeper of the park, he was exhausted. Each month when it was time to collect water and electricity fees, he had to wear his legs out. So far as reasonable people were concerned, you called on them once, and they paid. As for the unreasonable, you could call on them ten or twenty times, but they did not react. They had so many excuses. One moment they would say they were overcharged due to miscalculation, the next they would say they only agreed to pay for what they had used in their own house, refusing their community contribution share. Their argument was that they never came out of the house at night, and that they had thus never needed the street lamps to light their way in the park. Last month, there had been a six-hundred-*yuan* shortfall in electricity payments, and it was Liben who had made up the shortfall. Why should Liben have to do it? Because someone had complained about him, saying, "Does Liben live in Sakelu Park without eating or shitting? Why is he exempt from paying sanitation fee?"

Walking to the lakeside, I had a glimpse of the lake and found it dirty and smelly. More than once I had heard people describe the limpid beauty of its water, but how different the lake lying before me was from that in their descriptions! It confirmed the popular saying — better to hear about it than to see it.

"What are you doing there? How many times have I warned you that you mustn't do that?" Xiaolin suddenly yelled out.

Out of the bush appeared the heads of two girls. Apparently, they were washing clothes, and were startled by Xiaolin's yelling. Once they caught sight of Xiaolin, they took to their heels with their washing basins. Xiaolin looked on helplessly as they fled. He told me that this stretch of water had been one of Sakelu's attractions, but who could have anticipated that it was being transformed into a washing pool?

"Why did they want to wash clothes in the lake since there is running water in their homes?" I wondered.

"Can a dog stop eating shit?" Xiaolin said. "They claim that they are used to washing clothes in a pool. Of course, such a claim is only an excuse. They do so simply because they want to take advantage of the situation. It is free to wash clothes in the lake, but they have to pay if they use the running water in their home."

63

About three hundred meters away from the portal of Sakelu Park, Shuanhu was busy with some large-scale construction work, which was a three-storeyed structure co-funded by Shuanhu and his brother Shuanniu for business purpose. The building was constructed on land belonging to the neighboring village. Right now the second storey was under construction. It looked like the work would probably be completed in half a month.

I was strolling alone, when Shuanhu saw me and shouted my name. In response, I waved at him from a distance. He then jumped down from the scaffolding. Dusting off the patches of white lime on his clothes, Shuanhu walked towards me, his mouth slightly open.

As we approached each other, we both reached into our pockets for a cigarette. By the time I took out my cigarette case, he had already inserted a cigarette between my lips. Then we shook hands and exchanged the normal greetings.

Getting two little stools from the portal guard of Sakelu Park, Shuanhu gave one to me and sat down on the other — we sat face to face. With smiles playing over his face, he asked me whether I had seen Dalin recently. I told him I hadn't.

Shuanhu praised Dalin at length, claiming that, among all the people from Mazi Village with a population of a thousand strong including the old and young, Dalin was the smartest, while Liben was the most foolish. "Dalin has real foresight. It was a really remarkable exploit for him to have married such a fine wife," Shuanhu said.

Shuanhu admitted that because Third Aunt had once offended him, he had long thought about taking revenge on her entire family. However, he suddenly came to his senses: we all came from the same village, what was the point of taking revenge on your fellow villagers?

Shuanhu said he would like to visit Dalin and ask him to do him a favor — to help arrange a job position for Jidan.

According to Shuanhu, ever since Jidan was a child her dream had been to hold a paid governmental job; and now this wish of hers was growing stronger and stronger. Shuanhu said, "How blessed are those on a governmental salary! They do not lack food; they do not lack drink; in winter, they are kept warm by central heating; in summer, they are kept cool by air conditioning. If they reach leadership positions, they get free limousine transportation. More importantly, holding a leadership position is like owning a private business. But think of the horrors associated with running a privately owned business: to begin with, you have to invest money in it; secondly, you are personally responsible for the risk of that investment; thirdly, there's no guarantee that your business will make money; fourthly, even if it makes money, the money-making process is full of hardships and indignities. However, holding a paid governmental leadership position is a totally different story: although you make an initial investment, after that you always gain and never lose: banknotes flow in like rushing torrents, swelling from thousands of rivers and channels."

According to Shuanhu's account, there were other reasons to change Jidan's line of work. Firstly, Jidan's beauty was declining with the passage of time. Rotten teeth can hardly cope with steaks. Rusty sickles can hardly chop firewood. Jidan no longer had any strong advantages in her trade. Secondly, finding her a man to marry had become a pressing issue. Having first hung out here, then there, in the blink of an eye, she was now about twenty-seven years old. A woman of that age could no longer be called a girl; it would be more precise to call her a widow. But what type of household should she marry into, then? This was a tough question for Shuanhu. In fact, it disturbed him so much that his hair kept dropping out, as copiously as autumn leaves falling from trees. Just look at his hair — it had gone gray; you could count the individual strands. It was not that Jidan could not find a household that would accept her — Larz's dislike for her didn't mean she had become an unsalable commodity no one was interested in. On the contrary, numerous suitors were pursuing her; they followed her in an endless procession; each of them was burning to have her. Take, for example, the old fellow named Ganban[35] from Beigou. He had dared to aspire to marry Jidan, like an ugly toad who wished to marry a beautiful swan. Why hadn't he taken a look in the mirror and realized what he was! He had been stricken by infantile paralysis as a small kid. Ever since then he had walked with a limp, his whole body tilting from one side to the other — enough to knock over the walls on either side as he walked along. He was over forty years old, and was still without a wife. That such a person should indulge so wild a fantasy! Having fixed his lustful eyes on Jidan, he asked more than twenty matchmakers to come, one after another in close succession, to propose a match. One matchmaker had been exceptionally persistent. Though Jidan spat in her face, the matchmaker didn't mind it at all. Obviously she had received money from Ganban to go on this errand. She had kept coming again and again, attempting to persuade Jidan. Seeing that these matchmakers couldn't do the job successfully, Ganban decided to come in person. With a plastic bag in hand, Ganban staggered into Shuanhu's villa. Opening the bag, he exposed thick wads of banknotes. After that, he fell to his knees, with his torso straight up like a tree stump; he knelt in this pose for a day and a night. Well, he could have kept that up for as long as he liked. No one in Shuanhu's family wanted to speak to him! Had he expected that this trick would move their hearts? What a ludicrous fantasy! Later on, Ganban was the victim of a robbery and in consequence, threw himself off a gully cliff.

Well, there was, of course, an ulterior reason why Jidan had hoped to get a "rice bowl" in the form of a governmental salary — because Jidan had contracted a disease too embarrassing to name. This disease was unfortunate in terms of time and place. It was ill timed in that it came when the problem of Jidan's marriage was under discussion. It was out of place in that it contaminated the only context in which Jidan might bear fruit—could a marriage that only bloomed but never bore fruit be counted as a marriage? Moreover, Shuanhu was eager to have a grandson from Jidan.

Anyway, Jidan's disease was not easy to cure. They had visited many hospitals for therapy, but the condition did not get better. With respect to this matter, Shuanhu could not help cursing Liu Qi. He was sure Jidan had been infected by Liu Qi, who had had all kinds of diseases. In spite of his grave condition, Liu Qi had been very fond of playing around with girls — and he had played voraciously. Liu Qi had promised he would see to it that Jidan became a government official; he had vowed many times, with his hand pounding his chest to show his sincerity. But after having taken his pleasure, Liu Qi was gone forever, leaving poor Jidan behind shedding tears of sorrow.

Jidan had to take medicine all year round. But the price of medicine increased by leaps and bounds. Pharmacy stores were like bottomless pits: no matter how much money you dropped into them, you would see no lasting effect. The money Jidan had spent her youth to acquire had to be continually fed into that bottomless pit. Any common family with a sick woman to sustain would undoubtedly go bankrupt; they would never see the end of their troubles. But if Jidan became a government official, her medicare would be covered by the government, and she would be entitled to reimbursement for doctors' visits and for the large quantities of medicine. Thus the germs would not develop into a dangerous threat. Medicines versus diseases could be analogized with cats versus mice — the presence of cats kept mice under check.

Shuanhu claimed that if Jidan became a government official, well, he would be father of a government official; as such, he would have a sense of accomplishment and pride; when that day came, the gossips would have to shut their smelly mouths.

Shuanhu did not think that the prospects for Sakelu were very bright. He even hoped it would collapse as soon as possible. He was sure that such a day would come and he would live to see those silly people become laughing stocks.

He said, "Only when Sakelu can no longer sustain itself, and only when its residents are scattered like birds flying from a falling tree can people tell who are swan-geese and who are sparrows, while who are no better than mosquitoes or flies."

"Think about this," Shuanhu continued. "It is true that every household has been compensated, with sums ranging from thirty to fifty thousand *yuan*. Even if the money is used cautiously, how long can such an amount support a family? Years from now when people run out of money, what will they do? Will they expect Liben to give them more money? Just look how they have been comporting themselves. They walk with their heads raised as high and straight as millionaires. With money to spare, they do no more work; they do nothing but gather together to play mahjong. In Sakelu Park, almost every household has bought a mahjong table; nine households out of ten play mahjong; and the remaining one sleeps away the time thus saved, instead of making plans for their future."

Shuanhu said he was not as foolish as those people; he had made long term plans for his family: the three-storeyed building under construction would be used for business purposes; he was going to strike pay-dirt while Sakelu was still in its prime. According to Shuanhu, long before the building's foundation was laid, he had worked out an ingenious plan for its use — most of the space would be for rent; only a small number of rooms would be used by himself to set up his firm. As for the rooms for rent, he would fully respect the occupants' will — they could start shops, restaurants, hair salons, clinics and other businesses. Whoever wished to rent would be acceptable with the exception of one person, whom he would deny firmly even if that person were to pay a monthly rent of ten thousand *yuan*. That person was none other than Fugui, a self-declared sorcerer capable of handling ghosts.

He revealed that Fugui had approached him many times to discuss the possibility of renting a room, but he had always refused.

"Can you guess what Fugui wanted the room for?" Shuanhu asked me.

"To transform it into a temple so that people from the neighboring villages and towns would come to worship him, offering him money and goods," Shuanhu answered his own question.

According to Shuanhu, Fugui had dressed as a witch when he came to see him last time; seeing Shuanhu, the first thing Fugui did was intone "May Buddha preserve us" again and again, before going on to allege that he had been sent by divine Shining Virtue, who had sent instructions for Shuanhu not on any consideration to refuse a room to Fugui.

Shuanhu said that Fugui's appearance had made him flare up; that he had refused Fugui harshly, calling him a silly cock; that he had declared he wanted to fuck divine Shining Virtue's mother and grandmother.

Having let out most of the rooms for rent, Shuanhu would use the remaining ones to run a profitable cultural entertainment company. He wanted to know how it felt to be a boss. He had given the issue careful consideration: the inclusion of the word "cultural" in the company name would make it sound elegant. But actually, the company was no more than a brothel. It was not that he himself was a lecher. But the world was in such a degraded state that temptations to lechery were the only thing which would attract customers. Without customers, how could a business make a profit? Without profit, what was the point of running a company?

Shuanhu planned to make his business attractive to all sorts of people. In addition to song-and-dance hall and teahouse, he would furnish private rooms to cater to various kinds of demand. Level One rooms would be decorated like gorgeous royal palaces. Level Two rooms would be like those of a five-star hotel. Level Three rooms would be like those of an ordinary hotel. Level Four rooms would not be furnished at all — the floor would be covered with straw and there would be bedding cushions on top — you could call such a room a pigsty if you liked, or you could call it a public toilet if you liked. Level One rooms would receive only mysterious figures; according to Shuanhu such mysterious figures resembled flies, which were fond of foul-smelling substances and inclined to fly wherever there was shit; in view of the fact that Sakelu was an isolated and safe place far away from the city, those mysterious figures would definitely come swarming in. Of course, this type of room would go at a high price: the price for one night might be one or even two thousand *yuan*. As a general rule, the mysterious figures would not take price into consideration, since they would not be paying with their own money. Of course, Shuanhu's company would raise no objection to providing them with valid invoices. Level Two rooms would mainly receive successful business people, who were well off and were highly concerned to save face. However, because the business people paid with their own money, they would not spend it as carelessly as the mysterious figures. So they would be charged less. Level Three rooms would mainly receive ordinary customers. As for Level Four rooms, well, they were fundamentally intended to meet the needs of migrant workers and poor people. At the moment, there were not many migrant workers around the place, but just because they were scarce in daytime didn't mean they weren't plentiful at night. In the future, when night fell, rich people would come in cars, and migrant workers would come on tricycles.

With regard to migrant workers and poor people, Shuanhu would adopt magnanimous policies: as long as they paid a minimum fee of five *yuan*, they would be permitted to enter. However, they would only be allowed to look and not touch; those who paid ten *yuan* would be allowed to look and also to touch; whoever paid twenty *yuan* would receive full satisfaction. Shuanhu said that as long as he adopted a policy of "small profits but quick returns," migrant workers would never stop coming.

What was more, through inquiry and investigation, Shuanhu had found that in cities male prostitution was trendy too. "Aha, that men can be prostituted shows how chaotic the world has become," Shuanhu said. Consequently, Shuanhu decided that, if there was demand, he would open a room for male prostitution too.

As for the *xiaojie*, Shuanhu would put them into different categories, too. Each category of girl would serve the corresponding category of client. No break in the hierarchical order would be allowed. Of course, this advice had been given to him by Jidan, who had been working in this line for a long time. If she did not have PhD level expertise, then it was at least at Bachelor level. With Jidan's backing, Shuanhu was fully confident about founding this easy-money making company.

At the end of our chat, Shuanhu repeatedly stated that he would go and visit Dalin; that he would persuade Dalin to join hands with him in this project. To have Dalin as his partner would be like having a large tree as a support: the tree would prevent him from tumbling down, and would moreover provide him with comfortable shade. So why not have Dalin?

64

I accidentally encountered Dalin outside a tax bureau, while he was in the process of lecturing to six or seven persons who were nodding and bowing around him; his face was flushed with the pride of success. Having apparently failed to notice me, he was about to get into a shiny black car. Dalin had become fat. From head to toe his body had swelled up like a piece of risen dough. His face seemed to be suffering the effects of dropsy, and his eyes were almost submerged by the puffy flesh around them. His belly had bulked out so much that it looked like that of a woman eight months pregnant. I could not but pity him. To be an official was not easy! Just look at Dalin, and how his figure had changed since he had become an official.

I was wondering whether or not I should take the initiative and greet him. After hesitating for a moment, I called out, "Dalin!" Straightening his back, Dalin turned round and realized that it was me. He walked toward me, and after a few pleasantries dragged me into his car, before I could say anything.

Where the car was going, I did not know. Nor did I know what Dalin wanted me to do. I seemed to have been kidnapped, sitting in the car like a block of wood. I felt somewhat embarrassed and put upon. The air in the car seemed to have become inert, and I felt like I was about to be suffocated. Several times I wanted to ask the driver to stop and let me get out of the car, but each time, just as the words were on the tip of my tongue I swallowed them again. Dalin and I sat side by side, his face frosty, eyes looking forward. We had chatted briefly, but it was like the exchange of snipers' shots: the report of one was met, after a prolonged silence, by that of the other.

The car drove into an upmarket residential area and then stopped in front of a townhouse. The security guard darted up to help with the car door. When I got out, I asked Dalin what this place was. Dalin said it was his home, a smile playing on his lips now. I asked abruptly "How many homes do you have?" Dalin made no reply. He waved his hand, and the car drove off.

That Dalin's home was luxurious was par for the course. But, luxurious as it was, it was not elegant; to tell the truth, it was pretty vulgar. For instance, there were pictures of coquettish movie stars between the gilded pillars, but not a single item of painting or calligraphy could be found on the walls. It was only the piano in a corner that endowed the house with a touch of culture. Sitting on the velvet sofa, I could not help but recall when he first used the flush toilet in my home. He did not know whether he should sit facing inward or outward, nor did he know how to flush after he had used it. More than once he had declared his envy, saying that he would be content with a room of his own in Yuebei, someday in the future. But every dog has his day, alas. Compared with Dalin's luxurious villa, mine was too humble to be called a house. It was at best a hovel.

Having made a cup of coffee for me, Dalin forced me to take a bath. I protested, but he insisted, saying that the first thing any guests had to do was wash themselves clean and fresh. Because the air outside was dirty, epidemics were many, and bathing was very necessary to guard his home from viruses. I found such words rather harsh: how long had he been rich, that he felt he should put on airs like this? With a sour face, I stood up, determined to leave. Dalin grabbed me to stop me, and apologized repeatedly, admitting that he had a loose tongue, and hoping that I would not mind, since he and I were brothers, that a taxman was liable to speak rudely, and he had no doubt been influenced by his profession, etc.

These few soft words were enough to extinguish the fire inside me. I sat back on the sofa and took a Chungwa he offered me. Dalin declared that I did not need to take the bath because he knew I was not so dirty as to pollute his home; but this time it was me who decided I wanted to try the bath-tub he had bought at the cost of thirty thousand *yuan*. He made no further objection as I walked into the bathroom.

The bathroom was very spacious. I did not find the tub until I had gone round two corners, and once I found the tub I could not get water out of it, no matter how hard I pressed the button. I had to call for Dalin, who told me that I needed to enter a code. After a cursory motion of his hand below the mirror lamp, a stream of warm water sprayed over me. He gave me a few instructions and withdrew, but I went on making mistakes. I randomly picked up a towel, a fact he picked up on when he came in for an inspection. He said the towel, with a name embroidered on its back, was used exclusively by his girlfriend. I turned it around. Sure enough it had "Beanny" written on it. Dalin snatched it from my hand, and passed me a new one which had never been used. I expected him carefully to hide away the towel with "Beanny" on it, but to my surprise he casually tossed it into the trash bin. I asked what was wrong with it and why he threw it away. Dalin said I had soiled it and that he had no reason to keep it. Feeling duty bound to apologize to him, I kept saying "I'm sorry." Dalin mentioned the towel no more, but made a remark which it would take me several years to digest, "How come you look more and more like a farmer fresh in town!" Later when I washed my head, I mistook body lotion for shampoo. All in foreign languages, how could I understand them? But I did not shout for Dalin. After a quick rinse with water, I emerged from the bathroom.

When I was back in the drawing room, Dalin became extremely warm and elated as if he was feeling repentant for his words and deeds. He even ignored the ringing of his mobile, and when I rose to take leave, he tried hard to dissuade me from going. He stated repeatedly that he was honor-bound to reward me, because it was me who had given him shelter when he first entered the territory of Yuebei as a vagrant. He had acquired an azure sky of his own, and believed that I had played my part in helping him get it. He was no ingrate, and could not bear to neglect me when he was so prosperous. If he ate shrimp, I should be able to eat fish. If he drank Remy Martin, I should be able to drink Xi Feng[36]. If he shone like a red sun, I should be able to shine like a lamp.

I sat on the sofa and awaited Dalin's reward. To be honest, I was more of a disinterested spectator than a participant awaiting his reward. I wanted to see what was next on the program. It was not long before he came out of his bedroom with a stack of photos in his hand. These photos were obviously enlargements. He tossed them away as if they were poker cards, telling me that I might take whichever took my fancy. Taken aback a little, I proceeded to examine the photos, which were images of young women, fifty or sixty or so in number, all of them extremely tarty, in a thousand and one postures. They wore little, some even with the hair between their legs exposed. I asked who they were. He said they were all girlfriends of his.

All of a sudden, I was overcome by violent nausea. I tried my best not to vomit. I asked, "What do you mean by this, Dalin? Do these women in the photos have anything to do with me?" Dalin laughed at my airs and graces. What normal man was not captivated by beauty? He had some even sexier ones, but, sorry, he would not show them to me, and would reserve them for his own use. In his eyes, the women in front of me were all second-rate products. But that was only his personal opinion, for if compared with the rest of their sex, each of these girls was a beauty. I might be able to pick two, bring them home and live with them, and all at his expense. In other words, I could keep two mistresses and he would pay for them. For a human being, life was a matter of decades. A life was no more or less than a life, whether it was led in this way or that way. Why should one be so hard on oneself?

The man before me could not be more strange to me. Was this still the same Dalin who had been so timid and cautious? Was this the same Dalin whose heart had been as pure as spring water? What firing must a lump of mud experience before it turns into a brick? What rain and wind must a fresh fruit hanging from a branch endure before it drops onto the ground and turns into rotten dirt? How true it is that beans may become a delicious dish when well-cooked, but a poisonous one when under-cooked!

A bit horrified, I told myself that I must keep as clear of Dalin as I would of narcotics! I stood up, and prepared to leave. Dalin obviously did not notice the change in my mood, because he began to narrate how he had been wrestling with women. He conceded that he had married an idiot wife, but he was not upset because, after all, an idiot was easily fooled, so that he could plunge into love's river to his heart's content, and freely swim up and down. He claimed that though there were thousands of beautiful women in this world, he only wanted to make love to a hundred. Now he was gradually approaching this target. Li Tiantian, the woman he had ruthlessly deserted, had suffered until she was half dead. Apart from other things, an inspection for tax fraud on a daily basis had made her cry for her mum and dad. Li Tiantian had invited him to tea, but he refused to go. How could he go like Liu Bang to attend the Hongmen Banquet? It was clear that his purpose was to topple her, and that he had made up his mind to do so! At last, subject to a one-off fine of one and a half million *yuan*, she closed the business down, to lurk out of sight like an earthworm. She threatened to kill him, seemingly unaware how high the sky was! Very well, Dalin would wait for the arrival of her assassin! One cannot see his opponent's footmarks unless his opponent takes action and leave some footprints. Did she think she could kill anyone she wished? Life was a combat zone, after all. It was hard to predict who would dominate, and who would lose their life beneath the knife.

I said, "Dalin, as your elder brother, I'm obliged to warn you. How have you become a man like this? Don't you know you are descending step by step into the abyss? Or perhaps you have already fallen into it! You can ignore my words, but I have to say that you will pay dearly for what you have done today! Money and beauty are fascinating traps that sooner or later will ruin you!"

A scornful expression on his face, Dalin sneered at me, "Are you still living in the Qin or Han Dynasties? No wonder you have lived your life in frustration. It looks like your brain has been corroded! Beauty and money, are these not the targets that everyone strains for but seldom reaches? Why must a man primp himself up into being a sanctimonious hypocrite?"

I said, "Take my advice or not. It's up to you."

Dalin replied, "I take no-one's advice as an imperial edict, except my workplace superior's."

I said, "Wait and see."

He echoed, "Wait and see."

65

The truth of the saying "A person connected to a man of influence enjoys more favor" was borne out in my case. Due to my connection to Dalin, I had indeed received some benefits. For example, Xue Yulu had phoned me a couple of times; praising me as a golden reporter, she invited me to work again in the press house.

I explained that even though all my documentation had remained in the press house for the past six or seven years, I hadn't worked there for that entire period, and my salary had long since stopped. I asked her what my status would be if I returned to work there again: a full staff member or a temporary employee?

In her usual ambiguous style, Xue Yulu replied, "You come back first, and we'll talk about it afterward."

So I went to see Xue Yulu. The minute I saw her, she started talking about Dalin. She shared with me the funny things that had happened when they were together.

She said, "When we went out hunting, Dalin nearly shot a woman that was bending over to hoe her field. The bullet whistled past just an inch above her head, leaving the poor creature so scared that she collapsed onto the ground, and was unable to pick herself up for the next half hour."

She continued, "Dalin looked very funny when playing golf. He took firm hold of the golf club as though it were a pickaxe handle. No matter how patiently we taught him, he could not learn how to play the game."

Laughing good-humoredly, Xue Yulu went on, "When anyone hit the ball within one foot of the hole, we encouraged him to nudge it straight in. He hit the ball as though all his fingers were thumbs. Instead of bringing it nearer to the hole, he sent it farther away. We all burst out laughing; we laughed so hard that our sides and stomachs ached."

She claimed she really liked the way Dalin behaved when he got drunk, "He was a real man with magnanimous manners; he didn't shout dirty words to people; he'd rather lean against a wall than have other people support him as he walked along."

Xue Yulu exclaimed with emotion, "Good men are truly rare in today's world. No wonder so many women are enamored of him."

Xue Yulu dwelled dramatically on her friendship with Dalin; she told me that they had been spending a lot of time together, and that they were now bosom pals. Her implication could not be clearer: it was solely on account of Dalin that I, who had been abandoned like an orphan, was now being reclaimed by her, since he had asked her to take good care of me (of course she had learned that he and I were cousins). As a result, out of compassion, she had decided to call me back. She admitted that the press house had not done right by me, but by no means should she be held accountable for the wrong; rather it had been Baldy Sun who should be held totally responsible; Baldy Sun had had a wicked heart and a pair of evil eyes, which were always fixed on women's buttocks.

In her words, I had been as soft as a well-cooked noodle and had behaved in an unmanly fashion; and if I had had the courage of any of the heroes in *Outlaws of the Marsh*, I would have stabbed Baldy Sun five or six times. "Who did he think he was?" Xue Yulu said. "Tough as he was, could he survive a butcher's knife?"

I laughed behind my hand, saying, "Xue Yulu, if you hated President Sun so bitterly, why didn't *you* stab him?"

Xue Yulu replied that she was kidding; that she didn't really mean it; that in real life, knives should be the last resort in any conflict. She said that her own brother was a case in point, which could teach a bitter lesson; that her brother used to like to play with knives and clubs, and he ended up being ruined by them.

Once she began to speak about her brother Xue Lihan, she was almost struck dumb in anguish. She claimed that even though she had hoped to influence matters in his favor by publishing an article immediately after the incident, it had not saved her brother from legal consequences; that her family had had bad luck, for the prosecutor in charge of the case had been inhumanly severe; that, to make the matter even worse, Xiang Wenhua had been an incredible disappointment — instead of helping Xue Lihan for her sake or for Xue Lihan's sake, Xiang Wenhua had presented himself at court as witness for the prosecution. How could Xiang Wenhua have had the heart to see her brother spend the rest of his life in jail? Xue Yulu could not help sobbing. But after a moment, her tears gave way to abrupt laughter. She said, "Well, well, it was not so bad. Lihan's life was saved. So the case could be considered a success."

When hearing the name of Xiang Wenhua, my heart shook slightly. I might well have forgotten him if Xue Yulu had not mentioned his name. Several years had elapsed, apparently in the wink of an eye, during which I never seemed to have contacted him — I had not called Xiang Wenhua a single time in the past couple of years.

I asked Xue Yulu, "What's Xiang Wenhua doing now?"

Instead of answering my question, she wrinkled her nose and eyes, as if she were suffering a heart attack. My question shocked her so much that she nearly fell off her chair.

"Do you know nothing about it, or are you merely pretending not to know?" she asked.

"I don't know anything about it," I replied. "Honestly!"

With fleeting smiles playing around the corners of her mouth, Xue Yulu declared that my expulsion from the press house must have strongly disturbed my nerves and caused me to go into a trance, consequently I had reached the point of not knowing what was going on around me.

Her mockery of me did not bring me one inch nearer to an answer. Actually, as I passed my old office door on my way to Xue Yulu's office, I had strained my neck to glace inside, and had found my table taken by a girl with blond hair. I could not see her face clearly, since her head was bent down — she was cutting her nails, but I did see that she was sitting at my old table, while Xiang Wenhua's table was bare. As a matter of fact, that had not surprised me, since his desk had usually been bare. But the odd thing was that the table was covered with a thick layer of dust. In the past, even when Xiang Wenhua did not show up for a month or two, his table would always be kept clean. If ever Xue Yulu noticed that his table had become even slightly dusty, she would stand at the doorway and scold so loudly that the face of anyone in the room would burn with shame for not having cleaned it.

Once more, Xue Yulu asked me whether I really did not know what had happened to Xiang Wenhua, or if I was simply pretending not to. When she was certain that I had not been feigning, Xue Yulu stopped playing hide-and-seek, but straight-forwardly told me, "Xiang Wenhua is now a steadily rising political star! To be exact, he is director of the province's department of resources."

Nonetheless, Xue Yulu sighed with emotion, exclaiming that this high office was agony for Xiang Wenhua — an agony that was bringing him to the verge of breakdown. She said that since Xiang Wenhua left the press house, they had seen each other only once. For the sake of a legal case over an estate dispute, she had invited Xiang Wenhua to meet with her at Alibaba Teahouse to drink tea. Xiang Wenhua had honored her greatly by declining a number of feasts for her sake, and had got to the teahouse in good time. The mere thought of Xiang Wenhua lowering himself to drink tea in Alibaba had moved Xue Yulu to tears. True, Alibaba was a nice place, but such niceness was a matter of perspective. For low grade officials and common white-collar clerks, visiting Alibaba would be no debasing thing. But that the chief of the province's department of resources should so have identified himself with the common people! "How modest-minded he is!" Xue Yulu exclaimed.

After commending Xiang Wenhua, Xue Yulu called my attention to a fact that should have been as plain as daylight — she emphasized that though she did not mean to sing her own praises, she was just as modest as he was. She had attained a vice bureaucratic departmental rank only slightly lower than Xiang Wenhua's vice provincial departmental rank, and yet she had been ready to shake hands with a person of no rank whatsoever, hadn't she? Wasn't she right now having an easygoing conversation with a person who had been sacked? Hadn't she often visited Alibaba, which was frequented by the commonplace populace? Wasn't she modest enough? Sometimes she could not help feeling moved by herself! Sometimes she even worshipped herself!

According to Xue Yulu, being a leading official was not to Xiang Wenhua's liking. He could not have liked it less, in fact. He missed the time when he had worked for the newspaper. In the old days he would come to work or leave his office whenever he felt like it; he could fart as loudly as nature dictated, without being checked, if he wanted; he would doze off at his table whenever he pleased, with his head resting on his arms and his arms resting on the table, with his snore resounding loudly enough to shake the ground. But now, he felt that countless eyes were watching him; that he had to look serious and grave all day long; that he was without freedom to do as his heart desired. Having to wear his formal shoes and decent suits, which wrapped him up like prisoner-garb, he felt miserably uncomfortable. The expensive tie around his neck, especially, reminded him of a hangman's noose. In accordance with the habit he had formed during the period when he held his press house job, every day at four o'clock in the afternoon, every cell in his body would feel sleepy, so that fuzzy clouds seemed to float within his skull.

He simply could not break out of this catatonic state, no matter how hard he struggled. On several occasions, he fell asleep while his subordinates were right in the middle of making a work report to him; more embarrassingly, he snored loudly. Although some people laughed involuntarily, no one dared to awaken him. When he finally woke up, he wiped the dripping water from his mouth; certainly he felt mortified and embarrassed.

Xue Yulu said that for Xiang Wenhua the most unbearable thing of all was attending ribbon-cutting ceremonies. Almost every day he would be led by the nose to attend some. The maximum number of such events on a single day came to eight; he had to run to them one after another in rapid succession. When there were new hotels to open for business or new roads on which construction was to be commenced, when the foundations of new gas stations were laid, or new telegraph-buildings had been completed, or many other events of the type, he would be dragged along to lend prestige to them. He was fed up to the back teeth with it.

Xue Yulu claimed that ribbon-cutting ceremonies were, as a rule, among officials' favorite activities. Who in the world could be fed up with such events? However, Xiang Wenhua did not like them at all. What was more, he disdained the meticulously forged golden scissors the hosting institutions had commissioned. Xiang Wenhua once said, "What good are these golden scissors? They are still scissors, aren't they? Scissors are for cutting. They disconnect things that were previously connected. From whatever perspective I consider the issue, I don't deem ribbon-cutting ceremonies to be auspicious."

Xue Yulu said that Xiang Wenhua had disposed of his gifts of golden scissors pretty casually: he had given one pair away to his house maid, one pair to an old watchman, one pair to a coolie trishaw cyclist, and one pair to Xue Yulu herself when he came to drink tea with her at Alibaba Teahouse.

To Xue Yulu, the most unbelievable thing was that Xiang Wenhua had expressed the wish of returning to the press house to work again. This had appalled her. Was he being serious? Surely not. Xue Yulu had responded that the press house was a small and unworthy temple for a great god like Xiang Wenhua to dwell in. She then jokingly said that she would love to change jobs with him: she would love to work as the director of the department of resources, and Xiang Wenhua could take her place as the vice editor-in-chief. Hearing her suggestion, Xiang Wenhua was exceedingly pleased, saying again and again, "What a good idea!" It was as if the exchange could instantly come true.

Now while telling me about this in her office, Xue Yulu exclaimed, "Xiang Wenhua is an odd person! Absolutely, he is an odd person!"

66

After I returned to the press house, the first task assigned to me was to interview none other than Song Laowan in the detention house. It was said that someone had made a complaint to the municipal political and legal commission against him on account of sexual harassment. According to materials now in the custody of the press house, Song Laowan had twice harassed a young convict. The first time he had grabbed the convict's reproductive organ through his trousers, and the second time he put his hand down the convict's trousers and groped his buttocks.

The materials made me want to laugh. Was it really necessary to make such a fuss about such a trifle? But Xue Yulu did not take it as a trifle; she turned it into a matter of cosmic dimensions. She exclaimed, "Fancy one man groping another man, how disgusting that was! What's more, the harasser was an old man! Every human being has the right to privacy, convicts not excluded. Who would go to hell, if not Song Lanwan, the old villain?"

Naturally, I made mention of Xiaolin. I questioned why no one sought justice for Xiaolin, who had suffered much greater harm. Xue Yulu laughed at my naivety once again, saying that such was life. Life was the interior decorator, who chose colors based on the host's preference. That might lead to a cabinet being painted red today, green tomorrow, and black the day after tomorrow. Everything and its opposite were normal. Was Dalin not a migrant worker? How had he become a leader of the tax bureau today? Song Laowan had a hidden protector, but that person had now died in a traffic accident. Were these things not all normal? Society was true to its own nature, and it moved along its own orbit regardless of one's opinions. Life did not acknowledge blame, even if one was mortally offended by it.

I asked, "Hasn't Song Laowan been dismissed?"

Xue Yulu replied, "Can't a dismissed person be re-hired? When the wind falls, everything goes back to what it was before."

With a wink, Xue Yulu told me a secret: the decision to get rid of Song Laowan had been taken with the intention of removing Xiaolin's sense of grievance. The so-called male convict was no more than a pretext! He had stolen a motorcycle, but was granted immunity from prosecution and been sent home because of his co-operation in writing this material.

I asked who had plotted this matter.

"Plot or no plot, Song Laowan ought to be punished, since he had done evil." Xue Yulu said.

"Why was Song Laowan not punished right after he had committed the offense?" I asked.

Xue Yulu heaved a sigh, saying that she had been for publishing my investigation report, but President Sun had stopped her decisively, and I surely did not need her to tell me why. President Sun was happy whenever there was bad news. "With his son living abroad, and his daughter running companies, do you think his children achieved all that on the strength of their own talents? No, he fathered two idiots, but he made use of his power to roll them in gold, so that they looked bright and glittery."

I met Xue Yulu half-way, and suggested, indirectly, that detestable as people like Song Laowan were, President Sun and the like were even more detestable. They were fence-sitters, who would sacrifice principles for profits. The people they wrote about became prostitutes or maidens at the stroke of their pen, as at the stroke of a magician's wand.

Xue Yulu said I was too captious, an innate weakness that I had never overcome! I was neither a politician nor a hero, but a small potato struggling to grow. How had I presumed to take on so many responsibilities? That stuff about prostitutes and maidens was total nonsense! Whether people were prostitutes or maidens depended on what was required of them. When one was required to become a maiden, one became a maiden, even if one was a prostitute. When one was required to become a prostitute, one became a prostitute, even if one's hymen was still intact. Was this weird? No, not at all! Weird was he who considered everything weird! Amongst the students of history, who would not know that history was written by historians? But historians served their masters. It was impossible that they should have no inkling of their masters' intentions. Like a clump of mud, history could be kneaded into any shape. And in all that there was nothing weird!

As she went on, Xue Yulu became emotional. She said that misunderstandings had arisen between us, but misunderstandings were not the same thing as implacable enmity. At least she and I belonged to the same camp, now; in common parlance, she and I were family. Her close relationship with Liben, her recalling me to the press house, her need for support in her struggle against the editor-in-chief, all these things ensured that I belonged to Xue's Camp and not to Qian's Camp (Qian was the name of the present editor-in-chief). Now that we were family, she could not help but worry about me. How was it that, despite my many years on the road, I had made no progress? Had time not taken a toll on me? How could the solid rock of seven years ago still be the same solid rock now?

I said that though a tree might turn into oil or coal over a period of ten thousand years, a rock would still be a rock after an equally long term of time. So what chance was there of a rock turning into something else in a mere seven years? I said that I anyway did not want to change — not from a black bean to a pea.

Xue Yulu could not suppress a snigger, saying that she finally understood that the bronze pea described by Guan Hanqing the playwright — which no stone, nor hammer, nor iron wok, nor steel teeth could break — was a man like me!

I said that, at any rate, I would not go to investigate the case of Song Laowan. By now I was beginning to pity the old pervert a little. Xue Yulu said she had given me the opportunity to rise again, but apparently I was a fool unable to distinguish what was important. She had had great difficulties getting me back to the press house, had done her utmost to override all objections and overcome all difficulties, and had finally fished me out of the surging waves like a needle fished out of a river. She had got hurt for my sake, but still I let her down. Had my brain been eaten by worms, or was it corroded by sulphuric acid? What was the matter with me? No, really, what was the matter?

Xue Yulu was almost screaming. She slammed her mug down on the desk so hard that water spilled from it and wet the stack of documents nearby. I could see that she was really angry, from the way she stared out the window, for what seemed like an eternity. She did not seem to come to herself until a fly landed on her nose. As she went after that cunning little fly with a flyswatter, she grumbled, "I wanted you to write a sensational article, so that you might apply for a chief reporter position, but who knew that you were an empty sack incapable of standing up! Are you what people say — a piece of cheap meat unfit for human consumption? Think it over, which would be better, to do the interview, or to be down and out on the streets?"

I said I had thought it over. I was not going to do the interview, nor would I return to work in the press house again.

Xue Yulu waved her hand, which meant I could leave. I stood up, thanked her all the same, and walked out of her office. I felt like I was walking on air, a sense that I had never experienced before, as if I had been released from prison. There was a song I felt like singing, but as I could not remember its lyrics, I whistled it instead. The elated look on my face might have led onlookers to think that I had just received a bonus, and from the corner of my eye I could see the security guard who stood like a post at the gate was staring at my upper pocket with strange, unblinking eyes.

Once out of the gate, I saw a group of newspaper men assembling around an old lady, and the office director bending down to soothe her. The old lady was sitting on the concrete steps, with teardrops big as rice-grains on her withered, wrinkled face. Upon taking a closer look, I recognized she was none other than President Sun's wife. While President Sun was still alive, she had come several times to make trouble, weeping, shouting, and claiming that she had discovered the names of more than twenty women in his notebooks — these women, like large nocturnal rats, had emptied his pockets and shaken the foundations of the family! In the end, the humiliated husband struck her, and the wife, in return, left five bloody scratch marks on his face.

Having done interviews together before, the office director and I were fairly well acquainted. At the sight of me, he nudged me with his foot and asked whether I was back at work in the press house. I said I was not. He asked why not — because the issue of my job had been discussed and approved in the editor-in-chief's meeting. I said it was hard to explain in a few words, and that I would tell him later in detail. Then I asked what had happened to President Sun's wife; she seemed very upset. The office director said President Sun's wife was overstuffed with food. I asked what he meant by that. He said she had turned up, making trouble because President Sun had not been awarded the title of Expert of Outstanding Contributions. The application materials had been submitted, but he died before the appraisal began. And anyone who died forfeited his qualifications as a matter of course. However, Mrs Sun could not reconcile herself to the situation. She thought someone had been denigrating President Sun, maybe even scheming against the memory of an old comrade who had dedicated his whole life to the revolutionary cause! Does tea get cold after the drinker leaves? She refused to believe such a heresy and wanted the cold tea reheated. Weeping wherever she went, she worked tirelessly to have President Sun crowned Expert of

Outstanding Contributions, a crown, she thought, with which President Sun would be able to raise his noble head in the underworld, and about which she and their children would be able to feel particularly proud. As a tree lives through its bark, so does a man through his face. Just look at the prosperity of the beauty industry. People, men and women, young and old, were crowding into salons and wearing the doorstep thin. Even prostitutes spared no efforts to make up, and even punters knew that they should wear brilliant ties. They used their faces as screens to hide their twisted guts, and the lice crawling in their clothing: it was a canvas on which they could paint whatever they liked.

I uttered "ugh-ugh."

The office director asked why I uttered "ugh-ugh."

I made no reply, but once again uttered "ugh-ugh."

67

I ran into Zhao Xiaohui at the church's portal as he was coming out. Because his head was down, he did not see me as I approached him from the opposite direction. As I drew level with him, shoulder to shoulder, I intentionally put out my foot to trip him. He staggered but soon recovered his balance. When he discovered that it was me who had just tricked him, Zhao Xiaohui revealed his striking white teeth in a broad smile.

"You visited the church?" I asked him.

"Yes," he replied.

"What brought you to the church?"

"I came to get a testimonial," Zhao Xiaohui replied.

"What on earth do you need a testimonial from the church for?"

"I ran into some trouble," Zhao Xiaohui said.

"What kind of trouble?" I asked.

Zhao Xiaohui explained that he had got into the habit of reading the Bible; he could not go to sleep unless he read a couple of pages from it; the Bible had become his sleeping pills, without which he could feel no peace of mind; no matter how hard he tried to sleep, he just could not. He had only himself to blame. After having read the Bible one night, he had carelessly forgotten to put it away next day. Consequently, someone had reported on him to the county government, accusing him of being a Christian. How could a Christian perform the duties of township head? In what direction would a Christian township head lead the Gaotai people? The county government had sent delegates to investigate the issue, and they had drawn the following conclusion: it could not be affirmed with certainty that Zhao Xiaohui was a Christian, but it could not be affirmed with certainty that Zhao Xiaohui was not a Christian; in the question whether he was a Christian or not, it was up to Zhao Xiaohui to prove it. And the only way to clear himself was to ask the church to produce a written notification stating that he had never participated in any activities organized by the church — and the notification must bear a red stamp.

I invited Zhao Xiaohui to my place, where I brewed some tea for us.

While drinking tea, Zhao Xiaohui sighed with profound emotion over the difficulty involved in acting as a township head. He said that those who had never done the job could not imagine how bitter it was to do it, but now after he had had a taste of it, how he wished to withdraw from the office. "Just think," Zhao Xiaohui said. "My small township government alone has a staff of over one hundred and thirty people! Troubles abound where people are many. In the township government courtyard, gossip and discord keep arising and surging like torrents, enveloping the place in a foul atmosphere. What awful circumstances!"

Indeed, Zhao Xiaohui had wanted to redress the problems, but his initial mobilization meeting had ended in chaos. During the meeting, some people looked askance; some put on fake smiles to disguise their distaste; some were careful to leave implicit the real object of their explicit curses. The eyes of one female vice head blinked as if they were neon lights; she had almost become Zhao Xiaohui's nightmare. They had once dated one another, but ever since they broke up, she had embarked on an unrestrained campaign of vengeance by slandering him. She invented the following accusation: the vigorous violet plant at Zhao Xiaohui's windowsill had been watered with his urine.

The old saying "A lie repeated a thousand times becomes a truth" was proved right in Zhao Xiaohui's case. So long as it was only one person who spoke ill of him on a couple of occasions, he turned a deaf ear and dismissed it out of hand. But after that person had repeated the allegations hundreds or thousands of times, he discovered, when he attempted to refute them or to fight back, that the lies had piled up as high as the Himalayas. To his annoyance, he found that humans were not very different from chickens; one rooster's crow can arouse millions of others to crow; one hen's cluck after laying an egg can stimulate others, even when they are laying no eggs, to cluck too. For a while, denunciations of Zhao Xiaohui were heard everywhere at the work place. Whatever Zhao Xiaohui said, no one would listen or obey. The situation worsened to the point that if Zhao Xiaohui pointed to the east, people would make a point of going west; if Zhao Xiaohui said there shouldn't be too much vinegar in food, the cafeteria chef would make every meal exceedingly sour, as if it had been immersed in a vinegar vat. Of course, there had been some righteous people. For example, an old man advised Zhao Xiaohui to toughen up, to become as a knife, to become as a gun, to become as a fire, to become as a flood. The old man said, "People like that are walnuts, which must be smashed with force in order to take out the kernels. What will the world be like if mice are not afraid of cats? If you ask me what

I mean by 'toughen up,' I'll tell you: Liu Qi is a good example of what I mean. When Liu Qi was the township head, who dared not to smile in front of him? Who dared to gossip behind his back? Who dared to talk back? It is true he was grossly tyrannical, but wasn't his tyranny somewhat justifiable? If you are dealing with sand, with a gentle effort you can grasp it. But if you are dealing with rocks, you are compelled to break them with explosives."

In the old man's view, Zhao Xiaohui had been employing the "gentle pressure" strategy when dealing with rocks. He claimed that essentially Zhao Xiaohui had made the wrong call in these circumstances. "Well, Liu Qi could be viewed as an aberrant product of the place," the old man said. "However, without this specific soil, could such a specific plant have come about?"

Of course Zhao Xiaohui would not follow the old man's advice and assume Liu Qi's rigorous discipline ethic. He hoped to govern in a civilized manner, i.e., to deal with tough customers gently. But what frustrated Zhao Xiaohui was not just gossip or discord; his real headache was the shortage of funds. The county government decided the lump sum for the payment of staff salaries in accordance with their number. However, instead of providing the full amount, it only provided 80 percent. That was to say, although the total sum of the staff's monthly salary was approximately one million three hundred thousand *yuan*, a shortfall of at least three hundred thousand *yuan* had to be made good by the township government itself. How could the township government make good the shortfall? One way was to reduce staff numbers. But then who could he remove? Among the people who had entered the township government pay roll, was there anyone who was not related to some powerful personages? None. The distance of ten kilometers from Gaotai to the county town was a tricky one: you could call it far, but you could just as well call it near. Because of this, in many people's eyes, Gaotai had become a staircase leading up to the county town. Those hoping to use this staircase were coming in an endless steady flow, which you could neither stop nor turn back. With regard to this matter, Zhao Xiaohui had displeased quite a few important figures, and he had even displeased County Secretary Zhang Shutian, who had written him notes asking him to receive various people, and who had been disappointed when not all were successful.

In addition to reducing staff numbers, another method would have been to collect money from the farmers. Zhao Xiaohui had hated to do this. The farmers had earned every cent in the sweat of their brow, even in their tears and their blood. They toiled day and night, with their backs bent down. After they had been reduced to selling their pigs, goats and sheep for a little money, how could he have the heart to snatch that money from their hands? Nevertheless, could he afford not to do so? After all, money was not going to fall from the sky. If he did not collect it from the farmers, he would have nothing to pay the township government staff with. At any rate, he could not simply pick some leaves up off the ground and pass them off as bank notes. If he failed to pay them their salary, wouldn't they tear him to pieces like a pancake?

It had been a headache, a terrible headache. As a last resort, he had been compelled to mobilize the village leaders to collect money from the villagers. If one wished to extort money out of farmers, it was not difficult to find pretexts to tax them: besides such taxes as livestock butchering fee, woods fee, fruit industry fee, flood prevention fee, new fiscal terminology beyond the farmers' comprehension had been coined, for instance, family planning core fee, land value increment nurturing fee.

It was true the farmers were simple people, but that did not mean they were idiots; as a result, these taxes had triggered large scale unrest among them. The situation could be summed up in an idiom: "Instead of securing both a hen and its egg, you find that the hen has flown, and that its egg is broken." The farmers went, one after another, to the county government, and even to the provincial government, to protest and petition. The director of the county's bureau of letters & visits had been hospitalized as a result of being beaten up.

It happened that under the heavy pressure of these taxes, a family of four people from a neighboring township had killed themselves with pesticide. As a result of this incident, the county government ordered an abrupt halt to such practices. At the county's general assembly, Zhang Shutian announced his ultimatum, "Whoever keeps collecting money from farmers will be removed from office." Ugh! How innocent Zhang Shutian looked! It sounded as if this had not been the natural consequence of his own policies.

Now that collecting money from the farmers had been forbidden, how should Zhao Xiaohui deal with the shortfall of funds? When Liu Qi served as the township head, besides the afore-mentioned compulsory taxes, the other alternative methods could be summarized in one word: sell! Liu Qi had sold nearly all the properties owned by the township. Gaotai used to enjoy a nation-wide reputation for its forests, but during Liu Qi's tenure, trees on one hillside after another had been logged for sale, leaving the hills barren. At the end of Liu Qi's tenure, only a tiny piece of woodland remained — it was now being exploited for commercial purposes in line with a contract signed back in Liu Qi's time.

Liu Qi had sold four mines formerly owned by the township. For the sale of each mine, Liu Qi had got five million *yuan*. Nevertheless, when Zhao Xiaohui took over the office, the account books were in the red.

In Liu Qi's day, none of the mine owners had dared not to seek his favor. Whenever pay day came round, if Liu Qi rang a mine owner and vehemently denounced him, the guy would understand what he was after. He would obediently and respectfully send a money-filled bag to Liu Qi — and of course Liu Qi had the skills to make them do this. If any of them were audacious enough not to send money, his coal-truck would be barred from passing along the motorway in front of the township government complex.

But the moment Zhao Xiaohui took over the township headship office, all these mine owners put on a different face and began to behave differently. Knowing that Zhao Xiaohui was a gentle, soft-hearted person who would not deal with them harshly, these mine owners observed with complete indifference the pressing predicament which Zhao Xiaohui was struggling against. They behaved as if Liu Qi had been their kinsman, and now they were eager to see Zhao Xiaohui become a laughing stock.

Not long after Liu Qi's death, the county affirmed its ownership over all these coal mines. Then, while the county was feeling pleased with itself on this account, the municipal government incorporated the mines under its direct leadership. Nowadays, even if the township government ventured gently to prod the owners, they would go to the mayor to launch a complaint. This being the case, how could the township government dare to deal with them harshly?

Actually, twenty percent of the personnel salary was a mere fraction of the funds the township government had to raise. As a matter of fact, the township government's expenditure was so diverse that it was impossible to break it down clearly. Take guest entertainment expenditure as an example: it was a bottomless pit. To begin with, officials from the county government's various departments would come down, in turn, to inspect or do survey work. Whenever they came, the township government was obliged to entertain them with nice food and nice drinks. Moreover, ever since the news media had made Sakelu a hot news topic, swarms of officials and journalists had been flocking here from the province and from the municipality. How could the township government endure this? Even if the township government had owned a gold mountain, entertaining these guests, who kept flooding in, would have worn it down to nothing. As a last resort, the township government had to start entertaining guests at a restaurant on credit. When the credit amount got too high, the restaurant proprietor and his wife put on faces as long as a donkey's. The restaurant proprietor visited the township government again and again, holding out his hand for the bills to be settled. Whenever his trips proved fruitless, his wife would take over for him. Her usual policy was: first to cry; when this trick did not work, to shout loudly; when that failed too, to curse; when this turned out to be useless, to hug Zhao Xiaohui's legs in front of all the spectators. If Zhao Xiaohui remained unresponsive, she would take off her pants and wail, claiming that Zhao Xiaohui had attempted to violate her.

Who could have borne such strain? At any rate, it was beyond Zhao Xiaohui's endurance. It was too much for him! Really too much for him!

68

Concerning Zhao Xiaohui's trip to Yuebei, the obtaining of a testimonial from the church was merely a side task, the principal one being to obtain a sum of money from the province. He had come by bus. The township car, likely to fall apart at any moment, had been left in the garage courtyard, empty of fuel and in need of repair — due to lack of money. The luxurious SUV bought by Liu Qi had been driven off by his younger brother, and the law court was still looking for it. In the county town, Liu Qi had owed hundreds of thousands *yuan* to different stores, which then collaborated to sue the Gaotai township government. Having lost the case, the township government had to sequester the SUV in order to pay the debts, but the vehicle had been snatched by Liu Qi's brother, who claimed that the SUV had been bought by his elder brother with his personal funds. Look, it was his elder brother's name on the invoice, not that of the Gaotai township government!

Zhao Xiaohui had come to Yuebei to raise funds for infrastructure construction at the county's urging. Back from his visit to Shandong Province, Zhang Shutian gave all the county officials a report comprised wholly of how the local officials in Shandong requested money from higher authorities. He said one of the important responsibilities of grass-roots officials was to extract money from the provincial or central governments. Zhang Shutian's lengthy speech could be summed up in two sentences: he who can bring back money is a hero; he who cannot, a toad hopping on the ground!

Zhao Xiaohui had decided that he was a toad, or even worse, a sick toad. Other toads seemed to be very happy, hopping around from morning to evening; but he was different — depressed, hardly able to jump, his feet weighed down as though by a huge leaden ball. He felt that he was the very duck in the legend, unable to fly high or to get down from the chicken rack.

The person Zhao Xiaohui wanted to meet was Xiang Wenhua. Governor Xiang had promised to build a road to Sakelu, but for the last half-year no further action had been taken. The road was not just connected with Sakelu's destiny, but also connected with the overall development of Gaotai Township. Zhao Xiaohui's blueprint foresaw this road as starting out from the township government all the way to Sakelu. It would become a golden road, along which Gaotai Town would be constructed into a small city, and all the villagers from the township could build their houses on either side, provided they were economically affordable. An overall plan was necessary, so that the houses would be built in conformity with urban requirements. Once the city emerged, the masses of Gaotai Township would see the prospects of getting rich, and the township government would not have to worry about sourcing funds any longer.

"It's a good idea but it's not easy to put into practice," I said.

Zhao Xiaohui sighed, "By saying it's difficult, you make it very difficult. By saying it's easy, you make it very easy. Difficult or easy, it depends on whether you have money. Whether you have money depends on the say-so of some leader! If the leader isn't happy, you won't get a rag. If the leader is happy and writes you a note, funds will flow like the waters of the Yellow River." Zhao stressed the importance of strengthening ties with Xiang Wenhua, a ladder by means of which one might go up or down as simply as picking leaves on a tree.

I said, "Xiang Wenhua has been promoted. Will a promoted Xiang Wenhua still be the same as he was before? Will he still dance to your baton?" Zhao Xiaohui said he had dined with Xiang Wenhua the previous night. Zho Xiaohui lavished praises on Xiang Wenhua, declaring, "He is so nice, so good, a genuinely good man, without any airs. It is hard to believe that he, the son of the governor, is as simple and unpretentious as a porter!" Zhoa Xiaohui admitted to me that he had needed to summon up all his courage to call Xiang Wenhua. He had hesitated for half an hour, and had picked up and put down the receiver half a dozen times; finally a thought flashed through his mind: "There is no harm in trying. If rice is denied, the rice bag won't be held back." To his surprise, Xiang Wenhua still remembered him, and said that he had left a good impression on him. More gratifying still was that Xiang Wenhua did not turn down his invitation, stipulating only as a condition that there should be no one else in their company.

Zhao Xiaohui said the meal had almost turned them into friends of one mind, because they had many things in common, the biggest being that both were tired of officialdom and had a strong desire to evade it. That Xiang Wenhua might have such a desire had not occurred to Zhao Xiaohui, who could not really take it on board. He did not understand why Xiang Wenhua was still unhappy when his official rank was so high that he had only one superior and ten thousand inferiors. It was only too natural that Zhao

Xiaohui himself should feel unhappy, because the lowest administrative level lacked qualified personnel and sufficient funds. A small township head like him, surrounded by people dragging him this or that way, was struggling like an insect in a spider's web, hardly able to move. How could he have any great expectations? But Xiang Wenhua was different. Those he encountered all kowtowed and burned incense to him. When he asked for wind he got wind, and when he asked for rain he got rain. Why on earth would he be unhappy? Zhao Xiaohui speculated that there might be problems between Xiang Wenhua and his wife, but judging from Xiang Wenhua's tone, he did not think that could be the answer.

So the meal had brought out a certain fraternal feeling and quite a few gains for Zhao Xiaohui. Xiang Wenhua declared on the spot that his organization would carry out a cooperative scheme of poverty alleviation in Gaotai Township. The lowering clouds were dispersed, and Zhao Xiaohui's heart was instantly flooded with sunlight.

Zhao Xiaohui talked with me about Sakelu, and skeptical about its future as he was, said that he was generally optimistic. As long as the road leading to Sakelu got built, Sakelu would become a basic point of the newly flourishing city, and by that time the villagers would be able to feed themselves. In the meantime, Zhao Xiaohui still had plenty of complaints. He said that Meiteng resolutely refused — in contravention of their initial promise — to recruit folks from Sakelu, with the exception of the sweet-tongued Song Tongguo. According to them, the villagers were hog-wild, undereducated, and many of them had sticky fingers. To sort this matter out, Zhao Xiaohui had gone into a tug war with Meiteng, disputing every step in high-pitched quarrels. Meiteng agreed to take on thirty workers from Sakelu, on condition that the company have the final say on who got recruited, with the right strictly to appraise and to select the candidates! Zhao Xiaohui accepted the conditions, but to his surprise, after a dozen recruitment notices had been posted in Sakelu Park for a dozen days, no one came except for Xiaolin and Baolai. When Xiaolin reported the result, Zhao Xiaohui could not believe it, and blamed Xiaolin's inadequate publicity and mobilization. So he himself spent one day trying to persuade people to apply for the jobs, and he, too, returned empty-handed. The villagers as they sat at the mahjong tables apparently hated to be interrupted. When Zhao Xiaohui spoke to them, they hardly raised their eyes.

"Why don't you go to work in Meiteng?" Zhao Xiaohui asked. "There are people who would fight for an opportunity like this. It's yours for the taking, why do you refuse it?"

"It's toilsome to work in Meiteng!" the villagers replied as if they were reciting from the same libretto after a rehearsal.

"Toilsome? Do you hear that! Is that a thing for grown-up people to say? Is playing mahjong not toilsome? Is sleeping not toilsome? How can they forget their own past so soon? In the scorching sun or chilly wind, bowed to the earth, their backs to the elements, working day and night in order to scrape a living from the fields, is this not toilsome? Today they are only asked to operate machines in a factory, and they all cry 'toilsome' in unison!" Zhao concluded that the problem with the Sakelu people was not that of laziness, but that of degeneration. A poor man finds joy in getting a single *yuan*, but if you suddenly give him a million, who knows what he may become.

By chance, a visiting delegation came on the day Zhao Xiaohui arrived at Sakelu, but every household was playing mahjong and the sanitary conditions were terrible. What a shame! The water in the lake, which once rippled so clearly, had now become smelly, and people passing by had to hold their noses. Among the scenic trees in the courtyard, some had lost their crowns, some others had broken trunks. Worse, there was a couple fighting in the courtyard. The woman, who was wearing her hair loose, accused her husband of extramarital affairs, and vehemently cursed his ancestors; and the man was by no means a pushover either. He was not her equal in swearing, but his fists were naturally harder than hers, so that when he struck her one of her incisors fell out onto the ground.

Zhao Xiaohui said he was very supportive of Kang Yuanyuan's civic education school. There was an urgent need to get it opened. Without a timely intervention, Sakelu would become a sunken wreck.

69

As expected, Kang Yuanyuan's civic school reopened. But unexpectedly, the school principal was not Kang Yuanyuan, but Larz, who was pretty enthusiastic about the project. He vowed he would make the school a model of its type.

It was not long before bad news came to my ears: Larz had been frustrated to the point of tears!

As a result of much effort, a professor from the social sciences academy had been persuaded to give a lecture at the school. However, obtaining an audience proved to be more difficult. Eventually a dozen villagers were dragged along to the classroom. But during the lecture, these people left one after another in quick succession, so that in the end Xiaolin was the only person remaining. The lecture thus stopped before coming to its planned conclusion. Naturally enough, this greatly depressed Larz. Even more depressing was the fact that no sooner had he turned around from seeing the professor off than he found himself surrounded by the very people who had attended the lecture. Among these folks, some had merely listened to a couple of the opening sentences, some had listened to seven or eight sentences, and even those who had stayed the longest — with the exclusion of Xiaolin — had only remained in their seats for about ten minutes. But all these people now demanded that Larz pay them an allowance for attending the lecture. Larz's refusal sent them into a furious rage. Some reproached him loudly, some pushed or dragged him, some threw chalk in his face. Larz wept. Anyone would have in this situation!

After hearing about the event, I surmised that Kang Yuanyuan would ring me. My guess came true only a couple of days later.

"What are you doing?" Kang Yuanyuan asked me over the phone.

"Nothing special," I replied.

She laughed, and said she wanted to appoint me to a leader's position, but she wondered if I would accept it.

Jokingly, I replied, "Nowadays, it requires a bribe to obtain a leader's post. I do not have any money to bribe you."

Kang Yuanyuan said that her assigning me to a leading post didn't require a bribe, but only my acceptance, which would help her out.

I said to her, "You make your offer first."

She said she hoped that I would work as the liaison director of the civic school; that the job was to mobilize, organize and keep in touch with any prospective students.

"Why don't you simply call the position by its name — the director of the recruiting office?" I asked her. "Why go all round the houses?"

The civic school was located in the three-storied building constructed by Shuanhu. The construction work had just been completed, with the concrete on the walls still looking damp. Except for a hair salon, which was now open for business, all the other roller shutters were shut.

The civic school was on the second floor. With the wall between its two adjoining rooms demolished, the combined space was big enough to serve as a classroom. In the classroom, there were over twenty sets of newly purchased desks and chairs. Thus there was seating for more than forty people. A statue of Einstein stood squarely at the front of the classroom. Sayings of famous people hung on all four walls.

As I went there to examine the classroom, I came across Shuanhu. He had selected a room on the ground floor to be his office. Given that it was in the middle of being modeled and decorated, he was temporarily using a second-floor room as his office.

Even though the name plaque of his firm had not yet been put up, he already assumed the air of a big boss. In his office, two young women were waiting on him, doing such things as sweeping the floor, making tea, pounding his shoulders and massaging his back. Sitting behind a large office desk, he rocked back and forth in his soft leather chair. Wearing an outdated woollen overcoat over his shoulders, he looked exactly like a government official working temporarily in a village as featured in old time movies.

Shuanhu invited me to take a seat in his office. He told one girl to give me a cigarette and serve me a cup of tea, and then instructed the other girl, who was pounding his back with her fists, to thrust her hand underneath his coat to scratch his back, so as to ease his itching. He verbally directed her hand's movements to the left, to the right, upward or downward. When the girl failed to scratch the spots that were irritating him, he started to upbraid both girls. He drove them out, making them stand and contemplate amid a field of corn crops. The corn cobs had been removed from the stalks, leaving them exposed to the autumn wind. He claimed that his reason for sending the girls to ruminate in the corn field was that they should never lose sight of the question: which would be more tiring, doing farm work or waiting on Shuanhu? Once they realized that doing farm work was more tiring, they would surely cherish the opportunity of serving Shuanhu!

All of a sudden, a bureaucratic note began to make itself heard in Shuanhu's speech, and this note got badly on my nerves. He repeatedly drawled "this" or "that" in the way a lowly official of some sort would do when delivering a speech to people who had never experienced the world. After having performed his "this" and "that" drama, in the end Shuanhu resumed his normal tone. He scornfully laughed at the village's households one after another — each and every household, without exception, was mocked by him. When the topic of the civic school was introduced, Shuanhu pouted, with his lips protruding like the eaves on an ancient house.

"Civic school! Ha-ha-ha, even pigs would have laughed at the idea!" Shuanhu said. "Those visionaries! They must either have taken the wrong medicine, or have had their heads thumped with a wooden club! Only that would have made them so crazy as to imagine that they could change people's brains. Pumpkins remain pumpkins. Wax gourds remain wax gourds. They attempt to transform pumpkins into wax gourds? Fat chance! Kang Yuanyuan really is a crazy woman. After having eaten some exotic meals in America, she has learned to produce foreign farts. How disgusting! Larz is just as crazy. He looks like a brilliant young man, but then how come he does the bidding of a crazy woman? If the crazy woman jumps off a cliff, will he do the same thing? He doesn't fancy Jidan. So what? That only means that though he has eyes he cannot see. What's wrong with Jidan? She'll become a civil servant soon. Dalin has recommended Jidan to Zhang Shutian, asking him to help her. Dalin's word has really produced an effect. By now Jidan has filled out the admission form and the medical check-up form. She is now waiting for Zhang Shutian to sign the forms. Compared with Jidan, Larz is currently an unwanted dog. Now it is Jidan who doesn't fancy him."

Seeing that he could collect rent from the civic school, Shuanhu maintained an attitude toward Kang Yuanyuan and Larz which could still be regarded as acceptably polite. No matter how foolish or blockheaded Kang Yuanyuan and Larz might be, as long as they could pay the rent in good time, Shuanhu did not mind their foolishness or blockheadedness a bit. In this sense, the more crazy people there were in the world, the better, because they were the ones who stuffed his wallet. Look at these expensive tables and chairs in

Shuanhu's office! Hadn't they been purchased with the rent Kang Yuanyuan had paid?

Thump, thump, thump — someone was knocking at the door. I rose and opened it. Outside stood Larz, who told me that someone was looking for me.

I bid farewell to Shuanhu, who waved back.

As we were walking along the veranda, Larz told me it was Township Head Zhao who was after me. I looked down at the ground, and spotted Zhao Xiaohui standing by an old car, smiling at me with his mouth half open.

With Larz at my side, I went downstairs and shook hands with Zhao Xiaohui.

Zhao Xiaohui said that he had just inspected some road construction works; that upon learning I was back in the village, he had come here specifically to pick me up; that he was about to take me to have my favorite spicy fish.

"No, no, no! There's no need for that at all!" I declined. "Spare as much money as possible."

While dragging me and Larz into the car, Zhao Xiaohui said, "I've got some money now. Don't you worry. This car was at the mechanic's for three years, but now it has been fixed. That it's up and running is proof that I do have money."

On our way to the restaurant, I found that here and there, the road — which had once been the main road — had been cut apart and butchered, making driving impossible. Our car had to detour onto a field, however the field, too, was exceedingly uneven. Zhao Xiaohui steered very carefully. There were times when the car tilted so much that it nearly turned over.

Zhao Xiaohui said that thanks to Xiang Wenhua's generous help, he had just succeeded in obtaining a considerable sum of money, which had been specifically designated for road construction. However, by dint of arduous negotiation with Zhang Shutian, he had had the pleasure of seeing the latter eventually yield to his request, and agree to set aside one million *yuan* for the township government to settle its debts. Though this sum was by no means enough to offset all the debts, at least some of the most urgent had been cleared, and the overdue salaries owed to the staff had been paid. Additionally, part of the electricity utility fee and the telephone service charges had been prepaid. This meant that for the time being, the pressure had diminished a little. Though the pressure had been reduced by only a little, Zhao Xiaohui could feel easy for a while.

Looking out of the car window, Zhao Xiaohui vehemently vented his bad feelings about this road under construction. He declared that it would be a 100% cowboy operation. "The road base is filled with garbage fetched from a dump. What an unheard-of thing! What a monumental spectacle!" Zhao Xiaohui deplored.

"And don't forget," Zhao Xiaohiu continued, "garbage is porous. How can porous garbage make a solid base for a road? But the contractors are like tigers' bottoms, which the common people dare not offend. When it was time to determine who would get the contract to build the road, all the powerful delegates gathered together for an intense war. After fierce argument, the upshot was the following: each and every delegate ought to make some concessions, so that each and every delegate could have a part of the project. Because each delegate was backed by the power of his protector, and none could be slighted, it was decided that each one would be responsible for constructing a portion of the road. Consequently, all the involved parties started work simultaneously on their own assigned sections."

70

After discussing the matter with Kang Yuanyuan, we agreed to adopt a point-based system. This so-called system ruled that each time a Sakelu villager attended a lecture he or she would earn two points (one of which would be deducted if they left before the lecture was over); whenever they accumulated ten points they were entitled to a subsidy of one hundred *yuan*.

I printed off the rules and went to persuade the villagers, household by household. I did not know how busy they were until I had knocked at a few doors. They were so busy, indeed, that they hardly had time to receive me. It turned out that most of them slept in the morning, and would not get up even to wash their faces or go to the toilet until the sun had risen over the tree tops. Then, they cooked a perfunctory meal, ate it in a hurry, and before they could put down their bowls someone had popped his head in at the door, or their phones had begun ringing incessantly — with the sole purpose of urging them to be quick, as the other three mahjong players could not wait any longer.

But there were a few exceptions, for example, Baolai's family. Baolai was living in a villa at the northwest end of the park. This villa, surrounded by wild grass and frequented by hares, was dirtier than a pigsty during the production team period[37]; it gave off strong foul smells. Xiaolin said that Baolai was not in, that Baolai had spent all the compensation money on Qiuli's illness, and was now working as a coolie at a construction site, so he was not to be found at home during the daytime. Undeterred, I asked to have a look at Qiuli, to see if she was on the mend.

On the door of Baolai's house hung a huge lock. A pat on the door provoked a scream from inside the villa, which sounded like neither crying nor laughing. It seemed to have come from the depths of a grave, like a ghost's singing — enough to make one's hair stand on end. Xiaolin said it was Qiuli's voice. Since having her bones broken by the Shuanhu family, Qiuli had never again stood up. She was paralyzed, and chained by Baolai to the bedstead, where food was thrown to her. Around her were heaps of faeces and puddles of urine, on which she often sat. One of her legs festered with oozing pus and wriggling maggots. Amazingly, she was very fond of looking at herself in the mirror despite the state she had been reduced to. In her pocket was a piece of mirror that she had picked up somewhere, and she would take it out and look into it from morning to evening. She talked, laughed, even quarreled angrily with the image of herself in the mirror.

Unable to see Baolai, Xiaolin and I headed for Beiqiang's home. Beiqiang never played mahjong. He said he did not like it, the noise which always accompanied it made his head ache. He was raising birds, and had several birdcages hung in the balcony; in consequence he was always getting nagged by his wife because of bird droppings on the floor. He was especially satisfied with, and even took personal pride in, the mynah he was keeping. It could speak like a human, with almost the same fluency as a TV broadcaster. Beiqiang said that he raised birds for two purposes — recreation and investment. The mynah, for example. He had bought from an old man at the cost of one thousand *yuan*, but hardly had a few days passed when someone traced him to his home and offered him three thousand *yuan* for it. He did not sell it, though. He knew a thing or two about the bird market. If the bird was brought to the "Wise Bird" competition arena in Yuebei and was caught by a camera even once, its price would soar to one hundred thousand or so. Beiqiang coaxed the bird into giving us a live demonstration, and it did not disappoint. It brought its talent into full play. One moment it spoke Henan dialect, the next moment Sichuan dialect, and the next moment the dialect of northeastern China. It imitated a street-crier selling steamed cold noodles, and even managed Beiqiang's hoarse coughing, very comically. Naturally, with its thin sharp voice, it could swear at people very well, too.

To my surprise, Beiqiang was not on good terms with Liben, the mention of whose name always sent him into a rage. If you want to know, money was the cause of all the problems. It was true that when Liben returned home he gave Beiqiang's family several stacks of US dollars — equivalent to one million RMB — in the presence of many people. On account of this money, Beiqiang became grateful and obedient to him as a matter of course, boosting his flight whenever possible, and anxious not to clip his wings. But who could have expected that Liben was simply staging a play when he gave them US dollars in front of others. Soberly considered, it was nothing less than a swindle.

I said so far as I knew Liben was not that sort of man. Why would he deceive his elder sister and brother-in-law, since he could build villas for the villagers with his own money? Xiaolin agreed, saying that Beiqiang must have misunderstood Liben. Liben's lengthy sojourn in Xiaolin's home had made him aware that Liben was running behind with his expenses at that time.

Beiqiang said that after receiving the money they had given it back, and asked Liben to help them deposit it in a bank because they did not know how to do it. So Liben went to a bank and came back with a savings-book account which contained the money as RMB. He gave the savings-book to his sister, and that should have been the end of the matter. Who, however, could have expected that he would come back for the savings-book after some time — borrowing money from them, so to speak. He borrowed — all right; who does not have moments of difficulty? And it was all right to borrow once or twice, but was it still all right when one borrowed eight or ten times? Seeing the balance in the savings-book shrinking day by day, eventually almost to single digits, Beiqiang and Lifang had to ask him to stop, whereupon Liben quarreled with them. Lifang was so offended that she set fire to that savings-book, announcing that she would no longer own Liben for her brother, and that he, who was as cruel as a wolf, was dead to her now. Sick with anger, she lay in bed for three days and three nights without eating or drinking anything. Beiqiang seized a hatchet and almost went to kill Liben.

I asked why Liben needed all that money. After two coughs, Beiqiang said it was just that Liben was being generous beyond his means! The bird in the balcony echoed Beiqiang's coughs and words, "Being overly generous beyond his means!"

Xiaolin tried to defend Liben. He explained that Sakelu had exhausted Liben's money. A one-time billionaire had been reduced to penury. He would not have borrowed money from his sister unless he had been at the end of his tether. "Do you think he likes borrowing money? He has a soft heart, ready to help anybody in difficulty, but helping people means spending money. The money he has spent on the Baolai family alone amounts to sixty or seventy thousand. What are the chances of a bad loan getting repaid? Furthermore, driven by vanity as he is, he pretends that he is still wealthy and still splashing money about, even though he knows that nothing is left in his pocket. He doesn't always spend money to be generous, sometimes he spends it because he has no other choice. For example, he has spent quite a lot on the payment shortfall for Sakelu's electricity and water supplies — and so has Xiaolin under Liben's influence. Do you think Liben wants to do this? But Sakelu will have to shut up shop if he doesn't. Isn't the notion of a blackout in a villa area ridiculous? In order to save Sakelu from failure before it has had a chance to really get underway, he has to carry a financial burden as heavy as Mount Tai."

Beiqiang's discontent resulted from many more things than Liben's borrowing money. Finding a job was another issue. Since Liben could appoint Song Tongguo, an outsider and an ungrateful wolf, to be Meiteng's administrator, why couldn't he get Beiqiang a job there? By helping Beiqiang to a paying job to help with his sister's and nephew's survival, Liben could at least repair the sense of kinship damaged by his demands on the savings-book. But Liben had done nothing. He let Song Tongguo get a good position. Did Song Tongguo give Liben a cent of what he had earned? What was Song Tongguo? A dwarf in doing but a giant in speaking, with a tongue glib with lies. What did Song Tongguo have that had caught Liben's eye? Years of living in the United States had not turned Liben into a wiser man; on the contrary, he was becoming more and more foolish. Beiqiang said he looked down upon Liben. They should not put it about that Liben was as intelligent as a PhD, capable of penetrating the secrets of the sky or those of the earth. As a matter of fact, he had the IQ of a kindergarten child.

Xiaolin and I persuaded Beiqiang to have some understanding for Liben, saying that Liben must have had his reasons for recommending Song Tongguo to work in Meiteng. Beiqiang questioned, "What reasons but that Song Tongguo flattered him and had a statue built for him? Has Liben become Chairman Mao, worthy of that statue? And it's a shabby one, made of poor-quality materials; a gust of wind is enough to blow it over. Well, where is it now?"

I was tired of Beiqiang's endless accusations against Liben. After urging him and his wife to attend the lectures, I signaled to Xiaolin with my eyes that we should leave. Once out of Beiqiang's home, we turned to enter someone else's, which Xiaolin said was Fugui's villa.

71

We knocked at the door of Fugui's house.

As the door opened, an unusual atmosphere suddenly engulfed us.

It was Layue who answered the door. She was dressed in strange attire, with a red band around her head, and some colorful strips of cloth hanging down from her neck. With her face dyed purple and blue, Layue looked exactly like a witch.

She said that her father was not in; that he was away wandering like a cloud somewhere. The implication was that we had better not enter the house.

In spite of her reluctance, I followed her into the sitting room as she turned back.

I seemed to have entered a deep cave. Everything around me was black, and nothing was visible. After a while, the contents of the room began to emerge, and the faces of the people around me could be made out.

"Why is it so dark inside?" Xiaolin asked Layue. "The sun is shining brightly outside. But inside it's like a tomb."

"That's because of the curtains," Layue explained. "These curtains are black. And they are double-layered."

Layue asked us to wait a minute, so that she could go into the inner room for a candle. "Once a candle is lighted, the room will brighten up," Layue said.

No sooner had Layue entered the inner room than Xiaolin drew the curtains open. "What a crazy woman!" Xiaolin muttered. "When there's good sunlight available, what's the point of lighting a candle?"

The minute the curtains were drawn open, a fierce wave of strong light rushed in like an overwhelming tsunami, which instantly swallowed the darkness. When Layue, lighted candle in hand, beheld the bright light, she was so astonished that she screamed loudly. Terrified, she let the candle fall to the ground. Without stopping to pick it up, Layue dashed to the window to draw the curtains together. Xiaolin, who was standing in front of the window, stopped her, and after they had argued for a long while, Layue had to yield to Xiaolin's insistence.

Layue begrudged this concession, and she never stopped grumbling as she was making tea for us. She said it had taken a great effort to muster some spirit presence, but now it had been dispersed in the blink of an eye.

What could she say to her father? If her father knew that she was to blame, wouldn't he break her legs?

"Yours would be a good life if only you lived it well," Xiaolin said to Layue, "so why don't you? Why do you pretend to conjure ghosts in this contemptible way? Aren't you fooling others and yourself? Do you find that interesting?"

Layue received Xiaolin's remarks with some hostility. She deemed Xiaolin's words blasphemous; she claimed that all spirits had ears to hear, and their ears were so sharply sensitive that at a distance of even one thousand kilometers they could still hear what people were saying. According to Layue, if Xiaolin's remarks annoyed the divine spirit, the spirit would hold Fugui's household to account: the mere distorting of their mouths and eyes would be a mild punishment, a more grave one would be paralysis, and the most serious outcome of all would take the form of choking to death on their food, or getting run down and killed by a vehicle while taking a walk.

"Come on! You stop your nonsense!" Xiaolin interrupted Layue. "If what you said were true, these spirits' ears could outperform radar, and people would merely need to keep some spirits on hand to do radar's job. And who would need radar then? Have you ever seen any spirits? Are they male or female? Do they have two legs or three legs?"

Layue assumed a mysterious look. She claimed she had indeed seen a spirit; she saw it in a vision. The spirit was a cat with sleek white hair, which gleamed like glass: the cat first jumped onto her bosom, then crawled onto the pillow and hummed musical tunes in her ears.

Layue declared to us that her vision had proved to be real; for when she woke up, she saw a white cat crawling on her pillow.

According to Layue, the cat was the very one she had taken to her parents' home after she divorced Qi Guangrong, but it had never occurred to her that it was the incarnation of a spirit. When she told her father about the vision, he affirmed with conviction that the cat was a god. Consequently her household began to worship the cat: any family member who happened to be at home must *kowtow* to the cat every day.

"Where is the cat?" Xiaolin asked.

"Dead," Layue sobbed.

Layue said that she was to blame, that she was responsible for the death of the fairy cat; and that was why her father had given her three lashes with a whip and had punished her by making her kneel down before the cat's remains for one whole week.

Layue told us that she had actually done the awful deed with good intentions. She had given the cat nice food and nice drink, and its death was the result of her feeding it a lot of meat, which she had put aside for it. Having eaten too much meat, the cat became bloated, with its stomach almost bursting. Unable to digest the meat, the cat rolled over and over on the ground. In no time, it got sick. Soon afterward, it became terribly weak. It did not defecate for three days on end. Layue grew desperately anxious and restless, until an inspiration flashed into her mind: she should go to the clinic to buy some laxative!

So she did. The directions prescribed a dosage of one tablet, three times a day. Naturally, the dosage directions were for humans. But to show her great concern for the cat, Layue crushed three tablets each time and forced them into the cat's mouth. As the saying goes "The road to hell is paved with good intentions," and instead of getting better after taking the medicine, as Layue had hoped, the cat became stiff and died. Layue wailed and wept, as if the dead animal were her own father or mother. But no matter how mournfully she cried, the cat did not revive.

Fugui's house was decorated to look like a temple. A bronze Buddha was set in a niche facing the main door. Below the Buddha was a table. In the center of the table lay a sizable censer surrounded by various offerings of dried fruit and fresh fruit. In the censer, three sticks of incense were burning, each exuding its own trail of smoke, enveloping the room in a cloud.

"Why did you divorce, when everything was going so well?" I asked Layue.

At the mention of this topic, Layue seemed abruptly to fall from the summits of heaven into a dark abyss — she left the spirit domain and instantly returned to the plain human world. She said it was her father who had forced her to divorce; that the divorce had been against her will. She said she still felt quite attached to Qi Guangrong. From her half-veiled remarks, it could be inferred that Qi Guangrong, though not gifted in making money, had been gifted in making love to Layue; that Qi Guangrong's "junk," which was as stiff and penetrating as a diamond drill-bit, had been an agonizing pleasure for Layue; that she had enjoyed what he had done to her in bed— and now, when he no longer did it, she wished he would.

Layue said that the thought of those things had gnawed at her so fiercely that she had often buried her lonely head in the bed-clothes, and shed tears. As for why her father had pressed her to divorce Qi Guangrong, hadn't it been because of the piss pot? During the engagement, Qi Guangrong had promised he would give the piss pot to her father as soon as he found it. However he had failed to fulfill his promise, using the excuse that it could not be found. Their son Langwa was by now a teenager, and yet Qi Guangrong had failed to produce the piss pot. This was why Fugui had decided not to wait any longer. Then, when he learned that each and every inhabitant of Mazi Village would be allotted a certain sum in compensation, Fugui commanded that Layue go through the divorce procedure and move back to live in Mazi Village.

Layue told us: it seemed that her destiny was inextricably linked to the piss pot. No matter where she went, she could not escape its clutches. As for why she and Song Tongguo had become deadlocked, wasn't it due to the execrable piss pot again? For the sake of the piss pot, Song Tongguo had put so much pressure on her that she had nearly hanged herself. Song Tongguo had explicitly stated that if Layue came to him with the chamber pot, he would accept her, but if she came without the piss pot, he would never sleep with her.

To tell the truth, Layue had no idea what the pot looked like. She had spared no effort to find it — she had left no container in Qi Gongrong's house unsearched, and she had dug three feet down into the ground, but still she had failed to find the treasure she so dreamed of owning.

Nevertheless, Layue was pretty confident that she would eventually get hold of the pot, given that Langwa was now in her hands, though the court had decided that the boy be put under his father's guardianship. As she had announced to Qi Guangrong: if he wanted to have his son back, he would have to offer the pot in exchange. It went without saying that Qi Guangrong wanted his son back; he had come again and again for Langwa, but without success. Why? Because Langwa had been hidden away in the home of one of Layue's relatives. No wonder that, whenever he came to Sakelu to demand his son, Qi Guangrong had seen neither hide nor hair of the boy, and that made him flare up with anger.

"What is it about Song Tongguo which attracts you?" Xiaolin asked Layue.

Layue did not answer for a long while. Finally she said, "I'm drawn to his talent."

Layue confessed that she hadn't thought of Song Tongguo as anything special until he was enlisted by Meiteng; it was then that the image she had of him abruptly loomed larger. She exclaimed, "How marvelous Song Tongguo is! 'Manager Song' I should call him. He wears western-style suits! And leather shoes! What a superb manner he has! What an air of importance he has! You can bet that, in days to come, money will rush his way in gushes and torrents. Where else can a woman find a man like that?"

According to Layue, such an opportunity might never be repeated, so she must keep firm hold of Song Tongguo. But to her annoyance and dismay, Song Tongguo was the playboy-type, often surrounded by beautiful young women. Layue had stealthily followed and watched him. And how disgusted she was by what she saw! She saw Song Tongguo dine with two young women in the best restaurant in Kaiyang; these two coquettish women frivolously pinched Song Tongguo's cheeks; from time to time, they would even fall into his arms and flirt with him.

72

I mobilized more than fifty villagers, and all, both young and old, said without exception that they were coming for my sake. Overjoyed with these people, Kang Yuanyuan spoke highly of my abilities and promised that when she opened a similar school elsewhere she would definitely appoint me headmaster.

A couple of conflicts arose during the first lecture. The speaker, invited from Yuebei by Kang Yuanyuan, was a female PhD who had studied in Great Britain and later done research on psychology in the United States. Kang Yuanyuan and I had warned her that when she gave the lecture she should try her best to use the vernacular language — the more vernacular, common and easy-to-understand, the better. However, this delicate female PhD seemed unable to change the elevated tone to which she was accustomed, with English words popping out of her mouth from time to time. The contents of her lecture — starting from the most fundamental codes of behavior in daily life — were not in the least profound. For example, one should not relieve oneself just anywhere, nor spit just anywhere, nor forget to flush the toilet bowl after use, nor yell loudly in public premises, nor break wind in front of others, nor pick flowers or break branches, and so on and so forth. While she was speaking about the harm spitting did to people, Dapao gave a cough and spat a thick clot of phlegm into the aisle nearby. That really annoyed her, and she put on a stern face and shouted at him to stand up, as if she were criticizing a pupil. Would Dapao, stubborn as an ox by nature, meekly stand up when ordered to do so by this woman? No, he just sat there motionless, his red face averted. The woman PhD asked him angrily if he was resisting her on purpose. Did he lack even manners? What did he mean by spitting so shamelessly?

Dapao was irritated by the woman PhD. He answered her with the dirtiest thing he could think of, "You ask what I mean? Well, let me tell you. I mean to fuck your mother!"

Hearing this, the whole class began to boil out of control with human voices, as if a hornet's nest had been poked with a stick. The woman PhD bent down over the desk weeping, so that Kang Yuanyan and Larz went up to console her. Dapao left in annoyance, while others chattered in great excitement, denouncing the woman PhD for being too bossy, too inflexible.

"All that over a bit of phlegm! Did you have to make him look small like this? What's wrong with spitting? Is it your business where we like to spit? For thousands of years, our ancestors have been spitting like this, generation after generation. Should a little kid like you, kneaded out of urine and mud, dare attempt to change a practice passed down to us by our ancestors? Who do you think you are? Think about what you have just said. Is it reasonable for you to prohibit people from farting? Seal their anuses with mud, sew them up with needle and thread, or bung them with a brick if you have the skill! Wanting to control what emperors cannot! Can you do more than an emperor? You are old enough to have heard the saying: 'You can rule over heaven and earth, but you can't stop people shitting and farting!'"

After this outbreak, half of the class disappeared, and Kang Yuanyuan restored discipline to what was left. She first appeased the red-eyed woman PhD, and then apologized to the rest of the class on her behalf. The lecture resumed. Instead of specific details of life, the woman PhD changed her topic to a bigger one — civil rights and responsibilities. And it was obvious why. It was less likely to clash with the villagers if the topic was kept impersonal and distant. But she still got interrupted, this time by Tian Baolai, a man no one would ever have expected to do something like that. He raised his hand in protest, saying that the woman PhD was a traitor. When asked how he came to that conclusion, he eventually managed to provide a satisfactory answer, although he was so timid that he was often at a loss for the right word. He said that the woman PhD never stopped extolling America's virtues as if America's moon was rounder than China's and American farts smelled better than Chinese ones, and that when she talked about China, she shook her head, saying this was not good, and that was not right. Even if China was not good, it was her motherland; it had given her life and nurtured her. What right did she have to point her finger at it? No matter how poor one's parents were, as their child one must not despise them. That was the basic ethical principle which all human beings should follow.

Having wised-up by now, the woman PhD did not directly argue with Baolai. She sat quietly and listened with smiling attention. However, this policy did not pacify the outbreak; on the contrary, her forbearance caused the villagers to become more aggressive. They cursed the United Sates loudly and recklessly, saying that it was the wickedest country in the world, that the mother of its president had been fucked by a donkey, and that all of its people must die and die hard!

Initially, Kang Yuanyuan, who was sitting at the far end of the classroom, was reluctant to get involved in the discussion between the woman PhD and the villagers. She was even secretly delighted by it. After all, being able to argue indicated a certain level of awareness! But as the discussion went more and more off the rails, she felt compelled to walk to the front of the room and pat once or twice on the desk. The classroom at once fell quiet again. Kang Yuanyuan addressed the villagers present, saying that she was willing to discuss with them the topic in question on condition that there should be no swearing or obscenities in their speech. Kang Yuanyuan asked whether they accepted these conditions or not, and the whole class declared its acceptance.

After the woman PhD walked out of the classroom, Kang Yuanyuan sat down on the lecturer's seat. She invited the villagers to air their opinions, however, they all appeared to have become deaf, unable to hear her, and dumb, unresponsive to her proposal. After a few seconds of silence, Kang Yuanyuan called on Baolai, asking him why he hated the United States so much. Baolai had entirely lost the thrust of his diatribe, but faltered on with it anyway, "The United States practices hegemonism. It thinks it's the world's policeman, and invades other countries all over the world." Kang asked him calmly, "Don't you think this world needs to have a policeman?"

She had hardly got these words out when a villager interrogated her, "Are you a spy from the United States?"

It was this question which resulted in the final failure of the lecture. It seemed that the villagers were fully convinced that she was a spy, and that the spy sitting in front of them was a ferocious wolf about to devour them, its eyes watchful and its mouth wide open. Panic-stricken, the villagers fled desperately, out through the back door.

Kang Yuanyuan sat there like a block of wood, her face deadly white, her lips trembling. She could not utter a word for what seemed like forever, only heaving long-drawn sighs. Larz poured a glass of water for her, asking if she felt unwell, and whether she needed to go to hospital. Kang Yuanyuan made no reply, but slumped forward over the desk weeping bitterly.

Shuanhu came in. While all these things were going on, he had been standing outside the classroom, either craning his neck to look in through the window, or pressing his body up against the wall to listen. Shuanhu patted Kang Yuanyuan on the back to calm her weeping. Why did she weep like that? It was not proper for a PhD to look at things as a farmer would do! Then he switched the topic. He said whether the civic school was a success or not, he did not care, he only cared about his rent; he would not tolerate rent arrears of a single cent, even if that meant the school failing midway. Kang Yuanyuan stopped sobbing. She assured Shuanhu that she would pay the rent as stipulated by the contract. Shuanhu lit a cigarette, blowing out one smoke ring, and then another. Ho-ho-ho! He chuckled, asking if Kang Yuanyuan could be flexible in her ideas and try her hand at different methods of training. For example, she might train farmers how to raise cattle, how to grow medicinal herbs, and so on and so forth. It was futile to reach for the stars straight away. What farmers wanted were tangible benefits rather than thoughts! If you stood at the entrance of a village and shouted for its folks to come and learn — at no charge to them — some motto like that, no one would heed you, even if you shouted until your throat was cracked; but if you shouted at them to come and collect an empty bottle which could be pawned for ten cents, what would happen? The whole village would come out for it, and even the paralyzed would be tempted to do so. It was a waste of time to attempt to train people if one was ignorant of this simple fact.

Kang Yuanyuan said she did know what the farmers wanted, but she knew that what they wanted could not save them. To feed them fish was not the solution to the problem. What was urgently required was to teach them how to fish! Farmers must have their blood and brains changed if they would free themselves from the predicament which had troubled them for thousands of years. Shuanhu laughed at her, saying it was people like her, and not the farmers, who must have their blood and brains changed. He hoped that he could cooperate with her in the training of a batch of high-quality *xiaojie*. He planned to recruit a hundred, train them before they worked, and grant them work-permits after they finished the training. Only by attracting high-quality punters with high-quality *xiaojie* could Shuanhu enjoy the incessant rolling-in of banknotes with a broad smile on his lips.

73

Some time later, news came to my ears that Kang Yuanyuan had not only cancelled the Civic School in Sakelu, but had also got into serious trouble.

To everyone's surprise, on the day the female PhD was giving a talk, Song Tongguo came with a tape recorder and recorded every word the lecturer and Kang Yuanyuan said. Afterwards, he rang Kang Yuanyuan to blackmail her. She must give him a sum of money, otherwise he would make lots of copies of the recording and submit them to the relevant authorities.

Kang Yuanyuan's eyeballs almost burst out of their sockets in fury. She argued that she hadn't made any false statements. Was there any impropriety in her giving the United States as an example, seeing that it was the No.1 advanced nation in the world?

But nevertheless, in order to avoid trouble, she transferred ten thousand *yuan* to the bank account specified by Song Tongguo, who had actually demanded fifty thousand. She decided not fully to satisfy his demand; this ten thousand *yuan* was meant to pacify him so that he would cease his restless trouble-making. After finishing the transfer, Kang Yuanyuan continued to burn with anger, her belly causing her intense pain, as though her intestines were convulsing. I did not hear from Larz about this matter until Kang Yuanyuan had already been in hospital for a month. Her condition was getting worse all the time.

I went to the hospital to pay Kang Yuanyuan a visit, carrying a bouquet and a basket of assorted fruits. As I entered the hospital gate, a strong sense of guilt swept over me; I felt like a penitent. I was quite sincere in this, because I came from Mazi Village and I used to be one of the villagers. Even though I had fled from them, I was inextricably connected to them by ties of blood, which could never be severed. It appeared that Kang Yuanyuan's health had been destroyed by them, yet somehow this did not seem right: rather than being the principal wrong-doers, they seemed more like accessories.

After asking around, I was informed that Kang Yuanyuan had been transferred from a general ward to a cancer ward. Hearing this, I could not help shivering. I thought to myself, "Has she got a malignant tumor? If so, it is like sitting on a rock surrounded by raging torrents. A wind, or a wave, might suffice to sweep the poor creature into the sea."

Kang Yuanyuan was asleep. I sat in front of her bed and touched her hand.

Her hands used to be as soft as fresh bread, but now they felt as coarse as shriveled bark. Her once round face, which had so suited her name, was now sunken, making her cheek bones protrude dramatically. Her lips were ragged and red, as if they had been drenched with blood. Larz, half kneeling before her bed, was tending her, cleaning with paper napkin the sticky saliva issuing from the corners of her mouth.

In the corridor, Larz told me that Kang Yuanyuan had got pancreatic cancer and it had reached its terminal stage; that the main feature of this disease was pain; that even huge doses of pain-relievers and injection after injection of distalgesics scarcely diminished the pain. Whenever she was seized by a fit of pain, Kang Yuanyuan would bite the quilt so forcefully that her teeth went right through it, so that she ended up gnawing her lips bloody. According to Larz, the pain had been alleviated slightly in recent days, mainly thanks to the increase in the dosage of dolantin, which at least enabled her to have some sleep.

Larz said he couldn't bear this anymore; he really couldn't endure it any longer; even a man made of iron would have been overwhelmed by this endless travail. He complained that Kang Yuanyuan had never done anything neatly and definitively, and that her illness, which was so lingering and inconclusive, was very much in her usual style.

"Either live a happy life, or die a quick death. Why does she go on like this, half alive and half dead?" Larz groaned. Of course, Kang Yuanyuan had tried to commit suicide. It was in the middle of the night. She tied a silk scarf round her neck and hung herself from the bed frame. But her fellow patients discovered her at it and called for the nurses. Thus Kang Yuanyuan's hoped-for suicide had come to nothing.

According to Larz, the night it happened, he had not stayed in the ward to tend Kang Yuanyuan overnight; he had given himself a night off. He learned about the shocking incident the following morning when he entered the hospital. He rebuked Kang Yuanyuan for having done it, but in his heart he was resentful of the other patients for being such busybodies. Why had they deprived her of her right to escape from that bitter sea of pain?

Right now, the most urgent thing for him to do, said Larz, was to go to the marriage registration office with Kang Yuanyuan and apply for a marriage certificate.

"She has deteriorated so much. What difference does it make whether she is married or not?" I asked Larz. "Can marriage revive her?"

Shaking his head, Larz said, "It makes a big difference."

Above all, so Larz claimed, a marriage would fulfill Kang Yuanyuan's wish to no longer be a single woman.

According to Larz, Kang Yuanyuan had whole-heartedly hoped to marry him; she had expressed this wish many times, but Larz's ambivalent attitude kept delaying the marriage; now that she had come to the last days of her life, if Larz continued to obstruct the realization of her wish, could he still be called a man of good conscience? What was more, claimed Larz, the marriage would facilitate the disposal of Kang Yuanyuan's property. Once they were married and became legitimate husband and wife, Larz would have an indisputable right to inherit Kang Yuanyuan's property.

Larz told me that Kang Yuanyuan's property was much less than he had expected, and her bank book was now in his possession. When she first returned from abroad, she had had more than three million *yuan* in her bank account, in addition to other property. But even so large an amount could not withstand such wild expenditure. She had subsidized this project and that program; she had run, without success, a class here and a class there. Her hospitalization had made her financial situation go from bad to worse. Like a huge pile of snow melting in the scorching sun, the amount in her bank account was diminishing rapidly.

"Can you imagine how insignificant the balance is?" Larz asked me. "As little as one hundred and eighty thousand *yuan*! What can you do with such a small sum of money? For each extra day Kang Yuanyuan continues to breathe, twenty more pieces of one-hundred *yuan* bills must be fed into the cashier's window. We must also consider the cost of her cremation and the cost of buying her a tomb plot. Nowadays the crematory and the cemetery have turned into greedy pythons — dissatisfied even after consuming huge sums of money. Thank Heaven, Kang Yuanyuan has got this disease. If she had been healthy, in no time she would have squandered all her money and been reduced to beggary. She was too careless of money. She had given away money as though it were a handful of ashes."

Larz stated that, in the past, almost every time he walked down a street in Kang Yuanyuan's company, he witnessed her "discard" at least one hundred *yuan*. Those begging on the street — and it did not matter if they were real beggars or fake ones — would invariably receive some money if they held out their hands to her. The funniest thing of all, was that one day when they passed along the street, Kang Yuanyuan, finding that she had forgotten to bring her wallet with her, borrowed two hundred *yuan* from Larz and distributed the entire amount to the beggars. Later on, when lunch time came, they themselves had to sit on the street and go hungry, because they did not have even fifty cents left in their pockets to buy a piece of bread.

By telling these anecdotes, Larz wished to convey a key message: if you do not use your money carefully in periods of prosperity, you'll find yourself without money when you badly need it.

Larz did not have high hopes that he would inherit any money left over in Kang Yuanyuan's account. What he coveted were her two estates in Yuebei. One was a good-sized apartment in a pleasant neighborhood. It was worth something now, given that house prices had been rising steadily. The other was a courtyard complex of considerable historic value. Kang Yuanyuan's parents died fairly young, leaving her an orphan. When she was still a child, this estate was seized by her father's younger brother. After returning from America, Kang Yuanyuan launched a lawsuit against her uncle, which lasted six years. She won the lawsuit, but lost her connection to her kinsfolk. Her uncle's wife was as ruthless as a tigress. Every time they met, the woman would fall upon Kang Yuanyuan, tearing at her mouth. Kang Yuanyuan had not wanted the courtyard complex on account of its estate value; rather, she treasured it as an inheritance from her parents. In addition to the real estates, Kang Yuanyuan owned some bonds bought in the United States. But Larz did not know the password, nor did he have any idea how to convert them into ready cash.

The conversation between me and Larz was broken off by Kang Yuanyuan's painful groans. We hurried back to the ward and came to her side. Pain convulsed her features; her hands grasped aimlessly, and her feet kicked frantically. It looked like she was trying her utmost to restrain herself; however, I detected, to my surprise, some cryptic, transcendent smiles on her face.

Larz went out to call for a nurse. Sitting on the edge of the bed, I held Kang Yuanyuan's shaking hands with all my might. Struggling to extract her hands from my grip, Kang Yuanyuan strove hard to point at something beneath her pillow. Assuming that she might be in need of some napkin secreted there, I propped up her head with one hand and searched under the pillow with the other. There I found an envelope. I asked her if that was what she wanted. She nodded with an effort and muttered something in a feeble voice. Nevertheless, I understood her: she wanted me to put the envelope into my pocket and not to open it until I was out of the hospital gate.

Having left the hospital, and coming to a street intersection, I found a quiet place beneath a flyover bridge. I took out the envelope and carefully opened it. What I found took my breath away: within the envelope were a piece of paper and two strings of keys. Attached to each key was a scrap of paper bearing information about which room it could unlock.

It seemed that a gust of chill wind were sweeping over the surface of the piece of paper in my hand. Undoubtedly, these few lines served as her will.

The will was by no means complicated. The characters resembled a miniature mass of cripples walking against a strong wind.

Kang Yuanyuan wrote in her will:

> First, all my account balance goes to Larz, as a token of my gratitude for his looking after me.
>
> Second, my two properties — one at Apartment 301, Building 5, Defu Garden, Defu Street, the other at Compound -25, 117 Anmin Road — are to be administered by the management of the municipal civil administrative bureau. All revenues from the auction of these two estates should be used exclusively to help orphans and disabled children. My best hope is to build a child welfare house.
>
> Third, all my financial bonds in the U.S. are entrusted to my friend Tian Liben, and their revenues are to be spent on building a Hope Project school in Sakelu, Gaotai Township, Kaiyang County. I have finally come to the realization that people's minds are too resistant to be changed, once they have been shaped in a certain fashion. To cultivate promising citizens, the training must start with the kindergarten.
>
> Fourth, my body is to be donated to China Red Cross. If any part of it can still be of use, feel free to make it serve anyone in need.

No sooner had I finished reading the will than my mobile phone rang. The number indicated that the caller was Larz. He asked me why I had left without saying goodbye to him.

"I still had something to talk over with you. Why did you leave so hurriedly?" Larz asked.

He wanted to know what I had taken from Kang Yuanyuan. He said he had heard a warder say it seemed to be a check. "Isn't it plundering, to make off with her belongings when she is dying?" Larz asked.

He sounded increasingly aggressive and explosive. He urged me to come back to the ward and return what I had taken, or he would call the police.

Instantly, Kang Yuanyuan's will became a scalding hot potato. I wondered whether I should keep it or get rid of it. Just then, lightning forked across my mind and the figure of a person surfaced in my brain: it was none other than Xue Yulu. "Well, why don't I just hand the will over to the press house?" I said to myself.

74

The news that Dalin had been attacked with sulphuric acid by Li Tiantian did not reach me until he was lying in the mortuary. It happened that at the entrance to a luxurious restaurant, Li Tiantian, with a canning jar in hand, slipped ten *yuan* to a waiter, and asked him to send out Dalin from his private room. Li Tiantian claimed that she was named Ye, Dalin's wife. When Dalin came out to find Ye Lihua, out rushed Li Tiantian from behind a car where she had been hiding; she lifted the can and splashed its contents onto Dalin's face. Dalin fell down, rolled on the ground and cried in pain, hysterically. People in the restaurant darted for the doorway, came out, and formed a circle of spectators around him. At the boss's instruction, some called 110 to report the incident to the police, while others dialed 120 to call for an ambulance. The 110 police car arrived after the 120 ambulance had rushed Dalin away. Oddly, Li Tiantian did not take advantage of the chaos to run away, but stood there waiting for the police to arrest her. When she saw them, her first words were, "Shoot me as soon as possible!"

Having lain in the hospital for two days, Dalin died from organ failure caused by the acid-burns. It was strange that no one from the Ye family showed up during that whole period, no matter how many times the hospital called them and even sent for them. It was not just that they refused to show up. What was more, Old Mr. Ye, a doddering old codger by now, in the presence of the hospital people, sent a houseman to light a string of firecrackers outside the gate. The Ye household fumed with anger at the mention of Dalin, and railed at him because of his ingratitude. How could a young man who had once been honest have become as fierce as a wolf in the blink of an eye like that? They said for him to divorce Ye Lihua was one thing, but to covet the family villa was quite another. He had come to the Ye household with empty hands, but wanted to leave with plundered gold and silver. Seen in this light, Dalin's entry into the Ye family was a plot, more or less; the act of a weasel who said "Happy-new-year!" to a hen. After having grown rich, taken tours abroad, obtained a decent job and promotion, he had become so conceited and pompous that he began to see Ye Lihua as a burden! But without her, he would still have been a dirty migrant worker. Who did he think he was? To kick down the ladder after making use of it, to kill the donkey after taking advantage of it, to do things offensive to nature and reason! Aha, there was some justice after all, because heaven had snatched away a mad dog, ridding the Ye family of a pest. Why should they visit him, and attend the funeral of such a piece of garbage? As he had been absent from home for a long time, Ye Lihua, driven insane, was still in the mental hospital. Ye Zhonghua had been consulting with his "brothers" in the procuratorate, hoping that it would bring Dalin to justice — starting with his job, because all the documents concerning his official status had been faked. He would not stop until Dalin was put into jail. In Ye Zhonghua's words, it would be easier to kill Dalin, a man who had appeared out of nowhere, than to kill a fly with a swat. Now the problem was solved; everything was all right again. Li Tiantian had heroically rid the people of a scourge, so Ye Zhonghua no longer had to cudgel his brains about it. Dalin had met his doom without the Ye family having to move a single finger. What could be more exhilarating?

According to Xue Yulu, who reported on the case, Li Tiantian had taken up with and then parted ways with two men after Dalin, so that when she wanted to resume their relationship, Dalin ignored her and called her a bitch in front of others. More irritating still was that Dalin sent men to check her accounts and issued a sky-high fine on account of tax fraud. When she went to reason with Dalin, he mocked her as having the face of a fossil dinosaur. Li Tiantian closed her restaurant and sat around doing nothing from morning to evening. She could not read, sleep or eat. Even playing mahjong did not interest her anymore. In desperation, she took to drugs, but the more she took, the emptier and more meaningless she felt life to be. She thought of suicide, but felt that her death would be in vain if she died alone — and, naturally, Dalin was her first choice to accompany her. Since he had mocked her for having the face of a fossil dinosaur, she wanted to make him have such a face too, and also experience the agony of having his face splashed with sulphuric acid. Li Tiantian kept claiming that she had not intended to kill Dalin, and that what she had done was for his own good, and for the good of the many other women who had been betrayed. She hated to see him fooling around with other women, making this one cry today and that one weep tomorrow. He was a woman-killer, the cause of Taoqi's death, of Li Tiantian's bankruptcy and of Ye Lihua's insanity. And foolish women were waiting in line to be devastated by him! In spite of the fact that ten years had passed since he parted with her, the thought of him would make her shiver and lose the will to live. Dalin was like a pain in her bones. Her wish was very simple: to put an end to this pain.

Xue Yulu really let Li Tiantian have it, saying that she was a whore, who had brought death to one of her best friends. In her report, she described Dalin as a soldier who had died at his post. He was a righteous man who had braved an acquaintance's hatred and thirst for revenge when he detected her in tax fraud and issued the appropriate fine. That accursed woman was a drug addict, and a sex pervert ready to splash sulphuric acid onto another's face, though a victim of such an acid attack herself. Xue Yulu cried, teardrops streaming down her cheeks. I was completely taken aback by such a reaction to Dalin's death. In the end, Xue Yulu revealed the facts of her association with Dalin. There were some dubious economic interests between them; it was not just a matter of disinterested friendship. Each year Dalin would bring more than five million *yuan* in advertising revenue to the press house, whereof Xue Yulu pocketed five hundred thousand, because it was a house rule that ten percent of advertising revenue be given to whoever brought it to the press house. More important was that Xue Yulu and Dalin were planning a show, in which stars from Hong Kong, Taiwan and Japan would be invited to Yuebei with funds raised exclusively by Dalin. With Dalin's support, the show would be profitable, at negligeable risk. It could only succeed, it could not fail. Xue Yulu would instruct the media under her control to fan the flame, so there was no need to worry about ticket sales. If it had been a great success, she and Dalin could each have earned up to ten million *yuan*; if a modest success, three or five million *yuan* at least. Now the game was up. It was at this critical moment that the accursed Li Tiantian had chopped down the great tree Xue Yulu was holding onto, leaving her hanging from a cliff, unable to go up or down. What should she do? Just as the tea gets cold after the drinker leaves, so the sponsors had changed their minds before Dalin's body was stiff. She had tentatively called them, but six of the seven said that they intended to halt sponsorship, while the seventh was ambiguous in attitude only because he did not have the authority to make a decision when his boss was abroad. "Do you think these sponsors wanted to be ripped off? No, they only dreaded Dalin's power. If they had refused, Dalin would have sent men to their companies to check their accounts. If there were no checking there would be no problems; conversely, problems would definitely emerge from checking. There are two ways to handle the problem — to drink a toast and be a sponsor, or to drink a forfeit and accept unbearable fines! They were shrewd businessmen and of course they knew very well how to secure advantages and avoid disadvantages. If they drank a toast, they might get a friend out of it, but if they drank a forfeit, they might get an enemy out of it with endless troubles. Now the sponsors had cancelled their sponsorship, the show would be aborted, and the organizers would be guilty of breach of contract, the costs of which were two million *yuan* in damages for the actors and actresses."

With this, Xue Yulu burst into snuffles and tears again. She said that the Ye's probably would not share the damages since Dalin had had a tense relationship with them and had fathered no children on Ye Lihua. If they refused to help, she would have to pay the damages all by herself. How mortally wronged she would be! All the income brought by Dalin over the years would be consumed by the damages in a single hit! There were deficits which she would have to make good with her own money! She hated Li Tiantian, a hideous dog-fucked, pig-bred, wild-ass-screwed, pheasant-laid monster! Couldn't she have waited four or five months longer, if she had wanted to murder Dalin? That can of sulphuric acid had not just killed Dalin; it had nearly finished her off too!

In contrast to Xue Yulu, who was so depressed, Shuanhu seemed rather happy with Dalin's death. I saw him at Dalin's funeral when he came with his daughter Jidan, who cried, portentously but without tears, although she had spent a lot of time to summon them up. She said that thanks to Uncle Dalin she had become a real government employee, able to work in the youth and juvenile office of the county's labor union. A few days after she took the job, she was given a task: to tour primary schools delivering a speech with the title "How to Be a Human." Wasn't that a simple topic? To be a human was not the same as to be a pig! The biggest difference was that man loved makeup, while a pig never looked at itself in a mirror!

Shuanhu's main task was to take care of Xiaolin. Third Aunt had been kept out of the loop, so she was still unaware of Dalin's death. Xiaolin was the only representative of the family present at the funeral. He cried until his legs became unsteady, and he knelt down before his brother's remains for a long time. In order to console Xiaolin, Shuanhu said that crying could not revive a dead man, that no-one lived forever. What was more, how many people in this world could hope to die such a dramatic death? A worthwhile death!

Truly so! What more could one have demanded? — wasn't it gratifying that the death of a former shepherd and wood-cutter from the countryside had stirred half of Yuebei City? Enough, enough, he had achieved enough!

Shuanhu turned and whispered to me even as he went on soothing Xiaolin. He told me that Jidan's job had been sorted out, and that he had been preparing to thank Dalin, but before he could show his gratitude Dalin had been reduced to a heap of ashes. Though he heaved a sigh when he said this, Shuanhu made me feel how pleased he was to have saved a lot of thank-you expenses — as a faint smile was playing around his mouth.

Dalin's funeral was boisterous, the courtyard inside and outside crammed with people who were talking about seeing the hero off on his last trip. Wreaths were laid out from the hall to the road, a distance of a few kilometers. Two parking lots were filled with cars, and on the platform stood several rows of people in western suits and leather shoes, each face as grave and solemn as the eulogy. A certain VIP delivered a speech to the crowd, and out of his mouth poured such refrains as "living a great life and dying a glorious death."

75

In addition to being troubled by Kang Yuanyuan, I was also haunted by Tian Dalin — they weighed so heavily on my mind that I found it difficult to breathe. To tell the truth, they had not been connected to me closely, either financially or spiritually. However, strangely enough, I dreamed of them almost every night. In my visions, they were always running after me, and no matter how desperately I ran, I simply could not gain on them; I was running after a train, and they were running after me: I could not catch up with the train, and they were about to clamp my legs at any moment.

In time, I became afraid of night; I became afraid of falling asleep.

I tried many ways to cope with the problem: I slept with the light on; I slept with an insense stick burning in the house; I brandished a burning torch above and below my bed before I went to bed. But all these tricks proved useless. I kept on having nightmares just like before.

I had despaired of ever escaping them, and then I suddenly thought of the church. I decided to go and spend some time there: probably the church could stop the ghosts from haunting me.

Minister Gao had risen to the position of high priest; Xiaomao had become his assistant. Skinny and fragile, Minister Gao reminded me of a wavering willow branch. He spoke more slowly and mildly than in the past.

In sharp contrast, Xiaomao had grown stout and strong. The beard around his mouth made him so unlike the person he had once been that I hardly recognized him. Apparently Xiaomao still remembered me. He greeted me, fetched a bench for me to sit on, and poured me some water. The welcome he extended to me was as warm as a pleasant fire.

After Xiaomao withdrew from the room, Minister Gao closed the door from inside.

This room served as Minister Gao's reading-room too. The decoration looked solemn. On the walls were many crosses of various sizes, along with some pictures depicting the Passion of Jesus Christ. The old-fashioned table and chairs were painted black and shiny. On the table and on some chairs were neat stacks of books having to do with the Bible. On a plain single bed were some simple bed clothes. The only thing that looked modern was a radio set on the table. Minister Gao told me the radio was for him to listen to Bible broadcasts.

As always, Minister Gao looked shy. He often lowered his head while talking with others.

"Have you thought it through?" he asked me. "When will you commit yourself to our Lord Jesus?"

I replied, "The frantic turmoil of the world has burdened me more than I can bear. Like a lost child, I stand at the crossroads; I cannot find my way home."

Minister Gao said, "Every person is a lost child. The problem is that many do not know they are lost. Those so-called successful politicians and entrepreneurs seem to have brilliant lives leading to brilliant goals, but actually they are pitiable. The most pitiable thing about them is that they do not realize they are pitiable. They pursue success and fame, profit and gain. Some of them even forget the existence of God — they regard themselves as a god. God has long ago discerned their wicked thoughts; of course God has seen through everything in this world. He sent Jesus to the world to act as his agent to lead the people into the paths of righteousness. What a tragedy that the devil has transformed so many men into demons. These men are selfish, greedy, hypocritical and vain. They turn a deaf ear to the teachings of Jesus Christ. They are wandering ever farther and ever faster from the true path. They run after meaningless vanities. They fight for a valueless bone like dogs do. There are no flowers awaiting them. What awaits them is nothing but cold, hard walls and a bottomless abyss. They are doomed: they'll either knock their heads against the walls and be horribly injured, or they will fall off the cliff and get smashed to pieces at the bottom."

Minister Gao claimed that every person was a child of God; God had compassion for everyone; however, in the face of proliferating greed, even God was powerless to help; that was why in his visions he constantly saw God's face covered in tears.

Minister Gao continued, "This world can be both complicated and simple. If you think it is complicated, it is complicated. But if you think it is simple, it is simple. Isn't it like a tug of war between Good and Evil? As Good gives way, Evil advances. When God's sunlight does not shine over the earth, the devil makes bold to appear and acts as if he were God. How is it that wickedness is so rampant in today's world? Isn't Evil to blame? Evil was once imprisoned within a cage. However, the door seemed to have been opened and thousands of lesser evils to have escaped the cage; they stretched themselves, they waved their fists, they cheered, they hopped, they looked as if they were about to achieve world dominance."

Minister Gao cited Xiaomao as an example. Within Xiaomao, he said, two forces — Good and Evil, were always fighting for the upper hand; when Xiaomao had thought about committing a theft, Evil was getting the upper hand; and since Xiaomao had thrown himself into the arms of God, Evil had been diminishing by degrees, and Good had been quietly thriving; for the time being, Xiaomao was situated at the middle point of the rope between Good and Evil, with Good and Evil resembling two giants pulling with all their might at each end in order to win Xiaomao over; if Good slackened a little bit, Xiaomao would be pulled towards Evil; but if Good exerted himself a little bit more, Xiaomao would follow Good and perform good deeds. What had happened during the past winter had convinced him of the unstable condition of Xiaomao's soul; how surprised he had been to discover that Xiaomao had stolen a silver cross belonging to another minister.

When he learned about the theft, Minister Gao, instead of rebuking Xiaomao, summoned him to his reading room. He opened his drawer, took out a bronze miniature statue of Jesus, and gave it to Xiaomao. Calmly he told Xiaomao that the bronze image had a market value of about six thousand *yuan*, and that this sum would be enough for Xiaomao to buy lots of wine and cigarettes, or alternatively to enjoy several visits to night spots. Surprisingly, Xiaomao took the miniature statue and went away with it. For two days Xiaomao could not be found anywhere. But Minister Gao felt sure he would come back eventually.

On the tenth day, Xiaomao did return. As soon as he saw Minister Gao, Xiaomao fell to his knees, and presented him with the silver cross and the bronze miniature statue. He told Minister Gao that he had planned to sell the two articles and use the money to do some business — in donkey hides or pig skins, or in coal or cement; then, after he had made some money, he would take a wife and would repay Minister Gao for the shelter he had kindly extended to him; to be specific, he would buy a villa for Minister Gao.

Xiaomao told Minister Gao he had negotiated with a woman and they had agreed on the price of the two items. But while he was on his way back to the hotel to fetch them, Xiaomao suddenly realized he was being secretly followed by several hulking men, with knives hidden beneath their coats. Without revealing any trace of suspicion, Xiaomao went back to the hotel. He took his bag and dashed out through a side door, his heart thumping all the time as loudly as a diesel engine. These were only his first steps in the business world, but already he could see the perils and dangers. In that moment of bewilderment, sounds rose within him and reverberated in his ear. They were the sounds of prayers in the church; they were the parishioners' confessions of repentance. The sounds were calling him back. However, instead of going straight back to the church, he headed to the police station. After walking back and forth in front of the police station, Xiaomao called up all his courage; he entered and confessed his crime. Assuming that Xiaomao was making up a story, the policemen remained impassive and took no action. Later when they saw that tears were rolling down Xiaomao's face, the policemen could not refrain from smiling. They promised they would investigate. Then they let him go. Sometime later, Xiaomao rang the church and learned that when the police came to investigate, the minister, whose silver cross Xiaomao had stolen, claimed that Xiaomao had not stolen it; rather he had deliberately given it to him as a present.

With tears in his eyes, Xiaomao went back to the church. Upon arrival, the first thing he did was to kneel down in the nave to confess his repentance. At the sight of Xiaomao, Minister Gao gently patted the boy on the shoulder: all the time, Xiaomao remained kneeling and weeping. Without uttering a single word of condemnation, Minister Gao told Xiaomao it was God's glory that had protected him and had guided him back. From then onward, Xiaomao faithfully devoted himself to God, and Good seemed to have taken root in his heart.

I told Minister Gao about Kang Yuanyuan's condition and asked him if he knew any means to save her. He said Kang Yuanyuan's dreadful fate resulted from her not having listened to God's decrees; that in the eyes of God, what Kang Yuanyuan had done was like the work of an ignorant child playing with toy building blocks — something was built, but it soon collapsed; something was rebuilt, but soon that too collapsed; even if it did not collapse, it was of no use in spite of its colorful look and amazing height. Minister Gao claimed that there had been good paths for Kang Yuanyuan to take, however she preferred walking among thistles; that the Lord had made a message for the world, but instead of spreading the Lord's message, she had come up with some noises of her own and spread them; that her body, which had been captured by unwholesome desires, might have been possessed by Satan.

Minister Gao promised to go, in the near future, to the hospital to see Kang Yuanyuan; he would offer a prayer for her. He said he might not be able to save her body, but surely he could redeem her soul.

After spending some time with Minister Gao, I felt much relieved. As I rose to say goodbye, a figure suddenly appeared in the door. Wearing a mask and a scarf, this person had kept the collars of his cotton-padded overcoat up around his neck. In spite of the fact that he was completely covered, I recognized who he was: Zhao Xiaohui!

76

Zhao Xiaohui, after having visited Kang Yuanyuan in the hospital, came to the church to see Minister Gao. It was not proper for an official to visit a church, so each time he came he would first wrap himself up, leaving only his nose exposed. According to Zhao Xiaohui himself, he had become psychologically dependent on Minister Gao, and missed the tolling of the church bell and the peaceful face of Minister Gao whenever he was beset with problems.

Of course Zhao Xiaohui felt very surprised at Kang Yuanyuan's illness, and very sorry as well. But he soon changed the subject to the most recent problem troubling him. He was going to be removed from Gaotai Township! The county's organization department had talked to him with a view to appointing him the warden of Kaiyang Old People's Home. In other words, the Township Head Zhao of today would be the Warden Zhao of tomorrow.

Why should he, who had the merit of having earned credit for some officials and having improved the financial possibilities of others with the large sum of money he had secured from the provincial authorities, be driven off the stage of Gaotai Township? He was obviously aggrieved at the mention of these things. Each cigarette he smoked proked Minister Gao to constant coughing. I admonished Zhao Xiaohui that he should not smoke, because this was a holy place. He ground out the cigarette, but hardly had five minutes passed before he lit it again, apparently forgetting my previous admonition.

I invited Zhao Xiaohui to my place. He continuously emphasized the friendship between himself and me. Since both he and I were down and out in this world, what did it matter how far back our acquaintance went? In a flash, I was his bosom buddy, the only one on whom he could rely in this world. No sooner had I fetched him a glass of water than he began rattling out his stories.

It was clear from what Zhao Xiaohui said that Meiteng lay behind all of them. The first impression of Meiteng was of a delicious cake, but deeper acquaintance revealed a bitter dose of poison. On the day when production was officially started, a grand ceremony was held to which were invited opera troupes from the province and acrobatic troupes from other provinces. Xiang Wenhua attended the opening ceremony. Of course, all the county and municipal heads were present. Zhao Xiaohui and other township officials became mere helping-hands, which Zhao Xiaohui did not mind, knowing as he did that in officialdom each grade in the hierarchy had the right to crush all its subordinates. As a township leader, he was nothing more than a humble grain of dust before his superiors.

However, problems had been lurking in this chaotic situation. As the leaders were being ushered into their seats, quite unexpectedly, out of nowhere, rushed the head of the municipal civil affairs bureau at the venue. This guy obviously loved attending meetings, especially ribbon-cutting ceremonies. He always arrived uninvited. Each time he came, he would tell you that he was accidentally passing by.... Even an idiot could see that he came for the gifts given out at the occasion. But he was no ordinary head! He held in his hand, like a thick piece of meat, the poverty and disaster relief funds allocated by the state each year. And it was he who decided to whom the meat should be given, and how much should be cut from it. Zhao Xiaohui often had to kowtow to him. An invitation to a massage or to go having fun with a *xiaojie* could secure several thousand *yuan* in allocations. An invitation to him and his whole family to tour Inner Mongolia could induce him to transfer twenty or thirty thousand *yuan* onto the account of Gaotai Township. Now that he had turned up to this event, Zhao Xiaohui did not dare to treat him lightly. However, his presence posed problems vis-a-vis the seating of the leaders. All those who had come were masters, but they differed in size, height and figure. The least miscalculation could turn you into a loser for the rest of your life. On which shelf must Zhao Xiaohui place this master? To be specific, at whose right side or whose left side must Zhao Xiaohui place the head of the civil affairs bureau? As a rule, the left side was more honorable than the right. The seating for the leaders had been drawn up on paper beforehand and countenanced by Zhang Shutian. While others had been seated, the head of the civil affairs bureau was standing there as stiff as a sorghum stalk. And it was Zhao Xiaohui's own simplicity to blame. Without consulting Zhang Shutian, he had put the head of the civil affairs bureau to his left side. His reasoning was that, although the head of the civil affairs bureau and the county secretary of the Party committee were of the same rank, the former was still a leader of the municipality. Just as a maid from the royal family was more powerful than a magistrate, so a leader who came from the municipality had a larger government-office, and was justified in occupying a more honorable seat. Zhao Xiaohui did not realize that he had made an irrevocable mistake until he tried to let this unwelcome guest sit by the side of the county secretary of the Party committee. Zhang Shutian showed a great deal of reluctance to make the required room. His face fell, and the smile on it was gone all at once. There had been a speech for him to deliver on the agenda, but he now stood up and walked toward Xiang Wenhua and the municipal secretary of the Party committee. Having whispered a few words in their ears, he left in annoyance.

Later, Zhao Xiaohui learned that Zhang Shutian and the head of the municipal civil affairs bureau never acknowledged each other; they were as incompatible as fire and water. Once colleagues, they were now enemies who would rather die than share the same space. It was said that one had urinated into the teacup of the other who, not to be outdone, secretly placed a watermelon-peel under the first one's chair and caused him to fall down with a fracture. Since the incident at the opening ceremony, Zhang Shutain had always snubbed Zhao Xiaohui. Finally the day came when people from the organization department talked to Zhao Xiaohui and told him that he would be appointed to a more important post: the honorable warden of Kaiyang Old People's Home. In this home lived more than ten childless or widowed old people, in their seventies or eighties, among whom three were mental invalids. It was a bizarre place, with ominous *fengshui*. No warden stayed long before falling seriously ill. Of the four wardens before Zhao Xiaohui, none seemed to have come to a good end. The first suffered from lung cancer, the second bone cancer; the third was paralyzed, and the fourth had just been diagnosed with uremia. This run of bad luck had lent the old people's home a sinister reputation, with rumors flying about savagely. The most vivid of these was that the home was built above a grave in which a wrongfully killed man was buried. Because he was wrongfully killed, he could not close his eyes. He lay there with his eyes open, meditating dreadful vengeance, and wanting to bite whomever he saw. As a result, the four wardens had become his victims in succession, in spite of the fact that all of them had tried to fight back. They invited *fengshui* masters to deal with it, but all they could do was constantly change the direction the gate swung in. When the first warden took office, the gate of the old people's home was facing north. The second warden changed its direction and made it face south. The third warden made it face east, the fourth, west. If Zhao Xiaohui wanted to do something about the gate, he had only two choices — either dig a long tunnel to walk in and out, or make a hole in the roof with ladders inside and outside to climb up and down.

The consensus was, that anyone banished to run the old people's home was more or less on death row. When people got wind of Zhao Xiaohui's new appointment, they displayed various attitudes. Some took evasive action when they saw him in the distance, as if he were a chunk of radioactive material; some sorrowfully sympathized with him to his face but laughed out loud when they turned round to go; and some invited him to a drink which sounded like it was the last they would ever share. In Kaiyang, a place no larger than a peanut, folks who quarreled on a northern street could bespatter with their rabid saliva a person on a southern one. Could he expect to keep a low profile when he went to meet his doom in the old people's home? Discussions about him could be heard everywhere in the county town. Once, when he was walking down the street, minding his own business, a woman's high voice penetrated his ear, "Zhao Xiaohui? Aha, I heard he's going to take office in a coffin!"

Zhao Xiaohui was very upset and depressed. Though it was true that he was only thirty five or six, his sideburns had turned grey. He was going bald and he often found his pillow covered with shed hair when he got up in the morning. He wanted to flee, but where to? As for the township headship office, he was not sorry to lose it, and had more than once thought about resigning from it in the past. What he could not bear was the public gossip. As relating these experiences he just underwent, Zhao Xiaohui could not help but gripe about Liben, blaming him for helping set up an enterprise here and stirring up what should have been still water. It made no sense to go over previous difficulties and problems, since there were too many of them. He had more than enough on his plate with his present troubles, which were just getting underway, so it seemed.

That Meiteng was a great polluter caught Zhao Xiaohui off guard. He knew that making tires inevitably entailed pollution, but he had not expected that it would be so serious. A few days after Meiteng had begun production, the neighboring villagers began to feel its impact. The crops within a radius of three kilometers were coated with a thick layer of powder, while the fields without crops were covered as with an enormous black shawl. An even graver matter was that the air was filled with an acrid odor, somewhat sour, somewhat spicy. Baidou Village, a neighbor of Mazi Village, was the first to react. The mother of the head of Baidou Village had already been suffering from bronchitis, and the odd odor aggravated her illness. She died in hospital after all medical means had been exhausted. Hardly had her funeral ended when livestock in the village fell sick and began to perish one after another. As a result, resentment soon came to the boil. In response to a shout from the village head, the whole village fell upon the township government, some shouldering spades, others carrying picks or axes, like the army of a peasant uprising. They shouted Zhao Xiaohui's name, and demanded that he come out of his office to pay compensation for the dead mother and cattle. Zhao Xiaohui immediately reported the event to the county, but Zhang Shutian the county secretary of the Party committee had gone abroad, and the county magistrate was attending a provincial meeting. The vice county magistrate replied that the matter should be settled within the township. But how could the township cope with it? Zhao Xiaohui came out to have a word with the masses. But before he could open his mouth, a brickbat flew out of nowhere. Two streams of blood shot out of his nostrils. When the local police heard that Township Head Zhao had been attacked, they called the county criminal police brigade. In no time, several police cars were rushing toward Gaotai Township, sirens wailing all the way. The masses had an instinctive fear of people in uniforms, and seeing so many policemen out with batons and handcuffs, they felt that their legs buckling beneath them. They fled in a panic, forgetting all the vows they had made when they set forth from the village.

Zhao Xiaohui was not seriously hurt. Once the bleeding was staunched at the clinic, he was practically out of danger. The police were keen to make arrests in Baidou Village, but were checked by Zhao. He patiently dissuaded them from going. After all, the masses were the victims of all this pollution. They were so helpless, so pitiful! The common people in China were extremely submissive. They would never fight back unless they were beaten or kicked beyond endurance.

77

Zhao Xiaohui had already visited Meiteng once, in the hope of persuading them to take measures against the pollution problem. Thanks to the unbearably bad air quality at the firm's production site, the high-rank administrative personnel usually stayed at a hotel in Yuebei. That was why the highest ranking leader Zhao Xiaohui could find on the firm's property was Song Tongguo, who had been appointed head of production.

Song Tongguo assumed the air of a person flushed with success. Wearing a western-style suit and a pair of leather shoes, and with his pot-belly protruding, Song Tongguo spoke in a bureaucratic tone, his sentences full of official jargon.

Song Tongguo received Zhao Xiaohui in his office. He instructed the beautiful girl standing on one side of him to make tea and light a cigarette for Zhao Xiaohui, and ordered the beautiful girl on the other side of him to massage his neck. When the girls' jobs were done, he told them to leave.

Song Tongguo never opened a conversation without bragging and this one was no exception. He said that by now he had shaken hands with high-rank leaders in the provincial government; that he had been served and massaged by girls in Kaidehua, the top luxury bathhouse in Yuebei City; that he had dined in all the expensive restaurants scattered across this city; that among all the delicacies, the abalone was particularly special. According to Song Tongguo, it was said that eating abalone just once would enable the eater to live five years longer. "This means," he declared with pride, "I will live at least to a hundred, because I have eaten abalone more than ten times." He asserted that since he would eat more abalone in the future, he was not in a position to figure out how long he would live.

Song Tongguo could not help mocking the people of Sakelu. He said that even though he and the Sakelu people all came from Mazi Village, the quality of his life was dramatically different from theirs! He was at the peak of Mount Everest, while the other villagers were at the bottom of the Mariana Trench; he was a space craft that flew ten thousand miles each day, while the other villagers were ox-drawn carriages tottering along muddy roads; he was a wild goose soaring in the skies with high aspirations, while the other villagers were chickens wretchedly searching for food on the ground. In brief, Song Tongguo meant that the good quality of his life and the radiant glory of his person were beyond Sakelu people's ken; that in no way could Sakelu folks be compared with him. Just as a farmer toiling all year long could not comprehend how an emperor lived, no Sakelu resident could envision his life even if they strained their imaginations to the utmost.

Song Tongguo asked Zhao Xiaohui how much he earned each month. Zhao Xiaohui answered, "Slightly more than one thousand *yuan*."

Song Tongguo expressed his deep pity for Zhao Xiaohui, saying, "What can one get for a thousand *yuan*? It would hardly cover the money I spend to fuck a call-girl in a five-star hotel."

Song Tongguo told Zhao Xiaohui that each month he earned nine thousand *yuan*; that he received additional payments in kind and in cash at the end of each year; that with all his income streams added together, his total annual income could easily range from one hundred and fifty to two hundred thousand *yuan*.

"Does that count as big money?" Song Tongguo went on. "Well, so far as big is concerned, it's not *that* big. But so far as small is concerned, it's not *that* small. Whether it is big or small depends on whose income it is compared to."

In Song Tongguo's view, compared with the people of Sakelu, even compared with Township Head Zhao, his salary was high enough; however, when he ventured further abroad and saw how really rich people lived, he no longer felt he was rich — on the contrary, he felt ashamed. He said that a man working as manager in a foreign-financed firm in Yuebei had an annual income of eight hundred thousand *yuan*, even though he supervised a much smaller staff; that another guy working as a department director in a certain bureau of electricity, with whom he had once dined, could easily scoop an income of four hundred thousand to five hundred thousand *yuan* per year. "Compared with these people," Song Tongguo said, "far from having gained any advantages, I seem only to have suffered grave losses. Nevertheless, I don't envy them." He claimed that as an honest and down-to-earth person, he well understood that to have a potful of oil in one's hands was an opportunity to dip one's fingers in the grease.

Uninterested in Song Tongguo's boastful talk, Zhao Xiaohui steered the conversation in the direction of how to cope with the factory's pollution problem. But Song Tongguo was strongly averse to this topic; he even got a bit angry. He denounced Zhao Xiaohui, saying, "As the township head, why would you refuse to stand with the investors, but rather choose to take the side of the mindless, trouble-making masses? What are they? No better than a herd of pigs! The fact that you take them for human beings only means that you, the township head, have had your eyes poked out by a steel rod. It is money that these people want, isn't it? Aren't they grunting like pigs for pig feed? If some rotten vegetable leaves were thrown their way, they'd wag their heads with satisfaction."

Exceedingly indignant with Song Tongguo for his having referred to the villagers as pigs, Zhao Xiaohui asked him pointedly, "If the villagers are pigs, then what are you? You are only a manager hired to work temporarily for the factory. If you are fired, won't you revert to being a pig, too?"

In reaction to Zhao Xiaohui's explosive and fiery remarks, Song Tongguo rose to his feet and stood behind him. Patting Zhao Xiaohui on the shoulder, Song Tongguo addressed him warmly as "brother" to calm him down. Zhao Xiaohui eventually calmed down, and Song Tongguo explained that his calling the villagers pigs was merely a metaphor. "The metaphor might sound harsh, but is there any essential difference between these people and pigs?" Song Tongguo asked. "These people are a motley crew, who flock like crows. Can the *things* on their shoulders really be called human heads? No! They can only be called pig heads. Their heads are like soft reeds — when the east wind blows, they lean toward the west, but when the west wind blows, they lean toward the east. This trait makes them welcome to both sides in a war. Why? Because they are brainless, and they are therefore easy to provoke; and they take an empty promise for a true one. What do they get in the end? Nothing! They struggle for survival at the bottom layer of society. To eat shit is their destiny. If you gave them gourmet abalone, they would probably get the runs."

Seeing that Song Tongguo was once again straying from the subject, Zhao Xiaohui reminded him that he had come to discuss the pollution problem, and that all other issues were irrelevant.

"What's the point of discussing the pollution problem?" Song Tongguo asked. "Wasn't it because of pollution that Meiteng was set up in Mazi Village instead of in Yuebei? What's the use of the villagers' blubbering? Just leave them alone. At the start, they have energy to complain, but in time they'll get exhausted and stop grunting."

Song Tongguo said something to the effect that he would teach any villagers who dared to make trouble a terrible lesson. He disclosed that Meiteng had just done something remarkable: it had recently recruited ten highly skilled trainees from Yuebei Martial Arts Academy and set up a team to guard the factory. "Under such circumstances, who will dare to make trouble?" Song Tongguo asked. "Let those who don't care about their own lives come. Anyway, nowadays human lives are fairly cheap. Yes, human life is not worth much. A big company like Meiteng can well afford the pay."

It seemed that Song Tongguo even wished, in his heart, that someone would come to the factory and make trouble. If a man came along asking to be killed, the security force would surely be happy to oblige.

"Killing one would intimidate plenty of others," Song Tongguo explained. "This strategy is known as 'Kill one to warn a hundred.' If Meiteng is to have lasting peace, it is absolutely necessary that some unlucky guy learn how tough Meiteng is."

Seeing that his discussion with Song Tongguo was going nowhere, Zhao Xiaohui left. The smoke in the air choked him horribly. He kept snorting in spite of the fact that he had put on a gauze mask.

As he approached the township government compound, Zhao Xiaohui saw that the portal was once again in the process of being blockaded — not only by people from Baidou Village, but also by people from other villages, it emerged. They were making a babble of noise: one man said his corn crops yielded poor harvests; one man claimed his cows had stopped producing milk; one man bawled that his chicken had suddenly stopped laying eggs; one man thumped his chest and stamped his feet, whining that his child's blood test showed three "+" signs.

Zhao Xiaohui approached the crowd.

When the villagers saw Zhao Xiaohui, instead of tearing at him or beating him up, which was what he had expected would happen, the people all knelt down simultaneously, and some of them even touched the ground with their heads repeatedly and respectfully.

Zhao Xiaohui told his assistant to fetch a stool. Standing on it, he spoke to the villagers at the top of his voice. He said that the pollution problem was not just the villagers' concern; that it was his pressing concern too. He claimed that his heart was intimately connected to the hearts of the people; that he was making efforts to lessen the pollution; however to solve the problem, he must be allowed some time — three months at least and six months at most — because he needed sufficient time to cultivate various connections, so that he would be able to get the attention and backup of superior levels of government. Zhao Xiaohui called to the villagers to stand up. He told them that kneeling down like that was a manifestation of a backward feudalist mentality, and that citizens in the new era should stand up straight and fight for their own dignity.

After rising to their feet, the villagers elected some delegates to negotiate with Zhao Xiaohui. All the others scattered and left.

In the township government's conference room, the angry delegates expressed their indignation. They all expressed their hope that Zhao Xiaohui would make a report on this issue to the higher levels of government, with the result that Meiteng would be forced to move out. Zhao Xiaohui tried to calm the villagers down. He suggested that two strategies could be employed simultaneously to deal with the issue.

Strategy One: the villages in question should compose a petition and have all the villagers sign it. Then he would find the son of the provincial governor and ask him to submit the petition to his father.

Strategy Two: they should use formal channels. First, the township government would make a report to the county government, then the county government would make a report to the municipal government, then the municipal government would in turn make a report to the government level above it, which would do the same, until hopefully the problem would catch the attention of the national central government's environmental protection authorities, who would then order an investigation into the matter to solve the problem. With regard to the villagers' demand that Meiteng be removed from its present location, Zhao Xiaohui was explicit with the delegates, "It is impossible! Meiteng has invested so much in the project. What's more, it has been shortlisted as a key investment project. Will it be moved away just because you want it to be?"

Zhao Xiaohui predicted that it would not be Meiteng but the people living in nearby villages who were most likely to be relocated.

Like a stone tossed into a pond and creating enormous plumes of spray, Zhao Xiaohui's prediction caused considerable turmoil. The delegates exploded into sound and fury — they were at the point of yelling, and some among them, in exasperation, even stood up and beat their palms against the table. They asked why it had to be the villagers who moved? What on earth was the reason? They said that their fathers had lived on this land generation after generation, and that the land was their inheritance; so why should they be asked to leave? They declared that they were not jealous of the erstwhile Mazi villagers, who now lived in villas in Sakelu; that they did not wish to follow the example of the Sakelu inhabitants, who now didn't know where their fathers' tombs lay; that by no means would they leave their own land.

"In no way will we leave our own land!" They reiterated. "It's not a matter of money. Rather it's a matter of whether we disgrace our forefathers or not."

78

I did not know the date of Kang Yuanyuan's death. In fact, I did not know Kang had passed away until Larz started pestering me for her will. Around his eyes were additional black circles which seemed to have been artificially applied. He invited me to drink tea in Alibaba, saying that he needed to have a talk with me.

Once a waiter who had himself worked to serve customers at the Alibaba, this time it was Larz who was being served as a customer, and he did put on the airs that went with the role of patron; his legs resting on the tea table, his saliva flying about as he gave orders. Our waiter became unsteady on his feet at Larz's constant swearing.

No sooner had I taken my seat in the private room than Larz produced from his pocket a certificate, unfolded it and placed it in front of me. A glance at the characters told me that it was the marriage certificate between him and Kang Yuanyuan. The strange thing was that the date on it was exactly the same as the one on which Kang had passed away.

After upbraiding the waiter for spilling a drop of water on the tea table Larz ordered him to scram. Once the waiter was out of the room, Larz turned and asked whether I had had a clear look at the characters on the certificate. I replied that I had, whereupon he asked me what I intended to do about it. I shook my head, telling him that I did not understand what he meant. He loudly accused me of feigning ignorance. Then he lowered his voice to ask, if my wife — of course I did not have one, but as this was a hypothetical question, it did not matter — were dead, who ought to have possession of her will? I asked what made him believe that I had taken Kang Yuanyuan's will. Larz said he was neither blind nor deaf. What was more, there were others in the ward when Kang Yuanyuan gave her will to me, witnesses with eyes to see and mouths to speak; so how could he be fooled? In a menacing tone, Larz said that if I handed the will over to him, he would still regard me as his brother. If not, then it would be too bad for me. I would have to deal with whatever consequences might arise from the matter.

I said, "Larz, can you talk calmly? You are young in years but old in your way of speaking. You're in no position to threaten anyone. Since you and Kang Yuanyuan are legally husband and wife, I am going to be frank with you. The will is not in my hands. I gave it to Xue Yulu. Kang Yuanyuan addressed it to the civil affairs department, stating that she meant to sell her houses and to build one or two children's homes with the proceeds."

Larz replied that this building of children's homes required his consent, that he was Kang Yuanyuan's husband and had a say in the disposal of such houses as were their joint property. I said I was not responsible for that. It was on Kang Yuanyuan's instructions that I gave the will to Xue Yulu. If he wanted the will, he could go to Xue Yulu for it.

Larz began to swear at Xue Yulu, wishing to heaven that the will were in anybody's hands but hers. He said that she was extrodinarily greedy, that he had long experience of her greed. He recalled how calculating she had been, once she asked him to be her partner to provide sexual services to her; and they parted for a rather funny reason — the purchase of a sweater. One night Xue Yulu sweetly offered to buy him a sweater imported from New Zealand, but the next day she changed her mind, denying everything she had said, so he grabbed his bag and walked out. It was Xue Yulu who had robbed him of his virginity. Before that he had never had corporeal contact with any woman.

On the third day after my rendezvous with Larz, my mobile phone began ringing non-stop. The calls, coming every half hour on average, almost drove me out of my mind. Naturally, they were from Larz and Xue Yulu. Larz said Xue Yulu denied that I had given her Kang Yuanyuan's will and hurled all kinds of abuse at him. How he wished he could have grabbed her neck to strangle her! He said he had been surprised to find something abnormal when he went to examine Kang Yuanyuan's residential properties: the apartment had been rented out while the old house was being pulled down. Larz asked the tenant who the landlord was. The answer was Xue Lihan, who, so they said, had been seriously ill and was out on medical parole. It was Xue Lihan who had the keys to the apartment; but who would have given him the keys except his elder sister Xue Yulu? Larz believed that Xue Yulu had coveted Kang Yuanyuan's inheritance, so he appealed to the housing administration bureau. And then something even stranger came to light. The registration record showed that the owner of the estate was Xue Yulu rather than Kang Yuanyuan!

Xue Yulu, however, took a different tack on the phone, accusing me of lying and attempting to murder her because I had set a hooligan on her to obtain from her a will I had never given her. The hooligan had caused great harm to her by cursing and defaming her and by pointing at her nose in the work place. How could a woman of her dignity withstand such humiliation? Xue Yulu added that Kang Yuanyuan's will was indeed in her possession, but that it was given to her directly by Kang Yuanyuan rather than by me. As for what had been written, that was a secret between her and Kang Yuanyuan and nobody else had any right to inquire about it.

Having rung frequently over a period of three or four days, my mobile phone suddenly became mute. Neither Xue Yulu nor Larz called me again. This peace came too abruptly for a perturbed heart like mine to adjust itself to the new situation. I felt a bit disorientated. It was not until six days later, when the police knocked at my door to interview me, that I was eventually informed of the appalling crime which had taken place during these seemingly peaceful days. Larz had killed Xu Yulu!

Having gained admission to Xue Yulu's office, Larz produced a dagger and stabbed Xue Yulu eleven times in all! By the time Xue Yulu had been rushed to hospital, her pulse had stopped and her pupils were enlarged because of the excessive loss of blood. Larz was caught red-handed by the security guards of the press house. He was now locked up in a detention house.

It was natural enough that the policemen were rather rude to me. They suspected that I was Larz's accomplice and the main plotter behind the case, so they pounded my table, smashed my teacups, pinched my ears, pulled my hair, struck my neck with their fists, and kicked my calves with their feet. Although I gave an accurate account of the whole matter, they kept shouting at me "to confess all the facts." Fortunately, they did not take me away; they just ordered me to stay at home, subject to being summoned at any moment. I wrote an affidavit to this effect, whereupon they left and never returned. After half a month's house arresst I myself set myself free. I wanted to see Larz, and the wish to see him grew stronger and stronger. He was a lost child and rather pitiful, despite the fact that he was now a murderer. He had murdered Xue Yulu, and himself as well. Xue Yulu's death could be safely attributed to him, the definitely identified killer, but who was responsible for murdering him? My effort to visit Larz was to no avail; I did not manage to see him. Reports of his words and acts leaked out of the detention house, and they won my respect for this young man who was about to die. He had tried his best to exculpate me, claiming that the killing of Xue Yulu had been his act alone and nothing to do with me!

In stark contrast to the treatment meted out to Larz, the facts of Xue Yulu's death had been distorted in her favour. She was even adulated to a high degree. A newspaper reporter, who was said to be Xue Yulu's student, wrote a whole page account of her moving exploits, claiming that she had been murdered by a gangster on account of her unyielding integrity. How she hunkered down at her desk, to compose a magnificent psalm of life! Even more ridiculous was that a lyrical poem, attributed to her, was attached to the lower right of the report. Two lines of the poem imprinted themselves on my mind, never to be rubbed away —

> The heroine's tragedy, sets off our mediocrity;
> O mediocre people, we live only to insult thy temple!

79

The world is a series of difficult mathematical problems. After solving one, you find another waiting to be solved. There are always endless new questions ahead. Once you stumble into this mess, you will not be able to pull your feet out. One tiny decimal point is sufficient to trip up even an energetic person.

Never underestimate the importance of a decimal point, inconspicuous though it may be. The whole world might change on account of this small dot.

A decimal point is rather like a person's little finger, which may seem inconspicuous. However, one movement of that finger may turn the world upside down, depending on the point to which it is applied. If it presses on the ground, it leaves a fingerprint at most. But if it presses on a nuclear red button, well, everyone understands how horrible the consequences might be.

The point I would like to make is: one small mistake may lead to endless trouble.

Right now I was up to my neck in problems. Actually, they were worse than just problems. It would be better to say I was going through a critical test, which would determine whether I would survive or perish.

It had to do with Kang Yuanyuan's will. Though the will had but briefly passed through my hands, Xue Lihan believed that I was responsible for his sister's death. Over and over again, he had come to my place looking for me, demanding that I pay for the loss of his sister's life. He said that his father, who had already been afflicted by high blood pressure, suffered a cerebral hemorrhage at the news of his daughter's murder, and was now being treated in a emergency room; that his mother, after this incident occured, had been persuaded by force and trickery, to go to a relative's place in the countryside, and that the news was still being withheld from her: it was hard to tell what would happen to the old lady if she learned what had happened to Xue Yulu.

Every time when he came to look for me, Xue Lihan would bring along with him three bodyguards, who always stood behind him, with their hands clasped behind their backs. Though they spoke no word, they looked murderous.

Xue Lihan claimed that since I could be considered an intellectual, he preferred to use words rather than force when dealing with me. He said if it were not for the fact that I used to be his sister's colleague, he would have torn me to pieces. He declared that his dead sister would never come back to life, even if he took my life, thus his main purpose must be to force me financially to compensate his family.

Xue Lihan told me stories, in a dramatic manner, about his powerful friends: some were influential in the conventional world, while some others were mighty figures among underworld gangsters. According to him, his gangster friends had offered to come and see me, but he had stopped them for the time being. It was up to me whether to pay the debt with my own life or with money.

I asked him how much money would do.

Taking out a calculator, Xue Lihan sat down on a sofa and began calculating like a professional accountant. After a while he exclaimed, "A minimum of five hundred thousand *yuan*."

"If that is the sum, I'd rather you kill me," I said, "because I don't have that much money, and I don't know how to get it even by theft or robbery. So far as I can tell, I could hardly earn that much money in a lifetime."

Xue Lihan began to add up the bill item by item. He said that if his sister had not been murdered, she could have lived to at least 80; during the lost forty years how much salary she might have earned, and how many bonuses she might have received, and how much in the way of allowances she might have been granted. Moreover, were these the only kinds of income his sister was used to receiving? "In view of her position and talent, how much invisible income could she have expected to earn!" Xue Lihan said.

Xue Lihan asserted that his sister's existence had guaranteed a large but intangible fortune to his family: how much glory and wealth she would have brought to her siblings by way of her influence! What was more, his father would not have been hospitalized if he hadn't been affected by this event. Should his father die on account of this tragic event, it would mean an additional huge loss to his family. His father was only seventy-three years old this year. Judging by his constitution and health, was it impossible that the old man might live to ninety? Every extra year of his father's life meant nearly an extra thirty thousand *yuan* on the old man's bank account. "Just calculate!" Xue Lihan said. "The old man's premature death would mean a monetary loss of four to five hundred thousand *yuan*, wouldn't it?"

Xue Lihan emphasized that he had conducted an investigation about me prior to coming, and that he had found I was a pauper, and that this was why the amount was merely a *symbolic* one.

"If money is what you demand of me, I have nothing; if you care to have my life, it's yours," I said to Xue Lihan. "I entreat you and your men to kill me and let me die. Anyway, life is meaningless. While I was doing my studies in school and university, we all looked forward to the future with longing, thinking that there would be flower beds ahead. But after graduating, I unwittingly stepped into a dirty, muddy ditch. Soon afterwards, I was myself transformed into a mass of dirt and mud. Now that I have become dirt and mud, does it make any difference if the dirt and mud lives or dies?"

"Shut up!" Xue Lihan yelled. "Your emotional outbursts are getting too sarcastic — they are really putting my teeth on edge."

Looking about my house, Xue Lihan said, "You never stop claiming to be penniless, so how did you manage to afford a spacious house of over one hundred square meters? Your house is worth money, isn't it?" He then explicitly told me it would be acceptable to pay him with my house.

"How can this be possible?" I said.

"Why not?" he asked. Then with firm resolution, he said, "Nothing is impossible, let alone paying a debt with a house!"

I had thought that his claim on my house was not meant seriously. However, on the following day, when I returned home, I found it hard to get to my front door. It happened that, just as I set my foot on the stairs leading up to the third floor, I saw that the staircase was blocked with various odd articles. After taking a closer look, I identified these items as my belongings: the wardrobes were upside down; the chairs were leaning here and there; the bedding and clothes were knotted into a messy tangle under a pile of moulded coal; the looking glass lay broken in pieces; some photos and old letters were scattered around, like joss paper offered to the dead at tomb-sweeping festivals.

I tried my utmost to get to my door, in order to ascertain what had happened. When I looked into the house, I could not help gasping: inside, on either side of the door sat a young man, each naked from the waist up. Their muscles, which protruded massively, looked as hard as leaden balls. They held long swords in their hands, and their eyes radiated hostility.

I went back down the staircase and wandered off along the street. Two lines of tears flowed from the corner of my eyes. The pedestrians in the street were getting rarer and rarer; each of them was hurrying back home. Somewhere ahead of them, a warm light awaited their return. But which room could I call my own?

There were moments when I thought about reporting the matter to the police, but I knew well it would be wasted effort — the police would most probably declare the case an economic dispute, and then nothing more would come out of it.

It was then that I suddenly felt my biggest enemy was not Xue Lihan, but Liben. Without Liben, how would I have come to know Kang Yuanyuan! And without having come to know Kang Yuanyuan, how could I have got into such trouble!

Whatever emotion I was experiencing did not matter, for no emotion of mine could solve my problems, which were staring me in the face. The immediate problem was: where would I spend the coming night?

Almost spontaneously, I thought of the church; I seemed to see the kindly face of Minister Gao before me.

I hurried to the church. I moved so fast that beads of sweat stood out on my forehead. As I walked, my legs and feet began to feel feeble, as if I were a shameful deserter — but rather than deserting a battlefield, I was escaping from my own home.

When I reached the church, the service was already over. The nave was filled with people lying scattered on the ground. It was winter time. Outside the church, the ground was covered with ice. Nevertheless, many people inside were sleeping, huddled on the hard cement floor. A female beggar took off her coat and wrapped her child in it, leaving herself covered only with thin clothing. She seemed to have caught a cold, and was coughing uncontrollably.

Seating myself on a chair, I looked blankly at the image of Jesus hung on the cross. I could not help wondering: God sent Jesus as his agent to save mankind, but could Jesus really do the saving? His teachings had been taught for thousands of years in the world, how was it then that the world was still full of violence and conflict?

Just as I was getting lost in my thoughts, a wave of unrest swept over the hall. All the people, sitting or lying, abruptly rose to their feet and rushed in one direction, as if they had just heard a trumpet summoning them to a military march.

They rushed to a corner of the nave. There, it seemed that they were grabbing and snatching at something.

A short while later, people returned. Some were holding cotton-padded overcoats with both arms, happy smiles on their faces. Someone was carrying a cotton-padded coat under one arm, with an air of self-congratulation; someone had some bananas in his left hand, a bottle of drink in his right hand, and a pair of leather shoes tucked under his arm. But there were people who came back empty-handed. Naturally, these people were looking pretty sour. They muttered under their breath — it appeared that they were complaining about the person in charge of distributing the items, accusing him of being unjust.

Just then I heard a voice calling me. Raising my head, I saw Xiaomao, who was standing in front of me and smiling at me. I asked him what he was doing round here. He said he had just distributed the clothes donated by some believers to people who were seeking shelter in the church from the cold weather.

"Why are you sitting here so late at night? Don't you feel cold?" Xiaomao asked me.

"I'm now homeless. I have to find a place to spend the night," I replied.

With eyes wide open, Xiaomao asked me, "What has happened?"

"It's a long story," I said.

Tugging at my lappet, Xiaomao invited me to share his room with him.

80

Spring Festival passed, and so did the next one. Some among the residents of Sakelu Park began to borrow money here and there. Some could not afford their children's tuition, because they had lost all their money gambling. Some had spent so extravagantly that they now had no money to buy rice and flour. Some had been thrifty, but went bankrupt due to medical expenses incurred by the illness of a family member. The upshot was that one third of Sakelu Park's inhabitants were in economic difficulties.

Sakelu Park showed more signs of decay day by day — weeds spreading all over the court, the lake water so smelly that every household had to shut its windows, rubbish piling up everywhere, street lamps out of repair, roads full of pits and potholes. The only thriving population was that of the flies which seemed to be celebrating that Sakelu had become their territory, singing and dancing all day and night. In Sakelu a Peruvian mosquito, a vivid black in color and with extraordinary long legs, could be observed flying around, a mosquito which could rarely be seen elsewhere. Once bitten by it, human flesh would instantly swell into a bump the size of a ping-pong ball. A six-month baby died after a single bite. Everyone in Sakelu felt anxious about the lurking danger. Some women would not go out without donning a veil.

Inside and outside the wall were two different worlds. While the area of Sakelu itself had become increasingly desolate, that outside was experiencing a big boom; in a few short years, it had apparently developed into a small town. During the daytime, chaos reigned in the narrow streets crammed with people selling watermelons, vegetables, shoes and stockings, and their cries rose and fell. At night, when all the vendors made their silent retreat, various cars would arrive and park in long lines along either side of the streets. Business flourished in this recreation city, more or less in the way Shuanhu had predicted — scintillating lights, gabbling human voices, deafening music and yells. Wealthy patrons in ties with leather briefcases tucked under their arms came and went. They either got drunk in a private room, or folded a girl in their arms and carred her away.

As Sakelu's fame grew in Kaiyang, even tricycle riders knew that the best-looking girls lived there. At wine tables, "to go sakelu-ing after a drink" had become common parlance among hosts and guests alike. When acquaintances met, they greeted each other more and more often with the question "Have you sakelu-ed recently?" Sakelu had thus become a euphemism for doing that kind of thing.

Shuanhu asked me back to Sakelu and showed me around his recreation city. He arranged a girl for me. A plump bird she was, and I played about with her for a while, until I gradually lost interest on account of the smell exuding from her armpits. Actually, if it had just been the smell of her armpits I would have put up with it. But mixed with the smell of the pungent perfumes on her skin it almost choked me.

Upon my exiting the private room, Shuanhu asked me how I felt. I said that I felt pretty good. Sitting in his luxurious office, which had been decorated like a palace, Shuanhu began to blow his own trumpet. He said he had sampled all the girls and knew who was sweet and who was hot. It was not that he was lewd, but that he had a responsibility to his customers, since appearances could be deceptive. One could never tell whether a dish was delicious or not until it had been tasted, whether a bed was soft or not until it had been slept on for a night. He had, in fact, eliminated a considerable number of low-quality girls, retaining only the best. That was one of the main reasons why his business was better than the others.

Shuanhu's phone kept ringing all the time. He either answered with a brief "I am busy," or simply ignored it and let it ring. After he had sent away the girl who had served him, he shot the bolt on the door with a queer mystic expression on his face. It was not until he spoke, that it dawned on me what he wanted. He had asked me back because he wanted me to provide copy for him. Of course, I would not be writing for nothing. For each article I wrote I could play about with three *xiaojie*, free of charge.

I asked what kind of articles he had in mind. Shuanhu said that the previous year he had won a string of honors, like Outstanding Entrepreneur, Startup Star etc. His aim was to become a member of the political consultative conference of the county, then of the municipality, and then of the province. As for his greatest ambition, well, it would be needless to guess, wouldn't it? It was to go to the People's Great Hall to attend the national political consultative conference. His present contributions had more than sufficed for him to be a member of the political consultative conference of the municipality, however, the old fogeys whose buttocks had long occupied the seats of the county and municipal political consultative conferences looked down on him, even despised him; they would never ever let him in. The most annoying thing was that they were quite unyielding, insusceptible to invitations or gifts, and this made his head ache bitterly. Seeing him in a quandary, some able man had advised him to hire somebody to write a good article about how great he was, and how many dropout pupils and childless or widowed old people he had aided. He had not done anything like that, of course, but he would hurry up and do so in the near future. The article must be published in the newspaper so that those old fogeys' crusty brains would be bombarded by them. If it did not work the first time, he would have it published a second time. If it did not work the second time, he would have it published a third time…anyway, he was not short of money, and did not believe that there was any political consultative bastion which he could not conquer. Although the writing of such an article might not seem a difficult thing, it turned out to be a sticking point. He said he thought of me after he had cudgeled his brains for a few days. The prospect of transforming a useless black bean like me into a precious pearl dispelled the clouds over his heart immediately.

I kept silent, without giving a yes or a no. I was filled with regret at having done "that kind of thing" with the plump girl, a regret which, like an iron chain, had bound me hand and foot. Shuanhu did not seem to have noticed my change of mood, rattling on as before. He said that he had finally got some dirt on Zhang Shutian, a resource from which all sorts of good things could be extracted, like a treasure chest. To be specific, Xu Yuanyuan, the boss of Beigou Coal Mine, had invited Zhang Shutian to make merry in the recreation city, and the brainless old goat actually came, jumping right into the trap that Xu Yuanyuan had set for him. As might be expected, Shuanhu received him with the greatest consideration, attending to him as complaisantly as possible, and generally kissing his backside until he was beside himself with joy. The best private room, the best girl, the best cigarettes and tea…even the tissues were of the highest quality. It never occurred to the silly old goat that his room had a hidden camera, and that his dirty deeds had all been recorded on a disk. Now the disk made regular appearances in Shuanhu's entertainment repertoire. He offered to show me, but I stopped him before he could. He laughed at the old goat for having a short floppy penis, for performing so poorly in bed, and for having to wrestle for what seemed like half a day to force his dick into the girl's fleshy hole.

Shuanhu and Xu Yuanyuan, each possessing a copy of the disk, were prepared to play their trump cards at any moment, and were only waiting for the right moment. Getting firewood is not a problem, so long as the green mountains are still there, and sooner or later the disk would come into its own. At first, Shuanhu had wanted to extort money from him, but the thought of his daughter made him change his mind. He decided instead to use the disk to secure an official post for his daughter Jidan who was a labor union worker without any power, and who was often despised by the chairperson. Was it fair? No! But what was to be done about it? The only way was to become a leader! Within the magic circle of officialdom, even donkey dung would shine, let alone a gold ingot like Jidan. As to where Jidan should go, he had already had a plan for her — chair of the environmental hygiene office! "You mustn't laugh at it, just because it's a lowly office. Hidden under it are vast oil resources. So long as you know how to explore and mine, you'll find under the apparently bleak yellowish earth a vast sea of oil."

The fact that the environmental hygiene office was a profitable organization had been personally witnessed by Shuanhu. Last year, he brought home a plaque of Environmental Hygiene Advanced Unit for his company. This plaque had given him great inspiration. Shuanhu could not contain his excitement when he talked about it. At first, his company was not on the list. Inspectors from the environmental hygiene office came, saying that he had violated this or that regulation, writing him a ticket, and even issuing an ultimatum to shut down his business. Well, as an old hand, how could he not see through their tricks? They should have just let him know that they wanted money. Was it necessary to go all round the houses like that? They beat the mountain to shock the tiger, but said nothing specific beyond implying that it was time he paid tribute and burned incense!

Shuanhu had seen such performance too many times. It was an old trick which had been employed by the tax bureau, electric power company, industrial and commercial administration office, street administration office, as well as the environmental hygiene office. However, he wiped out these invaders one by one, each the victim of a single bullet, like so many Japs. To be more exact, he took them all down with two kinds of weapons — money and women. What man could stand firm against these two temptations? Shuanhu dealt with the director of the environmental hygiene office in the same way. As a result, not only was the shut-down notice nullified, but he and the director became good friends at the wine and game tables. How did his company stand a chance in the competition to get a plaque of Environmental Hygiene Advanced Unit, given only eight out of the eleven candidates would be chosen? It all depended on human effort, as the old saying goes. And the crucial question is always: is your head filled with brains or with shit? Those whose heads were filled with shit only knew that one was one, unaware that one could become two or three or even four.

Apparently, the director of the environmental hygiene office, who had become Shuanhu's friend, had a head filled with lube, greasy and slippery. He had all sorts of ways of making money. For example, he ordered in his own name fifty plaques of Environmental Hygiene Advanced Unit from a handicraft company and traded them privately — one thousand *yuan* each without receipt or invoice, cash on delivery. As a result, the plaques were seen everywhere — above the doors of groceries, of family-owned small restaurants, even of public toilets full of buzzing flies. The director claimed that he had only made fifty plaques, but Shuanhu believed the number was far greater than that — one hundred and fifty at least. A rough adding-up would reveal how much the director had milked from this single project. Of course, he was reported and removed from his post eventually. He had only himself to blame, really. Why did he have to show off like that? Why did he have to take all the spoils without sharing them with others?

Shuanhu said that having money was terrific. It was really terrific! Money could be used to buy power. Once venal officials had been bought by you, they became your workers, tamed and submissive, totally at your command. When you met with flood, they would build you a dam. When a pit lay in your way, they would fill it for you. You did not need to worry about anything since they and you were in the same boat. If the boat capsized, you fell into the water, it was true, but so did they. Naturally, they would try their best to keep the boat balanced without your having to raise a single finger.

The reasons that Shuanhu had to so value the chair of the environmental hygiene office were: the newly appointed director was going to retire; and, more importantly, it was an easy job. In other posts Jidan would most likely give the game away, revealing her incompetence because of her little schooling and limited literacy, whereas this one was a sinecure for four seasons of the year. How nice to get paid for days idled away with one's hands up one's sleeves!

81

Another place that was as busy as Shuanhu's firm was a newly constructed temple. Like Shuanhu's recreation city, the temple was packed with people.

Shuanhu's recreation city stood to the west, while the temple lay to the east. The temple was not large, and its architecture was coarse. With tile-covered roof and adobe walls, it looked, at first sight, like a cottage. The spacious area in front of its façade was made full use of: it was filled with tricycles, bicycles and dense crowds of people. Given that the temple had been built by Fugui, Fugui naturally became its presiding monk.

In the temple, there was an ugly-looking statue of Buddha. In front of the Buddha was set an alms-collection box, and next to the box was a huge enamel basin for worshipers to stand their lighted incense sticks. The pilgrims, after having performed the rites of kneeling and incense-lighting, would then drop money into the alms-box — the minimum amount was one *jiao*, but there was no upper limit. Whoever wished to find favor in the eyes of Living Buddha of Shining Virtue was obliged to go to the back of the curtain to meet him; the Living Buddha would touch the crown of your head, and move his holy hand three times anticlockwise round your head, and then three times clockwise. Once this was done, the glory of Sakyamuni Buddha would begin to shine into your body, presumably. According to Living Buddha of Shining Virtue, "Sincere faith helps your wish come true. To show your sincere piety to the Buddha, you must pay at least ten more *yuan*."

Outside the temple gate, there was another incense burner — a huge one. From afar you could see smoke rising, floating in the air, and enveloping the area. Next to the burner was another goodwill donation-collection box, half filled with banknotes of various denominations. Next to the box stood Layue, who guarded it in case someone tried to smash the glass box with a hammer and make off with the money.

No one could blame Layue for her concern, since an actual robbery had already happened. It had taken place the previous month; two lads had smashed the glass box with a hammer and taken all the money in it. As Layue related the story, tears ran from the corners of her eyes. At the same time, she condemned those who had dropped joss money into the box. She said, "How worthless these people were! To do such a thing was like cursing the Buddha."

Layue told me that when she reported the matter to her father Living Buddha of Shining Virtue, he did not get angry; and that after calculating on his fingers, the Living Buddha announced his prophecy as follows: the person who had put the joss money into the box would surely die within three days. How wondrous it was! Only one day after the Living Buddha uttered this invocation, in the afternoon, a middle-aged woman in a neighboring village was hit by a car and died. And who might that middle-aged woman be? None other, there could not be the least doubt, than the person who had put the joss money into the box! "You see, a perfect example of cause-and-effect retributive justice!" Layue exclaimed.

Out of sheer curiosity, I decided to go to the other side of the curtain to see Fugui. Seeing that I was heading towards the curtain, Fugui's nephew, a strong and hulking man who was responsible for maintaining order in the place, pushed me backwards with great force. I staggered, nearly tumbling onto the floor.

"You must pay!" he shouted at me. "Those who haven't paid mustn't advance by even half step."

"Where should I pay?" I asked.

He pointed at a person behind the curtain. Until this moment I had not discerned that Fugui's wife was sitting there cross-legged, with a thick wad of banknotes in her hands.

I smiled at Fugui's wife. She cast a glance at me, but otherwise gave no sign that she knew me from Adam.

I smiled at her once again, but she simply turned her head aside, and paid me no further heed.

Quite a few people who had paid were patiently waiting in the queue. A long row of grotesque people sat on a bench. The majority of them were women, particularly aged women — some leaned on their walking sticks, some sat in their wheelchairs. But there were grownup men, too, and fashionable women.

I requested Layue to take me straight into her father's presence. She agreed without hesitation. But just as she was raising the curtain, her mother stopped her and a confrontation ensued.

"What a wastrel you are!" the mother said to the daughter. "What do you mean by smuggling useless people in? Has he paid?"

Layue made her mother take a closer look at me so as to recognize who I was: a former Mazi Village resident, an old neighbor. She told her mother that I was now doing "big things" in the provincial capital, stressing that when she and her father had visited the city, they had lived in my house.

Her mother replied, "How could I fail to recognize him? I could do so even if he were burned to ashes. He is Black Bean. Black Bean is forever Black Bean. He lives in the capital city of the province, so what? Can the drinking of the city's on tap running water transform him into Green Bean?"[38]

The mother was determined not to make any concession in the matter of my entrance fee, though she made it clear that if I paid the fee, I would be placed before the others in the queue — for the sake of our shared ancestral village.

"It's not that I love money, but Buddha does," she explained. "Buddha is looking down from the sky. If you fail to pay, Buddha will not grant whatever it is your request of him."

I could not stand listening to the argument between mother and daughter over something as trifling as ten *yuan* any longer, so I fumbled a twenty-*yuan* banknote out of my pocket and handed it over to the mother. No sooner did Layue's mother see the money than she smiled. The smile was pleasant enough, but only lasted a second. Like a blooming peony that withers in the blink of an eye, the smile vanished instantly.

When the mother offered to give me change, I waved my hand to signal "No." At this, the mother promised she would tell Living Buddha of Shining Virtue to turn his hand round my head a few extra times.

"Gangway!" Fugui's wife shouted to the people in our way as she led me towards Fugui.

"Don't throw melon seed shells onto the floor," she roared.

After stumbling here and there under the escort of Layue's mother, I finally came into the presence of Fugui. She whispered into Fugui's ear something to the effect that Fugui ought to turn his hand more times than usual about my head, since I had paid double the money.

Sitting inside a partitioned-off niche, Living Buddha of Shining Virtue looked decent enough. He wore a kasaya robe and a string of beads around his neck. Eyes slightly closed, he was murmuring something that was virtually unintelligible. A young man was kneeling in front of him, confessing that although he and his wife had been married for four years, they remained childless; that his wife had become so depressed that she had left him and gone to live in her parents' house. The young man claimed that he had come to seek the Living Buddha's prophecy. What he wanted to know was: could he successfully get his wife back from her parents' place? Could he and his wife succeed in having a son afterwards?

According to the young man, his grandfather had been an only son, and his father had also been an only son, and he himself was an only son too; but now even this tenuous father-to-son continuity was in danger, and the whole family line was in danger of failing.

"In the foreseeable future, my family line will be cut off," the young man sighed bitterly.

Stretching up his neck, Living Buddha of Shining Virtue blew into the air three times. Then, with explosive abruptness, he knocked against the table and denounced the young man, "In your last life, you were a criminal who committed murder. You sinned horribly. What was worse, you got away with it!" Such were the terms in which the Living Buddha condemned the young man.

The lad defended himself, saying that he had never murdered anybody; that on the contrary, he had been very kind and he had never killed so much as a mosquito.

Living Buddha of Shining Virtue corrected the lad, saying that he meant he had been a murderer in his *last* life, not in *this* life. "Have you got magic eyes that allow you to see across thousands of miles? Or into your last life? Common people can at best see their present life. Only Buddha can see both your last life and your present life, and even your next life."

Living Buddha of Shining Virtue emphasized that some people might not have been human in their last life — they might have been a pig that loved to wag its head, or a colorful butterfly. If a pig had cultivated its virtues attentitively in a previous life, it might be reborn a human in this life. If a person failed to cultivate his virtues, he might be transformed into a mule or a donkey in his *next* life.

Seeing that I was listening attentively, Living Buddha of Shining Virtue assumed an ostentatious air and began to expatiate — he claimed that he had clearly seen his next life; that since he had whole-heartedly devoted himself to the service of the Buddha, and also on account of the fact that he had been kind-hearted, he would be destined in his *next* life to rule over a large territory.

Having knelt for a long time, the young man ran out of patience, and asked Living Buddha of Shining Virtue outright what he should do.

The Living Buddha told the lad to rise to his feet, to pay him one hundred *yuan* for a consecrated talisman, and then always to carry the talisman with him. According to the Living Buddha, once the lad obtained the talisman, his wife would come back to him in spite of herself, since the wave of light emitted by the talisman would, like a magic hand, grasp his wife's hair, scratch her footsoles, and make her eyeballs itch. As his wife could not withstand these forces for long, she would certainly come back to her husband. After she returned, she would feel the urgent need to rush into the young man's arms, and in time a baby would fall out from between her legs.

Living Buddha of Shining Virtue even prophesied what the baby would look like: its eyes would be rounder and darker even than those luminous pearls which light up at night; and round its naval lotus patterns would be imprinted; and over its forehead two whorls would grow.

These words made the young man extremely happy. He smiled warmly. But just as he was taking money from his pocket, he hesitated slightly. He muttered something to the effect that if the prophecy failed to come true, he would have wasted his money.

Enraged by the young man's skepticism, Living Buddha of Shining Virtue said, "If you want to buy, buy now; if you don't want to buy, don't buy. But don't waste my time. I need to help the next person."

Living Buddha of Shining Virtue explained that he was collecting the money on behalf of Sakyamuni; that he wouldn't embezzle a cent for his own benefit; that he would pass on all the money to Sakyamuni, who could undoubtedly be regarded as a kind of high-rank official.

"Sakyamuni needs to eat and drink to survive. Without money to ensure his survival, how can Sakyamuni deliver all the living creatures from their torments?" Living Buddha of Shining Virtue asked the young man.

The young man went through one pocket after another. When he had gone through them all and taken out all the money he had, his hands held only a small quantity of small change, which Living Buddha of Shining Virtue beheld with disgust. Snatching the money from the young man, the Living Buddha spread the change on the table and began to count it out. When he had finished, he asked the young man, "It's not enough. It only comes to seventy-seven *yuan* and sixty-six cents."

The young man mumbled that this was all he had; that he had no more money; that to tell the truth, he had taken this money in order to buy some medicine for his father. He groaned that his father was suffering from emphysema and coughed uncontrollably all day long, and how irritating it was to hear the coughs and how he would love to block his father's throat with cement!

"Well, let's forget about it!" the Living Buddha cut in. "Seventy-seven *yuan* is okay. Anyway, this is all charity work. Poor people really shouldn't be deprived of Buddha's compassion."

As he spoke, Living Buddha of Shining Virtue returned sixty-six cents to the young man. Then, with a wave of the hand, he signaled him to leave.

After the young man left, a lame woman entered. The Living Buddha glared at her, but instantly turned his head towards me. After asking me some pro forma questions, the Living Buddha told me not to leave — he said he was about to invite me to eat mitten crabs and to drink Maotai spirit in a Kaiyang restaurant.

"Have you ever drunk Maotai?" he asked me. "It is the brand our national leaders drink."

He said that in the past he had merely heard of this great brand and that to take a sip of Maotai used to be beyond his wildest dreams. But thank goodness, his luck had turned. Ever since he had become Living Buddha of Shining Virtue, many officials had come to ask him to tell their fortunes. As a result, gifts from these officials had piled up in his house, so that now drinking Maotai was as commonplace as drinking water.

Inhaling deeply, he said emphatically that Living Buddha of Shining Virtue was not Fugui, and that the difference was as great as that between today and yesterday, between a white swan and a black duck, between salt and pepper, between soy sauce and vinegar. Therefore, people should not look down upon him any longer.

According to Living Buddha of Shining Virtue, in spite of being called Fugui for the former half of his lifetime, he had neither grown *fu,* rich, nor become *gui*, elevated. But ever since he renamed himself Living Buddha of Shining Virtue, he had truly become extraordinarily rich and elevated.

"Why do you want to treat me?" I asked him. "And is it okay for a practising Buddhist to do this?"

Lowering his voice, Living Buddha of Shining Virtue told me that he was about to treat some officials of the county bureau of religions, something he did mainly for the sake of a title. He said that at his age, he should at least have procured the rank of *chu*.

"If you ask me what *chu* means, I'll tell you: it is a talisman!" Living Buddha of Shining Virtue said. "It will bring me a sense of accomplishment. It will also enable me to raise the fee demanded of the patrons. However, presently I have no rank at all. If I want to receive an exceptional promotion to the *chu* rank, can I do so without inviting the authorities to dinner?"

82

When Third Aunt learned about Dalin's death, she cried for three days and three nights. Early on the morning of the fourth day, her blood-pressure spiked, and by the time they had rushed her to hospital, her brain was already bleeding internally. After doctors spent half a day attempting desperately to rescue her, she managed to hold on to life, but was left paralyzed on the bed, unable to move or to speak. Xiaolin was the only one who could sometimes understand what she was talking about. He brought her back to Sakelu, having stayed in the hospital looking after her for over a month. Although he had used up all the family savings to cure her, Third Aunt's illness did not get any better. Even at home, she still needed to take medicines and have injections, so Xiaolin was forced to borrow money everywhere. In order to buy her a decent coffin, he was even ready to ask Song Tongguo for a loan — though the interest was bound to be extortionate.

Song Tongguo denounced Xiaolin as a fool. Why did Xiaolin remain in Sakelu — just waiting for death to intervene? He should give up being head of Sakelu — an unprofitable post into which he had sunk his own money. Was something wrong with his brain? He should be out earning money in his prime; earning money was an absolute value. Were it not for Third Aunt and her family's kindness to Luobo, Song Tongguo would not even bother growling at him like this. Song Tongguo was a factory manager now, and as such he was parsimonious with his words; no one could make him open his mouth if he wanted to keep it closed. Song Tongguo repeatedly stressed how kind Third Aunt had been to Luobo, but he still charged more than ten percent interest on the money he lent to Xiaolin.

Song Tongguo invited Xiaolin to join Meiteng as his aide — as the director of the factory office, to be specific. He said that with his training, Xiaolin would turn from a clumsy crab into an agile carp in the blink of an eye. Of course, he had his own reasons for having Xiaolin by his side, i.e. he would be able to make him pay back his loans. He could conveniently deduct money from Xiaolin's salary, which required his authorization.

Xiaolin let the house in Sakelu to the girls hired by Shuanhu's company. He took a room at Meiteng's dormitory for single workers and arranged accommodation for Third Aunt there. As he had to clock on and knock off on time, he engaged the services of a care-taker. He did not earn much at

Meiteng — less than two thousand *yuan*. After one thousand was deducted each month, he had only seven or eight hundred *yuan* left, and that had to go on Third Aunt's medicines, rents, water-and-electricity bills, the caretaker's fees, etc. Obviously the money was far from enough. In the end, he was counting the cents off one-by-one. And he waited a long time before he had his hair cut.

Xiaolin was greatly troubled by this economic deficit, but Song Tongguo painted a picture of a beautiful cake. Song Tongguo promised to promote Xiaolin to Assistant Factory Manager within a year, so long as he did the job well. Once Xiaolin became Assistant Factory Manger, his salary would be doubled. Xiaolin thought that any difficulties would be purely temporary, and that good things were awaiting him in the near future. However, in the event Song Tongguo's deeds had disappointed him a lot, and the idea of leaving Meiteng flashed again and again through his head.

Xiaolin felt strongly that Song Tongguo, serving Cao with his body, but with his mind in Han[39], had not invested any effort in Meiteng's management. Song Tongguo pushed everything onto Xiaolin, and only showed up on payday at the beginning of each month. He would first take a walk around the factory, then seated in his office, he would send for a few middle-rank executives and hurl abuse at them. These middle-rank executives had been officially recruited, including two PhDs, who had worked the hardest and most conscientiously. Song Tongguo did not abuse them because of their performance, but rather for their lack of respect for him. Other middle-rank exexutives nodded and bowed to him when they saw him, but the two doctors had faces like steamed buns made of unleavened dough, without a trace of a smile. Others would express their gratitude after they received their salaries, secretly slipping him a carton of high-quality cigarettes or a pair of famous-brand shoes; whereas these two had not bought him anything, not even a roll of toilet paper. So it was they who had targets on their backs. They should thank their lucky stars that he had not given them a good kicking.

Song Tongguo stayed in Yuebei most of the time. Every three days he would report to Boss Wang, saying that the prevailing situation was excellent, blooming like fiery-red mountain lilies. Of course, he never missed an opportunity to boast, with extremely exaggerated body language, how hard he had worked. He even claimed that he had once fainted in the workshop and was carried to the hospital — an incident he had invented and related almost fifty times, in order to prove how righteous he was and how often he had come up with new measures in management. Boss Wang looked at him, nodding with satisfaction, patting him on the shoulder, and bursting into laughter every now and then.

To flatter Wang Dawei was all Song Tongguo had to do. Once the audience with the boss was over, he was free to do whatever he pleased. He was a frequent visitor to luxurious restaurants, recreation cities, bath centers, etc., always in the company of young girls. These were trendy girls, each more voluptuous than the other, and each speaking more affectedly than the other. Frivolous in speech and manner, they were always leaving crimson lip-prints on his cheeks. Of these girls some were Song Tongguo's mistresses, and some were his goddaughters (of two days' date). When they were around he was so gallant, so generous that he looked rather like a big-spending playboy.

These stories were told by Song Tongguo's driver, with whom Xiaolin had been on good terms. What Xiaolin cared about was not Song Tonguo's rotten private life, but in which direction he, as captain, was taking Meiteng. Was the ship going to hit the rocks and be wrecked because of his maladministration?

Xiaolin had been out twice with Song Tongguo, and each time he came back he had thoughts of resigning. Ostensibly Song Tongguo was working for cooperation between Meiteng and other companies, but in fact he was trying to undermine Meiteng. He rented two rooms from a hotel to raise money there in Meiteng's name. Having had a leaflet designed and printed in large quantities, he hired people to distribute them along the streets. The words on the leaflet promised, treacherously, very high returns. Conspicuously placed on the leaflet was a picture of him with Governor Xiang, taken at Sakelu. He always carried this picture in his pocket, and he never forgot to show it when he was eating or chatting with other people — even when he was flirting with massage girls. And he often casually made up stories about his brotherly relationship with Governor Xiang, saying that when coming to Kaiyang, Governor Xiang stayed at his home rather than at a hotel, that Governor Xiang had no appetite for the fish, meat and fowl offered by the hotel, but only for the spinach noodles made by his wife.

Investors, consisting of laid-off workers, white-collar employees, and a few majestic-looking wealthy people, found their way to the hotel rooms. On arrival, they would first make inquiries, but refused to make a decision until they had ascertained that the on-going project was feasible. It was natural that Song Tongguo would be surrounded by a throng of people asking all sorts of questions. At the critical moment, he would produce from his pocket the deal-clincher — the picture of him with Governor Xiang. He held the picture high, and told them how Governor Xiang and he were relatives, and how Governor Xiang had shared a quilt with him when they slept on the same bed. He even hinted that Governor Xiang was the real boss behind the pooling company, and that the funds being raised would be used to build subways in Yuebei, where high investiment would most probably yield high returns. Backed up by Governor Xiang, how could the company lose a cent? How could it go bankrupt? Ridiculous! Absolutely ridiculous!

Many people were skeptical, but quite a few took out wads of cash on the spot. One old lady stood outside the door and discussed with her son the possibility of selling their own house to buy shares. How profitable it would be to invest money here for three years while one house grew into two! From their talk it was easy to say that their lives were not easy. Her husband was sick, her son was driving a taxi for someone else's firm, and her daughter-in-law had, in all probability, to get up at three each morning in order to sell breakfast by the roadside. However, the mother and son evidently thought that their sun was going to rise here, and with their faces radiant with hope, they could not help bursting into giggles.

Having overheard the conversation between the mother and son, Xiaolin came out of the room and patted the young man, who took the hint and followed him into the other room. Xiaolin found an excuse to send Song Tongguo's driver away and told the young man to think twice before they decided to sell their own house. The young man stared at Xiaolin in astonishment, asking if the money raisers were liars. Xiaolin said whether they were liars or not was up to him and his mother to decide. He only warned them not to play around with the money they had earned in the sweat of their brows, lest they should regret doing so in the future. The young man asked Xiaolin who he was. If that guy named Song Tongguo was a liar, was Xiaolin not his accomplice? As he was not sure whose word was true and whose word was false, the young man rubbed his chin and finally concluded that Xiaolin was deliberately undermining his chances of getting rich. How often would a man get a chance like that in a lifetime? Governor Xiang was, undeniably, a big, upright official; how could he fraternize with liars?

The young man would trust his own judgment. After the unconvinced young man had gone, Xiaolin was called back by Song Tongguo. It was eight o'clock in the evening. Calls of inquiry were still coming through, but occasionally, and only a few people were stopping by to pay. The money raised filled two cases full to the brim, each of which was locked with two iron locks which had been bought by the driver. Song Tonguo had eaten only two deep-fried dough sticks during the entire day and, whether as a result of hunger or fear, he was now shaking violently, his face dark blue, and his lips purplish. After he had taken two bites of the banana the driver had bought for him and drunk some water, he recovered his humor a little bit. He began to boast to the driver and Xiaolin, asking them what they thought of his capabilities. In half a day, he had collected three million *yuan*, which was a great deal of money. If he collected money at this rate for three consecutive days, why, what was to stop him becoming a billionaire?

Song Tongguo repeatedly declared that this money was not his own, but belonged to Meiteng. Something had gone wrong with its financing. How could he not feel worried when he saw that its capital chain was about to break? The boss of Meiteng was wise enough to appoint him, a capable man, as the factory manager; otherwise the whole company would have collapsed when it ran out of money. Song Tongguo imparted his experience to Xiaolin, while criticizing him because he was so weak as to be upset by a little family difficulty. He should model himself on Song Tongguo, who, with a few turns of his head and gestures of his hand, could make tides of money roll in his direction. People differed in intelligence, so the wise drew in the stupid and ate them. It was eat or be eaten! What was life? Life was just a matter of eating people and being eaten. As to the picture with Governor Xiang, there were those who might have kept it in their pockets so that it could not have earned a cent, there were those who might have framed it behind glass to satisfy their own vanity at most; but he was different, wasn't he? He could do wonders with it! The wonder had been achieved. What was the correct term to describe it? It was called "profit maximization."

As he babbled, Song Tongguo drew two thousand *yuan* from his wallet, which he divided in two and forced into the hands of Xiaolin and the driver, saying that it was for the hard work they had done.

83

One family after another ran out of money on account of this or that reason. Although the sound of people playing mahjong could still be heard coming from the neighborhood of Sakelu villas, if you entered the houses, you would find that the wagers were getting ever smaller. In the past, people wagering five *yuan* or even ten *yuan* had been deemed miserly, but now one and two *yuan* wagers were becoming pretty normal. For a tiny minority of players, the wagers were even as small as one or two *jiao*. If you asked them, "Why do you keep gambling when all the while you complain that you've run out of money?" the unanimous answer was, "What else is there to do but play mahjong? If we don't, we simply sit and do nothing, and that's so boring. Can a lively, able-bodied person sit inactive from sunrise till sunset? Who can do that? To us, playing mahjong is the only way to kill time and to fill the boring days that come one after another."

When Spring Festival was around the corner, many people expressed a wish to look for Liben. They would ask him what they were supposed to do, now that they had run out of money. What should they do, now that they could not afford wheat flour, cooking oil, meat, fireworks, and new-year-clothes for their children? Their argument was that it was because of the sworn promises Liben had made in the past that they had followed his advice and had moved out of Mazi Village; so now that they were facing the possibility of starving to death, who else should they go to see but Liben? And it was worrying that the cursed man had not been seen for seven or eight months. Had he by some chance holed up in a mouse furrow, to be nibbled to nothing by mice?

Liben could not be reached by mobile phone. So the villagers sent someone to go to the county town to look for him on their behalf. But this man could not find Liben either. People were really starting to get anxious! What should they do? Hell, what could they do? The voices cursing Liben could be heard everywhere around Sakelu.

Someone made a suggestion to these anxious people — namely, Shuanhu. According to him, the Sakelu residents should go and talk with Meiteng.

Shuanhu's suggestion did not seem groundless: Meiteng had, after all, occupied the land belonging to Mazi Village, so it was not enough that it merely arranged a lodging place for the villagers; in addition, it should provide a livelihood for the villagers, as well as for their offspring for generations to come.

The villagers had been unhappy with Shuanhu for various reasons — they were especially hostile towards him because he had opened his recreation city right across from the portal of Sakelu Park — but now his words were like a match that lit a lamp in the villagers' mind.

"That's right!" the villagers agreed. "Though Liben the trouble-maker is missing, the company remains. Would it be a problem for such a big company to support us — just a few hundred people? It gives Song Tongguo big joints of meat to eat, so can't it give us some bones to gnaw on? We all come from Mazi Village — no, come to think of it, Song Tongguo should never have been regarded as a Mazi villager; he is no more than an outsider. But why have we been living so differently from the way Song Tongguo does?"

Though the Sukelu residents talked like this among themselves, none of them ventured to go to Meiteng to advance such a claim, since they had learned that the firm had recruited some guards, who were good at martial arts. These violent-looking guards could be seen swinging their long steel whips, which cracked loudly.

Was it enough to restrain their hunger? Meals are a necessity for survival and one meal missing can make a man feel faint. Without money to buy wheat flour, should the residents just starve to death in their own houses? So on the eve of the Chinese New Year, almost all the Sakelu residents came out of their houses and assembled at the gate of Meiteng.

Meiteng's production continued as normal, with dense smoke spouting from the thick chimneys. But the management personnel were on vacation. Song Tongguo was nowhere to be seen.

Standing in front of the gate, the villagers shouted at the top of their voices. Getting no response from the company, people's anger grew as they shouted, and they began to dash bricks against the gate. However, no one answered from inside. Then on someone's initiative, all the people acted as one man: they pushed against the wall, which fell to the ground.

When they shouted, no one answered. When they struck the gate, no one answered. But now when the wall was smashed, some people appeared. Indeed, five guards had appeared from nowhere at the sound of the wall's collapse.

These guards had, indeed, steel whips in their hands, as the earlier rumor had claimed. The guards rushed into the crowd, their whips whistling frighteningly.

Seeing that they were in great danger, the crowd scattered rapidly. But a few men were too astonished to move a single step: they stood where they were, motionless.

Without uttering a word, the guards swung their steel whips to strike with maximum force these stupefied people. Horrible cries burst out as the whips came down on them. Groans mixed with cries trailed in the air. Some people fell to the ground, but instantly managed to pick themselves up and make off. Some people remained flat on the ground after falling down. But the guards took no interest in those people — it seemed that they had forgotten to deal with them. Instead the guards surrounded two men whom they beat with increasing vigor. The stamping sounds their leather shoes made could be heard even by villagers who were standing at a distance.

The two men who had been surrounded and beaten up were Beiqiang and Baolai. After the villagers dialed countless times, the police eventually showed up. But both Beiqiang and Baolai were found to be in a deep coma.

Then a 120 emergency ambulance arrived. A doctor got out, and immediately declared Baolai dead, and that Beiqiang's weak pulse was intermittent — his condition was critical.

The ambulance carried Beiqiang away, while the police car took the guards into custody, leaving Baolai curled up motionless on the ground, his face covered in blood.

The villagers gathered around Baolai. They called Baolai's name; they shook his head. No one believed he was dead. How could they believe it? How full of life he had been only just now, how could he have become a ghost in the blink of an eye?

But Baolai *was* dead. There was no doubt about it — his tongue stuck out of his lips and there was no breath.

The villagers became exasperated. They began by remembering and counting Baolai's various good deeds, but as the list grew longer and longer, fury possessed them. The males shouted angrily, while the women wailed loudly. Then they yelled, exclaiming that they would carry Baolai's body to Zhang Shutian and ask him to give them a live Baolai.

They had moved approximately three hundred meters, when their advance was barred by a fleet of cars moving from the opposite direction. The fleet consisted of seven or eight vehicles, including a hearse, police cars and armed-police cars, and some normal cars — some of which were carrying county officials, some township officials. Some people got out of the vehicles, took hold of Baolai's body and loaded it onto the hearse. Once the armed-policemen had forced a passage through the middle of the crowd for the hearse, it tore away at full speed.

A vice county magistrate had come along. At the top of his voice, he shouted to the villagers, "Calm down! Be quiet!" After he had shouted for a long space of time, the tumultuous voices of the crowd gradually died down. Standing on an elevated platform, he placed one hand on his hip and waved with the other. But when he eventually began to speak, instead of talking about Baolai, he changed the subject by asking, "What day is it today?"

Not understanding what the vice magistrate meant by this question, the villagers remained silent.

The vice magistrate's assistant answered loudly, "Today is New Year's Eve."

Waving his hand, the vice magistrate said, "Right! It's New Year's Eve! What are people supposed to do on New Year's Eve? People ought to enjoy their family reunion feast at home. People ought to burn incense and worship their ancestors. But see what you have been doing. You have come to Meiteng to make trouble and cause disturbances, making it impossible for any of us to enjoy a peaceful New Year celebration. I make this solemn declaration: you are now residents of Sakelu; you're no longer residents of Mazi Village. Mazi Village used to be your home, but since its requisition by Meiteng, it no longer has anything to do with you. You signed the document. Your signatures testify that you agreed to leave Mazi Village. You signed it black on white. Today, then, you have stirred up trouble on someone else's property. What is your justification for doing so? Therefore, I command all of you to go back to Sakelu, to return to your homes. Whatever complaints or questions you may have, wait till after the New Year festivities. You can then present them properly in the hope of a satisfactory answer."

The crowd did not scatter as the vice magistrate had expected. On the contrary, its boisterous noise totally drowned out his subsequent utterances.

"What does he say? Does he say we're no longer Mazi villagers? How can that possibly be?"

"How can he talk such nonsense! How can he talk out of his arse like that?"

"We were born in Mazi Village. We were brought up in Mazi Village. Even if we have moved out, our ancestors are still buried there."

"Our roots are in Mazi Village. No one can deny this fact. Like trees, men cannot live without roots."

Lifang kept bawling. Her wails, which pierced through the cold night, sounded extremely sad and shrill. She wailed ceaselessly, "Beiqiang, you're gone. Without you, how can I and our children live on? What can we do? What can we do?"

An office clerk from the county government did his best to console Lifang, trying to stop her from crying. He said that her husband was not dead — he was only injured and was being sent to the Chinese medicine hospital for treatment. He told her he would take her to the hospital so that she could look after her husband.

On hearing this, Lifang took hold of the clerk's lappet, as if she were clutching at a life-saving straw. She would not let go of it for a single second.

The villagers ceased their uproar. One at a time they asked their questions, and demanded that the vice magistrate answer. The questions were of various sorts:

"What to do with Baolai's body?"

"Will those guys who were responsible for Baolai's death be properly punished, so that the dead can rest in peace?

"What should we do, now that we don't have money to celebrate the New Year? What should we do, now that we have nothing to live on?"

"After the New Year festive season, can the government make arrangements with all those concerned, so that each Sakelu household can once again receive tens of thousands of *yuan*?"

Two men among the crowd dashed towards the vice magistrate. Patting him on his shanks from below the platform, they made the vice magistrate tell them explicitly whether Sakelu residents were Mazi villagers or not.

Seeing this, the political commissar of the county's public security bureau, along with two policemen, dragged the two men away. The political commissar fiercely denounced them, saying "What are you doing? Are you trying to stir up a rebellion? What difference does it make whether you are Mazi villagers or not? Mazi villagers or not, it doesn't mean you can go and live there. So why make such a big deal of it?"

The two men struggled to free themselves from the hold of the policemen.

They roared at the political commissar, "Shut your dirty mouth, if you don't know the difference. The difference between being or not being Mazi villagers is a huge one. If you people acknowledge us as Mazi villagers, that means we still have a claim to Mazi Village, but if you do not acknowledge us as Mazi villagers, we have nothing." Undoubtedly, their choice of the word "claim" was the result of Kang Yuanyuan's civic training program.

In spite of the brawls and jostles, as midnight drew near, and the sounds of some sporadic fireworks became audible, the drama began to wind down. The vice magistrate's car drew off. A car owned by the county government took Liben's sister and left. The police took away a number of people — including the two men who had called out the word "claim" — and drove off too. A dozen armed policemen remained. Yelling all the while, they drove the people towards Sakelu; they showed no mercy to whoever dared to disobey.

Nevertheless, low whispers could be heard coming from the crowd. If you listened carefully, you could discern that they were reminding one another of Kang Yuanyuan's good deed; they were yearning for her arrival. Like blind people, they could not see where to go. If only Kang Yuanyuan could come and give them her advice!

84

Beiqiang returned home while Baolai was still lying in an ice-chest at the mortuary. With his spleen removed, Beiqiang appeared thin as a rake, and stooped all day. As there was no reimbursement for Beiqiang's medicine bills, Lifang kept going around inquiring and begging for help, a thick stack of medicine bills in her hand. She was beginning to look like Xianglin's wife[40], her hair disheveled, her clothes untidy, and her hands gesticulating. She would stop whomever she met, be they known or unknown, five-year-olds or eighty-year-olds. Once she had their attention, she would begin to complain, saying that it was Liben whom she hated the most because he was the cause of all her family's present misfortunes. He was her brother, her closest kin, this man who had made her suffer; she had carried him in her arms, cared for him, kissed and loved him when he was a child. Who would have expected that he was such a wolf as to bring misery like this on her family! After that she began to curse the United States for its extreme wickedness. Her younger brother had been good in every respect before he went abroad; the years spent there had turned him into the kind of wolf which bit its own sister! Was the United States a wolf's den, then?

One month after the spring festival, the Sakelu people organized another mass petition. They gathered outside the county government and blocked the roads. The county leaders sneaked out of the back door of the courtyard, leaving only the office director to deal with the matter; he sent for Song Tongguo, and invited the village representatives to the meeting room for talks. Song Tongguo was apparently not in a position to make autonomous decisions; he called Boss Wang every few minutes. He just repeated what Boss Wang had said to him, like a megaphone. To sum up, the demands of the villagers were twofold. One was to seek justice for Baolai, and the other was that Meiteng should make arrangements for their future lives.

As to the first, no one objected, since the county leaders had stated clearly that the case would be handled in a serious way, and that whoever had committed the crime must pay for it. Anyway, locked up in the detention house, the assailants could not get away without being punished! As to the second, however, the two parties were greatly divided and in intense opposition to each other. The villagers proposed two remedies. Meiteng should either provide each villager with a one-off subsidy of thirty thousand *yuan*, or a monthly salary of no less than five hundred per capita. Song Tongguo ran out, and, on the basis of a discussion with Boss Wang, resolutely refused the appeals from the villagers. He sneered at the villagers for indulging in a lottery-fantasy. Why? Why must Meiteng give them money or pay them salaries? Was Meiteng such a soft touch as to give money to whoever wanted it? Meiteng had no relation with them, and all the problems had been solved before it started production. The agreement between the two parties was still there in black ink and white paper. Was it reasonable for them to start finding fault with Meiteng now, just because they had run out of money?

The villagers and Meiteng were a bad fit, like a tenon and a mortise of different sizes. A quarrel broke out in the meeting room. Several representatives took aim at Song Tongguo and questioned if he still considered himself a Mazi villager. Was he a toad which, because it had drunk a bellyful of water, could take on the form of a turtle? A Mazi villager sacrificing the interests of the Mazi villagers, what was he if not a traitor? Furthermore, they had heard that it was at Song Tongguo's secret command that the security guards had so violently attacked the villagers.

"Song Tongguo, you motherfucker, are you a human being or not? If you are, how can you do shameless things like this? Baolai has been beaten to death, but you, you bugger, are still wearing a human skin to enjoy life in this world. How can that fucking heart of yours be so black, so noxious?"

Some villagers pounced upon Song Tongguo and held him by his hair and collar, but the office director soon got them off him. Song Tongguo barely reacted. His mouth moved, but no one could hear what he was grumbling about. The indignation of the villagers troubled him, so that he patted first on the desk, then on his chest, saying merely that he was willing to draw on his own savings to support the villagers. He calculated on his fingers for a while, then decided that he was willing to donate five hundred thousand *yuan* to the villagers in total, each of whom would then receive about five hundred. But, as a wild goose leaves its sound in the sky after its passage through it, a man leaves his name in this world after his passage through it. For the good deeds done, the good name has to stay. His idea was to have a sculpture of himself erected by the lake of Sakelu, like the one of Liben. The villagers did not need to pay for it, because he could draw the funds from other sources. All they needed to do was acknowledge his benevolence.

Song Tongguo's words greatly softened the attitudes of the representatives, but they were still not satisfied. What could be done with only five hundred *yuan*? They began negotiating, but when the number reached one thousand *yuan*, Song Tongguo would not let it go any higher. He even threatened the representatives with cancellation of the entire donation if they insisted on taking a mile when he gave them an inch; they should learn how to put down the bowl after they had eaten enough.

The director of the county government office chimed in at this point, saying that meals must be eaten mouthful by mouthful, and that ways must be fared step by step. A watched pot never boils. One thousand *yuan* per person — three to four thousand or four to five thousand *yuan* per family — was not a small sum. The villagers could get by with this money, and their future living would be discussed after Zhang Shutian, the county secretary of the Party committee, came back from Europe.

The representatives thought that the director's words were reasonable enough, so they forced Song Tongguo to write a brief letter of commitment and put an end to the negotiations. By the time they came out, the villagers had completely disappeared. The roads had been cleared, and, unlike earlier, there were policemen on patrol. After many inquiries, the representatives finally learned from a tricycle man that the villagers had been driven to a deserted construction site, so the representatives headed for it in a hurry, with Song Tongguo following behind. He said that he wanted to apologize to the villagers in person.

Once there, the representatives were immediately surrounded by the villagers, most of whom, on hearing that they could each get one thousand *yuan*, agreed that this was a fairly good outcome, in spite of the dissatisfaction shown by some of them. Half a loaf was better than no bread, after all. It was better to have, rather than not to have, this one thousand *yuan*! And one thousand *yuan* for trouble-making was far better than raising crops in the sweat of their brow! Once the money was spent, they could always come back to make trouble from time to time. It was not bad to live by making trouble! For one thing which Sakelu people did not lack was time.

Not many villagers noticed that Song Tongguo had arrived, but he had. He climbed up to the unfinished building and shouted "Dear fellow villagers!" The crowd gradually settled down, and looked up at him. Song Tongguo made three silent kowtows to them, then began tearfully to relate how he had failed to take care of them, how he was ashamed to look them in the face. The only way he had to reward them, to atone for his sins, was to take out all his savings and distribute the money among them, thus proving that it was for them that he had been working in Meiteng all these years. Baolai was his brother, and the loss of Baolai had struck him so bitterly that he had not been able to eat or sleep for three days.

Once they had heard Song Tongguo's confessions, those who had been denouncing him only a moment before, seemed to have changed their minds, and said that he was not a bad guy. It seemed that they had looked at him sidelong and calumniated him as a liar all the time. What, of all that he had said, did not warm the cockles of one's heart? He wanted to take money out of his own pocket and give it to the villagers; what was that, if not a living Buddha?

Some of the villagers tried to persuade Song Tongguo to come down from the building. "Don't cry, don't cry. You've done enough for the Sakelu villagers. On the contrary, it is the Sakelu villagers who have wronged you. They always looked side-long at you, always thought you were an outsider, and locked you out of their hearts. It is they who ought to kowtow and apologize to you!" Some of them even went so far as to climb up by him and prevail on him to come down, to come back to be among the villagers. How they missed him during the long time he was away! It was a great honor for Sakelu that it had nurtured a great manager, and who among them would not welcome close contact with the great manager?

Down came Song Tongguo, greeting this person, shaking hands with that one. And he even flirted with one woman. He waved goodbye to them, after which the crowd dispersed, seemingly in great joy — some to go shopping in Kaiyang's high street, some to burn incense in the Confucian Temple, and the rest to return to Sakelu in a great hurry.

Two months flew by. However, Song Tongguo's commitment was just a scrap of paper. The villagers wistfully looked forward to its fulfillment. One wanted to marry off his daughter but the wedding was delayed time and again; one borrowed money for his child's tuition but the agreed repayment date had to keep being postponed, and as a result he had to break off relations with the creditor; one had a sick child in a hospital that threatened to suspend medication if the bills were not cleared; one waited for the money to buy grain, on the verge of starvation. Some cursed in anger, while others stamped their feet with anxiety. They looked up to Song Tongguo as to the moon and stars, but he was the kind of savior who neglected to send charcoal on snowy days. Several representatives commuted between Sakelu and Meiteng, without catching a glimpse of him. When they called him, no one answered. When they asked people in Meiteng about him, they nodded in absent-minded ignorance. The representatives had no choice but to wait for him to show up, taking turns day and night outside Meiteng's gate. They believed that the moment would come sooner or later when Song Tongguo, as the factory manager, stepped through that gate.

On the fifth day, the villagers on watch saw Meiteng's real boss, thin and lanky, with an ant's build. Of course, they did not dare to approach Boss Wang; they only looked on from a distance. Their intuition told them that something strange was going on at the company, because the boss came in the company of some leaders from the county government, in addition to five or six policemen in two police cars, all with grave expressions.

Soon the villagers on watch got inside news which was a real bolt from the blue. Song Tongguo had vanished with Meiteng's huge funds! As to where he had gone, even the police had no idea!

85

A smell permeated the neighborhood of Sakelu. As time passed, it grew in intensity, until eventually people found it unbearable. The smell was too strange to name. You might call it a pungent odor, but that did not quite do it justice. You might call it an acrid odor, but that did not seem quite right either. It was a blending of the two, resembling the smell of a gigantic cesspool. The smell was so strong that even those with sinus problems could smell it. Many people had physical symptoms: some suffered dizziness, some became nauseous, and some even lost their appetite.

Where was the smell coming from? Although plenty of people searched high and low, they did so in vain. At their wit's end, they called the anti-epidemic station. Slow, as always, in coming, the anti-epidemic station people showed up after a long interval, detectors in hand. They entered Sakelu. They sneezed. Instantly they declared the smell was from some decayed dead body.

"Did anybody die recently in this place?" they asked.

"No one died lately," people replied. "Baolai died, but he has been interred. He was buried deep on a turtle-shell shaped plateau about two kilometers away. Could the smell of his corpse come all the way here?"

At that moment, someone remembered Baolai's wife Qiuli, and said, "Baolai was interred six months ago. How has Qiuli managed since then? Her cries could be heard in the aftermath of Baolai's death. But why is it so long since we last heard her cries?"

This villager's words reminded people of Qiuli. It dawned on all of them that it was highly probable that something had happened to Qiuli. Busy with earning their own livelihood, the villagers had collectively forgotten her.

A handful of villagers escorted the anti-epidemic personnel to Baolai's house. The closer they approached, the stronger the smell grew. At a certain point, they found that the intense smell was so disgusting that they could hardly go on. The anti-epidemic personnel put on their gas masks; the villagers either put on masks, which they had borrowed from one another, or covered their noses and mouths with towels. The crowd shambled up to the façade of the house. They forced the door open. Instantly, a shocking scene presented itself to them: Qiuli was dead; her body had decomposed horribly; her face had become unrecognizable; her torso seemed to have been devoured — the intestines were completely exposed. A closer look revealed that a host of maggots were wriggling in the abdomen. And next to her corpse, several rats lay dead.

Frightened out of their wits, all the people who had beheld the scene screamed and ran away as quickly as their legs could carry them. The anti-epidemic people sprayed some disinfectant onto the corpse and departed too.

The villagers discussed what to do with Qiuli's remains. The discussion went on and on, but no one was willing to get involved in Qiuli's business. They said, "Qiuli didn't have a normal mind when she was alive. Now, having died such a death, won't her ghost be violent and vicious? To get involved in her business is like thrusting your fingers between revolving grindstones, isn't it?"

Several people thought of Fugui simultaneously. Even though Fugui was considered to be an utter fraud by the Sakelu people, nevertheless, they still wanted to put him to the test, so that they could see how he would deal with it. Didn't Fugui have a talent for fooling around with spooky conjuring? Now a real ghost had turned up, he must demonstrate the ability he claimed to have.

At the very moment the crowd was talking about him, Fugui arrived. Having heard of Qiuli's death, Fugui came with the others to see what the situation was. On his way, he kept coming across people who were talking about him. Every doubt people had expressed about his tricks came to his ears. Fugui was now dying to impress the villagers with a demonstration of his courage. He had seen all sorts of grotesque people before. He had beheld all sorts of grotesque corpses before. "What is there to fear?" he asked the villagers. He invited the people to follow him. He said he would perform rites for Qiuli near her corpse.

None of the people followed Fugui. Instead they stood in a group, trying to see from afar if he could improvise a solution.

In a short while, the same Fugui who had valiantly set off to confront Qiuli's remains, rushed back in a state of agitation, with his face deathly pale, his tongue faltering, his lips quivering. He remained speechless for a long while.

"What's the matter?" the villagers asked.

With enormous difficulty Fugui eventually pulled himself together, and said, "What a horrible thing! It's too horrible! The Sakelu residents are heading for a big disaster!"

"Why do you say that?" the villagers asked.

Fugui explained that the ghost he had just encountered was a green one — the most frightening type, which even Sakyamuni Buddha was powerless to overcome. He said he had dealt with black ghosts, white ghosts, red ghosts, and blue ghosts, but he had never dealt with a green ghost. Today he had just had his first experience with a green ghost, and to make things worse, it was the green ghost of a person who had died of starvation; his encounter with such a doubly formidable ghost had really shocked him out of his wits.

Picking up a round piece of clay, Fugui drew a line on the ground. He advised people against crossing the line, saying that anyone who did so might well run into the green ghost face to face, which would certainly bring them grave misfortune, so they could expect at best to collapse with an illness and be confined to bed, at worst to kick the bucket immediately.

As he said this, Fugui knelt down on the line and murmured some invocations intelligible to no one, holding his hands together palm to palm.

Then, Fugui rose to his feet. He set about instilling into the heads of the people the notion that the accelerating decline of Sakelu was due to the fact that an unpleasant, crazy woman used to inhabit the park; that the Sakelu residents had suffered from poverty and ill luck entirely on account of this woman; that since this crazy woman had so casually taken off her pants, her bad body odor had submerged all the positive masculinity in Sakelu; that the Sakelu residents had been too kind to the woman; that the Sakelu residents should have got rid of this trashy woman as soon as possible; that they should have clubbed her to death.

The frightening warning line drawn by Fugui was soon crossed. The person to cross it was Shuanhu, who was followed by a pick-up truck carrying an empty oil tank and a group of young men, who were standing at the back. These young men were employees in Shuanhu's company. In addition to being nimble-handed and fleet-footed, these young men were bold and daring. They wrapped up Qiuli's remains in a reed mat and stuffed the lot into the oil tank. After filling the tank with lots of lime, they moved the brimming tank away.

Shuanhu told people that Qiuli's remains had badly affected his business; that it had brought bad luck to the residents of Sakelu, too; that he was offering to deal with the remains for the sake of helping the community.

When people asked him where he was about to move the corpse to, instead of answering, he just reassured people that there was nothing to be uneasy about. He said the corpse was so dirty; he couldn't sell it for profit.

That evening, the Sakelu residents learned Shuanhu's true reason for getting rid of Qiuli's corpse, since a group of people had just been seen entering Baolai's house and knocking around with hammers. When asked what they were doing, these people answered that they were decorating the house for Shuanhu.

"Why does Shuanhu want so many houses?" the Sakelu residents wondered. "Can he take Baolai's house for himself simply because he wants it?"

The villagers thought that if things went on like this, Sakelu would descend into chaos. Consequently, some people wanted to form a delegation to go and argue with Shuanhu, only to discover that hardly anyone wanted to join them. *How mighty Shuanhu is now! A direct collision with him would end in crushing failure, like an egg going up against a rock. When an egg goes up against a rock, does the egg escape injury by sheer force of will?*

At the mention of egg, people inevitably thought of Shuanhu's daughter Jidan, whose name meant *chicken egg*. Truth to tell, Shuanhu's daughter should no longer be called Jidan, but Tiedan, *Iron Egg*. By now, she was the director of the county's environmental hygiene office. What was more, she had been married to a man more ferocious than a wolfhound: he worked in the county town as the captain of a hotel's security corps. Who would dare to provoke this family?

Additionally, Shuanhu lent out extortionate loans, which the majority of villagers had taken. To get the loans, collateral was required. But what could the villagers use as collateral when they did not have any land or income? Their house was all they had to mortgage. Any provocation of Shuanhu would put their houses at risk, and defending Baolai's house would be a very serious provocation indeed. If Shuanhu, by some dirty trick, compelled a debtor to pay back the loan, wouldn't the debtor, pushed beyond endurance, hang himself?

A variety of rumors grew concerning the whereabouts of Qiuli's remains. Among them there was one which sounded vivid and plausible — that Qiuli's corpse had been carried to a hunting-dog training center to feed the beasts; and that after having eaten Qiuli's dead body, three expensive hunting-dogs died. Whether this rumor was true or not remained uncertain because there had not been any eyewitness. However, the hunting-dog training center did sue Shuanhu in court — the Sakulu residents knew this because the lawyer employed by the dog training center had come to Sakelu to take pictures, and, while doing so, was attacked by Shuanhu's men.

86

About a month previously, posters proposing the purchase of villas began to appear on every wall of the Sakelu courtyard. No buyer's name was provided, but there was a contact number. When villagers called the number, they could not help gasping in horror. The number was one of Shuanhu's company's! In other words, the buyer was none other than Shuanhu!

And why did the villagers gasp in horror? The reason was very simple. Two families had sold their villas to Shuanhu, but the sum they received could, at best, be termed "meager." They had borrowed money at usurious rates from Shuanhu and were pressed for payment of their debts. However, Shuanhu did not confront them in person; he just sent two strong lads, from outside the neighborhood, to harass the two families every day. As a rule, the lads did not say a word, but their actions alone were enough to frighten their timid hosts. When the host ate, the lad would eat with the bowl and chopsticks he had robbed him of; when the host took a walk, the lad would take a walk along with him; when the host went to the toilet, the lad would follow him to the toilet; and when the host went to sleep, the lad would go to bed with him, sometimes even lying between him and his wife. A few days later the two families, unable to bear this anymore, begged Shuanhu for mercy, soft words pouring out of their mouths. In the light of their difficult situation, Shuanhu proposed buying their villas. They had no choice but to accept his proposal. They had thought that they could get a sum of money large enough to build a thatched house; however, when the time came to settle accounts in earnest, they all gaped in surprise. The loan was only two thousand *yuan*, but in less than a year both the principal and its interest so multiplied that the debtor had to repay nearly twenty thousand. Cheap as a rural villa was, it none the less depreciated in value, and with the poor environment as an additional problem, a villa was hardly worth twenty thousand *yuan*. Was there any difference between selling it to Shuanhu and giving it to him free of charge? It would be a blessing if they could give it to him free of charge; but to their annoyance they discovered, that even after they gave it to him for nothing, they would still owe him a few thousand *yuan*. Luckily, Shuanhu was a generous man. Either because he had taken into consideration that they were his fellow villagers, or because he had been touched by their bitter wailing, for whatever reason, with a flourish of his arm, he wrote off the money that they would have had to pay him. Was he not benevolent enough, not merciful enough for them? In addition, he even gave each family five hundred *yuan* so that they could pay for their journey out of Sakelu.

What a heart-breaking scene it was when the two families took their leave! In a drizzling rain, the whole village turned out to see them off with swollen red eyes, the villagers ranging from old folks over seventy to small children three or four years old. On both sides of the road they stood, having turned out, as it seemed, for a funeral rather than to bid farewell. No one knew where they were off to; even they themselves did not know. They could not even answer the most pressing question of all: where were they going to put up for the night?

Of course, there were villagers who would sell their villas of their own free will. Beiqiang was one of them. Afflicted by back-aches and leg-aches, he needed help when walking but no one offered any, so he had to carefully edge forward against the wall or hobble on a walking stick. He was so thin that he looked distorted. However, he was more worried about his wife than himself. After they returned to Sakelu from the hospital, Lifang did nothing for a whole year except this: a stack of hospital bills in hand, she would wander away and disappear for days or even months. Their home was in a mess, and dust covered the desk, tea table and wardrobes like a flannel blanket. Spiders had woven webs in the cracks in the walls; lice crawled thickly in dirty clothes and quilts and sent off gusts of foul smell; and the corpse of that once cute white cat, which had starved to death half a year before, still lay under the bed. Sometimes Beiqiang summoned up the energy to get himself something to eat, but more often than not he went without food from morning to evening.

Xiaolin had called on Beiqiang several times. Every time he went he would bring Beiqiang some daily necessities he had purchased for him. Apart from Xiaolin, no one ever stepped over Beiqiang's threshold. Suffering on account of Liben's wickedness, Beiqiang naturally bore a grudge against him. Now, besides Beiqiang, all the people in Sakelu gnashed their teeth in hatred at the mere mention of Liben. Since they could not find him, they diverted their hatred toward Beiqiang and Lifang. Beiqiang could often hear insinuating curses from outside his windows, and he felt more acutely the repercussions of the small acts of others. Sometimes it was a worn-out shoe flying in through a window, sometimes it was an iron ladle head or a brickbat. The lock on his gate was damaged, and articles in his home often went missing for no good reason.

How could such a life go on? Not having money was bad enough. Worse was the mental disease from which he supposed Lifang had been suffering. Worse yet was that he and his family had to withstand all kinds of insults and threats. Beiqiang lost all hope in life. He had been so fearful of death, but today he was afraid of being alive. He made the effort of putting a nylon rope around his neck, only to find that he was too weak to hang it over the lintel of the door. And so he hesitated between life and death, not knowing which was better for him. There was a problem which would not leave him in peace: who would care for his daughter if he died? Who would care for Lifang? Rely on Liben? Was that not a sheep putting its faith in a wolf? His daughter had been sent to study abroad by Liben, and each time she called home Beiqiang had to tell her a pack of lies, about how healthy he and her mother were, how happy life at home was, etc. He cried; he cried at the thought of his daughter. When she returned home from abroad, was she supposed to find that her father had hanged himself and that her mother had gone mad?

Leaning on his walking stick, Beiqiang stumbled to the courtyard, where he caught sight of Langwa, who had now grown as tall as a corn stalk. A meal box in his right hand and a plastic bag with fried cakes in his left hand, Langwa was on his way to deliver a meal to his grandfather. Beiqiang shouted him to halt, and told him to pass on a message to his grandfather, to the effect that a man called Beiqiang wanted to see him and that he might make a trip to Beiqiang's home. Langwa did not say anything. He cast a glance at Beiqiang, his eyes full of trepidation as if he had seen a monster. He was so nervous that he fell prone on the ground, food scattering in all directions.

That night Fugui walked into Beiqiang's home; obviously Langwa had done his duty. Fugui did not take off his kasaya robe even after work. On arrival he could not help but yell in alarm, saying that Beiqiang's house was full of ghosts and was hardly suitable for any human being to live in. Look, there was a blue ghost hiding behind the door, a black one lying prone under the bed, a white one looking into the mirror in the bathroom, a green one gobbling a steamed bun with chili sauce in the kitchen. In total, there were over thirty ghosts in Beiqiang's home. Just now they were having a meeting, but one of them slipped out of the venue to hold Beiqiang in its arms. Their meeting, though, was disrupted by Fugui. They regarded Fugui as mice regarded cats. What was Fugui by profession? He was born to catch ghosts! Once they recognized him, which of them would not take to his heels at his approach? Why did those who had just gathered to listen to their leader flee when they saw him? Because they were afraid of him! Liu Qi used to boast in front of others that all the pigs knew him when he was a butcher. Fugui refused to be convinced, even if all Liu Qi's boasts were technically true. It was one thing to overcome simple-minded pigs. Liu Qi needed to catch a ghost in order to prove that he was really capable. The only thing that mattered was the ability to catch ghosts. Fugui firmly believed that he was the one endowed with that ability.

Fugui was right away seconded by Beiqiang, who thought he must be onto something, because he too could feel the presence of ghosts right at that moment. Perhaps it was because a certain ghost had crawled into his head that he felt headaches? Perhaps it was because a certain ghost had blown air down his back that he felt a chill all over it? Perhaps it was because a certain ghost had drawn his hamstrings that he felt weak in the legs? Perhaps it was because a certain ghost had scratched his armpits with long nails that he felt them itch? Good grief! It turned out that he had been living under the same roof with ghosts all the time. It was no wonder that he had been down on his luck all these years.

Fugui further explained that Beiqiang's house had been built on the grave of a pedlar, who remained one in the nether world. Wherever the pedlar went, a crowd of ghosts would follow to look on. As he no longer travelled from street to street, the pedlar slipped into Beiqiang's house and opened a supermarket which attracted ghosts, coming and going the whole time. Among the ghosts Fugui identified a familiar figure. "Guess who it is. Qiuli? No! Luobo? No! Dalin? No! Liu Qi? Yes, Liu Qi! Him and no one else!" A shameless man, Liu Qi had resumed his old trade as a butcher, killing pigs and selling pork. He looked monstrous, and often unzipped his pants to pee in the room. Just a sniff would tell you how strong the room smelled of urine! And whose was it, if not Liu Qi's odor?

"What should be done?" Beiqiang asked.

"Exorcise the ghosts!" Fugui replied.

"How?" Beiqiang asked.

"Very simple. Set fire to the house. The ghosts will either have to escape the raging flames or be burned to death!" Fugui replied.

87

Once more I encountered Zhao Xiaohui at the church. This time he was determined to be a believer. One does not need to perform any formalities to believe in God. Whoever believes in God may come here.

Zhao Xiaohui said that even Jiaoda, the Jia family's old servant in *A Dream of Red Mansions*, had lived a luckier life than his. It took him aback that Jiaoda believed the stone lions set in front of the entrance to the Jias'Mansions to be clean. He claimed that whenever he caught sight of a stone lion, he seemed to see all the dirty business it concealed, as if he were wearing x-ray glasses.

"Yes, dirty business is everywhere," Zhao Xiaohui exclaimed. "To a great extent, a person's rise or fall depends on it." Zhao Xiaohui asserted that as a person who hated such dealings, he had no choice but to give up playing the game.

In Xiaomao's dormitory — actually the commune dormitory which Xiaomao and I shared — Zhao Xiaohui looked very gloomy and his head hung low.

Xiaomao was comforting Zhao Xiaohui, to whom he said, "If you convert to God, you'll have nothing to agonize over; you will forgive this world and the various sorts of people who live in it." In Xiaomao's view, all the cheating and flattering people got up to, no matter if they were in business or in officialdom, were in essence done to make a wretched living; and these people's souls had been possessed by the Devil. However, they were unaware of this. They did not really know what they were doing.

Zhao Xiaohui claimed that, to be honest, he himself had never imagined he would end up in such a situation; that when he first came to the old people's home, he had indeed planned to run it well, and had paid no mind to the rumor that it was an ominous place. He began his tenure by hiring some vehicles to take the old people to the bath city to have a bath — they had not taken a bath for donkey's years. Bony and skinny though they all were, the lice wriggling in the seams of their clothes were exceptionally big and fat, so that their skins were spotted red on account of the bites, and quite a few of them had festering sores. After the bath, each of them was given two new suits of clothing: their old clothes were gathered together and buried. After having done this, Zhao Xiaohui headed for the county's civil affairs bureau to apply for funding.

Before he took over at the old people's home, it was already heavily in debt.

The first day he went to his new office, the creditors instantly surrounded him.

These creditors were owners of department stores, clinics and other firms, and each of them had a handful of IOUs in his hand. In addition, some former employees of the old people's home, of both sexes, rushed into his office clamoring their demands for overdue pay. Zhao Xiaohui sent for the accountant, who showed up to say that there were only eleven *yuan* on the account; and that these eleven *yuan* were there only to prevent the bank from closing the account.

The accountant complained that he had paid a number of bills for the old people's home from his personal funds; that right underneath the glass panel over his office table there were several IOUs signed over to him by the former warden.

What choice did Zhao Xiaohui have, but to pacify the debtors? He told them that he had just started and was not yet acquainted with the situation. He promised that when he knew what was going on, he would certainly pay the debts. "To pay off debt is a moral principle which no one should question," said Zhao Xiaohui. He promised he would keep his word.

The old people's bath and clothes had been paid for by Zhao Xiaohui out of his personal funds. But he did not have a lot of money saved. It appeared that funding had become a crucial issue for the old people's home — money was water, while the old folks were fish; without water the fish had but one prospect: death! Driven by the urgency of the situation, Zhao Xiaohui paid a visit to the county's civil affairs bureau, which was responsible for allotting funds. He hoped that the bureau could relieve him in his hour of need.

Director Hao of the bureau was older than Zhao Xiaohui by a couple of years. An acquaintance of Zhao Xiaohui's, he used to pat him on the shoulder and call him "brother," declaring that he had a brilliant career ahead of him, and predicting that in eight or ten years' time he would probably rise to the office currently occupied by Zhang Shutian, and that when that day came, Zhao Xiaohui would reign supreme. "Every dog has his day, as the old saying goes," he said. "An obscure and tiny reptile today may well turn into an enormous python tomorrow."

But once Zhao Xiaohui was appointed to run the old people's home, Director Hao's behaviour changed dramatically in his regard. His face seemed changed, as in a slide show, when a new picture replaces the last. When he encountered Zhao Xiaohui on the street, Director Hao even pretended not to know him. When he was accosted by Zhao Xiaohui, instead of looking him in the face, he looked upward and muttered a reluctant "eh" in sign of recognition.

So now when Zhao Xiaohui went to see Director Hao for funding, he naturally received no encouragements from him. Director Hao complained, saying that Zhao Xiaohui's precursors had all been ungrateful; that none of them had understood the rules of the game. He asked Zhao Xiaohui sarcastically, "What do you want the money for? Didn't you have a knack for obtaining funds? You even know the son of the provincial governor, so why are you pretending to be in penury? What's your purpose in coming to the civil affairs bureau to cry about how hard up you are?"

Naturally, Zhao Xiaohui refuted all this energetically. Their voices grew increasingly loud, and their arguments became increasingly explosive. Director Hao patted his palm on the office table, and in a fit of anger, he grabbed his mug off the table and dashed it at Zhao Xiaohui, who dodged instinctively. Pang! The mug hit the glass panel of a book cabinet, so that it shattered and fell in pieces onto the floor.

Having beaten a hasty retreat from Director Hao's office, Zhao Xiaohui returned to the old people's home. He felt extremely gloomy, as though he were imprisoned in an airless room made of iron: he had difficulty in breathing, as though he were about to suffocate. He spent a sleepless night. The following morning, no sooner had he entered the portal of the old people's home than the mobile phone tucked into his waist began ringing. The caller was the secretary of the county's discipline inspection commission. The secretary confidently asserted that Zhao Xiaohui had beaten up Director Hao.

When responding to the secretary's accusation, Zhao Xiaohui did not soften his voice at all. Instead, he interrogated the secretary, "How did you come to this conclusion without an in-depth investigation? On what grounds do you claim that I, Zhao Xiaohui, have beaten up Director Hao?"

The secretary accused Zhao Xiaohui of slandering him. "How can you say we haven't conducted any investigation?" the secretary asked. He said that the commission would never permit one official to do violence to another official with impunity. "What a wicked thing for the director to be beaten up in his own office!" the secretary exclaimed.

According to the secretary, the discipline inspection commission had taken immediate action; they had set up a special team to investigate the case thoroughly. The secretary claimed that it had already carried out an on-the-spot investigation and taken note of eye-witness testimony; that all the eye witnesses had testified to the fact that Zhao Xiaohui had beaten up their director. Months later, Zhao Xiaohui learned from a vice director of the civil affairs bureau that anyone who testified that Zhao Xiaohui had beaten Director Hao was given a bonus of one thousand *yuan*. Under these circumstances, who would scruple to take the money?

On the phone, the secretary ordered that Zhao Xiaohui present himself at once to the discipline inspection commission for interrogation. But instead of going to the discipline inspection commission, Zhao Xiaohui came to Yuebei. His original intent had been to go and see Xiang Wenhua. However, since Xiang Wenhua was otherwise engaged, their meeting was postponed for one or two days. Without any other place to go, Zhao Xiaohui came to the church.

To our surprise, while conversing with us, Zhao Xiaohui expressed his admiration for Liu Qi. He said, "If Liu Qi hadn't committed murder, no one would have dared to do anything to him. In this world, everyone picks a weaker person to bully. If you seek to act the gentleman, or to win people over with your good sense, or to play games according to the rules, you will end up fermenting bitter wine for yourself!"

"Do you think I have no idea how officialdom works?" Zhao Xiaohui continued. "Actually, I'm pretty familiar with the text and the tone of bureaucratic theatre. But I just can't bring myself to play along. Even under threat of death, I still couldn't bring myself to do that! On the whole, I attribute it to the over-tender heart I inherited from my parents."

Quite naturally, Zhao Xiaohui mentioned the volatility of Kaiyang officialdom. He said that some delegates from the province's discipline inspection commission had come down and talked with the county secretary of the Party committee Zhang Shutian, who was serving his fourth term in office. The general view was that Zhang Shutian did not have many more easy days ahead.

According to Zhao Xiaohui, such rumors had been rife in the county town for a while, and people had been heatedly discussing the matter. Those who used to cling to Zhang Shutian were in a panic; they turned as one man and formed ranks around the county magistrate. They employed two methods to please him: one was to visit him at his house with no delay, and the other was to condemn Zhang Shutian with harsh words. One rumor claimed that it was solely thanks to the county magistrate's secret machinations that Zhang Shutian had been targeted by the province's discipline inspection commission. Even idiots knew that the two leading officials had been at odds — Zhang Shutian had rendered the county magistrate as futile as the ears of a deaf person. Consequently, the county magistrate had mobilized all the forces he could summon, and had tried every means in his power to push down Zhang Shutian. Zhang Shutian was condemned as an outrageous grafter who had not even hesitated to turn a profit from the construction of a public toilet. He was also denounced as a lecher — the proof being that a whore-like opera actress had been promoted again and again, and in no time had become a vice director of a bureau, for no other reason than that she had established a connection with Zhang Shutian.

"And further evidence of Zhang Shutian's lechery is his affair with the adulterous Jidan," Zhao Xiaohui went on. "Jidan is half illiterate. In a public speech she delivered, she mispronounced 'Terra-cotta Army Figures' as 'Terra-cutter Army Figures.' However Jidan was once seen sitting flirtatiously on Zhang Shutian's lap during work hours. But that did not stop her putting on a grand air whenever she preached spiritual civilization to other people. It was like a madam in a brothel preaching virginity. How funny it was! What great irony!"

With regard to Jidan, Zhao Xiaohui had a long story to divulge. His facial expression looked so odd that you could not tell whether he was laughing or crying. He said that on the third day at his job in the old people's home, Jidan paid a visit. She brought two men along with her, one carrying a copper sign board, the other a hammer. Without entering the gate, they set about nailing the board engraved with words "Advanced Hygiene Unit" onto the top of the gate frame. After they had put the sign up, the two men left, while Jidan stepped into the courtyard and came to Zhao Xiaohui's office. In a straightforward way, she told Zhao Xiaohui that since his assumption of the present office he had done an excellent job, and as a result the old people's home had been nominated an Advanced Hygiene Unit. If he would be so kind as to go to the portal and take a look, he would find that this was true: the honor plate had been hung up. And the next thing Zhao Xiaohui ought to do was pay up the money! Of course, in view of the fact that Zhao Xiaohui had once worked as the head of Gaotai Township and had been a friend of her father's, she would do him a favor and demand two thousand *yuan* only, while all the others were required to pay three thousand *yuan*.

Zhao Xiaohui, taken aback, ran to the portal to have a look. Indeed, the sign was up there!

"Why have you raised the price?" Zhao Xiaohui asked. "I heard it cost one thousand *yuan*."

Jidan wore an air of self-satisfaction, and claimed that the increase in the charge reflected her good performance in her job. She said that as a newly appointed director, she would be despised if she failed to achieve something. But what kind of achievement? The most important kind, of course, was to increase the money the department made. But how could that happen without increasing the price of the sign boards?

Zhao Xiaohui said, "I have no money for that! Please remove the plate!"

The smile on Jidan's face withered instantly. In an angry voice, she said, "The plate has been put up! By no means shall it be removed! If you have the money, pay now! If you do not have the money, borrow and pay now!" Jidan added that she was determined to procure the money by any means necessary!

Looking determined and grave, Zhao Xiaohui said he was serious — he really couldn't raise the money; even if Jidan threatened to take his life, he still couldn't raise the money.

Seeing that Zhao Xiaohui's attitude was growing tougher, Jidan softened. Suddenly she changed tack — she began to speak in a coaxing voice; she called Zhao Xiaohui "Old Brother Zhao." With her fleshy hands she patted Zhao Xiaohui on the back, pinched his cheeks, claimed that she had been in love with him for many years, but that she had never had the courage to express her admiration for him, on account of the huge gulf between them. But in her mind, she said, Zhao Xiaohui was her Mr. Right: what a glittering treasure he was in her mind!

When she saw that her coquetry did not work, she started to cry. She cried so bitterly that she knocked her head against the door frame. Her cries attracted the attention of the old folks, who came, in twos and threes, to see what was going on. Some of the old people reproached Zhao Xiaohui, saying, "How can a big man like you bully a slip of a girl like this?"

Seeing he was cornered, Zhao Xiaohui agreed to what Jidan had asked for. As he had no cash at his disposal, he had to write her an IOU.

88

Zhao Xiaohui was bent on obtaining an audience with Xiang Wenhua.

"Whast for?" I asked.

"First, to get funding for the old people's home. Second, to seek a powerful protector."

According to Zhao Xiaohui, a protector was indispensable for anyone wishing to take a single step forward in society. Even if a protector could not propel you like a rocket does a satellite, he could at least extinguish fires for you. People in the world were quick to adjust their reaction to you. When you were down they pretended that they had never known you, whereas when you were prosperous they came in droves to cosy up to you, calling you brother, or even claiming that you were a relative, no matter how distant! If you did not have a protector, a problem the size of a sesame seed could be manipulated by your enemies so that it would ferment and expand like a hot air balloon at their disposition; and that seemingly sesame-seed-sized problem could easily transform into a bullet aimed straight at your heart, and destroy you instantly. However, with a protector standing behind you, things would be different, and a problem as big as the sky could be nullified. A phone call from your protector could make a withered tree come into leaf, a cycas tree blossom, a dumb man speak, in short, the impossible possible.

I asked Zhao Xiaohui if he still wished to stay in officialdom. Zhao Xiaohui said that he did not know what he should do. Before him was a high wall, behind him a steep cliff, above his head an iron cap, and below his feet a knife's edge. There was only one place left which still looked welcoming, but when he came near he found that it was a grave of livid aspect, gaping like a fanged mouth. He told me that Xiang Wenhua was the last straw for him, and that what he was doing could be termed either "trying his luck," or "kicking his last."

However, Xiang Wenhua immediately rejected Zhao Xiaohui's invitation. He hung up before Zhao Xiaohui could finish his words. Embarrassed, Zhao Xiaohui said he wondered if he had offended Xiang Wenhua in some way. He pondered for ages without figuring out anything. I took out my phone and dialed Xiang Wenhua's number. To my surprise, Xiang Wenhua's attitude toward me was very positive; he even made brief jokes with me, saying that he would like to put some time aside to treat me to tea, so that we could reminisce over the good old days in the press house. He said he was sick of his present life. Surrounded by hypocrites and worked on by crafty people, he found that the life he was currently living could not be more tedious.

It seemed that Xiang Wenhua was in a good mood, so I lost no time telling him that Zhao Xiaohui wanted to see him, and it was my hope that he could offer him a little help. Unexpectedly, Xiang Wenhua opposed an absolute veto. He said he would not see anyone from Kaiyang County. When I asked him why, Xiang rebuked me bitterly, saying that I was the reason that he and his father first began their association with the Kaiyang people — an association which had caused deep harm to both of them. I asked what specific harm there had been. Xiang Wenhua did not disclose it, saying only that he would tell me when we met.

Three days later, helpless Zhao Xiaohui left in disappointment, but I met Xiang Wenhua. He kept to his bed in a hotel, absent from work on the pretext that he was sick. He was exhausted — utterly exhausted — and yawned at the mere thought of a pillow, but when he did go to bed, he had difficulty in falling asleep. So he thought of me, and called me for a chat.

Wrapped in furry white pyjamas, Xiang Wenhua greeted me at the door with a big yawn. The moment I stepped into his room, he set out the parameters of our chat: no talking about serious matters; instead, we should stick to gossip concerning neither of us, such as funny anecdotes about the relationship between men and women. As instructed, I told him a joke about circumcision in an African tribe, but found that he was not amused. I went on with a rather blue joke, when I suddenly heard snorts from him, thick and thin. He seemed to have fallen asleep leaning on the sofa, his head tilted to one side. Forty or fifty minutes later, he opened his drowsy eyes and asked why I had stopped telling stories. I asked who would listen while he was sleeping? Xiang Wenhua looked rather surprised, then denied that he had been sleeping. He said that he had been listening all the time, only that I had suspended my narration.

Back from the toilet, Xiang Wenhua seemed to have forgotten the conditions that he had set, and diverted the conversation to serious matters. He said I did not know that Kaiyang and Sakelu were two major sources of his headaches. Or more exactly, they were not the sources of his own headaches, but of his father's. It was his father's headaches that were the cause of his own. Was it wrong for his father, as a governor, to inspect Sakelu?

No! Was it wrong for his father, a friendly governer, to have pictures taken with people when they asked for that favor? No! However, the devil is in the detail: a small picture taken with the villagers had brought a sea of troubles to his father. On the strength of this picture his father was accused of backing a fraudster. One man from Sakelu named Song something-or-other — "Song Tongguo," I supplemented — had made use of a picture taken with his father to raise money, and the number of defrauded investors came to three to four hundred. When Song Tongguo ran away with the money, these victims gathered to block the gateway to the provincial government courtyard, demanding an audience with his father. They carried streamers, shouted slogans, distributed leaflets, and did not balk at attacking and slandering his father. Imagine the fatal damage to his father's good name! His father ordered the public security department to track down and catch the fraudster and made arrangements to pacify the victims, but petition letters still flew to Beijing.

Hardly had the first wave retreated when a new one broke. By the time the billowy sea of protest raised by the fraudster's victims had subsided, groups of Sakelu residents had crowded into the petition office of the provincial government. As if abetted by some conspirator, each of these folks had a picture taken with Governor Xiang in his pocket. After they had tearfully finished telling their stories, they would kneel down in the square in front of the provincial government compound, holding aloft their pictures taken with Governor Xiang. Those who did not know the truth would naturally attribute the suffering of the villagers to Governor Xiang. Alas, what a tough job it was to be a governor! With no one to share the misery of his heart with, the governor could only swallow his own broken teeth, so to speak. Xiang Wenhua said that he felt sorry whenever he saw his father, a man who had been afflicted with a hundred and one diseases but could hardly find time to lie in the hospital for a few days, and who occasionally sighed how much he envied watermelon vendors on the roadside. Xiang Wenhua believed that his father was telling the truth rather than groaning about an imaginary illness.

I was as much stunned to hear Xiang Wenhua mention the self-immolation of a certain villager, as I would have been by a blow to the head from a hard club. The one who had burned himself was from Sakelu. He was apparently disabled in the leg, always limping on a crutch as he walked. Reports from the public security bureau of Kaiyang County said that he had a mental disorder. Yes, his wife also had a mental disorder! He had set a fire to his villa before he came to immolate himself in Yuebei. He died an ugly death.

I enquired if the man who had burned himself bore the name of Beiqiang. Xiang Wenhua replied that he did not know what he was called, and that he did not care who he was; but he was clear that the man was disgusting. After a pause, Xiang Wenhua muttered that the man seemed to be a relative of Tian Liben. "It must be Beiqiang, Liben's brother-in-law," I shouted. "But how could he have done such a senseless thing? I heard that his wife had become a mental invalid, but never that he was!" I kept silent for a long time before I was able to pluck up courage enough to ask Xiang Wenhua what had become of the man who had burned himself.

"He died! What else?" Xiang Wenhua said coldly.

89

Meiteng had completely stopped production — as I heard from Xiaolin. He had proposed a meeting with me in a park in Yuebei. Like a spy coming to meet his contact, I identified him in the depths of a wooded area. The birds' chirpings sounded remarkably loud in those otherwise silent environs. Looking out through the cracks between the trees, I saw many pairs of lovers near and far — some were hugging each other, some were lying entangled on the ground.

After handing me a cigarette, Xiaolin chainsmoked nonstop. He puffed one gust of heavy smoke after another. The smoke blurred his features from time to time.

"Anything gone wrong lately?" I asked him.

Xiaolin did not react to my question until I had asked him several times. He heaved an abrupt sigh, then fell into prolonged silence again.

Losing my patience, I urged him, "Whatever the matter is, just speak up! Don't waste time."

After his lips had opened and closed repeatedly many times, Xiaolin eventually said that he was being pursued by the public security police.

Astonished, I asked, "How come?"

Shaking his head, he told me he had been suspected of playing a role in Song Tongguo's fraud. Song Tongguo had asked him to collect the money which had been raised, and Song Tongguo's chauffeur, who was now in prison, denounced him as an accomplice. That was why the province's public security bureau had issued a notice, ordering public security officers across the province to spare no effort to capture him. This time he would not escape jail. Even if he grew wings, he could hardly fly far enough away.

"Has Song Tongguo's whereabouts been discovered?" I asked.

"No, so far there's no news about his whereabouts," Xiaolin replied.

Xiaolin told me that somehow Song Tongguo had managed to transfer thirty million *yuan* out of Meiteng's bank account. The subsequent disruption of Meiteng's funding had resulted in the complete stoppage of production. Although the machines had ceased to roar, and the chimneys had ceased to vomit smoke, the firm's administrative office was still busy. Actually it was tumultuous in there. The American share-holders sued the Chinese shareholder, holding the Chinese shareholder responsible for his poor supervision as well as for his improper appointment of Song Tongguo to the manager's post. As the two parties were sorting out the accounts, physical violence broke, despite the presence of lawyers. Meiteng's courtyard had offered a more chaotic scene. It was fully packed with people. The workers, whose pay was overdue, seemed to be rioting. They sequestered the car owned by the chairman of the board; they took away anything they thought had value — the machines were dismantled, with load upon load of iron parts transported by tricycle to reclamation depots to be recycled; the two gorgeous stone lions at the factory gate were nowhere to be seen now; the landscape trees had either been uprooted and taken away, or chopped off in the middle. Together with the workers were some former business partners who had supplied Meiteng with raw materials. They thumped their chests and stamped their feet in frustration, for Meiteng owed them enormous sums. They denounced Meiteng, cursed Meiteng, and vowed they would fight to the end even though it would mean their common ruin.

Xiaolin asserted that various factors had contributed to Meiteng's failure, for which Song Tongguo was not wholly responsible, though he had indeed aggravated the situation and delivered the fatal blow; that before Song Tongguo precipitated the disaster, crisis was already looming. First of all, given that Meiteng had bribed Zhang Shutian, it did not have a moment's peace once Zhang Shutian was sent to prison. The new county secretary of the Party committee adopted a circumspect attitude with respect to this matter, as if it were an epidemic disease which would doom whoever came into contact with it. Moreover, since Zhang Shutian had been wearing Meiteng like a shining silver costume to show off his own face to advantage, the last thing the new secretary wanted to do was add brilliance to such a costume. He would rather promote his own fame by setting up a new project. As a matter of fact, he had been focusing his attention on a newly introduced Thai joint-venture.

According to Xiaolin, even an insignificant electrician had been able to inflict unbearable pain on Meiteng. Every time he came to Meiteng, the electrician put on the angry face of an infuriated king. He would cut off the electricity as he pleased, leaving Meiteng no option but to suspend its production work from time to time. The electrician claimed that he had been infuriated by Meiteng's decision not to entrust him with the circuit installation project. Additionally, Meiteng was ignorant about established practice and was exceedingly stingy; only when he threw the circuit break — and this made him even more fuirious — did Meiteng think to give him a few insignificant gifts, such as a carton of cigarettes, or a flat red-envelope — when he opened the envelope, he found a single Old Man Portrait bill[41]. "Buh!" the electrician muttered complainingly. "Meiteng calls itself the No.1 big company in Kaiyang, but how mean-spirited it is — as tiny as a shot glass! How miserly its gifts are. This amount is as inconsiderable as mosquito shit. The amount is minuscule! What a loss of face!"

What had irritated the electrician even more was that Meiteng had reported him to the county's electricity supply bureau! "What's the fucking use of reporting me?" he shouted. "If I didn't have connections in the electricity supply bureau, how could I have got the job in the first place?"

Xiaolin admitted that popular repugnance at Meiteng's pollution was also a factor which could not be ignored. The inhabitants in the neighboring villages never ceased complaining and petitioning. Their letters of complaint flew hither and thither, and eventually caught the attention of the national environmental preservation bureau, which ordered the provincial environmental preservation bureau to investigate the problem and deal with it. The provincial environmental preservation bureau, in turn, glued seal badges to one after another of Meiteng's workshops. To tell the truth, Meiteng resembled a huge structure built on sand; its collapse was inevitable. What had surprised people was that the collapse should have come so rapidly.

Xiaolin said he was going to give himself up to the public security bureau. The scariest thing was the quite unbearable life he would have to lead in prison. His greatest anxiety was that he might be sent back to the farm where he had been before. If that happened, he sincerely feared that Song Laowan would molest him once more! If Song Laowan still worked there, did he have any chance of coming out alive?

"Does Song Laowan still work in that farm?" Xiaolin asked me.

"I have no idea," I said. "As far as I know, Dalin was thinking about doing away with him. As for what came of it, I know nothing. "

"Have you received any money from Song Tongguo?" I asked Xiaolin. "If you haven't, why should you give yourself up to the police?"

Xiaolin lowered his head, which seemed weighed to the earth. He did not answer me. When he finally looked up, I saw that his face was wet with tears.

"What's wrong?" I asked.

Unable to control his emotions any longer, Xiaolin sobbed. Then his sobbing gave way to full-throated wailing. After a long while, he pulled himself together, and said that if he had received any money, he would not have felt so immensely wronged — on the contrary, he would have felt he deserved all he got!

"If I had got money, wouldn't I have used it to pay for my mother's medical treatment?" he asked. He told me that to procure the insignificant sum of three thousand *yuan* for his mother's medical treatment, he had been compelled to sell the villa house for a knock-down price to Shuanhu, who was so pleased with the transaction that his face erupted into broad smiles.

Xiaolin told me Third Aunt was dying. Having no home of her own after the villa was sold, Third Aunt had been taken to her nephew's place. She was housed in a place he felt too shameful to reveal to anyone. You could call *that place* a cattle pen or a pigsty: initially it had been used as a family cattle pen, but after the cattle were sold, it served as the family pigsty. In order to make room for Third Aunt, her nephew had been obliged to sell two piglets cheap.

According to Xiaolin, it was obvious that Third Aunt was hopelessly ill. At one moment, she seemed to be in this world, and at the next, in the nether world. She kept murmuring a sequence of names which Xiaolin could not grasp. Only when she called Dalin's name did Xiaolin see some light shining out of her gloomy eyes.

Xiaolin told me that when he first retired from military service, he looked forward yearningly. He aspired to fly like an eagle, soaring in the blue skies. Alas! Who on earth could have imagined he would end up a wretched chicken! A chicken whose feathers had been completely plucked out!

"Is this what I call *my life*? Is this what I came into this world for?" Xiaolin convulsed with rage, tears in his eyes.

I wished I could comfort him. But what could I say? I chose to be silent; I just smoked one cigarette after another.

Xiaolin entreated me to do two things for him — he said that was why he had asked me to come here. The first thing was: if Third Aunt passed away during his imprisonment, I should take care of her funeral and interment; her coffin and clothes for that occasion had been prepared and were laid aside in Fugui's house. Xiaolin told me that Third Aunt owned a silver bracelet; it was part of her dowry and one of her fondest belongings. She treasured it so much that she had worn it only once — and that was on her wedding day. After that, she never wore it again, not even on her birthdays, when she only took it out to feel it with tender love. Xiaolin told me that the bracelet, along with Third Aunt's mourning portrait, had also been laid aside in Fugui's house.

The second thing Xiaolin entreated me to do was the following: if he were wrongly sentenced to jail, he hoped I would hire a lawyer to plead his innocence. He said that despite the injustice done to him, he firmly believed that the truth would ultimately come to light; that the law would do him justice; that his good name would be restored.

I gave him my promise to help.

Rising to his feet, Xiaolin said he was leaving to surrender himself to the police right away; that the existence of a fugitive was too agonizing.

The last rays of the sun were penetrating through the branches and leaves, and fell on Xiaolin's back. Seeing his vanishing figure, grievous waves of indignation suddenly began to sweep over my mind.

Xiaolin staggered ahead, limping forward like a drunk.

90

Inexplicably, Liben's phone call occasioned a feeling of happiness in me. Was he not the theatre director who had put on first one play in Mazi Village and then another in Sakelu Park? Although late on the scene, he might still, if he used all his strength, be able to turn the tide, transform base metal into gold, and save Sakelu from the ignominy of complete collapse. However, my happiness disappeared once he told me that he was sick and in the fifth ward of the medical university hospital.

The fifth ward was a big one, somewhat like a dormitory for migrant workers. Spacious as a classroom, it was tightly packed with twenty beds and crowded with patients, carers and visitors. What a chaotic scene! Patients, men and women, young or old, were groaning here or howling there, while nurses shouted reproaches in through the door from time to time.

Liben was curled up rather forlornly at a corner near the window. He was on a drip, with a worn-out look on his face. Flakes of whitewash dropped from the cracked walls from time to time. Two spiders were crawling about in a web in the corner. Something dirty had condensed on the window panes so that the image of what was outside became a mottled blur.

Liben said his disease was not a serious one: it was only a gastric ulcer, from which he would recover after two days of intravenous injections. I asked how he could live in such an environment. He said that this ward was cheap and that the beds cost only two *yuan* each day, that the patients were either farmers or urban paupers, who paid little and were naturally repaid with poor service. He had to swallow hard and repeatedly before he could tell me why he had phoned me. He wanted me to advance him some money for his medical bills.

I asked him if he had really been reduced to such poverty. Looking embarrassed, he said that he was in temporary difficulties, and that everything would be all right once he was out of hospital. He revealed that he was negotiating a new project, and once he secured it he would not have to worry about money again. I asked why he had disappeared for nearly a year. No one could find him. Where had he been? Liben said he had been in the United States lobbying for Sakelu's future, hoping that he could secure financial aid through an international relief fund, but unfortunately he came back empty handed. I said that countless people were looking for him, and that everybody missed him. A smile played round the corners of his mouth. He said, "Really? Am I that important?"

Naturally, Liben asked about Sakelu. Had the road to the outside world been built? Had the drainage pipeline been laid? Were the disputes with the neighboring village on their way to being resolved? And so on and so forth. I urged him to take care of himself first of all, and he could make a trip to Sakelu after he was out of hospital, and then he would know and understand everything. With a sigh, he said that he felt intense sorrow for Kang Yuanyuan. How could she have died so unexpectedly? She had been preparing to build a school in Sakelu. He said it was a pity that all her good will was gone with the wind, and that the Sakelu kids had to go to school in the neighboring village. However, things would change, if only gradually. He had contacted an NGO in Australia who showed great interest in Sakelu after receiving the photos he had taken. They arranged for an Australian newspaper to give him a full-page special interview. An obscure man in China and in the United States, he had acquired a name in Australia, where children wrote to him, women presented flowers to him, and old couples applauded him. When he checked his mailbox, thousands of letters flew out to greet him, most of which cheered him on, though a minority expressed doubts about the existence of Sakelu. The Australian NGO wanted to cooperate with him in order to set up Sakelu as an international example.

Liben's intermittent narration sounded absurd to me. Like a somnambulist, he seemed to be in the grip of unrealistic fantasies. I did not think that he was aware of the present state of Sakelu, but I did not want to shatter his dream. On the contrary, I was happy for him to live in his dream forever, so I interrupted him and changed the subject, leaving him still intoxicated by his delusions about Sakelu's prospects.

I talked about religion. I asked Liben if God and His paradise really existed? Liben replied that he firmly believed in God and Paradise. He said he believed that human beings were God's creations. When that Darwin guy claimed human beings had descended from monkeys he was obviously talking nonsense. What a ridiculous thing to say! How could this idea have been accepted by so many people? A little thought could debunk the theory. If Darwin was correct, the monkeys we saw should all look different, with some still monkeys with short tails and red buttocks, while others should be endowed with a few human features; some, further on the evolutionary road, should be on the frontier between monkeys and human beings; and, finally, some should be near to human beings, albeit with some monkey characteristics still detectable. But what was the real situation? They were two distinct types of animals without anything in common, like vehicles running on two different tracks. That human beings had descended from monkeys was something that even pigs would not believe, but many foolish people would! In spite of that, in the eyes of God, these foolish people had merely been led astray, and were worthy of sympathy.

I said that I doubted human beings had evolved from monkeys, but I also doubted that human beings had been God's creation. There was no evidence showing that human beings had evolved from monkeys. Was there any evidence showing that human beings had been God's work? In my opinion, human beings had evolved from nothing other than but human beings. Given that the Earth was a planet suitable for various species to exist, it was no wonder that thousands of species of life came into being, among which were tailless human beings. In the process of evolution, human beings became increasingly clever, increasingly nimble, increasingly sly and more villainous. Once they became masters of the earth, they revealed their brutal nature and exploited other forms of life to the utmost, keeping only those which could be put to use, such as cows for farming, mules for carrying loads, cuckoos to announce the harvest, crickets to satisfy man's lust for merry-making…and they killed without mercy those animals who got in their way. As a result, a large number of species died out, and those left over were on the brink of extinction.

I was just getting engrossed in my own speech when I felt someone pat me on the back. I turned to find that it was Liben's neighbor signaling me to be quiet. Lying on the neighboring bed was a little boy who had just had an operation, and he was still unconscious on account of the anesthesia. All sorts of rubber tubes in his nose and mouth revealed how serious his condition was. The boy's mother, in old clothes and with a haggard face, was sobbing on the edge of the sickbed. She tried hard not to cry out loud, but the handkerchief in her hand became so wet that it looked as if it had just been picked out of water.

It was the boy's father who had patted me on the back. His eyes were dull and his face emaciated. A piece of cardboard beside him aroused my interest. There was some string attached to it, so it was obviously meant to hang somewhere. A surreptitious glimpse at it revealed it to be full of poorly-written characters; it turned out to be an SOS message, bewailing that their child's lung cancer had used up the family's last cent, and that having borrowed from every single relative, they were now forced to appeal to the kindness of passers-by for help.

I tried to talk to the boy's father, but he had hardly spoken a few words before he burst into tears. He told me that he would go begging in the streets every day with the board hanging around his neck. He would kneel down on the sidewalk, constantly kowtowing to people as they went to and fro. However, due to the proliferation of so many fake beggars, people were increasingly indifferent, so his net profit was not much, hardly more than one hundred *yuan* a day. What could be done with one hundred *yuan* in the hospital? It was not even enough for a small bottle of intravenous medicine! They had no choice but to sell their house. Then the boy's maternal uncle sold his house too, and with his contribution they managed to chip in enough money for the boy's operation. The boy ought to have been wheeled into the ICU after the operation, but was forced to stay here because there was no more money left.

I asked where the boy was from, and his father said that he was from Kaiyang. I shuddered, then hurriedly asked him which part of the county he was from. "Gaotai Township" was the surprising answer. I had no courage to press on, afraid that the names "Mazi" or "Sakelu" might come out of his mouth. But though I stopped asking questions, the boy's father did not end his account. He said a rubber factory named Meiteng had been built in the neighboring village, resulting in unprecedented pollution in his own. The fields yielded much less grain, and in the little that was harvested toxins were found! Many villagers fell ill, and three suffered from various forms of cancer, his son being the youngest. He was brimming with hatred. He hated Meiteng. He hated the man who had introduced Meiteng — this wolf! — into their land. He was so full of hatred that it made him grind his teeth loudly! How he wished he could kill them with a knife or an axe!

I consoled him, after which I turned away, not saying anything. This conversation between us had all been picked up by Liben, so his face congested into a high pink. I sent for the nurse, and after she had changed bottles for Liben, I went to the bank to withdraw some money. I put some money on his hospital account, and took leave of him, urging him to be cooperative; then

I left the hospital.

I did not expect that Liben would so soon follow me out of the hospital. When he called to tell me, I was completely shocked. I asked him why he left the hospital. Since the hospital fee had been paid, what need was there for him to slip out of the hospital? Liben started tripping over his tongue, as he told me that he had just donated the money which I had transferred to him to…none other than the little boy in mortal need of money. The little boy was in danger of his life, but he was not. He only had to bear a little pain in the stomach, which would perhaps soon get better. "Do you remember that when we were small, we used to bear discomfort stoically when we got sick, didn't we?" Liben asked.

I swallowed the reproaches which he so richly merited, such as that he should not donate the money I had given him on any pretext whatsoever. At any rate, he had spent that money on saving life rather than doing wicked deeds. What's more, the little boy came from my hometown, and he was so pitiful.

Liben told me how ashamed he had been. He said that when he heard the father's words and saw the mother's tears, his heart was torn apart. He wished that he could tell them the truth and confess to them that he was the man they hated, but he did not have the nerve. As to whether the little boy's disease had anything to do with Meiteng's pollution, that was another matter; but one thing was certain — Liben would do his utmost to save him.

91

Once again, Liben disappeared. I did not know what had happened to him until two months later. He was in hospital again.

Unlike his last hospitalization, which had been due to a gastric ulcer problem, this time it was cerebral hematoma – the result of the beating he got when he revisited Sakelu.

He had gone to Sakelu alone, without informing anyone beforehand. When he got there, he was taken aback by what he saw: two bulldozers, like roaring monsters, were pulling the villas to the ground. Many villas had been completely demolished, leaving piles of debris on the ground; some villas had been reduced to broken walls, in danger of collapsing at any moment; a very few villas still stood as they had done. Some strangers, both male and female, were delving among the debris, searching for recyclable bricks, broken wooden planks, ragged clothes, and so forth.

"What's going on here? What has happened? Where have the villagers gone?" This was sequence of questions which occurred to Liben. He asked the scavenging people, but they either said "I don't know" or simply shook their heads. After stopping a bulldozer, Liben eventually learned that the machines had been hired by Shuanhu.

"What right does Shuanhu have to chase the villagers out of their houses? What right does he have to pull down these villas?" Liben shouted. In great anger, he commanded that the bulldozers instantly desist from this savage deed. But would the drivers listen to him? They only listened to those who hired them and paid them.

They said to themselves, "Who is this guy that comes from who knows where? Is he asking for a good hiding? What right does he have to stop us from carrying out the work?"

Liben was burning with anger. The two bulldozer drivers were burning with anger, too. They had contracted to do the job, and whoever stopped them doing it was preventing them from making money. Naturally, neither their words nor demeanour were pleasant.

Seeing a stranger standing in front of his bulldozer and attempting to block it, one of the drivers shut down his machine and picked up an iron handle. He was about to hit Liben on the head.

From past experience, the driver knew that this trick would be effective. A number of people had previously attempted to stop them from getting on with their work, but every time he picked up the iron handle, people became timid, and their legs turned to rubber. The soft are afraid of the hard. The hard are afraid of the brutal. The brutal are afraid of the desperate. Is there anyone who does not take his own life seriously? Threatened, nine people out of ten shielded their heads with their arms and fled as fast as possible. Only very few wanted to see which was harder, their heads or the iron handle. "Aha, you want pain, then you'll get it — you just wait!" the bulldozer driver thought to himself.

Of course, before the driver hit an intruder on the head, he calculated the force he would use, so that the victim would feel unbearable pain but not suffer permanent damage. Were he to exert his full strength, the thick, hard, crooked iron piece would definitely cause the victim's blood to spill in all directions, like a watermelon hit by an iron hammer.

As expected, the sight of the up-lifted handle frightened Liben. He became deathly pale. He stepped backward, and said he would go and see Shuanhu. The driver could not care less about whom the guy would go and see; all he wanted was for the trouble-maker to leave the site. Looking at Liben's retreating back, the driver laughed with self-satisfaction.

Putting away the handle, the driver returned whistling to his engine booth seat. The bulldozer rumbled and sprang back to life, and another wall was shoveled to the ground, to the accompaniment of a renewed roar from the engine. The collapse of the wall caused a loud noise and waves of dust.

Liben wanted to see Shuanhu. But it was no easy matter. Shuanhu ran his business in his inner office room. In the outer room, which served as the reception space, all the sofas were occupied by people waiting to see him.

Once inside the reception room, everyone who wanted to see Shuanhu was required to sign in a registration book. Then the receptionist would go into the inner room to ask Shuanhu whether he would receive the visitor or not. If Shuanhu nodded his head, the receptionist would issue a number to the person and instruct them to wait for their turn.

The door to the inner room was guarded by two sturdily-built bodyguards, one on either side. One of them was especially eye catching. For one thing, his hair was dyed orange. For another thing, his hairstyle resembled a turkey standing arrogantly atop his head, dominating the clean-shaven skin surrounding it.

The reception room was pretty spacious and luxurious. All sorts of people were to be seen waiting in the room: there were aged, even senile, people as well as seventeen or eighteen years olds; there were well groomed people as well as a few raggedly dressed ones; there were people in western style suits, in government official-style costumes, in the industry & commerce administration officer's uniform, as well as in the police uniform. It was very quiet despite the fact that there were thirty or forty people in the room: some were reading newspapers, some were dozing, and some were engaged in their own thoughts. Only occasionally did sporadic coughs break the quietness.

After helping Liben register, the girl receptionist went into the inner room with his personal information. To Liben's surprise, Shuanhu refused to see him. This refusal came in a pretty mild manner: he claimed that he was very busy now, and that if Liben would be so kind as to wait, he could come back to see him in three days' time, but that if Liben didn't have the patience to wait three days, he should just tell the receptionist what he intended to say and ask her to pass the message to him.

Liben wanted to barge in and interrogate Shuanhu in person, "Why do you let the bulldozers demolish the villas? Isn't that an act of plunder? When such a terrible thing is happening in the plain light of day, why does no one intervene?" Liben wanted to ask Shuanhu these questions and others besides…However, since he could not produce a numbered permit, he was pushed back by the bodyguards as he approached the door. At his wit's end, Liben departed in low spirits.

After leaving the reception room, and seeing that the neon lights in the recreation city were on and glimmering in broad daylight, Liben was pretty curious. Before he had taken more than a couple of steps in that direction, he was suddenly surrounded by a handful of street girls who had been observing him for some time. They pulled his lappets, tugged his tie, twisted his ears and even pinched his cheeks, each vying with the others to proclaim that she was the best, prettiest, and most entrancing of them all.

Liben told them explicitly that he suffered from sexual impotence; that he couldn't perform that kind of act. However, none of them took him at his word. One of them called Liben stingy ghost, another said she knew how to cure him of the problem — as long as he did the deed with her just once, the thing between his thighs would be forever hard and penetrating. Liben endeavored to get away from these women — the strong odor they exuded made him almost faint. But it was no easy matter to free himself from this entanglement. One girl rubbed her gigantic, half-veiled-and-half-naked breasts against Liben's chest, while another forcefully put her arms around his neck and kissed his cheeks.

Finally Liben succeeded in getting rid of these street girls. Hailing a tricycle taxi, he instructed the driver to take him to the county town. Under his directions, the driver parked at the gate of the public security bureau. As he stepped inside the gate, Liben came across a departmental director of the bureau, who had once treated him to a feast. At that feast, to thank Liben for having recommended one of his relatives to work in Meiteng, the director had raised his cup and exclaimed that this toast was a testimony to the establishment of brotherhood with Liben; that thenceforward he would revere Liben as his older brother.

Today, however, this younger brother looked as if he had completely forgotten his older brother. Passing by Liben, his own shoulder almost rubbing against Liben's, the younger brother showed no sign of recognition, as if they were utter strangers. As Liben called out his name, he turned around, cast a glance, then without saying a single word, turned back round again. He entered a room, and slammed the door behind him.

Liben could hardly bear such rudely cold treatment. Not long before, he had been a favorite celebrity in Kaiyang — wherever he went, he used to be surrounded, admired and flattered by crowds, even warmly invited to dinner and drinking parties by them. How many people had felt honored to know him! How many people had abased themselves before him! How many people had seized him by the arm and begged him to have his picture taken with them! He had only been absent for one year, how was it that all these Kaiyang people's faces looked so cold? His friends were avoiding him; his acquaintances were no longer acquaintances. It had been three days since he checked into a hotel in Kaiyang. During that time, he had made more than one hundred calls, hoping that someone would come to talk with him, so that his depression might be dispelled. But his hope was futile — no one showed up.

Undeterred, Liben knocked at the younger brother's door. When he entered and identified himself, the younger brother looked a bit embarrassed, explaining that he had not recognized Liben just now. The fact that Liben had become skinnier did not stop the younger brother proclaiming that Liben had put on weight. The fact that Liben's hair had become sparser did not stop the younger brother saying it was more abundant. After some tedious greetings, the younger brother began to glance at his watch from time to time, which was his way of saying "It's time for you to leave."

Without further ado, Liben told the younger brother that he was there to report a case.

"What is it?" the younger brother asked.

Liben said that Sakelu Park was being brutally demolished, and that the residents were nowhere to be found. He hoped the public security bureau could stop this, and set up an investigation.

Hearing what Liben said, the younger brother laughed, his face looking as pleasant as a yellow chrysanthemum blooming on a bright autumn day.

"Do you live in a world of your own, or in dream? Which law does the demolition of Sakelu violate?" the younger brother asked. "Shuanhu has acquired the land legally. The demolition of the houses is legal. All the necessary paperwork has been completed beyond reproach. How can it be called an illegal violation?"

Taking a paper napkin out of his pocket, the younger brother wiped the snot running from his nostrils, and said, "In reaction to the demolition, some people engaged in disturbances, some appealed to higher authorities, some threatened suicide, some acted like shameless villains. In sum, these people have been up to all sorts of tricks. But all the disturbances have calmed down now, haven't they? No matter how high the sea-swell rises, it eventually subsides; no matter how high grasshoppers may jump, they cannot withstand the stamp of a human foot. A person should know his own weight. Everyone should behave himself and conform to the conventions."

After offering his advice, the younger brother asked Liben what had got into him, that he wanted to stir up an old issue that had already been settled? What did he want to achieve? Did he aim to make money or just stir up unrest for its own sake?

Liben, in line with his incorrigible habit, began a lecture on citizen rights, which bored the younger brother so much that he turned his head further and further backward. Seeing that they were talking at cross-purposes, the younger brother claimed that he had some urgent matter to attend to, and that he would have to show Liben the door.

92

Liben had visited many departments, and had consulted many documents which showed that the demolition of Sakelu had been countenanced and approved by various parties. The documents also showed that after Sakelu was demolished, an amusement park would be built on the site. Much larger in scale, the park was expected to attract a great many customers from Yuebei.

Wherever he went he protested so loudly that he got a sore throat. One of his key points was that, although Kaiyang County, where Sakelu was located, had every right to dispose of it, Sakelu was the realization of Liben's blood and dreams, and had been built with his private capital. How could they justify changing its function without prior permission from the investor? Millions in capital crumbled to dust, thousands of people gone into exile, who would not be indignant at the thought of such things?

No one was interested in Liben's protests. People went about their business as usual. In despair, he returned to Sakelu once again. This time there needed no great effort to meet Shuanhu who, for his sake, had put aside other things and reserved a private room in the recreation city. To his surprise, the man who had once been a country bumpkin was dressed like a rich overseas Chinese just back from abroad, to make him — who really was an overseas Chinese just back from abroad — look like a migrant worker. Shuanhu had oily black hair, and a smooth, moist face which seemed to have been carefully beautified, though wrinkles were still detectable; the western suit he was wearing looked neat and stiff. It seemed that Shuanhu did not care what Liben had on his mind. He started the conversation with a discussion of his tie. He let Liben guess how much it had cost him. Liben shook his head, saying that he had no idea. Shuanhu laughed at him, saying that Liben had indeed wasted his time in the United States, where there were beggars as well as millionaires! One careful look at the tie hanging from Shuanhu's neck would suffice to help Liben to new knowledge! "What is it? It is a Pierre Cardin, the most expensive type, the one they call Golden Pierre Cardin, costing six thousand *yuan* apiece! Expensive, right?" Yet for him it was a bagatelle. He had bought eight at a single purchase — five for the leaders who had always supported him, and three for himself. He had been silly enough in the past to disparage those who wore ties, thinking that they were stupid dogs trying to pass themselves off as wolves. Now he had changed his mind. He realized that a tie was very important to a man because it was a symbol of success. He then lamented the lack of real gold ties on the market. Were there such a thing, he would be the first to buy. How grand it would be to buy a tie like that and to have it hanging before one's chest!

Shuanhu changed the subject and asked Liben who the most successful person in Mazi Village was. Liben went with the flow and said it was Shuanhu, without doubt — an answer which satisfied Shuanhu completely. Drunk with self-regard, he patted his own leg twice, Liben's thigh once, and praised Liben for being mentally alert though physically disabled; he had put those many years of study in a foreign country to good use. Mice could not fly even if you picked them up by their ears and threw them up into the sky. That was their fate. Like pigs or dogs, they were born to eat shit. Only a few people broke away from the pack and grew wings for flight. And one must not forget that the flights themselves differed, since that of the mosquito and that of the wild goose had nothing in common. In Mazi Village only four persons were able to fly — Shuanhu, Liben, Jidan and Black Bean. Black Bean was a sparrow, unable to fly far or high. Now in the provincial capital, Black Bean was said to be such a failure that he had even lost his job. Liben, whom Shuanhu had admired so much, had turned out to be a migrant bird. Seemingly busy and on the move, Liben would achieve nothing in the end, not even a cozy nest. As for Jidan, she was a seagull, welcomed wherever she went. As an official, Jidan's biggest gain was that she, like a net, had caught a school of oil-rich fish. Her achievement did not depend on how much money she had raked in. Shuanhu had discovered a new admiration for this sociable woman, who was so flexible in her diplomatic tactics. She asked this leader to act as her father today, that leader to act as her brother tomorrow, and as a result more than half of the leaders and heads had become her relatives. Therefore, who would not wish to take special care of her? Of course, there was only one *really* big shot to emerge from Mazi Village; none other than himself! A goshawk by name and nature, he soared in the sky, braved rain and wind, and created a spectacle without parallel. He so admired himself that it was practically worship. He was convinced that he was awesome, really awesome! Although he had more money than he could carry, he was still dissatisfied, because his name was not well known yet. He was clear-headed enough to know that he had not earned a good name in the world at large. Many people abused him, many people condemned him, and many people spread rumors about him. Celebrities were bound to face jealousy and hatred. However, who that had a lot of money did not wish to have in addition a good name? From the girls he hired, he had learned the importance of face. These girls, with a lower body dirtier than a public toilet, were very careful about the application of powder to their faces, paying good money for it. If a prostitute knew that she must take care of her face, how much more should Shuanhu, the noble entrepreneur? As a tree lives by its bark, so does a man by his face!

Was there any way to make one's face shine like gold? Having pondered this question for a long time, Shuanhu had concluded that it was advisable to follow three basic strategies. First, he would donate money for the building of schools. To be specific, he planned on building a school named after himself, exclusively for the children of poor families. Above the blackboard of each classroom would be hung a large picture of himself, to which all the children would have to salute before classes began each day, and shout slogans and compliments, to show their admiration for him! With the passage of time, would he not come to stand like a mountain in the minds of the pupils? Once the children were captured, their parents would have to put their hands up and surrender. How could Shuanhu not know these people by now? He knew them as well as his own fingers. To be frank, they were just like pigs. A little food would make those who were grunting angrily at you a moment ago lick your boots at once. It was true that he was ignorant of the principles of missile construction, but no one could say he did not know ordinary Chinese people. He knew the so-called "people" all too well; muddle-headed, and with their eyes closed, they were used to drifting with the tide and repeating the words of others. When they hated you, they would denigrate you as if you stank worse than dog shit; but if you gave them a matchstick, they would immediately forget that they had slandered you, and in a different tone eulogize you as more fragrant than a flower.

Second, he would strengthen his investment in media. As long as you spent money, the media would trumpet your praises. The media was not as pure as people thought, and its deceptive tricks were inexhaustible. Shuanhu knew the power of the media. People would change their opinions of him once the media began bombarding them with favorable reports, and it would not be long before they began sighing, "Ah, we didn't realize what a good guy he is! It seems that we never really knew him, that we blamed him unfairly, and that we have wronged someone who is almost an angel!"

As for the third strategy, Shuanhu appeared a little bit shy about it, and hesitated between revealing and concealing. But Liben kept at him, until he had to empty the bag. It was a strategy more profound than the previous two. The first two were nothing but short-term measures, while this one was a long-term strategy which could make him immortal. This grand strategy had him laughing under his quilt at night. The strategy would take a few years, and included three stages: first, ask a master to write a biography of him; second, ask a sculptor to make a stone statue of him; third, have a temple built dedicated to himself.

He had intended to hire Black Bean to write his biography, but was afraid that he would squint at him through a door slit and conceive him as being flatter than a pea. Furthermore, Black Bean knew everything about him, and that might be detrimental to his glorious image. Many people had knocked at his door, eager to write for him. Pen-pushers like that were more docile than sons once they were on the payroll. If you insisted your hair was green, they dared not describe it as blue. If you wanted the black mole on your forehead to look like the sun, they dared not describe it as the moon. Some said biographies should present a true picture of life; were they not fooling ghosts? In order to show his life story in a good light, Shuanhu, who had never read a book in his life, had visited several bookstores and carried back a sack half full of biographies. After he had finished reading them, he came to the following conclusion: so-called biographies are, more often than not, false! A look at the characters in those biographies led one to wonder — was it true that all of them were tall and perfect? The biographers did not seem to be describing men with normal bodies. No man could live without eating, drinking, urinating, shitting, and sleeping, but none of those biographies ever featured pissing and shitting. Were those people actually gods, not mortal human beings? Didn't they snort? Didn't they sometimes have piles? None of those things could be found in the books! Therefore, Shuanhu's conclusion was that all these gods had been created by people!

Since man could become great through unrestrained propaganda, Shuanhu, too, wanted to be inflated into a hot-air balloon, blown big and full, floating in the air, to be looked-up to by thousands of upturned faces. He wanted to experience the feeling of being hailed and worshipped. He admired ancient kings because they could order anyone to die, or have anyone's head cut off like a watermelon. All subjects who saw them must kneel down, all courtiers must flatter them, and all beautiful women congratulated themselves on winning their favor.

Shuanhu wanted to build himself a temple, and place a stone statue of himself in its hall. The statue would have two uses — in his lifetime it could be a place for people to burn incense and kowtow, and in the future it could be a place for coming generations to offer sacrifices. All men must die, kings not excepted. For most people, death was final. They were swept away like grains of dust by a gust of wind. However, it was different when one built a temple for oneself, because in so doing one could be immortalized. Were it not for Confucian Temples, people would not know that a man named Confucius, who had been dead for thousands of years, had ever lived. His contemporaries might not accept him, Shuanhu, but who could say if people might not regard him as another Confucius in a thousand years' time?

While Shuanhu was delivering these pronouncements, Liben gently snored.

93

When the topic of Sakelu's demolition was mentioned, Shuanhu's countenance became hideous. The verbal conflict between Shuanhu and Liben soon gave rise to physical confrontation: they wrestled all the way from the room to the parking lot outside the recreation city. As they fought on the spacious parking lot, the scene attracted a great deal of attention.

How could such a thing be tolerated? On the boss's home turf, someone was holding him by the collar. Had the bodyguards been hired in vain? Were all those employees paid for nothing? Well, their boss and a stranger were involved in a fight, so what better opportunity for them to impress their boss than right now?

Instantly, the bodyguards rushed over, and so did the personnel from various posts. They forced open Liben's hands and freed Shuanhu from his grip. Then several men surrounded Shuanhu and escorted him away. In the meantime, those who remained — who were the majority — surrounded Liben and fell upon him as one man. They beat him and kicked him. In no time, he lay flat on the ground.

Shuanhu, who had not gone far, shouted to his men to stop the beating. He said the man they were attacking was an American; they only needed to teach him a lesson, which they had already done.

"If the American is beaten to death, won't the incident cause an international dispute?" Shuanhu said to his men.

"All the American imperialists are paper tigers; they cannot take a hard beating," Shuanhu went on. He explained that it was his vehement hatred of American imperialism which had led him to beat this particular American.

As the crowd dispersed, Liben picked himself up off the ground with difficulty. Blood was oozing from a wound on his head — the result of it hitting the ground as he fell down. One of his legs seemed out of control. Every step forward caused him acute pain. Just as he was at his wit's end as to which direction he ought to take, a figure appeared in front of him. For Liben, this person was like a ray of light in a dark night.

That figure was a nun. As Liben had been beaten by the mob, she was there, watching. When all the others departed, she did not move; she kept on watching. As Liben attempted to rise and move, the nun, seeing that Liben was having difficulty standing, moved toward him and gave the impression she wished to offer aid. However, she quickly withdrew her hands.

Blankly, Liben gazed at the nun, who suddenly burst out laughing. And what she said astonished Liben, "You are so tough and lucky! Can't believe you are still alive after such a beating!"

Liben murmured, "You look familiar. But I cannot remember who you are."

She burst out laughing again. She said it was no wonder that Liben couldn't recognize her; actually, when she first put on the habit, even her son Langwa failed to recognize her.

The name "Langwa" brought it all back to Liben.

"Are you Layue?" Liben asked.

"Yes," the nun admitted. "But I'm no longer called Layue. Now I'm called Nun Lotus."

Liben asked her why she had chosen to become a nun.

She said it was her father who had forced her to; it was against her will.

"Where is your convent?" Liben asked.

Layue did not reply. Instead she urged Liben to waste no time in having his wound dressed. "Look how badly you are bleeding! The blood has stained your ear red."

Following Layue, Liben arrived at Fugui's temple. As always, many people were there. In front of the stone Buddha, the air was permeated with incense smoke.

Fugui had been confirmed as abbot. Since then, he had no longer performed diagnostic and healing activities — his nephew had taken over the job.

Almost uneducated, his nephew hardly knew how to write, and, to overcome this problem, had taken to drawing various signs on scraps of paper. If he drew a particular number of eggs, it signified that just such a number of sheets of joss paper must be burned; if he drew a particular number of iron rings, it meant that just such a number of bank notes must be offered to Fugui; if he drew a certain number of horizontal lines, the person must run around his own ancestral graveyard for just such a number of rounds; if he drew a certain number of vertical lines, the person must thrust into the mounds of his ancestral graves just such a number of bamboo sticks covered with red paper; etc. etc.

There were always dimwits who could not understand what Fugui's nephew meant — they often took the iron rings for eggs, and they believed they were required to burn joss money before the Buddha's image when they were supposed to offer bank notes to Fugui. When encountering people like this, Fugui's nephew always flared up with anger. He would invariably rebuke them at the top of his voice. Sometimes, rebuking did not do justice to his anger, and in exasperation he would kick the dimwits.

Fugui kept to a small room and did not go outside. Bad health was one reason for his seclusion. But a more important reason was that he did not want to expose himself to public view. Now that he had been promoted abbot — the absolute authenticity of which was confirmed by the red certificate issued by the religious affairs bureau, he thought he would definitely be taken seriously. An abbot was at least equivalent to an official of *chu* rank. This meant he was almost on a level with the magistrate of Kaiyang County. If a county magistrate forgets his dignity, but associates with cobblers and grocers, could he still be esteemed as the top official of the county? Consequently, Fugui kept himself to himself, not exposing himself to the riff-raff. Of course he would receive distinguished guests in person — for example, key officials or wealthy bosses. But such kinds of people were very rare. There was hardly one such patron every two months.

After they entered the temple hall, Layue took a handful of dried wormwood, burned it and applied the ash to Liben's wound. Using some adhesive bandages and a piece of gauze, she neatly bound Liben's wound. After she was done dressing the wound, Layue began to ask Liben questions, as if she were interrogating him at an interview.

"What do you do in the United States?"

"I do some volunteer work," Liben replied.

"Are volunteers classified into different levels or ranks?" Layue asked.

"No. They are not," Liben replied.

An awkward expression appeared on Layue's face. After hesitating for a moment, Layue instructed Liben that when Abbot Shining Virtue asked him this question, he must claim that he had a rank, and that his rank was one tier higher than *chu* level.

"What is the point of telling a lie?" Liben asked Layue.

"Don't ask," Layue said. "You just answer Abbot Shining Virtue as I instruct you."

It was utterly dark in the room in which Fugui resided. Stepping into it,

Liben could discern nothing at all. He was overwhelmed by a disgusting sour smell, so strong that it nearly suffocated him.

Liben heard Fugui cough and expectorate. He heard Fugui ask Layue, "Who is it that you bring in?"

Instead of answering her father, Layue struck a match and lit a candle that stood on the window sill. In the dim light, Fugui's form gradually emerged.

Fugui lay huddled on his bed. Seeing it was Liben, Fugui managed to sit up and leaned against his piled-up quilt. His face resembled a skull, and his countenance was as sallow as dark yellow paper. He stared at Liben for a long time, his fishy eyes filled with puzzlement.

In a feeble voice Fugui asked Layue, "Who is this person you bring?"

Patting her father on the head, Layue said, "Are you feigning muddle-headedness or are you really muddle-headed? Don't you recognize Liben?"

After softly repeating "Liben" for many times, Fugui eventually remembered who Liben was — wasn't that the guy who had been to America and returned with a bagful of American dollars? Wasn't that the guy who had come up with the fancy Sakelu idea, and funded its construction?

Fugui was pretty displeased with Layue for having taken Liben to see him. He rebuked Layue, "Have you lost your mind? Is Abbot Shining Virtue a nobody accessible to anyone?" He said something about Abbot Shining Virtue's rank being the equal of the *chu* level, and that it had, in ancient times, afforded whoever possessed it the privilege of being carried around in a sedan chair. He reproached Layue with not recognizing the value of agate, or failing to tell the difference between gold and nickel coins.

During this denunciation of his daughter, Fugui could not help sobbing. His tears and snot mingled as they flowed down, and left a sticky mess on his collars. Layue mopped her father's face, and his coat, with a corner of the quilt.

Quivering ceaselessly all over, Fugui refused to be cleaned. He declared his own snot and saliva were Buddha's sweet liquid essence. What a shameful waste it was to wipe it away! The best thing would be to have a worshipper come in and pay money to suck up the discharge — and whoever sucked up and swallowed the discharge would be blessed — and would not only live a splendid life in this world but also have free access to Elysium after death.

Disregarding her father's nagging, Layue wiped the muck away. No sooner had she finished cleaning than Fugui said that he wanted to urinate.

Bending down, Layue pulled out a basin from under a table and lifted it up in front of Fugui. There was already some urine in the basin — that accounted for the acrid smell in the room.

Fugui undid his belt and took out his thing. Carrying the basin and holding it beneath Fugui's thing, Layue turned her head away.

Everything was ready. But like a person with nothing to cry about, who none the less attempts to cry, Fugui, after making persistent efforts, ended up squeezing out only a few tiny drops of urine.

Unable to bear the bad smell and the funny atmosphere, Liben withdrew from the room and stood outside the door. Before long, though, Layue asked him in again, saying that her father had something important to tell him; that he must come in and listen carefully.

As soon as Liben came in, Fugui asked him if he felt greatly honored.

"I feel cornered, and hopeless for the future," Liben said. "Under such circumstances, what on earth would make me feel honored?"

Fugui was displeased. After a fit of coughing, he interrogated Liben, "You get to see an eminent monk so easily, without paying a cent. Doesn't that make you feel honored? How many people have bowed down and pleaded to see me without success! How can you take Abbot Shining Virtue so lightly?"

Fugui's look had exasperated Liben from the beginning, and this bragging only aggravated him further. His voice full of sarcasm, and his head nodding ceaselessly, Liben replied, "I do feel honored. I feel greatly honored, as if I were meeting the president of a whole country."

Fugui laughed happily. He was so cheerful that for a long time he would not shut up. He went on with his bragging, claiming that he could foresee everyone's life in the next world; he knew who would enter Elysium and who would struggle eternally in a sea of bitterness and anguish. He declared that all the Mazi villagers except him would become ghosts after death — but that he would become a god. According to Fugui, ghosts were divided into a hierarchy of classes; different classes were allocated to different layers of the hell; the higher a layer was, the less pain the ghosts suffered, but the lower a layer was, the more pain the ghosts suffered; the majority of the Mazi villagers would be doomed to the eighteenth layer, which was actually a huge caldron full of boiling oil for frying ghosts: the oil was on fire; it boiled, rolled, heaved. One ghost after another was dumped into the caldron to be fried. Like grasshoppers, the ghosts desperately struggled, cried, grieved, and yearned to die. However, unlike humans, who could die when they were sick of living, ghosts couldn't die no matter how disgusted they were with their existence. No matter how hard they might try to commit suicide, they continued to exist as ghosts. The Mazi villagers were unworthy of their ancestors. They violated holy ordinances. Thus they were destined to go to the eighteenth layer. If they were not so doomed, then who would be? They hadn't followed in their fathers' path; they had allowed the land to be lost which their fathers had acquired through hard work, the land their fathers had passed down to them. The most sinister thing was that nearly all the households had lost their ancestral graveyards. Some graves had been levelled by bulldozers and buried underneath concrete. The bones in other graves, after being dug out by excavators, had been scattered here and there like sticks of kindling.

"If you wanted a perfect example of a disgrace to one's ancestors, then this is what I'd point to!" Fugui said. "No. It is more than a disgrace. It is nothing less than fucking over one's ancestors!"

Nevertheless, Fugui was pretty pleased with his own future, which was, more or less, a comfort to him. He said he would go to Elysium. There in Elysium, among the spectacular edifices that looked more gorgeous than royal palaces, a throne was certainly reserved for him. As he came in and went out of an edifice, the porters on either side of the door must take off their hats to salute him, and multitudinous beauties would look at him with alluring eyes. When he reclined on his comfortable, gilded chair to take his ease, there would be people doing various things for him: some would massage his feet, some would waft him with fans, some would pound gently on his shoulders, some would massage his back. How superbly comfortable he would be! How perfectly wonderful it would be! But he would not indulge himself; he would do his utmost to save his family members, who were suffering in hell. It wouldn't be very difficult to accomplish. "Just think about this," Fugui said. "Don't the brothers and sisters, uncles and aunts, nephews and nieces of those who have been accepted into royal palaces, benefit as a result? As the saying goes 'When one becomes an immortal, his chickens and dogs fly to heaven along with him.' That's how things are in this world. In the nether world, no doubt it's the same."

Fugui's plan to deliver his relatives was as follows: once he rose to power in Elysium, he would assign them to important offices — it would be best to put them into provincial governorships. If that was too difficult, he would at least procure township headships for them.

Whenever he mentioned Song Tongguo, Fugui could not help shaking. His utterances became unclear. Sometimes, he confused Song Tongguo with Qi Guangrong. According to him, Song Tongguo was a male prostitute, so was Qi Guangrong; Song Tongguo had taken possession of the piss pot, and then refused to give it to him; he had been Song Tongguo's father-in-law for more than ten years — to no advantage! That piss pot meant a lot to him! If he could go to see Sakyamuni with the pot in his hand as a gift, how high he would rise in Sakyamuni's estimation! That pot would not only signify his high status, but also his honor. It would be a proof of his exceptional background. "Once Sakyamuni receives the pot, won't he show me favor?" Fugui asked.

"But unfortunately, Qi Guangrong fled. He couldn't be found anywhere," Fugui sighed. "What a pity that no trace of the pot could be detected!"

94

The news that Liben had made an appearance near Sakelu soon reached every corner of Kaiyang. The news was relayed by the Sakelu villagers, as they dispersed, over the whole county, and in no time they learned everything there was to know about him — that he was living in a small hotel named Mule in the county town, on three pot-noodle meals a day.

Just as there are no abuses without abusers, so there are no debts without debtors. If the disasters which had befallen the Sakelu villagers were a tree, the person who planted it was Liben. If their misfortunes were a river, its source was Liben. They looked for him because they wanted to restore their happiness, or, if they could not restore their happiness, they could at least make him answer for all their misfortunes. If he knew what was good for him, he would give them a large sum of money; otherwise, he could expect a severe punishment! They hated him so much. How they wished they could tear him into pieces and boil his flesh in a saucepan!

The villagers secretly coordinated with each other, and agreed to get even with Liben at some future time. If they did not have him in an armlock right now, then only because they wanted to include as many victims as possible in order to take vengeance on him. Some of the villagers had gone to work in other provinces and would need time to get back. But what if the duck flew away in the meantime? If Liben heard about their plan and fled, wouldn't all their previous efforts be wasted? The more assertive villagers formed a council to arrange for someone to watch him, in order that the villagers might always be informed of his whereabouts. At the first sign that he might be going on the run, the villagers in Kaiyang could take immediate action without waiting for those in other places to return. If Liben took a bus, they would block him at the bus station. If he was picked up by special car, they would intercept him at the entrance of the expressway from Kaiyang to Yuebei.

The villagers pooled a small amount of money, just enough to pay Dapao's twin nephews to come over and shadow Liben. The elder of the brothers was named Yidan, the younger Erdan. They checked in at the Mule Hotel, and the room they chose was opposite Liben's. They recognized Liben, but Liben did not know them. They longed to avenge their maternal uncle, whose family had had to take shelter in their home. Just as utensils are bound to knock against each other, so discord was inevitable between their mother and their aunt if they were living under the same roof. The aunt used to accuse the mother of bullying her, and had threatened to commit suicide several times, driving the mother to the verge of a heart attack. Wasn't Liben, the fake foreign ghost, the root of all the unrest in their family? These dogged brothers kept a close eye on him, carefully observing his comings and goings. When Liben went to have his shoes mended, they went to have theirs mended. When Liben took a walk along the river, they also took a long walk along the river. When Liben bought cigarettes in a shop, they too bought cigarettes in the shop. When Liben went to the county government, they squatted down by the stone lions outside the gate. Even when Liben went into a toilet, they either followed him into the toilet, or strolled around outside.

Liben had noticed their presence. He took the initiative of asking what they were by trade. They replied that they were salesmen for medicinal materials. Having heard that the medicinal materials market in the United States was bullish, and that its prices were for the time being advantageous, they were considering going into business with him to mass-export such items. Liben seemed to believe them, and went to their room from time to time to chat with them. He told them that he was not much of a businessman, but that he could introduce his friends in the United States to them, who would let them know whether there was any chance of cooperation. From then on, wherever he went, he would invite the brothers to go with him. He bemoaned his loneliness, and was distraught that he was treated like an alien in his own hometown, that friends from the old days had turned into strangers.

The twins suggested that they all go to the target range the day after next, after breakfast, and examine a medicinal herb there. As the herb was rare, it was extremely expensive, and, if shipped to the United States, it would be worth its weight in gold. The herb grew on the mountain by the target range, but the mountain, with thick forests and rampant grasses, was said to be the haunt of leopards, and human beings rarely went there. In this environment the herb continued to grow in its original condition, and by exploiting this good luck they and Liben stood to make a fortune.

No matter how the twins played up the herb's price, Liben would shake his head and say he was not going. He told them that he was not out to make money and that his only reason for staying in Kaiyang was to wait for a lawyer from Yuebei. He called that lawyer nearly every day, urging him to come as soon as possible. At first, the lawyer was not too happy with the deposit that Liben had transferred to his account, but he would not say so directly, stressing in a roundabout way that he was neither a graduate fresh from university nor a beggar on the streets, etc. Liben could see what he was driving at — the money given him was not enough. Later, the lawyer stopped complaining about the money, but never stopped moaning on the telephone about how busy he was — with one lawsuit after another to attend to, and not a minute of free time. He would come, anyway; he would find time to come because what he valued was not the money this lawsuit would bring him, but rather its social significance. It was inevitable that a lawsuit against the government would attract the media. If the media paid attention to the lawsuit, they would pay attention to the lawyer; if they paid attention to the lawyer, his fame would spread far and wide. With the rise of his fame, there would be more lawsuits for him to prosecute, and his charges could go up like a boat on a rising tide.

The lawyer reassured Liben that patience, more patience, and even more patience, would pay, but by now Liben's patience was practically at an end. His heart, as if on fire, had fixated on this lawyer whose thunderings, however, never heralded rain. But he forced himself to continue waiting for the day when the lawyer would eventually emerge. The lawyer was his last chance, so he could not afford to give him up easily. Once the lawyer came, he could discuss with him how to sue Kaiyang government for its illegal demolition of Sakelu. If Kaiyang government lost the case, Liben's only demand would be that it rebuild Sakelu on a different site with government funds, and relocate the villagers in exile so that they could resume their lives. Such a demand was by no means exorbitant. Shuanhu might or might not be listed as the second defendant, but Kaiyang government should certainly be prosecuted. Sakelu had been built on a piece of legally approved land, and the certificate clearly specified a seventy years' lease. How could it be changed at will, as if it were just a game? Furthermore, Tian Liben was the principal investor, and yet, though he was the legal owner of the property, he had neither been informed of its demolition nor given any compensation. Was this reasonable? What kind of behavior was this? He could not allow such absurd savage things to stand. No, absolutely not, none of them!

Liben's narration left a fairly good impression on the twins. They offered to treat him to a drink in a small restaurant. A plate of peanuts, a plate of stir-fried potato shreds, that was all there was to eat with the liquor. The liquor was rather cheap, three *yuan* for half a liter, and it was so strong that he could not help sticking his tongue out after a single sip of it. The twins, however, enjoyed it very much. After briefly urging Liben to join in, they began to drink to each other, cup by cup. A kind of rivalry seemed to set in between Yidan and Erdan, as neither would give in, one ridiculing the other for his mosquito's stomach while claiming that he himself was the better drinker. As they went on, they became more talkative, gesticulating merrily with hands and feet. After a short period, one bottle was taken away empty, and it was not long before the second was drunk almost to the dregs. Eventually, Yidan could not hold on any longer, and after a hysterical bout of vomiting he subsided, with the assistance of the proprietor, onto the sofa near the counter, his head drooping to one side, but Erdan, a bottle held tight in his hand, kept on talking — mumbling, to be exact, for his tongue was by this time as stiff as buckram. Liben failed to get the bottle off him no matter how hard he tried. Erdan emptied the upturned bottle straight down his throat, and threw it onto the ground. With a crash, the bottle broke into pieces, which flew in all directions.

The proprietress was very unhappy, and some of the other guests cast contemptuous looks at Erdan. Liben apologized to the proprietress as he helped a waitress to sweep up the shards. Erdan yelled to the proprietress to get him two more bottles of liquor. He declared that he had admired Wu Song[42] from childhood, who had drunk eight bowls of liquor before embarking on a journey over Jingyang Mountain. It was nothing for him, to drink so small a quantity. To be or not to be a hero, that was a question of drinking capability!

The proprietress refused to sell Erdan more liquor, on the pretext that it was sold out. Erdan swore bitterly at the proprietress, saying that the black mole on her neck was the mark of a procuress, that she had been born a whore, and had started the restaurant only after she could whore no more, etc. The proprietress did not brook any further argument, but she presented the bill to Liben. Liben paid up, but he had difficulty getting the two brothers out of the restaurant. Yidan was fast asleep, while Erdan was talking nonsense.

Erdan reached towards Liben and said that he had something to say to him. He stood up, teetered a few steps, and pressed down on Liben's shoulders to force him to sit down in a chair. Liben asked what on earth he wanted to say. Erdan wandered off into a world of mists and clouds. Although he drifted from topic to topic, his main purpose was to lament his untimely birth. If he had been born in the period of Three Kingdoms, he would have been Cao Cao[43] for sure. If he had been born during the Chu-Han War, no doubt he would have been Xiang Yu. If he had been born in the Ming Dynasty, he would have been Li Zicheng, etc. What a pity that he had been born in a time so peaceful that he, a hero by nature, had no stage on which to demonstrate his prowess; and that he had to live as obscure as a loach, with his tail pinned between his legs! Had he not practiced martial arts since his childhood, in order to disappear into the maquis? Now all he could do was throw wine bottles, to vent his pent-up resentment.

Liben tried to bring back Erdan's wandering tongue to the present, so that Erdan would betray himself concerning Liben. He suspected that the two brothers must be hiding something from him because their eyes were constantly shifting. They claimed that they were medicinal materials salesmen, but they lived in the hotel, doing nothing for long periods of time, and never actually purchasing medicinal materials.

Now that they were drunk, Liben asked Erdan what he and his brother really were. Were they really vendors of medicinal materials? Erdan sneered at Liben, saying that Liben had a wooden head that turned at others' command. They had deceived him, and the fact that he had believed them proved that they had had the potential to be qualified spies. The state really was taking gold for sand. What a pity that such talent had been wasted! Why couldn't it appoint them to the most important posts? If sent to Taiwan as undercover agents, they would, by dint of their capabilities, swindle the so-called president, the one named Ah Bian, out of his senses. Once Ah Bian was seized, the mainland and Taiwan would be reunited without resorting to the use of any weapons.

Listening to Erdan's divagations, Liben managed to catch his meaning at last. The Sakelu villagers were conspiring to get even with him. The twin brothers' attempt to induce him into going to take a look at the so-called rare medicinal materials was, in fact, an attempt to get him into a meeting with the Sakelu villagers.

Erdan admitted that Liben did not seem to be a bad guy. In addition, motivated by the friendship he was beginning to feel for him, he dissuaded him, in a roundabout fashion, from going the next day, as it would certainly do him no good. Ha-ha-ha, was he not talented? He was both a secret agent and a double agent.

Liben asked for details of the time and place which the Sakelu villagers had decided on, for meeting; then, clenching his teeth, he said that he was determined to go! What was there to be afraid of, since he was going to meet his brother and sister villagers, and not fierce terrorists?

95

Liben made his way all by himself to the target range, which was next to a reservoir. He had intended to go there along with the twin brothers. However, when the sun had climbed above the top of the hotel building, the room where the twin brothers lodged was still utterly quiet.

When he peeped in through a narrow gap between the window curtains, Liben made out Yidan sound asleep, but Erdan was not there. Liben asked a waitress where Erdan had gone. With a scornful look on her face, the waitress said, "Erdan, as his name implies, really is a silly trouble-maker[44]. Because of him, we none of us slept last night."

According to the waitress, some time past midnight, Erdan had screamed and rolled on his bed, complaining of a stomach-ache. The waitress brought him some painkillers. He took several tablets, but the medicine did not help. So the waitress and her colleagues had to move him to the closest clinic, where he could get intravenous drip therapy.

As she related the story, the waitress stressed again and again that Erdan had been so heavy to carry, and that they had knocked such a long time before the clinic door eventually opened.

Given these circumstances, Liben decided to go to the meeting alone.

Hiring a motorcycle taxi, he told the driver his destination.

Liben had been hearing of the target range since his childhood. It had been infamous on account of the fact that strange things often happened there. For instance, a little girl who had gone missing near her own house was found dead half a month later at the target range, with her ears gone and her mouth sewn up with thread. Not to mention the hunter who had — as people supposed — been wounded by a leopard that haunted the woods adjoining the target range. It was strange, though, that the leopard, instead of biting any other part of his body, concentrated exclusively on his crotch, so that more than half of his reproductive organ was bitten away. When Liben was a boy, the target range had been a place of horror for him. When adults in the neighborhood wanted to stop their children crying, their most effective threat was: "If you keep crying, you'll be abandoned at the target range."

The target range was already in existence during the early years of the Republic of China, perhaps even before the Republic of China had been founded. Later on, it was put to good use for militiamen and militiawomen to drill on. Young men and young women selected from the surrounding villages crawled on the ground, shooting at the woods. Still later, the militiamen and militiawomen began to build a dam, which, when it was eventually completed, stopped a winding creek not far away from the target range.

After the resounding reports of shotguns, the roar of shouted slogans, and the thunder of explosive blasts, the target range seemed less terrifying to people. Nevertheless, few people frequented it on account of a rumor which had gone round. According to the rumor, the range was an ominous place. Whoever visited it would have bad luck. Women who came back after a visit to the place would conceive only girls but not boys. Any man who visited the place would suffer from a sore waist and aching legs, and afterwards every part of his body would go wrong: what should be hard would no longer be hard, what should be soft would no longer be soft.

Liben had been wondering why the villagers had chosen to meet him at the target range, rather than going straight to the hotel to find him. "They know which hotel I live in. Why would they prefer the range, which is so far away, to the hotel, which is so near, to meet me?" he wondered.

The motorcycle, having completed a bumpy journey along a zigzag path, finally climbed onto the target range. What Liben saw astonished him. Numerous pieces of red cloth were blowing in the wind. They were all over the place. Some were hung over trees, some were spread out on the grass, some were worn over people's heads or around their bodies. It was dazzling to see.

To tell the truth, "pieces of red cloth" was too general a term to describe these items, since some of them could be distinguished as red bed-sheets or red sweaters, and there were even quite a few diapers made from worn-out red clothes. The motorcycle driver told Liben that the people were using the red items to exorcise evil ghosts; that the only color ghosts feared was red; that red could scare ghosts so much that they would flee in all directions at the sight of it.

When Liben appeared among the crowd, cries of shock burst out, as if he were a ghost who had come to do mischief. But when the people realized that this fellow was none other than Liben, whom they had been anxiously awaiting, somebody shouted, and this triggered a general outburst in unison from the crowd. Mingled with their cries were insulting remarks, and this fusion resounded in the air.

The people who first closed in on Liben were women. They condemned him in wailing, drawn-out voices; they twisted and pinched his arms and neck. A middle-aged woman, whose name Liben could not recall, spat hatefully onto his face.

Many other women, one after another, followed her example — only they did it more rudely and more violently. Some tore and ripped his clothes, some pulled and tugged his hair, some crawled onto the ground biting his feet, some jumped up slapping his face. In the meantime, all the men stood around, babbling curses. Though they did not speak with one voice, the message was all too clear: *Even if we kill and dismember you, our grievances cannot be assuaged.*

Liben apologized nonstop. Again and again he said, "I'm sorry! I'm sorry!" But his apologies were to no effect. He wanted to ask the villagers to calm down and listen to his explanation; he wanted to tell them how he had striven to defend their rights, so that they might have confidence in their future. However, he felt his throat swelling and fuming. No matter how hard he tried to speak, he simply could not get anything else out.

Liben felt dizzy — golden stars seemed to float in front of his eyes. He fell to his knees, hoping that this would make the villagers stop beating and humiliating him. Nevertheless, the villagers did not ease off in the least. On the contrary, they acted more violently: some hit Liben on the head, some kicked him about the waist. The funny thing was that those who were currently beating him seemed insatiable; they wanted to keep Liben as their own exclusive target, and had no intention of giving way to other people. Naturally, this caused the others present to feel dissatisfied and to complain, "What have we all come together for today? We are here to punish the traitor of Mazi Village, aren't we? In this matter, each and every one of us has a part to play—because we all have a bellyful of grievances to make good. But, of course, there are always people who love to take more than their share. They take advantage of their physical strength and push other people aside, cutting off access to Liben. Is this fair?"

To deal with this unfair situation, Dapao rose from amidst the rabble and took a stand on the elevated clay platform. Shouting loudly and waving his shovel-like palms, he ordered people to quiet down and listen to him. Gradually, the crowd did calm down; the beating and kicking stopped. People lifted their heads, waiting to find out what fart Dapao was about to crack off — he had been nicknamed Dapao because he farted a lot; his loud farts would burst out like a volley of cannonballs shot by artillery.

Dapao began by praising himself and his two nephews, saying that if it hadn't been for his own outstanding wisdom, if it had not been for Yidan and Erdan's skill in luring the enemy into the trap, the villagers wouldn't have been able to catch Liben. He declared, "Liben normally runs as fast as a rabbit! You could see him running, but you could not catch him. It's a good thing that he has now been securely hooked, the slippery fish. But when we punish this poisonous fish, we should choose the right strategy. We mustn't inflict punishment on a whim. If we beat and kick him as we please, we might easily kill him."

Dapao suggested that Liben be made to kneel down in the centre of the range, that people line up in an orderly queue to thrash him one by one, that every person hit no more than once, because one hit by each person was already more than Liben could bear.

People generally agreed that Dapao's suggestion was a good one. In short order, the crowd, after considerable pushing and shoving, formed a long queue. Though there were people who jumped the queue, which roused lots of protests, after some quarreling and arguing, the mood quietened.

Several young men dragged Liben to the middle of the range. Liben remained in his kneeling pose.

Dapao assumed the role of commander-in-chief. He appointed five villagers to help maintain order. As soon as he announced "Start," the people began to approach Liben in order and struck him in turn. Some struck with great might, some with less force; some struck with hammer-like fists, some with feather-like palms; some struck seriously, some perfunctorily. A very few people felt sorry for Liben. One of them even took out his handkerchief to erase the blood issuing from Liben's nose. By contrast, some people hated Liben so much that they wanted to smash his head; instead of delivering one blow, they struck five or six times in succession. When one person was told he had gone over his limit, he claimed that he was punishing Liben on behalf of all those who had died in desperation. "Since we moved out of Mazi Village and settled down in Sakelu, so many people have died premature deaths," he said. "Do you think those people would let this swindler off?"

Another man did an exceptionally odd thing. As he approached Liben, instead of raising his hand to strike, he took out the thing in his crotch, and in the full public view directed a jet of urine onto Liben's face.

Liben could hardly kneel up any longer. There were moments when he saw only black, and he kept collapsing. But the men who had been appointed to watch over him propped him up each time. Presently, the only thought in Liben's mind was death — to die quickly, as quickly as possible. What right did he have to go on living in this world? The incessant blows had made his face swell, but slowly and gradually, he ceased to be conscious of them. He felt that his head was like a beehive that had just been poked by a rod; it seemed that numerous bees were flying and humming around him. Down he fell. It was like when a power-cut interrupts a movie midway through, and the colorful screen abruptly goes black.

96

Yidan and Erdan were completely at odds on the issue of whether Liben had jumped into the reservoir himself or had been pushed in by others — though the dispute did not arise until Liben had been dragged out of the water by the brothers and rushed to the county hospital for emergency treatment. Now Liben was out of danger. Except for a brain hematoma and some soft tissue injuries, there were no major problems. However, his mental state was very bad. His eyes dull and his lips tightly-clenched, he was lying on the sickbed like a puppet, mute, absent-minded, and completely unresponsive.

What a day for the twin brothers! Once they had sobered up, they found that Liben was gone. Having looked for him in vain, they headed for the target range, ready to apologize to the villagers — to say that they were sorry, that it was due to their negligence that the cooked duck had flown away. They were even prepared to accept a beating from their maternal uncle Dapao. But what a surprise! That there should have been such an idiot in this world as Liben who, like a moth, had hurled himself into the fire.

When they arrived at the target range, there was not a soul to be seen. A few red ribbons scattered by the wind were hanging and fluttering among the thorns. Apparently, many people had been there, to judge by the numerous footprints left all over the tender meadow. A fat owl perched on a honey locust tree, shrieking.

The brothers followed the owl's shrieks to the reservoir, and were astonished to find a man lying prone on the bank. After they turned the man over, they were even more astonished to find that it was none other than Liben, who was still half immersed in water. The posture of Liben suggested that he had struggled to crawl out of the water, fainting on the shore for lack of physical strength.

The brothers called for an ambulance to transport Liben to the county hospital. Hospitals attached importance to no man, but only to money. As there was no treatment without a sufficient deposit, Erdan sought aid from a martial-arts contact, a boss who, upon hearing that the man Erdan wanted to save was a Chinese American, drew a thick stack of money from the bank and gave it to Erdan without hesitation. Erdan's martial arts contact was thirsty for capital to invest in real estate development, so he was thinking that he might stake a small amount of money now for Liben's big money in the future. Which Chinese American did not have a bulging purse?

Liben woke from a coma of twenty-four hours, but the man became dumb the moment he woke. Whatever questions the brothers asked, he showed total indifference and refused to answer. Yidan insisted that Liben had been pushed into the water, while Erdan said that he had jumped into the water of his own volition. The two brothers argued until their ears turned red and their faces purple. They made a bet in the end — the loser would have to buy the winner a pack of cigarettes worth of five *yuan*. Both of the brothers wanted Liben to talk so that they could decide to whom the pack of cigarettes would go. But Liben uttered nothing; he only stared blankly at the ceiling.

Erdan began to relate how they had made an effort to save Liben, how he had gone all out to borrow money, and how he had been given many a cold shoulder by stingy bosses, and so on and so forth. Still, Liben showed no sign of gratitude. Erdan lost his temper, and so did Yidan. The two brothers angrily thwacked their palms against the bed board, so hard, in fact, that the son of the man in the next bed was disgusted because his father, an old man who was suffering from heart disease, needed to have good rest. So the brothers stopped thwacking the bed, but started to denounce Liben instead, one following the other, as though they were performing a crosstalk. They said that Liben was a cold-blooded animal, that they had saved a drowning wolf who did not know to thank them etc.

When darkness fell, Liben produced from under his pillow a slip of paper which had been written at a time unknown, and presented it to Erdan with a trembling hand. Erdan took it, but saw nothing written on it. He scrutinized it right and left, and finally discovered on its upper right corner a faintly-written telephone number. Erdan dialed the number although he did not know whose it was. At once, in the nave of the church, the mobile phone in my pocket began ringing. I normally never answered my phone during prayers, but it went on ringing insistently. I ran into the courtyard, took the phone out, and found sixteen unanswered calls.

I learned from Erdan of Liben's present situation. Erdan, in a casual but unrelenting fashion, exaggerated the seriousness of Liben's medical condition, warning that if I delayed there was a risk that the next time I saw Liben, it would be as a corpse. In a panic, I went to consult Minister Gao, who was composed as ever, and repeated the words he had said many times previously,

"Liben is a lost child." I asked Minister Gao if there was any chance of Liben returning to the right course. Minister Gao sent me to Kaiyang so that I could bring Liben back to the church. Liben would awaken to God's light.

In a car provided by a fellow believer, I hurried to Kaiyang Hospital, along with Xiaomao. I first went to find the doctor. I had intended to inquire into Liben's case, but the young doctor responded only with complaints. He took me to be one of Liben's family, which, as he kept saying reproachfully, had not acted in accordance with established practice. His words, in practice, were no challenge to my comprehension. He was actually telling me that he had saved a gravely ill person for no recompense. He even tactfully hinted that if a patient's family was too stingy, then it would be the patient who would suffer! A patient in the hands of a doctor, was like a piece of dough in the hands of a chef who could turn it into steamed buns or noodles, or just let it go moldy.

The doctor's words unleashed an irrepressible fury in me. How I wished I could give him a quick slap, but I had to forbear, because I knew full well that, as a Christian who had been baptized, I should watch my conduct and refrain from blind impulses. As instructed in the Bible, I must forgive everything, forgivable or unforgivable! What's more, as he had said, Liben was now like a piece of dough in his — the chef's — hands. How could I afford to offend him? Therefore, in a flattering tone, I asked him to let Liben leave so that I could transfer him to another hospital. The doctor asked if Liben was really an overseas Chinese. I assumed that he would show mercy to Liben, for fear of making a negative impact on the world, so I repeatedly emphasized that Liben's identity as an overseas Chinese was true beyond question. A radiant smile played around the corners of his mouth, which did not open until a long moan had faded away. He said that all overseas Chinese were wealthy! Though he said it in a muffled tone, I could still make out what he meant: a wealthy man should in any event give something, if only as a token of kindness! If old farmers gave him one or two hundred *yuan* just for curing a cold, then how much more should an overseas Chinese, whom he had saved from dying, repay? I begged the doctor, telling him that Liben had lost everything on account of his failed investment, and that he scarcely had a few hundred *yuan* in his pocket, never mind a few thousand. The doctor grimaced, his face as gloomy as the weather before rain. He waved his hand, saying "Stop talking about this matter. That's all for it. I am very busy.

How can I have time to waste my breath here?"

The doctor stormed off, very much annoyed. He disappeared in the blink of an eye, as if he had evaporated. I searched for him everywhere, asked everyone I met after him, and finally found him in the boiler room. The attendant there was the doctor's relative, so the doctor often used the room to bargain with medicine salesmen. It so happened that the doctor had just received a kickback from a salesman when I arrived at the boiler room. He was saying goodbye to the salesman, while tucking a thick stack of banknotes into his underwear, his face frothing with smiles like soap bubbles. I grabbed the doctor mid-step, as he was about to leave. He shuddered for a second, but when he saw who it was, a queer smile appeared on his face. He asked what I was doing, and what I meant by grabbing him by the arm?

I said that I was not doing anything, that I only wanted him to undersign a hospital transfer for Liben. With a twist of his lips, the doctor accused me of being brave from a safe distance. Was a permit something that anyone could obtain if he wanted one? What was a patient? A patient was money! A patient was economic benefit! A doctor's salary and bonus were directly dependent on the number of patients under his care. Without patients, the doctor would have to eat dust, wouldn't he? At first, he had had six patients, but they slipped away one after another, leaving only two including Liben. He had to keep a close eye on these last two. Could he afford to let them go? In a word, anything might be negotiable, but not permission to leave the hospital or transfer to another one!

I followed the doctor into his office. It seemed that no one had been in there for several days, and there was a thin coat of dust on the desks and chairs. The doctor asked why I was constantly following him. He was busy, had many things to deal with, and did not wish me to interrupt him. I said that I did not want to disturb him either. So long as he agreed to discharge Tian Liben, I would be off straight away. He said that the matter was not up for discussion.

Seeing the futility of all this, I racked my brains for another method. I asked the doctor if he knew a man by the name of Leopard in Yuebei. He said yes, of course, who did not know Leopard? Leopard was more famous than the governor. I told him that I was Leopard's brother, an extraordinarily close one; that the first time Leopard went to jail, it was I who had fished him out; that being a trustworthy person, Leopard was loyal to me and would sacrifice his life for me; and that the little boy behind me was none other than Leopard's younger brother. The doctor said as far as he knew Leopard had been arrested because he had killed someone. I replied that that story was intended for public consumption. In reality, he went in at the front door only to be stealthily released at the back. Having controlled the underworld in Yuebei for twenty years, he had far-reaching and wide-spread influence, and who dared to touch him? Leopard had offered to come in person, but I had stopped him. However, I could still call on him in case of trouble. Meanwhile he had let his brother come with me, for fear that I might be bullied or encounter any problems I could not solve on my own. I warned the doctor that if he refused a toast, he would have to drink a forfeit, because Leopard went into a rage at the drop of a hat, and at his command two cars full of roughnecks would arrive at Kaiyang in no time. To these men, the only way to earn credit and rewards from Leopard…was to bring human legs to him.

So saying, I took out my mobile phone, pretending to be dialing Leopard's number. Ashen-faced, the doctor immediately pressed his hand over my phone to stop me. "I'll let Tian Liben go, all right?" he said repeatedly. "I'll let him go. Between brothers there is no problem that can't be resolved."

97

After lying in bed in the church for more than a fortnight, Liben regained most of his physical and mental health. He could get off the bed and move around. His moody expression began to lighten. He spoke to people more and more. Occasionally, I could hear him arguing with Xiaomao over international affairs. Regarding Xiaomao as a muddle-headed inferior, he mocked him, saying that he worshipped Jesus without knowing in which country Jesus was born.

Xiaomao, of course, had a ready retort. He loved to live his life in muddle-headedness; like a contented sleeper, he did not want to be wakened. What was bad about muddle-headedness? To some extent, it was a source of happiness, because it could transform complexity into simplicity, disorder into order. It was like a big snowfall, which covered everything in the world, making miscellaneous things assume one single white color.

Xiaomao claimed that he now turned a deaf ear to all external events, and that he was single-mindedly obsessed with reading the Bible. "I only care about which words in the Bible I don't know how to read yet, and which sentences I can't understand yet," Xiaomao said. "As for other things, what do they have to do with me? I couldn't care less, not if the heavens fall down or the earth falls apart."

Xiaomao used me as a counter example to prove his point. He claimed that at night I always turned from side to side in bed, having difficulty falling asleep; that even after I fell asleep, while I was dreaming I talked nonsense without knowing it. "Isn't that the result of his minding too many things that are none of his business?" Xiaomao asked. "How tiring it is to live a life like that!" He said that, irrespective of whether *I* felt tired or not, just looking at how I lived my life made *him* feel tired.

After sharing the same room with Xiaomao for days, their exchanges became more and more unpleasant; consequently, Liben proposed to move in with me.

I lived in a detached room. The polite name for it would be a bedroom, the rude name, a toilet. In fact, it had once been a toilet. After I came to live there, the church hired a team of artisans, who built a new toilet in a different part of the courtyard and transformed the old one into two separate rooms, one of which was a utility room, the other of which was my bedroom.

After living with Liben, I found that his temper was getting increasingly erratic. He did smile occasionally, but most of the time he was moody. For example, he might be in the middle of humming a song, and all of a sudden flare up, smashing a vase or a tea cup on the ground. Or, while he was conversing with you, he would give you the impression that he was talking to himself — he would repeat things a dozen times, and then ask you reproachfully why you were so unresponsive.

Sleeping in the same room with Liben was both embarrassing and terrifying. Like him, I could not fall asleep until long after I had gone to bed. After a period of restless torment, I would finally fall into a trance sometime after midnight, only to be woken up by his shrill cries, which made me sit up straight in bed and quiver all over. They sounded like the wails of a ghost or the howls of a wolf. In fact, they were more like a sharp knife cutting into my lethargic head. However, when I looked at him in the other bed, I often found him sound asleep, as if nothing had happened.

Sometimes, in my dreams I felt myself tied up by a thick cord around my waist. I tried my utmost to struggle free. I wrestled and wrestled until I woke up and found that what was holding me was not a cord, but Liben's arm. God knew when he had got onto my bed and under the quilt. Like a newly-wed husband, he held me close in his arms, as if I were his wife. Occasionally, I felt that his hand was maneuvering — he would rub and knead my reproductive organ as if it were a fluffy toy. When this happened, I would feign sleep, but fits of disgust shot up from the bottom of my heart.

Often, when I woke up in the middle of the night, I found Liben's bed empty. I would turn on the light and glance around the room for him, but he was not there. "Where can he have gone?" I would wonder. I would call him at the top of my voice. I would run outside to look for him. At first, my calls always woke Minister Gao and Xiaomao, who would often join me in the search. Later on, when my calls had become a familiar event, Minister Gao and Xiaomao grew less sensitive; they no longer accompanied me in this pointless activity. I was left alone to call and seek him, with an electric torch in my hand.

Naturally, the first place where I looked was the outhouse. During all my previous searches, I had found him there only once. I found that instead of relieving himself, he was naked, and using a wooden stick to play with a dung beetle in a moonlit corner. When he heard my scolding, he looked at me in confusion, as if wondering why I was ruining his friendship with the dung beetle. After we returned to our room, I was hoping he might say a word of apology to me. But to my surprise, he embarked on a long philosophical discourse on the existence of dung beetles, claiming that they were one hundred times happier than human beings.

In most cases, I found him in the most unlikely spots, for instance, on the cutting board in the kitchen, or amidst the ash by the furnace, or under a pew in the church nave, or some other strange places. Sometimes he was in his senses, but sometimes he was sound asleep.

There were rare occasions when Liben looked fairly normal — he had a clear mind and a rich sensibility, which made it impossible for you to detect any abnormality in him. For instance, one night when neither of us could sleep, we started chatting about our childhood as well as our experiences in recent years. It was I who cried first — for the loss of my job and of my house. Though I knew that in the eyes of God my cry was shallow and meaningless, I did not care — I just cried as much as I wanted to. My crying, like a burning fuse, touched on the most tender part in him, and set his internal fuse on fire in turn: he cried too. His voice was particularly loud and strong, with a longdrawn-out melody, as if his howl would go on without end, like the thousands-mile-long Changjiang River. The sounds of his cry exceeded mine. I stopped crying. All of a sudden, I felt it somehow indecent and insipid for a man to cry. Liben went on crying at the top of his voice, his features twisted, his face soaked with tears and snot.

For a moment, I wanted to comfort him. But on second thoughts, I changed my mind, believing that perhaps a hearty cry would be better for his health. So I let him be; I was interested to see how long this man who had made a name for himself for being tough, would cry, and if there were more tears in his body than petroleum in the earth. So I just listened in silence, with my head drooping. In the deep, silent night, Liben's howls sounded exceedingly loud and far-reaching.

Liben did not stop for a whole hour. He said he couldn't have held back any longer — like a woman with ten babies in her womb at once, he had felt terribly burdened and desperate and urgently needed to give birth. Now that he had cried, he said, he felt much relieved, as if the babies had been born. As time passed, Liben talked more and more. Drawn along by the things he spoke of, he was thrown into convulsions from time to time. Over and over again, he was choked with sobs.

He said he had deemed himself a savior, but now he saw clearly that he had been a destroyer. Yes, a destroyer. He was a Nazi. He was a tornado, which destroys what shouldn't be destroyed and sweeps away what shouldn't be swept away. He was more vicious than Hitler. He was viler than a demon. He was the source of all evils, the root of all disasters. He was disgusted with himself; he couldn't be more disgusted with himself. He had, with his own hands, ruined his hometown. He had not only scattered his fellow villagers to unfamiliar places, but had also lost his own spiritual home. When in America, how he had missed his hometown! That nostalgia had been a fire burning brightly in his mind. Or rather, it had been a powerful illness raging in his body, often driving him to tears. Every path and road, every house and cottage, every trail of smoke rising from the households' kitchen chimneys, every crop of grass — all of these hometown things were warm and sweet in his memory. With the hometown standing behind him, his life seemed to have had a fixed point of support. But…but now the hometown was buried under cement. The mountain was no longer the same. The river was no longer the same…. There was no doubt but that he was a destroyer! Since he returned to his hometown, many people had died a miserable death. Many people were reduced to misery. Kang Yuanyuan, a once passionate lover of life, had got cancer and died of it. His own sister and brother-in-law, who had been dearest to him in the world, had died with confusion and a grudge against him in their hearts — they didn't die in peace. Also, he had ruined the bright prospects of two young men, Xiaolin and Larz. Even Song Tongguo had been his victim.

"Song Tongguo used to be a simple country fellow. What has made him conceited and greedy?" Liben asked. "Wasn't it I who cooked up the cauldron of pitch he jumped into? Now he is wandering in alien lands like a tramp, hiding out here and there. Oh, what an unbearable existence that is!" he deplored.

Liben was getting really excited. He yelled and murmured alternately, his lips shivering, his voice husky. He got out of breath. At certain climactic moments, he struck his fist heavily against the bed board; he even knocked his head against the wall. In a loud voice he called himself an annihilator who had ruined his own hometown, his own relatives, his own friends, and himself. As such an annihilator, how could he have the face to still live in this world?

Liben confessed that when the villagers beat him, he had not felt angry with them, instead he had only wished they would beat him to death then and there. However, it dawned on him that if he *had* died then and there, the villagers would have been held accountable, and some of them would have had to face criminal charges and fresh misfortunes, so in desperation he jumped into the reservoir. His hope was that he would drown as soon as possible, so that he would be completely free of his miseries. But contrary to his wish — probably because he had committed too many evils — even the God of Death refused to receive him. The villagers, in great confusion, hurriedly yanked him out of water and pulled him to the bank. Thinking that he was dead, the villagers were frightened out of their wits and fled desperately. It turned out that he had just been in a coma — he was not dead.

Liben admitted he had complicated emotions about Yidan and Erdan. On the one hand, he thanked them for the kind help they had extended to him. On the other hand, he resented them for having done something that was none of their business. "Why were they such busybodies? What was the point of extricating me from the grip of Death?" Liben groaned. "Death puts everything to an end. Isn't it wonderful?"

"Calm down, please!" I said to Liben. "There's always hope. Don't think of death all day long!"

I told Liben that an investigation report I had composed concerning the current situation in Sakelu had been published in a journal for internal information; that the report had attracted Governor Xiang's attention; that it had shocked him grievously. It had been said that the governor had summoned the leading officials of Kaiyang County to Yuebei, and rebuked them fiercely. Furiously patting his hand against his table, Governor Xiang demanded that the Kaiyang officials act immediately to redesign and rebuild another Sakelu, so that the residents could be rehoused, and their livelihood could be planned in the long-term.

"Three months ago, the Kaiyang authorities recalled Zhao Xiaohui from the South, where he had worked after leaving his office," I said to Liben. "Zhao Xiaohui is now taking direct charge of this project. He called me to say that the land requisition paperwork for New Sakelu has been completed, the only problem which remains is who will invest in the project."

"Are these things true? Or are you telling a story?" Liben asked me.

"They are definitely true. I heard it from Xiang Wenhua. How can it be a story?" I asked him reassuringly. "Xiang Wenhua told me that his father had taken the journal for internal information home; that the goveronor was so indignant over this matter that he ate his dinner absent-mindedly and perfunctorily."

Liben said nothing more. He lay on the bed, with his head buried in his quilt. He seemed to have fallen asleep.

I turned off the light and went to my bed. Given how tiring it was to sleep under the same roof with Liben, I felt relieved to see that he was quiet.

For me, sleeping resembled diving. Just as I was plunging beneath the surface, and in a trance-like state, I heard Liben call me.

"What's wrong?" I woke up in terror.

"Could you do me a favor?" Liben asked me.

"What is it?" I asked.

"Time for going back! Time for going back!" Liben repeated these words many times, as if he were speaking them in his dream. He said that before going back to America, he would like me to accompany him on a tour to Mazi Village. This would be his last visit to the village, and he would never go there again in his lifetime.

"When would you like to go?" I asked him.

"Tomorrow evening."

"Why evening?" I asked.

Liben said that in the evening it was less likely that he would meet acquaintances: he feared to meet acquaintances.

Then, in a half-veiled manner, in broken words, Liben claimed that the reason why he preferred evening was that he wanted to see Mazi Village in moonlight. "After being violated and disfigured, I wonder how the once pleasant village looks now," Liben said.

"No problem. I'll go with you," I promised. "Isn't your hometown mine, too?"

98

The moon was hanging in the sky, along with black clouds with which it seemed to be playing hide and seek as it first ducked coyly behind them, and then floated in carefree fashion outside. There were even times when the moon retreated between two clouds, like a shy young woman trying to cover her face with a blue veil, thus making herself all the more conspicuous.

With the ins and outs of the moon, its light on the ground became alternatively bright and dim. Liben and I set out from the county town of Kaiyang on a tricycle. It was already midnight when we reached Mazi Village. To be precise, this place was called Meiteng rather than Mazi Village, but it had always been Mazi Village for us at the conscious or subconscious level. We each carried a bag on our backs, in which, besides bread and water, were thick stacks of joss paper. There were many varieties of this, among them joss money in various denominations, ranging from one hundred million to ten or five. We bought all denominations, afraid that our ancestors would not know how to spend the large ones, if they were short of the small. Liben and I felt a sense of guilt toward our ancestors, especially our parents who had brought us into this world and brought us up, and this guilt, like a heavy debt increasing at compound interest, must be repaid in one way or the other. Since Meiteng had been based here, the once-green fields were covered by concrete, and piles of steamed-bun shaped graves had disappeared completely. Like all the other Mazi villagers, we were unable to locate where our parents had been buried. If the joss paper was burned in the wrong place, then it would go to the wrong account, and others would draw the money while our ancestors would still be poverty-stricken.

In addition to joss paper, there was also a digital camera in Liben's bag. He wanted to take a few pictures and bring them back, to soothe his nostalgia. We walked aimlessly in the village in the moonlight. The so-called village should rather be called an industrial park, which should itself rather be called rundown town. Occasionally, amid the dead silence, dogs in the residential quarters could be heard barking.

After Meiteng had ceased production, the electricity bureau cut off its electricity supply on account of its huge electricity bill remaining unpaid. The streets were blacked out, and the factory was deserted. In the residential quarters, the abler workers went out to make a living, while the rest had to get by with candlelight. Meiteng was dark at night, lonely during the day. No birds flew in the sky, no frogs croaked on the ground, and passers-by were rarely seen — just a couple of suspect looking guys, who prowled around, poking their heads into odd corners, on the lookout for anything that might have survived the depredations of earlier thieves.

For Liben and me, our first priority was to find the graves of our respective parents. As far as I could remember, Liben's parents were buried not far from mine. His mother passed away in his childhood, while my father took an eternal farewell to the world when I was six years old. As children, we used to visit tombs together. We were two little naughty buddies competing in the matter of sacrificial articles, and the odds were ten to one that Liben would be the loser.

In the moonlight, which was dim but intense, we went from place to place till our legs were weary, but we still could not confirm the specific positions of the graves. We were invariably different or even sharply opposed in our memories. We quarreled whenever we could not agree with each other, both of us with too much to say. Liben argued that the graves of our parents were under the warehouse area, where individual warehouses formed a large area of their own, but I did not think so, insisting they were under the goods yard. I argued that the goods yard was close to the administrative area, that if they were not under the goods yard, they must certainly be in the administrative area. These were the only two possibilities. Liben accused me of being too conceited, and I told him he was.

As we could not come to a compromise, I said to Liben that we had better burn the paper where we each thought the right place would be. Liben made no reply, but I had already made my way to the administrative area. The gate of Meiteng had been gone for a long time, and even the walls had holes in them here and there. In the court, the concrete floor was full of pits and hollows, while the enormous garden was overrun with weeds. The office building stood there like a huge skeleton, with twisted doors and broken glass.

Walking into this yard was like walking into a boundless cemetery, and horror wrapped me tightly like a great shroud. I knelt down before the office building and took out the joss paper from my bag. I drew a big circle on the ground with a piece of chalk I had brought with me, put the joss paper into the circle, and ignited it with a lighter. With a few words to the effect: "Dad and mom and grandpa and grandma, come quickly to take the money," I made three kowtows before the flaming joss paper. Then I fled like a defeated wretch before it was even half burned. I was so scared that it seemed that countless ghosts were standing by my side, baring their teeth at me. It was not until I was out of the gate that my heartbeat began to slow down. I let out a long-drawn breath as if I had accomplished a death-defying task.

I wanted to rejoin Liben as soon as possible. On that chilly and lonely night, I felt like someone deserted on the barren surface of the moon, and Liben was my only available companion. However, he was not where I had left him. Where had he got to? I remembered his insistence that his parents were buried in the warehouse area, so I headed in that direction. Once I entered the warehouse area, I regretted it. The area was vast, half a kilometer from north to south! The colossal warehouses, each right next to the other, extended farther than the eye could see. I called Liben's name, as I fumbled my way forward. Liben did not respond, but my calls echoed back and forth among the warehouses, which made my hair stand on end.

I had almost given up, when I heard someone sobbing faintly. It seemed that the sobs were drifting on the wind, one moment to my left, another moment to my right, then right in front of me, then from behind my back. I could not make out where these faint sobs were coming from. But I felt more at ease, because I knew the sobs undoubtedly had something to do with Liben, and they at least suggested that he was in this area.

I searched up and down, and finally began to home in on the sobs. Just in front of a warehouse on the western side, I saw joss paper burning, and the silhouette of Liben who was kneeling down on the ground by the fire. I could hear his heartbroken wailing clearly now. I checked my steps because I did not want to interrupt him; but to my great surprise, it was himself he was mumbling about, not his parents. He was making confessions to his sister and brother-in-law, imploring them to forgive him. He said he would go to the netherworld and slave for them to atone for his sins, if only they would not hate him and would continue to be his sister and brother-in-law. He called his own name, begging himself to accept some money, so that he could lead a fairly comfortable life in the netherworld. "Alas, Liben, others may have joss paper burnt and sacrifices offered to them after they die, but you, you childless spendthrift, who will burn any for you? You are a homeless ghost!"

Hearing the somewhat bizarre things Liben was saying, I walked up to him and patted him on the shoulder. His sobbing, like a fast running train, was not easily halted, but his voice weakened and dropped, descending gradually, like an ebbing tide. Eventually, he stopped sobbing completely and rose slowly to his feet. As he did so, his unsteadiness on his feet revealed how weak his legs had become, the result of either kneeling too long or being burdened with too much grief. But for the timely support of the wall, he would have fallen down.

I asked Liben what it was he had been trying to say through his sobbing. He did not answer me, only looking up at the moon. I had to press him repeatedly before he opened his mouth. He flatly denied, however, that he had sobbed out his own name, saying I must have been misheard. I did not push him any further on the question, since he was obviously loath to answer it, and asked him instead what we should do next. Liben said Mazi Village had actually gone. It had disappeared forever from this planet and what we saw and touched now was nothing but a facsimile. If there were any traces of Mazi Village of yore, they could be found in two places — the old locust tree nicknamed Old Mom, and Three-River Bay. Liben suggested that we go to these two places, which might give us some consolation.

I had no objection. Besides, since my only motive for making this trip was to accompany him, I would go wherever he wanted to go. However, we had to turn back midway. The zigzag path, untrodden for so long, seemed to have decayed. Leek-like sedges grew out of its bed, and these, as they withered, produced a surface slippery as ice, too slippery to walk upon in fact. Liben fell down several times, and I did twice.

A sleeping owl started up at our approach. Its shrieks were alternately long and short, sad and sharp, as they reverberated in the deep valley. The once-beautiful Three-River Bay smelled of death, like an immense mortuary. To our horror, gusts of foul odor enveloped us as we approached. The smell became fouler and fouler, till we almost fainted.

Liben asked what the smell was. I said it was the waste water. He was skeptical, saying it was winter, and that Meiteng had been out of action for nearly two years, so how could there be any waste water? I dissuaded him from going down to have a look. In addition to the unbearable smell, the view down there would certainly be a depressing one. Three-River Bay, having been stripped of its green grass and clear water, was now a large pool of waste water the color of soy sauce. Weeds and trees around it were withering and dying one after another. "The Three-River Bay of memory and the Three-River Bay of reality have long been mismatched," I said. "For the sake of our good memories, we'd better turn back."

Liben sat in silence on the ground for a long time. Then he stood up and turned back. Up on the bank again, I reminded him that the tree nicknamed Old Mom might no longer exist. He said the tree was still in existence, and he was certain of it! He claimed that he had made a point of impressing on the boss of Meiteng that the tree must not be cut down, and that it must be protected from possible damage with iron railings. He said he had seen with his own eyes when the Meiteng workers were sinking piles and building fences around it.

Sure enough, Old Mom was still there. Even in the moonlight its imposing form stood out in the distance. Liben was getting a little excited, and I was too. He quickened his pace, as did I. The tree that had lived on through generations of Mazi villagers, had been planted by our forefathers' forefathers, and had thus become the symbol and witness of the village. Old Mom was almost too old, indeed, too ancient. Perhaps she had not lived one thousand years, however, it was no exaggeration at all to claim that she was eight hundred years old.

The railings around Old Mom were long gone, so nothing hindered us from embracing her. Liben hugged her and kissed her as if he had just been reunited with a long-lost lover. I hugged her too, but I suspected she lacked the vitality of other ancient trees I had seen. It seemed to be a concrete pillar, not a tree. The trunk felt so stiff, so cold against my face.

Liben had a different feeling. Totally immersed in some fantasy, he caressed Old Mom with his hand, and rubbed her with his face again and again, with tears welling up in his eyes. I called to him several times, but he turned a deaf ear.

I decided to climb Old Mom to see if she was still alive. When we were small, adults earnestly and repeatedly warned us that all other trees could be climbed, but not Old Mom! Old Mom was a sacred tree, and anyone who climbed her would court misfortune — in the best case in the form of scarlet swellings all over the body; in the worst case, in the form of death. The Shuanhu family claimed that Qiuli's sickness was due to the fact that she had squatted down under Old Mom and peed. On Old Mom's neck, I reached for a tilting branch. A living branch should be soft while a dead one would crack. The branch I broke cracked so smartly, that a gentle twist would make it snap into two or three pieces. I could not believe that Old Mom had died, so I climbed higher and tried other branches. Sure enough, the moment I grasped one it cracked. I grasped another, and it cracked too.

I shouted to Liben, who was under the tree, "Old Mom has died!" Liben did not come out of his reverie until I had shouted four or five times. Refusing to believe me, he looked up to accuse me of talking nonsense. I broke off a few of the thicker branches and dropped them down so that he could examine them in person. He picked them up and snapped them one by one. There followed a long period of silence. I asked Liben whether he was convinced this time. He did not speak, but only looked up at the moon. At that moment there was no moon in the sky; drifting black clouds had merged into a gigantic barrage which entirely engulfed it.

I slowly slipped down from the tree. I said to Liben, "We thought we had touched Old Mom's body, but we never thought it was actually her icy corpse!"

As day began to break in the east, I said it was high time we got back. Liben showed no desire to leave, saying he did not want to go, and that he would like to stay a little longer in the land of his hometown. He would let me return first. I laughed at his denseness, "Is this our homeland? Then where is our home? And where is our land?"

I left, as I could not make Liben budge. The tricycle which had brought us here was still waiting at the crossroad. The driver was very angry because he had not expected that he would have to wait in the cold wind for a whole long night. He nagged on and on, spitting nails. I knew his only purpose was to ask for more money. Without a word, I paid him the amount he was demanding. I told him to return before noon to pick up my companion Tian Liben and take him back to the county town. He should be near the old locust tree. The tricycle driver said it would be no problem, and before we parted I wrote down my telephone number for him.

Back to Yuebei, walking into the church, I thought I could get some real sleep in Liben's absence. A whole night without sleep was really too much for the body. Just as I was lifting the quilt, and my head was about to touch the pillow, when my mobile phone rang. It was the tricycle driver, who gave me some shocking news. Liben had committed suicide! He had hanged himself from the old locust tree with his trouser belt!

There was a lingering fright in the tricycle driver's voice, but he still managed to ask, repeatedly, who would pay him for this futile trip to this lousy place. He had searched through Liben's pockets, but found only one *yuan* and fifty cents!

THE END

Notes

1 Kang: a heatable bed made of earth or brick.

2 Luobo: the name means turnip.

3 Huaihua: the name means locust tree blossom.

4 Liang Qiuyan: the female protagonist of the play with the same title in the 1950s.

5 Gangan: the name means long and thin pole.

6 Fengshui: literally meaning wind & water, *fengshui* is the Chinese art or practice or belief in maintaining and creating harmonious surroundings which are vital to human survival and development. The core idea of *fengshui* is the harmony between humanity and nature.

7 CPPCC: the Chinese People's Political Consultative Conference, one of the two institutions of China's political system.

8 Reform Through Labor: a system to regulate convicts in China.

9 Red envelope: meaning gift of money, it is so called because it is usually packed in a red envelope.

10 Jidan: the name means chicken egg.

11 Chicken: in Chinese vernacular language, chicken also has the meaning of prostitute.

12 Lei Feng (1940-1962): the soldier in the People's Liberation Army who has been regarded as a model volunteer helper in China.

13 Laowan: the name literally means old bowl.

14 Hongmen Banquet: a famous banquet during the Chu-Han War (206 BC-202 BC), held at Hongmen by Xiang Yu, King of Chu, who was supposed to kill his rival Liu Bang, King of Han, later the first emperor of the Han Dynasty.

15 Monkey King: one of the three disciples of Priest Sanzang in *Pilgrimage to the West.* Before making the pilgrimage in the company of Priest Sanzang, Monkey King had risen in revolt against Emperor Jade when he was slighted in Heaven, proclaiming himself Great Sage Equaling Heaven.

16 Jin: weight measurement in China. 1 *jin* is equal to 500 grams.

17 White Dew: one of the 24 solar terms used for guiding agricultural activities.

18 Pao Ding: a legendary butcher who was able to skillfully cut up an ox. The story first appeared in *Fundamentals for Nourishing Life* by Zhuang Zi (C.369 BC-C.286 BC).

19 110: the emergency call number for police in China.

20 Liang: weight measurement in China. 1 *liang* is equal to 50 grams.

21 Shu: an ancient name, now short term for the Sichuan Province.

22 Xiaojie: the word used to mean a young lady, especially a young lady from a well-to-do family, but is now a euphemism for prostitute in parts of China.

23 Xishi: one of the renowned Four Beauties of ancient China. Her beauty was said to be so dazzling that while leaning over a balcony to look at the fish in the pond, the fish forgot to swim and sank below the surface.

24 Diaochan: one of the Four Beauties of ancient China. Diaochan is a heroine in the well- known Chinese literary classic *Romance of Three Kingdoms*.

25 Northern Wei Dynasty: a dynasty which ruled northern China from 386 AD to 534 AD.

26 Li Zicheng (1606-1645): a rebel leader who overthrew the Ming Dynasty in 1644 and ruled over China briefly as the emperor of the short-lived Shun Dynasty before his death a year later.

27 Yuan Shikai (1859-1916): an influential figure in the last years of Qing Dynasty. Yuan Shikai played an important role in the events leading up to the abdication of the last Qing Emperor, his autocratic rule as the first formal President of the Republic of China, and his short-lived attempt to restore monarchy in China, with himself as the Hongxian Emperor.

28 Dapao: the name literally means cannon.

29 Ding: a bronze vessel with two loop handles and three or four legs. It was a symbol for a state and its sovereignty in ancient China.

30 Wang Shuo (1958-): a contemporary Chinese writer.

31 In Chinese language, hemp and pockmark are homonyms.

32 Yangko: a folk dance popular in North China.

33 Dong Zhongshu (179 BC-104 BC): initiator of the exclusive worship of Confucianism in the Han Dynasty.

34 Dali: the name means great reason.

35 Ganban: the name literally means dry plank.

36 A well known brand of liquor.

37 Production team: an organization for rural economy in China, lasting 1958-1984.

38 In many rural areas in China, people do not have the convenience of using running water from water faucets at their houses. They have to travel some distance to draw water with buckets from springs or wells, carry water home and keep the water in a vat. Therefore, having running water from faucets marks a major difference between the city and the country.

39 In 200 AD, Guan Yu, general and sworn brother of Liu Bei, was defeated and detained in Cao Cao's army, but he remained loyal to Liu Bei who was with royal blood of the Han Dynasty.

40 Xianglin's wife: a character in *The New-Year's Sacrifice* by Lu Xun. She went mad after she had lost her job and her child.

41 Old Man Portrait bill: one-hundred yuan bank note. The Old Man refers to Mao Zedong.

42 Wu Song: a hero in *Outlaws of the Marsh* who killed a tiger on Jingyang Mountain.

43 Cao Cao: statesman, strategist and poet during the period of Three Kingdoms (220 AD-280 AD).

44 Erdan: the name literally means second egg, while his older brother Yidan means first egg. Erdan in vernacular Chinese also means crude, rash, silly.

About the Author

An Li (born 1962), is a Chinese writer who has dedicated himself to presenting real life and to revealing the truth behind it. Acclaimed as "the kingdom of thought, the mason of language" due to his profound insight and masterful technique, he has become a special phenomenon in contemporary Chinese literature.

About Chax

Founded in 1984 in Tucson, Arizona, Chax has published more than 240 books in a variety of formats, including hand printed letterpress books and chapbooks, hybrid chapbooks, book arts editions, and trade paperback editions such as the book you are holding. In 2021, Chax Press founder and director Charles Alexander was awarded the Lord Nose Award for lifetime achievement in literary publishing.

The Face of Time is Chax's second publication of books from Shaanxi, China, authors.

Our address is 1517 North Wilmot Road no. 264, Tucson, Arizona 85712-4410. You can email us at *chaxpress@chax.org.*

Your support of our projects as a reader, and as a benefactor, is much appreciated.

You may find CHAX at *https://chax.org*

Composed in Adobe Garamond Pro and Optima fonts. Adobe Garamond Pro is adapted from the 16th Century font designed by Parisian engraver Claude Garamond. Optima was designed in 1958 by German typographer Herman Zapf. Notes are composed in Gill Sans, designed in 1928 by British artist and designer Eric Gill.

Book design by Charles Alexander.

Printed and bound by KC Book Manufacturing.